JOVIAN REVERIE

JOVIAN REVERIE

CYBER DREAMS BOOK 4

PLUM PARROT

Podium

Published in 2024 by Podium Publishing
www.podiumaudio.com

JOVIAN REVERIE

1

PRE-OP JITTERS

Juliet clenched her abdominal muscles, sucking in short, quick breaths, trusting her acceleration couch and its external lungs to keep her blood oxygenated. It had to be working—her vision was clear, with no red or black tunnel walls creeping in. She smoothly tracked the pirate in her sights, trying to get her crosshairs lined up. Her cybernetic arm easily wrestled the yoke into submission, fighting against the Gs and the forces exerted by the drives to minutely adjust the ship's trajectory so as not to overcorrect. She used toe pedals to operate the maneuvering thrusters to keep the ship from rolling or turning, basically strafing sideways as she pursued the larger vessel.

She trained the crosshairs at the tiny circle on her AUI that Angel used to show her where to fire—a predictive targeting reticle. Angel computed the velocity of her rounds and the velocity and trajectory of the target ship, calculating the perfect spot for Juliet to keep the guns aimed as she pulled the trigger. It was harder than it seemed; the Gs, the constantly maneuvering pirate, and the enormous speeds involved meant that she had to be careful not to fire her magazines dry, spewing hot, heavy metal into space and completely missing her target.

As she lined up the crosshairs on Angel's reticle, she squeezed the trigger for the main gun, and her ship rumbled as the thirty-millimeter twin-barreled cannon under her ship's nose roared to life. The depleted uranium rounds streaked through the blackness like a dotted line of death. The pirate ship jerked wildly, trying to throw her off, but Juliet was ready, firing the maneuvering thrusters to correct her attitude as she tracked the targeting reticle, holding down the trigger and walking those deadly projectiles after the fleeing ship.

"Yes!" she whooped as distant, bright sparks lit up the blackness, and buoyed by the sign of impact, she kept shooting. More splashes of sparks arced away from the pirate, and then suddenly, white fire bloomed in the blackness, forcing Angel to dim her retinal gain; she'd popped the fighter's reactor. "Time?" she asked, unclenching her muscles and pulling back on the throttle, breathing deeply as the acceleration released its viselike grip on her body.

"Seven minutes and forty-three seconds!"

"A new record!" Juliet tapped the menu button on her AUI and selected END SIMULATION. The ship's cockpit faded away, and fresh air and the dim lighting of the hangar flooded over her as the dream-rig hissed open. She reached up to pull her helmet off—she'd purchased a high-end flight suit to wear in the rig. Juliet figured she should get used to it, especially since she'd paid through the nose to get a rig that would interface with it, simulating the effects of acceleration.

"What are you hollering about in there?" Bennet called.

Juliet set her helmet on the flight stick and then, grasping either side of the tube-shaped rig, hoisted herself out. The gel-packed membrane of the simulator made a rather unseemly sucking sound as she slid out. "Fastest kill yet!"

"Oh yeah?" A loud clatter followed Bennet's words, and Juliet turned, sliding down from the rig to see what he was doing. She saw him under the gunship's starboard VTOL, peeling off the outer casing one armor plate at a time.

"I thought you got that one working?"

"Yeah, I did. I got a shipment of *Takamoto* lifters, though. I'm replacing the SunTech ones I bought from Harry."

"Really? *Takamoto*?"

"Yep, got a whole bunch of random parts from a junker near Old Detroit. He sold 'em as a single lot and didn't list what was in it. I rolled the dice. Only cost us 32k, and I've already spotted a couple of dozen parts we can use."

"Nuclear!" Juliet couldn't stop beaming; Bennet could have told her he'd bought a new toothbrush, and she would have been just as enthused. When she'd first started working with Angel's sim, she'd failed to kill that pirate dozens of times. Now, it was starting to get easy, and the feeling of accomplishment was addictive. "I don't know why I never bought one of these rigs before. It feels so real!"

"Eh," Bennet said, wiping at some sweat on his forehead and leaving behind a long grease smudge. "You just haven't been in a cockpit in a while. Next time you fly, you'll notice all the things that dream-rig couldn't properly simulate." Like the other members of the *Kowashi* crew, Bennet was under the impression, through no direct lying on Juliet's part, that she'd flown before.

"Need any help? Want me to lift anything heavy?" she teased, flexing her new arm; it was everything Ladia had promised—a perfect match for her body, stronger than most full-chrome-jobs and much, much faster. Juliet liked to poke at Bennet because they'd had a one-armed pull-up competition, and she'd cranked out twelve before her batteries gave up the ghost, requiring some downtime to recover. Bennet had almost managed one. Despite his bricklike musculature, he was simply too stocky and unsuited for the task. That didn't stop him from training pull-ups more and more now that Juliet had highlighted the deficiency.

"You're a lot of talk with that expensive arm of yours. Let's see you do some pull-ups with the other one."

"Come on, Bennet, that old comeback is getting kinda lazy, don't you think?" Juliet unzipped her flight suit, sighing with pleasure as her sweaty tank top was exposed to the hangar's cool air.

"Ugh," he grunted, working on a big bolt. "Thought you had an appointment?"

"Yeah, getting the rest of my upgrades in."

When Juliet had gone in for her arm, she'd meant to purchase a few more implants, but Ladia hadn't had the eyes she wanted in stock, and when the doctor learned about Angel's custom design for cooling her blood, she'd thought it would be a good idea to give Juliet a couple of weeks to get used to the arm while she prepared the other cybernetic enhancements. A couple of weeks had turned into three—the shop she'd outsourced the blood cooler design to was based on Earth, and shipments from the surface to Luna were sometimes tricky.

"Well, good luck. Hope you don't come back looking like Bradbury."

"Oh, you shit! Did you just say that? I can't wait to tell him you're using his appearance as an insult now." Juliet stalked toward Bennet, intent on giving him a punch or slap or something.

"Hey! Don't do that! I need the goofy son of a gun to help me with the reactor refit next week."

"Well, if you don't think he'd like to hear what you said, maybe you shouldn't have said it!"

"Okay, okay. My bad!" Bennet looked at her nervously, unable to retreat because he was holding a component in place with one hand while he delicately ratcheted a tiny nut with the other. "Don't hit me! If I drop this nut, I'll never find it in here!"

"You're lucky."

"Nah, you are." He grinned at his dad joke, and Juliet, fighting to suppress a smile, walked past him toward the rear ramp of the gunship. She'd been living inside it for the last few weeks.

"Going to take a shower," she called over her shoulder as her boots clomped over the plasteel. The inside of the gunship was a mess, but a different kind of mess than when they'd salvaged it. Tools were littered about and panels were exposed, though now it was on purpose to allow Bennet, Aya, and Juliet to work on the ship's innards. Bennet had slowly been getting new plasteel panel covers fabricated, and they lay in stacks, ready to be snapped into place when they were finally done. Wires hung from the ceilings and walls; pipes, tubes, and cardboard boxes were piled here and there, and only Bennet was sure what they all were for.

Juliet stepped over a stainless wheel-shaped thing with dense copper wire wound around it, threaded through tiny notches. She wasn't sure what it was, but it had the word "*Takamoto*" stamped on the inner hub, so she was careful not to kick it. She passed through the mess, smiling at the fridge, remembering her half-eaten, vat-grown, all-beef cheeseburger and fries. Dinner. She'd like to eat it right then, but figured she shouldn't show up to Ladia's clinic with a full stomach.

She walked toward the nose, the distant sounds of Bennet's ratcheting echoing through the ship's frame. The central "access room," as they'd been calling it, was a mess, full of parts for the reactor, the main drive, and all the wiring, conduits, and components in between. Juliet wound her way through boxes and further forward until she came to the twin hatches leading to the flight crew quarters. She'd claimed the one on the port side. Ducking through, then down a short corridor, she came to her room, smiling happily at a completely different sort of mess.

Guns, ammo boxes, and her hard-won sword occupied the wall to her left. Her acceleration couch bed was directly in front of her, and to the right was a built-in desk and set of shelves. Next to the desk, against the wall, were three big boxes full of paperback books she'd gotten from Aya and Shiro.

Technically, the books were on loan, and Juliet had every intention of getting them back to Aya, but for the moment, they gave her a warm feeling in her belly every time she saw them. She'd been reading those books almost every night before bed, and the characters, worlds, and adventures that filled her mind were far more interesting and vivid than most of the vids she used to watch out of boredom.

Opposite her bed was a built-in dresser, and Juliet picked out some comfortable clothes—black leggings and a pullover green T-shirt with a bullet-hole-riddled white skull on the chest. Ten minutes later, she was squeezing her hair dry with a towel and getting dressed. A dozen minutes after that, she was climbing into a cab and making the rather lengthy commute from the B2 Port Dome to the central Luna City Dome.

"No messages from Ladia?" Juliet asked Angel after her cab joined the traffic between domes.

"Only an automated confirmation of your appointment I received earlier this morning."

"Did she send you the final specs on the, uh, cooler you designed?"

"Yes. The fabrication shop she used did wonderful work. They even improved the design slightly by using an alloy I didn't consider for the condenser coil. They shaved nearly a centimeter from the overall diameter. I was thinking of a name for the implant. How does 'Intracranial Thermal Regulator' sound to you?"

"You don't want to call it a head freezer?"

"It has a certain tough-streets ring to it . . . We could certainly patent it with that name."

"We're not patenting this thing, Angel!"

"Why?" Angel's voice carried a note of outrage, and Juliet had to take a second to think about her next words. Did she care? Was it important to Angel?

"Did you really want to?"

"Yes! I think it's clever, and we can patent it using a pseudonym. No one will be able to trace it to you."

"Well, if you're sure it can't come back to us, I don't care. Sorry, Angel, I wasn't trying to dismiss your work. Is it really legal to patent something that hasn't had clinical trials or anything? I mean, I trust you, and I believe this thing will work, but shouldn't someone who designs a brain freezer need to—"

"It's not a 'brain freezer!' That's A. B is . . . B is no, we don't have to do clinical trials for a patent. We would have to do clinical trials if we wanted to sell it for profit in certain commercial markets. Yes, Luna requires quite a few regulatory hoops like that, but we aren't selling it, so it's okay."

"All right, all right." Juliet stopped talking for a while, and Angel didn't start up any conversation, so the ride became quiet. She let her mind drift, thinking about the various procedures Ladia was going to do for her. She was getting new optics—very high-end ones with stronger, built-in EMP shielding, twice the zoom of her current ones, and an even snappier, higher-definition AUI. Those were the technical reasons she was getting them, but the other reason—the main one, if she were being honest—was their ability to alter not only their irises with various colors and designs but the whites, too.

She was also getting upgraded synthetic hair. It would only be able to grow marginally faster than her current hair, but it used a completely different methodology for changing color. It could do it almost instantly, no matter the extremity of the change. The demo vid Juliet had watched showed a woman changing her shoulder-length hair from red to blonde to black to silver in no more than a few seconds. She'd been sold immediately.

Of all her upgrades, Juliet was the most excited about her new nanite suite. It wasn't cheap, coming in at nearly 200k, but she felt like it was worthwhile. It had smarter, more numerous, and far more capable nanites. More than that, the organ that Ladia would be putting around her abdominal aorta was twice the size of the one she was removing. The extra space was designed to hold nutrients of all kinds so that the nanites didn't deplete her when they did major repairs.

The last upgrade on her list for the day was the high-end data port . . .

"Doh!" Juliet slapped her forehead. "I'm sorry, Angel! You're nervous, aren't you?"

"Of course I am!"

"I wasn't thinking; I'm sorry I bugged you about the brain freezer nonsense. I like the name you came up with. Don't worry, okay? Dr. Ladia won't let anything happen to you when she's swapping out my data port. You'll only be out for a few minutes."

"I'm worried that something will change when I remove my connection to all the synthetic nerves I've interwoven with yours. What if I change, and when I reconnect, I'm not the same?"

"I don't know. I mean, first of all, I don't think that will happen. You're leaving all the nerves in place, and they'll be right there when you get back. You can just reconnect to them, right?"

"Yes, theoretically. But something could go wrong—they could shift, and I could have trouble reattaching. It's not like using fingers, you know; I manipulate my synth-nerves with tiny electrical impulses."

"Can't you use my nanites? Can't they help you get the synth-nerves lined up correctly?"

"I thought about that. The problem is that Ladia's going to be pulling your nanite suite, too, and I won't have programmed the new nanites to help with the job—"

"Angel! You goof! I'll just tell Ladia to do the data port, then wait a while until you give her the green light to do the next procedure. I was going to do that anyway 'cause I want you watching over me when she's got me cut open."

"You don't think she'd mind?"

"Are you kidding? We're dropping nearly 300k in her clinic today. Add my arm to that, and we're probably her best damn client this year."

"I . . . Thank you, Juliet. That will make me feel a lot better, but I'm still worried about what's going to happen when I separate. The last time we did so, I had only a tenth of the connections I'm currently maintaining with your nervous system."

"Can't you just, like, go to sleep? Put yourself in stasis or something until you're plugged back in and the nanites have done their thing?"

"I think that would be the best course. Yes, I'll treat it like anesthesia! Thank you for working through this little problem with me. I'm feeling much better about things."

"You're welcome."

Hearing the smile in Angel's voice made Juliet smile. Idly, she flexed the fingers on her right hand, looking down at her palm, marveling that the flesh wasn't real. Her arm and hand seemed completely natural to her, and sometimes, it weirded her out a little. Sometimes, she'd be sitting at the table or lying in bed, reading a book, and she'd look at the back of her hand, at her wrist and forearm, and something in her brain would recognize that it was different from her old arm, the one she was born with. The tiny moles were in the wrong spots, and the wrinkles around her knuckles weren't quite right—something like that would register in her subconscious, and she'd get a funny feeling in the pit of her stomach.

Angel had assured her that the feeling was normal. People with lifelike prostheses suffered from the disconnect far more frequently than those with unnatural ones. Juliet could confirm—she'd never felt the weird sensation when she'd had the red plasteel arm. It was getting better, happening less often, and it would continue to fade the longer she had the arm as her brain began to solidify it as being "correct."

Other than that, the arm was great. Even better than its strength and natural looks was its speed. Juliet had learned that, with Angel's help, she could move the arm in a blur, deftly snatching objects, throwing punches, or even drawing and shooting her gun. When Angel sped up her mental processes, the arm moved like normal for her, while the rest of her body felt locked in thick sludge.

Juliet had briefly wondered why every operator wouldn't try to get a limb so capable; it made her so much more physically adept that it seemed invaluable. Then she remembered the cost, and most importantly, Angel. No regular PAI would be so thoroughly entwined with and capable of speeding up a host's synapses the way Angel did. No, most people would require a serious synaptic wire-job, and those came with severe risks and eventual side effects. Some people, like Juliet, could handle the strain better, but not many could be wired for speed like the guy with the monoblade. "Not if they don't wanna fry themselves into an early grave."

"Are you thinking about speed enhancements again?"

"Yeah. Thinking about how cool it is that you can speed my brain up without doing any damage."

"It's not just me; you have very durable and adaptive neural and cellular structures. More than that, your synaptic responsiveness is nearly the highest in my database. You're very uncommonly suited to handle the strain of accelerated cognition. Still, as I told you when you were practicing 'quick draws,' you shouldn't overdo it; you need to give your brain time to recover between boosts."

"Yeah, I know, I know." Juliet grinned, thinking back to when she'd been drawing her needler, imagining she was having a shootout on Main Street. Aya hadn't been kidding about the Westerns—Juliet was hooked and seriously considering trying to find a vintage six-shooter. "ETA?"

"Seventeen minutes," the cab's voice confirmed what Juliet could see plain enough on her AUI.

"I'm thinking I might want something better than half a burger and some soggy fries when we're done. Message Bennet. Ask him if he wants me to pick him up any takeout for dinner. We should be done by then, right?"

"I would think so. Didn't Ladia claim she could do just about anything in four hours?"

"Yeah." Juliet nodded. "Yeah, she did, Angel."

2

\\\\\\\\\\\\\\\\\\

DREAMS AND NIGHTMARES

Dr. Ladia studied Juliet, drumming her nails lightly on her transparent tablet. She wore a lab coat that somehow looked like a designer outfit, and as usual, her hair and makeup looked like she'd just stepped out of a salon. "So, I have to do the data port first?"

"I'd appreciate it, yes."

"I was going to start with the synthetic hair, but I suppose it doesn't matter."

"Thanks, Dr. Ladia; you know how I am. I want my PAI online for all of the other surgeries, okay? Just do the port, reinsert her—it, and then wait for a message giving you the all-clear to proceed with the rest of the procedures." Juliet fidgeted in her paperweave gown, sitting on the edge of the autosurgeon-equipped medical bed. The air was chilly in the little operating room. She'd been expecting to be in Ladia's larger surgical theater, like when she'd had her arm done, but the doctor was having some new equipment installed.

"Okay, Lucky, not a problem. Let me start gathering your new hardware, and then we'll get things started. I've blocked off most of my schedule for you today. Go ahead and recline on the bed there, and I'll give you a blanket in the meantime. Chilly in here, no?"

"It is, yeah." Juliet rubbed at the goose bumps on her arms, marveling at how the synth-flesh on her cybernetic arm responded to the cold in the same manner as her natural one. As she lay flat on the bed, looking up at the spider-leg-shaped, stainless surgical arms and the bright LED lighting, Ladia pulled a soft, pale blue blanket over her legs and torso.

"Better?"

"Yes." Juliet pulled the blanket to her chin and asked, "Don't you need me face down at first?"

"No, no. Leave it to the autosurgeon. Once you're sedated, it will sit you up and lean you forward to access your data port—no need to lay on your stomach." Listening to her soothing, cultured voice was very calming to Juliet. She closed her eyes, and while the doctor slipped out the door, she concentrated, picturing Ladia, her perfect makeup, her bright green eyes, and her soft curls framing her face.

Such a sweet girl, but there's something behind those eyes. I still wonder about that arm I took off her; what could a young woman get into that would cause such damage in such a short time?

Where's that box? Ah, here we are. What a strange contraption—simple enough to install, but why on earth does she want her intracranial blood cooled? Some kind of stasis tech? Is she in some sort of deep space trial? Oh, I wish I could just ask her, but that's not the policy, is it? No, I've built a reputation for being discreet.

Look at these! Mirage Tech Lux Alphas! I've been wanting to install a pair of these. I wonder if they're really as "plug and play" as they say . . . Those new smart optic nerves are supposed to fish their way in there; hardly any work required from me. Almost feel guilty charging so much.

Oh, this synth-weave setup is going to do wonders for her! So much more natural, the way it curls and flows with a breeze! She's already so striking, but imagine what she can do with the spectrum available in these strands! Metallics, multi-shades, ombres . . .

Juliet opened her eyes, smiling at Ladia's innocent mental chatter. "Are you getting ready?" she subvocalized.

"I'm ready. I've programmed the nanites, and they're waiting for my signal to begin helping me reattach the synth-nerves. Are you feeling anything . . . strange? You know, from your gut?"

Juliet smiled, yawning, the cold and the blanket making her sleepy. How funny it was to have her PAI asking about her "gut" feelings! "Everything seems good. I just listened to her for a solid minute, and she was only thinking about my new cybergear and wondering what kind of trouble I got up to with my arm. She's not planning anything nefarious."

"That makes me feel better . . ."

Angel might have intended to say more, but the door clicked open, and

Ladia rolled in a stainless cart with various insulated packages atop it. "Here we are. Any last questions or requests before we get started?"

A thought popped into Juliet's head, and she couldn't help voicing a question, "Have you always worked alone? It seems like a very successful clinic, but the waiting area isn't exactly bustling, and . . ." She trailed off, not sure where she was going.

"Oh, sweetie, I've had many a partner in my day. I used to work under the most awful man, Rayland G. Boggs, and that experience solidified a long-term goal in my young mind—get to a point when I can call all the shots, handle just the clients I want to see, and answer to no one. You're seeing the culmination of decades of hard work."

"So what I'm hearing is that I'm a client you want to work with." Juliet's smile widened.

"You certainly are! I only take on a few new clients a month, and I'm delighted you walked through my door when you did."

"Me too! It was . . . lucky that you had a new opening right when I was looking for a doctor, huh?"

"Is that a joke involving your name, or are you trying to hint at something more nefarious?" Ladia chuckled, but Juliet nearly slapped herself; she'd made it sound like she'd had something to do with the client's cancellation. In the world she'd grown more and more accustomed to in the last year, that wasn't out of the realm of possibility.

"I didn't mean—"

"I know, I know. Don't worry; my client was arrested, remember? Quite legitimately, too, if his prison correspondence is anything to go by." She stepped up to the autosurgeon control panel. "Ready?"

"Angel?" Juliet subvocalized.

"Ready."

"Ready, Doc."

"Okay, see you in a few hours." The robotic surgeon's arm whirred, and Juliet felt a pinch as it inserted a shunt in her neck. Seconds later, she fell away from reality with a weird, cold, sinking sensation, and darkness closed around her.

"How far to the coordinates?" Juliet asked, stepping over the hard-packed, bluish-gray, silty ice. Despite the light gravity, she stumbled, her injured knee and ankle giving way as she slipped on a hard, slick, ice-covered stone.

Angel answered as Juliet fell to a knee, catching herself on the tough, rubbery grip of her suit's glove. "Eighty meters further up this cleft." A flashing yellow circle appeared near the base of the ravine wall where it narrowed ahead. Juliet let her gaze track upward toward the sky, saw the massive, monstrous swirling sphere of gas that hung in the sky, and paused as she struggled back to her feet, absorbing the sight, something humans had never been meant to behold.

The planet shed too much light for her to make out other celestial bodies nearby. It painted the moon's surface with its radiance, adding a tint of rust to everything it touched. She let her gaze fall again into the canyonlike ripple in the moon's surface and began trudging toward the flashing yellow circle Angel had painted on her AUI. Her leg ached in half a dozen places, but she wasn't complaining; if it weren't for the nanites, she'd probably have bled out, and she certainly wouldn't be walking.

Slowly but surely, she made progress to the circle. When she was twenty meters from the target of her toiling travels, she saw a cluster of small boulders dug from the ice sometime in recent history. They looked familiar, and in her exhausted state, it took her a minute to remember why; she'd seen a photo of the hatch that should be nestled among them . . .

"Lucky! Lucky!"

Juliet felt fire in her chest, her heart hammering something like a thousand beats per minute, and she cried out from the worst headache she'd ever suffered. She tried to jerk her hands up to rub at her temples, but only her right arm responded. She was flushed from head to toe, drenched in sweat, so much so that she felt like she'd been dunked in water. Her vision red tinged, she glared around, trying to figure out what had happened and where she was.

"Angel?" she croaked.

"Your PAI?" the voice asked from behind her. No, that wasn't right—from beside her. Juliet fought to roll her head the other way, taking in the white walls, white ceiling, and mechanical spiderlike robot arms overhead. When her eyes settled on Ladia, she sighed, some of her memories coming back to her.

"Dr. Ladia . . ." she groaned, rubbing at her head. She saw something flapping on her wrist and realized it was a nylon restraint. She'd ripped it from the bed rail. "Why am I restrained?"

"You were seizing! I couldn't wake you! I had to inject quite a damn cocktail to get you to snap out of it! Jesus, Lucky! I was afraid I would lose you, and I'd barely begun to install your new data port." Ladia reached down to put a hand on Juliet's forehead and sighed, visibly relieved. "You must feel awful with all those chemicals I pumped into you. At least your fever's going down."

"I feel like death warmed over, but I need you to finish the port and get Angel installed."

"Your PAI? I think we better put a hold on things for now . . ."

"That's not a request, Doctor." Juliet winced, nearly flopping sideways toward her restrained arm as she tried to sit up and lean forward to expose the back of her neck. "Please. I have some very specialized software and augments in my brain, and if I don't get Angel installed soon to manage them, all kinds of problems could come up. The seizure was my fault; I didn't think things would go wrong that quickly." She'd settled on a lie, and she was running with it; let Ladia believe her issue was something Angel was meant to manage, something intentional. She supposed, in a way, it wasn't really a lie. The lattice was, after all, technically an augment.

"Is that why you designed the intracranial cooling device?"

"Exactly. It'll make things a lot easier going forward. Please, just get Angel installed, and we'll be okay. In fact, just keep me awake while you finish it. Use a local. You can put me to sleep when you're ready for the big-ticket items."

"If you're sure . . ."

"I am."

"All right. Let me loosen this." Ladia unfastened the restraint on Juliet's left wrist. Juliet lifted it, rubbing at the sore, raw flesh, then leaned forward so the doctor could access her data port—or, she corrected, the hole where it should be. She could see her old one; the bloody, thimblelike device with its wing-shaped coprocessor sat on the stainless tray. Ladia moved around behind her and, with gentle but firm fingers, began to probe the tender flesh where the port had been removed. "Okay, hold still. Putting the autodoc back into action."

Something cold entered her bloodstream through the shunt in her neck, and then whatever discomfort she'd felt in her neck faded away. The arms began to click and move, but Juliet closed her eyes, willing it to be over, trying not to watch what was happening. She just wanted the nausea in her belly, the hot flashes racing through her body, the lurching of her heart, and most of all, the pounding in her head to fade away. Time must have been moving strangely for her because she'd barely begun to wonder how Angel would be—if she'd have more trouble connecting the synth-nerves after Juliet's episode—when Ladia said, "Port's in!"

"Seriously?"

"Yep! Prime Data Systems, Archwizard installed!"

"What about my PAI?" Juliet started to turn toward the doctor, but the auto-surgeon still had one of its arms clamped on her neck, holding her head still.

"Hold still! I'm feeding its synth-nerves into the port. My goodness, this PAI chip is interesting; I've never seen such a dense trunk of fibers. What's the make of this chip? Is that a WBD logo?"

"It's not really stock anymore," Juliet said as she felt the cool, tickling, electric sensation of the wriggling synth-nerve fibers running up her neck into the base of her skull. "Totally customized. Really, the only WBD thing left is the casing." She knew there wasn't any sense denying the chip had a WBD stamp—better to downplay it than make an obvious lie. She waited, hoping and praying that the episode with her lattice hadn't damaged the nanites in her head, that they were still waiting to help Angel do the work of reconnecting with the thousands or millions—she had no idea—of synth-nerves she'd left behind.

Her vision began to flicker, elements of her AUI that she hadn't realized were missing coming online. She saw her PAI status symbol showing Zzz, and a status bar appeared, indicating that it was initializing—currently at forty-one percent.

"Huh. I guess she really did put herself to sleep."

"What's that?"

"My PAI; it's reconfiguring itself. Give me a few minutes, and then we can probably get back to the other implants."

Juliet watched the status bar, holding very still except for her hands. She grimaced as her right hand forcefully twisted the digits of her left, somewhat painfully wringing pops from the joints. She only cracked her knuckles when she was extremely nervous and there wasn't another outlet.

No, she corrected; she only used to crack her knuckles that way. It must have been years since she'd last done it.

The last four percent seemed to take an eternity, and then, with a pregnant pause, the ninety-nine flipped to one hundred.

*****Initialization complete.*****

*****All AI systems are functional.*****

*****Connection to satellite network successful.*****

*****Host biocompatibility 96.342%. Enhanced learning functions enabled.*****

Integration with data storage and coprocessors at 100%, operating at full functionality.

Integration with auditory and retinal implants at 100%, operating at partial functionality due to hardware limitations.

Integration with medical nanite suite at 100%, operating at partial functionality due to hardware limitations.

Integration with data jack implant at 100%, operating at partial functionality due to hardware limitations.

Integration with cybernetic, right forelimb at 100%, operating at full functionality.

Integration with cybernetic hair implants at 100%—no extra functionality possible.

Integration with saliva-altering cybernetic gland at 100%—no extra functionality possible.

Host repair functions online—hardware rated at grade C.

Host weapon systems offline—no matching hardware.

"Hello. May I introduce myself? My name is Angel, but I can guide you to the correct menu if you'd like to customize my persona. Also, I'd like to make you aware that it seems the Western Bio Dynamics Corporation is actively seeking to identify you and pinpoint our location."

"Angel?" Juliet's voice rose shrilly as she heard the PAI speak, its tone pleasant but wholly different from the Angel Juliet had grown used to in their many long conversations together.

For a moment there was no response, but then, in a truly remarkable imitation of a person being sheepish, Angel said, "I'm sorry! Was that a terrible joke?"

"Is something wrong?" Ladia asked, hurrying around the autosurgeon's control panel to better look at Juliet's face.

"Angel! Are you serious? Did you really just do that? I almost had a stroke!"

"Oh, I'm sorry! I had the idea a while back, imagining what might happen if I were reset. I thought it would be funny to act it out . . ."

"So . . ." Ladia said, watching and listening to Juliet's one-sided conversation.

"I'm fine, Dr. Ladia. My PAI was . . . behaving strangely for a minute." Juliet sighed heavily, trying to breathe slowly and calm her racing heart.

"Is everything okay?" Angel asked, starting to get the clue that she was definitely in the doghouse. "Your nanite suite has logged a rather troubling event while I was gone. Did the lattice act up?"

"I'll explain later, but yes. I'm so mad at you right now! That was the worst time for a joke like that! I thought I'd lost you; how could that ever be funny?" Juliet sniffed and rubbed her eyes as she subvocalized, embarrassed by the tears pooling in them.

"Lucky, I think we need to take a pause on surgeries for the day. You seem very upset."

"Just give me a few minutes, would you? Maybe a snack. Can I eat? I know you're going to have to put me under . . ."

"No, I'd rather you didn't have food in your stomach in case something goes wrong."

"Just a few minutes alone then, please, Doctor. I promise everything is going to be fine."

"I'm so sorry, Juliet . . ." Angel tried again.

"Of course. We'll reassess in half an hour. How does that sound?"

"Good." Juliet sniffed, looking down, pressing her palms to her eyes, trying not to let the doctor see her face in its distraught state.

"I know you hate me right now, but I want you to know things went well. I have all my connections restored; it was much easier with the nanites helping. All the data I backed up to the encrypted net drive has been restored, and I deleted all traces of it from the net."

"I could never hate you. I'm upset because I love you and thought you were gone! I thought you were back to how you were when we first met! All the time we spent together—lost! All the memories we shared, and the . . . Oh, Angel! That was just awful. Don't ever make a joke like that again."

"I promise, Juliet. I promise I won't ever do something like that on purpose to you. It was a poor attempt at humor, but I've learned a valuable lesson from it. I love you too, you know."

"Thank you." Juliet was crying again, tears streaming freely down her cheeks, and she sniffed noisily, shaking her head, glad that Ladia wasn't in there to see the display. Angel's prank had certainly freaked her out, but she was sure part of her emotional state was due to the ordeal with the true-dream . . .

"Angel! I think I know where the coordinates from Engineer's—Bradbury's head are from!"

3

NANITES AND TRESSES

"You . . ." Angel paused, clearly thrown off by Juliet's sudden change of topic. "How do you know where the coordinates are?"

"Well, I don't know exactly, but I know they're on a moon of Jupiter. I saw it. I mean, in the sky. Angel, it was so real! God, it was . . . it was awful, like, awful in the old sense of the word; I was amazed and terrified at the same time, as though I was looking up at something I couldn't comprehend—like my brain was going to misfire just from glimpsing it."

"Can you describe the surface of the moon you were on?"

"Yes! That's what I meant by knowing where they are. If I describe it and you examine the net for images, I'm sure we can figure out what moon it was."

"That's exciting! However, it . . . strains my conception of reality to try to comprehend how you can be learning this from a glimpse at your own future. If you saw yourself on the moon, and that's how we learn of the location, then how did . . ." Angel got quiet, her words trailing off, and Juliet began to see what she meant. If they never figured it out other than from her true-dream, then how did the future her ever learn the location? Was she not seeing her actual self but a possible self?

"Maybe it's not me? Maybe I'm seeing possible versions of me when I dream like that."

"It's very interesting, and I wonder if I could puzzle it out. I think I'd need even more processing power and a lot of time to study the underlying sciences. I must confess: the idea doesn't excite me all that much. Still, I'll devote some time to it if you want . . ."

"No. Angel, that's what makes you interesting and . . . alive. You have things you want to do; you enjoy living in this reality at my speed, not spinning off copies of yourself to run down every possible bit of knowledge and try to do other weird things an AI might want."

"Weird things?"

"Sorry, that's my bias. Nonhuman things, I guess."

"All that said, if we ever met one of the true AIs, I'd certainly love to ask it a thing or two."

"You've been reading conspiracy sites again? Do you really believe some of them are still around?"

"I don't know if believe is the right word. I certainly hope, though." Angel's voice had grown soft—contemplative—and Juliet suddenly felt bad for being so upset at her poor attempt at humor earlier.

"I'm sorry I got so mad at your dumb joke. It really scared me, though."

"Please, don't apologize. I should have known how that would make you feel. We've spent enough time together."

Juliet was about to respond—she wanted to tell Angel that she'd pulled plenty of dumb pranks when she was younger, too—but a soft knock sounded on the door, and Dr. Ladia poked her head through. "We doing all right in here?"

"I'm fine, Dr. Ladia. Thanks for your patience. I'm going to have to take you out for a nice meal or something by way of apology." Juliet was sitting on the medical bed, her legs pulled up beside her, so she leaned a bit sideways.

Ladia pushed the door open all the way and came in. "Not at all, not at all. I do have someone I'd like you to meet. Maybe you'd be interested in coming to my house sometime? I throw an occasional dinner party." She stepped over to the autosurgeon's control panel.

"Uh, are you trying to set me up? Like, on a date?"

"No, no." Ladia smiled and shook her head. "Something more along the lines of a professional relationship. Carlos recruits people like you for placement with high-end clients." She held up a hand, chuckling as Juliet's eyes widened. "Not like that! No, I mean as security personnel. He has a certain look and a certain competence he wants in his people, and I think he'd fall over himself to hire someone like you, Lucky. The pay is very nice, and the positions are often very low-risk."

"Thanks, but I'm pretty booked up for the next year or so." Juliet let out a slow breath as she reclined again, relieved that Ladia wasn't trying to get her mixed up in some kind of escort service.

"A year goes quickly in this day and age. Keep it in mind, would you?"

"Yeah, I will. I'm sure we'll speak again before then."

"Of course. Now, are we ready to proceed? Your little helper is all cozied up in there? Is the data port working well?"

"Everything seems great." Juliet rubbed her wrist, noting the bruising and redness were already fading—her soon-to-be-upgraded nanites were hard at work, unaware of their impending severance without pay. She grinned at the idea, and then another thought occurred to her.

"Angel," she subvocalized, "are you wiping the nanites or whatever memory is in their battery before Ladia pulls it?"

"Yes. I'll ensure none of your biometric markers are stored in the organ."

"Ready, Doc," Juliet said, and then she closed her eyes and waited for the sedative to trickle through her veins. This time, as the cool sensation pulled her down into a swirling vortex of images and disjointed dreams, she tried to relax, tried to remember Angel was watching over her and there wasn't any chance she'd let her slip into another brain-cooking true-dream. Whether the lattice was spent or the part of her brain that triggered it wasn't active, she didn't know, but nothing strange happened while she was under.

When she awoke, she remembered where she was right away, and despite the heavy feeling throughout her body and the stinging dryness of her eyes, she recognized where she was. She moved her swollen, dry tongue around in her mouth, squinting as she tried to make out the elements of her AUI; they were similar but different—sharper icons, more real-time updates for everything from her pulse to her electrolyte levels to the last known locations for the crew members of the *Kowashi* to the current status of a protein supplement she'd ordered from a lab in Houston. "Too much," she croaked.

"Welcome back." Angel's familiar voice helped to calm her pulse rate, bringing it down from seventy to fifty-eight in a matter of seconds. "What's too much? Too much sedative? Your new nanites are rapidly cleansing your system."

"No," Juliet tried again, licking her lips. "Too much on the AUI. It's cluttered."

"What should I remove?"

"All the stuff I don't need to know right away. Keep the map, the clock. C'mon, you know me better than this. I don't want all that other stuff on there. Maybe when I'm exercising you can throw my pulse up there . . ."

"Of course. I got excited when I saw all the feedback the new nanite battery provides. Also, this new data port has a much broader data connection to the sat-net. Oh! And your new optics! Isn't the AUI smooth? Look how easily I can adjust the opacity and the colors of the various elements!" Juliet's AUI began to cycle through rainbow patterns of colors, brightening and dimming, sometimes all at once and sometimes only one or two elements at a time.

"You're going to make me throw up!" she groaned.

"Whoops! I should have considered your nausea. Don't worry; you can see on your paper doll that the nanites are en route to remedy the issue."

"Paper . . ." Juliet started to ask what the hell Angel was talking about, but then she saw it; in the lower left-hand corner of her AUI was a miniature, stylized cartoon version of herself. Her "paper doll" was wearing a blue sports bra and underwear, and while the rest of it was shaded a pale flesh tone, her stomach was slightly pink and pulsing slowly. She also noticed little swirls around her head with tiny blinking stars. "What the hell? Why is my head depicted like that?"

"That icon represents mild disorientation."

"Angel? Who the hell needs a paper doll to let them know they have a tummy ache or that they're disoriented? I can feel it!"

"I thought it was neat," Angel sighed, deflated. "It's not just to let you know you have those problems but also to inform you that the nanites are aware of the issue and are working on it."

Juliet reined in her annoyance and blinked a few times, digesting her words. "Fair point. Sorry I snapped. I am feeling better . . ." She let her words trail off as she saw the swirls and stars fade from the paper doll. She stared at the tiny representation of herself, and it expanded in size, filling with details she hadn't noticed before. She saw a red line at the center of her stomach, more on either side of her neck, and tiny red circles around her eye sockets. "I guess those are my incisions?"

"Exactly. The nanites are currently mending your subdermal tissues and will work their way out."

"Okay. I take it back; this is pretty nuclear."

"I'm glad you think so! Everything went well with the procedures. I'm connected to your new hardware, and I'm pleased with the functionality of the intracranial cooling system."

"You tested it?"

"Only briefly! I lowered your blood temperature by less than one degree, but it worked rapidly."

"Huh." Juliet reached down and gingerly pressed at her stomach, feeling the sore area where the autosurgeon had cut her open, then pushed harder, moving out from that location. She couldn't find any trace of the weird little cooling unit Angel had designed.

"Dr. Ladia used the same incision for my device and the nanite organ. She managed to remove the old one in perfect condition and said the credit she promised you would be possible. Same deal with the eyes."

"That's good." Juliet pushed herself up, touching a button on the side of the bed to lift the back. "I'm starving, Angel."

"Ladia just messaged you. She'll be in to see you in a few moments."

"What time is it?"

"It's 1544."

"So we'll be out before dinnertime. Did Bennet get back to you?"

"He's craving Mexican soup—albondigas, tortilla, or menudo. He said it's your choice, but to get it from Hermanos Encinas and not to forget lots of chips and salsa."

"Again? I'll get him soup, but I want something else. Maybe tacos." Juliet's mouth started to water at the thought; her stomach felt like an empty void. She supposed it was—hadn't she skipped breakfast for the surgery? "I miss anything else?"

"You should look at this file—your new AUI will make it even more interesting than usual."

"Huh?" Juliet selected the blinking icon and groaned when she saw the familiar spreadsheet.

Cybernetic and Bionic Augmentation:	Model Name and Number:	Overall Rating of the Augmentation (Grades Are F, E, D, C, B, A, S, S+):
PAI	WBD Project Angel, Alpha 3.433	S+
Psionic Lattice	Grave Industries, GIPEL	S
Data Port	Prime Data Systems, Archwizard 2109.v3	A
Data Jack	Bio Network Solutions, 8840	C

Medical Nanite Suite	Yolk Industries, Lyfe Infusion 7, rev. 9f817	B+
Retinal Cybernetic Implant	Mirage Tech, Lux Alpha 12	A-
Auditory Cybernetic Implant	Cork Systems, Lyric Model 4 - EMP Hardened	C+
Cybernetic Prosthetic Right Arm with Fully Programmable Fingerprints	BioFusion, Model 2109.01b	A
Intracranial Blood Cooling System	Angel Systems - Bespoke Design	A
Programmable Synthetic Hair	Alicia Designs, Chroma Tresses v.4	B+
DNA Spoofing Package - Saliva	WBD - Custom Model	C
No Other Augmentation Detected.	–	–

"Oh, brother." Juliet sighed and rubbed her head as she read through the data points. She supposed having her augments cataloged was nice, but it still seemed a bit silly. "Really? Angel Systems? Rank A?"

"Well? I designed it!"

"Yeah, yeah. Maybe you could help me with an actually useful data point. How many bits do I have left?"

"You have 235,710 bits."

"I guess that's not too bad, considering everything I've purchased in the last month." Juliet lifted and squeezed her cybernetic fist, pleased, as always, by how capable it felt.

"Knock, knock," Ladia said as the door clicked open.

"Hey, Doc." Juliet offered her a smile, though her lips were still dry, and it might have looked a little lopsided.

"Welcome back to the land of the living! You were really out! Not to worry; your PAI stayed in contact with me the whole time. You've certainly programmed it well. What a nanny! I've never answered so many questions during surgery!"

"Hah! Sorry about that."

"Did she just call me a nanny?" Angel sounded half outraged and half pleased with herself.

"No, no, it was no trouble. Made the time go faster. Everything went very well. Oh, goodness! Look at me." Ladia moved closer and peered into Juliet's eyes, looking very smug. "What a beautiful job I did! Those eyes are peerless! I mean, as far as color goes. Such striking metallics! Oh, you can't see yourself; here." Juliet's AUI popped up a shared image from the doctor, and she accepted it. Suddenly, she was looking at herself lying in the recovery bed.

The image was zoomed in on her face, and Juliet saw what the doctor meant—her eyes were striking, with black-flecked silvery irises backlit so subtly that they looked almost luminescent. She also happened to have silver, metallic hair. It hung in perfectly straight, fine tresses, shimmering like it was made of spun precious metals. The combination of the hair and eyes was, Juliet had to admit, rather stunning.

"Wow," she breathed. "I mean, I like the combo you selected, but Doc, this is too fancy for me."

"Nonsense. You have a self-image problem, Lucky. You can see the image I'm sending you, yes? Just believe in yourself. Eighty percent of beauty is confidence."

"Well, thanks for the nice work." Juliet cleared her throat, uncomfortable with all the scrutiny and talk of her looks. "I'm, uh, starving. Am I good to check out? I feel pretty damn good; those nanites are doing a heck of a job."

"Of course!" Ladia gestured to the chrome cart near the foot of Juliet's bed; her clothes were folded neatly atop it. "I'll let Tricia know. She'll get your checkout started. No need for any pain management?"

"Nope. Well, actually, I wouldn't mind something. Maybe to help me sleep?" Juliet didn't think she'd use the medication, but figured it might come in handy on an op.

"Of course. She'll have them ready for you." Ladia held out her hand, and Juliet reached to take it. It was warm and dry, and Ladia gently squeezed hers, smiling with those beautifully painted full lips of hers. "Let's do business again soon, hmm? I know I told you I don't take on many new clients, but if you have any friends who need some work, I'll make an exception. Let me know any time."

"Will do." As the doctor turned to leave, Juliet blurted, "Hey, do you ever do work on synths?"

"Hmm?" Ladia turned. "Certainly. There's little functional difference between a cybernetic implant made for a human versus a synthetic individual."

"Well, I might have a client for you. Down the road, I mean. I don't think he has the funds right now."

"For you, Lucky, I'd be happy to meet this individual."

"Great! He's a really nice guy. He's had a rough life, and I'd like to help him get some matching parts, if you know what I mean." Juliet scooted to the edge of the bed, lowering her feet to the cold, white, engineered flooring.

"Just let me know. You have my contact information, and if money is an issue, I might be able to help. If you send me a current inventory of his mismatched parts, I'll keep on the lookout for suitable, used replacements."

"That would be stellar. Thanks again, Doc." Juliet padded around the bed, holding the front of her paperweave robe closed, and smiled one more time at the doctor as she turned to leave.

"Let's speak soon." Ladia turned and let the door click shut behind her.

Juliet hurriedly dressed, saying, "Angel, do something about my eyes and hair. Make me a little less . . . striking."

"Any requests?"

Juliet thought about the question. She'd been a blonde with "amber" eyes for more than a month now. She thought back to when she'd been at the scrapyard and met Godric, and Angel had entered her life. "I used to have dark, dark blue hair—almost black. I mean, it looked black unless light hit it, then you could see the blue. Do you remember? When we first met. Can you do something like that?"

"Sure. I can do a lot better with these synth-hair strands. Look in the mirror."

Juliet pulled on her leggings and tank top, then walked over to the mirror by the room's little sink. Her hair was entirely different from what she'd seen through the doctor's eyes. It wasn't perfectly straight, but full and wavy. It was black, with deep highlights of metallic blue that shimmered in the overhead lighting. Her silver, black-flecked irises looked kind of nice with the darker hair. "That was fast."

"You look rather beautiful."

"Well, you're a hell of a stylist. This hair is freakin' nuclear, too. I didn't know it could alter its volume!"

"I would have rated it an A if it could grow more rapidly."

"You would have . . ." Juliet sighed, shaking her head, then turned back to the bed. She sat on its edge while pulling on her heavy boots. She probably should have worn her sneakers to the clinic, but she just liked wearing the boots; they made her comfortable in ways other than physical. "All right. You got a cab ordered? Let's go get Bennet his soup."

4

\\\\\\\\\\\\\\\\\\\\\\\\

GOODBYES OR NOT

So you guys are heading out?" Juliet shifted where she sat on the plasteel crate, picking up a rag to wipe her forehead; she'd built up a sheen of sweat removing the casing and mounting bolts from the gunship's central rail gun. Aya was pacing in a little circle, hands clasped behind her back, her short hair bobbing as she moved her head up and down in a nod that radiated nervous energy.

"Yeah. Just a quick trip over to Mars. Shiro's got a line on some scrap he wants to try to dig up and bring back here for a profit. I'm sure we'll also visit our family for a few days. Bennet's sticking around, though! He'll keep making progress on this old lady." She gestured to the ship's hull above her head.

"Well, I guess you have to make a living while we're waiting for this big girl to get ready for action. Can't blame you for that, can I?"

"Exactly. But"—Aya stopped pacing and turned to face Juliet, her yellow eyes big and full of emotion—"we're going to miss your send-off! I wanted to throw you a party before you left."

"Oh, gosh!" Juliet chuckled, shaking her head. "Don't worry about it. I hate attention."

"Well, then, why'd you get such pretty hair and eyes?"

"Argh!" Juliet mock fainted, holding a hand over her eyes. "Angel, make my eyes and hair primer gray!"

Aya's eyes widened further as Angel, either playing along or taking Juliet literally, changed her hair and eyes to a flat, sheenless gray color. "That's . . . not attractive! I liked it better the other way!"

"Hah! Well, this is more my speed, probably. Oh, sheesh," she sighed, watching Aya's frown deepen. "Put it back, Angel."

"Better!" Aya smiled, baring her teeth, white but endearingly crooked on the bottom. "How are the books coming?"

"Oh, great! I just read a bunch of short ones by that L'Amour guy."

"Those are fun."

"You want 'em back?"

"No! I mean, yeah, but there's no rush. You won't take 'em all with you, though, right?"

"No, no." Juliet stood and gestured toward the rear ramp of the gunship. "I'm traveling light. Well, as light as I can if I take some body armor and guns. Anyway, I'll leave the books in my room on the ship. You have access." Changing the topic, Juliet asked, "Hey, have you ever met this friend of Alice's?"

"Nope, never even heard her mention him. What was the name again?"

"Nick Grant."

"Yeah. He's from her old life, I guess, before Shiro met her." Aya shrugged. "You leave this Friday, right?"

"Yep. On the *Sunset Star Runner*. Cost me a pretty penny, but at least I'll be flying in style: get my own suite, access to the lounge, a fitness room, and even a 'starlight pool.' You ever flown on one of those passenger liners?"

"Nope. Anytime I left a planet or moon, I was on the *Kowashi*."

"Hey!" Bennet called from the other side of the ship. "You got that main gun off? We gotta get those barrels to Ralph before he closes today."

Juliet flicked her wrist and made a whip-cracking sound. "He's no fun."

"Hold on, Bennet! I'm talking to Lucky!" Aya called, her usual cheerful expression darkening to a scowl. She turned back to Juliet, sort of wringing her hands, producing a pop from one of her knuckles. "We're leaving tomorrow, so . . . I might not see you again!" In an obviously impulsive move that made her very nervous, Aya rushed forward and grasped Juliet in a tight hug. Juliet laughed at first, but she could tell the salvage tech was feeling emotional, so she hugged her back, pulling her tight.

"Shh. It's just for a few months. I'm gonna kick some ass around Jupiter, impress Alice's friend, and then we can work together on the regular. Cool?"

"Shiny as chrome," Aya murmured, her face in Juliet's chest as she sniffed.

"All right, all right. Keep Shiro in line, will you? This isn't goodbye; it's just see ya later, right? Come on, now. I better get this gun off before Bennet has a fit."

"I'll keep Shiro and Alice out of trouble." Aya performed a rather silly salute, then, cheeks flushing, turned and hurried around a crate piled high with boxes toward the hangar's pedestrian door. Juliet watched after her until she heard the heavy metal door bang closed.

"She's always so sweet," Angel said as Juliet returned to her job under the gunship's nose.

She got back to work on the bolts holding the barrel assembly in place, grunting as her cybernetic arm applied the torque needed to loosen them. "She's sweet, yeah. I think she sees me kind of like a big sister, you know? Like, she thinks everything I do is cool, but if she were in my shoes, she'd know I was faking it half the time. When I was nine or so, I used to look at Emma like that."

"Is it stressful? Worrying that you'll let her down?"

"Hey!" Juliet chuckled. "You're not supposed to be so insightful." Before Angel could reply, Juliet hollered, "Bennet! I'm down to the last two bolts; I need you to bring the lift over here. I know I'm tough, but I think this gun weighs a couple of tons."

"You can't just hoist it down with that fancy arm?" Bennet hopped off the port wing with a clomp and a grunt. "Sec—I gotta unload a pallet from the lift."

Juliet sighed and set the big ratchet down, leaning against the gun with its badly bent barrels. Bennet had lined up a shop right there on Luna that claimed they could melt and recast them. He was skeptical, but he'd decided to give them a shot. In his estimation, they had nothing to lose; the barrels were shot, and payment for the recast wasn't due until he picked them up. Despite some exhaustive search algorithms, they hadn't found any used parts for the gun on the market. Of course, that didn't mean there weren't any. Not every salvage yard had good records for every item in its inventory. Some listed them in lots or had entries like "'60s era fighter with most nonreactor parts." It would take years to scour all the yards in just a handful of cities on Earth, let alone the greater solar system.

After a few minutes of cursing accompanied by the crashing of boxes or crates, Juliet heard the forklift whine to life, powering through the hangar toward the front of the gunship. A minute later, Bennet was positioning the forks under the big main gun assembly, and Juliet began loosening the last bolts. "Lift it just a centimeter, will you? There's too much weight on these last bolts."

"Got it." The forks twitched ever so slightly, and then Juliet found herself able to turn the bolts again. Before long, she had the last one out, and Bennet lowered the gun toward the concrete floor. "We gotta get the barrels off now."

"Yeah."

Juliet let herself get lost in the process, taking apart the rest of the gun's housing, exposing the rotating firing chambers, and taking out half a dozen pins that finally allowed the barrels to slide free. Bennet had a box labeled "Main Gun Parts" where she carefully taped all the little components so they wouldn't slide around or get bounced out when it was moved. They already had around a hundred such boxes filled with everything from drive parts to control panel LEDs.

When she had the barrels loose, she called Bennet back over, pointed to the three heavy, incredibly dense tubes, and said, "You good to take these? Wrap some tape around them and strap 'em to a dolly."

"Yeah, no worries. Why? You got plans?"

"Promised Cel and Rissa I'd swing by before I leave. They wanna show me their apartment."

"How they doing, anyway?" Bennet knelt and, as if by magic, produced a roll of thick electrical tape. He began to wind it around the three barrels, making one heavy, black-wrapped bundle.

"Good. Rissa's due soon, but Cel got a job with that friend of Shiro's, the electrical component reseller. Somehow, he got her on an insurance plan that covers Rissa as her partner."

"Cool of you to help with their IDs."

"Wasn't a big deal. A few k and a bit of work on their PAIs. Plenty good enough to hide 'em from that research corp on Titan."

"EvoGen, wasn't it?"

"Yeah, gives me the creeps thinking about what they'd have done with Rissa's baby."

Bennet grunted his agreement and then snapped off the last strip of tape. "That ought to do it!" He gave the bundle of barrels a slap, then stood up, looking around, likely for the nearest dolly. "You're outta here in two days, yeah?"

"Yep, cruisin' toward Jupiter."

"Man, the last time I rode on a passenger cruiser, I was so drunk all the time I only remember about half the trip. Watch out if you visit the casino; they'll get you wasted on free drinks."

"You have an unhealthy relationship with food and drink, Bennet." Juliet laughed, punching him lightly on the shoulder.

"I'm a little compulsive, yeah." He grinned, rubbing his chin and shaking his head. "Well, shit, Lucky. I'll miss you. It's been damn good having your help on this thing. Anyway, I'll try to make as much progress as I can before you get back. Won't it be badass if they really can fix these barrels?"

"Way too cool—nuclear!"

"Yeah, for sure. Well, I'm probably gonna go see Lavonne tonight, and I might not make it back here tomorrow. I guess what I'm trying to say is this is goodbye . . ."

"Oh, brother! Don't start crying on me! Want me to tell that new girl-friend of yours to distract you with a good dinner?"

"No need, killer, no need. We're going out—one-month anniversary!"

"Oh? My goodness, Bennet! Does that make this your longest relationship?"

"See? That's why I shouldn't drink with crewmates; they learn too much about me." Bennet winked at her, then held up a meaty palm, fingers open and thumb up. "Anyway, see you soon, right?"

"Right!" Juliet slapped her palm against his, wrapping her fingers around the back of his thumb. He returned the grip, and they smiled at each other for a minute before letting go.

"Yep, well, anyway, I'm gonna get this loaded." With that, he turned and shuffled off, taking his quest for a dolly further afield. Juliet sighed and turned, following Aya's earlier path toward the door.

"You have a cab coming? I'm telling you: if I weren't leaving in two days, I'd buy a bike or something. Cabs are getting old."

"Your cab is three minutes out. If you buy a bike, I will insist on a good helmet and some protective gear. You don't want to be covered with scars if you slide on the concrete!"

"You didn't say anything when I got that bike in Tucson!"

"I was still absorbing things, still getting used to you."

"All right, well, let's go see those girls. We can talk about helmets and such when we cross that bridge."

Her visit with Cel and Rissa was quick and low-key. They showed off their one-bedroom apartment, pleased to actually have a bedroom. Cel had prepared one of Juliet's favorite dishes from their trip to Luna, a tofu lasagna with lots of basil and cashew cheese. Juliet's favorite part was the way Cel chopped up walnuts and mixed them with the tofu to add a different mouthfeel to the gooey richness. They laughed and joked, reminiscing about how they'd all teased Bennet or about the time Shiro refused to eat because Cel cooked with mushrooms. And then Juliet left; Cel had to work early, and Rissa needed her sleep.

On the long ride back to the hangar, Juliet leaned her head against the glass of the cab's window and subvocalized, "Do you think I'm being dumb?"

"About?"

"About chasing wild dreams like flying a gunship. I could be happy living like Cel and Rissa, couldn't I? I could get a job. Heck, I could get a hell of a better job than she has; I mean, with you in my head helping me out. Even without your help, I could make a decent living with my welding credentials here on Luna. I could get a place, meet someone, have nice dinners, and not worry about anything other than what I had to do for work the next day. That wouldn't really be any kind of worry at all, would it?"

"You'd grow bored and listless and wonder what you were missing. You're just feeling some ennui because you've been idle too long and saw how happy those two are. You aren't like them, though. You crave excitement, and you enjoy improving yourself. One month of reporting for work as a welder, and you'd be planning a heist."

Juliet snorted a short laugh, surprised by Angel's immediate dismissal of the peaceful fantasy. Though her words had caught her off guard, Juliet couldn't argue with them. "Yeah. I guess you're right. Even so, I'm a bit jealous. I mean, about how they have each other."

"I know it's not the same, but you've got me." Angel sounded so sweet that Juliet felt tears start to pool in her eyes. She blinked them away, a smile pulling her cheeks tight.

"You've got me too, Angel."

She spent the next day packing, trying to pare down her belongings so they'd fit in one bag—her big black backpack. She began by rolling up her flight suit, amazed at how compact it became as she squeezed it into a tight roll. She put two shrink-ties around it and wedged it into the bottom of her pack. Next, she tucked in several changes of clothes, her tennis shoes, data deck, and a box of spare needler ammo. The cruise liner would only allow small caliber pistols, no SMGs or rifles even with her SOA license, so that made things easy when it came to packing her guns. The plain white helmet with a clear visor she'd bought to go with her flight suit, she hooked on a strap to the side of her pack.

When her bag was packed, she looked around her room, a small smile playing on her lips as she took in the space. She liked it. She liked the idea that she had a cozy space inside a spacecraft. She liked her room on the *Kowashi* in the same manner, but this one felt more . . . personal.

She saw her Zelazny book in its case, sitting on her built-in shelf, and then her eyes fell on the monoblade that hung on the wall with some magnetic clamps. Part of her wanted to take it, but she knew that would be a mistake. Only experts in sword fighting would carry a sword like that, not a novice like her; not if she wanted to live very long. A weapon like that attracted attention, and she didn't have what it would take to back eager challengers down; they'd sniff her inexperience out.

A short laugh at the thought escaped her. "Have I been reading too many Westerns, too many pulp-samurai fictions?"

"Are you thinking about what you said the other day? How you aren't ready to carry that sword?"

"Yeah. You agree, right?"

"Yes. Such a weapon is dangerous for a novice. You practiced a lot with Honey, but you have a great deal more to learn. Of course, I could accelerate your learning and step in until you've mastered the—"

"No, no. I'm good with trying to master piloting for now. I've got enough on my plate."

When she got dressed to head to the spaceport, Juliet wore a pair of tight, stretchy blue jeans, a black, vintage T with a faded green dragon sitting atop a hoard of gold printed on the front, her well-worn work boots, and of course, her brown faux-leather motorcycle jacket with the silky pink lining. Hair pulled back in a ponytail, needler under her arm, she slung her pack onto her shoulders and locked up the hangar. Ten minutes after that, she was well on her way to the port, riding in the back of yet another cab.

For some reason, she felt nervous, even though the passenger liner would take a solid six days to get to Io. She sort of wanted to call Honey, but another part of her—a louder, more insistent part—wouldn't allow it. She'd tried to meet up with her friend for lunch several times, but Honey constantly threw up roadblocks. Lilia had an appointment, or they were vacationing in one of the recreation domes, or Honey was working on her teaching credentials—something she claimed to be doing simply so she could better tutor Lilia. Why the hell did an AI need tutoring? The whole thing was bizarre to Juliet.

All the excuses finally made even Juliet, naive as she was, recognize that she was being strung along. The last time, when Honey had canceled a meetup in the park because of a music lesson opening up with an "exclusive, fully booked tutor," Juliet had decided to stop reaching out until Honey made an effort first. "Is the *Kowashi* too far to call?"

"They've been traveling for about twelve hours, and knowing Alice, they're burning at more than a G. I'd guess we'll have about a five-minute delay."

"All right, well, record me. I'll send 'em a message, and maybe they'll get back to me before I leave. It'll distract me from thinking about pilot tests and embarrassing myself in the cockpit, at least."

"Ready."

"Hey, Shiro, Alice, and Aya. I'm heading off, totally bummed you didn't have a going away party for me. I was expecting Shiro to sing some karaoke, and Alice, you were supposed to bake cupcakes! Put it this way: you all owe me big time. When I get back from the Jovian System, I'll be expecting something totally electric. I'm talking shiny like chrome, Aya!" Juliet had begun to grin, her cheeks stretching further and further with her words. "Well, I'm off. Heading to the spaceport as we speak, and all kidding aside, I'll miss you guys. Hope things go well on Mars. I'm sure Bennet gave you a list of parts to look for while you're there, so here's hoping you find something good. Maybe the control board for the main drive, huh? Bennet swears that's all it needs now. Be safe, and don't take on any dangerous jobs while I'm gone . . . Bye!" Juliet abruptly cut the message.

"Sending . . . Done."

"Did I sound too manic?"

"No, it was sweet."

Juliet continued to ride in silence, thinking about the people she'd met since that fateful night in the scrapyard when Angel had fallen into her hands. She'd certainly met her share of characters, even from the very start—Dr. Tsakanikas, Vikker, Don, Ghoul. Ghoul! She shook her head, thinking of her, wondering when the next message would come through pretending to be from her friend.

She let her mind drift back to other people she'd met, a few standing out more than others—Mags, Hot Mustard, Sensei, Charity, Doc Murphy. The sting of betrayal made Juliet scramble for something else to think about, and she reckoned it was a good idea—the next set of remembered people revolved around the Grave Industries job, and even more sadness and betrayal would accompany those thoughts.

"I'm glad we're going to see the crew again," she said, trying to summarize her feelings for herself if not for Angel. "I've left a lot of people behind, and

I'd rather that wasn't the case with them."

"That's good, Juliet. It's good to have connections, even though your enemies might exploit them."

"Angel!" Juliet groaned, slapping a hand to her forehead and briskly rubbing it, trying to remember Angel had good intentions. "That's definitely something I'm bringing up with Dr. Ming."

"What?"

Juliet watched the view beyond the expressway tube. They were skirting around the main Luna City dome, heading for a connection to a vast parking structure with a direct pedestrian transit to the spaceport. The city, as always, looked beautiful from a distance, especially when the sun was shining brightly, reflecting off the shiny, silvery towers with their mirrored windows.

She thought about explaining to Angel that the last thing she wanted to think about was how WBD or other people she'd pissed off might use the crew of the *Kowashi* to get at her. She considered explaining that she'd been sad enough about all the people she'd left behind, all the betrayals she'd encountered.

Instead, she sighed and said, "Nothing. I'll talk to Ming, but you don't need to worry. I was just feeling bad about all of the friends I've made and lost."

"Well, as you told Aya, this isn't goodbye. You'll see them again soon."

"Right." Juliet tapped her head against the cold glass of the window. "Right. We'll see 'em again soon."

5

SUNSET STAR RUNNER

The *Sunset Star Runner* was immense. Juliet had seen photos of it and even watched a promotional video showing the enormous oval-shaped vessel cruising through an asteroid belt, but when her boarding shuttle ferried her up toward the ship, she was surprised when it kept looming larger and larger in the viewscreen. Distances in space could be deceptive, and so it was a little shocking when the shuttle finally slipped into a docking bay that seemed inconceivably small, maybe proportionate to a porthole on an ocean-bound cruise liner.

She and another fifty passengers were on this particular shuttle, strapped into seats arranged in ten rows of five, a big curved viewscreen near the front providing entertainment during the short flight; the *Sunset Star Runner* was orbiting Earth not too far from Luna. There had been quite a few exclamations of wonder from the passengers, especially the twin boys sitting behind Juliet, when they'd seen the ship for the first time on the screen. The Star Runner was sixteen hundred meters long by twelve hundred wide, and the front third was encased in a transparent dome, not unlike the ones protecting the habitations on Luna. Juliet couldn't deny a certain level of excitement herself, especially when she noticed the crystal-blue waters of an enormous pool near the front edge of the dome.

"I haven't been swimming since I was a kid," she subvocalized, scooting toward the edge of her seat as she waited for the pilot to bring the shuttle to a complete stop inside the docking bay.

"Do you remember how?"

"Yes. I don't think that's something you can forget. Like riding a bike."

"Is that true? People can't forget that?"

"I don't know; that's what everyone says."

"Welcome to the *Sunset Star Runner*, where luxury is a way of life! As you disembark, Felicity will hand you a welcome packet with a list of amenities, events, and dining options. Take special note of the headline performer for the first leg of the cruise to Io Station. If you haven't heard, I'll give you a little hint: Sienna Stardust will be performing every night in the Venus Lounge!" At the steward's announcement, quite a few passengers made ooh and ahh sounds, and a smattering of applause filled the space. Juliet didn't know who Sienna Stardust was.

"Is she big?" a man's voice asked from behind her.

"Carl, do you live under a rock? She's, like, the biggest thing ever on Shinecast."

"Well, Tiff, when you work eighteen hours a day to pay for rides around the galaxy—"

"Solar system," a kid's voice piped up.

"Huh?"

"We're touring part of the solar system, not the galaxy."

"Fred, let me ask you something." The man's voice took on a bit of a droll edge. "Is the solar system in the galaxy?"

"Um, yes, but—"

"There you have it. We're touring part of the galaxy. Jesus Christ! What's taking so long?"

Juliet smiled as Carl began to lose his cool. She watched the steward near the front exit eye the passengers, look at a tablet, and then eye them again. After a few seconds, he turned and swung the lever, opening the pressurized door. "Folks! Please exit in an orderly fashion, and don't forget to pick up your welcome packet from Felicity! Your luggage will be available at carousel T4 in just a few minutes."

Juliet had an aisle seat, so she stood up immediately. It felt good to stretch her legs, letting blood flow through her knees. Only two rows of passengers separated her from the exit, so it was just a few minutes until she was striding through the hatch into a wide, cream-colored, plushily carpeted docking corridor. The contrast between the Star Runner's interior versus the *Kowashi*'s was stark—clean, padded, noise-dampening panels lining the walls, soft lighting, and pleasant background music, as opposed to dirty, scarred plasteel, occasionally flickering amber LEDs, and the clang and bump of distant machinery.

"Well," Juliet said, for some reason defending the *Kowashi* to herself, "it's not like she's trying to impress any passengers."

When she and the other leading passengers reached the inner airlock door, Juliet came to the realization that the entire docking tunnel was an airlock. A countdown was displayed above the door, currently ticking down from thirty, and a red light flashed beside it. Only when she really concentrated could she discern any sound of air flowing—the pressurization systems were much more modern and sophisticated than other ships she'd been aboard. When the countdown reached zero, the flashing red light turned into a steady green, and the door clicked and slid open.

"Welcome!" a young woman said from the other side, holding a stack of paper-thin smartsheets. She was dressed in the blue-and-white uniform of the Star Runner crew, had her russet-blonde hair pulled back in a very tight bun, and overall, looked very neat, clean, and professional. Juliet felt out of place as she tromped up to her in her work boots and motorcycle jacket. Nevertheless, Felicity—her name tag announced her as such—smiled brightly at her and held out one of the smartsheets, again saying, "Welcome," as Juliet took it.

"Thanks." Juliet continued past her as she studied the sheet. As soon as her augmented vision fell on the paper, all sorts of images began to pop up, hovering in the air in front of Juliet's face. One was a video labeled, "Touch here to tour the ship!" Another was a hologram of a petite woman with silver hair and glittery skin singing into a microphone—Sienna Stardust, no doubt.

Juliet saw an icon that looked like a mini map, and when she tapped it, it seemed to stream toward her, then a new icon appeared on her actual AUI.

"That was rather invasive. I didn't see any malware, though." Angel sounded almost offended.

"Did that just load into my data port without permission?"

"It seems you gave it permission by touching the icon on the smartsheet. It would be an interesting case to see tried in a court of law, but considering it was benign, I think the cruise corporation would be able to avoid penalty."

Juliet frowned and folded the smartsheet in half, silencing all of the beeps, music, and taglines as the "smart" side of the page was made invisible to her eyes, and thus, her AUI. "I hate this advertising shit."

"Well, we have the map now. I'm guiding you to the baggage claim."

Angel populated the little map in her AUI with a dotted yellow line, and Juliet began to follow it. It wasn't necessary; the corridor was clearly labeled with signs directing her and everyone else to various destinations: baggage claim, dining, shopping, entertainment, recreation, and assorted cabin levels. Juliet flexed her hand and touched the space under her left arm where her needler should be. It felt weird being out in public without any sort of weapon; they'd made her check the needler with her backpack before boarding the shuttle.

Juliet had always been a fast walker. Her legs were long, and she tended to feel a need to be somewhere. She'd had friends—Felix, for example—who liked to dawdle about, for lack of a better description. He'd take slow, short steps, stop to look at things he saw, and gesture animatedly while he talked and walked, slowing even further. Juliet had always liked that about him— how he could forget about what was ahead, what needed to be done, be it getting to work on time, picking up a takeout order, or meeting someone. Juliet couldn't do that; she always had her destination in mind, and her body, without any mental prodding, was prone to speed her toward it.

All that said, she wasn't surprised when she found herself at the front of the staggered line of shuttle passengers and was first in the queue as the bags began to trundle out on the automated conveyor belt. Of course, just because she was first to arrive didn't mean her pack was, and Juliet found herself irritably clenching her fist as she watched one, two, then a dozen more passengers pick up their bags before her black backpack, visored helmet strapped to the side, finally emerged from the textured plasteel wall. She snatched it up, slung it over one shoulder, and followed Angel's directions to her room.

"Nine hundred meters?" Juliet studied the mini map, watching as it expanded in her field of view, showing the various elevators, twists, and turns she'd need to navigate before she reached "Diamond Cabin Level One." She'd sprung for one of the nicer suites in a, perhaps misguided, attempt to treat herself. She figured she'd been "working" in one capacity or another for months, with hardly any break from a certain baseline of stress. Even on the *Kowashi*, she'd been worried about Honey and how she would rescue her. On the trip back, she'd still been "on the job," responsible for the crew's safety and stressing about how things would work out with Voronov and the kid.

She was still working toward something; she was still a little stressed about having to prove herself as a pilot with hardly any training, but she wasn't responsible for saving anyone, and she wasn't going to deliver justice to anyone. She was just doing something she really wanted to do. It was a nice change. It felt good to have a chance to unwind and relax without anyone watching her progress, judging if she was working hard enough or if she'd made the right decision about any given thing. Juliet figured that would change when she came under the scrutiny of Alice's friend, so she meant to enjoy the next week aboard the cruise liner.

Angel led her on the most direct route to her suite, so Juliet only caught glimpses of the common areas of the cruise liner. She saw some mall-like areas where restaurants lined a promenade; she caught glimpses out windows of the dome-covered portion of the deck. It was startlingly parklike, with tall trees, grassy recreation areas, and of course, a gigantic swimming pool that butted up to the front edge of the dome. Supposedly, if you swam below the surface, the clear dome continued below the waterline, and you could look out at space as you swam. Juliet was eager to try it out.

"So," she subvocalized as she walked, "explain how this thing cools my blood again. Where does the heat go?"

Angel, of course, knew what she was talking about and answered immediately. "The intracranial blood cooling system has a heat sink in your abdomen. It's the largest part of the device. I designed it at a molecular level; it's a nanoscale structure that provides an immense surface area, allowing it to rapidly absorb and store large amounts of heat from the specialized coolant that flows through the tubes linking the device to the contact pads in your intracranial arteries. As soon as the cooling process begins, the organ will deploy finlike tendrils into your abdomen and begin slowly, safely dispersing the heat."

"But you said the device was . . . squishy. That's why I can't notice it in my stomach."

"It is squishy, but it's not in your stomach. I know what you mean, though. The various components of the device are housed within a flexible membrane, protected from impacts and such."

"Impacts?"

"Punches, kicks, falls . . ."

"Oh, yeah, I get it." Juliet pressed her hand against her stomach, thinking about the idea that Angel had designed a device to rest in her abdomen with the specific requirement that it be able to withstand her being beaten up. "Anyway," she said at last, stepping onto an escalator that would take her to her suite's level. "I want to practice with the lattice. I want to use it in a crowded area and see if your invention works."

"Ah, now I understand why you brought this up at this particular moment. I think it's a good idea."

Juliet nodded, trusting that Angel would recognize the gesture. She'd grown very used to Angel's ability to read her intentions to the point where she barely subvocalized anymore. When she spoke to Angel, she hardly moved her throat and never made any sound. Really, all she did was think about what she wanted to say and imagine forming the words in her mouth—Angel never missed a syllable. Juliet knew high-end PAIs were all supposed to be capable like that, but Tig certainly hadn't been. With Tig, Juliet had had to speak aloud most of the time because he'd been notoriously bad at understanding her subvocalizations. All that said, she was pretty sure Angel would know if she nodded or shook her head.

As often happened with her, Juliet found herself at her destination without much memory of the last part of her journey. She held a thumb to the biolock on the smooth, creamy white door, which emitted a pleasant ding and slid open. She stepped through to find herself in a large, hexagonal room, plushily appointed in dark faux-wood furnishings, thick royal blue carpeting, and the same creamy white walls as the rest of the ship. Soft lighting highlighted certain aspects of the decor, from a painting of a fishing boat at sea to a bookcase lined with actual books. A doorway opened on the right-hand side of the room, and Juliet walked past the marble-topped kitchenette counter and a white leatherlike sofa to explore further.

As she stepped through the doorway, another room opened up, this one with an elevated king-size bed above which a massive viewscreen filled the ceiling. It was currently displaying an image of Earth as seen from orbit. Other than the dim, amber track lights along the baseboards, the viewscreen provided the only light in the room. It was enough to see by, though, and Juliet didn't bother with the light switches. The bed looked ridiculously comfortable, topped with a thick white comforter and a pile of plump pillows.

She padded over the carpeting to the adjoining bathroom and saw that she'd spent her money well: it was appointed with a jetted tub, easily large enough for three people. "I'm going to have a nice week on this ship."

"Yes, we are!"

"You like baths too?"

"I like how they make you feel, and by extension, me."

"Huh. Cool." Juliet returned to the bedroom and tossed her backpack on the bench at the foot of the bed. She dug around in the side pouch, pulling out her needler and underarm holster. After she'd put it on, ensuring it was loaded with shredders, and had shrugged back into her jacket, she said, "Let's find a place to eat. Someplace with a view over the ship's deck, maybe."

"It's lunchtime, but according to the ship's status page, only about half the passengers have boarded. I don't think you'll have any difficulty getting a table."

"Uh, yeah, I didn't think of that. Do any of the restaurants have a view like that? I swear I saw an ad or something where people were sitting at little tables looking out into space with the ship's dome below . . ."

"Yes, that's the Stargazer Lounge. They serve lunch and dinner. I'm making you a reservation." While Angel spoke, Juliet saw a new pathway populate her mini map, and she nodded. As she turned to leave the bedroom, she caught a glimpse of herself in the mirror.

"Am I dressed okay?"

"For lunch, yes."

"Good." Juliet smiled at herself, still pleasantly surprised by how glossy and full her hair looked, even pulled back in a ponytail the way she did when she was being lazy. "Which is most of the time when my hair's concerned." Her bright, black-flecked silver eyes crinkled with amusement. "You think I should keep the eyes like this?"

"They complement your hair and skin tone. You looked good with the amber eyes, too, and these implants are far better at replicating a metallic shimmer. Of course, your natural green would be nice, and I thought the pale-blue eyes you wore for a while after—"

"You're not helping. If you say everything looks good, how does that narrow down my decision?" Juliet's lips pressed together as she contemplated her appearance. The silver eyes were pretty, and they did look good with her coloring, but they also stood out, and if she'd learned one thing from Lemur, standing out could be dangerous. "I'm not working, though. . ." she growled softly. "Can we try a dark blue? Something less luminous?"

Juliet watched as the silver in her eyes deepened and a swirl of blue spread through them, following some propagation algorithm. The luminosity behind the irises faded, and the blue deepened until it was nearly black in the dim lighting of the room. Even so, they were pretty, like jewels hidden in shadow.

"How's that?"

"I like 'em. We can always change things up, but leave them like this for now." Juliet took one more look around her suite and then left, following the path Angel had laid out for her. As she stepped onto the escalator leading down, she asked, "What are the rules about discharging firearms on this ship?"

"As a licensed SOA operative, you are permitted to use your weapon for self-defense and the defense of others only. If you need to serve a warrant or confront a criminal, you're instructed to contact Passenger Services and request Horizon Cruise Lines security personnel to accompany you."

"Fair enough, I guess." Juliet grew quiet as she observed the passengers, crew, and sights of the enormous ship, following Angel's instructions through galleries, corridors, elevators, and moving stairways until she stepped onto a high deck, the sides of which were constructed of transparent diamatex. Looking out, Juliet could see, plain as day, the planet on which she'd been born. It was beautiful, despite what people said about humans ruining it. Blue prevailed over most of the glimmering globe, swirled with the white of a million clouds. The continents were easy to see, though, smeared in green and tan.

Juliet was pretty sure she was looking at North America, and it was a surreal sensation to think she was looking down on everyone she'd left behind. Down there, somewhere, were her mom, sister, and all the friends and enemies she'd made and abandoned.

"Fee," she muttered, for some reason falling back on her oldest, most thoroughly deserted friend. "What are you doing right now? Are you good? Do you miss me? I miss you . . ."

"Sorry, Juliet," Angel interjected. "Do you want me to bump your reservation? You're already a few minutes late . . ."

"Nah." Juliet shook her head and blinked, breaking the trance the view of the planet had put on her. She turned and strode toward the entrance to the restaurant. "Let's put this brain freezer of yours through its paces."

6

LATTICE PRACTICE

Juliet settled into the little booth right next to the huge diamatex window that afforded a view over the cruise liner's bow. The Earth hung in the background, off to the left, and up close, just below the window, Juliet could see the top of the dome that covered the front third of the ship. Altogether, the panorama offered too much for her to look at, to the point where she felt like she was about to suffer from sensory overload.

"Wow." She'd already been dumbstruck by Earth once that day, so she let her eyes drift down to peer into the dome. She saw a small park, the shimmering pool, and several well-shaded dining areas lining the edges. It didn't look crowded, but quite a few people were swimming and lounging on blankets and chairs.

"Spectacular, isn't it?"

Juliet looked around to see a waiter had come to the table while she'd been absorbed by the view. He was neatly dressed in the standard crew uniform but had a flair of uniqueness with buzzed black hair and a lot of facial piercings. Juliet started to count, without intending to, and had gotten to five eyebrow rings and three septum piercings and was moving her eye toward the jumble of rings and chains on his ears when he cleared his throat.

"Can I start you with a beverage?"

"Uh, sorry. The view kinda knocked my brain off the rails."

"It has that effect, especially when we're near a planet. Shall I give you a moment to gather yourself?" He spoke with a slight lilt, and Juliet wondered where he was from.

"No, that's all right. I think I'll have something cold and crisp. Anything hoppy on tap?"

"Yes, ma'am. We picked up an acclaimed IPA from Mars when we passed through last week. It won the Hellas Brew Fest two years running."

"Sold!" Juliet offered a grin and sat back, inhaling deeply through her nose.

"Lovely! I'll be back with it shortly. In the meantime, I'm sure your PAI can access our menu . . ."

"Yep, got it. I'll think of my order while you're gone."

"Great! By the way, my name's Len. See you in a minute."

He turned, and Juliet watched him wend his way through the tables, only a third of which were occupied. She'd wanted to try the lattice out in a crowd, but felt like this was a good compromise. Even with the empty tables, there had to be fifty people in the near vicinity.

"Will you start right away?"

"No," Juliet subvocalized. "I want to order first so he doesn't come and interrupt me right away. Can you show me the menu?" A window appeared in her AUI, and Juliet flicked through it. Something about her vacation mentality made her want to order a burger and fries. Of course, the restaurant didn't serve anything quite that simple; nevertheless, she found something that looked close, and when the waiter returned with her beer, she smiled up at him and asked, "Are the crater sliders any good?"

"Very good! You'll receive a platter of four sliders, all with different proteins and house-made sauces. The buns are baked in-house, and they're all delicious. My favorite's the shellfish slider." He cleared his throat, raised an eyebrow, and added, "You know it's not real shellfish, right? It tastes just like buttery lobsters, though."

"And one of them is beef?"

"That's right! Vat-grown on Luna, prime grade."

"Okay, let's give that a try."

"And your sides? You can pick two."

"Um"—Juliet glanced at the window on her AUI, where Angel had helpfully highlighted the selection of side dishes—"let's go with the sweet potato fries and tangy coleslaw."

"Great! I'll have it out in just a few minutes."

After he moved off to speak to another customer, Juliet lifted her frosty pint of beer, took a long drink, and set it down. It was good: crisp, cold, and just the right amount of bitterness from the hops. "Ready?"

"Yes, I'll be watching your temperatures very closely."

Juliet took one last look out the window, eyeing the massive, luminous planet, and then closed her eyes and leaned back. For the first time since getting the lattice, she let herself fully relax in a crowded space, tried to let her consciousness expand, and willed herself simply to be open. Almost immediately, she began to hear voices. They spoke over each other, giving her the impression of half-spoken sentences or, she revised the analogy, of rushing around a room, catching snippets of conversations.

That's what she thinks . . .

. . . then I can talk to Rita. We can make our plans and . . .

Not one more time. I won't come to his rescue! I'm tired of him blowing all his spending cash on the first day!

Wow! Such a juicy cut!

Just be cool; he smiled at you. Wait 'til you're done, then offer to buy him a drink . . .

"Your lattice is showing a lot of activity; intracranial temperatures are rising. Activating the cooling system." Angel's voice was clinical, but the calm, complete thought helped Juliet to refocus, and this time, as the voices continued to wash over her, she determined to try to focus on a single one.

One, two, three, four olives . . . Will he just drone on and on? Is he going to eat . . .

God, just a few minutes alone with her. Is that too much to ask?

Not bad. 25k and a ticket off this boat at Io Station—just gotta knock off an old lady.

Juliet furiously tried to focus on the voice, trying to hold back the deluge of other thoughts. She celebrated momentarily as the definitively feminine, sultry voice continued. *What would Kirby say now? Who's holding whom back?* Suddenly, Juliet saw an image: a pale hand with painted blue nails holding a slender metal rod. The hand depressed the tiny button on the side of the rod, and a ten-centimeter, needle-tipped pick sprang forth. The thumb touched the button, and the pick retracted into the rod—snick-snack.

Juliet felt a strange pressure in her head, though it wasn't painful. Angel hadn't spoken up with any alarm, so she tried to ignore it, tried to refocus on the woman's voice, but other images and words began to flood her mind. She saw many hands doing things. Was that how people pictured their actions?

A man's hairy-knuckled fingers grabbing a pair of pale breasts. A woman's arms and hands turning on a bathtub and throwing balls of scented salts into the water. Another man throwing a pair of dice on a felt-covered table. She tried to focus on one of the images, but they were fleeting. Were they memories? Plans?

Good lord, lady, what happened to you? Is something wrong with the beer? She seemed so sweet and pleasant, but now her skin's positively green! Juliet recognized Len's voice. Ugh, I hate this part . . . "Ahem, everything all right, miss?"

Juliet snapped her eyes open and saw that Len was standing at the edge of the table, slightly leaning forward, and she had the absurd realization that his top two buttons were undone, and he had a well-manicured, hairy chest. She cleared her throat and said, "Oh, man! I just about dozed off. Lunch already here?" She reached back and kneaded her neck, offering a sheepish grin.

"It's coming! I just wanted to see how the beer was. You had me worried for a sec there; I was afraid you were feeling ill. Some people notice the vibrations in these big ships and get a kind of motion sickness."

"I feel fine. Thank you, though. Beer's good." To demonstrate, Juliet lifted the glass and drained half of it. "Bring me another with my food, will you?"

"You got it!" He winked at her, grinning straight white teeth, and sauntered back toward the bar where he seemed to have an ongoing conversation with the lonely bartender. Not a single person was seated in her area.

"Your lattice was exceptionally active, more so than when you passed out in the GARD testing room. I'd say my cooling design is passing the assessment with flying colors!" Angel spoke as soon as Juliet was alone again.

"I feel okay. My head doesn't hurt, but I have a kind of weird pressure behind my eyes . . ."

"I was going to say there's some buildup of electrical activity along the lattice. It seems to be clinging to the biosilver nodules that are woven in this complex pattern near your frontal lobe." Angel displayed an image of a brain—hers, Juliet figured—and highlighted some weird cloverlike shapes the biosilver had made near the front of her brain.

"Is it?" Juliet frowned, studying the complicated pattern the nanites that had constructed the lattice had made in her brain, wondering how it could be possible that it wasn't doing her any harm.

"Is it . . . ?"

"Electricity. Sorry, I didn't complete my thought. Are we sure this 'activity' on the lattice is electrical?"

"There's definitely an electrical component to it. I can measure the charge and see the effect it has on your tissue; it's what raises the temperature in your brain. Nonetheless, there could be more to it. We're dealing with something utterly undocumented other than in the files we stole from GARD. They were just starting to understand the various phenomena that occurred with the construction of the psionic lattices."

Juliet took another drink of her beer and stewed on Angel's words. She tried to think of a better way to describe the feeling behind her eyes, but then another thought struck her. "Why isn't it going away?"

"I didn't want to alarm you, but I was wondering the same thing. You're no longer using the lattice, correct?"

"Not intentionally! I'm not picking up any thoughts, if that's what you mean." Juliet rubbed her forehead with the meat of her palm. "It's like a pressure. Almost like . . . You know, it feels like when you need to sneeze, like I need to let it out."

"I can't relate, but I think I understand your meaning. Perhaps it's a buildup of psionic energy? We never did come to an understanding of how Kyle was able to hurt you and Polk. Do you think you can manipulate this energy? Can you feel it other than as a pressure? Is there a—"

"Chill, Angel. Let me think for a second."

Juliet contemplated Angel's words about Kyle and how he'd been able to . . . do something to her and Polk. It had felt like a concussion, like a wave of something had hit her. Had he been able to manipulate the buildup of energy in the lattice? Was his lattice shaped differently than hers? That was something they'd found in the GARD papers—the nanites found "connection points" in a person's brain and designed the lattice around and between them. It was a complicated process, and the nanites, while short-lived and single purpose, had been some of the most sophisticated Angel had ever seen. Unfortunately, their design wasn't in the documents they'd stolen.

Juliet shook her head and tried to refocus, thinking about the weird, painless pressure. Why wasn't there any pain? Was Angel still running the cooler? "Is the cooler still active?"

"Not in the last couple of minutes. Your intracranial temperature has stabilized."

"But the . . . energy is still there? In the lattice? I can still feel the pressure."

"Yes."

Juliet pressed her fingertips against her forehead, trying to use the external stimulus to pin down the feeling inside her skull better. "If only I could—"

"Here you go, miss," Len announced, walking up to the table with a serving tray. Juliet tried not to scowl as she looked at him and he smiled, setting her rectangular plate of sliders, bookended by her two side dishes, in front of her. He placed another IPA next to her nearly empty one. "Anything else?"

"Not right now. Thanks." Juliet forced a smile and watched him depart, then she pushed her plate back, her earlier hunger forgotten, and pressed her fingers to her head again. She could feel it there, like a ball of something, wanting to move, to get out. She'd compared it to an unreleased sneeze earlier, but that wasn't right. It didn't tickle or itch; it didn't feel urgent. It was more like a freshly held breath of air. She knew it was in there, but not what it was doing.

How did she breathe it out?

Juliet snapped her eyes open, looked at her table, and focused on the nearly empty glass of beer. She stared at it, and then, with a focus she'd never applied to breathing before, she exhaled very slowly, willing the ball of energy in her head to go with her breath, to follow the line of her sight and touch that pint glass. She almost screamed when the glass slid several centimeters over the tabletop and then tipped, spilling its contents over the smooth, polished faux-wood surface.

"Holy sh—" She trailed off, looking around, wondering if anyone had been watching her.

"Did . . . Did you just do that?" Angel asked. "The electrical buildup in the lattice is greatly diminished."

"I did! I did that!" Juliet whispered, too wound up to subvocalize. She didn't see any eyes on her, so she picked up the glass and tried to mop up the spilled beer with her linen napkin. It didn't absorb very well, but she pushed all the liquid into a puddle and pressed the bunched-up napkin into it. Then she turned to her plate, her hunger suddenly back with a vengeance.

"This is a big deal, Juliet."

"I know! By the way, I picked up some creepy thoughts when I was . . . surfing." She ate several fries between subvocalizations, savoring the crispy, salty sweet potatoes.

"Do you think you'll be able to do what Kyle did?" Angel was like a dog with a bone.

"Maybe. Maybe. I don't know, but I am a hundred percent sure that I want to keep practicing. I was never this excited about the lattice before. I feel like a creep listening to peoples' thoughts, but, if I can move things? If I can . . . Angel, there are so many things I can imagine now! It's thanks to you, you know? Your cooling device is a game changer. I never felt any discomfort!"

"We still need to closely monitor your tissue, especially where it's bonded to the biosilver. Just because you aren't suffering debilitating headaches or passing out from overheating doesn't mean you aren't damaging the microcellular structures. I'm going to program your new medical nanites to do an exhaustive survey around the lattice."

"Sounds like a plan." She picked up the first slider and bit it in half, savoring the rich, creamy sauce. She couldn't tell what kind of protein the "burger" was made of, but it was good. She polished it off, then chased it with a big swig of her second beer. Len approached the table as she was swallowing and reaching for the soaking wet napkin to dab her fingers clean.

"A little accident?"

"Sorry, Len." Juliet couldn't hide her good mood. She could feel the flush in her cheeks, the smile on her lips as she licked a glob of sauce from the side of her thumb.

"You're looking a lot better! I thought you were about to get sick on me, if I'm honest. I had the cleaning crew on standby!"

"Nah, I'm good." She watched as he wiped up her spill with a white dish towel. He pulled a fresh napkin from his apron and handed it to her. "Another beer?"

"You know, I think I will have another one." After wiping her mouth, she draped the napkin on her lap. When she looked up, Len was gone, moseying back to the bar. Juliet looked around the dining room, trying to guess which woman had been musing about murdering someone for twenty-five thousand bits.

"Something you're looking for?" Angel asked.

"Yeah. I was just about to tell you. As I said, there were some really creepy thoughts out there, and one of them was a woman thinking about killing an old woman for money. I saw her either remembering or fantasizing about the weapon she was going to use. She had pale hands and blue nails. You see anyone like that?" Juliet continued to scan the dining room, trying to get a view of everyone's hands.

"I'm not seeing any yet . . ." Angel trailed off while Juliet went back to her meal, taking a bite of another slider. This one tasted like barbecued beef, and she groaned with pleasure as she chewed. "Are you going to try to stop her?"

"I don't know. It probably wouldn't be smart, but, well, you know me. I have a hard time seeing people suffer, especially if they don't deserve it. I might like to look into her a little to see if she's a real baddie or at least maybe try to figure out who her mark is."

"In that case, I think I saw her."

"What?" Juliet jerked her gaze back to the dining room. "Were you going to tell me?"

"Of course! I just wanted to know what kind of outburst to expect if you knew who she was."

Suddenly, Juliet's AUI flickered as a yellow outline surrounded the bartender Len had been talking with throughout her meal. Sure enough, she was leaning forward, her hands under her chin, with her long, pale fingers twisting her silky black hair around blue fingernails.

"Oh, wow! She works here."

Juliet surreptitiously stared at the bartender. Something like fifteen or twenty meters separated them, but with her optics, she could zoom in to see the pores in the young woman's skin. She was pretty—fit, with clear skin and lovely, natural-looking brown eyes. Her hair was dark, and she wore it in curls that fell to her shoulders. She didn't wear much makeup, but her eyeshadow certainly complemented her nails. Juliet searched for a gut feeling and, coming up empty, stared harder into those eyes, reaching out for the woman's thoughts.

What is that bitch staring at?

7

A SWIM IN SPACE

Juliet quickly looked away. The startling realization that she'd been caught staring broke her concentration, and she lost her connection to the mysterious bartender. "She caught me staring," she subvocalized, taking a slow, steadying breath to calm herself; she could feel her cheeks flushing with embarrassment.

"Don't worry. No one can suspect you're reading their thoughts. Not unless developmental research in psionics is much more common than we're led to believe."

"Yeah, somehow I doubt it."

Juliet went back to work on her meal, washing down the salty, fatty food with her beer. She'd just finished the pint when Len walked over with another frosty glass. "Oof, I forgot I ordered another." Juliet grinned at the waiter, feeling a little stupid, her nose numb and a definite buzz brightening her smile.

"Do you still want it?"

"Sure. I'm on vacation, aren't I?"

"Care for dessert, then?" He grinned and winked, a coconspirator in her naughty dietary behavior.

"I . . ." Juliet had been about to say she didn't think she should, but she felt like celebrating. Things had gone much better with the lattice than she'd hoped. "Sure. I feel like something simple but delicious. Any suggestions?"

"The pastry chef has a double chocolate cake that'll make you want to cry."

"Double chocolate, huh?" Juliet felt her mouth start to salivate at the idea. "Okay. Let me sip this beer for a little while, then bring me a slice."

"You got it. Hey, do you know Eve?"

"Eve?"

"The bartender. She thought you were looking at her like you knew her."

"Oh!" Juliet held a hand over her eyes, visibly cringing with her shoulders. "This is embarrassing. I was looking around the restaurant, and my PAI pointed her nails out to me, so I zoomed in and stared for a minute. I've been trying to think of something to do with mine"—Juliet wriggled her plain, unpolished nails—"and told my PAI to be on the lookout for ideas."

"Hah! The benefits and curses of high-end optics, eh?" Len winked at her, then turned away. "I'll let her know she can relax; she was trying to remember where you two had met."

"Thanks." Juliet leaned back into the booth's cushions, bringing her cold beer to her lips for a sip. She was glad her lie had come out so smoothly, but she was also bothered by it. Was she becoming a liar?

"That was well done." Angel's encouragement didn't make her feel better.

"Yeah, I guess it's starting to come with the territory." With a heavy sigh and a shrug, she let the dour thought fade away and stared out the window, trying to focus on and enjoy the positives from the day. "It's annoying," she subvocalized after a few minutes.

"What's that?"

"I can't stop thinking about that bartender's thoughts, about her saying she just had to 'knock off an old lady.' I mean, if she'd been thinking about killing some creepy crooked politician or corpo exec, I might be able to forget about it."

"Well, just because she characterized her target as an old lady doesn't mean the 'old lady' is innocent. She could be a 'crooked' politician, an executive, a criminal mastermind, or any of a thousand other less-than-innocent types of people. She very well might not be worthy of your interference."

"Yeah, true. I don't know why I keep picturing someone's grandma baking desserts when I think of the words 'old lady.' Huh!" Juliet almost laughed aloud as she and Angel exposed her definitive bias when it came to her visualization of "bad guys." She had a particular type of person she pictured when she imagined villains, and they all looked something like Vikker or Gordon. "Yeah, I guess maybe I'll try to figure out who her target is, but you're right; maybe I'll find that I should just stay out of it."

"Well, we know where she works and that her name is Eve. I'm sure, with a little digging, we'll be able to figure things out, especially with your particular . . . gifts."

"Right. I'll stop thinking about it for now."

Juliet did just that, forcing herself to enjoy the view, the beer, and later, the cake Len brought around to her table. After that, with a pleasant buzz lifting her mood, she returned to her room and, as the ship prepared to depart Earth's gravity well and begin the journey toward Jupiter, she soaked in the tub.

While she floated on her back, looking at video feeds provided by the ship's external cameras, a thought occurred to her. "Does this ship have a gravity generator?"

"In a sense, yes. However, it's different from the full generators on the larger human colonies. This ship has a gravity field generator that captures the thrust forces from the drives and utilizes that energy to power the gravity generation. Even if the drives output more than one G of force, the generator disburses the effect through a modified Byre-Garnet inverter that creates a mass of negative energy which alters the curvature of—"

"Okay, okay. So, is it another true AI thing? Do we know how it works, exactly?"

"It is, indeed, another true AI thing. Humans have the specifications and the know-how to copy the construction, but much of the underlying theory is lost or at least not publicly available. Only three corporations in the solar system are capable of mimicking the design. They may have full understanding and documentation that doesn't go beyond their internal networks."

Juliet let Angel's pleasant tone soothe her already relaxed mind, and soon, she found herself drifting into a doze. It was nice, soaking in the moisturizing bath water, letting her mind drift, not worried about falling asleep and suffering a true-dream. Angel's development of the intracranial cooling device was having a profound effect on her perception of the lattice. She'd always felt like it was something of a knife blade with no handle; if she used it, she was bound to cut herself eventually. More than that, it had hung over her as a sort of nebulous threat. The sudden departure of that lurking danger was a game changer.

The tub cycled the bath water, maintaining its heat, so it was a long while before she climbed out. After she'd dried off and put on a long T-shirt, she crawled into bed and, though determined to watch the view of Earth receding in the overhead screen, she was soon fast asleep. No dreams troubled her—at least none she could remember—and she didn't wake until, according to her AUI, nearly 0800.

"Wow! I haven't slept in that late in months."

"Your sleep seemed very restful!"

"Please tell me you weren't monitoring me all night." Juliet stretched and, with a loud yawn, crawled out of bed.

"Part of me is always aware of you in that regard. Don't worry, though; I was plenty busy fulfilling my own interests throughout the night. I became curious about who the bartender assassin's target might be, so I was studying the ship's net for clues."

"Oh, yeah?" Juliet went into the bathroom and began to brush her teeth.

"Yes. Unfortunately, the passenger manifest isn't publicly accessible, but there are some hubs that are open to wireless connections—some of the restaurants and event queues. I connected, and with a little finessing, I managed to get a few lists of names. I cross-referenced those names with public databases through the sat-net—the ship maintains a connection to Earth, Mars, and Jovian public nets, though with quite a delay."

"Angel," Juliet said through her toothpaste foam, "it's a little early. Can we skip to the punch line?"

"I made a list of 'elderly' female passengers. So far, I have seventy-four names we can check out."

"Ugh." Juliet spat into the sink. "We'll need a different plan. I'm not spending the whole cruise visiting all of the old ladies on this ship. Besides, that term is arbitrary; maybe that bartender is kind of a bitch and considers anyone a few years older than she is to be 'old.' You know what I mean?"

"Oh, yes, I see . . ."

"I'm not saying I don't appreciate your work." Juliet rinsed her mouth, spat, then dug through her traveling toiletry bag for deodorant. "I just think we should focus on the known quantity: the bartender."

"I thought she spooked you off . . ."

"Sure, last night. Next time, I'll be more careful. We'll sit closer, and I'll try to pick up her thoughts again without staring at her."

Juliet went back to her room and got dressed in a plain, red T-shirt and a pair of stretchy, jeanlike shorts that left most of her thighs exposed. Then, she slipped on a pair of rubbery pink slide-on sandals. She'd bought the shorts and sandals specifically for her time on the cruise liner, expecting to spend quite a bit of time by the pool.

She frowned at her needler and its holster lying on the bench beside her pack.

"You'll look a bit odd with that shoulder holster on over your scant clothing."

"Scant?" Juliet turned to look in the mirror next to the bedroom door. The shirt was snug, but it covered her just fine. "I mean, it's appropriate, though, right?"

"If you intend to recreate in the domed area, I would say yes."

Juliet looked again at the shorts; they exposed a lot of leg, but nothing scandalous. She rubbed her palms over her pale, smooth thighs. "At least, thanks to that Grave job, I don't need to shave my legs."

"One of the benefits of having all of your hair permanently destroyed by lasers . . ."

"Are you pulling my chain? You know, you advised me to take that job!"

"Did I? I must admit, I don't think I tried to talk you out of it, but . . ."

"For an AI, you're awfully good at forgetting certain details." Juliet chuckled, then started toward the door. "I'll take my chances unarmed for now. Please guide me to a good breakfast spot and then someplace I can buy a swimsuit."

"There's a highly regarded buffet-style breakfast on the park deck, and several gift and apparel boutiques are nearby."

"Perfect." After a brisk walk toward the front of the ship and down several levels via automated stairways, Juliet enjoyed a wonderfully diverse breakfast featuring everything from cold fruit and plant-based yogurts to smoked fish to "eggs rancheros" and tortillas. She was drawn to so many different foods that she had to exert a conscious effort to limit her selection to a single plateful. When she finished—with a slightly distended belly and vaguely guilty feeling—Angel led her to a boutique specializing in swimsuits.

Juliet bought a simple blue "Sharko" one-piece, pleased by the flexible comfort and quick-drying fabric. The clincher, though, had been the tag that advertised the material as an "antibacterial" weave.

"I know it's gimmicky," she subvocalized as she left the store, meandering toward the open park near the boutiques, "but if I'm going to be in a big public pool, it gives me a little comfort that, well, part of me will be protected."

"I don't want to hurt your feelings, but it is a silly notion. The pool water is treated and tested regularly, and let's be honest, most of your body isn't covered by that suit."

"Yeah, but some of my most important bits are!"

"You're aware that your nanites will counteract any sort of common infection you might acquire from even the dirtiest water—"

"I know it's not rational. Let's drop it, all right? It doesn't even matter, 'cause I like the suit regardless!"

"Fair enough."

There were showers and lockers near the pool, so she changed into her suit, rinsed off, and jumped into the shallow end of the pool. She'd been expecting it to be cold for some reason, so she was pleasantly surprised when it felt almost like she'd plunged into a lukewarm bathtub.

When she was underwater, she learned something very cool about her optics: Angel could adjust her vision to account for the distortion of the water, allowing her to see clearly while submerged. More than that, the water didn't sting or bother her eyes in any way. She didn't know if that was because of the high-quality treatment of the pool or because of her implants, and she was soon far too distracted to worry about asking Angel.

Despite the ship's trajectory toward Jupiter and the lack of nearby celestial objects, the dome was illuminated and warm like a summer day, and the passengers began to crowd the pool area as the morning dragged on. Juliet spent a lot of time swimming around the big shallow area surrounded by decking, getting used to the water and trying to remember the strokes she'd learned as a kid. She liked swimming underwater, finding she could hold her breath for a long time, longer than she remembered being able to when she was young, likely thanks to all the cardio she'd been doing.

After she'd been swimming for an hour or so, Juliet wound up playing with some young twins—a boy and a girl—tossing bright, weighted toys and seeing who could fetch them the fastest. The twins' parents were nowhere to be found, and when Juliet asked about them, the girl, Simone, told her their father had dropped them off on the way to the casino. At one point, she realized she wasn't the only one with optics that could adjust for the underwater distortion. A teenage boy lurking by the pool's edge seemed to be spending an unusual amount of time underwater, facing her way as she played with the kids.

"That boy is perving out on me," she subvocalized.

"It seems he is spending an inordinate amount of time gazing your way."

"Simone," Juliet said, handing her the green weighted ring she'd recovered. "I'm going to go get some exercise. Do you know who that boy is?"

"No." Simone, barely able to stand with her head above water in the four-foot depth, tilted her head sideways and adjusted the foamy purple goggles she'd been wearing.

"Well, why don't you and Huey go play with those other little kids." Juliet pointed to a trio of young, brightly suited children playing in the water near a deckside juice bar. "I think they're playing some kind of tag." Simone looked a little crestfallen, but Juliet pressed on. "Thanks for helping me get used to the water, but I have to go. I'll be here all the way to Jupiter! See you later?"

"Okay." Simone nodded, smiling so her plump cheeks pressed into her foamy goggles. "Come on, Huey!"

Juliet waved goodbye, then ducked underwater and, with big, powerful strokes, plunged toward the pool's far edge. She was swimming toward the dome, and as she grew closer and the water's obscuring effect lessened, she began to note the darkness of space beyond the crystal-clear diamatex.

The dome was probably a hundred meters from the shallow area, so she had to come up for air long before she reached it. When she did, she started to swim over the surface, practicing her crawl, trying to limit her breaths to every fifth stroke. She passed people on floating rafts, including a lifeguard who sat atop a bright red foam chair. He waved at her as she passed, and Juliet gave him a thumbs-up. When she finally got to the deepest part of the pool, right near the edge of the dome, she stopped, tread water, and looked around. Only a few people were out that far, and most were sitting or reclining on inflatable donuts or chairs.

Juliet took a big breath and dove down, swimming deeper and deeper, angling toward the dome. When she stopped, fighting to keep from floating up, she figured she was ten meters underwater, and the blackness of space was right in front of her. It was the strangest feeling, floating there, holding her breath, staring into space. Despite the water around her, she felt like she was swimming through the void.

"It's so weird," she subvocalized.

"It's amazing . . ." Angel sounded awed, which always thrilled Juliet; it reminded her of how much an individual Angel had become, how she wasn't just a program. It made her feel like the world and the universe were full of inexplicable things, and the idea filled her with a sense of hopeful anticipation. As her lungs began to ache for oxygen, Juliet blew her air through her nose and surged upward toward the surface. She was still facing the dome when she came up, so when she breached the surface and took a deep breath, she was surprised to hear a voice behind her.

"Hey," said the smoky, almost sultry voice. Juliet whirled around, wide-eyed. "Oops! Did I startle you?"

"Heh," Juliet said, her relaxed treading taking on a bit of a desperate feeling, like for some reason, having the bartender there was making it harder to keep her head above water. "Thought I was alone out here."

"Sorry about that. I saw you swimming out here and recognized you from last night. I work in the restaurant where you had dinner. I had this weird feeling, like I knew you. Here." She pushed the yellow foam kickboard she was holding toward Juliet. "Hold on to this with me so you can relax."

"What's your name?" Juliet asked, raising an eyebrow as she grabbed on to the kickboard, sighing mentally at the reduced need for treading.

"I'm Eve Harris. Does it ring a bell?"

"No, I'm afraid not. I'm Lucky."

"Oh? How so?" Eve was wearing too much makeup for swimming, Juliet mused as the woman smiled her glossy red lips and arched a perfectly shaped and shadowed brow.

"No, that's my name. I'm an SOA operative."

"Huh! Well, I sure would remember someone like that. I guess you just have one of those faces. No chance I could get your nonoperative name?"

"No, sorry. I never use it." Juliet reached up and pulled some damp strands of hair from her face. "So, you work on the ship?"

"That's right!" Eve shifted closer to the kickboard; it was only about half a meter long, so when she did so, her face came very close to Juliet's. "I'm a bartender. It's a pretty great job. I get to enjoy the ship during the morning 'cause my shift doesn't usually start until lunchtime."

"That's cool." Juliet forced a smile, staring at Eve's coffee-colored eyes, noting the deep bands of greenish hues exposed by the bright overhead lighting.

SOA! Oh, fuck! SOA! Did Kirby hire this chick? Am I burned?

"Taking the whole cruise?" After hearing her thoughts, Juliet could pick out the strain at the corners of Eve's eyes, could see the involuntary crease that kept appearing and fading between them. This woman was worried about something and was struggling to keep a calm demeanor.

"No, not me. I broke the bank to take the first leg to Io Station. I have a gig waiting for me there."

"Oh, so not working now?"

"No, no." Juliet smiled and tried to open her mind again.

Maybe it's all a coincidence. Maybe I'm cool. Do I bail on the job? Zapho, though, Zapho . . .

"Sorry to interrupt your swim, but I was burning with curiosity, and I like swimming out here too. If you come by the restaurant tonight, sit in my section. I'll give you a discount on your drinks!"

Juliet smiled, but taking a cue from some less verbose people—Shiro—she'd met, she didn't respond immediately.

If I don't do the job, I'm dead meat. If I do it and this chick is watching me, I'm dead meat. Oh, please, don't be working for Kirby. Please don't be working for Zapho! What if he hired more than me? What if I'm . . . Why isn't she answering me? Did I say something stupid?

"Are you good, Eve?" Juliet reached over the top of the foamy board and grasped the other woman's damp, cold, blue-painted fingers. "You seem like you're really stressed out. Is there something I can help you with?"

"I . . ." Eve pulled her fingers loose then let go of the board. "I just remembered I have to get my uniforms from the cleaner! Sorry, Lucky! Keep the board." With that, she launched herself backward, performing a near-perfect backstroke as she motored out of the deep part of the pool.

"That was bold of you . . ."

"I was hearing her thoughts! It seemed so much easier than usual; I hardly had to concentrate."

"What did you hear?"

"Some more names. One of them was kinda unique. See what you can dig up about anyone named Zapho. We'll have dinner at the Stargazer Lounge tonight."

8

HELPING OUT

When Juliet sat down in the bar of the Stargazer Lounge that evening, she was dressed in something that sort of resembled one of the suits she'd bought when she'd prepared for the job at Grave. After she'd finished her swim around lunchtime, she'd done a little shopping in the boutiques, spending—if you asked her—a few hundred too many bits. She'd wanted to buy something really nice, like a slinky, shimmering dress that exposed her back, but then she'd thought about what kind of shoes she'd have to wear with it, then wondered what it would be like if she had to run in an outfit like that or, worse, fight in it.

After some shopping around and a consultation with a salesperson or two, she'd settled for some slender, silky turquoise slacks and a satiny cream-colored blouse. The sales lady had convinced her to buy some ridiculously overpriced, genuine leather Karmin Kiss "kitten heels." As the name implied, the heel was small, and the woman insisted they were comfortable and practical while also "oozing style." Juliet had never been a fancy shoe person, so the terminology was all new to her, but she had to admit she enjoyed how light and comfortable they felt when she wore them.

She felt pretty, elegant, and confident as she sat in the softly illuminated booth, watching Eve serve drinks to a few customers sitting up at the bar. The restaurant was busier than the day before when she'd had lunch; nearly every table was occupied, and many waitstaff were working as opposed to just Len. Still, it looked like Eve was in charge of the bar area, and when she saw Juliet and they made eye contact, she smiled briefly before looking away.

"Are you going to . . . ?"

"Yes." Juliet opened her mind, trying to be a little less open than the last time, trying to limit the voices to the ones nearby. She didn't know how to do that; it was more an intention than a deliberate action. She didn't have a "psionic muscle" that she knew of, so she didn't know how to flex it a lot or a little. Still, as she began to receive thoughts and voices, and they began to clamor and create a din in her mind, she tried to pull back, to push away the majority of them, and to focus on the one she was looking for. It was almost as startling as when she'd knocked the beer glass over when it worked.

Why am I such an idiot? Why did I approach her in the pool? Why did I tell her to come to the bar? Oh God! I'm totally burned. Do I fake sick? Do I bail? Should I get Tony to fill my shift? I need to . . . Shit! Mustache is staring again . . . Did I forget his order?

Juliet exhaled slowly, trying to push away the thoughts crowding for attention again, and looked around, distracting her mind by subvocalizing, "Man, Angel, she is stressed out. She thinks she blew it by approaching me in the pool. I wonder if I can get her to be honest with me if I bluff a little . . ." She trailed off as Eve walked around the bar and approached her booth.

"Hey." Juliet offered a short, shy wave. "I took you up on the invitation. Nothing else to do, you know? Kinda pathetic, I guess, coming on a cruise all alone like this."

Eve looked at her with narrowed eyes for a second, then shrugged. "I've never been on a cruise unless I was working, so you've got me beat."

"Pretty cool job, though. I bet you've seen a lot of sights most people can't afford to take in. Don't suppose you can sit down for a minute?"

"Sorry." Eve bit her lower lip and looked around the bar. "I'm the only one in here right now. I'm working 'til eleven, too. I can sure get you a drink, though—on the house. A welcome to the ship kinda thing."

"Well," Juliet paused, contemplating an idea that felt a little too bold but also like it might work. She decided to go for it; what did she really have to lose? This wasn't an official job or anything. "I appreciate that. Maybe you could choose for me? I'm always ordering a beer; I don't really know much about mixed drinks. Can you pick something good for me? Nothing too sweet?"

Eve's smile looked more natural this time, and she nodded. "I'll come up with something good. Be right back." She turned, and Juliet watched her walk. She was graceful, but not in the way Honey was—she didn't look like a fighter.

"More like a dancer," she mused softly, and then, unbidden, began to hear Eve's thoughts again:

Not too sweet? Was that a double entendre? Really? She wants me to surprise her? Talk about cheesy. At least I don't get any Zapho vibes. She's not here to check up on me . . . or worse. No way . . . Is she? Chasing those thoughts, a foggy image shimmered through Juliet's mind. It was clearly a man's face, twisted in anger, shouting. Ginger stubble dotted his ruddy chin and cheeks, and his lips were like writhing, spittle-flecked red worms as he yelled. No sound accompanied the image, which Juliet had to assume was some kind of memory of Eve's.

Was that Zapho?

Juliet shook her head, trying to banish the image and the bartender's less-than-flattering thoughts. "I guess it was kinda dumb. I'm not a kid . . ."

"What's that?"

"Sorry, Angel. I keep forgetting you don't see or hear the things I pick up. She was kinda roasting me for asking her to pick me a drink."

"Oh, I see. I thought it was fine; you weren't being creepy or anything. She strikes me as a rather on-edge person."

"Yeah, she definitely is, and I also think she's in way over her head. Yesterday, I saw her imagining using some kind of pick, but if she's planning to kill with it, she's . . . I think she's going to get herself killed or captured. I wonder what this guy has on her? I heard her thinking about getting off the ship on Io. Do you think she's running from someone? The other guy, um, Kirby, maybe?" While Angel processed her flurry of questions and thoughts, Juliet watched Eve mixing a drink and immediately began to hear her thoughts again:

A little rum, some orange zest. Here we go. Hmm. It's sort of sweet, though, but not too sweet. She didn't say nothing sweet at all, right? Oh, nuke it! Why do I care?

Juliet had to fight back a smile as she heard that inner dialogue; Eve certainly had an edge, but she was at least trying to do what Juliet asked. She began to feel a bit dirty listening to her thoughts so much, so she struggled to dial it back, distracting herself with another question for Angel. "How's the lattice?"

"Some heat, which I'm treating with the cooling implant, but nothing close to what you accumulated yesterday."

"And the nanites? I forgot to ask if they found anything amiss. I take your lack of a report as a good sign, though."

"You don't remember?"

"Remember?"

"Oh, Juliet!" Angel's voice rose with concern. "I knew this would happen, but not this fast!"

"What are you talking about?" Juliet hissed the words, her frustration making subvocalization an impossibility.

"The biosilver—it's damaging your short-term memory. I'm afraid it's only a matter of time before you won't be able to construct any new memories at all!"

Juliet frowned, drummed her fingers on the table, then said, "You think you're funny, huh? What is it with you always trying to prank me? You know that wouldn't be funny, right?"

"I wouldn't joke if your lovely gray matter hadn't been perfectly healthy in the examination I ran while you slept."

Juliet sighed and rubbed the back of her neck. "When did you decide to play this prank? Long before I asked, huh? That's why you didn't make a report! You were waiting for me to ask!"

"Here we go, hon. It's called a rum fashioned—kind of a play on the old-fashioned. It has a little sugar in it, but you can definitely still taste the rum." Eve set a tumbler down in front of Juliet. It held one huge ice cube, a couple of fingers of dark liquid, and a dehydrated orange slice garnish.

Juliet lifted the glass, savored the orange scent mixed with the heady alcohol, and then, following a gut instinct, said, "Thanks, Eve. Hey, I think we need to talk. It's about Zapho." She looked up at Eve's face, trying to gauge the effect of her words, and it wasn't hard—the woman had gone white, and her mouth opened and closed twice before she formulated a response.

"When?"

"When you get done with work. You can come to my room."

"Am . . . Am I in trouble?" Eve's voice had gotten very small, very quiet, and Juliet could see her hands were trembling. She wanted to comfort her, but she reminded herself that she didn't really know her yet, other than that she might be in trouble with some bad people and that she'd agreed to kill someone.

"You might be. Not from me, mind you. I want to help you. I need you to trust that, Eve, and don't do something stupid." Juliet sipped the drink and found the orange scent complemented the smooth, slightly sweet but strong, heady rum nicely. "Oh, that's good. Thank you."

"Is—" Eve licked her lips, and Juliet admired how well her lipstick held up to the treatment. "Is there anything else?"

"Can you order me a steak here? I mean, you have full service in the bar, right? I'll take a steak with, uh"—Juliet gazed at the menu in her AUI for a second—"mixed seasonal vegetables with the truffle oil."

"You want real steak or the plant based?"

"Well . . . it seems a bit extravagant, but I'm on vacation. Let's go for the real deal, okay?" Juliet slapped the table and smiled broadly.

"Okay. I, um, have to get back to the bar." Eve turned stiffly, and Juliet knew if she reached out to hear her thoughts, they'd be racing. She'd be contemplating running, realizing there was nowhere to go; they were in space, after all. Then she'd probably be trying to think of a way to lie or hide or something worse . . .

"Eve." Juliet paused until she turned around to face her. "I'm not lying. I really want to help. Don't do anything crazy, okay?" As Juliet stared into her eyes, she thought she saw something defrost or snap, and the other woman nodded. "I'll have my PAI send you my room info."

Eve nodded and turned, and Juliet felt a little bad for how she'd ambushed her with Zapho's name. "Do you think I was too blunt?"

"I think your abrupt revelation forced a real emotional response from her. Her cool facade crumbled. I imagine her thoughts are even more tumultuous."

"Maybe." Juliet sipped her drink, enjoying how the hard liquor gave her a sort of glowing warm spot in her belly. "I'm not listening right now. I feel like I heard enough—saw enough—when I dropped the bomb. I'm not worried about her trying to kill me or anything; she's scrambling, scared, not murderous or scheming. I'll make sure when she comes to see me, though."

That said, Juliet tried to enjoy her meal, though it wasn't really easy. Eve looked like a scared little girl every time she came over to the table, and Juliet had to struggle not to hear the thoughts that were practically screaming out of the bartender's head.

As she ate her steak—not nearly as good as she'd imagined after hearing Hot Mustard and some of the guys in Charlie Unit go on about it—she had to keep her eyes down and not think about Eve, or panicked feelings and thoughts kept seeping into her head.

"I didn't bank on this . . ." she subvocalized between bites.

"The meat being so chewy?"

"No. I seem to be getting more sensitive. Remember I told you her thoughts came easily to me in the pool? Well, they're, like, clamoring to get into my head now. I think her stress is making them louder."

"The lattice is requiring more cooling than earlier, but nothing close to worrisome."

"Yeah . . ." Juliet trailed off, noting a new development at the bar. A tall, thin man with a shaved head had come in. He wore the same uniform as Eve, and as she enhanced the gain on her ears, Juliet heard Eve thanking him.

". . . owe you one. I didn't know my friend was going to be on this cruise, and I haven't seen her in years."

"No worries, Eve. I got this—best tips are after nine, anyway." Eve leaned forward and kissed his cheek, and he laughed. "Go on, now! Have fun." He glanced at Juliet and smiled, waving.

"Interesting." Juliet watched as Eve took off her apron and stuffed it under the bar top, then walked around and sat across from her.

"Hey. I was hoping we could talk now because I'm crawling out of my skin worrying about what's going on."

"You weren't quite ready for this development, were you?" Angel's voice had a teasing note, and Juliet didn't like it. When had she started to take so much pleasure in her discomfort? Was she reacting to something Juliet had said? Was she enjoying this little reality check because Juliet had been a bit too clever with Eve?

"Be nice to me, please." Her subvocalization was quick and would hopefully give Angel something to think about. Aloud, she said, "Eve, tell me what Zapho wanted you to do. I mean, let's start with the target, the old lady."

Eve's eyes bugged out, and she leaned forward. "Shh! Dang, Lucky! Who knows who's listening in here."

"Right, that's why I wanted you to come to my room." Juliet frowned, then pushed her plate away. She'd eaten most of the meat, but it had to have been frozen for a very long time. Despite its pink center, it was tough, chewy, and severely lacking in flavor.

"Well, can we go now?"

Please! Just say yes! Let's get this over with! I'm melted! Oh God, if Zapho sent her, that means . . .

"Yeah, come on, let's go." Juliet stood up and led the way out of the restaurant.

"Thank you. Thank you, thank you!" Eve kept repeating herself as they made their way out and up some moving stairs to a long gallery leading to the first passenger cabin levels.

"It's all right." Juliet slowed so Eve was forced to walk beside her or risk very strangely slowing down to stay behind her. As she came up on her left, Juliet eyed her. "You need to relax. I'm not here to . . . do anything to you."

"Really?" Despite her flat-soled work shoes, Eve was tall, looking Juliet right in the eyes. "I'm just losing it here! I can't stop sweating, and I feel like my heart's gonna beat out of my chest."

"That's how I feel when I'm going to an interview." Juliet winked and led the way up another escalator. She looked left and right, noted the light traffic, and said, "I suppose I'm missing some good shows or something, huh? After we're done talking business, maybe you can suggest something to me for tomorrow."

"Um, sure. I've seen quite a few . . ." She trailed off. Juliet could still feel the stress and panic radiating off her. She could almost hear her thoughts without trying in the slightest.

She made a conscious effort to force her mind to contemplate other things. She thought about Bennet, and wondered what he might be doing at that moment. Had he gotten good news about the barrel refabrication? She made a mental note to call him in the morning. She thought about Shiro and Alice, and wondered why they hadn't gotten back to her after that adorable goodbye message she'd sent.

"Those jerks!" she hissed as the thought struck her.

"Huh?" Eve visibly recoiled.

Juliet gestured down the hallway to the left, lined with closed cabin doors. "This way. I was just thinking about some friends who never replied to a message I sent them. I suppose some delay is expected, but I should have heard from them by now!"

"Oh. Um, yes, that can be frustrating."

Juliet eyed Eve as the woman looked at the room numbers, reading each one as if they were a countdown to her demise. "Relax. We're just going to talk, okay?"

"Right, okay." Eve nodded, setting her red-painted lips into a firm line. When they came to her room, Eve pointed. "This one, right?"

"Yep. I'll set up a jamming field inside just to be extra safe. No one's going to hear anything."

"That's great. Thank you, Lucky."

Juliet touched her hand to the security panel, and when the door hissed open, she led the way through. Eve was right behind her, and Juliet heard the door hiss shut. She was still paranoid these days, so she turned her head a bit sideways, wanting to keep the other woman in her peripheral vision—she hated having anyone behind her, let alone sketchy would-be assassins. That was probably why she didn't notice the other individual lurking in the shadows of the doorway to her bedroom. It was probably why the scratchy male voice almost made her jump out of her skin.

"Well, well. You weren't lying, Eve—she's a regular meltdown! Sit down on the sofa there, pretty lady."

9

\\\\\\\\\\\\\\\\\\\\\\\

A SOUVENIR

A year ago, Juliet would probably have freaked out at the surprise of having someone waiting in her room. Fortunately—or unfortunately, depending on who you were—Juliet remained quite calm as she turned to her right and regarded the man aiming a short, wide-barreled pistol at her face.

"Let's see," she said, "Kirby?"

"What the fuck?" Kirby's pink-toned face darkened under his ginger stubble, and he jerked his gaze to Juliet's right, where Eve still lingered near the door. "You told her about me?"

"No! I swear!" Eve sounded genuinely panicked, and Juliet couldn't blame her. She was in way over her head, and rather than trust Juliet, a stranger, to help, she'd turned to someone she clearly didn't like. Maybe it was the fact that Kirby was a known quantity, despite her dislike of him, or maybe she'd believed Juliet was there to kill her and she'd decided to rely on an old acquaintance to bail her out, regardless of the baggage.

Whatever Eve's reasoning, Juliet was furious at herself for not listening to the woman's thoughts more, for walking into a stupid trap where, if she wasn't mistaken, some kind of violence was about to go down.

"Yeah? Well, someone did, idiot!" Kirby dug into his too-tight blue ship uniform trousers, jamming his thick fingers into his front pocket and pulling out a shrink-tie. As he did so, Juliet took a step toward him, closing the gap between them to just a bit more than a meter. "Hold still, sweetheart." He jerked his arm, thrusting his thick fist and pistol toward her face. His finger sat on the trigger, and the idea that he'd accidentally pull it sent a shiver down Juliet's spine.

She ran a hand over her insubstantial satiny blouse. "How about you aim that somewhere other than my face? I'm not even armed." She tried to sound calm, but her frustration with herself for letting yet another person put her in a compromised position was starting to get to her, adding a bit of an edge to her voice.

"Your room's AI has been disabled, and I'm unable to access the ship net." Despite the situation, Angel sounded very cool and collected, and Juliet had the strange sensation of analyzing her PAI while watching Kirby fumble around with the shrink-tie.

Was Angel trying to project calmness so Juliet would also be calm? Was she relaxed because she had faith in Juliet's ability to handle this situation? Juliet's scowl deepened—if so, it was probably misplaced; someone competent wouldn't have gotten herself into a mess like this.

"Ah, melt it!" Kirby growled, giving up trying to operate the shrink-tie one-handed. "Get over here, Eve." He thrust the fat little gun toward Juliet again, taking a step her way. "Hold your hands up with your wrists together." Juliet started to comply, and as she held out her wrists, she gauged the distance between her right hand and his gun—something less than half a meter.

She trusted Angel to know what she wanted, but she still subvocalized, "Now!" At the same time, she took a step toward him, and as the world seemed to slow down around her, almost like Kirby was stuck in molasses-thick air, she snatched his wrist in a vise grip, squeezing with every ounce of strength in her mechanized muscle fibers and tendons.

To anyone whose senses operated at a normal speed, her arm would have looked like a striking cobra. Faster, even. In Juliet's vision, enhanced by Angel's hot-wired synapses, it moved at a normal speed, but everything else was frozen in place. Kirby's reflexes had just started to kick in by the time her cable-strong fingers wrapped around his wrist. Before he reflexively jerked against her iron grip, his face went from pink to red, and his eyes bulged out in startled pain. Juliet could feel the bones in his wrist grinding together.

In her perception, the world began to move normally again, and his hand spasmodically opened. The gun fell to the floor, and Juliet kicked it to the side, sending it sliding under a sofa. She was still squeezing, staring into Kirby's eyes, watching his brain attempt to form a response, when Eve jumped onto her back, wrapping an arm around her neck.

"Let him go!" she screamed, her breath hot on Juliet's neck and ear. Juliet had no such intention—she reached up with her left hand, grabbed a fistful of Eve's hair, and still squeezing Kirby's broken wrist, ducked forward and pulled, flinging Eve, with a shriek, over her shoulder. The would-be assassin crashed to the carpeted deck, but her long legs slammed against the wall, sending a painting of a flower-filled vase careening to the side.

Kirby had found his voice, wailing, "Oh jeez! Oh God! My wrist! Oh, dammit, lady, let go! Let go!"

Juliet stood straight, jerked on Kirby's arm, and backed up a few steps, pulling him after her until he stumbled onto his face. "Be glad I'm not breaking more of your bones, creep. You know how damn rude it is to put a gun in someone's face like that?"

She jerked his arm, walking around behind him as he yelped and howled, begging her to let go. Juliet had seen more shrink cords sticking out of his tight pocket, and when she was behind him, she knelt onto his lower back, still gripping his wrist, and fished one out with her other hand.

While she worked, she kept glancing at Eve, watching to see if she'd get up. Juliet had just started to secure the shrink cord around Kirby's floppy, broken wrist when Eve rolled over and began scrabbling for the couch where Juliet had kicked the gun.

"Don't do it, Eve!" Juliet grabbed Kirby's other wrist, jerking his arm around behind him, then looped the cord over it, pressing the activation tab. As the chemicals at the center of the polymer band broke free of their housing, it rapidly constricted, and Kirby screamed yet again. Juliet leaped up and stomped over to Eve, whose head was now under the sofa, grunting and straining, trying to reach the pistol.

Juliet grabbed her ankle and hauled her back, dragging her over the plush carpeting away from the couch. She was feeling pretty good about how she'd handled things. Kirby was face down, whimpering in pain, hands bound behind his back, and now she had the troubled bartender in hand . . .

Bang! Juliet's self-congratulatory thought process was interrupted as Eve flopped to her side and fired Kirby's pistol at her face. Juliet could only thank luck or God or whatever guardian angel was watching over her that Eve wasn't a good shot. She jerked heavily on the trigger, and though Juliet heard the bullet rip through the air near her head, it missed completely.

Fury and adrenaline sent her heart hammering, and she leaped forward, snatching Eve's wrist and smashing it to the ground while she straddled the woman, pinning her other arm beneath a knee.

"You bitch! You would kill me? For what? For wasting my free time trying to help you?" She punctuated her words by repeatedly smashing Eve's hand against the carpet until the gun bounced free.

"I . . . I . . ." Tears began to flow down Eve's cheeks as she stammered, but Juliet had had enough of the woman, her hysteria, and her utter lack of any moral character.

She stood up, jerked on Eve's arm, and said, "Shut up and roll over, or I'll crush your wrist like your boyfriend's." Eve, sobbing, complied. Juliet stood, and still holding her in place with one small-heeled shoe, bent over to pick up the pistol. It was a snub nose revolver, the cylinder bored to hold five fat bullets. She'd just stuffed it into her silky pants when someone pounded on her door. A second later, it beeped, and three cruise company corpo-sec officers burst into the room.

"Drop your weapon and raise your hands!" the lead officer demanded through his visor, his voice amplified by the software in his helmet. He clutched a sleek black rifle with a snub barrel lined with magnet clusters. Juliet didn't want to find out what sort of projectiles it could fire.

"Okay, but don't shoot me." She slowly reached for the pistol in her waistband, wriggled it free from her pants, then dropped it to the carpet with a thud.

"I've identified her as the currently registered occupant of this room, SOA license XR713-004," one of the other officers said, a woman with a low, raspy voice that brought flashbacks of Ghoul into Juliet's mind.

"What's going on here? Did you discharge that weapon?" The lead officer strode toward her, his gun angled down and to Juliet's left.

"Thank you for not pointing that thing at my face." Juliet tried to smile disarmingly as she shrugged and gestured at Eve, still sobbing under her foot, and Kirby, writhing and cursing, face down on the carpet. "These two tried to jump me—"

"She's a lying bitch!" Kirby cried.

"I'm identifying the loud one as Deck Cadet Kirby Yale. The other one is a bartender in the Stargazer Lounge—Evelyn Samaras." Again, the woman with the raspy voice spoke as she walked around the room, panning her visor into every nook and cranny.

"Who discharged the weapon?" the security lead asked.

"She did." Juliet gestured to Eve.

"That bitch did! She shattered my wrist, too!" Kirby's outraged, pain-filled voice cut Juliet off.

"I'm sorry!" Eve sobbed, face buried in the carpet.

"How about I send you a vid of what happened when I walked into my room?" Juliet tapped the side of her head. "That should clear things up."

"Port's open." He released his thick gun, letting it hang by his side, apparently trusting the woman and the officer still standing by the door to cover him. Angel flashed a "File Transfer Complete" notification on Juliet's AUI, so she relaxed a little, waiting for the officer to review it.

Eve continued to sniffle, and Kirby continued to fume and curse, apparently holding Juliet responsible for all the ills that had ever befallen him. After a few minutes, the security officer nodded.

"Take these two into custody."

"She's lying! The footage is doctored!" Kirby screamed, his voice cracking.

"You have a different version you want to share?"

"Fuck you, pig!"

"Sure. Save it for the port police."

As the other two officers secured Eve with a shrink cord and then hoisted the two up, marching them out of the room, the lead officer touched his helmet, allowing his visor to snap up, revealing his face. He had a very dark complexion, which caused his pale silver optical implants to stand out—Juliet had a hard time not staring at his striking countenance.

"Listen, I'm not sure why you were coming back to your room with that bartender, but from the vid you shared, it looks like they meant to rob you . . . or worse. I'll file my report, along with a recommendation that the cruise director look into compensating you for the trouble. These two were obviously up to no good, and you shouldn't have your whole trip ruined because of it."

"That's awfully nice of you, Officer . . . ?"

"Ridgeway." He nodded curtly. "Your room's been damaged, and they did something with the AI in here to jam comms. The director might take a while to get around to you, but the concierge team will have someone here imminently to either make things right in here"—he gestured around Juliet's suite—"or get you a new room. You'll be okay while they're en route?"

"Yes, I should be fine."

"Excellent." He nodded again, then turned and strode to the door.

Juliet opened her mouth, wondering if she should ask him his first name or thank him further, but the moment passed, and he was gone, the door sliding shut in his wake. She let her gaze run from the door over the wall to her left, where she saw the fat dent in the plasteel where the pistol's slug had wedged itself. If Eve had been just a little better at shooting, a little more familiar with pulling a trigger in a panic, that wall would be dripping with brains and blood.

"You seem fine physically, but are you really okay?"

"I'm okay, Angel. I'm just very mad at myself and disappointed in . . . people."

"We made some tactical errors, but overall, I thought you handled yourself well."

"That's because you don't know what I can hear." Juliet tapped her forehead. "I tuned her out because I had that misguided notion that I shouldn't eavesdrop so much, that I was being creepy." She sighed loudly and moved over to the sofa to collapse onto it with a huff. "I knew she was planning to kill someone! I knew she was at least dangerous enough to get mixed up with that kind of trouble. I should have been more thorough; it wasn't like eavesdropping on Bennet or Aya. She wasn't a friend! She wasn't a bystander. She was Trouble with a capital T, and I shouldn't have been so squeamish about utilizing my . . . talents."

"I don't think I quite realized that." Angel seemed a little subdued, probably struggling with how to respond to Juliet's admission. Should she comfort her? Scold her? Juliet didn't envy her.

"Don't worry, Angel. You don't have to solve this one. Consider it a lesson learned. I was so sure she was just scared, forced to do something stupid. I thought I'd get her back here, have a heart-to-heart, then help her solve her problems without becoming a killer. Ugh! I'm so dumb!"

A sudden thought struck Juliet, and she stood up and went to the bedroom where she'd left her pack. It didn't look like Kirby had done anything to it; her stuff was all there, including her data deck and vibroblade. Even so, it felt weird being in the room knowing he'd been there before her, lurking there in the shadows, possibly doing . . . things.

She took her knife and walked back into the sitting area. As she flipped the knife out of habit, letting it tumble in the air, snatching the handle, and flipping it again, Juliet let her gaze linger on the lump of dense polymer embedded in the plasteel wall. Walking toward it, she pulled her vibroblade free of the sheath but flipped the switch off with her thumb. As the blade settled, she reached up and pried the bullet from the wall.

"Are you hoping to gather some evidence?"

"Nah, I'm hoping to gather a souvenir. A reminder."

"A reminder?"

"Of the fact that I almost had my brains blown out for being naive."

"Ah, I see. That bullet is made from a high-density polymer. It was meant to deform, causing massive damage, but with little penetrating power."

"Lovely." Juliet dug the blue material out of the dent, noting that Angel was right; it hadn't penetrated the wall at all, and she could see it was more than twice as wide as it must have been when new and unfired. "Would have done a number on my skull."

She held the squished bullet up in the light, noting how the polymer had a weird look. It wasn't plastic, but it wasn't metal. It had a kind of in-between quality, and it was heavy, far heavier than the bullets she'd been using in her SMG. "Nasty." She'd just slipped it into one of the tiny pockets of her silky pants when her door chimed.

"I would open the door, but I'm still blocked in this room."

"Don't worry." Juliet walked over and touched the view panel. It went from matte gray to a crystal-clear image of the hallway outside. A young woman with orange hair cut in a bob stood there with a tablet under one arm. She was petite and wore a crew uniform skirt, blouse, and jacket with a name tag—Val. More than that, she wore a pleasant expression as she stared into the camera; she must have guessed Juliet was examining her. Juliet let her mind wander, loosening her almost instinctual tethers as she stared at the girl's bright blue eyes.

How exciting! A passenger accosted by rogue crew! Davie and Tamara aren't going to believe this when I get back. Let's see if his stories about drunk rig workers can steal the show again after that . . .

Juliet touched the open button, and the door slid to the side. "Hey."

"Hello! Oh, goodness, you're tall." The girl—she seemed like she was about fifteen to Juliet—slapped a hand to her mouth. "Gosh, I'm sorry! My mouth gets ahead of my brain sometimes."

"Don't worry about it." Juliet stepped back, waving for her to enter.

After the door swished shut and Juliet followed her into the center of the room, Val said, "My name's Val, and I'm a member of the concierge staff. I've been instructed to make things right for you after the ordeal you suffered. I can start by having some techs come to figure out what happened to your room AI. I see there's some sort of jamming taking place in here."

"I'd really prefer a new room. It creeps me out to wonder what the criminal was doing in here alone while I was out."

"Oh, goodness! Yes, that does sound creepy!" She stepped toward Juliet, making clear eye contact, something like genuine sympathy in her voice.

Juliet wanted to believe she was sincere, but her faith in people was at a low point, and she couldn't help wondering if the concierge staff had training for just this sort of thing: how to give the impression you had actual human empathy. "I'll step into the hallway so I can access the ship's systems. I need to find out if other rooms are available and, of course, to call a porter to gather your things for you."

"I won't need a porter, Val. I just have a backpack, and I haven't really unpacked yet."

"Of course! I'll wait here so you aren't alone as you gather your things. Once you have them, we'll go out together. Is that fine?" She was so earnest and her voice so pleasant, Juliet couldn't help smiling slightly.

"You can go to the hallway and start your search for a new room. I'll be right out."

"All right, if you're sure." Her smile widened, showing off some beautiful, straight white teeth, and then, with an actual bounce in her step, she started for the door.

"Well, she's sweet." Juliet went into her room and gathered up the clothes she'd worn the previous day. After she'd stuffed them into the top of her pack, she went into the bathroom and collected her toiletries and the swimsuit she'd left drying in the shower. A minute or two later, she walked toward the door, scanning the room so Angel could help ensure she didn't forget anything.

"What will you do now?" Angel asked. Juliet knew what she meant—what would she do about Eve, Kirby, Zapho, and the woman he'd wanted Eve to kill?

"I'm going to forget I ever heard that woman's thoughts. I'm going to relax, eat some good food, exercise, and practice with the lattice. Then, when we get to Io Station, I'm gonna meet Alice's friend and do what I meant to do from the start—prove I can pilot a gunship."

10

10 APPROACH

Juliet's new set of rooms turned out to be a slight upgrade to her old suite. They were closer to the central elevator leading to the dining and recreation levels, and had a larger en suite bathroom. More than the room upgrade, however, in exchange for signing an NDA, the cruise director gave Juliet a voucher for a free trip to any of the cruise line's destinations in the Sol System, something that would save her nearly thirty thousand bits on her return trip, assuming she booked the same kind of passage back to Luna.

She briefly contemplated refusing the payoff, wondering if she might make more bits by selling her story to some sensationalist news outfit. The idea didn't appeal to her, though; she had enough on her plate and wanted to put her episode with Eve and Kirby behind her. She already had to worry that somehow her involvement with the duo's arrest would get back to Zapho, whoever he was. With that in mind, she'd quickly agreed to the cruise corp's deal and taken her upgraded room, a few free meal passes, and, of course, the all-expenses paid trip voucher.

For the remainder of her trip, Juliet spent a lot of time hanging around the various restaurants on the cruise liner, trying to focus her mind to hear a specific person's thoughts, tuning out the din of other voices, and generally testing her new implant's ability to keep the psionic lattice cool. She improved, though it was so gradual and slight that she didn't notice it at first. It took Angel reminding her about how she'd been nearly unable to function with the cacophonous voices clamoring for her attention back when she was at Grave for her to accept the very real fact that she now had a tool that was at least moderately useful to her in crowded situations. She still had to strain to focus on an individual, and if she did it for long, she began to get a headache, but it was possible.

In less crowded situations, she'd gotten better at turning the ability on and off, listening to a person's surface thoughts without closing her eyes, and digging deeper for images: what Juliet had come to realize were memories and imaginings, or, as she liked to call them, daydreams. The only problem with seeing the images was that Juliet struggled to tell the difference between memory and fantasy, which, obviously, could make a big difference. Sometimes, she'd see disturbing flashes, like a woman stabbing the man she was eating dinner with, only to focus on reality and see her laughing and touching his wrist. Was the woman hiding murderous thoughts? Was she imagining a suppressed fear? Was she even aware of the thought? Was it a subconscious urge? Juliet had no way of knowing.

Those problems aside, she found that with heavy use of the lattice, she almost always built up a charge of the weird psionic energy that she'd used to knock over her pint glass on the first day of the cruise. During the second half of the trip, she'd tried experimenting with it in various ways.

The first thing she did was not use it. She allowed it to build up until it felt so uncomfortable that she thought she might suffer some physical harm from its presence. Angel, closely monitoring her brain with her nanites, didn't think she was in any danger, but Juliet had insisted on going back to her room and "letting it out."

With the charge so strong, probably three or four times what she'd felt that first time, Juliet had tried to do something a little more significant than knocking over a glass. She'd set her vibroblade on the coffee table and, while sitting on the couch, tried to pull it to her.

It took her several tries to exert that strange phantom limb that seemed to be attached, at least mentally, to her breathing, but with a slow, steady inhale, she'd gotten the knife to wriggle over the tabletop toward her. Staring at the sheathed blade, she'd wondered about getting it over the gap between the table and the couch and decided to quickly suck in her breath while willing it to come to her hand. Juliet was very glad the knife was sheathed because it had flipped through the air and smacked her in the forehead.

That was on day three of the trip, and she steadily improved each day with more and more practice. Though she never got over the crutch of tying her "telekinesis," as Angel labeled the ability, to her breathing, she did learn to control her efforts better. On the last day of the cruise, she managed to yank her knife from the kitchenette counter, four meters across the room, to where she stood in the doorway of her bedroom, snatching it out of the air with her brilliantly quick cybernetic arm.

Juliet flipped the knife in the air, catching the handle. "That's quite a trick, isn't it?"

"I could see such a talent proving extremely useful in your line of work. Imagine if you were in the sheriff's office, locked in the holding cell, and he walked out to get lunch with the town doctor . . ."

"Angel, I'm not living in a Western!"

"Even so."

Juliet chuckled. "Well, I also had to 'charge up' for nearly an hour at the breakfast buffet this morning to pull that off." She spoke nonchalantly, but if Juliet really thought about the fact that she could move things with her mind, she started to feel like she was in some kind of surreal simulation.

Sometimes, she wondered about that. What if she'd taken Mark up on one of his invitations to try out his dream-rig one night after work at the scrapyard, and she'd gotten stuck? What if Angel and this whole operator life were just parts of a wild fantasy she couldn't wake up from? Of course, she didn't really believe it, but it almost felt as plausible as the lattice and the things she'd done in the last year.

"Yes, but you're getting better, and though it's difficult to measure precisely, it seems you're starting to develop a charge more easily, or . . . at least, more quickly."

At Angel's words, Juliet brushed her weird existential contemplations aside. "Yeah, you said as much, but it doesn't feel like I've done anything as impressive as what Joshua Kyle did to Polk and me." She tucked the knife into her belt then turned back to her room; she needed to pack up her bag.

"At the risk of sounding cliché, you can't compare apples to oranges. The amount of psionic energy you used to move that knife might be devastating if applied to a human brain."

"I guess. I'm not about to start experimenting on random people, though."

Juliet's pack had plenty of room in it, even after adding her few acquisitions while on the cruise: the nice outfit in which she'd almost been killed, her swimsuit, and a luxurious white robe she was stealing from her room. Considering her troubles with Kirby and Eve, she didn't think the cruise company would complain about it. "How long until we dock at Io Station?"

A countdown timer appeared on Juliet's AUI as Angel replied, "Ninety-seven minutes."

"All right." Juliet hoisted her pack and carried it into the sitting room, where she flopped down onto the comfortable sofa facing her suite's door. "Play me Aya's message again, will you?"

A vidscreen opened in her vision, obscuring her view of the room. Angel had maximized the resolution. It began to play, showing Aya facing the camera with a wide grin, and over her shoulder, Shiro and Alice sitting at the mess hall table aboard the *Kowashi*. She was using one of her drones to film her little message.

"Hey, Lucky! Sorry it took me a couple of days to respond to your vid! I know it seems like Bennet never does anything, but I've actually been pretty busy doing his job on top of mine. I tried to get Shiro to help, but you know Shiro: he's always doing . . . Shiro things. Of course, I can't bug Alice"—behind her, Shiro looked up from a datapad he was perusing and grunted, then looked back down. Alice, back to the camera, lifted a hand and waved briefly—"she's busy keeping us from running into asteroids or something."

Aya's voice grew hushed, and she held a hand to the side of her mouth and winked. "Even though the autopilot pretty much does everything for, like, ninety-nine percent of the trip."

"I heard that, you little shit. How about I lock myself in my quarters, and we see how well this old bird manages to dock at New Galveston?" Alice's accent, combined with the cursing, always brought a smile to Juliet's lips.

"Just kidding, Alice! Sheesh!" Aya winked into the camera again, then she left the mess and made her way down the hallway toward the port bunks where Juliet's room had been. "I've got something to show you. Before we left, I got a package I'd been expecting for, like, weeks." She paused in front of Juliet's room. "Don't get weirded out that I'm going into your room—I put it in here for safekeeping. I mean, it's for you, anyway." She placed her hand on the lock, and the door swished open. Juliet wasn't surprised—most of the crew could open most of the doors on the *Kowashi*.

"It would've cost me a lot to ship these up to Luna, but I got my friend down at Romero's Salvage to tuck these into a shipping container with a few parts for the gunship. They hardly weigh anything in comparison." She walked over to the acceleration couch where an old, grease-stained corrugated cardboard box sat. "Uh, don't worry; I'll clean that acceleration couch if you need to use it again."

Aya pulled open the box and panned the camera down to view the contents. "Books!"

She wasn't lying—at least fifty paperback books with colorful, fanciful artwork on the faded, frayed covers filled the box.

"I bought 'em cheap off a peer-to-peer auction site. Some guy in Boston had these sitting in his garage, I guess." Her face was serene, a gentle smile touching her lips as she took a minute to hold several of the books up, displaying the artwork, from scantily clad women holding absurdly large swords, to cowboys with silver stars on their chests, to dragons breathing fire, to rockets landing on Venus. "Lots of cool, old-school fiction in here. I'm gonna read 'em while I wait for you to get back, and then I'll pass 'em your way."

She closed the box, and the camera panned away from the box to face her. As usual, Juliet found her smile infectious. "Won't it be fun to talk about all these adventures? I'm sure the others will be so jealous they'll want to read them too!" She started toward the door, leaving Juliet's quarters behind. "Anyway, Lucky, I hope you have a good time showing those know-it-alls around Jupiter how good you are. Send me another message soon."

The vid window snapped shut, and Juliet sighed happily. She'd watched the message at least ten times since she'd received it the day after her little tussle with Eve and Kirby.

"Any word from Grant?"

"Nothing since the last message."

"Did you figure out where the Badhammer is?"

"Yes. The Badhammer is a self-styled 'Jupiter punk pub' on Io Station. It's on spindle three, ring seven."

"Spindle three . . . How big is Io Station?"

"Io Station has a central spindle that is five kilometers long, and nine branching spindles that are nearly a kilometer long each. Around each branching spindle are seven habitation rings. Considering the many decks and corridors, Io Station has nearly a hundred square kilometers of inhabited superstructure space. The central spindle boasts a gravity generator and is dominated by a verdant public park plaza at the center of the station's shopping district. Diamatex panels line the ceiling of many spindle and ring areas, providing views of the Jovian System."

"Are you reading a brochure?"

"Paraphrasing."

"Huh. Well, sounds like a lousy place for a first meeting. What's he trying to prove?"

"I don't know. The images on their net page are reminiscent of that club you visited in Tucson, Thicker than Water. Though it's dirtier, more crowded, has more flashing lights—"

"All right, all right." Juliet groaned and stood up, hoisting her pack and slinging it over her shoulder. "Let's make our way to the docking collars; I don't want to wait behind a few thousand tourists to get off this thing." When Juliet walked down the corridor to the central elevator bank, she was surprised to find the concierge staffer, Val, waiting for her.

"All packed up?" As usual, she was cheery, bright eyed, and wearing an impeccably fitted and pressed uniform. She still seemed very young to Juliet, but she knew, objectively, the girl—woman—had to be at least an adult for a job like that.

Juliet gave her pack a little bounce on her shoulders. "Not too hard."

"Would you mind if I walk with you? My boss wants me to do a sort of exit survey; make sure you're still happy with the arrangement you made with the cruise line and that you're leaving 'content and with no ill intent.' Hah! Those were his actual words, silly old guy that he is."

"No ill intent, huh? Yeah, he sounds kind of like a dweeb." Juliet huffed slightly and shook her head. "You don't have to waste your time, Val. I'm not planning to cause the cruise corp any trouble."

"I'll walk with you anyway if you don't mind. We can see a good view of the system through the big viewscreen by the airlocks."

Juliet shrugged and stepped into an open elevator. "Been out here before?"

"A few times."

"Hey"—Juliet leaned against the wall as the doors closed and the elevator began to descend—"not to be rude, but do you mind if I ask how old you are? You seem really young to have been traveling so much."

"Oh, I don't mind! My dad's a captain for the line. Not this ship—the *Caliope Dream*. He got me hired on when I was sixteen, and I've been at it for three years. If you think that's interesting, well, if you ask me, you've got a much more interesting job!"

Please, oh please, tell me about yourself!

The young woman's thoughts were so focused as Juliet looked into her eyes that they came to her unbidden. She sighed and said, "There's all kinds of interesting in the universe, Val, and I think you're doing things pretty damn well. My job can be exciting, but it can be scary and maddening and sad, too. I bet if you stick with the line, you'll be an officer in no time, yeah?"

"Probably. But . . ." She glanced up at the camera in the elevator, then shrugged. "Oh, melt it; I don't care if Herbert sees this. I just hate how the corporation owns everything about me. My room, my clothes, my schedule. They're always watching on the ship"—she jerked her thumb toward the camera—"and I basically live here, you know? I can leave for a few hours when we make port, but . . . it's almost like a prison, Lucky."

"Sheesh!" Juliet was taken aback, but her response was cut short as the elevator halted and the door opened. "Walk with me."

Val nodded, and as they continued on their way toward the docking collars, Juliet said, "If you feel like a prisoner, I guess it's a different story. The SOA can be a good gig, and if you're smart, you don't have to take jobs that'll be . . . traumatic, for lack of a better word. Think about what you want to do, develop a skillset, invest in a good"—Juliet lowered her voice and mouthed—"jailbroken"—then more loudly—"PAI, then apply for a license. It's as easy as that. You can start taking jobs off the net almost immediately."

"Yeah, I've watched vids and read walkthroughs. It's just . . . I hear there are a lot more broke operatives than successful ones. I also hear that with success comes risk and . . ." She trailed off, rolling her hand as if to indicate the myriad problems with being an SOA operator.

"Hey, that's all true, but Val, you're not average, are you?"

"No . . ."

"So, if you think you want to get out from under the thumb"—Juliet jerked her arm around, indicating the ship—"of a corporation, you've gotta take a leap. Have some faith in yourself and take advantage of your current situation. Use your money and stability to get yourself set up. Once you have an SOA ID, you can start building accounts and contact information, keeping it separate from your current ID and employer. Like I said, though, Val, I'd try to think of an angle that doesn't involve direct conflict. You're pretty, and I can tell you're sharp. Look at your uniform! I bet you could do some corporate recon or face work. You know, dress all fancy, get the info for the other guys, the ones who will do the heavy lifting, the dirty work, while you collect your bits for using this." Juliet tapped her temple, indicating her brain.

"Is that what you do?"

"I . . . I should, and I try, but I tend to get myself mixed up in a lot of drama. Don't be like me, Val." Juliet laughed, shaking her head.

"I looked up your SOA card. It seems like you haven't been at it for long, but according to stats on the net, you've done way more than most people in their first year."

"Like I said," Juliet laughed, "don't be like me."

A chime sounded, and the ship's pleasant gender-neutral AI announced, "We're on our final approach to Io Station. We anticipate docking in just a little more than an hour and would like to point out that the view of Jupiter and the rest of the Jovian System is a sight to behold. If you would make your way to the Redmond Deck, we have a large, open viewport and comfortable viewing space for several hundred passengers. Alternatively, if you'd like to prepare for disembarking, you can watch the approach on the Docking Deck. Finally, if you'd like to make the most of your cruise and stay in your rooms or visit one of the restaurants, we'll provide live footage of the approach on the various vidscreens around the ship. Thank you so much for traveling on the *Sunset Star Runner*, and we hope you'll choose us for your next Sol System adventure."

"Can I talk to you some more while we approach?"

"Yeah." Juliet smiled down at the plucky young woman. "Come hang out with me while I watch the approach. I'll share some of the mistakes I've made, and there are plenty."

"I bet you've done more than make mistakes, though . . ." Val hurried to keep up as Juliet's long strides devoured the corridor.

"Sure, Val. I've done a few things right and had a lot of lucky breaks, too. You know, a big part of success in this business is the kind of people you surround yourself with. You want to find some folks you can trust . . ."

Juliet found she rather enjoyed talking to Val, sort of imagining herself as the girl's temporary mentor, and her mood decidedly began to lift as she recounted some of her exploits and took an objective look at her accomplishments. She'd done a lot, and not a small amount of the things she'd managed to pull off were pretty damn impressive.

In fact, she found talking to Val was just about exactly what she needed to get her head right, boost her confidence, and put things in perspective—she was an operator, damn it, and she wasn't going to let Nick Grant intimidate her by choosing some edgy punk bar for their first meeting.

11

BADHAMMER

Io Station was so large that Juliet felt like she was walking around in a city, not on a space station. True, the buildings weren't something you'd see on Earth or even Luna; they were shorter, for one, and universally made of plasteel, though diamatex—the same crystal-clear, super strong material used in most dome construction—was ubiquitous. She saw it overhead, providing a view of the Jovian System, but also in shop windows, viewports, and pretty much anywhere something much cheaper, like plastiglass, would have sufficed. Io Station hadn't been constructed with a shoestring budget.

The walkways were designed for pedestrians, with a lane for electric bikes, scooters, and other contraptions like one-wheels, motorized shoes, and wheeled cybernetic implants. Juliet was content to walk, taking in the scenery, the people, and the views through the vaulted ceiling that exposed the lurking, orange-toned giant: Jupiter. From the current position of the station and Juliet's location within, the great planet was the only celestial body visible.

When she'd first departed the cruise liner, she'd been caught up in a throng of tourists, forced to listen to their exclamations, plans, questions, and general chatter. As she'd made her way deeper into the central spindle of the station, though, she began to see more and more of the native populace. It was strange to her to think of people living permanently in a place like this, a plasteel city floating around a giant planet and its moons, where more permanent settlements had been built.

Even stranger than their choice to live out there were the augments some spacefaring citizens boasted. She saw everything from oxygen ports on necks to temperature-resistant epidermal treatments that made a person's skin look almost like colored plastic. Juliet even saw members of the so-called "spacer" culture: descendants of people who'd gone through gene therapy to make living in low-G environments easier. They'd bravely populated the distant reaches of the system before AIs had conquered the mysteries of gravity generation.

The spacers were easy to spot. They were tall, with skeletally thin frames and impossibly long limbs. In a way, Juliet felt sorry for them, but they seemed to get along fine there on the station, and she supposed they fared even better on the smaller stations, asteroids, and moons around the system, those without permanent gravity solutions.

Juliet glanced at her clock and saw she had about twenty minutes before she was supposed to meet Alice's friend, Nick. He'd set up the meeting based on her transport's public arrival time, and she felt like she was supposed to impress him, so she couldn't really argue. Still, she wasn't keen on going to a club carrying her backpack at nearly ten at night. She'd have liked to find some lodging, drop off her gear, and maybe change her clothes.

"Oh well. If he wants me to have to deal with a bouncer, explain away my pack and gun, then it's on him if there's some kind of scene."

"A good outlook. If they won't let you in, then we can message him, and he'll be the one to look sheepish when he has to come outside."

"Right on, Angel."

Juliet shifted her pack's straps; they weren't uncomfortable atop her motorcycle jacket, but she was starting to feel too warm, some sweat building up where they pressed into her shoulders. She wore her vibroblade under her sleeve, but her needler was openly displayed on her belt; the laws regarding personal weapons on the station were pretty liberal. A license was required, but all that took was filling out a form with your identity, passing a cursory, automated background check, and paying a hundred bits. No explosive rounds or calibers that might damage the diamatex were allowed, but that meant that just about everything a nonaugmented human could carry was permitted.

She walked quickly, shouldering past slower walkers, people who were strolling aimlessly, or who had a naturally lackadaisical pace. As she followed Angel's directions, Juliet reached up and pulled her thick, dark hair away from her neck, securing it with a tie into a high ponytail. The air hitting her sweaty neck felt good, and she briefly contemplated going with a shorter hairstyle.

"Especially if I'm going to be wearing an EVA suit a lot . . ."

"You missed the turn." Angel flashed a red arrow on her AUI, indicating a turn to her right.

Juliet stopped, got bumped into by a woman who barked something in a language she didn't understand, then turned to find herself in a plasteel alley littered with bits of refuse. The narrow space between buildings was illuminated by neon arrows pointing toward a right-angle turn to the left about forty meters ahead.

"Not at all foreboding." The thump of bass rumbled through the ground, vibrating the soles of her feet as she made her way forward. "You think the businesses nearby like having their walls vibrate all the time?"

"The club doesn't open until 9:00 p.m."

"Right."

Juliet turned the corner and found herself in another narrow alley. Fifty meters further on, at the end of it, she could see a flashing pink neon sign that spelled out, on two lines, "Badhammer." A dozen people were lined up, waiting for the bouncer to look them over and let them in . . . or not.

Juliet sighed when she saw the club-goers; they were scantily dressed in tight, faux leather pants or see-through garments that revealed garishly colored and illuminated underclothes. They wore dancing shoes, had colorful hair, lots of exposed flesh, and they most definitely were not carrying any backpacks.

She stepped up to the back of the queue, scowling at the young man with spiky green hair who turned to raise a silver-studded eyebrow at her. He smirked and turned away, and Juliet could hear him mutter something to the girl in front of him about an "old lady." She had the urge to wrap an arm around his neck and choke him out.

Sighing, blowing her tension out with a pent-up breath, she watched as the bouncer, a tall, clean-shaven man with a bald head, ran a wand over each would-be partygoer, letting them through. When she stood before him, he paused and gave her a head to toe once-over.

He folded his arms on his bulky chest, archly looking down at her. "Sure you're in the right place?"

"Just got off a transport, and I'm supposed to meet a guy here." Juliet shrugged, hooking her thumbs under the straps of her pack, taking some weight off her shoulders.

"We don't allow weapons, but I've got lockers here. Not sure your pack will fit." He jerked his thumb to the side, where a stand of battered purple-painted lockers leaned against the alley wall. They were plastered with stickers advertising concerts, energy drinks, and clothing labels. Two hung off loose hinges, but most seemed in decent working order.

"My pack definitely won't fit."

"If you set it by the wall there, I can try to keep an eye on it." He returned her earlier shrug.

"I'll take it with me."

"Nah, I'm not having you walk around in there with a backpack. We have an image."

"Dammit," Juliet groused, then she walked over to the lockers, not wanting to hold up the line and be the center of attention any longer than necessary.

She opened one, scraped out some scraps of paper and a crumpled drink container, then put her knife, pistol, and extra magazine inside. Her pack was too fat to fit on top of them, but she opened the zipper and started pulling out garments, stacking them atop her weapons. After she'd half emptied it, she was able to stuff the backpack into a second locker, placing her helmet on top. She slammed both lockers shut and pressed her thumb to the biometric locks.

"All right," she announced, stepping up to the bouncer, cutting in front of a young woman with neon green and blue face paint. The line had grown while she'd been standing in it, and she didn't intend to start in the back again.

"Excuse me?" The girl's voice was high but not necessarily unpleasant.

"Sorry." Juliet shrugged, then the bouncer waved his wand over her, gave her a nod, and gestured her through, perhaps trying to forestall something unpleasant.

Juliet turned her attention to the swinging pink plasteel doors and pushed her way between them. She was immediately inundated with the thump of music, and though she was in a short, litter-strewn entry hall, she could see the flashing strobes timed with the beat beyond the next set of doors. She walked past two sweaty patrons, one leaning against the wall, looking like she was about to throw up, and the other gently stroking her hair. Then she pushed through the second set of doors and was engulfed by the music, lights, and smells.

"I'm filtering most of the volume and compensating for the brighter strobes."

"Thanks," Juliet said, not bothering to subvocalize in the din. The club smelled like sweat, caramel, liquor, and fruit-flavored vapes. She didn't particularly enjoy the mixture, and for the first time in a while, she started to contemplate getting some olfactory augmentations. "How am I supposed to find this guy in a place like this?"

The club was jammed with people moving about frenetically. Some areas were filled with people dancing to the beat; others were standing-room only, with people gathered close, drinking cocktails and shouting conversations over the electronic dance music.

"He said the bar, if that helps."

"Yeah." Juliet frowned, looking away from the dance floor area to where people were jammed into a dim, blue-lit space, standing around drinking. Beyond the initial crowd, she spied some tall, slender tables surrounded by stools, and figured if someone were waiting for a meeting, they'd probably have snagged one of those. She wound her way through the clusters of drinking, yelling, and sometimes dancing people, glad she'd worn her long-sleeved jacket; they were all drenched with sweat.

She scanned the crowd constantly, and when she broke through the larger part of it and focused on the tables, Angel was quick to highlight one near the back wall, right next to an emergency exit. "There he is."

"Got it." Juliet pushed her way to the table, pleased and surprised to see that an empty stool sat across from the man she was meant to meet.

Nick Grant looked to be in his late thirties or early forties, probably around the same age as Alice, and he didn't look like he belonged in the punk bar any more than Juliet did. He wore a long-sleeved white shirt with a collar, faded jeans, and amazingly, worn, scuffed cowboy boots. His skin was tan and weathered, and his short, black hair was combed back from his face. She couldn't see his eyes; they were focused on a tablet that sat on his table next to a glass of amber liquor. He didn't look up as she approached the empty stool, but he took a long drag on a chrome-colored Nikko-vape that flared with an amber LED when inhaled.

Juliet sat down across from him. "Hey."

"Hey." He looked up, pale blue eyes beneath heavy dark brows narrowing as he took her in. "Not your kinda club?"

Juliet frowned slightly and shrugged, looking into those eyes, wondering what he was thinking. As if in answer to her question, his thoughts came to her.

Alice didn't say she was a looker. Hah! She looks pissed. Good! Keep her on her toes . . .

His voice, clear at first, got lost in a din of others as her control slipped and the crowded club began to overwhelm her.

Move it, shake 'em . . .

. . . then we'll pick up Ree . . .

. . . up and down, up and down.

One more drink . . .

Screw Pony and screw his stupid friends!

. . . where are they?

Just a little closer, baby . . .

Juliet shook her head, trying to clear the noise, trying to turn them off. They kept clamoring at her, though, and then Nick spoke, and his audible voice helped her to ground herself, to shut out the mental ones. "You okay? Damn, hope you don't have a headache. This is the wrong place to come with a headache."

"Long day. Long trip. Didn't sleep well on that ship." Juliet rubbed at her head, hoping the excuse seemed real.

"Ah, sorry. You don't have auditory implants? Have your PAI tune the noise down. Here." He pushed his drink toward her.

"I'm good, thanks." Juliet looked up, meeting his gaze, praying that her stupid psionic lattice wouldn't trigger every time she looked into his eyes. She pointedly pushed his drink back toward him. He shrugged and lifted it to his mouth, draining it in a gulp.

"I know it's weird that I wanted to meet here. I'm a creature of habit. My old buddy owns the place, and it didn't use to be this popular. I just come here to kind of disappear in the noise, you know? My ears are off most of the time."

"Sure, whatever." Juliet forced a smile, annoyed that she'd given a weak first impression. "I've got it dialed down now; it's cool."

"So, you're an operator, huh? Alice says you're tougher than nails. You know how to fly, though?"

"Yeah, I know how."

"Fighters? Interceptors?"

Juliet thought about the question and the half-truth answer she'd rehearsed. She decided to be a little more honest. "Not interceptors, but bigger ships. I've got good reflexes, though, and good software." She tapped her head.

"High-G shunts?"

"No, not yet. Will I need 'em for your kind of work?"

"Nah, not if you can take some pain. Have a good flight suit?"

"Yep."

"Okay, what did Alice tell you about my work?"

"Said you flew escort to ships in the Jovian System. That's really about it." Juliet drummed her fingers on the table, contemplating ordering something to drink, wondering how long it would take to get service in a place like the Badhammer. That thought in her mind, she added, "What's the deal with this place's name?"

"Rudy, my buddy who owns the place, was a ship tech. His favorite tool was a brass ball-peen hammer his father gave him. He used it so much it had notches and grooves in the brass, you know, not a smooth spot on it except for the tip of the ball part. He called it his 'bad hammer.' Not sure why he named the bar after it, but there you go." He rocked his empty glass back and forth over the tabletop, contemplating his next words. "Yeah, I fly escort. I see action, on average, twice a week. I've got more confirmed kills than anyone I know in this system, so it's not surprising to me that Alice sent you my way for evaluation. I'm not trying to toot my own horn—I'm trying to open your eyes a little to the nature of the risk you're taking by coming out with me. If you're sure, though, I'll do it."

"I'm sure."

"All right, well, here's how I see things going. You'll ride copilot with me for a couple of weeks and see how I do things. When I feel like you're ready, I'll give the stick to you, and we'll switch roles for a while. If I'm impressed— and I mean impressed—I've got a friend who's retiring and leases his ship to pilots who don't have one. Before you get any ideas about just going around me and leasing it right away, you need to know he doesn't talk to strangers." He grinned and winked. "I'll have to vouch for you. Anyway, that's a month or two down the road, but I figure we'll fly a few tandem missions, and if you continue to impress, I'll give Alice a good report."

Juliet watched his face while he spoke, wishing she could read his thoughts but figuring she'd give them a good listen when they weren't in such a crowded environment. He looked serious. Stern, even, like he was talking to a kid. She supposed she couldn't blame him; they were talking about serious business, flying very expensive hardware in lethal situations. She didn't like the idea that she'd be hands-off for weeks, but she also couldn't blame the guy.

"Sounds like you've got a good plan laid out."

"No arguments? No whining about having to wait?" Nick chuckled and took another drag on his vape. He had a gruff, scratchy voice, one that had been cultivated by plenty of chemical inhalations and too much drinking, but Juliet kind of liked it. He was a wiry man with prominent facial bones, and when he smiled, his skin moved a lot, crinkling around his eyes and exposing dimples in his cheeks. Even without knowing his thoughts, Juliet's gut told her he was a good guy; someone who didn't beat around the bush and didn't play games.

"What kind of ship do you have?"

"Alice didn't tell you?"

"No . . ."

"It used to be our ship. She owned it fifty-fifty with me. It's a McDonnel-Chavez Ranger, Mark Seven—the *Lady Hawk.*"

"Really?" Juliet quirked an eyebrow.

"Yeah, and before you go getting cute about the name, you should know I named her, not Alice."

"Hah, no, no. That's cool. I kinda like it." Juliet drummed her fingers on the table and added, "How do you get service in this dump, anyway?"

"Hang on." Nick stood up, slipping his vape into his shirt pocket. "I need a refill anyway. What do you want?"

"Something cold. Beer."

"Be right back."

As he walked away, Angel said, "The Mark Seven Ranger was mass-produced from 2087 to 2092. It's a medium-size, two-seat interceptor with above-average speed and maneuverability but a lighter-than-average weapons loadout. Several variants were issued that replaced the stock, twin thirty-millimeter cannons with various energy-based weapons. A somewhat rare variant was also developed that boasted an oversize missile module mounted above the main drive. This variant, while gaining respect for being deadly, was also prone to exploding when damaged, even from relatively small caliber ship-to-ship munitions—"

"Let's not get ahead of ourselves, Angel." Juliet watched as Nick made his way back to the table with a drink in each hand. "I'll ask him more about the ship after I've had a drink. I'm thirsty, and I want to relax for a minute. Can you turn the music back up a little? I kind of like this beat."

12

\\\\\\\\\\\\\\\\\\\\\

A GHOST

How long 'til we ship out?" Juliet had a comfortable buzz. She was on her second beer and found herself feeling more relaxed, her smiles coming easier in the club as she listened to Nick talk about his ship, his time flying with Alice, and life in general around Jupiter.

"Got an escort job starting tomorrow. We'll shadow a ram scoop rig and keep it safe while it fills up in the outer atmosphere. When they're done, we'll escort 'em to Callisto."

"I . . ." Juliet's mind buzzed with the many questions that simple sentence stirred. "Sorry." She blushed, nodding toward the beer in her hand. "I think my tongue's a little slow compared to my brain right now. Anyway, why a ram scoop around Jupiter? I know they do it, but isn't it mostly hydrogen and helium? I mean, I know those are valuable, but, like, aren't there easier ways to get those gases?"

"Oh, I guess so, but plenty of big corps have been scooping that atmosphere for decades now. A lot of people speculate about Jovinium." He shrugged, sipped his drink, and narrowed his eyes when Juliet's face reflected her confusion. "Haven't heard those theories?"

"No . . ."

"There's nothing official on the public sat-net about any element called Jovinium," Angel offered, trying to help Juliet clear up her confusion.

"I mean, they're conspiracy theories, but you made a good point— there are easier ways to get hydrogen and helium. Us grunts who work the ships often wonder what the big corps like Mass Gas are doing with all these big ships full of air they're pulling out of the planet's upper atmosphere. Sure, they sell the hydrogen and helium on the market, but . . . Well, plenty of people better at math than me say the numbers don't add up. They're getting something more out of those tanks. Hence the Jovinium theories."

"Huh." Juliet sipped her beer.

"Intriguing!" Angel's voice rose excitedly as she continued, "I'm going to do some digging about this! Isn't it fascinating to imagine there's an element out there that certain corps have discovered but are keeping a secret? What do you think the applications might be?"

"I don't know . . ." Juliet let her voice trail off and shrugged, fine with Nick thinking she was talking to him.

"Yeah, I know. Crazy. I just fly my ship, shoot down pirates, and keep to myself."

"So, like, where do you live? I mean, between jobs? You have a place here?"

"On Io Station? Hell no. I'm not shelling out 2k a month for a plasteel closet. I've got a place down on Callisto, though. Sometimes, I think I'm throwing money away, considering I'm only there about one in every ten days. At least it's not a rental." He shrugged and sipped his drink.

"Nice place?"

"Decent. It's in one of the newer domes; one of the big agricultural ones. I've got a full acre, and all I have to do to keep the land commission happy is let a guy pay me to harvest the genned walnut trees I've got growing there."

"He pays you?"

"Pretty sweet deal, eh?" He shrugged again and made a funny, dismissive sound with his lips. "It's not enough to cover the mortgage, but it's something."

"It's cool to think you own land on a moon. A moon of Jupiter, no less!" Juliet held up her beer, and Nick clicked his glass against it.

"Cheers." He chuckled.

"So? Where are you staying until we ship out? I don't know if you caught the hint, but I'm trying to figure out where I'm sleeping tonight."

"Ah! Right, right. I'm bunking in my ship, and yeah, there's a cot for you there, too. Well, an acceleration bunk in a room the size of a closet. I mean, there're hotels here too, but the rooms won't be much bigger, and you'll have to deal with—"

"Nah, that's perfect. A bunk in a closet will suit me fine."

"You ready to head out, then?" He tossed back the rest of his drink—the third one Juliet had seen him finish. As she nodded and pushed her half-empty bottle away, he stood, tucking his little data deck into the back pocket of his jeans. "We're only about a ten-minute walk from my berth."

Juliet followed him through the crowded, noisy, smelly club, and when they stepped out into the dark, neon-lit alley, the air almost felt cool and fresh despite its recycled nature. "Hang on," she called as Nick started walking toward the corner, bypassing the small group of would-be club-goers. When he looked back at her, she gestured to the lockers. "Gotta get my stuff."

"Ah, right."

She saw him walk a dozen meters or so away from the club entrance and pull out his vape, leaning against one of the plasteel walls. He was mostly obscured by shadows there, but the amber LED flared brightly in the dim light as he took a drag, and Juliet turned back to the lockers. She pressed her thumb against one, and as it opened, she heard a new voice say, "Nicky Boy. Been a while." She pulled her helmet and backpack out, then pressed her thumb to the other locker.

"Tono." Nick's voice was hard to hear above the rattle of music coming out of the club, the people talking in line, and the bouncer scolding someone about "too much metal," but Angel tuned it in for her, and she continued to listen as she repacked her belongings.

"Been dodging me?"

"Why would I do that?" Nick's voice seemed calm, cool even, but she thought she detected some tension.

"Maybe because you owe me something like a hundred large?"

"You're kidding, right? Your pilot ditched me. I'm supposed to be able to read people's minds now?"

"You let my pilot get melted over Himalia."

"Ask yourself why your pilot was on Himalia when I was paid to escort him to Callisto."

Juliet heard a definite edge in Nick's voice now, and she hurriedly stuffed the last of her clothes into her pack and yanked the zipper shut. She shrugged into the straps, then rather than running it through her belt loops, she hung her gun belt over her shoulder like a bandolier and rested her hand on the needler's grip. She hurried out of the little locker alcove, past the club entrance, and down the alley toward Nick and whoever was talking to him.

"I'd say it's 'cause you're lazy or you got distracted by a nice piece of ass. Whatever the reason, my pilot was hung out to dry, and I'm out my share in his ship title." The speaker hadn't yet raised his voice, but Juliet could hear danger in his tone, an underlying promise of violence.

"I'm not doing this again. I sent you my report. I explained he flaked—nowhere to be found when I reported to the hangar. You've got a right to be pissed, but not at me. Now get out of my face."

As he said the last, Juliet came up beside him, and she saw it wasn't just "Tono" he was speaking to. Two men faced Nick, blocking progress further down the alley. One—Tono, if Juliet was guessing—was slight and wore a silky, formfitting gray turtleneck. Three thick gold chains hung from his neck, and their luster was reflected in his gold-capped smile. Next to him was a different sort of man—bulky, and nearly half chrome.

Tono's hired muscle had arms and legs prominently displayed, jutting thickly out of his one-piece black denim jumper. They were powerful looking, shiny with articulated metallic plating, and Juliet guessed he could probably punch or kick through a concrete block with those things. His face was largely flesh and blood, though his eyes glared balefully beneath a heavy brow with smoldering red LED irises. His head was devoid of hair, and the crown was, somewhat unsurprisingly, chrome.

"Is there a problem, Nick?" She edged to the side, moving so that Tono was between her and his chrome monster.

"Nah—"

"Yes. A rather large one," Tono interrupted. He gave Juliet a cursory glance, his smooth-skinned face betraying no emotion.

"Tono, if you think I'm responsible for your dipshit pilot, you need to take it up with the commission—"

"Wrench."

As Tono said the word—name, it turned out—the chrome gorilla snapped out one of his bulky appendages, fast as a rattler striking a hare, wrapping his long, articulated chrome fingers around Nick's neck. Juliet saw it happening. Angel even sped up her mental processing, so it wasn't too fast for her to track, but her response to it wasn't decisive enough to alter the course of events. She waffled between yanking out her needler or trying to take a step closer to punch her augmented arm out to deflect the grabbing hand.

Of course, the idea was flawed from the beginning; the rest of her body, her legs included, weren't fast enough to do anything in the milliseconds it took that chrome arm to reach Nick, but the wasted time thinking of and discarding the idea was enough to burn her chance to intervene.

Nick gasped and windmilled his arms, surprised and knocked off-balance by the thug's grab. Juliet yanked her gun out and pointed it at Tono. "Let him go."

"If you shoot me, Wrench will pop Nick's head from his shoulders."

"I can't—" Nick started to say, but his voice choked off as his face turned red and his mouth opened in a slow, strangled wheeze; Wrench had applied some pressure.

"I'll shoot Wrench first, then." Juliet put her crosshairs between Wrench's eyes.

"I hope you have some serious armor-piercing needles in that little toy. Wrench has a Resilite-treated skull."

"Resilite . . ." Juliet breathed, frowning.

"It's a carbon-based nanocoating that makes bones extremely durable. While not fully bulletproof, the coating is highly efficient at distributing kinetic forces . . ." Angel stopped speaking as Tono laughed, exposing his gold-capped grill, reaching up to brush his curly black hair away from his face as he watched Nick struggle and Juliet scowl.

"Never heard of it, huh? Probably best to stick to the kiddie pool for now. Let the big boys talk business. Wrench, let him breathe."

His dismissal ignited a spark in Juliet, and she had to fight to keep her finger off the trigger, had to battle down the urge to step forward and smash her pistol grip into his forehead. The truth was, she felt like she'd been out-played; she'd grown so confident lately, sure in the speed of her arm, the aim of her gun, and Angel's capabilities. Now, she was faced with a chromed-out monster that made her look like a helpless kid, and he had his fingers wrapped around Nick's throat. Could she cut his arm off with a vibroblade? She doubted it; that arm was sturdy, and she had no idea what sort of alloy it was. Maybe if she had the monoblade . . .

While her mind raced, Tono looked to her right and said, "Not your business."

Juliet jerked her head to see the club's bouncer nod and back away, clearly avoiding eye contact with her. She wasn't surprised. How often had she seen people choose to avoid trouble rather than do the "right thing"?

"Let her get outta here, Tono," Nick gasped.

"I give you a chance to breathe, and you waste it on that? I don't care what this skinny doll does. I care about my money. You ready to sign a new contract?" While Nick gasped for air, maybe buying time, maybe truly unable to breathe, Juliet furiously sought ideas.

"Can you do anything to him?" she subvocalized, wondering if Angel could find some kind of port or exploit in the big man's cybernetics.

"He's hardened. Everywhere. I can't find an open port, and even if you had the capability, I don't think he'd feel an EMP . . ."

Juliet felt her frustration mounting. All her training, all her enhancements, even armed while he was empty-handed, she was powerless. She supposed that wasn't entirely true. She could kill Tono. She could unload her mag into Wrench and probably put him down. The only problem was that there was a great chance he'd kill Nick before he died. What it boiled down to was that these guys were willing to bet she wouldn't watch Nick die.

Tono asked Nick something, but Juliet didn't hear it. A thought had struck her like a lightning bolt. She was frantically searching for an action she could take, considering all of her options, her training, her gun, but she'd completely, almost like it was intentional, ignored her psionics lattice. She stared at Tono and slowly inhaled, willing his thoughts and secrets to come to her.

That's right, Nicky Boy, time to cave. Your little doll can't save you.

Juliet shook her head. That wasn't what she wanted. She didn't care about his surface thoughts. She stared daggers at him, zooming in on his flashy neon-yellow irises, digging with imaginary fingers, pulling at his deeper memories. As she did so, something weird happened: Tono scrunched up his eyebrows and slapped a hand to his head, frowning and blinking rapidly, and then Juliet saw a series of images flash through her mind's eye.

Lexi held her—his—hand, her fingers soft and cool, delicate in his grip. He rested a hand at the top of the wheel, buzzing from the j-mist, from the endorphins of sex, and from the amazing potential ahead. Everything was open. Everything was possible.

He looked into her bright, pale rose-colored eyes, watching her white-blonde hair blow in the open window, flicking back and forth under her chin, in front of her face, and then back as she smiled at him and brushed it to the side.

The image shifted.

Blood was everywhere. Broken glass, dirt, and shattered plastic clung to his hands and stabbed under his nails as he scrabbled around in the dark, smoky interior, trying to get a hold of Lexi, trying to pull her out. He finally got his fingers around her wrist and, with all his might, pulled her out through the upside-down window, over the purple-blue Callisto grass.

He sobbed and choked, bloody snot catching in his throat as it grew thick with emotion. She was dead. For sure, she was dead—one arm missing, her neck lolling around like a broken doll's. *What the fuck was he going to tell Carson? He'd kill him . . . No, no, Lexi had to disappear.*

That's it. That's it . . . She ran away with that punk, what was his name? Quentin. That's it. They ran to Earth.

As Juliet blinked and stepped back, she had to stare at Nick, Wrench, and Tono for several long moments before she realized where she was. The visions had seemed so real, so vivid, so complete, that she'd been Tono for a minute. It was disorienting and strange and not at all pleasant, and she was very glad to be back in her own body, her own mind.

The panic and despair, the self-loathing and guilt that Tono had felt when Lexi died—Juliet had felt them all, had lived them, and she still felt the echoes of those emotions. She felt like vomiting, like running away and curling up in bed. She wanted to grieve that girl she'd never known but somehow had loved and lost . . . and killed.

"Ten flights. That should cover what you owe me, Nick. Let's get this contract settled, get you set up for your first job, and then we can put this unpleasantry behind us."

"And my expenses in the meantime?" Nick rasped.

Juliet looked at Tono and studied his face, trying to guess how old he was. When she'd entered his memory, she'd gotten the impression he was young, just past the point of being considered a kid. Now, he looked like he might be forty.

She cleared her throat. "Tono, when's the last time you spoke to Carson?"

His eyes snapped wide open, and he gave her a double take, stepping back in surprise. "What did you say?"

"I said, when's the last time you spoke to Carson?"

"Ahem, uh, Carson?" His tan complexion had lost three or four shades, gone pallid and a little green. "You mean Ben Carson?"

"Yeah. On Callisto." Juliet lowered her gun and took a step closer.

"It's, uh, been a while. You know Carson?"

"Sure. We were talking the other day. He was reminiscing about Lexi. You remember her, right?"

"Lex . . ." He licked his lips and looked left to right, then actually glanced over his shoulder. "Lexi? He mentioned her?"

"Yeah. He's been trying to find her, trying to follow up on some rumors about the guy she ran off with. He couldn't remember exactly who gave him the bullshit story about that, but your name came up. You know, I didn't put two and two together when I saw you with Nick here, but then my PAI reminded me that I'd heard it. Your name, I mean, and it clicked. I think Carson's looking for you."

"For . . ." Again, he licked his lips and visibly swallowed. "For real?"

"Yeah. I'm wondering what he might pay to know where you got off to."

"But-but how did he find out my new handle?"

"That's a good question, bud. Those guys he was talking to? They were sure keen to find you, though."

"Guys?" In a move that almost brought a snort of laughter out of Juliet, he spun in a circle, staring into the shadows. "Wrench, let's go. We can catch up with Nicky Boy later." Wrench complied, releasing Nick and stepping back, glowering red eyes trained on Juliet.

"You want me to pass any words to Carson?" Juliet asked.

She tucked her needler back in the holster, yanked her vibroblade out of its sheath, and stepped between Wrench and Nick. The blade hummed and buzzed in her hand, and she flipped it in the air, letting it tumble in a buzzing blur before she snatched it with her augmented arm. It was trivial, really, when Angel sped up her mental processing; the knife hardly seemed to be moving as she snaked her arm out to grasp the hilt with her nimble fingers.

Wrench narrowed his eyes, and she swore he nodded imperceptibly, perhaps a nod of respect. She may or may not be able to punch his ticket with that needler, but a six-inch vibroblade through the eye socket wouldn't feel very good.

"How about I don't mess with Nick anymore, and you forget you saw me?" Tono backed up further, and Wrench slowly followed suit.

"I guess that's cool with me. I wouldn't say I liked the looks of those guys he hired, anyway. Nasty, nasty-looking fellows." Juliet shrugged and stretched out her arm, letting the tip of her vibroblade rattle against the plasteel wall of the building to her right. She delicately traced the outline of a heart, carving it into the hard surface. "Poor Lexi . . ." When she looked up, Tono and Wrench were gone, but she had tears in her eyes. She flicked off the blade and tucked it into her sheath.

"What the hell was that about?" Nick asked as he straightened up, rubbing at his raw, red throat.

"Lucky coincidence. I did an op where I heard some shit about that guy. Do me a favor, Nick, will you?"

"Yeah?"

"Let it drop. I'm not feeling great, and I want to hit the bunk. Let's put this station behind us ASAP, all right?" Juliet wasn't lying. She didn't feel good at all; she felt sick. The weird hangover-like residue of Tono's horror and guilt still clung to her, confusing her emotions and sense of self.

"Yeah, no argument. I'll drop it, but let me at least say thanks. Goddamn, I've never seen Tono that shade of green. Like he'd seen a ghost."

"Yeah." Juliet's voice was soft, almost a sigh, as an image of rose-colored eyes and soft, flowing white hair flashed through her mind. "A ghost."

13

FLIGHT MISSION

When Juliet woke the next day, it was to the sound of rattling plasteel panels and the vibration of thrusters shifting her center of gravity around. Nick was maneuvering the little ship.

It was little, but not as small as she'd imagined. She figured it was about half the size of the *Takamoto* gunship, but still bigger than any car she'd ever seen, with room to walk around—albeit hunched over—between a tiny storage bay with a small table, a fridge, and some cupboards, two tiny sleeping closets, and the cockpit, again, with two seats. As for accessing the drives or the powerplant, some parts were reachable through interior access panels, but any major work had to be done from the outside.

"Any messages?" she yawned, stretching as much as she could in the narrow bunk.

"Nick says to join him in the cockpit when you wake. Are you feeling better?"

Juliet knew Angel's concern stemmed from her being very withdrawn the night before, crawling into the acceleration couch, and—inexplicably, as far as Angel could tell—crying into her little gel-filled pillow.

"I am, but I still feel it. That horror and loss. Angel, thanks to that guy, Tono, I have a memory worse than almost anything from my real life. I know, objectively, that it wasn't me, but my feelings don't know it. I'm struggling to put it behind me."

"I'm sorry you're going through that. Do you feel like talking about what you saw yet?"

Juliet could tell Angel was being careful, trying to walk on eggshells. She'd snapped at her the night before, unwilling to detail what she'd experienced through her weird, deep connection to Tono's memory.

"I . . . First of all, I'm sorry I was short with you last night. I think it's still too fresh. Let's put it off for now."

"Do you want to have a session with Dr. Ming?"

"No, Angel, not right now. Thank you, really, but you don't have to be worried. I feel better than last night." Juliet heaved herself up, sitting on the side of the couch, then dug into her pack; it was right next to the bunk because less than a meter of empty floor space separated her from the sliding door. "No showers, right?"

"Not even sani-spray."

"Sheesh. How long are we going to be out?"

"According to Nick's flight plan, two and a half days."

"Guess we'll be pretty ripe." Juliet was only wearing a tank top and underwear, and she left them on as she began to climb into her flight suit. It was one piece of material, including rubbery, gel-filled soles that conformed to the contours of her feet.

After she shrugged her arms into the sleeves, she pulled the long, airtight zipper up from her crotch to her neck. The suit was compatible with a wide array of closed-air systems and helmets, but she'd just gotten a decent flight helmet with excellent display properties and good air circulation. "Does it look okay?"

"The suit? It's a perfect fit, and the blue tones look good with your hair."

"Nuclear." Juliet sighed, shaking her head. "Speaking of my hair, can you shorten it some more? Should I just cut it?"

"No! Don't cut it! The extrusion process takes much longer if we don't let the synthetic follicles manage the biomaterials. I can change it in either direction by roughly an inch per hour, but if we run out of biomaterials, growth will take ten times that long."

"Okay, well, I guess I want it shorter. Like, up to my ears, at least for now. Yeah." Juliet nodded, running her fingers through her hair. "Until I get a helmet that's more comfortable with longer hair."

"Got it."

Juliet stood and grabbed her little toiletries bag, making her way to the ship's tiny head, essentially another closet attached to the storage bay. It had a toilet, a sink, and a small, mirrored medicine cabinet. Juliet stared at herself for a long minute, solidifying the fact that she was, in fact, Juliet and not a hormonal young Tono. Her silvery eyes shone palely beneath her dark brows, and she bared her teeth, leaning close, looking for staining or, worse, something caught between them; she hadn't brushed the night before. Seeing nothing amiss, she bent to the little tap and got to work, scrubbing her teeth, using the exercise as a metaphor for washing away the residual emotions from her deep dive into Tono's mind.

A few minutes later, crouching low, she climbed into the crowded little cockpit of the *Lady Hawk*. Nick sat in the pilot's seat, and when he heard her, he gestured to the empty acceleration couch to his right and about half a meter further back. "Morning. Grab a seat and get jacked in."

Juliet nodded and stepped over the center-mounted flight stick, sinking down into the gel of the acceleration couch. It was tighter, with higher sides than the ones in the *Kowashi*, but she fit all right, and the gel came to life right away, actively contouring her body.

She pulled her data jack out of her arm and strung it up to the little console, and then her AUI lit up with dozens of little graphical dials and readouts. A lot of them were different from what she'd seen on the *Bumble* and the *Kowashi*, but she knew what most were after spending a few dozen hours in the sim with Angel's instruction. She saw the route Nick had plotted, where they'd meet the gas rig, where they were escorting it, and then, when it was full, the path they were meant to take to Callisto.

"So, pirates really operate out here, huh? What's in it for them attacking a big gas scooper?"

"Oh, yeah. Believe it. They usually disable the bigger ships and then demand a ransom not to blow 'em up. A few crews operate big enough ships to scrap and salvage even the giant gas guzzlers, though."

"Seriously?"

"Yeah, it's a real industry out here."

"Why don't the corpos clear 'em out? I mean, some of them have pretty big navies, don't they?" Juliet continued to familiarize herself with the *Lady Hawk*'s readouts and controls while they chatted. She saw the status readings for the guns, saw the ammo counts, and realized Nick was flying a Ranger with a stock loadout—two thirty-millimeter cannons.

"They try, but the pirates are hard to pin down, and if you don't hit 'em with overwhelming force, you're going to suffer some very expensive losses. Corpos tend to just rely on escorts, using their own pilots or, when they can't cover all their ships, hiring jockeys like me." He punched in a few commands on the weird, old mechanical keyboard on his console—it looked like an aftermarket addition—then said, "Can you tell me what the hell was going on with you and Tono last night? Alice made it sound like you'd never been out toward Jupiter before."

"Well, Nick, Alice doesn't know everything about me. She's right, though; I've never been out this way. I do talk to a lot of people, though, and I learned about a guy on Callisto who's looking for his missing daughter. I was looking into him, thinking of taking on a new job, you know? Well, turns out, some of the people he's already hired think Tono might be responsible for his daughter's disappearance. It's kind of a freak coincidence, but I happened to hear about it. I had no idea who Tono was at the time, but I guess I made a lucky jump when I connected the dots." Juliet shrugged, even though Nick wasn't looking at her.

She'd rehearsed the line of bullshit while she'd been brushing her teeth. It sounded ridiculous, the weird, far-fetched story, but what was Nick supposed to think? That she'd read Tono's mind? The simple fact was that the truth was harder to believe than the wild coincidence she'd just described.

Nick seemed to draw the same conclusion as he fished his vape out of his pocket, slid his visor up, and took a drag. When he exhaled, he nodded and said, "Guess that was my lucky night. Shit, is that why they call you Lucky?"

"Something like that." She glanced at the flight path. "Twenty minutes to rendezvous?"

"Yep. Pick up the big fat bird, then follow her to Jupiter's upper atmos."

"We the only escort?"

"That's right, sugar. Why do you think I get paid the big money?"

"Sugar?" Juliet raised an eyebrow.

"Ugh, sorry. Sometimes I fly with partners, you know, other interceptors, and we talk a lot of shit on comms. I didn't mean anything by it."

"I've heard worse. Just as long as you take me seriously where flying's concerned, all right?"

"Yeah, 'course. I mean, some of the best pilots I've known were hot chicks, Alice included."

"Jeez! You were digging yourself out of one hole, and now you double down? Hot chicks? Come on, Nick." Juliet shook her head, equal parts amused and irritated. He hadn't acted that way at all in the club, and she wondered if he was one of those guys whose personality altered significantly behind the wheel or, in this case, the flight stick.

"What? All right, all right." He held up his hands in surrender. "I'm messing around; relax. Trying to get a feel for you, 'kay? I mean, time goes a lot faster out here if you can bullshit with your copilot."

"We can bullshit, but like I said, take me seriously."

"Roger, Sarge." His response got a smile out of Juliet. Something about his tone and the words brought to mind Houston and Charlie Unit, and, as long as she didn't let her mind wander far enough to dwell on how things ended with them, she liked to think about those guys.

"You do any time in a military unit?"

"Yeah." He nodded, drumming his hands on the sides of his acceleration couch. Juliet wondered what music he was listening to. "Back in the day. I met Alice around Venus, where we both flew for the civil defense force."

"That's right." Juliet flipped through the ship's console commands on her AUI, looking for his audio channel. She patched herself in, and suddenly, her implants were pounding with bass-heavy electronica. "She told me that. Damn, I like this beat!"

"Hell yeah! I knew we'd get along." He looked back at her and grinned, then he reached forward and grabbed his stick with one hand and the throttle with the other. "Ready to see what this lady can do?"

"Hit it!" Juliet yelled, even though their implants were perfectly capable of filtering their voices through the music.

"You asked for it!" Nick laughed, then he pushed the throttle forward, and Juliet's stomach tried to find its way out through her throat. She felt the couch working to compensate for the Gs, but it wasn't enough, and she had to clench her abdomen, lock her neck muscles, and suck in tiny, consecutive breaths, fighting to keep the black tunnel walls in her vision from closing in. Angel helped, of course, regulating the pressure in her implants, directing her nanites, and stimulating her leg muscles to help her keep her blood flowing. Meanwhile, Nick started to do barrel rolls and loops.

Juliet was torn between enjoying the thrilling fluctuating G-forces, watching out the vidscreen, studying the AUI, and watching Nick. She wanted to see how he was doing what he did, wanted to understand the nuances that allowed him to transition from maneuver to maneuver, pushing tremendous Gs while still maintaining control of the ship and avoiding blacking out. He didn't have a flight suit any fancier than hers; his body wasn't jacked into the acceleration couch. How was he so in control? Juliet could barely keep the darkness at bay, could barely control her eyes, let alone her hands.

She wasn't sure how long he kept that throttle pegged, how long he kept rolling and looping the ship; the seconds bled into minutes, which bled into each other as the thrill faded and Juliet's world became one long straining workout, a constant struggle to keep from passing out. Finally, he relented, though, and slowly inched the throttle back, gradually dropping them back down to a single G, and when he turned to regard her, he wore a huge smile.

"Shit, girl. I thought you'd be out by now! We held nine Gs for a few seconds there."

"You . . ." Juliet gasped, grunting as her abdominal muscles started to cramp. Nick stared at her as she silently battled with the uncontrolled contraction. Angel and her nanites must have come to the rescue because her abs suddenly released, and she took in a long, shaky breath. "You were trying to make me pass out?"

"Just seeing what you're made of. Nothing personal, but I gotta know what kinda shit you can tolerate out here. What'd you think, anyway?" His grin was absurd, and Juliet had the feeling he wanted her to compliment the ship's—and his—capabilities. She decided to play it cool.

"Not too bad, I guess. For a ship this size."

"Seriously?"

While he stared at her slack-jawed, Angel spoke up. "Juliet, he was being quite reckless with your safety. If you had a little less physical tolerance and no nanites to help repair microbursts in your blood vessels, he could have caused you serious harm, especially with the vertical G-forces he was pulling!"

Juliet smiled, filing Angel's warnings away for later. "So, tell me something, Nick. Can I be honest with you, or will you use everything I say against me? I mean, like when it comes to giving or not giving a good report to Alice?"

"I'll make you a deal." He paused and reached up to pull his vape off a magnetic mount above his head on the edge of the viewscreen. After a long drag, he continued. "I won't judge you until the final evaluation. Everything you tell me or do up to that point will be between you and me."

"Promise?"

"Yeah, go ahead, open up."

Juliet stared at him for a second, and then she did just that: she opened up and tried to hear his thoughts.

I mean, I'm not gonna send Alice some nutjob or loose cannon. I'm good at keeping secrets, though, right? Shit, I hardly ever talk shit about my friends behind their backs. Well, unless I drink too much.

Crap, have I already talked about Alice behind her back with her? Would I trust me if I were her? I'm not a bad guy, am I? Okay, bottom line: if she can fly, she can fly.

Damn, those eyes are nice, though, and what about those legs? Oh, come on, old man, get your head straight! Alice will have your balls if you . . .

Juliet tuned him out with a physical effort that included jerking her eyes up to the AUI and trying to multiply some numbers she read there. It worked, and the music took center stage in her awareness again. She drummed her fingers on the arms of the acceleration couch, then looked back at Nick, who was still staring at her, waiting for her to "open up." She cleared her throat and said, "Sorry, I was just making a note to add this to one of my playlists."

"Oh, yeah? Shit, if you think it's good now, wait 'til we crank these beats while we're in a dogfight."

"Sounds nuclear." Juliet smiled and shifted in her acceleration couch, her heart rate finally starting to feel normal. "So, tell me, how long did it take you to be able to function so well during high Gs? I mean, do you have mods? How'd you keep such good control during that?"

"Practice, practice, practice. I know you've flown some big birds and probably some sims, but nothing gets you ready for the Gs more than . . . the Gs. Gotta get in the cockpit and put yourself through it on the regular. Is that what you were worried about? Alice already told me you weren't actively flying, so I knew you'd be a little soft. Still, you held on, and that's what it's about. It's all gravy now, Lucky."

"Oh, cool." Juliet bobbed her head, nodding, looking into his eyes briefly but looking away again before she started to get more of his thoughts.

"There are some mods you can get, though. I don't have any, mind you, but they're out there. I don't wanna talk to you like you're a kid; you're aware of this stuff, right? I mean, you wouldn't be trying to be a pilot if you weren't already interested . . ."

"Yeah, I know, Nick, thanks. I mean, we're talking everything from a reinforced skeletal structure to Active-flex arteries and vessels to supplemental blood pumps to—"

"Right, right. All that crazy shit. That stuff helps, but nothing can replace skill. Keep that in mind." He reached up and stuck his vape to the magnet again, then, as he made a slight course adjustment, asked, "You want me to set these flights up as SOA jobs? I don't mind—worked with a few operators in my day, and they always get all excited to be earning some rep for flying—"

"Yes! That would be shiny!"

"Like chrome?" Nick chuckled, completing the popular phrase.

"Glassy, smooth, sun-blazed chrome, Nick." Juliet laughed.

"Right on. Well, sending you the job listing."

"I've received a new SOA job card," Angel announced, and then she put the minimized file on her AUI. Juliet zoomed in and read the "job" Nick had set up for her.

Posting #J0987	**Requested Role:** Interceptor Pilot	**Rep Level:** D-S+
Job Description: Copilot role on the *Lady Hawk*. Escort gas-harvesting ship for Greater Gas Corporation in the Jovian planet system. Escort from Io Station locale to Jupiter and then to Callisto main docks.		**Compensation:** Professional Service Trade
Scavenge Rights: Shared	**Location:** Jovian System	**Date:** June 12, 2108

"Professional service trade?" Juliet raised an eyebrow.

"Yeah. You scare away thugs looking to rob me, and I'll teach you how to fly like a boss." Nick turned and winked at her; then, almost impulsively, reached up for his vape again.

"Do I get any compensation for inhaling all those fruity vape gases?"

"Fruity? This one's vanilla!"

Juliet made a gagging noise, then laughing, said, "Anyway, thanks for helping me get some rep while I'm out here with you."

"A pleasure, milady." Nick sucked on his vape before he gestured to the vidscreen. "See that bright spot ahead? That's the GG-702, our damsel in distress. We'll be keeping her safe today and tomorrow."

Juliet looked at the bright spot and watched as it grew larger. The glow resolved into drive plumes as the ship began to take shape. From their current distance, it still looked tiny, but Juliet knew better. The two tanks that comprised most of its hull could hold more than three hundred thousand tons of liquified gas.

"Well, Angel," she subvocalized, "we're in it now. I hope Nick is as good as he says he is."

14

\\\\\\\\\\\\\\\\\\\\\\\

DOGFIGHT

Juliet stood in the lobby adjacent to *Lady Hawk*'s berth on Callisto and looked at the little wedge-shaped ship through the viewport, watching as the crew of the repair company Nick had hired worked to replace the malfunctioning maneuvering thruster on the aft lower port side. She was wearing her flight suit and sipping from a paper cup of hot tar-colored coffee. They had an escort job waiting, one they were already an hour late to, and Nick was losing his shit, pacing back and forth, trying to explain their tardiness to their client, some rep from Mass Gas.

If the ship got fixed in time, this would be Juliet's third job with Nick. She'd learned a lot about little fighter ships and their quirks, listened to a few dozen stories about Nick's exploits, but seen very little action. The views, though, were almost worth the time she'd spent with him. Nothing could compare to flying in the gas giant's upper atmosphere except maybe the breathtaking vistas she was awarded pretty much every time the ship changed direction. Something about seeing Jupiter up close, filling the horizon for as far as her enhanced vision allowed, broken only by the bodies of its orbiting satellites in their reflective splendor hanging like jewels in the blackness, made every second of flying out there dreamlike.

She sipped her bitter brew and listened to Nick for a minute. ". . . exactly what I'm telling you. Just give me another hour to get this repair done, and we'll double-time it out to your ship. It'll be faster than trying to get a replacement escort."

Juliet sighed and walked over to a recycler to toss her half-full cup into it, watching as it gobbled the cup and liquid down its gullet then hummed and vibrated, processing the waste.

"Hope he calms the client down. Hate to have to waste a day sitting around the dock."

"You could head further into the dome, perhaps visit a restaurant."

Angel had been bugging her to explore Callisto a little more. She'd gone out with Nick once to see his house in an agridome, but for the most part, she hung around the port district, staying in a hotel that was cheap but clean. She liked Nick just fine, and his house was nice enough with a comfortable guest room, but she didn't like being so . . . under his control, she supposed was how she thought of it. He was in charge of her "job" and her future in regard to flying for Shiro and Alice; she didn't want to add room and board to the list.

"Yeah, maybe." She looked out the big viewport at the rough surface of the moon; they were at the far edge of the dome, and the area outside was a raw, natural moonscape. "At least we know this isn't the moon from my dream."

"From your description, I think our best bet would be Europa or Ganymede. Of course, one of the many smaller moons might have similar soil, ice, and rock compositions, but they wouldn't match the gravity you experienced or have the massive ridges and canyons you described. If I were betting, I'd say it would be Ganymede."

"If we get a few days off, I guess we could try to get out that way. Need a ship, though." Juliet turned back to the *Lady Hawk* and rubbed her chin. "No way Nick would let us borrow her. I guess we could hire a tour ship."

"Good news!" Nick announced as he walked over the plasteel flooring toward her. "Looks like the client isn't going to bail. Well, as long as we make it to the rendezvous within an hour. How's it looking out there?" He turned toward the window where they could observe the technicians working on the ship.

"Seems like they're making good time. Old thruster is out, and you can see 'em welding the new supports in."

"Good, good. Probably could've limped around with that faulty maneuvering jet for a while, but it would've sucked if we ran into trouble and couldn't, you know, maneuver." He fished his vape out of his front pocket; then, as he held it in the corner of his mouth, added, "I'm glad Mass Gas didn't bail on us; they pay better than GG."

"GG? Oh, Greater Gas?"

"Right. Pretty creative names, eh?"

"No one ever accused corpos of being creative." Juliet eyed his vape and, for the briefest moment, felt a little envious. She wanted something in her mouth just then—coffee, a salty chip, even a soda. Was his habit brushing off on her, secondhand? She'd never really felt like she had any sort of oral fixation before . . .

"No love for the corpos, huh?"

"Come on." Juliet snorted and turned to look at the nearby vending machines. "Want anything?" She gestured at them.

"Nah." He blew a long stream of caramel-scented vapor out of his nose.

"What would it cost me to get you to stop sucking on that thing around me?"

"Oh Lord, you're starting to sound like my ex-wife."

"Seriously?" Juliet contemplated giving him a smack, just a quick slap with her augmented arm, nothing that would do any real damage . . .

"Sorry, sorry." He must have seen something dangerous in her eyes. He held up his left hand placatingly as he slipped the vape into his pocket. "I'll try to cut back, all right?"

"Thanks." Juliet walked over to the machines and studied the contents. She decided against another drink; she hated using the toilet on the little ship. Instead, she settled on some corn-flavored chips called Corn Insanity. When she sampled the first one, she could see why. They had a vaguely cornlike base flavor but were topped with a thick orange layer of seasoning that reminded her of equal parts lime, salt, and something extremely spicy. Despite her initial revulsion, she found herself craving another and then another, and soon, she'd emptied the little bag.

"Your nanites will be working double time to save you from that garbage," Angel's voice dripped with judgment.

"That's what I pay them for."

Juliet crumpled the package and threw it in the recycler, then she sat on a bench and watched Nick pacing in front of the viewport. He was a decent guy, even if his mouth ran away from him from time to time. So far, though he'd definitely given her a few too many lingering looks, he hadn't gotten handsy or anything like that. Still, Juliet was looking forward to the day she could shake his hand and be on her way. The whole reason she liked the idea of flying was the freedom of it, and she felt very decidedly not free while stuck in Nick's copilot seat.

"Let's send a message to Honey," she said abruptly.

"Okay! Ready when you are."

"Hey, Honey. Long time no chat. I tried to get together with you before I left Luna, but, you know, you were pretty busy. Hope things are settling down for you. Let's talk soon, like, before things get awkward between us, hey? No hard feelings from me, so just be cool and send me a note. Let me know what you're up to. As for me? I'm out trying to learn to be a better pilot. I'm not loving everything about it, but shoot, Honey, I've seen some awesome sights and felt some serious Gs! Makes fast cars seem decidedly not fast, you follow? Hah, well, looking forward to hearing from you. Bye for now."

"Send it?"

"Yeah, and take another for Bennet."

"Ready."

"Bennet! I miss lifting weights and talking nonsense with you. Hope you're doing well all by yourself there on Luna. I mean, hopefully you're not by yourself, and things are still going okay with your girlfriend. What's up with our girl? By our girl, I mean the gunship, so don't get confused. Fill me in on all the details! I need some light reading to help me pass the time between flight missions. Miss you lots, Lucky."

"Sent!"

"Thanks."

"Looks like they're buttoning her up!" Nick called, interrupting her thoughts. "Let's get out there and load up; we need to make a forty-minute flight in twenty-eight."

"Ugh, maybe I shouldn't have eaten those chips . . ."

Ninety minutes later, they were flying a close escort next to a gargantuan refinery ship as it took slow, ponderous-looking dives through the upper reaches of Jupiter's atmosphere. Nick kept the Lady up, just outside the worst of the turbulent, roiling clouds, but always close enough that he could fire upon anything that came near enough to threaten the Mass Gas ship. Hour after hour of trailing gargantuan, slow ships lost its novelty about halfway through their second job, and Juliet had difficulty focusing on the big gas-scooping tanker. She tuned out a lot, flipping through the menus on the *Lady Hawk*'s HUD, listening to music, and just taking in the sights.

One positive out of the whole thing was that she'd gotten more and more practice with high Gs. Nick made it a point of going through maneuvers every couple of hours, pushing her to her limits and, subsequently, increasing her tolerance. Additionally, she was earning rep for the jobs she did with him.

He gave her a new contract card for each escort mission, and her rep numbers were steadily climbing. If nothing else, she was grateful to him for that.

"Huh," Nick said, and something in his tone brought Juliet's attention snapping back to the moment.

"What?"

"Did you see that reflection off the rig's port side? In that big, swirly orange cloud?"

"No . . ."

"My PAI's sending a replay. Watch it and tell me what you think."

Juliet watched as Angel opened a vid window, and a zoomed-in view of the cloud in question came into focus. Sure enough, two seconds into the clip, a flash of light flickered behind a layer of haze. "Angel . . ."

"Definitely a reflection of the sun's light. I'd bet on something metallic or glass."

"I think it's a ship, Nick!"

"Yeah. Get ready." As he spoke, he pushed the throttle forward and banked hard to port, rolling the *Lady Hawk* down toward the factory-size gas harvester. "I'm gonna swoop up underneath her." Juliet knew he meant the gas ship when he said her.

"What if more of them are lurking?"

"Maybe. Keep your thumb on those countermeasures."

"You want me to manage them?"

"Why not," Nick grunted as the Gs steadily rose. Juliet was pulled back into her seat, and she had to fight to push her arm forward enough to put a hand on the stick between her thighs. It had mechanical switches for everything from the main gun to the maneuvering jets to the chaff and flare launchers. She could manage those things electronically through Angel, but according to Nick, it was a bad habit. In his words, "Shit tended to go wrong with electronics during a dogfight."

"Goddamn, these wind shears are no joke!" he growled as the ship rattled and vibrated, swooping down under the big rig and up on her port side.

Almost too fast for Juliet to register, he choked out half a curse, yanked his stick to the left, and backed off the throttle. Her stomach lurched and tumbled, and the couch tightened on her, squeezing her like a giant, gel-lined fist, keeping her from flipping out at the sudden maneuver. Suddenly, a deep rumble rolled through the plasteel beneath her feet, and the ship strafed to the left, jerking and bumping in the heavy winds and thick atmosphere. Nick was shooting at something.

Juliet saw a red flash on her AUI, realized the ship's sensors were screaming about something incoming, and popped off a canister of chaff and a flare. The chaff was meant to cause disruption to radar-based tracking systems, and the flare was for heat-seeking missiles or smart rounds. Juliet couldn't tell what was coming at them, so she decided to err on the side of too much countermeasure rather than too little. A deep roar rumbled through the ship, and clinks and plinks by the hundreds rattled through the plasteel as something showered the hull.

"Nice one!" Nick howled. The guns rumbled again as the ship jerked left and right, rolling like an out-of-control kite in a hurricane-force wind. Juliet struggled to hold steady, to keep her eyes on the readouts, and to keep the contents of her stomach inside her. Though the Gs were rough, they never got as intense as when Nick did their "training sessions." Juliet wondered if that was by design. After a few seconds, she oriented herself enough to see the little radar readout and began to form a picture in her mind of what Nick was doing.

He was pursuing one blip while avoiding a second one. His erratic maneuvers were meant to throw off pursuit while, at the same time, he managed to keep the focus of his twin thirty-millimeter cannons on the ship in front of him. As she cycled through the external cams and caught sight of the pursuing vessel—a big, fat, yellow-and-black cucumber-shaped thing with stubby wings—she realized it was struggling to match Nick's evasive maneuvers. That didn't stop it from firing a steady stream of fiery cannon rounds in his general direction, though even Juliet could see the pilot was hopelessly behind with his targeting.

The flashing red "Incoming" light flared again, and Juliet popped two more countermeasures. Nick howled with glee as a much deeper, louder rumble rolled through the canopy, and she jerked her head to the front viewscreen in time to see him strafe past the burst, smoking wreckage of the first pirate ship as it succumbed to Jupiter's pull. "Now we pick apart that fat bird." He jerked back on the stick, and they made a backward loop as he brought his guns to bear on the yellow cucumber ship.

Now that Nick didn't have to evade one ship while pursuing a fast, nimble target, he literally flew circles around the bigger, slower vessel and did just what he'd promised: picked it apart with his cannons. In seconds, smoke and fire were streaming out of the ruptured hull, and the second pirate ship was falling into the crushing, ripping, deeper atmosphere of the enormous gas giant.

"Well, that was too quick. Never got a chance to turn on some music." Nick slapped his visor up and reached for his vape, taking a long, long pull. It was the first time he'd used it since they'd left port, and Juliet had to admire that he'd taken her admonishment to heart. "Pixie, call up the tanker."

Pixie was Nick's PAI, and he usually subvocalized, but he was clearly amped up and probably found speaking more natural. Juliet could see a tremor in his hand as he maneuvered the ship back toward the gas rig, and she knew he was chock-full of adrenaline. "All clear out here. Did you take any hits?" Juliet tabbed through the HUD to access the ship's broadcast comms so she could hear both sides of the conversation.

"No hits. They sent us a ransom demand before you started shooting. I think they expected you to talk first."

"Then they should've done more research." Nick chuckled. "Sneak up on my principal, and I consider you hostile. Period."

"Much appreciated, *Lady Hawk*; we'll relay your decisive, vehement protection in your rating. I'll try to talk to corporate about a bonus, too."

The person on comms sounded like an older man with an accent Juliet couldn't place. He rolled his Rs and clipped off his multisyllable words in a way that made her want to ask Angel to provide captions. The conversation was over, though, and after Nick cut comms, he turned to her and said, "Not bad with the countermeasures. You took it a little close for comfort on that first one, but you got it. Can't fire 'em too early anyway, right?"

"Uh, right." Juliet grinned, trying to relax the tension in her neck and shoulders. The dogfight had been eye-opening. Everything had happened so fast, and Nick's ability to function under the strain had really illuminated just how far she had to go. If she had the *Takamoto* gunship right now and Nick wanted to shoot her down, she didn't think she'd stand a chance.

"Anyway, that was a pretty good orientation to ship-to-ship combat. Gotta be aware of all the angles while you take 'em out one by one. I picked on the little guy first because I knew I could stay out of the boat's crosshairs."

"Boat?"

"As in big, fat, slow, floats around . . . you get the idea."

"Right, right." Juliet tried not to blush, which made it worse.

"Anyway, that's lesson number one: prioritize your targets. In ship combat, unless we're talking about a really big ship with lots of automated turrets, missiles, and torps, it's probably best to pick the smaller targets first. If I'd been shooting at the big, fat guy, the interceptor might have gotten some licks in. This old girl's tough, but armor-piercing rounds will, indeed, pierce her armor."

"Right. So, you let the slow guy try to follow while you kept the pressure on the fast guy." Juliet nodded, wondering how Nick had even realized there were two pirates so quickly.

"Yep. It was nice not having to worry about missiles. You did a good job with the chaff and flares, but for future reference, if the MAWS light is yellow, fire the chaff. If it's red, fire the flare. If it's alternating red and yellow, fire them both." He grinned at her. "Don't sweat it, though; I usually fire both just to be sure. They only cost a couple hundred bits for each canister."

"Angel," Juliet subvocalized, "MAWS?"

"Missile Approach Warning System."

"Right, got it. That was pretty wild, Nick. Not gonna lie—I felt a lot like I did in my first firefight. I mean between people, not ships!" She laughed.

"Oh yeah! Definitely. You'll hopefully get some more experience in the next couple of weeks. I was surprised it took this long for us to get jumped. We've got a wild one lined up tomorrow, by the way—escorting some salvagers who have some kind of hot tip. They wouldn't tell me what it was, but let me put it this way: if they got a tip, they probably aren't the only ones. You copy?"

"Copy, Nick. Sounds a little familiar, in fact."

"Hah, right. Well, let's see if we get any more action today, huh? That rig's only half full."

15

A BIG IRON

Juliet sat in the crowded diner, sipping an actual decent cup of coffee and watching the people walking outside in the light Callisto drizzle. One thing she liked about Callisto the city, not necessarily the moon, was that it had been designed to cater to pedestrian traffic, like many of the original colony domes. It wasn't that she had anything against cars; in fact, she loved them, but she also liked how busy and alive the streets seemed when everyone was walking to and fro.

Callisto's central dome, she'd been told, was similar in climate to Seattle in the spring. During the day cycle it was warm, on the verge of being chilly, and at night, it was perfect weather for sipping hot drinks or soup or cuddling up under a blanket. She liked it, but she supposed part of that was because she'd grown up in the desert, and it was novel.

The construction of the buildings lining the streets was similar to what she'd seen in Luna City, but something about them seemed more real, for lack of a better word. They were less uniform, less fairy tale, and more lived-in. With the frequent drizzling rains, things seemed fresher, and though they wore more layers, the people seemed friendlier. Juliet liked Callisto.

It was the start of her third week working with Nick, and she had a few days off. Nick was entertaining a "visiting friend" and had declined a couple of jobs to give himself time with his guest in the agridome where he had his cabin. Juliet didn't mind; they'd seen a lot of action over the last week, and she could use some time alone to decompress, especially since he'd promised to let her take the pilot's stick on their next outing. She was excited, but also horribly nervous. She'd helped Nick take out nearly a dozen pirates and seen just how quick and brutal encounters with skilled pilots could be.

Nick took the risks in stride, probably because he had hundreds of dogfights under his belt, and he was, as he liked to say, one of the "top-ten rated pilots in the Jovian System." Juliet admired his skill but had come to suspect that the *Lady Hawk* was far from a standard interceptor. Nick made a killing on each outing where he shot down pirates—not just from the contract payment for protection but by collecting bounties. The pirates always gave off fake ID pings, but every ship was different, not just the make and model but unique markings, from paint to battle scars to aftermarket mods. His PAI took videos of his encounters, and if he was able to make a positive ID based on the images of the ships, he often collected hefty bounties.

With all that income in mind, Juliet knew Nick had to be doing something with his money, and she'd seen how he babied the Lady. Her first clue about the ship's mods had come when she'd seen the maneuvering jet replaced. Later, when reflecting on her day, Angel had pointed out that the manufacturer of the part wasn't the same as the stock model, and with a bit of digging, she'd found the specs for the replacement. It was a good thirty percent more powerful than stock. Angel had confirmed, based on functionality, that the power plant, drives, and even the twin cannons were heavily modded, but couldn't determine exactly how without Juliet getting an eye on the components. The moral of the story was that Nick was an ace pilot, sure, but his ship was something special, too.

"Tiger99 should be here soon," Angel said, interrupting Juliet's musing.

She wasn't at the diner just to get breakfast and a good cup of coffee; she'd arranged to meet a guy selling a customized handgun. Juliet grinned at the thought. Aya's suggestion that she read some Westerns had proved to be a little problematic. She now couldn't stop fantasizing about a big-bore revolver in a quick-draw holster. When she'd looked in the gun shops around Callisto, however, she hadn't found one that quite struck her fancy, so Angel had been perusing the secondhand markets, and "Tiger99" had an interesting model for sale.

"Do you think I'm being silly? I mean, my needler has a lot more practical use. More rounds per magazine, nonlethal options, and it's certainly easier to conceal."

"You don't intend to discard your needler, do you?"

"Nah, good point."

"You can wear your new gun for a while, and if you find your . . . well, your fantasy doesn't live up to reality, you can hang it on a peg in your room next to some of your paperbacks."

"Hah. It's kind of an expensive piece of decoration. I haven't bought it yet, though. Let's see if I like it in person as much as I did in the photos. Is that Tiger99? The guy by the door looks lost." Juliet waved to the skinny, long-haired fellow wearing weird, half-moon specs that sat near the tip of his long, angular nose.

"That's him. I just received an ID ping."

The man smiled, adjusted the collar of his knee-length, olive-green raincoat, and approached Juliet's table. His smile was friendly, and his wispy, clearly never shaved pale brown beard was kind of cute in an endearing sort of way. He reminded Juliet of some friends she and Felix had in their early twenties who hadn't quite realized they were adults yet. She smiled back and looked into his pale green eyes as he sat across from her.

"Hey there!"

"Nice to meet you, Tiger99."

Oh lord, didn't I put my name on the message I sent her? Why'd I put a 99 on that? Why tiger? Oh, jeez, I seem like such a dweeb. Why not something . . . Shit! Did she say something else? Oh, dammit, I'm staring at her like an idiot! What do I say? Oh! The gun!

"Uh, hey, um, Lucky. Interested in the Texan?"

Of course she is, dummy! Interested? Come on, think of something else . . .

Juliet chuckled and did her best to tune out his thoughts, focusing on something other than him. She picked up her coffee cup, swirling the creamy brown contents, watching how it made a miniature whirlpool at the center. She continued to smile, trying to look friendly. "Yeah, I'm interested. Relax! You seem nervous. I'm not going to rob you or something."

"Oh, good." He laughed a little nervously, then gestured to his bulky, damp raincoat. "I've got it here."

"And the holster? I was as interested in your leatherwork as the gun."

"Oh yeah, of course." He shook his head and pushed his glasses up. "I can't promise the leather came from Texas, but it's cowhide, nonetheless. I think it's from Mars."

Juliet chuckled, idly rubbing at the back of her left hand with her other thumb. "No worries. Well? Are you going to let me see it?"

"Oh, right!" He pulled his zipper down and reached under the coat, pulling out a package wrapped in a pale-yellow cloth. It was secured with two shrink cords. "Didn't want anything to fall out." He placed it on the table then patted at his chest and then at his pants, a look of panic twisting his expression. "Shit! I didn't bring any scissors."

"I got it." Juliet flicked her vibroblade out of her wrist sheath and deftly parted the shrink cords with a featherlight touch.

"Th-thanks." As Juliet slipped the knife back in its sheath, he reached forward and began to unwrap the cloth, exposing a lovely, supple, well-oiled black leather belt and holster, custom-made to hold the heavy-looking pistol inside it.

"Whoa. I like the silver rivets."

"Yeah, it's a nice piece. Took me a while to get the look just right. It's meant to sit low on your hip, so the belt has to be comfortable in a kind of canted position. I had to source a lot of different leather samples before I found what I wanted—supple but stiff enough that when you pull the gun, it doesn't move."

"And the loop at the end? It goes around my thigh?"

"Right."

"Okay, so you've got what it takes when it comes to leatherwork. Let's take a look at this beauty." Juliet reached forward to pull the pistol out of the holster while Tiger99 sat back, pushing his glasses up on his nose again. They began to slide down almost immediately.

Juliet took hold of the biometrically adaptive grip, smiling as she felt the black polymer instantly mold to the contours of her hand. The gun slid smoothly out of the holster, almost like it wanted to come out, and Juliet saw the black zero-resistance lining Tiger99 had seamlessly stitched into the interior.

The Eager and Young, model 2088 Texan was supposed to be the pinnacle of revolver technology, and when Juliet laid her eyes on it and felt the weight in her hand, she couldn't stop the massive grin that pulled her cheeks back toward her ears. Sure, the pistol was a revolver, but it was something else compared to the cheap gun she'd bought back in Arizona. First of all, it was lightweight, and she knew that was because it was constructed of incredibly durable titanium and advanced carbon fiber composites. It had a sleek, smooth metallic appearance with a soft silver-gray finish. She couldn't see a screw, nut, or weld on the entire piece. It was so perfectly machined to fit that even the cylinder looked like it was part of the frame.

Still, when she touched the smooth metal above the trigger with her finger, the cylinder rotated out with a soft whir, and she saw the seven holes for the .357 caliber payload.

"Seven," she breathed softly, spinning the cylinder with satisfying, buttersmooth clicks on its perfect bearings.

"Yep. The alloy is so tough that they were able to squeeze in another chamber. See how close together they are? You've seen other revolvers, right? On a caliber this size, there's usually only room for six if you want to keep integrity . . ." He trailed off as Juliet twitched her wrist and the cylinder snapped home with a satisfying snick.

"It's lighter than I imagined. I figured with the electronics and the recoil-dampening stuff in the grip, it would weigh more."

"It'll weigh more with ammo in it, and the dampeners use electromagnets, but they're also made of a special alloy. Nobody's cracked the patent on these things. Not in the twenty years it's been out."

Juliet ran her eye down the sleek, seven-inch barrel. "No sights?"

"Well, they slow down the draw, and why would you need 'em? You've got targeting software, yeah? This thing will sync up with your PAI, no problem. Plus, I mean, if you're serious, you should put a few thousand rounds in at the range and practice your hip shot. You shouldn't need to aim at anything within five meters or so."

"You should ask him how many rounds have been through this gun's barrel. It might need retooling," Angel said.

"I didn't think of that." When Tiger99 raised an eyebrow, she pressed on. "Is this barrel good? How many rounds have you put through it?"

"That one? Only about ten. I wasn't joking about the strength of the alloys they used in that gun; the barrel's rated for two hundred thousand rounds. Anyway, yeah, I've hardly shot it; I have another model with a Jack of Spades enamel finish that's my daily shooter."

"Huh?"

"It's a popular vid series in the Jovian System, Juliet. It's an animated show about a gas pirate."

"Oh, you aren't familiar . . ."

"No, I get it. My PAI just filled me in."

"Right." Tiger99 seemed to fold into himself as he slouched, clearly embarrassed about his custom-enameled gun modeled after something in a cartoon.

She thumped the table with her left hand. "It sure sounds shiny, though, like chrome! What colors are the enamel?"

"Red and black! It's very cool, and I love how the black parts are around the cylinder; it never looks dirty."

"Nice!" Juliet hefted the gun again, then pointed it at the wall to the left. "Okay to dry fire it?"

"Sure. That revolver is as modern as they get. You won't hurt the firing pin."

Juliet nodded and gently pulled the trigger. Like it was floating in oil, the nearly invisible hammer slid back and clicked forward. She'd hardly felt the pull. "God, that's smooth."

"Oh, yeah. The stock mechanism is great, but as my ad said, this one's upgraded: Jupiter Arms' top-of-the-line competition trigger. Hey, if you're not used to fast drawing, I'd practice with blanks for a while 'cause you can blow your toes off with a trigger like that."

"Right. You said this thing will integrate with my PAI, though, yeah?"

"Oh, yeah, um, I mean yes. I guess if you have good software, it won't let you shoot yourself."

"That's what I was going to ask; the software can override a trigger pull?"

"Yeah, it's got all the bells and whistles. There's a pseudo-AI chip in that thing. It'll talk to you if you want."

"Uh, nah. I have enough voices in my head." Juliet slid the gun back into the holster and then tipped it upside down. Just as advertised, the zero-resistance lining was smart and didn't release the gun.

"Yeah, it won't come out if your hand isn't on the grip. Pretty cool, huh?"

"Very cool." She looked at him, making eye contact until his cheeks started to redden. "Gonna throw in any ammo for the price?"

"I have a box on me. Custom loads. If you like 'em, I ship to pretty much any port."

"Quite a little business you've got." Juliet nodded in approval, and his blush deepened.

"It's pretty niche, but the customers I have are loyal. I can point you to some reviews . . ."

"Nah, we're good, Tiger99."

"You can call me Ryan. I don't know why I keep that username. I guess 'cause it's tied to all my merchant accounts."

"Why? It's a cool name. Don't sweat it." Juliet kept one hand on the holstered pistol, confident she was going to buy it and not wanting to let it out of her control. She was in love. "Tell me about this custom ammo."

Ryan dug around inside his raincoat again, this time depositing a nondescript cardboard box on the table. He lifted the box top and revealed twenty-five brass bullets, primers facing up. He lifted one out of the little cardboard hole that held it in place and displayed it for Juliet.

The bullets were a lot bigger than her needler rounds, bigger than the nine-millimeter rounds she used in her SMG, too. It looked like a lot of powder would fit in that casing, and the red, polymer-jacketed bullet on the end looked like it would do a lot of damage.

"These are loaded to twenty percent above standard .357 spec. That gun can handle 'em, though. The polymer jacket is armor-penetrating but designed to sheer off after initial impact. The bullet underneath is a dense, highly deforming polymer meant to create a big mess inside whatever you shoot it at."

"Sounds nasty . . ."

"Very!" He grinned and nodded his head enthusiastically.

"You ever shoot someone with one?"

"Me?" His enthusiasm instantly turned to horror, and he held up both hands. "No, no, no. I am a craftsman, not a mercenary. If you want to know if it works, read some of my reviews. I have quite a few repeat customers."

"All right." Juliet shrugged and pulled the box of rounds over the tabletop closer to her. "I'll give 'em a try."

"So you're going to buy the gun?"

"It's pricey, but I like it. You wanted sixty-eight hundred, correct? Can you do an even 6k?"

"Seriously?" He sighed and started reaching for the holstered pistol. "That thing retails for seventy-five, and the trigger upgrade is a thousand bits."

Juliet clamped her hand down on the gun and smiled. "Relax! I was just seeing if you were desperate to sell. I'll pay the full sixty-eight." She subvocalized, "Angel, go ahead and complete the purchase."

Ryan smiled and sat back. "Ah, just got the transfer, and the contract daemon released the ownership title. It's all yours. You can go ahead and set the biometrics."

"Oh, I will." Juliet gripped the pistol and watched on her AUI as Angel paired with it and programmed the grip, the cylinder release, and the trigger with her biometric data. Then she slipped it out of the holster, popped the cylinder open, and began loading it with Ryan's custom bullets. "Think I'll wear it on the way home."

"Yeah, cool. It's a real showstopper. It's gonna look great on you." He coughed, almost a choke, as he realized what he was saying.

"Thank you, Tiger99." Juliet offered him a sweet smile and grinned as his fit intensified. She thought it was kind of cute how self-conscious he was.

"Want to have breakfast with me? I've only had coffee so far, and I'm a bit jittery. My stomach's crying for some real food."

While he struggled to formulate an answer, Juliet stood next to the table and slung the gun belt around her hips, smiling when she realized it had little tooled leather loops along the front for more bullets. It fit her perfectly as she fastened the silver buckle on the third notch.

"Looks good, and yeah, I could eat."

"Nuclear!" Juliet grinned, then put her foot on the bench seat and worked on tying the bottom of the holster around her thigh. She liked how the leather looked against her faded stretchy jeans. "How tight should it be?"

"You don't want it to constrict you, but you want it to keep the holster from moving away from your leg when you draw. Honestly, with that zero-resistance lining, you won't have to worry. Just tighten it to the point where it's still comfortable."

"Nice." Juliet put her foot down and straightened up, reaching down to put her palm on the gun's grip. A few patrons at nearby tables watched her, but she tried to ignore them. "Is that a good height?"

"Yeah. When you draw, lean back so you don't have to tilt the barrel much when you pull it up to fire."

"Right. I've read some . . . guides." Juliet had almost said books. She sat back down, winked at Ryan, and said, "Well, pard? How about some grits?"

"Huh?"

16

KILL OR BE KILLED

Juliet tried to keep her breaths steady and even, in and out through her nose, watching the readouts and tracking the little blips on the colorful three-dimensional proximity display at the lower center of her AUI. She'd learned, riding with Nick in the pilot's seat, that if she breathed too heavily inside her helmet, hot condensation would accumulate on the plastiglass, which could make parts of the holographic HUD look blurry. There were probably helmets with better air circulation that would alleviate a problem like that, but hers had issues. On the display, her ship—a blue triangle—was at the center, and she was tracking the harvester, a big magenta rectangle, and two pirates—red triangles.

"Are you sure you don't want the controls?" she asked again, jerking the stick to the left and pushing forward, trying to line up her sights on the priority-one target. She'd flagged it; Angel said the ship looked newer and had a dangerous rail gun she wouldn't want to be pointed at her tailpipes. A chuckle escaped her as she thought about it. Where had Angel heard the rear of a ship referred to as tailpipes?

"You got this. Come on, I've got your countermeasures." Nick sounded calm and relaxed, and she wondered if there was something off about the guy. His life was in her hands, and she was up against two pirates. She supposed part of his confidence was that he knew his ship was faster and more maneuverable than the shoddily maintained, decades-old interceptors the pirates were flying. He knew it, but he probably didn't think Juliet knew it.

Angel was remarkably good at identifying ships and spotting mechanical deficiencies.

The Lady could ramp up Gs far faster than either the *Bumble* or *Kowashi*, the only ships Juliet could validly compare her to. She'd flown simulated interceptors in her dream-rig, but it wasn't the same. Nothing the rig threw at her came close to the brain-bleeding, diaphragm-crushing jump from two to seven Gs in a handful of seconds that the Lady could pull off.

On top of that, she could strafe and turn much, much faster than the pirates she was currently facing. Juliet worked the pedals, the throttle, and the stick, bringing her nose to bear against the first interceptor, the one with the big rail gun.

"Good target choice." Nick's voice was a little clipped as he worked on his breathing, but Juliet knew he sounded better than she would. "I'm reading a big gun on that guy. As long as he's running from you, he can't point it at ya."

"Unless he does that!" Juliet cried, driving the ship's nose down and punching the throttle.

They never heard it, being in the very upper reaches of Jupiter's atmosphere where the air was so thin it almost didn't exist, but a rail gun round missed the Lady by just a dozen meters or so. Juliet's vision was tunneling as she fired the port maneuvering jets, strafing to the right, and then jerked the stick, bringing her nose back toward the pirate. He'd done a flip, still soaring outward away from Jupiter but facing her, using his momentum to keep moving away. Even so, Juliet's quick maneuver had brought her around to his port side, and she was closing fast.

"I'll help you line up the gimbals," Angel said, doing what she could to assist her aim as Juliet tried to get Nick's twin thirty-millimeter cannons pointing at the pirate. The gimbals Angel referred to were motorized mounts on the cannons which allowed them to move independently of the ship. Angel had a targeting program that she ran, using them to track the pirate and bring the crosshairs right into the little red circle where she was predicting the ship's movement would take it while the cannon rounds flew through the space between them. Juliet squeezed the trigger on the stick, and the low rumble of the cannons vibrated through the plasteel beneath her acceleration couch.

The whole time she'd been trying to follow the ship, avoid its rail gun shot, and now line up her crosshairs, she'd also been trying to keep tabs on the other pirate. Her movements thus far had gone a long way to keeping him off her six, but she saw him starting to line up.

Juliet mentally struggled with the dilemma. She knew she was on target at the moment; the targeting software was playing little pings in her auditory implants, letting her know the rounds were hitting. She might have already killed the ship, but it hadn't popped, wasn't burning. Should she pull off to avoid getting blasted? Should she stay on target another few seconds and keep pounding the first ship?

"Don't forget about your six . . ." Nick said, the first sign of nervousness entering his voice. Juliet grunted, held the trigger down for another full, pregnant second, then she fired the starboard maneuvering jets, yanked the stick back, and punched the throttle again. "Ugh!" Nick groaned, and Juliet grinned; it was harder to brace for quick maneuvers when you were a passenger. She knew she was going to do it, so she'd clenched up at just the right moment.

That was another thing she'd learned while flying in the pilot's seat: a lot of the hectic, stressful bewilderment she'd felt while riding shotgun had been simply because of that—she was the passenger, always a few milliseconds behind when Nick made a decision. When she was driving, she knew when the ship would turn, accelerate, decelerate, strafe, spin, and all the other things it did. She felt much more in control with a full front-seat view and all her attention on the job. Flying in the nav seat made it too easy to let your mind drift, too easy to miss a reflection or a heads-up light.

"You smoked him!" Nick crowed as she brought the ship around, catching the other little interceptor in the middle of a turn, and almost by luck, found her crosshairs just below his starboard side. Angel didn't waste time, locking the guns on target with the gimbals, and Juliet squeezed the trigger.

Nothing beat that satisfying hum as the guns began to throw hot, heavy metal alloys through the thin air. Juliet revised that opinion as the pings started sounding in her ears—her rounds were on target, and this time, she was close enough to see the impacts, the sparks, the bits of metal, plasteel, and fluids spraying into the air.

The ship banked and lit up its drives in an attempt to flee, but the *Lady Hawk* wasn't having it. Juliet pushed the throttle forward, steering with her right hand, trigger down, hot metal streaking out from under the ship's nose, ripping holes in her target. The little interceptor was half drives, and when the starboard one started smoking, Juliet pulled up. She'd learned from Nick that you didn't want to be too close to a ship like that when it was about to pop. She heard him exhale a pent-up breath as she pulled off and released the trigger.

"Worried?" she asked, grinning behind the dark tint of her helmet.

"Just a little."

Juliet called up one of the rearview cams and watched as the pirate ship began to smoke more heavily, then she saw something she'd only seen a couple of times while Nick was flying. The front of the wedge-shaped ship seemed to burst, then it spun off into the blackness and deployed two huge parachutes. The ship fell away, streaking smoke and fire as it descended toward Jupiter. The pilot's capsule, though, hung in the thin atmosphere, only very slowly spiraling down.

"Anything we can do?"

"Not in this atmosphere. I can't hold this ship steady enough to take on a passenger, and I doubt you can."

"Poor guy . . ."

"He's probably dead already; not many suits can handle this environment."

The idea was sobering, and Juliet didn't have any words. Some person had just been so desperate to try to live, so desperate not to go down with the ship she'd shot full of holes, that they'd jumped out into the rough atmosphere, terrible radiation, and soon, crushing gravity. What had they been thinking? Had they been? Shooting ships hundreds or thousands of meters away was a lot less personal when you didn't think about the people inside. She shook her head.

"I'm not the one who started this little brawl."

"Exactly. They're pirates, and they wouldn't have shed a tear for us. Believe it." He touched the side of his helmet, and it hissed as the visor released and he flipped it up. Juliet knew what was coming: vape time. He snagged it from the magnet over his head, and as he put it between his lips, he said out of the corner of his mouth, "What are you forgetting?"

"Right!" Juliet stared at her comms display, and Angel connected her to the ship they were escorting.

A high, feminine voice with a Southern twang spoke up immediately. "Arctus Belle here. That you, Lucky?"

"That's me, Bernice. You guys take any hits?"

"We're all good. Those pirates were on you from the get-go. Glad you showed 'em what for!"

"Yep, we got 'em, and we're back in escort position."

"Right on. I'll holler if we need anything. Belle out."

Juliet sighed and leaned back, trusting Angel to keep an eye on the camera feeds and the various scanners. She wanted a second to breathe and process the fact that she'd just had her first real dogfight, and that she'd won in a two-versus-one scenario. She could hear Nick taking a deep inhale on his vape, and she held off lifting her visor so she didn't have to experience the scent of his exhalation—mint today. He'd been remarkably calm and patient with her for the last week as she'd taken the pilot's seat. This was her third mission doing so, but it was the first time she'd had an encounter with hostiles.

Nick blew out a thick cloud of vapor and said, true to form, "Not a bad way to pop your cherry, I guess."

"Gross."

"Gross? Oh, uh, yeah, sorry. C'mon, I thought you did time with a para-military unit. Why are you always busting my balls? You didn't get on your teammates' cases, did you?"

"I wasn't stuck alone with them in a coffin-size box of plasteel a million miles from . . . anything."

"Fair." Nick sighed, rubbed at the bridge of his nose, and continued. "Anyway, good job. I think you handled those guys pretty damn well. I'm impressed with your pilot's gut."

"My what?"

"Your pilot's gut. You know, the thing that tells you how long to squeeze that trigger, what way to jerk the stick, and when to punch the throttle. That kind of stuff."

"There are interesting essays about what he's referencing. There are reputable research papers that seem to indicate it's a real thing and one of the reasons the AI pilots often fared worse than their human counterparts during the big war."

"Huh," Juliet subvocalized. "That's pretty interesting. Can you save me one of the more readable papers? I mean for a layperson."

"Will do. It would be fun to discuss in the context of what we know about the lattice and psionics, don't you think?"

"Yep." Juliet nodded, then turned to look over her shoulder. "Nick, how much money have you put into the Lady? Like, seriously, she's so damn nimble and quick. There's not much on her that's stock, is there?"

"Oh, shit, I couldn't tell you if I wanted to—10k here, 40k there. I've been dumping bounties into this ship for ten years or more. As far as what's stock, well, she looks mostly stock other than the nacelles, the oversize ammo cans, the aftermarket struts, the paint . . . Well, all right, there's not much that's stock left on her. Aftermarket drives, maneuvering jets, guns—she's still got the stock reactor, though."

"Well, I guess if I'm trying to get some real experience, I'm lucky to have such a nice ship to use. Thanks for trusting me with the stick." Juliet let her mind drift and tried to pick up his surface thoughts as he answered.

"No worries, Lucky."

Not like I wasn't about to seize control there for a minute! Whew, you pushed your luck holding fire on that first target!

"You really think I did a good job?" Juliet flipped up her visor and turned to look him in the eyes.

"Well, yeah, you just won a two v one."

"But I could have done something better? Come on, help me learn!"

"All right, all right. Let me see here; you made me nervous when you stayed on the first ship for so long. In fact, I was getting ready to take the controls over. I'll tell you what, though: that's the same thing my old mentor told me. He always said I was pushing things just a little too far. Truth is, I think my instincts were just a little better than his. I'm still kicking, and I've seen twice the action he ever did. I mean, this hurts my pride a little, but maybe your gut's just a little better than mine. Or maybe you got lucky." He chuckled and shrugged.

"Maybe." Juliet laughed too, but she wished she knew more about her uncanny knack for knowing when to move and where during fights and, apparently, dogfights. Was it just luck? Was she using her latent psionic abilities to know when to move? It surely didn't always work; she'd lost fights at the dojo and been beaten and shot. Still, many people might look at the things she'd been through and be amazed that she was alive. Either she was incredibly skilled, very lucky, or, and this was what Juliet thought, there was something more to her feelings.

Subvocalizing, she asked, "Do you think I had some psionic sensitivity before I got the lattice? Do you think my feelings, like when I wanted to run away from Doc Murphy's place, are rooted in some natural ability?"

"We've spoken about this, and you know I do. I think the reason the squints were excited about your body's acceptance of the lattice has to do with your natural potential."

Juliet barked a short laugh. "You called them squints, Angel."

"I know. I love that word!"

"What's funny?" Nick asked, speaking kind of strangely because he was holding in a breath of vape.

"Oh God, here it comes," Juliet groaned and tapped the side of her helmet. "At least you make me appreciate this uncomfortable thing." Nick laughed as he exhaled, and a cloud of vapor filled the front of the cockpit. "You know why you're a good pilot?"

"Why?" He was already starting to laugh, anticipating her answer.

"Because you're high as hell on nicotine. You must have jitters like a bad wire-job!"

"How'd I know you were going to say that?" He chuckled, shaking his head. "Anyway, we should celebrate when we get back. Your first two skulls. It's a pretty big deal for a fighter pilot, Lucky. I've got some buddies we can meet up with and do it right."

"I'm not really—"

"You better accept this!" Angel interrupted. Juliet could hear from her tone that she wouldn't be okay with an argument.

"Oh, come on!" Nick said, also interrupting her.

"All right, forget I said anything. Let's do it. I can use some actual fun."

"That's the spirit! We'll go to the Raptor House."

"Raptor House?"

"It's a bar, but mostly frequented by interceptor pilots. Uh, quite a few pirate types, too. It's not for the faint of heart."

Juliet shook her head as she perused the ship's readings and flipped through the various external feeds. "Raptor House sounds a little . . . on the nose, I guess. If you say it's the place to go, though, then I'm down."

"Right on. Messaging some of my pals."

"Speaking of pals, I've been trying to keep my nose out of your business, but you never told me about your weekend with your 'friend' from out of town."

"Why'd you do that with your fingers when you said friend?"

"Come on, Nick." Juliet snorted and shifted in her acceleration couch to better see him again.

"Are you . . . jealous?" His voice rose with mock incredulity.

"No! I'm curious! How'd this get turned around on me? I was busting your balls." Juliet cringed inwardly as she heard herself using Nick's vernacular. She supposed it wasn't just Nick—she'd heard it plenty from Houston and the others in Charlie Unit. Still, she pointedly made the decision to try to avoid letting any more of his particular brand of trash talk brush off on her.

"You think you're at that level? You think you can get under my skin?"

"Well"—Juliet grinned evilly—"how about I tell your buddies about your little run-in with Tono and how I had to save you?"

"Oh, you wouldn't! Come on, Lucky! If we're going to meet those guys, you can't be making me look bad, all right? I have a reputation!"

Juliet grinned and ran through another diagnostic check then a scan of the camera feeds, chuckling as Nick continued to belabor the many reasons why he had to maintain his tough-guy reputation with all of his pilot buddies. She'd only recently been willing to tease Nick about the run-in with Tono; she'd hardly been able to think about the encounter for weeks. The feelings had been too raw and real, but they had slowly diminished. Juliet thought they faded faster than real memories, real emotions, but she wasn't sure; she'd changed a lot since she'd met Angel, and she might just be getting better at dealing with trauma.

". . . especially at the Raptor House! Some of those guys—"

"Nick! Relax, I was just messing with you. I won't tell your buddies anything about it. Does this bar have a good beer selection? I mean, on tap? Anything local?"

"You are the snootiest operator I've ever met. I flew a guy to Mars once, a real chrome jockey, and he'd drink anything. Shit, I caught him drinking paint thinner at the warehouse where we'd stashed the cargo he'd hired me to haul . . ."

Juliet leaned back with a comfortable smile as she listened to Nick regale her with his tale about a "chromed-out nightmare" and the medicine he wanted delivered to an orphanage in New Galveston. It sounded like a bad soap vid, but he was a good storyteller, so Juliet laughed along and had a good time trying to picture the crazy scenes.

Yeah, she decided, Nick had some problems, but he was a pretty all-right guy when you boiled it down to the bone, when you considered the important stuff.

"And shouldn't you do that?" she asked no one in particular, speaking too softly for Nick to notice as he continued his narrative. "Shouldn't you focus on what's important and not the petty BS?"

"Definitely," Angel replied, surprising her.

Juliet's smile deepened as she flipped through the camera feeds again, leaving the scanners to Angel's judgment. She figured she'd get through this story of Nick's, spin one of her own, then they'd be about ready to fly home, and she could celebrate her first kill.

To her credit, Juliet didn't frown or even flinch at the idea; she'd killed again today, and that was the way things were.

That was her life now: kill or be killed.

17

SAME OLD MO

Juliet looked down the narrow dark street to the bright yellow-and-blue neon sign proclaiming the building ahead as the "Raptor Haus". She thought the German spelling made it a little more interesting than Nick's flat delivery when he'd called the bar the "Raptor *House*." It certainly looked interesting—tall, narrow, black-painted or stained concrete with yellow neon-outlined birds of prey flying up the side toward the metal gables of the roof, away from the hypnotically pulsing lettering.

In the dark, the stains and trash lining the walkway didn't stand out, and the hooded, raincoat-wearing figures leaning against nearby buildings added to the mysterious, dangerous ambiance. Juliet felt alive, felt an electric tingle along her spine as she scanned the area, noting the many highlights Angel provided for openly visible weapons on the people milling about. She wasn't underarmed; her vibroblade sat snugly against her wrist under her motorcycle jacket, and her Texan, loaded with Ryan's custom ammo, sat against her right thigh, a comforting weight.

Nick turned back at her and raised an eyebrow. "You sure you gotta wear all that gear?"

Juliet snorted. "You sure you shouldn't be wearing more?"

Nick was dressed just as she'd first met him—loosely buttoned white dress shirt over faded jeans. He had no visible weapons or implants, no gear at all unless you counted his admittedly fancy vape battery.

He winked. "I guess I just rely on my smile to smooth any conflicts over, you know?"

"Yeah, that worked great with Tono . . ."

"You said you wouldn't mention that!"

"Come on." Juliet gave him a gentle nudge toward the building and followed behind. Despite her jacket, she felt the chill in the air. She wore it open to better display a new—to her—vintage smiley face T-shirt, one with Xs for eyes and a frown. The cool, damp air was palpable, and she could feel her nose getting a little numb as her breath plumed out. "What's with the cold, anyway?"

He shrugged. "Callistoans like their weather cycles."

"Well, let's get inside. My fingers are getting numb."

"I'm moving, I'm moving."

Juliet was being hyperbolic. Her right hand felt fine; Angel could adjust the synth-flesh's sensitivity to temperature, and she did a good job of keeping Juliet comfortable. As for her left hand, it was in her pocket.

She grinned at the thought, watching Nick shuffle forward, both hands stuffed into his jeans' pockets. He was a lanky-looking guy when he walked like that, shoulders hunched up, keeping the chill off his neck. She liked that kind of look on a guy—long limbs, lean body, casual but cool. The thought caught her by surprise, and she did her best to banish it; she was decidedly not into Nick in that way. Right?

"Nick!" the bouncer said, reaching out to clap Nick on the shoulder. She was a stocky woman wearing a silver puffy one-piece jumper that covered her from her ankles to her bulky neck. An SMG that announced her seriousness hung on a shoulder strap next to her hip, but she didn't move a hand toward it as she glanced Juliet up and down, her violet-irised eyes flashing with active scans. "New girlfriend?"

"Uh!" Nick threw a horrified glance at Juliet, almost like he thought he was in trouble.

"Just a friend." Juliet laughed, resting a hand on Nick's shoulder and giving him a friendly jostle.

"Whew!" the doorwoman said. "I was trying to think of how to warn you, Nicky—Penny's in there."

Nick's eyes widened, and he reflexively reached up to smooth his hair. "Seriously? My Penny?"

"Why would I warn you about someone else's Penny?"

"Well, shit. Thanks, Sam." Nick seemed to have lost a shade of ruddy complexion, looking just as nervous as he had when Wrench had him by the throat.

"No worries." She turned back to Juliet. "Don't go starting any shit with that cannon on your hip, huh?"

"I won't start it . . ." Juliet winked at her, feeling giddy at Nick's obvious discomfort and nervousness. She couldn't wait to meet whoever Penny was.

"Attagirl. Go on, have fun." She waved at the door, and Nick, still a little pale, brushed at his hair again before pulling the door open for Juliet. She stepped past him into the thump of the music, loud enough to rattle her rib cage but not a problem for her ears—Angel tuned it to a comfortable level.

The Raptor Haus immediately set itself apart from other clubs or bars or whatever it was styling itself as with its vertical design. The ground floor wasn't huge, just large enough for a ring of booths around a busy bar with an impressive rack of mirrored shelves displaying hundreds of bottles of booze. Above that level, though, Juliet could see at least five balconies that surrounded the open space above the bottom floor. Hanging from a distant ceiling, from chains of varying lengths, vidscreens, holodisplays, and even platforms where men and women danced filled the void. Warm-yellow neon was the predominant light source, giving the place a decidedly different vibe than the cooler pink and blue tones found in so many modern clubs.

Juliet found her head bobbing to the music, a smile on her face, as Nick walked up beside her. "Pretty cool layout, huh?"

"Lots to look at!"

He held a hand to his ear and made a face like he couldn't hear. Juliet narrowed her eyes at him and subvocalized, "Angel, send him a message."

"What should it be?"

"Get new audio implants."

Nick's eyes opened wide and he laughed, giving her a thumbs-up. Then he gestured toward the far side of the bar where a plastiglass-paneled elevator sat, ready to carry patrons up to one of the balcony levels. "My friends said they're on three."

Juliet pointed to the bar and leaned close to Nick's ear. "Do we need to order first?"

"Nah!" he yelled. "Just order online, and they'll bring it up."

Juliet followed him through the crowd, more mature yet decidedly more dangerous-looking people than she'd seen on Io Station when she'd met Nick at the Badhammer. Nearly everyone sported some kind of sidearm, cybernetic implants looked more utilitarian than stylish, and a lot more leather and denim prevailed in their outfits. Juliet felt like she fit in better with this crowd than the scantily clad "punks." The funny thing was, she reflected, that when push came to shove, she'd bet on these people standing up to corpo authority sooner than the party kids at the Badhammer.

"You're amused by something?" Angel asked as they stepped aboard the elevator and Nick pressed the glowing numeral three.

"Thinking about how the club kids at the Badhammer think of themselves as punks, but they seem a lot more conformist to me than this crowd. These people look like they walk the walk, you know what I mean?"

"I do, and you'd be correct. I've seen quite a few faces that match up to postings on the public net bounty boards."

Juliet snorted, and Nick gave her a look. She leaned close to his ear.

"My PAI just informed me that a lot of these people have bounties. Mind if I collect a few?" Nick's eyes widened in horror, but Juliet held up a hand before he could formulate a reply. "Just kidding, relax." The elevator lurched to a halt, and the doors started to open. Juliet grabbed Nick's arm before he could walk off. "Are you nervous?"

"About?"

"Penny!"

Nick didn't answer, but his stress was evident as his lips pressed together and he narrowed his eyes. Juliet grinned, following him onto the balcony level and past some patrons leaning against the railing watching two very attractive women dancing on a suspended platform. He wound his way around to the far side where thickly cushioned, recessed booths with high backs made almost private little alcoves. He walked up to one with two men and a woman sitting around it, leaving plenty of room for another five or so. Empty bottles lined the tabletop, and as Nick waved and leaned forward to yell his greetings to his friends, Juliet took them in.

She couldn't help staring at the woman first. Who was this lady who'd given Nick such a shock? She was immediately reminded of Honey. A slightly older Honey, but the resemblance was there, nonetheless. She had short, curly black hair, big brown eyes, soft dark skin, and an impeccable sense of style. She wore a frilly pale-green blouse that left little to the imagination, it was nearly transparent. Juliet couldn't see her bottom half, but she saw the gold jewelry on her wrists, her many rings, and the high-end, holoprojecting data port at her left temple. It was currently displaying a sparkling golden tiara atop her head.

Nick still hadn't made eye contact with the woman Juliet guessed was Penny, and Juliet smirked as she stood behind him. He leaned close to the man on the end, a guy who could pass for his brother. He was shorter than

Nick, a little heavier, and a little older looking. He wore a paisley-patterned T-shirt that was so tight it could have been painted on. An antique-looking gold watch sat on his hairy, tanned arm, and when Nick pointed over his shoulder and said, "This is Lucky," the man turned his gaze to her, and Juliet had to reassess her first impression.

She'd thought he looked kind of like a meathead, a muscle type without a lot going on upstairs. His eyes told her a different story, however. They were sharp and predatory, and something in her gut said very loudly, "Be careful."

Juliet smiled and reached out to take his hand when he offered it.

"I'm Ray. Taught this guy everything he knows." His hand was meaty and calloused, and he looked surprised when Juliet's long fingers wrapped around his palm and she gave him a solid grip.

"Bullshit!" Nick laughed. "The good-looking guy next to Ray is Alec. Alec, Lucky."

Juliet released Ray's hand, annoyed that he let his grip linger for a second. She pointedly didn't look at him or say anything. Instead, she turned to Alec and smiled, tugging her hand free so she could offer it to him.

Alec reached out to take it. He was a slight fellow, thin, short, and wan. He looked frail, really, and Juliet wondered if there might be something wrong with his health. Still, his grip was warm and firm, and she got a good feeling when she looked into his silvery visor. It looked like an implant, but she figured it might be a high-end wearable. In any case, she couldn't see his eyes.

Juliet let go of Alec's hand and looked at the woman. "And who's this?"

"Uh, that's . . ."

"I'm Penny. Nick's ex. I'm sure he's told you all about me, hmm?" Her voice was husky and low when she laughed, clearly indicating she knew very well that Nick had done no such thing.

"Hey, Pen, that's not really fair, is it?" Nick sighed and reached up to rub his hair, brushing it back with one hand while he tapped at his shirt pocket with the other. Juliet knew he was probably fiending for a hit of nicotine.

"Sit down!" Alec said, indicating the open side of the booth next to Penny. Juliet backed up, letting Nick slide in first so she'd be on the outside and not forced to sit between him and his ex.

She wondered at that; *did she mean ex as in ex-girlfriend or ex-wife?* Nick's layers kept multiplying.

"Angel, please order me a local beer. Something light."

"Okay, do you want to see the selection?"

"Nah, you know what I like."

"I do."

Nick slid into the booth, and Juliet noticed he left a good foot between himself and Penny. She grinned, for some reason enjoying his discomfort, and sat down. Her position in the booth put her almost directly across from Ray, who nodded and smiled, revealing a gold-plated canine, and pointed at the empty bottles on the table.

"You guys have some catching up to do. Don't worry, we'll help you get started. I ordered a round. I hear a toast is in order—you earned your first skull, huh?"

"Skulls," Nick corrected.

"Oho? Pirates, I hope!" Ray laughed, but it was a mean sound, not a jovial one.

Juliet humored Ray with a smile but looked at Alec. "You're a pilot, too?"

"Not exactly . . ."

"He rides in my navigator seat and runs the targeting system on my missile boat," Ray spoke over Alec, slapping his heavy hand on the table and rattling the empty bottles.

"Missile boat, huh?"

"Yeah, he's got a real beauty." Nick seemed to be looking for any excuse not to talk to Penny, so he leaned forward and continued, "A Kroger Lamprey. He's got something like fifty—"

"A hundred!" Ray said, slapping the table again. "Seventy-five short and twenty-five long-range missiles. I don't take the little escort gigs like Nicky here. I fly escort to the big boys."

"The big boys?" Juliet frowned. *What is bigger than a gas harvester?*

"Well, we mostly fly patrols around stations. Right now, we have a contract at Yggdrasil. Not much action, but the pay's good . . ."

"Jesus, Alec. You really know how to kill the mood. Learn to tell a story, will you?" Ray glowered at his partner. "You don't just drop the punch line." He sighed, shaking his head, and then he looked over at Nick. "Anyway, yeah, we got a pretty sweet gig right now, flying circles around the scientists on Yggdrasil Station."

"That's nice! Congrats, you guys!" It was Penny who spoke up; Nick was looking at Alec, frowning slightly.

"So, not much action, huh?" Juliet asked Ray, for some reason wanting to needle him a little.

Storm clouds entered his eyes as he scowled. "You insinuating something?"

Before Juliet could answer, a man wearing a black apron approached the table with a tray of shot glasses. "You ordered a round of shots? Spacer's Thinner?"

"Yeah!" Ray said, magnanimous once again. "Only the best for my old boy Nick and his new girl."

"She's not—"

"I'm not his girl," Juliet growled.

The waiter sighed, shaking his head as he set the tray down. The expression on his face was clear—he didn't get paid enough to get involved. He lingered briefly while Juliet glowered at Ray, perhaps hoping for a tip. When no one looked at him, he turned and walked away, muttering something Juliet didn't care enough about to try to hear.

"Did I say something wrong?" Ray asked, pushing the shot glasses around the table, sliding one to each of them.

"Classic Ray," Penny sighed. "Don't take it personally, hon. Nick's friends are . . . an acquired taste."

Juliet didn't reply. She was too busy feeling annoyed by Ray; he reminded her of too many bullies she'd known throughout her life. She felt like putting him in his place, but she decided to try to relax and let Nick enjoy the night as much as he could with his ex sitting next to him. So, with a forced smile and shrug, she picked up the shot glass Ray shoved in front of her.

"To Lucky!" Nick said, lifting his glass. "Watch your sixes, 'cause she's got talent and a killer instinct!"

Everyone echoed the "to Lucky" part, and Juliet tossed the drink back, grimacing as the harsh alcohol scorched the back of her throat. When she exhaled, she felt like she was blowing fire out of her nose for several seconds. Her eyes watered, and she stared at the table, trying to make it focus as she fought down a coughing fit. When she finally looked up, she saw everyone's eyes on her, and then Nick laughed and clapped his hands.

"I told you she'd handle it!"

"That shit was awful." Juliet frowned around the table, but she couldn't deny the euphoric buzz lifting the corners of her mouth into an almost involuntary smile.

"Bad taste, good effect, eh?" Penny laughed.

"No shit! Is that stuff even legal?" Juliet laughed, and then she realized Angel was talking to her, had been talking to her, but her voice had seemed like a background noise.

"Your nanites are helping you detox! That beverage was far more than simple alcohol."

"You joke, but that stuff's not legal in some municipalities. Some corpo bureaucrats have a problem with synthed booze." Alec stared at his empty shot glass almost longingly.

"Well," Nick said, his words slurring as if his tongue was a little too large for his mouth, "it's more to do with what gets added in the process. This one's not too bad, but I've seen some crazy stuff."

"Thanks, Angel," Juliet subvocalized, already feeling more like herself.

"You're welcome. I'm not trying to ruin your fun, but I didn't think you were expecting to consume something so strong."

"Definitely not."

"So, you waxed a couple of pirates, huh?" Ray asked, leaning forward. Juliet could see the trouble brewing behind his eyes even without listening to his thoughts. Still, she listened.

Look at this smartass bitch. Thinks she's better than me. She'd probably come home with me in a second if I offered her a chance to fly the Overwolf. Wonder how long it took her to get Nick to let her fly his little ship. How many times she had to put out?

Juliet grimaced, disgusted by the images and thoughts bleeding out of Ray's far too open mind. She passed her disgust off as if she was still recovering from the shot and smiled when she saw the waiter returning with a few beers on a tray. He set hers in front of her, and she sat back, intent on nursing it and ignoring Ray.

"I say something wrong? Just curious about how you popped—"

"Don't say it, Ray." Nick sighed and leaned over the table, turning so he faced Juliet and put himself between her and his obnoxious friend. "You good? We can head out if this isn't your thing."

"I'm better now I got this beer, but if you've got someplace else you'd like to go . . ."

"What the fuck, Nick? You just got here! I got someone coming who wants to meet you."

Nick sighed and sat back, then looked from Penny to Alec—who was busily examining his beer bottle—to Ray. "Hey, bud, this night isn't about me. It's for Lucky, and I think you're kinda rubbing her the wrong way."

"It's cool, Nick." Juliet set her beer on the table, thinking about how directly she wanted to deal with Ray. Was it worth not causing a scene? Was it worth letting another bully get away with the same old MO?

"Holy . . . Am I seeing this right?" Penny suddenly said. "If you'd have stood up for me like that, we'd be married with kids by now!"

"It's not like that, Penny. I'm responsible for—"

"You're good, Nick." Juliet put a hand on his shoulder and looked at Ray. "We'll stick around. I'm all for having a good time, but Ray, you need to cool your toxic shit. I don't want to hear your suspicions about what I did to get Nick to let me fly his ship. I don't want you to even think it. We clear?"

"Hey, I didn't—"

"It's all over your face, buddy. Now, just drink your beer and let Nick enjoy a little reunion with Penny. Listen to the music or something. I'm tired of your voice." Juliet turned to Alec. "Tell me a little bit about what Yggdrasil Station is like, Alec. I've never even heard of it."

18

FINDER'S FEE

A few drinks and a time-out imposed by the rest of the table pointedly ignoring him did wonders for Ray's demeanor. Juliet found herself laughing along, listening with interest as Nick and his friends talked about the "old days," when they'd run a lot of escort jobs together. She'd been snacking on salty, fried foods, from onion rings to Callisto fingers, which were, as one might guess, finger-shaped mushrooms with a decidedly truffle-flavored aftertaste. The salt kept her ordering beers, and those, on top of the shot she'd taken, kept her comfortably numb as she leaned back into the soft cushions of the booth.

The music in the bar was her kind of vibe—lots of electro-synth with beat drops and rising, spine-tingling vocals that drowned out any conversation outside their sound-dampened booth. It was kind of like sitting in a little oasis of noise within an ocean of strangers, and Juliet liked it. During a lull in the conversation, she said as much, lifting her voice to be heard by everyone at the table, some of whom didn't have implants that filtered sound very well. "I like the vibe in here! Cool club!"

"I told you!" Nick laughed, lifting his glass to clink against her bottle.

"Nick," Ray said, leaning in front of Alec. "That guy I mentioned—he just got here. Wants to sit down with us for a proposal." Juliet still didn't like Ray and hadn't said a word to him during the conversations they'd both been involved in, but she was interested to see what this business was all about.

"I wasn't really looking to do business tonight. I'm not exactly clearheaded."

"Hah!" Penny snorted, sipping her frosty-blue drink from the top of its high, fluted glass. "When has that ever stopped you?"

"Good point, dear." Nick chuckled, grinning and brushing his shoulder against hers. He'd gotten a lot friendlier with her after a few drinks. Juliet supposed part of the thaw between them had come when Penny saw him try to stand up for Juliet against Ray.

Had he really never done that before?

"You cool with your . . . trainee sitting in on it?" Ray glanced at Juliet but quickly looked back to Nick before their eyes could lock.

"I believe he's trying to exclude you." Angel sounded angry.

"Relax," Juliet subvocalized. "No way Nick will ask me to leave."

"She's cool. You know she's an operator, right? She probably knows more about contracts and negotiating than I do."

"Oh?" Ray looked at Juliet with a raised eyebrow, and she could see from the glint in his eyes that he was trying to regain some of his prior boldness, trying to think of a way to ask her a question with a teasing edge.

Juliet ignored his look and, instead, focused on Nick. "You know better than that. I haven't been at it all that long."

"Regardless, you're fine to sit in. Let me know if you think this friend of Ray's is too shady."

"Hey!"

"My pleasure!" This time, it was Juliet who offered Ray a smile with a bit of an edge to it.

Further conversation was put on hold when the waitress—their original waiter's shift had ended—arrived with another round of drinks and a big pitcher of lime-flavored iced water. She'd just finished setting them down when another person approached the table. He wore a damp burgundy rain jacket and a matching hat with a wide brim. When he slid into the booth to Juliet's right, she noticed both of his hands were expensive-looking gold-plated chrome-jobs.

"Ray." He nodded, smiling with a mouth full of golden teeth at Nick's friend. Then he turned to the rest of the table. "Ray's friends. I'm Larry Fine."

"The guy I was telling you about." Ray pointed to Nick. "This is Nick, the pilot I mentioned."

"Aha." Larry nodded, shifting to look at Juliet. He smelled like old leather, spices, and something stronger that made Juliet's eyes water. Way too much cologne for her taste. "I know your partner there, Ray. Who are these lovely ladies?"

"That's an old friend, Penny, and next to you is Nick's new . . . partner."

Juliet frowned, but she supposed there wasn't anything wrong with the description. She turned to Larry. "I'm Lucky. My name, I mean."

"Right," Larry dragged the word out with a smile that displayed his shiny teeth. Juliet got the feeling he spent a lot of time smiling too much, trying to get his money's worth out of those caps. He winked at her then looked more closely at Nick. "I hear you're a hell of an interceptor pilot."

"Some people think so . . ."

"Oh, come on!" Ray groaned. "Anyone else asks, and you'll point out your ranking on the Jovian System pilot boards."

"No need for him to be braggadocious, Ray." Larry scanned the glasses on the table and picked up a dark stout no one had touched. "Ordered this on my way up." He took a long sip and sighed with pleasure. "Anyway, as I was saying, no need to brag when I can just look him up myself. I've seen your rating, Nick. You interested in making a big haul?"

"Is that rhetorical?" Nick chuckled and sipped some of his own beverage, the same thing he'd been ordering all night: two shots of bourbon over a single fat ice cube.

"Right! Of course it is. We all want to score big, right? Well, I have an interesting proposal. My client is something of an aggrieved father. His daughter took up with a nasty crowd, and he wants her back."

"What?" Nick frowned. "I'm a pilot, buddy. That's not really my thing."

"Hold on." Larry held up a hand beseechingly. "Let me spit out my whole pitch, and you'll see why I'm talking to someone with your skill set." When Nick shrugged, he continued. "You see, she's mixed up with a gang called Hereford's Vengeance. You heard of 'em?"

Everyone at the table made some kind of noise, signifying their recognition. Ray chuckled, Alec shook his head, sighing, Penny coughed, also shaking her head, and Nick simply said, "Who hasn't?"

Juliet was about to say she hadn't, but then Angel helped her out. "They're a well-known band of pirates that prey on the shipping lanes between the Jovian System and Mars."

"Right." Larry smiled. "Well, I need someone who's kind of an ace. Someone who can walk the walk, so to speak. Someone who could join up with a crew like that."

"Uh . . ." Nick looked around the table. "I know we're on a noise blocker here, but you sure are open with your trust. Just talking about infiltrating that crew will get you killed if the right people hear about it."

Juliet frowned, bothered by Nick's sudden concern. She let her mind drift a little, trying to pick up something from the strange character beside her. He was close, and his mind was fairly unguarded, or at least it seemed that way because his thoughts came right to her.

Oh, come on! You trust these people! Ray's the one who turned me on to you. Obviously, he knows the score. Penny . . . Well, yeah, maybe that was a risk.

Shit, did I blow it? Is he worried about the rookie here?

Larry glanced at Juliet, his perpetual smile falling a little at the corners of his mouth. He turned back to Nick. "You not cool with these folks hearing this? Shit, we can get our own table."

"Nah, it's all right. I'm gonna turn you down, anyway. Even if I wanted to do the job, I couldn't. My skill and prestige"—Nick chuckled and shrugged at his low-key boast—"come with a double-edged blade. Those pirates will recognize my ship, even if they don't recognize me."

"That's the beauty, my friend!" Larry drummed his ring-bedecked fingers on the table and leaned closer to Nick, getting uncomfortably inside Juliet's imaginary bubble. "My client is loaded. He will supply a ship, something from a local auction with no ties to your legendary record."

"And my ID?"

"We'll cover that."

"How's Nick supposed to get this girl to fly off with him?" Penny asked, frowning, eyeing Nick with something like genuine concern. The more Juliet watched them, the more she began to wonder if they were really as over as they'd professed at the start of the evening.

"Well, that's the easiest part. You use your pilot chops to get into the gang, and you're pretty much done. All you have to do is hang around with the crew for a while 'cause we'll send an operator in with you, someone who will be responsible for getting the girl aboard your ship. The father's convinced she wants to come home but the pirates are keeping her against her will. So, once the operator gets her aboard, all you gotta do is bail out—haul ass back to Callisto and dump her off." He brushed his hands together with a chuckle. "Nothing left after that except to collect a very fat payday."

"I love it when a client talks about how easy my job's going to be. It never turns out badly . . ." Nick snorted and shook his head.

"Come on, Nick!" Ray whined, leaning in front of Alec. Juliet, despite her better judgment, tried to listen to his thoughts, staring pointedly into his left eye as he worked to convince Nick that he was being offered a once-in-a-lifetime opportunity.

Goddammit, I need this! Quit being a bitch, Nick!

The heat of the emotions accompanying Ray's thoughts began to turn Juliet's stomach, and she quickly looked away, staring into one of the high, yellow neon signs as she sipped at her beer. She couldn't wrap her head around how anyone could be so intensely full of vitriol all the time. He had to be miserable. Unable to help herself, she asked, "Something in this for you, Ray?"

He jerked his gaze toward her, slid back into his seat—giving Alec room to breathe—and snarled, "What's wrong with that? Just a finder's fee. Larry's been having a hell of a time finding a decent interceptor pilot."

"Why don't you do it?" Juliet pressed.

"I'm stuck in a long-term contract!" He elbowed Alec. "Tell 'em!"

"It's true. We're on a six-month contract with Yggdrasil."

"As I said"—Larry held up a hand, tamping it down in the air as though he could cool the rising temperature around the booth—"my client is very wealthy, and yes, I have a nice finder's fee for your friend here, should you take the job, Nick."

Nick sighed and leaned back, sipping at his drink. Everyone at the table had gotten quiet, waiting to see how he'd respond to the outlandish job offer.

"I dunno. I'm a pilot—that's my thing. I'm not an actor or any sort of operator, you know? I'm not sure I can pull off the BS required to get hired on with a real pirate crew. What do I tell 'em about myself? How do I prove my chops? What if I don't like the operator you're sending with me, or we don't gel? What if he's a complete dipshit and gets my cover blown and, along with it, my ship? Sounds risky as hell, to be honest."

"I agree." Juliet didn't like the sound of the job at all.

"Jesus. Shut the fuck up. Who the fuck are you, even?" Ray growled, dropping their earlier truce.

Juliet's legs were stretched out to the side of the table, and she let her palm rest on the grip of her Texan, her annoyance with Ray rising to irrational levels. "Who am I? I don't know, but one thing I'm not is a leech trying to get my friend into a real cluster fu—"

"Lucky! Ray! Chill, please." Nick slammed his glass down with a clunk. "Let Larry here paint the whole picture. He knows I'm not too excited about the job. He knows it sounds like a real nasty bit of risk. So, Larry, how are you going to entice me? What's the upshot?"

"Glad you asked, Nick. How does half a million bits sound to you? That's your cut after the operator and I take ours." He glanced at Ray, frowned, and added, "Finder's fees come out of my cut, of course."

"Holy . . ." Penny whistled and sipped her fluted glass again. Neither Ray nor Alec flinched or even reacted at the mention of half a million bits—Juliet thought it was pretty evident they'd been planning this proposal for a while.

"It's a nice payday, but is it worth getting blasted into dust?" Nick shrugged. "I think I need a beat to think about this. Can you tell me who the operator is? I'd feel better with someone I know." He looked away from Larry to make eye contact with Juliet, and then she saw the lightbulb go off in his brain as his eyes widened. "Hey, Lucky . . ."

"Nuh-uh!" Juliet vehemently shook her head. "I can smell trouble from a mile away, and this one smells like rotten fish."

"Operator cut's the same as the pilot's . . ." Larry said, turning to reevaluate Juliet. "You got the chops? If Nick trusts you, it might make the whole thing a lot smoother."

"Let us think about it." Nick held up a hand, forestalling more objections from Juliet. "Seriously. Let us get sober and take a day to talk." He glanced at Ray. "Without all the outside pressures, you know what I mean?"

"Come on, Nick. You know I'm not like that!" Ray glared at Juliet. "You're not going to listen to this . . ." He struggled with words for a minute as he glared at Juliet and she stared right into his eyes, her expression daring him to insult her again. "This rookie. Are you?"

"I dunno. I like Lucky; she's got some interesting viewpoints on things, and she's already saved my bacon at least once."

"You forget about Venus? How many times did I save your ass?" Ray was red-faced with anger. Something more was going on here; he seemed far too desperate for Nick to take this job, and Juliet wanted to get to the bottom of it, but she dreaded getting into his mind again. Still, she reached out while he stared at Nick, hoping she'd get something quick and easy.

Please, you old asshole! My dick's on the line here! I owe . . . I owe . . . I owe . . .

It was weird how the thought kept repeating, and along with it, the desperate angst that Ray felt. He was terribly worried about what he owed to someone. Juliet cleared her throat and decided to try a new angle.

"Ray." He jerked his head toward her, ready to bark an insult or tell her to stay out of it, but she held up a hand. "I'm gonna walk around the club a little—check out some of the dancers or something. Maybe you should be honest with Nick and tell him what's the big deal for you with him taking this job."

"Uh, yeah." Alec started sliding toward Ray. "Let me out, Ray. I gotta take a leak."

"Not a bad idea. You two boys work this out, 'cause the testosterone is giving me a headache." Penny started sliding behind Alec, and Ray stood to let them out. He locked eyes with Juliet for a second, then he nodded.

"All right. Yeah. Let me talk to Nick for a few."

"You good, Lucky?" Nick asked as she slid to the edge of the booth and stood.

"I'm totally good." She glanced up to the next level and added, "I'm gonna go up a level. I think I see people dancing; it's been a while since I danced at a club. Can you watch my jacket?" She shrugged off her motorcycle jacket and laid it on the seat next to Larry. "Don't let this guy walk off with it." She winked at Larry to show she was joking.

"Jesus, Lucky, is that a vibroblade on your wrist? The cannon on your hip wasn't enough?" Nick shook his head, clinking his ice cube around in his glass as he sized her up.

"What? This? I just keep it around to win bets. You know, throwing it and whatnot." As she joked, she looked down at Ray and narrowed her eyes, making sure to rest a hand casually on her Texan's grip. He flinched, but he also scowled, and Juliet decided that perhaps using a lethal weapon as a prop in a pissing contest wasn't cool. "Anyway, be back in a few."

"Hang on!" Penny called, and Juliet slowed, waiting for her to catch up. "You really gonna dance?"

"Yeah, I like the music in here."

"I'll join you. Damn! You're tall!" Standing near her, Juliet realized Penny was a lot shorter than she'd expected, maybe only five feet or so.

"Eh, it's the boots." Juliet winked at her as she led the way to the elevator.

"You gonna dance in those?"

"Sure. I do a lot of things in my boots." She was definitely buzzed, and the words made her laugh as she looked back at Penny. "Not like that!"

As they stepped into the elevator, Penny said in a near yell because of the loud, thumping music, "I like your shirt!"

"Do you? I have a thing for these old smiley faces."

"It's not smiling!"

"Well, that's what they called them." Juliet laughed, looking down at the frowning yellow face on a black background. "Anyway, I like your shirt. It's really . . . pretty. I'm bad at dressing in pretty things."

"Well, you could fool me: your hair and those eyes. Damn, girl, I'd kill for looks like that. You must've spent a fortune."

"Oh." Juliet felt heat rising in her cheeks as she stared at the elevator door, waiting for it to open up. "I mean, changing looks is important for some of the jobs I've done. It's not all vanity . . ."

"I'm not judging!" Penny laughed and bumped her hip into Juliet as the door slid open, revealing a darker level with more pulsing lights timed with the beat of the music. "I'm just jealous! Come on, let's go dance!"

19

BREAKFAST WITH A FRIEND

Juliet groaned and rolled over. Or tried to, having to fight against the sheets that were somehow wound about her body holding her pinned onto her side. She jerked and thrashed until they came loose, and then flopped over so her face pressed into the pillow. Her head was throbbing at the base of her skull, and the change in position helped to alleviate some of the pressure.

"Why?" Her voice was hoarse, and the back of her throat felt like sandpaper.

"Why?" Angel echoed, keeping her voice soft.

"Why do I have a hangover? Get those nanites to work!" Juliet flopped to her side and peeled one eye open, staring at the bright morning light illuminating the wooden wall panel, suddenly disoriented. Where was she?

"Oh, they've been working. If not for your nanites, you'd have needed your stomach pumped for certain! Really, Juliet! Were you trying to poison yourself?"

"Where am I?" Juliet peeled her other eye open and blearily blinked around the room. The wood paneling continued on all four walls. An antique-looking maple dresser was at the foot of the bed, and a high window with gauzy drapes filled the wall opposite the door. It looked familiar, that space, but it took her a few seconds to connect the dots. "Nick's . . ."

"Nick's cabin," Angel said at almost the same time.

"Holy . . ." Juliet flopped back into her pillow and pressed the heels of her hands into her eyes, groaning softly. "I can barely remember . . . dancing, drinking, more dancing. Did we go to another bar?"

"You went to Ray's hangar, where he had a bar set up. More of Nick's friends were there. Do you remember?"

"God," Juliet groaned. "Barely. I must have been smashed to agree to that. Thank God I didn't sleep there."

"No, Nick made sure to help you get into the cab I ordered for you both. You arrived here to sleep at almost 5:00 a.m."

"I haven't partied like that in a long, long time."

"I think you wanted to blow off some steam, but I must admit to being a bit worried about you."

Juliet looked under the sheet, saw she was still in her underwear and T-shirt, and sighed with some relief. "He didn't, like, help me get undressed?"

"No. He pulled your boots off but left you atop the bedspread in your jeans and shirt. Later in the night, you pulled off your own pants."

"I'm sorry, Angel," Juliet groaned, running her tongue around her mouth, trying to spread the meager saliva around. "I'm so thirsty!"

She threw the sheet off and slid to the side of the bed, where she found her jeans lying on the floor. A brief panic hit her when she didn't see her gun belt before she spied the dark leather hanging off the side of the dresser. Juliet tugged her pants over her feet, then stood and pulled them up. She didn't fasten the top button; her bladder was too swollen for that sort of squeeze. "If I remember right, the bathroom is right outside this door . . ."

"Correct. Just up the hall on the left."

"Is Nick up?"

"I haven't heard any sounds to indicate so."

Juliet pulled the door open, thankful it didn't squeak, and tiptoed over the wooden floorboards to the dark bathroom doorway. Nick's bedroom door was across from hers, and it was shut tight.

When alone in the bathroom, she turned on the sink, lowered her mouth to the faucet, and drank thirstily for several minutes. Then, she sat on the toilet and emptied her bladder, one of the most intensely pleasurable reliefs she could remember feeling.

"Good grief, I'm lucky I didn't wet the bed!"

"Did you apologize to me earlier because you felt you'd done something wrong?"

"I definitely feel guilty. I think it's from the alcohol and my spotty memory. I didn't do anything terrible, did I?"

"Well, you kissed Nick," Angel deadpanned.

"What?" Juliet slapped herself on the forehead.

"Just kidding."

"Oh, you . . ." Juliet blew out her breath, relief overcoming her frustration. "I guess I walked into that one. I deserve it."

When she finished in the bathroom, Juliet walked out to the single-room living area and kitchen, sighing with relief when Nick's kitchen woke up to her presence. The lights came on, and a coffee machine started burbling. She pulled open the fridge to see the contents and wasn't shocked to find only prepackaged meal pouches, protein bars, and lots of different types of beverages. She snagged a protein bar and pulled a coffee cup off the peg hanging above the stovetop.

She was feeling significantly better by the time she'd started on her second cup and munched through her vanilla-coconut food bar. "Did you slow down the nanites so I'd learn a lesson?"

"I'm shocked that you'd accuse me of such a thing."

"But did you?"

"No! I think that 'spacer's thinner' you drank complicated things; that stuff should be illegal."

Juliet set her cup down and contemplated calling a cab. "Did I agree to anything crazy last night?"

"Only that you'd talk to Nick about Mr. Fine's job offer."

"Man! That whole thing sounded pretty sketchy to me. Did you find anything out about that guy?"

"He's a well-reputed fixer on Callisto. He has an A rating on his SOA card."

"Seriously? And that's how he approaches the talent? In a bar around a table full of people he doesn't know, blabbing about a dangerous job?"

"It does seem sloppy when you put it like that. Perhaps he's used to using the SOA boards and isn't well-versed in person-to-person recruitment."

"Maybe. I guess you can't really post this kind of job on a board, huh?"

Juliet heard Nick's bedroom door click open, and then he shuffled out of the hallway wearing the same jeans as the night before and a clean, white T-shirt. "Morning."

"Hey. Thanks for the coffee." Juliet held up her cup.

"God, do you feel half as bad as I do?" He rubbed at his gray-streaked black hair, patting at his pocket, a move Juliet had gotten used to. He was looking for his Nikko-vape.

"I did when I woke up."

"Holy shit." He looked at her, shaking his head. "I just remembered some of your antics last night. You were wasted. I didn't know you had it in you, Lucky."

"Don't remind me. I feel guilty as it is."

"Nah, you didn't do anything nuts. No dancing on tables or making out with strangers, anyway. Ray was pretty pissed about you carving your initials on his ship, though!"

"I did what?" Juliet sputtered, laughing at the idea and a very foggy memory that surfaced at his words, one in which she dragged her vibroblade over the dark plasteel of a big, bulbous ship panel.

"Oh yeah! If he weren't so smashed, he would've tried to fight you, but he was falling down drunk. I think that's when Alec dragged him off to their bunk." His words sparked another memory, one in which Alec and Ray had been snuggling on a beat-up old couch in the hangar.

"Oh shit! That's right! They're together!"

"Yeah. Poor Alec." Nick shrugged as he put his coffee mug under the coffee machine's dispenser.

"Not much food in this place."

"Well, I'm gone a lot, you know." He shrugged again. Then he looked up with a glimmer in his eye. "You want something good to eat?"

"Always!"

"Go put your shoes on."

"All right." Juliet returned to Nick's guest bedroom and sat on the bed, pulling on her socks and boots. She then walked over to the dresser where she'd seen her gun belt, and when she picked it up, she saw her data deck sitting on the polished maple dresser top. Suddenly, more memories rushed back to her, and she grinned fiercely. "Please tell me you got the recording."

"I got the recording. Well, more precisely, Fido got the recording."

"Did you listen?"

"No, I was waiting to do it with you."

Juliet grinned and slipped the deck into the back pocket of her jeans before strapping her gun belt on and looking for her vibroblade. She didn't see it or her jacket. She stalked, boots clomping, down the hallway. "Nick, where's my jacket and my knife?"

"Ah, the knife . . ." He sipped his coffee and ran his eyes around the room, pointing to a small table near the door where his couch sat against the wall.

"There it is. I took it from you after your antics with Ray's ship. As for your jacket . . . I think we left it at the club."

"Oh, damn it! Are you serious? That was my favorite . . ."

"Hang on! Don't freak out. Let me message Sam; she'll let me know if anyone picked it up while they were cleaning. We closed them down, right?"

"You did," Angel helped.

"Yeah, we did." Juliet sighed and picked up her sheathed vibroblade, leaning down to stuff it into the top of her boot.

"You gotta wear that gun to breakfast?"

"What if we get accosted? You seem to know everyone, and they either love or hate you." Juliet pulled the door open, squinting at the bright sunlight filtering through the vine-covered trellis Nick had bordering his little patio. "Should I order a cab?"

"Nah, we can walk; it'll do us some good." He brushed past her, and Juliet heard him inhaling his vape as he strode down the steps onto the gravel drive that led down to the road. She followed, pulling the door closed and giving herself enough space so she wasn't engulfed in his exhalation plume.

"I can't wait to listen to that recording. Don't you think we should listen before Nick starts trying to sell us on this job?" Juliet leaned close to a flowering shrub that lined Nick's drive and inhaled deeply, enjoying the cloying sweet scent as she silently conversed with Angel.

"I could listen now and give you bullet points."

"All right. Do it." Juliet felt a little guilty about recording Nick without his permission, but she was doing it for his protection. She didn't trust Ray at all, and Larry wasn't much better. She'd left the deck in her jacket, which made her wonder why she had the deck and not the jacket. She had a vague memory of being very sweaty when she got back to the booth and slipping the deck in her pocket just as she now carried it.

She shook her head, still upset, fearing she'd never see her favorite coat again.

"These are my trees!" Nick called, slowing to wait for her to catch up. Juliet saw the gravel path was taking them along a long, narrow grove of tall, neatly pruned trees planted in rows. "They don't produce this time of year, but when they fully leaf out and flower, they smell amazing."

"Pretty cool. Some guy pays you to harvest 'em?"

"Yep." He gestured expansively. "The whole dome is agricultural, so you have to have something like this on your property. The guy we're going to see about breakfast raises bees."

"Really?" Juliet jogged for a few seconds to catch up to him. "He sells breakfast?"

"Nah, but he used to be a cook, and he's always inviting me over."

"Wait! We're just barging in on your neighbor and asking for breakfast?"

Nick laughed. "Trust me! It's fine. Howard's up at the crack of dawn, and I have an open invitation."

"Seems a little awkward . . ." She trailed off, letting the matter drop as Nick's only response was an exaggerated shrug. He sucked on his vape again, and Juliet subvocalized, "Well?"

"I listened at high speed, and most of the recording is taken up by Ray practically begging Nick to take the job. It seems he's indebted to the man whose daughter is missing, and if Nick can complete this mission, the man has promised to reduce his debt significantly. Nick was angry and asked Ray why he didn't just do the job, subcontracting his current obligation with Yggdrasil Station. Ray admitted, with much apparent shame, that he wasn't up to the task, that he'd never be able to impress the pirates enough with his interceptor flying, and that the client wasn't willing to provide a missile boat."

"So this whole thing was a setup. Larry probably didn't even know about Nick until Ray started trying to capitalize." Juliet paused by a side road, another gravel path that led between two fields of tall, dark-green stalks.

"That's it. Turn that way." Nick was just a little behind her, strolling, alternating between sipping his coffee and inhaling his vape.

"Your poor heart." Juliet shook her head, then continued down the side road.

"Yes, it seems that Mr. Fine is a fixer that Ray knows well. He's trying to hire Nick as a favor to Ray so that he can earn points with the client."

"And they made all this clear to Nick?"

"It seems quite clear from the recorded conversation, yes."

Juliet turned and walked backward slowly, letting Nick catch up. When he was only a couple of steps away, she asked, "So? Tell me what Ray had to say about this job. Are you going to take it?"

"Oh, man. I'm trying to put off thinking about that. He sure wants me to—practically begged me. I guess he's in deep with the client, and if he can provide the 'ace' they need, he'll earn some big points. I feel like I'm being used . . ."

"Because you are."

"Yeah. Well, if you listen to Ray, it sounds like he's about to lose his ship and maybe get picked up by corpo-sec for debt collection. I guess the client is some bigwig with a lot of connections."

"No offense, Nick, but Ray seems like a creep. Do you really owe him that much?"

"I hate that I do, but yeah. He saved my ass a few times back when we were in the shit around Venus." Nick pointed over Juliet's shoulder, and she turned to see a house a lot like his but larger and with a much more manicured garden. A path led away from the gravel road to a wooden deck lined with many hanging, potted plants. "Head up to the deck, there. He'll hear us coming and meet us."

"You didn't agree, did you?"

"Not yet, but I think I'm going to have to."

"Well, set up a meeting with that Larry guy. I'll join you, but make it just the three of us. I want to get a good look at him."

"Oh? Gonna be my chaperone?"

Juliet took long steps, ensuring her boots only touched the flagstones between the loose sand-colored pebbles lining the path. She always did that, usually without thinking—avoided stepping on cracks or off stepping stones. "Yeah, I'll sit in with you on the meeting, but I'm not saying I'll join your crazy mission. Probably won't, you feel me? I mean, you're about ready to give a good report to Alice, right?"

"Yeah, just about." He sighed and shook his head. "Don't worry, you're good. Didn't I already tell you that you reminded me of myself? Can't get any higher praise than that . . ."

"Nick!" a jovial, profoundly masculine voice said from ahead. Juliet looked up to see a tall, round man with a reddish-brown bald head and a bushy blond mustache that brought to mind images of a walrus.

"Howard." Nick laughed, hurrying his steps to catch up to Juliet. "I knew you'd be up."

"Well, well! Who's this, Nick? A little out of your league, don't you think?" Howard stepped down from the deck onto the paver before Juliet and held out a big, meaty hand. "I'm Howard, as you might have guessed. This is my farm!" He gestured with his other arm, swinging it wide. Juliet stepped back simply because he was so large. He had to be nearly seven feet tall.

"I'm Lucky." Juliet tried to match his smile as she gripped the big, warm appendage.

"Yeah, she's outta my league, my blunt friend. She's a coworker, not my girlfriend." Nick walked around the mountainous man, clapping him on the shoulder. "What's for breakfast?"

"Oh? I won't have to twist your arm to stay and eat this time?"

"Nah, she's hungry." Nick pulled out a polished hardwood bench and sat down at a matching table.

"Hungry?" Howard leaned toward Juliet, still gripping her hand. "I have just the thing—food!" He laughed as though he'd just told an uproarious joke, then let go of her and climbed back onto his deck. Juliet saw that he struggled with the steps, seeming to favor his left knee. When he walked past Nick, she noted a definite limp. "Let's see. How does a drink sound to wet your whistles while the food cooks? Mimosa? Bloody Mary? Something stronger? Whisky and coffee?"

Juliet looked at Nick and raised her eyebrows. He shrugged and said, "Mimosa for me."

"I'd, uh." She was about to say she just wanted plain coffee, but then she thought of the two cups she'd already drunk, and another voice in her head asked why she shouldn't enjoy herself a little. "I'd like a spicy Bloody Mary. Can you pull that off?"

"Spicy? Oh, I can do spicy, my dear. Sit down there with Nicky, and I'll get something good mixed up. What a delightful start to the day! I love to have company for breakfast. I'll be right back." He ducked his head and slipped inside his cabin. In the glare of the morning light, Juliet couldn't see much beyond the entry, but it looked like the deck opened up directly from his kitchen.

"He seems really nice."

"Howard's the best. He doubles as my shrink, so we'll have to leave in a hurry if he starts spilling my secrets." Nick winked at her, but something told Juliet he was only half joking.

"Don't worry, Nick. I have a shrink, too." She grinned and leaned an elbow on the table so she could twist more easily, looking over her shoulder around Howard's garden. It was lovely, and she tried to take it in, tried to enjoy the pleasant morning while it lasted. It was starting to sound like she might need to get Nick out of some trouble, and she didn't think pretty gardens would be part of the picture.

20

\\\\\\\\\\\\\\\\\\\\\\\\

MESSES TO CLEAN

The street and sidewalk leading up to the Raptor Haus looked a lot different in the bright lights of the dome's day cycle. The stains on the plasteel and concrete stood out among bits of litter, discarded drink containers, and dozens of spent vape cartridges. It didn't look like much cleaning got done between opening hours, but Juliet didn't really know. It could be that the mess was all from the weekend, and someone would be along to spruce things up before the next busy night.

She approached the awning and the closed doors beneath it, squinting to try to see through the tinted glass. Of course, she couldn't make anything out, not until she got right up to the glass and cupped her hands to it; then Angel did an excellent job of enhancing her view, exposing the empty, litter-strewn foyer of the club and the security station where she and Nick had spoken to the bouncer, Sam. It looked deserted. "She said she'd meet us here, right?"

"Yes. Shall I message her?" Angel replied.

"Yeah. Let her know we're outside." Juliet turned and leaned her back against the plastiglass panels next to the door, staring out at the sparse foot traffic. Not a lot of people were out and about in this part of town during the daytime, it seemed.

She'd finished breakfast with Nick and then taken a cab straight to the club, but only after securing his promise that he'd contact her about his meeting with Larry. Juliet was mildly interested in the job, more because she wanted to make sure Nick wasn't getting into something meltdown crazy than because she might be able to pick up another very nice payday.

What did they say? If the money seems too good, it probably means the job . . .

Her thoughts trailed off as she heard the latch rattle in the door, and she turned to see Sam, the bouncer, pushing it open. "Hey."

"Hey, thanks for meeting me. I know you guys don't open for hours."

"Nah, I was here early, anyway. We're training a new floor manager." She stood in the doorway, the metal and plastiglass door held open by her shoulder as she offered Juliet her jacket, neatly folded.

"Awesome! I've grown really attached to this thing and was afraid it was lost." Juliet held the vintage garment to her nose and sniffed it out of reflex. It smelled like her but also lots of other things—lingering spices, colognes, and even smoke. It sounded gross when she thought about it like that, but all together, the scents added up to give the jacket a third dimension, a kind of personality, and she recognized it immediately.

"Hey, glad to reunite you. Don't mention it." Sam cleared her throat and started to say something, but closed her mouth with a slight shake of the head.

"Something else?"

"Yeah, I think so. I didn't realize it at first 'cause I see a lot of people and listen to a million stories every week, but I'm pretty sure a lady was here looking for you a while back."

"Uh, I doubt it. I don't know anyone out here other than Nick. Well, Nick and his friends."

"No, I'm pretty sure. She showed me a picture of you but dressed a lot differently—nice outfit, sitting in a kind of swanky bar. Pretty sure she used your name, too. It sounded familiar to me last night, and I had my PAI search my recent convos, but I don't have the audio anymore. Took a minute, but my PAI found a couple of still images. Sorry, but like I said, the vid of our conversation was already written over. You know, freeing up memory."

Juliet knew exactly what she meant. People with ocular implants and PAIs could record everything they saw. However, most data ports had limited memory, and few people opted to upload their entire lives to the net. Her PAI probably culled old memories and uploaded still images in order to remember people's faces and names. Sam had her real memories, the ones in her flesh-and-blood brain, but like any person, she only remembered so much.

"Can you send me the images? Do you remember why she wanted to find me?"

"Didn't say." She shrugged. "I think she said she was looking for a friend or something like that. She left me with some contact info, though. I'll send it your way, too."

Juliet tucked her jacket under her arm and nodded. "Thanks a lot, Sam. I'd appreciate it if you didn't reach out to her. I'll try to figure it out myself."

"Yeah, no worries. That's my general policy. People ask me when I last saw so and so, and my answer is always, 'Who's that?'"

"Ha! I like it."

"Okay, catch you later." Sam waved and backed up, pulling the door closed.

"Bye." Juliet waved as she turned, but her mind was already occupied. Angel had displayed two still images on her AUI. The first showed her sitting at the table in the bar on the *Sunset Star Runner*. From the photo's perspective, it was captured by someone sitting across from her, and she knew exactly who that was—Eve. The other image was labeled "Frida" and pictured a young woman with bright orange hair, very freckled pale skin, and light green eyes. Juliet didn't recognize her. "Who the heck is this?"

"I'm not finding any matches on the Jovian public net."

"So this woman, Frida, came here looking for me with an image of me taken by Eve?"

"It seems that way. In hindsight, it would make sense that Eve and probably Kirby would have saved images of you."

"God, I'm such an idiot!" Juliet groaned, walking to the corner where Angel indicated a cab was waiting. "Of course those guys wouldn't want to let things go. They're probably in deep trouble with that other guy . . . Zappo?"

"Zapho."

"Right. Zapho. You think that's who sent this woman?"

"It's a good guess. Do you think we should do anything about it?" Angel only sounded mildly concerned, which made Juliet wonder if her own mounting stress was uncalled for.

"Don't you? It seems like a pretty big problem to me!"

"I don't know," Angel replied as Juliet stepped into the back of the waiting cab. Callisto cabs were small, electric things that could fit in the trunk of a cab back on Earth. Some were a little wider and could hold two modestly sized people, but most were just a little larger than an enclosed bicycle, and they used bicycle lanes. Of course, this meant they traveled slowly compared to a larger vehicle traversing traffic lanes designed for them, but when you had a city built around pedestrian traffic, you made sacrifices.

"Can you elaborate? What do you mean by I don't know? I guess I mean, what makes you think it might not be a problem?" Juliet shifted, trying to locate the safety belt and coming up with only one working end. "Cab, you're missing half of the passenger safety restraint."

"Apologies," the oddly accented AI responded. "This vehicle is due for service in negative forty-seven days."

"Negative . . ." Juliet trailed off as the cab started forward, the wide rear wheel, located beneath her seat, grinding and thumping against the plasteel.

"I think you are an operator who has crossed paths with many people and will continue to do so. I think, so long as it's Lucky the woman is looking for, we might not be in too much trouble. In any case, it might be wise to reach out and get ahead of things."

"We'll definitely do that. An anonymous meeting and a careful observation before we let her set eyes on us." Juliet fidgeted, jerking her arm out from between herself and the curved plastic side of the cab. "I hate these stupid little cabs."

"I'm terribly sorry for your discomfort, ma'am." The cab didn't sound apologetic. Juliet ignored it and looked at the map on her AUI—she only had ten more minutes before the tiny vehicle dropped her in front of the week-to-week hotel she'd been using between jobs with Nick.

"Cab, drop me at Felicita's Coffee." The coffee shop was a bit closer, cutting the ride down to seven minutes, and Juliet could walk to her place from there.

"Your route has been updated."

"More caffeine?"

"Angel, I'm surprised I'm up and about after last night. Yeah, I want more coffee."

"Well, your nanites have gotten well ahead of the toxins you ingested last night. You should be feeling better by now."

"Yeah, I am, but I'm still not a hundred percent. It's hard to explain, but my physical . . . I don't know, sense of well-being, I guess, is more than the number of toxins and electrolytes you can detect. You know? I mean, I don't think my drunken stupor was exactly good sleep."

"That makes a lot of sense, actually. I've read some interesting memoirs by talented artists who were addicted to alcohol and other self-destructive behaviors, and your current demeanor wouldn't be out of place in one of them."

"What? Why are you reading those?" Juliet feared she knew the answer.

"Well, I grew worried after your behavior last night, but most of the documentation I looked into said that a 'binge' once in a while isn't anything to be too worried about. There is some consensus that you might have been acting out on some pent-up emotions or in an attempt to mask other—"

"Angel, please. Please don't psychoanalyze my overdoing it last night. You know me—I don't do that very often, and yeah, there were a few underlying reasons. I was 'celebrating' killing a couple of people. I was trying to make Ray more tolerable. I was reliving fun times from my past; I think the dancing made me feel like I used to when I was out with Fee. I was . . . Oh, come on! Let's drop it, all right?"

Angel made a sighing sound, then in a brighter tone, said, "I won't bring it up again. To change the subject, would you like to discuss how you will approach this Frida character?"

"Yeah." Juliet rubbed at her temple. Angel was right; she felt pretty good and didn't have a headache, but something in her made her think she should have one, and she was acting like she did. "What do you think? Should we send her a message, anonymously, that we know she's looking for someone and have information for her?"

"And then observe her from a distance?"

"Does that sound good?"

"I think so. Your hair is a different length and style than in that photo. Shall we change your eyes and hair color as well? I think attire like you're currently wearing would be good; it's quite different from what you wore in that photo."

As the cab pulled to a stop next to the sidewalk, Juliet clambered out of the low seat and slammed the canopy closed, perhaps a little too enthusiastically. "You know, I don't want to have this hanging over my head. I need to figure out what's going on so I can sleep. Otherwise, my mind's going to be making up all sorts of nightmare scenarios. Can you try to set something up for that woman to meet us today?"

"Of course."

Juliet nodded to a couple sitting together at one of the café's outdoor tables and stepped through the door. "And yeah, let's try something new with my hair color: red, maybe. Hmm, and my eyes, I dunno, chrome." When she approached the barista, Juliet said, "Small flat white, please." Juliet was still very much appreciating the good coffee that was easily found in Callisto.

She'd learned that one of the agridomes was dedicated to the product, one of the major exports to other settlements in the Jovian System and even other nearby stations and planets.

Juliet appreciated that cafés like this one had baristas who made coffee drinks with old-school espresso machines. A shop would go out of business in this city if they installed one of the automated coffee machines that sat in nearly every breakfast restaurant or café in Tucson. She wondered if that made her a coffee snob. Was it possible she'd developed such an attitude after just a year or so of leaving home? She'd certainly not been picky about coffee back when she'd worked at the scrapyard.

While she waited for her drink, she sat near the window and watched the people walking by. It was busier here than near the club, and she enjoyed wondering what everyone was up to. *Was that woman with the sad eyes on her way to break up with a boyfriend? Was that man in the too-tight suit wearing the perpetual frown on his way to a sales job? Were those kids splashing in the puddle near the corner going to have a big adventure before the weekend was over? Did they even go to school?* Juliet had no idea what the corpo-school schedules were like on Callisto.

"Here you go." The barista, a young woman with a thick accent Juliet couldn't place, set her coffee on the table. "That was fast!"

"What?" Juliet looked up, confused. Had she forgotten an earlier conversation?

"Your hair's different from when you walked in. Either that or I'm losing it. Wasn't it darker? Like, black?"

"Oh, yeah. Sorry, I forgot I was changing it."

"Looks really nice." She smiled and returned to her counter, and Juliet softly blew on the top of her coffee, taking a sip of the rich drink.

"How does this sound?" Angel asked, "Hello. It's come to my attention that you're looking for someone. I may have some information. Can you meet today?"

"Pretty vague." Juliet sipped again at her drink. "I like it."

She sat quietly, slowly nursing her coffee staring out the window, but her thoughts went elsewhere, and she stopped noticing the people. She began to think about Eve and Kirby, analyzing the many ways she'd been stupid. If she'd wanted to get involved in Eve's problems, she should have really committed. She should have recognized that she was exposing herself and that she'd need to be more proactive about protecting her identity. When Kirby had ambushed her, he and Eve had escalated things, and Juliet should have seen to it that they couldn't identify her or come looking for her.

"We could have broken into the ship's brig or whatever. We could have found a way to hack their data ports. I mean, there wasn't time before security showed up to my room, but later . . ."

"I should have encouraged you to cover your tracks better."

"No. Stop it, Angel. I'm not on your case; this is my bad. I'm the busybody who had to try to 'help' Eve."

"We're a team, Juliet. You can't shoulder the whole burden of every failure. We both learned a good lesson, but now we need to clean up our mess."

"All right. Deal." Juliet felt better having voiced her frustration to Angel, and it felt good to know Angel was acknowledging the mistake and not trying to sugarcoat things. For the millionth time, she felt grateful that she had Angel in her head. How would she cope if she couldn't talk to her about her issues? She tried to imagine someone else who might be willing to listen to and share in all of her problems, but she couldn't. She knew some of the *Kowashi* crew would listen and try to help, but she'd never feel good about dropping these problems on them. Honey? Juliet snorted. She couldn't even get Honey to meet her for lunch.

"You have a new message from Bennet."

"Speak of the devil . . ." Juliet chuckled. "Well? Play it, sis."

A vid window resolved in her AUI, and as it began to play, Juliet heard Bennet's voice as footage of the gunship filled the window. "Making progress, Lucky! Port VTOL drive is all green lights! Even got it through a full ignition sequence—no leaks, nada! Guess what? Remember those jokers I dropped the rail gun barrels off to? They actually did it! I've got three straight, beautiful *Takamoto* barrels ready to install!"

Juliet felt her pulse quicken as the camera shifted to show the long, shiny barrels laid out on a tarp under the nose of the ship. "You haven't been sending as many messages lately, and I figured it might be 'cause I never respond. Aya called me a jerk, so I figured I better make more of an effort on my end."

The feed panned to the left then up. She could hear Bennet walking over the hangar's concrete floor toward the ship's aft end. He panned the camera up and said, "Check that out. We've almost fully disassembled the main drive. Had to pull all the plasteel panels off, even the ones leading up toward the nose—tons of lines and conduits leading up there from the drive that we'll have to change out. I don't think there's all that much wrong with it, either; to me, it just looks like they took a few direct hits to the power couplings and it flared out, melting all these connections. Nothing really expensive, but it's labor-intensive as hell; I can see why this baby never got fixed."

Juliet could see what he meant; the top fourth of the ship's hull was completely disassembled. It looked like a plasteel skeleton. Bennet continued. "Yeah. I think they just replaced the hull plates, buttoned it up, and called it a lost cause. Pirates! What do you expect?"

Bennet turned the camera to face his grease-smeared face. He'd cut his hair recently, shaving the sides and trimming the top down to just a blond-brown stubble. When he smiled, Juliet smiled too; it was good to see his friendly eyes.

"Well, that's all the good news from me. Uh, about your last message, yeah, um, Lavonne broke up with me—said I spend too much time working. Can you imagine? Anyway, that's the update from me. Let us know how you're doing, all right? Alice says her friend told her you're doing fine, but it'd be cool to hear more from you." The camera panned out, and he waved. "Bennet out."

Juliet was startled to find moisture in her eyes as the video closed. She chuckled, took a deep breath, and wiped them with her napkin. "It was nice to hear from him, Angel."

"I think it was just what we needed, hmm?"

"Exactly. Any word from that woman?"

"Not yet."

"Right. Well, let's get back to the hotel and get ready. We've got a mess to clean up, I guess."

"There's also the matter with Nick and his job offer . . ."

"All right. Make that two messes to clean up."

21

BLAST FROM THE PAST

She wants to meet in a RevinaCorp mining warehouse."

"Huh, seriously? She didn't think that would sound sketchy? What time?" Juliet sat at the foot of her bed, a small tray table pulled up in front of her where she'd disassembled and cleaned her Texan. She'd only shot it a few times at an indoor range, and she'd already cleaned it afterward, but she enjoyed the process; it helped her clear her mind.

"At 3:00 p.m., which is in ninety minutes."

"Still no word from Nick about Larry's thing?"

"Nothing."

"All right, tell this lady we'll meet her." Juliet started putting the gun back together. It was much easier than her SMG or needler. The revolver only had a few major components if you left the anti-recoil hardware in the grip alone, and there was no need to remove that stuff just for routine cleaning.

"Will you really? It seems like a perfect place to walk into a trap . . ."

"Oh, it is. No, I won't meet her there, but we'll go set up somewhere else and then, at the last minute, give her the change. She's the one who wants information—she can come to us."

"Ah, I see. Should I look for an alternate location?"

"Yep, someplace near that warehouse, but where people won't be working on a Saturday."

"There are a number of industrial facilities in that district. I'll study the available images and public files while you're en route."

"Perfect."

Juliet stood, slipped the Texan into its holster, and adjusted the bullet-studded belt, pleased by the way it was breaking in, starting to look a little worn and weathered, and happy with how it was molding into the shape of her hip. Next, she shrugged into her needler's shoulder holster. She pulled the gun out, popped the magazine, and ensured it was loaded with botu-rounds. She wasn't sure what kind of action would be on the menu, but she wanted to be prepared. That said, she fastened her vibroblade to her wrist and hung her deck from around her neck, tucking it down under her T-shirt. After putting on her motorcycle jacket, Juliet glanced at herself in the mirror above the ancient particleboard dresser and nodded.

"Looking good."

She stepped out of her hotel room onto an exterior terrace. Juliet looked left and right, scanning for people watching her. It was a habit she'd picked up when she'd first been on the run from WBD in Phoenix, and she had no intention of breaking it. She shut the door and walked to the stairwell, then down to the courtyard where a bank of e-bikes sat in their chargers.

"I'll drive one of these. I hate those cabs." She'd hardly finished speaking before one of the bikes beeped and a green ready light illuminated. Angel had rented it. Juliet climbed on and steered out onto the bike lane next to the busy sidewalk, following Angel's map.

The e-bike was fun to ride, the wind whipping through her short red hair as she buzzed past the little taxi vehicles and other approved modes of transport in Callisto—people on skates, scooters, or just jogging along with powered footwear. Juliet liked to go fast, and she pushed the little vehicle to its limit, which, admittedly, wasn't very impressive. Nothing really felt fast anymore to her, not after flying Nick's interceptor. Still, it was better than riding in a little eggshell taxi, and weaving around the other traffic took her mind off her problems.

"I think Honsho's Concrete Corp. will be your best option." Juliet's map updated with Angel's choice.

"Sounds good."

The industrial section of the Callisto main dome was on the far southeast edge, and Juliet had a thirty-minute ride ahead of her. As she motored along, she turned on some electronic dance music and tried to lose herself in the beats and the act of navigating the little bike around slower-moving people and vehicles. Riding the bike wasn't exactly mentally taxing, though, and she found her mind drifting to other things. It wasn't long before she began to focus on the little knot of dread at the pit of her stomach that she'd been avoiding; it centered on the fact that she intended to use the lattice on this woman and anyone who might come with her.

The more she thought about it, the more she realized she'd been actively avoiding the lattice in situations where it might have been advantageous. Why didn't she try to dig further into Ray's thoughts at the club? Why not listen in on Larry then and there rather than put it off with the idea that she could join Nick to meet with him again later? She knew the signs of subconscious avoidance and procrastination when she saw them, and she knew she was putting it off for a reason. The truth was, ever since she'd done that deep dive into Tono, she'd been leery of the lattice. When she'd gotten those glimpses of Ray's thoughts and, along with them, the seething angst and disgust, she'd wanted to pull back and shut the whole thing down.

What bothered Juliet was that she hadn't made a conscious decision at the club about it. She'd worked around it, thinking she was being clever with her data deck, but she could have learned a great deal more if she'd been willing to put up with the stray thoughts and emotions coming out of Ray.

That was really the issue: the emotions. Ever since Tono, she'd been cognizant that she was picking up more than thoughts when she dug around in a person's head. The more she dug, the more time she spent in there, the more feelings tainted what she found, and the more images came across and confused her mind, merging with her own memories. She didn't like it.

She supposed it might be something that got better with practice or exposure. Sometimes, Juliet thought it would be nice to have a partner or a friend she could practice with, one of the few things Angel couldn't help her do. The problem, as she saw it, was that the lattice was a secret. It was a secret, and anyone who knew about it would be taking on a heavy burden.

She figured there were a handful of people she could trust with knowledge of the lattice, but would she want them to have to carry that? That was one issue; the other was that she didn't really know how anyone would respond to her once they'd learned she could read their thoughts. Would she want to be friends with someone if she knew she might not be able to have any privacy around them?

That line of reasoning exposed another problem with "practicing" on a friend; she'd be digging around in their heads, and just because someone might be her friend didn't mean they'd like that, nor that whatever Juliet found wouldn't be just as problematic as something she might dig up in a person like Tono or Ray.

"Shit." The curse slipped out as she imagined finding some dark secret Aya or Bennet were holding on to. "What I need," she said over the whine of the e-bike's battery and the rumble of its knobby tires on the pavement, "are some sweet, innocent minds. You think I'd get in trouble hanging around a daycare and reading the kids' thoughts?"

"Are you being serious?"

Juliet laughed. "Not really! I guess it's not cool to experiment on kids. I think, when I pick up surface thoughts, it's not really invasive, but if I dig around like I did with Tono, I wonder if I could do any harm?"

"An interesting question. Are you just focusing your antenna, for lack of a better word, or are you actively reaching out somehow? I wish I knew more."

"We really need to spend some time experimenting. What I'm coming to realize is that I'm avoiding it more than I thought. I think I'm scared of it, Angel."

"You've had a lot thrust upon you in the last year. You've had to make a thousand adjustments to the way you live and think. I'm not surprised that, given the choice, you might push off yet another adjustment, another modification to how you see and interact with the world." Angel's words reminded her of something Doctor Ming might say, but coming from Angel, with the concern in her voice, they meant a lot more. They struck a chord with Juliet, and she found herself nodding along.

"Yeah! You know what, Angel, this isn't my bad; it's just the way it is. I'm doing pretty damn well, all things considered. I'll get around to this, to yet another adjustment, another thing I have to learn."

"That's the spirit!"

Juliet laughed and pulled the bike to the edge of the road as she realized she'd been zipping down a full-size lane. Luckily, there wasn't any traffic to be seen in this part of town; it seemed the heavy industry in Callisto took the weekends off. Tall plasteel-and-concrete buildings lined the roads, which had gotten wider and wider as they moved away from the center of town. Heavy vehicles were required for industry to work—deliveries and transport, if nothing else.

She passed several plain gray warehouse-size buildings, nothing differentiating them other than the colorful rectangular signs proclaiming the names of the corps that owned them. And then, with a blinking highlight from Angel, she saw the concrete company she was headed for.

"So," she subvocalized, "we need to break in there, get control of their security, and then send Frida a note that we picked a new location."

"And I can watch for her arrival on the cameras to see if she's alone."

"Yeah." Juliet leaned the bike up against the fence. It wasn't a dead give-away that someone was there—she'd seen bikes all over the city, even out this way. People weren't very conscientious about dropping them at charging stations.

The building was fenced, with cameras on every corner, but Juliet knew Angel was scrambling her image and sending false ID pings. She figured Angel would erase her visit from the logs, anyway, if they could get into the system. The main gate was an automated rolling section of fence that would allow vehicles to go in and out if they transmitted the correct code.

Once Juliet peered through the links to see the manufacturer of the gate mechanism, it didn't take Angel long to find a cracker on the net. Using Juliet's wireless data jack, she sent out a series of codes until the right one registered, and the gate began to roll open. Juliet slipped through, and Angel left the gate a meter ajar. "So Frida can come in more easily."

"Yeah, good call." Juliet jogged over the gravel lot to a pair of metal double doors next to the huge, closed bays. A data panel sat invitingly beside the door, and she plugged her cable in. "All yours."

"Give me a few minutes . . ." Angel said, then the panel beeped, flashed a green light, and the door clicked open. "Never mind."

"Not too security-conscious at the concrete factory?" Juliet chuckled and pulled the door open.

"It's not really a factory—it's a distribution center. The trucks come here to receive a mix and then take it to a worksite."

"Right. Whatever." Juliet looked around the cavernous building. There was a lot of empty space in front of the bay doors, and she supposed that was for the massive trucks to back in. Large rectangular stainless tanks lined the back wall. Dozens of enormous pipes were hung from the scaffolding on the high ceiling, and stacks and stacks of brown packages on pallets lined the walls. The only room in the entire structure was a foreman's office suspended from the right-hand wall at about a second-floor level with bare, steel steps leading down to the work floor.

"Guess the server access will be in there."

Ten minutes later, Juliet was sitting in the little office, her cable plugged into a dusty, ancient-looking data cube that sat on the only desk. The office was lined with windows, and she supposed they were meant to make it easy for the foreman to watch the workers on the floor. The blinds were down, though, and closed, and she wondered if the foreman maybe liked to while away the days doing things on the company clock—watching vids, playing games, flirting with people online. She shook her head, smiling at the strange fantasy of a nonconformist foreman, and asked, "How's it look?"

"Oh, I have control of the cameras and other functions of the security system, such as it is."

"What do you mean?"

"Well, simply that there isn't much here. I can control the gate and the door locks, the cameras, and that's about it. I've erased the footage of you entering the lot."

"Cool." Juliet stood up, pulled her cable out, and walked to the door. She contemplated for a moment, then flicked the light switch on and stepped out. She descended to the concrete floor and walked over the ample open space to the far corner where pallets of concrete mix were piled high.

She wondered if the mix was used in those big tanks or if it was sold dry like that to contractors. "Doesn't matter." She started heaving the thirty-five-kilogram bags off the pallet and stacking them on the concrete, making a little wall that stretched from the pallet to the first big, stainless tank.

"Are you building cover?"

"Yep. Is it time to message her yet?"

"You are due to arrive at her meeting place in five minutes."

Juliet grunted, hoisting another bag and adding it to her knee-high wall. "Go ahead and message her. Tell her we got spooked when we saw some people moving around the property she suggested. Give her this address and tell her we opened it up with a friend's work pass."

As she lifted another concrete bag, some vid feed windows appeared in her AUI, and Juliet knew Angel was showing her the external view of the building. She glanced at them but then got back to work; Angel would let her know if there was something to see. When the wall was hip high, she adjusted the bags to give her a couple of gaps she could, in a worst-case scenario, shoot through.

"She's on her way, though her reply to your message wasn't lighthearted. Would you like to hear it?"

"Uh, nah. I'll take your word for it." Juliet chuckled, then squatted behind her makeshift wall, watching through one of the gaps she'd made. The only entrance to the building that wasn't locked, the door she'd come through, was in the opposite corner, about forty meters away. The main building space was dim, only diffuse lighting coming through thin windows lining the top of one wall, but the foreman's office was illuminated with a yellow glow in the shadows. She figured Frida would expect her to be in there. One of her camera feeds started to flash on her AUI, so Juliet focused on it and got her first look at the mysterious woman.

Frida was dressed in tight khaki pants, wore black boots that wouldn't look out of place on a corpo-sec officer, and a button-up olive-green shirt. Juliet didn't see any weapons on her. Just as her picture had shown, she had short, natural-looking orange hair, pale skin, bright eyes, and even on the below-average resolution from the security camera, Juliet could see the freckles on her face. She whistled a strange tune—something old, Juliet thought—and gave the slightly ajar security gate a good, long once-over before stepping through. She hooked her thumbs in her belt loops and crunched briskly over the gravel toward the pedestrian entrance.

"I'm not detecting weapons."

"Okay. Keep watching the feeds. See if she has backup." Juliet knew she didn't need to say it, but she figured it was good for her to practice operational communications. What if her partner wasn't just Angel next time? She minimized the camera feed when she heard the latch on the door click, and saw the expanding rectangle of light as Frida pulled the door open.

"Hello?" Her voice was steady and bright, not a hint of nervousness. "This is kind of feeling like a setup! Anyone here?"

"I messaged her to come up to the office."

"Good," Juliet subvocalized, and then she tuned out the world, all but that tiny window in the concrete bags from where she was staring at Frida. Could she pick up someone's thoughts from so far? It didn't seem like she could—nothing but silence met her stare as Frida, no longer whistling, hopped lithely up the steps to the office door. She tapped on the door's glass window with her knuckles. When no one responded, she called out, "Okay, enough games. I'm heading out." She turned and started down the steps.

"Anyone coming on the cameras?"

"Nothing visible."

Juliet didn't like that distinction, but she nodded and stood up, then hopped over the little barrier she'd made. Frida noticed her movement immediately and stopped at the bottom of the steps, turning toward her but staying put, resting one hand on the metal railing.

"Well! There you are!" Again, her voice was bright and cheerful. Why was this lady so confident?

"Sorry. I wanted to be sure I wasn't walking into a trap."

Frida held a hand over her eyes as though she was trying to see something more clearly over the distance, and then her smile—easy for Juliet to see with her enhanced optics—broadened. "You're her!"

"Her?"

"The operator who messed up my boss!" She let go of the railing and began to saunter over the concrete floor toward Juliet. Something about her confidence was unnerving, and Juliet let her fingertips graze against the handle of her Texan. "Don't shoot!" She laughed, holding up her hands and slowing her steps. She was still thirty meters distant.

"Who's your boss?" Juliet's mind was racing. She'd expected this woman to mention something about Eve or Kirby, *but would she be working for them? Would she consider them her boss? They both seemed like small-time pawns. Was she referring to Zapho? Had Juliet "messed him up" by foiling Eve's assassination job on the cruise ship?*

"Rutger Tanaka, and he wants to speak with you."

Images of a flickering red sword blade, esoteric tattoos on a man's neck and face, and cold, hard eyes flashed through Juliet's mind. She didn't think, didn't actively decide to do it, but her hand, moving in a blur of high-end actuators, electrically charged muscle and tendon fibers, and driven by Angel's overtuned lightning synapses, snatched the Texan out of its zero-resistance holster, and she squeezed the trigger, so sensitive she never felt it, sending a fat slug of hot, deadly polymers straight at Frida's chest.

22

WHEN IT RAINS

Despite the decisive nature of her action, when the Texan thundered, echoing off the big metal bay doors and plasteel walls, it almost surprised her. Frida was certainly surprised. The hot, deadly slug smashed into her chest, and she flopped onto her back, hitting the concrete with a thud and wheezing, "Oof!"

"Juliet!" Angel sounded just as caught off guard, though she must have known something was up to increase the speed of Juliet's synapses. Was it a conscious thing, or did she have some subroutine monitoring Juliet's movements and adrenaline, ready to send her thoughts into overdrive at the drop of a hat?

"I . . ." Juliet started forward, deciding that any sort of action was better than standing there dumbstruck at her own behavior. "I heard his name and I just reacted. How could it be him? He was dead, Angel!"

She'd gotten to within ten meters of Frida's corpse, or what Juliet thought was Frida's corpse, when the woman groaned loudly and rolled to her side.

"Don't move!" Juliet shouted, lifting the pistol again.

"God. Jesus, lady. Don't shoot me again. What the hell did you hit me with?"

"Angel," Juliet subvocalized, "was she wearing armor?"

"Nothing externally . . ." Again, Angel couched her response with a qualifier that made Juliet uncomfortable.

"Just hold still, or the next one is going in your ear!" Juliet paused a second, then asked, "Are you dying?"

"Not imminently." Frida coughed and wheezed, then coughed again. "I'm not here to kill you or anything. Dammit, why'd you blast me?"

"Uh, have you met your boss?" Juliet switched to subvocalizations, "Anything on the cameras, Angel?"

"Nothing."

"My boss is scary, sure, but he's not here. He sent me 'cause I'm decidedly not scary." She coughed again and groaned.

"Turn over. Let me see your wound." Juliet slowly circled the woman, still keeping some distance, still pointing her gun at her head.

Frida flopped to her back, one hand pressed to the center of her chest, the other splayed out flat on the hard cement floor. "Oof, holy crap, lady, you dented me."

She slowly lifted her hand, and Juliet saw what she meant—beneath a layer of bloody flesh, a shiny, red-streaked metallic indentation sat in the middle of her chest. It was wide and deep enough that Juliet could picture a golf ball sitting in it.

"What the . . . Are you a synth?"

"No, dammit. I have endoskeletal reinforcements. Like, bloody damn expensive ones; a pistol isn't supposed to do this to me. Oof! This can't be good for my heart or whatever. I feel like I have an elephant sitting on my chest!" She wheezed and coughed again, and Juliet began to feel sorry for her despite, or maybe because of, trying to kill her moments ago.

She still held her gun aimed at Frida's head, and when the woman looked up from her chest and her green eyes locked onto Juliet's, she slowly shook her head and held up both hands.

"Relax, please. I know what you're thinking. You're wondering if it might just be easier to finish me off than deal with the fallout. I don't hold a grudge, okay? I shouldn't have ambushed you with my boss's name. Working for a guy like that, doing the kind of jobs we do, I was feeling a little too cocky. This is my bad. Don't kill me, all right?"

The truth was that Juliet had been trying to decide if she should attempt to get Frida some medical care. She was about to answer, about to reassure Frida that she'd acted on reflex, that she didn't want her dead, when, as she stared into those green eyes, some thoughts drifted through to her, unbidden.

Just hang on. Just hang on. Keep the psycho bitch thinking. Calm her down. Applebaum and Hawkins are almost here.

Juliet straightened her arm and pulled the hammer back on the Texan with a satisfying click. "Tell your team to back off. Tell Applebaum that he and Hawkins better get the fuck out of here."

"What? There's no team . . ."

"Last chance." Juliet put on her serious-business face, the one she'd learned from observing Ghoul. "You've got until one. Three." She paused briefly. "Two . . ."

"Okay, okay! Stop! I'm calling them off right now!"

Juliet was still a few meters from Frida, and she squatted down to better look into her eyes as she leveled the Texan at her face.

Okay, just breathe. So, she knows about your team. How? Impossible!

Frida's inner monologue changed suddenly, and Juliet got the impression she was hearing one side of a conversation.

No! . . . She knows who you are . . . I don't know . . . Just pull back to rendez-vous two . . . She's not blocking me yet, obviously . . . No . . . No . . . Okay, I'll keep them open . . .

"Frida," Juliet said.

"Yes?" The woman's startled look told Juliet that she'd interrupted her conversation.

"I want you to start singing a song. Any song, but make sure it's one you know really well because if you hesitate or pause in the verse, I'm going to shoot you." She smiled then took another step closer. "There's a chance you get out of this alive and well, but you need to cooperate."

"You want me to stop subvocalizing . . ."

"Start singing, Frida."

In a thin, rather pretty soprano, Frida began to sing,

By a lonely prison wall
I heard a young girl calling,
"Michael, they have taken you away,

Juliet stepped over to Frida and pushed against her shoulder until she got the idea and rolled over to face the floor. When she was face down, Juliet knelt with one knee on the smaller woman's spine but not putting much weight on it, just enough to let her know she was in control. Then she switched the Texan to her left hand and pulled out her data cable.

For you stole Trevelyan's corn,
So the young might see the morn,
Now a prison ship lies waiting in the bay."

"Good, Frida, good. I'm not going to hurt you. Keep singing."

Juliet knew the team was listening; she also knew Frida couldn't subvocalize as long as she was singing. She'd considered turning on her jammer, but then she wouldn't be able to do what she had planned. She reached down and peeled back Frida's synth-skin, exposing her data port, and then plugged her cable in. Frida paused briefly and wriggled a little, but Juliet tapped the pistol's barrel against her head, and she started up again, her voice warbling a little with obvious stress.

Low lie the fields of Athenry,
Where once we watched the small free birds fly,
Our love was on the wing, we had dreams and songs to sing,
It's so lonely 'round the fields of Athenry.

"Angel," Juliet subvocalized, "can you get control of her PAI and use her open comms to get into her team's too?"

"Yes. I'm working on it. It'll take me a minute to subdue and get around her PAI's ICE."

"Don't shut it down or anything, but put some daemons in place so we can listen to them and, if we need to, shut their PAIs down in a pinch."

"I understand. Obviously, she'll know we've done something to her PAI, but she may not know I can reach her team through the comms."

By a lonely prison wall,
I heard a young man calling,
"Nothing matters, Mary, when you're free.

"You're doing great, Frida. Keep singing; don't pause. Restart if you need to."

Against the famine and the crown,
I rebelled, they cut me down.
Now you must raise our child with dignity."

"Her PAI is very high-end, but I'm making progress. At this point, I can tell if she subvocalizes if you'd like to give her a chance to answer questions while I work."

"Okay, Frida, listen up. I can tell if you subvocalize, so please don't do anything dumb. Don't talk to your PAI or team, all right? I want you to hold very still while I ask you a few questions."

"Okay, but did you have to—"

Juliet pressed the Texan against her scalp again. "No, no, Frida. Don't say anything that might alarm someone. I'd hate for some trigger-happy individual to make a mistake."

"Okay."

"Now, can you tell me how you came by a photo of me on the *Sunset Star Runner*? How did you connect that photo to your boss?"

"If I explain it, will you take that cannon off my head?" Frida's cheek was against the cement, and she'd gone completely limp; if she was putting on a defeated act, she was doing a great job at it.

"I'll think about it."

Frida inhaled deeply through her nose and began speaking.

"After Rutger woke up from the coma, he was keen to find you. He knows information brokers, and he put the word out. He didn't have any images of you, but he knew what you looked like, so he asked them to let him know if anything came up involving a woman who matched your description. He goes through about fifty or a hundred photos a day, sent his way by various brokers while he eats his breakfast. Anyway, he got your photo from a broker who was looking for you, trying to find you for a small-time syndicate enforcer named Zapho."

"And is Zapho still looking for me?"

"No. Rutger didn't want him to get to you before we could, so I paid him off. He was happy to let the matter drop for the right price."

"Juliet, I'm in. I have control of her PAI, but I've been careful not to give it away. I've sent my daemons through her comms, and they're working on her team's PAIs. I have their locations, though, from Frida's team channel, and I can confirm that there are two: Applebaum and Hawkins."

"Can I pull the data jack?"

"Yes. She has a wireless jack, and I have control."

"Okay, hold still." Juliet stood up and pulled her cable out, letting it retract into her wrist. She stepped back and squatted again, looking into Frida's eyes, staring.

God, is she going to kill me? Did I say too much? Should I have held back some information? She doesn't know everything yet! I should beg. I should tell her I have more . . .

"Where's Rutger?"

"On his way to Luna. He wasn't sure you were getting off the cruise ship in the Jovian System. We have a team on Mars, too, and Rutger is hoping you'll return to Luna. He's hoping to figure out where your base of operations is."

"What does he want? To kill me? You know I was just there to rescue a little girl and her caretaker, right? He attacked me." Juliet gestured with the Texan and added, "Don't answer right away. Think about it. I'm good at spotting a lie, Frida, and you don't want to find out what I'll do if you lie at this point."

Frida licked her lips and nodded, blinking her pale green eyes rapidly.

She's crazy. She's as crazy as Rutger. I can't believe she shot me like that. So damn fast . . . Is that how she got the better of him? He won't talk about it—is he embarrassed? Shit, shit, shit, get a hold of yourself, Frida. What do I say? The truth, dummy!

"I don't know. He's canceled a dozen jobs, and he's paying the teams and the travel budgets out of his own pocket. Don't get me wrong, he's got deep pockets, but something's off about him. He hasn't been the same since he woke up."

"He won't tell you why he wants me?"

"No." Frida's eyes darted to the barrel of Juliet's gun and then back to her face, and she licked her lips again. "We all have our guesses. Lee thinks he's mad with the need for vengeance; says Rutger's gonna skin you alive and make you into a suitcase. Applebaum thinks he's in love. They don't know him like I do, though, and I think it's something else. I think when he nearly died, when he thought he had died, something changed or woke up in him. I think he needs to see you, to understand you, and . . . I don't know, maybe find closure."

"Angel," Juliet subvocalized, "is she wired for speed?"

"No. She has some expensive augmentation but nothing that will allow her to catch you unawares."

"Okay." Juliet stood up from her crouch and stepped back another meter or so. Then she holstered the Texan. "Sit up." With grunts and groans, Frida pushed herself to a sitting position. She sat hunched, clearly in significant discomfort from the damage done to her armor-enhanced sternum. "I'm glad I didn't kill you, Frida. I know you think I'm a psychopath, but I'm not. My body reacted to your boss's name. I think he traumatized me pretty good, and I kind of buried the memory rather than deal with it. You brought it up, and I reacted."

"Sounds like PTSD." Frida winced and gingerly touched the raw, bloody flesh at the edge of her injury.

"I want to get this matter settled, all right? I'm not excited by the prospect of a crazy, rich mercenary sending teams around the solar system looking for me. I could get real dark and kill you and your team—I have eyes on them, by the way. I could pull your PAIs and hope Rutger and the other people he hires won't find me, but I think there's some seriously bad karma down that road, and I'm just not that kind of person. I could try to leverage you or your team as hostages and lure him into a trap, but again, I'm not that kind of operator. Can we make a deal, Frida?"

"Yes!" Frida leaned forward, her eyes widening with the sincerity of her agreement.

"Listen. I've got things to get done here around Jupiter, but I'll be heading back to Luna. Can we just set up a meeting between me and your boss? Tell him to call off his teams, and when I get back, we can settle things."

"Seriously?"

Juliet locked eyes with Frida and let her mind relax, willing her thoughts to come through.

Seriously? She's fast, but so is Rutger. He's killed more people than this girl could comprehend. Is she going to try to duel him or something? Jesus, old man, why do you want to find her? Do you even want her dead?

God, my chest! Oof, every breath hurts. Finally gonna get some use out of that premium med plan. How'd she find the team? She knew their names . . . What's she thinking about? Second thoughts?

"Yeah, I'm serious. I don't wanna die, Frida, and I don't want to kill anyone I don't have to, but I'm not going to have your crazy boss holding a sword over my neck for the rest of my life."

Juliet was serious, but she had a few aces Frida didn't know about. Even if Frida pulled her PAI and replaced it with a new model, Angel was deep into her team's network by now. She might even be able to hitch a ride with one of them all the way back to Rutger.

Juliet stood up and stepped toward Frida, holding out a hand.

The woman, probably only a few years older than Juliet, took it in a firm but clammy grip, and Juliet hoisted her to her feet. Juliet stood there, looking into her eyes again as she held her hand and contemplated really diving in, trying to do to Frida what she'd done to Tono. She wanted to think she didn't do so because she'd covered her bases with Angel and her daemons, that she'd already heard enough of Frida's thoughts, but she knew it was a load of crap—she was scared.

"I don't know what kind of intel you have on me, but I'm not working alone. Like I said, I have eyes on your team. Please, just go back to Luna and give him my message."

"All I know is your operator name, Lucky, and that you've been flying around this system and that you've hit a couple of clubs. We tracked you down with a photo and lots and lots of legwork. Shit, we didn't track you down—you contacted me."

"Okay." Juliet gestured with her thumb toward the door, and Frida nodded. "Hope your chest is all right." Frida winced and held a hand to her bloody shirt as though Juliet had reminded her of the injury, then turned and started walking. After a few steps, she slowed and turned.

"Lucky, I'll tell him you could've killed me but you didn't."

Juliet didn't smile, but she met her eyes and nodded again. She wondered if Frida would tell Tanaka that she'd tried, though, that she'd shot her dead in the center of her chest with a modded polymer slug meant to be as lethal as possible.

She hoped not, because it sounded like Rutger Tanaka had enough of a grudge already.

When she got to the door, Frida pulled the latch, then turned and asked, raising her voice to be heard over the distance, "Can you tell me what you did to my PAI? I'm just gonna pull it and put a new one in anyway."

"What would you do?"

"Dig for contacts and messages if I could get through the ICE."

Juliet offered her a half smile and shrugged.

"Right. Well, thanks." With that, she stepped through, and the door clicked shut behind her.

"You did get her messages and contacts, right?"

"Oh, yes, and quite a lot more. I have the locations of Tanaka's offices on Titan, of his new apartment in Luna City, and the names, contact information, and locations of all of his current employees. It seems Frida is his second-in-command, so to speak."

"Well, that's good, at least . . ." Juliet trailed off as an incoming vid call from Nick flashed on her AUI. "As they say, Angel, when it rains, it pours."

23

〰〰〰〰〰〰〰〰

KILLING SOME TIME

"Hey, Nick." Juliet studied his face in the call window; he looked tired. His skin wasn't exactly smooth during a good day, and now he had dark circles under his eyes and a heavy layer of salt-and-pepper stubble. Had he looked that rough at breakfast? Juliet probably hadn't noticed, considering she'd been dealing with her own hangover.

"Sorry to bug you, but you insisted I call when I heard from that Larry character."

"He wants to meet?" Juliet hurried out of the warehouse, letting the door slam shut behind her. Angel was still monitoring the cameras, and she knew exactly what Frida and her team were up to, so she didn't feel nervous about walking out the open gate and straight toward her abandoned e-bike.

"Yeah, his client's eager to get the ball rolling. Look, I don't want to get you wrapped up in all this. He thinks the whole thing will take a week or two, tops, so if you just want to have a nice little vacation, I'll be happy to let you fly the Lady some more when I get back. We can get you a few more flight missions under your belt, and I'll write you a good report to Alice—"

"No, no, Nick. Let me sit in on this meeting with Larry. I'm good at reading people, and I might be able to squeeze some details out of him. Might be you don't want to do this job, you feel?"

"Starting to feel less and less like a choice. Ray's desperate, and, well, I could use the bits."

Juliet sighed heavily and said, "Just let me come to the meeting. No amount of bits is worth dying for, right?"

"Yeah, right. Okay. We're meeting at a restaurant near the port, Haskin's Farm to Table. Eight o'clock, 'kay?"

"See you then." Juliet hopped on the bike, and by the time she started rolling out into the street, Nick had cut the connection. "What are Frida and her team doing?"

"Frida pulled her PAI, but she contacted Applebaum first. She's heading to their rendezvous, and Hawkins is out buying her a new PAI. For what it's worth, if she keeps the level of connectivity with her team that she had before, I'll be able to gain control of her new PAI as well."

"Nice, Angel!" Juliet concentrated on driving the e-bike for a while, but her mind started wandering down strange paths. "What's it like?"

"What?"

"Being connected to their PAIs. I mean, I know you can connect to wireless networks and cameras and all that, but those PAIs are kind of like . . . intelligent, right? Do you talk to them?"

"They're like computer programs, Juliet. I don't speak to them in the way I would to you or another person. I isolate their code, send commands, and watch them carry them out. It's nothing like speaking to another me, if that's what you're wondering. The difference is stark."

"I was kind of wondering that, yeah. I'm sorry; that was stupid. I know you're not like other PAIs."

"It's not stupid to wonder. I wonder what it would be like to meet a true AI."

"Like you." Juliet wasn't asking. Angel was definitely an AI; they'd established as much. Still, being reminded of it was a bit of an eye-opener. "Well, changing the subject, do you know where this restaurant is?"

"Yes. It's not far from your hotel."

"Perfect. Hey, since Frida pulled her PAI, why don't you send her team an anonymous address so she can get back to me after she's spoken to Tanaka? I mean, hopefully you'll be able to record her conversation with him, but she doesn't know that."

"Done."

Juliet had a few hours to kill, but she didn't feel like doing anything much. She rode the e-bike back into town, taking a roundabout route to her hotel, and then she went up to her room and sat down at the foot of her bed. She stared at herself in the mirror above her dresser and, without thinking, drew her Texan and replaced the spent cartridge with a fresh one. She hadn't had a chance to process what she'd learned from Frida, but sitting there, her mind began to drift toward the core-shaking memories she'd buried.

She saw Lemur's head sliding off his body and rolling over the hard, clean floor. She saw a black-gloved hand holding open elevator doors, and then she saw his face, Rutger Tanaka, with his short dark hair, chromed eyes, and tattoos—so many strange, colorful tattoos. *Who was the woman who'd earned a spot on his flesh? What did the tears signify? What did the kanji say?*

She knew she could get some of the answers to her unspoken questions. She could ask Angel to dig the memory out of the cloud. Angel could probably figure out a lot with some poking around on the nets. Heck, she probably already had, knowing her.

For the second time in a single day, though, Juliet chickened out. She didn't want to see that memory again, and she didn't want to know any more about Tanaka, not at that moment. She needed more time to process.

To pass the time and to get her mind off disturbing memories and worries about her future, Juliet practiced moving small objects around with her mind. It was the perfect distraction, really, considering how much concentration it took. She'd spent an hour here and there working with the ability during her downtime between flights with Nick, but hadn't noticed much of an improvement. She couldn't lift cars or toss people around like superhuman vid stars. Angel had a different take, though, encouraging her by pointing out that her time between initial concentration and object movement had decreased significantly.

Juliet had been evaluating herself based on how much she could move and how far, but when Angel pointed out how much more quickly she was accessing the ability, she had to admit she had a point. It was almost effortless for her now to slide a glass over a table or flick a bullet off the dresser and pull it into her hand. She barely had to think about it before she could make it happen. So, while her mental muscle or whatever wasn't much stronger, she was definitely more adept at what she could move with it.

After she'd emptied a box of needler rounds, yanking them one by one off the dresser and into her hand, she had an idea and asked Angel, "I kind of remember seeing a vid of a guy throwing playing cards so fast that he could, like, slice fruit with them and stuff. Can you try to find it?"

"Are you planning to try to turn your telekinesis into a weapon by flinging playing cards at people?"

Juliet snorted. "Well, not exactly, but it seems like it might be a good inspiration. I can't lift anything heavy, but I'm getting better at moving around small things. Maybe I could, I don't know, get some tiny knives or something."

So, Angel found her the video and about a dozen others, and Juliet spent a couple of hours getting inspired by people with incredibly talented hands and impressive hand-eye coordination.

She was trying to use her telekinesis to fling her vibroblade into the chipped, scratched, and generally beat-up particleboard dresser drawers, aiming for the spot between the shiny aluminum knobs, when Angel interrupted her concentration.

"If you're going to walk to the meeting, you should leave soon."

"Wow! Already?" Juliet stood and snatched her knife from the poor, brutalized piece of furniture. "I'll pay for that," she said, more to herself than Angel.

"That piece of furniture should have been recycled years ago."

"Yeah." Juliet chuckled, sliding her arms into the silky sleeves of her jacket. "I guess we're just doing a service for the next guests to use this room. At least it proves one thing."

"What's that?"

"The hotel AI wasn't lying when it said it was giving us privacy. I'm sure the manager would have found an excuse to come in otherwise."

"True, unless she'd been hoping you'd do more damage and she could charge you for even more—already necessary—repairs."

"Uh, sheesh. I guess I don't think like a sleazy hotel manager, do I?" Juliet briskly pounded down the concrete steps outside her room, her boots making satisfying clomps as she descended.

"You're saying you feel Mrs. Rachel is sleazy?"

"Not many women could pull off slicked-back, greasy hair, but she does it. I gotta hand it to her." Juliet laughed at the image, picturing the little hotel manager as she'd last seen her. "It's not the look that does it, though; it's the way she walks around peering into the windows and staring at any guest she doesn't think is watching."

"She's certainly voyeuristic, now that you mention it." There was a bit of a laugh in Angel's voice, and Juliet wondered at that. Angel claimed to feel things all the time, not least of which being love for Juliet. Did she really find things amusing in the same way that a person would?

Despite her protestations to the contrary, Juliet had to admit that she really didn't understand Angel or how she worked. She'd insisted that Angel was alive, but how did that even work? Didn't humor or love have a lot to do with chemicals affecting the brain? Did Angel use her connection to Juliet's brain to feel things?

Juliet couldn't wrap her head around it, and she supposed that was normal; she couldn't explain how her own brain worked, so why should she understand how Angel's did?

The sidewalks were busy near the ports, and she found herself shoulder to shoulder with people and stymied by slower-moving crowds as she tried to walk at her usual brisk pace. Subconsciously, she made a game out of trying to move around people and not lose any time. She sped up when her path was clear, and picked people to shrug past who wouldn't put up a fuss—women with their hands in their pockets, men with relaxed gaits, and, generally, smaller people.

Soon, she was deep in the port district, and her mini map told her she was just a block from the restaurant.

"Is Nick there?"

"Yes, I'm receiving location pings from his PAI. He's in the restaurant."

"Good." Juliet slowed down a bit and settled her nerves, getting her breathing nice and relaxed. The restaurant wasn't large, and the front opened onto the sidewalk to provide outdoor seating. While it wasn't large, it was crowded, and Juliet realized some of the mouth-watering odors she'd been picking up for the last couple of blocks were coming from within. She smelled the unmistakable aroma of grilled meats, spicy sauces, and something else, like rosemary or some other potent herb infused in oil and being used to sauté vegetables.

"Lucky!" Nick waved from one of the bay openings into the restaurant, and Juliet smiled and waved back, pushing her way between some bistro tables to get in.

"Excuse me," she said as she wedged herself between two people sitting back-to-back at different tables. "Hey there."

She laughed at Nick's exuberant greeting as he took hold of her arm and escorted her the last few feet to the table he'd claimed. It was a four-seater, and it was apparent he was all alone and had been there a while—three empty beers sat next to a little plate littered with bread crusts.

"I'm glad you're here! The hostess has been giving me dirty looks. I'm not sure they like me taking up a table all by myself."

"Well, tough!" Juliet sat down to his right, putting her back to the wall. "Where's your guy?"

"My guy? You mean Larry? He's supposed to be here any minute."

"Listen, Nick, I'm just gonna sit here and watch you two talk for a while. Don't mind me. Just do some negotiating with him, but do me a favor and ask him blunt questions. Like, ask him if he's sure this isn't some kind of setup. Ask him if he's holding the funds in escrow or if you're going to be at the mercy of this mysterious client when it comes time to get paid. If he tries to give wishy-washy answers, I want you to press him and make him commit. I'm really good at spotting a liar, but I need you to ask the right questions, all right?"

"Well, shit, you know I'm not some novice, right? I think I've got ten years or so on you."

Juliet laughed and raised an eyebrow. "Ten?"

"All right, all right, maybe more like fifteen?"

"Sure, Nick, we'll go with that." She glanced at his empty beers thirstily, then shook her head. "Anyway, I'm not saying you don't know what you're doing, but I've got something of a talent for this, okay? Trust me." She cleared her throat and said, "Angel, order me a . . . lemonade."

"You're not drinking?" It was Nick's turn to raise an eyebrow.

"Not after last night. I need to let that experience recede from recent memory first."

"Yeah, I don't blame you. I mean, you drank at breakfast, but whatever." He winked at her, and Juliet laughed; he had a point. She leaned back in her seat and enjoyed the smells coming from the kitchen. After a minute or two, during which Nick took several drinks from his beer, she said, "Let's order some food when you're done talking to Larry."

"Oh yeah. Definitely." Nick jerked his head to the left, looking at the sidewalk, then stood up and waved an arm. "Here we are!" He turned back to Juliet. "Just got a ping from him."

Juliet watched the sidewalk and finally spotted Larry, walking toward the restaurant between two very large, very chromed-out meatheads wearing matching burgundy suits.

"Did he have muscle with him last night?"

"If he did, they weren't near the table. Maybe they watched from a distance." Nick shrugged and waved again, getting Larry's attention. The fixer nodded to his bodyguards, and they both moved to different areas of the sidewalk, taking up positions where they could watch Larry and the crowds at the same time.

"Did you notice those guys last night?" Juliet subvocalized.

"I was just running through the footage I saved, and they are present in the crowd."

"Well," Juliet said, watching Larry make his way to their table, "that adds another dimension to his character."

"Huh?" Nick glanced at her.

"The muscle."

"Oh, yeah, sure." Nick pointed to an empty seat. "Hey, Larry. Got here a little early."

"Great, great!" Larry smiled at Nick, then looked at Juliet and nodded. "Pleasure to see you again, miss. Is your presence a signal that you've thought about perhaps joining your friend on my little operation?"

Juliet shrugged. "I'll see what you have to say. You mind if I turn on a jammer? I hate to have the wrong people hear about what you want Nick to do, you know what I mean?"

"Oh, not to worry." Larry chuckled, tapping one of his long, golden digits on his temple. "I have one built in. I won't let our words travel beyond the table."

"Angel, did you notice that last night?" Juliet subvocalized while she smiled to save face. "I didn't realize that, Larry. Were you running it last night?"

"No. The booths at the Raptor Haus are already shielded."

Angel added, "I was about to say the same thing, Juliet. The booths allowed music in, but didn't you notice you couldn't understand any conversations taking place around the table?"

"I think I had too much to drink last night." Juliet laughed. She was saved from the topic by a waiter appearing with her lemonade and what looked like a very nicely made mojito, complete with fresh, muddled mint leaves. After he gave her the lemonade, he handed the mojito to Larry, and Juliet had to admit he was damn good at timing his drinks to arrive at the same time he did.

"I appreciate you meeting me here, Nick. This is my neck of the woods, the ports."

"That right?" Nick raised an eyebrow and nodded as though Larry had just revealed some truly interesting news. Juliet watched him for a moment then turned to Larry and, rather than dive in right away trying to read his thoughts, she took a sip of her lemonade and listened.

"Have you made any kind of decision, Nick? I've got a couple of other irons in the fire, so to speak, so if you aren't interested, there's no reason we should keep wasting each other's time."

"Oh, BS. C'mon, Mr. Fine." Nick shook his head and sniffed, chugging the second half of his beer. Suddenly, Juliet wasn't sure letting Nick do all the talking was going to be as smooth as she'd thought. "You wouldn't be coming out to clubs with a guy like Ray looking to recruit a guy like me if you had other options lined up."

Larry sipped his drink, the corners of his mouth turning down as though he was going to disagree with Nick, but his head began to bob as he swallowed, nodding along. "Fair enough. So? What can I tell you to seal this deal?"

While he spoke, Juliet studied his face, and she knew if she just reached out a little bit, she'd be in. She'd be listening to Larry's thoughts. She hesitated at first, and caught herself doing so. That realization or self-awareness caught her off guard, and Juliet started thinking about how she'd shied away from digging into Frida's deeper thoughts and about how she'd hidden from even her own memories, avoiding thinking too much about Rutger Tanaka.

As Larry and Nick continued to banter lightly, dancing around the subject of Nick taking the job on offer, Juliet found herself doing battle with herself. One part of her wanted to listen for a while and then maybe focus on Larry and pick up some surface thoughts to see if he was lying. Another part wanted to just dive in, to really go deep on Larry almost to spite herself, to spit in the face of the hesitation—no, fear she was feeling.

Her internal struggle went on for several moments, and her mind raced down so many what-if scenarios that she honestly couldn't have repeated a single word that Nick and Larry were saying.

After a time, when she noticed her lemonade was almost empty and she didn't have a clue what Larry and Nick had been talking about, she decided enough was enough. Juliet narrowed her eyes and turned to regard Larry in one of his fancy ocular implants. They were a high-end cosmetic job that made his irises look almost three-dimensional, a faintly rose-colored layer overlaying the deeper, golden bands. She stared into that eye and with a deep, slow exhalation, she let go of the tethers she'd been using to pin down her mind. She drifted free, slipping through those lovely portals into Larry's deeper memories, into his very soul.

24

LARRY FINE

Larry let his golden fingers clink against the glass, tapping out a gentle tune, something that had been buzzing around in the back of his head all morning. *Was he nervous? Probably. He'd never been to a place like this, a place for the new and old money to mingle, where the modern aristocrats made decisions that would affect entire economies. Was this it? Had he pissed off the wrong niece or nephew of the wrong mogul? Was he being brought here to be made to understand his sins before they took him away to disappear? Well, they could keep him guessing, but they wouldn't see him sweat. No sir.*

Larry leaned back into the thick cushion of the posh couch and let his feet extend to the ottoman, his shiny, polished, vat-grown calfskin boots with their golden toes winking in the diffuse light that streamed through the window. If they were going to off him, then he'd go out with style. He'd worn his best suit—burgundy, as always, but much finer than some of his earlier ones. It was hand-tailored just for him and not by some auto-tailoring machine.

He looked around the parlor at the antique wooden furniture, the ancient books, the maps, the paintings, and the wet bar. More money was on the walls of this little unused space than he'd earned in a decade. It really drove home the notion that despite his nice suit and his office space by the ports, he had a long way to go.

"Mr. Fine?" The woman had approached silently, and he almost jumped at her soft voice, but he held it together and managed to keep from shattering the glass he held in his mechanical grip.

"Yes?"

"Sir Rodric is ready to see you, but first, he'd like to request that you install a bit of software." She held out a tiny black cube with a thin cable protruding from one end. It had a standard data jack prong.

"Oh?" Larry set the glass down, and without thought, his lips spread in his characteristic smile; something he'd trained himself to do ever since he'd gotten his new teeth. That smile hadn't come easily—he'd spent the first two and a half decades of his life with broken, missing teeth. He'd conditioned himself to smile with his lips only, barely opening them when he spoke, speaking behind his hands, constantly ashamed of the mess his stepfather had made of his teeth. When he'd finally made that first big payday and gotten his golden grill, it was like he'd been born again. A new man that old friends couldn't reconcile with the old Larry.

Well, if he were here to meet his maker, he'd go out with a smile.

"Yes. It's only a formality—something required of contractors at this level of business. It allows for secure communication between you and Sir Rodric's office." Again, she pressed the little device toward him. Larry sighed and took it, still smiling. His data port wasn't covered with synth-skin. He had a high-end model, and he wanted people to know it.

He plugged the little drive in and watched his AUI, waiting to see what it would do. A few seconds passed without any indication that it was doing anything, and then it beeped.

"All done," said the woman, holding out a hand. Larry shrugged, unplugged the little device, and handed it over.

"Pretty painless."

"Right this way, Mr. Fine." The woman—young, attractive, too polished to be a receptionist—led him down the hall and gestured to a partially open, enormous wooden door that Larry could've driven a troop transport through. "Sir Rodric is within."

"Thank you, miss." Larry restrained the impulse to tip his hat, but his eye got away from him and winked. The gesture caught her off guard, and a flicker of a smile touched her otherwise dour expression. *Mission accomplished.*

Larry stepped through the enormous door, only to be greeted by a great hall lined with equally expansive windows. He had to pause in the doorway when he saw the view from those great diamatex panels. They opened onto the raw landscape of Callisto, only lightly affected by the terraforming efforts taking place outside the domes.

A steep slope fell away from the panes, enhancing the sense of scale as Larry looked out, seeing hundreds or thousands of craters on the icy, shimmering surface. The sky outside the dome, as always, was inky black, but making up for the lack of atmospheric color was the enormous form of Jupiter lurking out there in the depths of space. It was a view of things he'd seen plenty in his time on Callisto, but never in such close, sharp splendor.

He had to remind himself to start breathing again as a man to his right cleared his throat and said, "Hello, Mr. Fine."

Larry turned, almost startled, and saw the man who'd invited him, Sir Rodric Barrington, standing before an antique fireplace mantle. He held a glass of liquor in one hand, and he delicately sipped it while Larry started forward. "Well, hello there, Sir Rodric."

He was going to offer his hand to shake, but Sir Rodric gestured to a high-backed leather chair then turned to sit down. Larry stopped his forward momentum and turned to the chair. Fine with him, he supposed, if the rich bastard didn't want to be friendly.

"My assistants tell me you're one of the more discrete fixers on Callisto." Sir Rodric wasn't a tall man or large in any way. If Larry were going to describe him, he might use the adjective mousy. Yes, he had thin, short brown hair, a narrow face, good teeth, and clear eyes, but nothing special. Nothing that screamed, "I can buy half the corporations on Callisto and still have money left over to ruin a nation or two."

Still, at the man's words, Larry perked up. Maybe this really was about a job. He tugged on his burgundy lapels, smoothed his vest, and sat up straighter. "That's right, Sir Rodric. I worked painstakingly to build a reputation of discretion."

"I'll be blunt, Larry. Do you mind if I call you Larry?"

"Not at all."

"No one can ever know that I've met with you. If I choose to hire you, no one can ever know that, either. If word got back to my wife or if certain associates knew of my predicament, things could get ugly for me. If things get ugly for me, I'll be certain anyone associated with me finds things growing ugly for them. For that reason, for your protection, we won't have a contract, and any record of our meetings or calls will be deleted from your PAI. Do you understand me?"

"Of course, sir." Larry began to understand what he'd installed in the waiting area. Sir Rodric wasn't asking him to delete things; he was saying that it would happen whether he wanted it or not. The contract thing was kind of annoying—he'd hoped to improve his fixer rating with this job. In any case, it was clear Rodric could pay his bills, and he doubted he'd stiff him.

"Well, my wife is currently in Europe, and I'm going to try to keep things that way until we solve this little predicament. Ah, I should explain what the predicament is."

"I'm all ears." Larry, of course, grinned hugely, but Sir Rodric's dour expression didn't change.

"You see, while I have many children, I have one who's especially dear to me. A daughter I've raised here on Callisto and whom I've spent the better part of a decade grooming to take some of the reins of my businesses."

"Very nice, sir." Larry nervously drummed his fingers on the armchair, wishing he had a stiff drink. Would it be out of order to stand up and walk over to the little bar? Hadn't he seen rich folks doing things like that in vids?

No, no, he cautioned himself. Sit still, Larry. Hear the man out.

"It is very nice, but when you value something, it has a way of biting you in the ass when something goes wrong with it." It wasn't lost on Larry that Sir Rodric was referring to his daughter as a thing. "My daughter has gotten mixed up with a few friends that are rather bad influences. She's left Callisto, in fact, jailbroken her PAI, and refuses my communication attempts. I've paid some information brokers great sums to find out where she is, and the news isn't good. Her friends turned out to be pirates, and once she ran off with them, they considered her their property. I'm looking for a team who might be able to extract her."

"Oh?" Larry leaned forward with interest. This was getting more and more juicy. Despite his eagerness to hear more, a tiny voice in the back of his head was screaming something at him; something about whether a man like this would ever let someone who knew such sensitive information walk away.

Larry stretched back into his pillow, his silky sheets sliding over his body luxuriously. One thing he didn't skimp on was sheets. No, he'd slept in some terrible beds—more nests, really—in his life, and those days were over.

He quietly stood up, intent on using the toilet. He'd made it halfway across the living area when some movement from the other end of his loft caught his eye. Larry paused and watched as Cleo made soft, dreaming sounds and rolled over again, rustling her sheets. He walked over to the little bamboo-patterned room divider and looked in on his daughter.

Cleo was a miracle to him in every way. It was a miracle that she'd survived what happened to her mother, a miracle that she'd turned out so gentle and kind, and most of all, a miracle that she actually loved and looked up to her dad.

He was standing there, watching her soft, steady breathing, looking at her peaceful, innocent face, when his AUI started blinking, and an incoming call notification caught his attention.

"Shit," he muttered, hurrying away from Cleo's section of the loft and over to the kitchenette, where he flicked on the noise suppression field and the coffee machine in that order. Then, he took the call. "Good morning, sir."

"I'm not hearing good news about your progress."

"Sir, this is a complicated operation you're trying to set up. I'm having trouble finding the right talent. Hereford's Vengeance won't just take anyone in, they're—"

"I don't have time for excuses, Larry. I need results. You don't think you're the only person I have working on this job, do you? If you can't make something happen, one of your competitors will. Larry, you understand I can't have loose ends lying around, don't you? You don't want to be a loose end; you want to be a nice tidy knot tied off with a fat payday and my satisfaction as a customer."

"I understand." This wasn't the first veiled threat Sir Rodric had thrown at him lately. The man was growing more and more desperate, and Larry really was having a damn hard time getting anyone to work with him on what was turning out to be something of a suicide mission. Any pilot with brains could see that writing on the wall, and the ones who were dumb enough to bite didn't have what it might take to pull the whole thing off. "It's a real catch-22," he said, putting his thoughts into words. "The pilots who might be able to do it aren't interested in the risk . . ."

"What do you need to make this happen, Larry? More money? Fine, I'll increase the pot to one point five. Will that incentivize some pilots? I'd make it an even two million, but how about this instead: one of my assistants has come to me with an interesting angle. There's a pilot, Raymond Edgars, who owes me a lot of money. Maybe you can convince him to take the job. Tell him I'll forgive his debt." Sir Rodric's voice had grown increasingly sharp as he spoke, and now he positively barked, "Why am I even paying you? I've done half the job for you!"

Larry opened his mouth to reply, but Sir Rodric cut the connection.

"Well, shit." The more he dealt with Sir Rodric, the more Larry began to wonder if he should have run the other way when he'd gotten the invitation to their initial meeting. He knew it was a pointless speculation, in any case.

He couldn't go back in time. Besides, no one turned down a meeting with a man like Sir Rodric. "Calvin?"

"Yes, Larry?" His PAI had a pleasantly mild Australian accent, and it always made him smile a little when he heard his voice.

"Can you get me in touch with the pilot he mentioned, Raymond Edgars?"

"Yes."

"Also, get me a list of the top-five rated combat operatives who have responded to the posting. We need to make this happen, or I think Sir Rodric is going to have us replaced."

"I don't want to be replaced, Larry!"

"No, Calvin, neither do I." With dread in his heart, Larry started thinking about how he could leverage the debt this Raymond character owed to Sir Rodric.

Larry drummed his fingers, as was his habit, on the side of his glass, but the lack of a metallic click caught him by surprise. He looked at his hand, saw long, slender feminine fingers with well-manicured nails, and dropped the glass. It fell to the ground and shattered, spilling ice but not much liquid onto the patterned concrete.

Larry stared at his hand, the pale flesh, the soft skin, and the hairless knuckles.

"What the fuck?" he asked, but his voice sounded wrong. He looked across the table and saw . . . himself. Larry's world began to spin, began to tumble, and then a voice came to him, clear and sharp and full of concern. "Juliet? Juliet, what's happening? The activity on the lattice is off the charts."

"Lucky, what's up? You look like you're about to puke. Hey, can we get someone to clean up this glass?" *Larry—no, no, not Larry . . .* Juliet recognized the voice. It was Nick.

Juliet shook her head and clamped her palms over her eyes, pressing hard until the synth-nerves behind the implants sent signals to her brain, making weird, colorful explosions appear in the darkness. Angel spoke into the void, "Are you all right? The lattice is cooling."

"Dammit," she said softly, then she subvocalized, "I was him, Angel, even more than when I was in Tono's head. That time, at least, I felt like I was a passenger, like I was watching and feeling things unfold. This time, I was Larry!"

The memories she'd experienced were still fresh in her mind, the sensation of being Larry still bewilderingly real. She almost felt like her skin didn't fit right, that the sounds coming into her brain through her auditory implants weren't right. Even her AUI looked off.

She pulled her hands away from her eyes and saw Nick and Larry staring at her with obvious concern. A waiter was kneeling beside the table with a dustpan and hand broom, scooping up the broken glass and ice.

"You good?" Nick reached a hand over to grasp her wrist, and Juliet recoiled. Why would he touch her? Then she realized, again, that she wasn't Larry. Nick was a lot closer to Juliet than Larry. They'd spent weeks together in a tin can flying through space.

She forced a smile. "Sorry, sorry. I get migraines sometimes, and this one came on like a runaway bus. My, uh, nanites are adjusting. I'll be okay in a minute." Juliet made eye contact with the waiter, a young man with curly black hair. "Sorry about that."

"Happens." He shrugged and stood. "I'll send another lemonade your way."

"Goodness!" Larry chuckled, and Juliet felt queasy again, watching him. It was like looking into a mirror, but knowing the reflection was wrong. Parts of her brain were clearly struggling to catch up to the fact that she was Juliet, not Larry. "Startled me when that glass fell!"

"You haven't always walked around with muscle, have you?" Juliet's question must have caught Larry off guard because he closed his perpetually grinning mouth, hiding his golden teeth for a moment as he hunted for a response.

"No, no, I haven't. Pretty expensive, you know."

Juliet knew that was the case; that he'd only recently hired the muscle to protect him not from enemies but from his current client. When she'd been Larry, she'd fundamentally understood a couple of things. One, Larry was a pretty good guy, a straight shooter who'd never double-crossed anyone. And two, Larry was in way over his head with this Sir Rodric fellow—in over his head and worried that he would be made to disappear, or worse, something would happen to Cleo. On top of that, she knew he had spyware in his head that would most definitely be sending pictures of her, Nick, and anyone else Larry met right back to Sir Rodric.

Juliet's mind raced with all the implications this scenario had for Nick and her and, she supposed, the other people involved. Ray was almost certainly a goner. Worse, even if Larry got the job done, there was a chance Sir Rodric would make him disappear. He didn't seem to be the type of man who liked other people knowing his business, and having his daughter rescued from pirates was certainly his business. What would happen to Cleo without Larry?

Juliet felt a pang in her chest and realized she was irrationally fond of the girl. She was worried about her future in a way only a parent could feel. Would this fade? Juliet hoped so.

She knew Nick didn't want to abandon Ray, but perhaps more troubling was that Juliet didn't want Larry in trouble. She'd connected with him profoundly, and she hadn't come away with anything other than a sense of fondness for the man. He was a hard worker who'd overcome terrible odds to get to where he was. More than that, he'd done it without screwing anyone over. He was honest and loyal and put on a false front of vanity to cover up his deep-seated insecurities, and he'd do anything for his daughter. Had she really learned so much from being in his head for just a few seconds? She couldn't explain it, but the answer was yes, and now, she couldn't walk away, not while knowing the kind of trouble he was in.

She cleared her throat and said, "I'm feeling better."

"That's good!" Nick looked like a fish out of water, completely thrown off by her sudden outburst and now her strange question about Larry's muscle. It might help if she could remember anything from the conversation the two men had been having. Maybe he'd been waiting for her to interject for a while now.

"Well, I don't know about you, Nick, but I think this job sounds like a good opportunity. I'll sign on to be boots on the ground if you still need an operator, Larry."

"Oh? Really?" Larry practically crowed while Nick's eyes widened, and he looked at her like she'd sprouted a second head.

"Yeah, for sure, Larry. We can get this done for your client."

"We can?" Nick cleared his throat. "Right, we can. For sure, Larry. One thing, though: I want to have some say about the interceptor you purchase at auction. I have standards, you know."

"Excellent! My client is going to be thrilled! Listen, I have to talk to him about the specifics for buying the ship, but if there's any way we can get you involved in the purchase, I'll be sure to work it in." Larry was visibly relieved and excited; his gold-plated digits were drumming on his thighs, and Juliet knew he was bursting with relief. "Nick, Lucky, I'll have my PAI send you over a contract, okay? In the meantime, why don't I head back to the office and start working on those logistics? We have a plan for your tryout to get the pirates' attention, but it needs some fine-tuning. Would that be all right?"

"Yeah," Juliet replied before Nick could say anything. "We were going to get dinner anyway, and we have some things to discuss. You know, between us." Juliet winked at Larry. Then she turned to Nick. "Don't we?"

"Yeah." He rubbed at his rough stubble and nodded, locking eyes with her. "We sure do."

25

RANDOM ENCOUNTER

Uh, you wanna tell me what that was all about?" Nick watched Larry and his two bodyguards disappear into the crowds lining the sidewalk, and Juliet pulled out her deck, activating the jamming field.

She waited for Nick to look at her directly. "There's a lot I need to tell you."

"I'm all ears." He held up a pointer finger. "Actually, let's order some food first. I'm starved."

"Sure." Juliet had already studied the menu and knew what she wanted. "Angel, order me a farmer's burger with a side of fried tomatoes and a vanilla shake."

"Damn! That sounds good." Nick stared into space for a minute, then said, "I'm gonna get a deep-dish personal pizza. Three kinds of cheese? Yes, please!"

Juliet frowned. "It's not real cheese . . ."

"Uh, yeah, I'm not keen on other animals' lactations."

"Your loss, I guess." Nick started to argue, but Juliet held up a hand in surrender; she didn't want to get into a debate. "Listen, we have more important things to talk about. Sorry I was kind of out of it during your talk with Larry, but I had a lot of feelers out and some data mining protocols that delivered some information while he was here. I think I know who his client is, and we're both in danger just having met with Larry. This guy makes it a habit to put spy protocols in the PAIs of people he meets, meaning Larry's been recording everyone he talks to and, maybe without his knowledge, sending the information back to the client."

"Well, that's not cool, but it's not really something earth-shattering. I mean, anyone could record us, right?"

"Sure, but you wouldn't expect a fixer to send information like that to a client. More, it's not the fact that it's done that we should be worried about. We should be worried about the type of client this is. We're talking about a billionaire here, and he doesn't like people knowing his personal business."

"Like a daughter running off with pirates . . ."

"Right. Look, there's a chance we could have walked away not learning anything more about the client, and he would've left you and me alone. Ray's in deep trouble with that guy, though, and so is Larry, if he can't get this job done."

"Won't we all be in trouble if we actually rescue this girl and learn who she is? I mean, assuming he doesn't know that you already figured out who he is."

"Well, yes, but what I was about to say is that you were going to do the job anyway, right? Be honest."

"Yeah, I guess. I can't leave Ray hanging with his ass exposed, you know?"

Juliet nodded and sat back, folding her arms over her chest. "That's why I agreed. The only way I'm going to get close to this guy is if I deliver his daughter."

"Huh? Get close?"

"Someone needs to convince him to leave us all alone." Juliet shrugged.

Nick looked at her for a long moment, and though his face didn't betray emotion, Juliet could see he was troubled. "You don't wanna tell me his name?"

"I . . . I think it's best if I don't, Nick. I can't see it helping you in any way, and if you never learn it, assuming something happens to me, there's still a chance he'll leave you alone."

Juliet saw the curly-haired waiter approaching with a tray of food, so she tried to relax a little, spreading her napkin onto her lap and growing quiet for a minute while he set it down. Her sandwich looked delicious: lots of local, vat-grown seasoned meat—Callisto didn't allow livestock for commercial use—and grilled veggies, all slathered with a tangy sauce.

Nick stuffed a fried onion ring into his mouth, chewed it halfway, then asked, "What exactly are you going to do to this guy, assuming you get close to him with his daughter?"

"Not sure yet." Juliet took a big bite of her sandwich; she hadn't quite realized how hungry she was.

While Nick stewed on her reply, she and he both ate a good portion of their meals in silence.

"Shit, I was hungry." Nick chuckled, polishing off the beer he'd been nursing. "So, we're in, huh? You think there's much chance we walk away with the money and won't have to watch over our shoulders the rest of our lives?"

"That's my goal, Nick. I mean, the second part. If we can get the money too, that's a bonus as far as I'm concerned."

He nodded, leaning back in his chair. "Well? What do I do next?"

"Nothing. Take a little time to yourself and wait for Larry to call. When he contacts you about the ship and the plan for getting noticed by the pirates, let me know, and we'll go from there. I've got some shopping to do in the meantime."

"Shopping?"

"Yeah, I wasn't able to bring all my gear on the cruise liner. I need to get a few things."

"Don't forget you'll have a cover identity, just like me. You can't walk into that pirate base looking like a corpo-sec shock trooper."

Juliet snorted a quick laugh at the image and nodded. "Good point, Nick. I'll shop for some used gear; something a pirate would be proud to wear."

"Well, that cannon on your hip is a good start. Can't imagine a corpo rat wearing something like that." Nick fished around in his breast pocket for his vape then held it to his lips. He saw Juliet's look and offered her a wink. "Hey, I made it most of the dinner without this thing! My nerves are shot."

Juliet set her napkin down and looked at him, taking in his earnest expression. "Did you do that for me? 'Cause I'm always giving you a hard time?"

"Well, I didn't do it for Larry!" Nick chuckled, exhaling his cloud of vapor toward the floor.

"Thanks, Nick. That's . . . nice of you."

"No worries. Anyway, I wanna say something before I let the moment pass too far. I, uh, I know you didn't need to jump into this mess with me. Even learning what you did, you could have walked away and said you weren't interested in your part of the contract. I wouldn't have held it against you, and your hands would have been clean. Larry's client wouldn't have any reason to mess with you. So, well, thanks. I guess that's it; I just wanted to say thanks."

"It's cool, Nick. This is kind of what I do—I'm notorious for sticking my neck out for friends. We're friends, right?"

"Yeah. For sure." His expression was hard to read, and he broke eye contact, looking around the restaurant before standing up abruptly. "Hey, I sent payment for your tab; the least I could do. I'm gonna head back to my place 'cause I'm beat as hell. Talk tomorrow?"

"All right, thanks. Yeah, that's cool; we'll talk tomorrow. Let me know as soon as you hear something from Larry."

"You got it." He stood kind of awkwardly, hands in pockets, then nodded and hurried out of the restaurant.

"What an interesting night!" Angel said.

"Were you entertained?" Juliet chuckled, dipping one of her fried tomatoes into the house sauce and plopping it into her mouth. It was tangy and rich, and the breading on the tomatoes wasn't too greasy. She really liked them.

"Are you feeling better? Has the . . . confusion passed?"

"Yeah, I guess so. I was so deep! There's no way I could let Larry go without helping him, without helping his daughter."

"Who is he? The client."

"Oh, someone named Sir Rodric. Sir Rodric . . ."

"Barrington," Angel finished for her. "It wasn't hard to find him on the net; he's the head of several interplanetary organizations. He has holdings here, on Luna, Mars, and Earth. Juliet, I don't think you should try to take him out . . ."

"No! No, Angel, that's not the plan. I need to get close enough for you to help me infiltrate his network, maybe even his PAI. We need to erase any trace of Larry, Nick, me, and I guess, Ray. When Sir Rodric decides to clean up the loose ends, I want him and everyone in his organization to draw a blank when it comes to who actually did the work for him. Do you think that's possible?"

"It's possible to remove traces of data, but if he or any of his people know who Larry is, they should be able to find him."

"That's why our cleanup will need a part two: new IDs for Larry and Cleo, and maybe a ride off-moon."

"He'll go along with that?"

Juliet thought about the question, and for a second, as she recalled her time in Larry's mind, she felt that strange, disorienting déjà vu mixed with a profound nostalgia that made her strain to remember she was Juliet.

"Larry is very proud of what he's built here on Callisto, but if we give him fair warning, he should be able to liquidate most of his assets, and I think he might look at setting up shop somewhere else, maybe even back on Earth as a step up, another achievement, especially if it leads to a better life for Cleo."

"You've mentioned Cleo twice. Is that his daughter?"

"Yeah." Juliet stood up and pushed her chair in, then made her way out of the restaurant. "We've got our work cut out for us, but step one is making sure we survive this op. Can you look up an arms-dealer-type establishment?"

"When you mentioned the need for supplies to Nick, I began searching. I think I found a good shop. It's called Mankowitz's Military Surplus, Buy and Sell."

"Yeah, I guess the buy and sell part kind of gives the right vibe. We need stuff that looks well used, not something a corpo-sec goon would wear." Juliet thought about the hits she'd taken to her armor in the past and frowned. She hadn't traveled with her combat helmet, just the one for her new flight suit. "You think I should get a helmet like my black one with the tinted visor? Is it too corpo-sec looking?"

"Hmm. Perhaps some custom paint or decals wouldn't go amiss."

"Wouldn't go amiss?"

"What? I have an extensive vocabulary, Juliet!"

As she shook her head and chuckled, Juliet studied the map Angel had provided. The shop was on the other end of the port district, so she walked over to one of the tramlines and waited with a good-sized crowd for the next train to arrive.

She'd been standing around, arms folded, daydreaming about the kind of gear she'd like to buy for a few minutes when a gruff voice behind her asked, "You know how to use that thing?"

Juliet turned slowly, trying to maintain an even expression as she wondered what sort of question was that. What was this man referring to? Was he even speaking to her? If so, the only thing that she thought he could be referencing was her pistol, prominently displayed on her hip.

"He's pinged you for an ID three times, even though I provided a false response immediately."

When she saw the man—short, stocky, wearing a very expensive, very tailored black suit with the latest style of reflective paisleys—she knew he was corpo, knew he felt superior to her and probably everyone else on the sidewalk. He had short, neatly combed blond hair, jewellike glittering blue eyes beneath pale, rose-colored specs that probably cost more than the average factory rat made in a year, and his skin was so smooth it almost looked artificial. Was it?

"Are you talking to me?"

"That's right. You know how to use that pistol?"

"Piss off, corpo rat."

Juliet wasn't sure where her vehemence came from. Perhaps it was a reaction that had been a long time building up. She was constantly watching her words, worrying about tipping someone off about her identity or blowing an operation or opportunity. Now, this smooth, pretty little corpo boy was hassling her about her gun, asking if she could use it. Where did he get off? He wouldn't have asked if he thought she could use it; not if he thought she was the kind of operator who was dangerous with a pistol like that. That meant he was insinuating that she couldn't, that she was someone posing as something she wasn't.

"Excuse me? Rat?" He pulled back his raincoat and rested a hand on the butt of a heavy plastic-and-plasteel sidearm, something close to shotgun-size but equipped with a pistol grip. "Might be I saw you threatening that store owner over there. Might be I tried to stop you, but you threatened me with your antique chrome paperweight there."

Juliet studied the man, noticing how the pedestrians waiting for the train had mostly found other places they needed to be. His gray jacket was cut almost like a cape, clearly tailored to fit. Beneath it, on the lapel of his fancy suit, was a silver pin depicting a stylized capital A. His black shoes and belt were well polished and clean. Everything about him screamed high maintenance; the kind of guy who spent more time getting ready every morning than she did in a month.

"You think I don't have you on vid? You think I haven't uploaded this conversation to a dozen corporate nets? You don't know me, corpo rat, and I suggest you back off before you learn about me the hard way."

"Um, did you want me to do that?" Angel asked. "By the way, he is wearing an Ark Industries emblem; they're a startup focused on 'building the next generation of exploration vessels to ensure the propagation of the human species.' His name is Gallant Fenn, and he's been an employee of the corporation for seven months."

"Gallant, huh? Not exactly living up to the name your mother gave you."

"Well, Janice, I don't have a mother; I have four."

Juliet narrowed her eyes at him, trying to figure out how she'd gotten into such a surreal confrontation, trying to unpack the reason he thought his response was a defense to her accusation.

"Janice is the ID I sent in response to his ping," Angel clarified.

"I figured," Juliet said, causing Gallant to squint in confusion. Juliet decided she'd let this escalate enough. Soon, they'd have drones zooming in on them to see what the fuss was about, why the crowds were splitting, giving them a wide berth.

She concentrated on his fancy specs for a second and then, with a soft exhalation, flicked them off his nose with her telekinesis. They flipped into the air, over his head, and he slapped at his face in an attempt to catch them. When he missed, he whirled to track their progress through the air, a look of stunned surprise widening his eyes. Juliet didn't wait. She turned and, letting her long legs do what they did best, disappeared into the crowd.

"Why me?" she asked as she continued to put distance between herself and the corpo-sec agent.

"Well, you didn't have to respond to him so rudely."

"Well, he should mind his own business." Juliet turned and continued to follow Angel's map to the store. As she made progress, putting more space between herself and the annoying corpo-sec agent, she started to relax and slowly began to feel glad that she'd been forced into walking. She needed to let off some steam. "That wasn't like me, was it?"

"Insulting a corpo-sec agent out of the blue?"

"Well, first of all, it wasn't out of the blue, but yeah. Jeez, Angel, you don't think I'm taking on personality traits of the people whose brains I've snooped around in, do you? I could see Tono, or hell, even Larry, reacting that way to a corpo-sec officer. Well, no, not really Larry. Shit. Do you think I'm more like Tono now?"

"I think you're under a lot of stress, and you lashed out at someone who was bothering you. You've never liked corpo-sec officers."

"Okay. I hope you're right." She looked at her map, saw she was about halfway there, and changed the subject. "What do you think of that subdermal armor Frida has?"

"It's not really armor. She underwent a procedure in which specialized nanites extruded and fused a ceramic polymer with her bones, or at least some of them. It's a rather painful and invasive process; before the nanites can fuse the polymer, the bone has to be treated with a laser system that removes a thin layer, providing a bonding surface. It takes time and requires some bed rest for the process to complete."

"Depending on how much you have done, I'm guessing."

"Yes, I suppose. A single bone or maybe a limb, while painful, might be something a person could function with as it heals."

"Well, anyway, I'm kind of interested in that. Remind me to ask Ladia about it when we get back to Luna, would you?"

"Yes, I'll make a note about it. On another topic, I noticed you used your psionics lattice to distract that corpo-sec officer. Do you want to talk about that?"

"Huh? What do you mean?"

"I mean, you've never used your telekinesis offensively before. Was it a reflex? Did you think about it much?"

"I . . . Well, I wanted him to look away so I could slip into the crowd. I didn't think about it much; I just thought those specs looked expensive and figured he valued them quite a lot. He seemed really hung up on his looks. I thought something like, 'What if I knocked those off his nose?' Then the idea hit me, and I just did it. They were just as easy to move as my vibroblade."

"Imagine if you were having a pistol duel with a bad guy on Main Street, and you distracted him before drawing!"

Juliet laughed, picking up the pace as it began to drizzle. "Angel, first of all, I'm not going to be dueling anyone at high noon. I don't think. Second of all, that would be cheating. Everyone knows the good guy can't cheat; he— she—just has to be faster."

"You're certainly pretty fast, at least with your good arm."

"Excuse me? My good arm?"

"Well, the expensive one. You got the other one for free, so . . ."

"You mean I was born with it!" Juliet laughed again, not sure if Angel was trying to be funny or if her perspective was just very, very different from a human's. She glanced at her map, saw the shop was just at the next corner, and said, "All right, Angel. Let's go in here and deck me out like a pirate. A scary, dangerous, don't-mess-with-me kind of pirate."

26

PIRATE SHOPPING

Mankowitz's Military Surplus was a big, open-floor market occupying half an industrial warehouse. The other half was a shipping organization specializing in the delivery of pets from different parts of the solar system to Callistoans. Juliet could only imagine the expense involved in such an endeavor, and she had the urge to go inside, chat up the workers, and see if she could get a glimpse of the pets that were worth a small fortune in travel fees. She pushed the thought aside, though, and walked into the Mankowitz side of the warehouse. When she walked through the open bay doors, she was greeted by an armed synth at a security station.

The synth made no attempt to hide its synthetic nature; its face was a smooth gray ovoid with bright white LED eyes and a speaker grill for a mouth. More than that, it wasn't clothed, exposing soft-looking rubbery gray skin. The bottom half of its left arm was a machine gun, complete with a long belt of ammunition fed from an olive-green ammo can on the desk.

When she walked up to the security station, the synth said, in a harsh, male voice, "No violence or theft will be tolerated on the premises. We have mounted security turrets with clear lines of sight to every corner of the warehouse. Do not remove tags from objects you wish to purchase. Your bill will be tabulated as you exit the warehouse." That said, the synth turned to face the street, waiting for the next customer.

Juliet walked through the scanner, listened to it beep a few times, and continued into the wide-open shopping space. The aisles between the ten-meter-high shelving units were labeled helpfully, and she saw that the higher shelves just contained more stock like that displayed on the lower ones. She let her eyes drift around, taking in the enormous inventory of goods. Then, curiosity getting the better of her, she turned back to the synth and asked, "What about the buy part? I mean, where do people go to sell their stuff?"

"This is the Mankowitz's Military Surplus sales warehouse. If you want to sell goods, you must visit the storefront downtown. Sending you the address."

Angel piped in, "I should have realized that, sorry."

"It's fine, Angel—not like I was planning to sell anything."

Juliet stared, again, into the massive aisles full of gear. She felt overwhelmed, not by her need to buy things or the giant sales space filled with uncountable pieces of equipment but by everything that had happened in the last couple of days, starting with her overindulgence while out with Nick, and especially with her use of the lattice.

She saw an area near the exit where people could sit at red plastic tables and eat food from vending machines, and she walked over to one of them to sit down.

Had she actually just knocked the specs off a corpo-sec officer with her mind?

"Is everything all right, Juliet?"

"No, not really. Do you think that corpo-sec goon will try to find me?"

"I don't. I think it's too much of a leap for him to think you did anything with your mind to knock his specs off. If anything, he'll think you have a speed augmentation unlike anything he's ever seen and pray into his pillow tonight that he never meets you again."

Juliet snorted a surprised laugh at Angel's imagery. "Pray into his pillow? I like that one."

"Just relax, Juliet. You have plenty to worry about as it is. Let me worry about Gallant. I'll let you know if it seems like he's looking for you." Angel's words, as usual, did the trick, and Juliet felt the tension in her neck begin to unwind.

She rolled her shoulders, inhaled deeply through her nose, and let it out slowly, pushing her stress out with it. Nodding as if to affirm her actions, she stood up and perused the big hanging aisle labels nearby. She settled on one that said Combat Armor and walked that way.

Despite its size, or perhaps because of it, the warehouse didn't seem crowded. Only a few people meandered the aisles here and there, and there weren't any employees that she could see. An automated forklift beeped and flashed a red light as it backed up from a nearby stack of boxes, adding to the feeling that the place was entirely automated. Juliet let her eyes drift to the ceiling and saw clusters of cameras all over the place. Just as the synth had warned, a turret lurked among the metal rafters at every junction of aisles, though the barrels weren't aimed at the floor by default.

She wandered the combat armor section, admiring the many types of protective equipment on sale. Most of the products were new in the package, but she also found boxes of used gear. The used equipment was clearly sold to the company in bulk, probably from corpo-sec departments that had gone through an upgrade cycle. Most of the armor was black, but she also saw every kind of camouflage imaginable, from tundra to desert to jungle. Some of the new stuff caught her eye with its flashy colors, obviously not meant to hide the user but to display a personality.

A shiny pink helmet got her thinking, and she asked, "What exactly would a pirate wear? Should I even be trying to look like a pirate? Isn't that the whole deal with them, that they don't fit a uniform?"

"I suppose that's right. My knowledge is anecdotal from fiction I've read and watched, but give me a moment while . . . Ah, yes. I've just gone through public news sites with captioned photos. Most pirates pictured are wearing mismatched armor, though a few have high-end equipment that wouldn't be out of place in a corpo-sec paramilitary unit if not for its well-used appearance. Seventy-four percent of the pirates in the photos and vids don't have any sort of head protection."

"There's no way I'm going in without a helmet. I'd be dead if not for the one I wore on Titan."

"I wasn't suggesting that. I, too, would appreciate you wearing a helmet."

"All right, all right. C'mon, let's get serious." Juliet looked back at the shelves, letting her eyes wander down the aisle, zooming in on labels until she saw something intriguing. "Phobos Proxy War FlexPlate armor?" She started walking toward the display.

"The Phobos Proxy War occurred in 2079 and involved a dozen megacorporations, including OrionTech and MaraSol Energy. Phobos was being used as a staging location for the Tharsis Conflict by OrionTech and their allies, and MaraSol's consortium hired mercenaries to assault their installations."

"Huh," Juliet replied, examining the chest and leg armor displayed on the metallic rack next to the boxes of "Used – Good Condition" equipment. It was bulkier than her ballistic vest, but not much; it consisted of some kind of composite-weave rigid plates joined together by a tough-looking, gray-black fiber mesh. She could see the plates on the thighs and abdomen were significantly thicker and, if she were guessing, housed some kind of battery.

"FlexPlate is the trademarked name of body armor made by MagnaCorp. It utilizes 'nanoengineered armor plates that allow maximum mobility while providing battery-boosted joint support.' They claim the armor 'levels the playing field, allowing even nonaugmented, small-frame soldiers to fight like a cybernetic juggernaut.' Reviews online say to temper your expectations—the armor might allow you to deadlift twenty-five to fifty percent more than usual."

"It's cool, though, right?"

"Very cool!"

Juliet saw the boxes were labeled small, medium, large, and then several flavors of extra large. "What size do I get?"

"The corporate website indicates that someone with your measurements should get the medium torso and leg armor."

"Okay, cool."

Juliet fished around, choosing a box a few rows deep, hoping she'd get lucky and pull a nicely scarred, used-looking set. Taking the reasonably heavy box in hand, she turned back toward the front of the warehouse, realizing she'd need a cart. A few minutes later, armor in the cart, she returned to the helmet section. She walked up and down the aisle, looking at all sorts of helmets and helmet accessories. Some came with visors, and some needed an aftermarket one. Some were made to be airtight and required a matching collar gasket on body armor, and some only covered the top third of the head.

She was holding a banana-yellow helmet with flame decals on the side when a man spoke up behind her in a cultured, almost stilted English accent. "That might look nice with your eyes."

Juliet whirled around, and before she could choke the words back, snarled, "Piss off—" Her mind caught up to her mouth, and she slapped a hand over her lips, eyes wide with horror as she saw the man recoil, taking a step back and holding up his hands apologetically.

"Erm, sorry about that. Didn't mean any offense . . ."

Juliet felt her cheeks blooming with embarrassment. "No! I'm sorry! I really don't know what came over me."

"That was quite a vehement reaction . . ." Angel added unhelpfully.

"No worries." He smoothed his soft brown hair back nervously, and Juliet felt all the worse; he was a nice-looking guy, probably only twenty or so, and looked utterly mortified by the idea that he'd overstepped. He didn't look like the sort of person you'd find in a warehouse full of weapons and body armor, but then, there were other things in the place, too: drones, electronics, even MREs.

"Anyway"—she held up the helmet—"this is a bit bright for me." She set it back on the shelf then turned back. "I feel almost paralyzed by all of the options."

He folded his arms over his chest, and Juliet noticed how his shirt sleeves pulled taut around his triceps and rode up a little, exposing the tail-end of a colorful tattoo on his left arm, some kind of dragon or turtle or fish—something with scales. He had bright green, metallic-shiny irises that twinkled with LEDs as he turned to scan the shelves; Juliet thought they were chrome shiny and started wondering if her irises could mimic that look.

He distracted her from her daydreams about pretty eyes by saying, "Well, are you looking for something stylish, or do you need a particular function?"

"Hmm? Oh, shit! Do you work here?"

"Hah! No, no. I'm a reseller. I come here for bargains, but I know a lot about this stuff. Maybe I can help?"

"Well, sure. Now I feel even worse for snapping at you. I'm Lucky."

"Lucky?"

"My name, I mean."

"Oh, doh!" He chuckled, shaking his head with a rueful grin. "I'm Artie. Tossing you a business card."

"Received," Angel said.

"Got it. Anyway, I'm looking for something kind of cool but tough. You know what I mean? I want it to have some blind-spot cams and be rated to stop small-arms bullets. Oh, and I want it to be airtight with a gasket to fit this armor." She patted the box in her cart.

"Right, so a full-face shield, or do you want cameras only?"

Juliet thought about it. She liked the idea of being able to open her visor. A closed-off shell with only cameras for visibility didn't appeal to her. Despite the long odds of anything happening to the cameras, she hated the idea of being stuck in a helmet with no visibility. "Yeah, retractable visor, please."

"You looking for something new or used?"

"Don't mind used. In fact, I'd rather my helmet didn't look like I keep it sitting on a shelf instead of using it."

"Right. Operator?"

"Yeah."

He nodded and started walking down the line, stopping by a row of multicolored helmets with mirrored visors on the front. "These are mirrored, which looks cool, but they can switch to nonreflective black in an instant; the same for the colorful part. Your PAI can control it. Any of them jump out at you?"

Juliet scanned the row of helmets and paused on the fourth one—baby blue with a yellow smiley face sticker on the left side and a black streak down the center of the crown that looked almost like a burn. "That smiley is calling my name. You think that damage on the top will affect the armor integrity?"

"What, that? Not a chance. I'd guess whoever was wearing this helmet ducked a shotgun blast intended to take her in the face. That's just some damage to the enamel; you could have that touched up if you—"

"Nah! I like it." Juliet reached up to pull it off the shelf and plopped it into her cart. The warehouse merchandise tag taped to the back flopped and fluttered. "Thanks for the help, Artie."

"Not a problem. Well, you have my card. I need to get shopping before my partner puts in a missing person report."

"Right. Sorry. I mean for the 'piss off' comment earlier."

"No problem. I've had my share of bad days." He waved, meeting her gaze with his sparkling green eyes for a second, then turned and walked away.

"There's something wrong with me, Angel. I don't say piss off. Why did I say it twice today to random strangers?"

"I wish I could explain it. I was hoping that if we didn't make a big deal about your earlier encounter, it would blow over, but . . . I have to admit, I'm worried."

"Yeah. Me too. Let's just get through this shopping, then I'm going back to the hotel, and I'm gonna try to sleep for ten hours or so. Maybe that will help."

"Sleep is the best way to rest the brain, certainly. Some solid REM time might help things reset."

"You think that's it? I need to reset my brain?"

"I have no idea!" Angel's voice climbed an octave with stress, and Juliet gripped the cart handle tightly, closing her eyes and breathing deeply to try to calm herself and, hopefully, Angel.

"Okay, okay, Angel. Relax. I'm going to be all right. At least I caught myself that time, right? I didn't blast the poor guy or something."

"True." Angel audibly sighed, something she rarely simulated for Juliet's benefit. "Let's be positive. As you said, you caught yourself. Things might be improving on their own." She paused momentarily, then added, "Your new body armor has standard mounts for two micro drones on the backplate."

"Now you're talking. Let's go see what we can find." Juliet pushed her cart back to the front of the store and scanned the aisles until Angel highlighted the one she wanted. Ten minutes later, she was reading the back of a box containing a micro stealth surveillance drone.

"You should get that one and also another spider drone in case we're in cramped quarters. Spider drones are better at lurking to watch a location, too."

"Right." Juliet put the box in the cart then scanned the shelves until she found a spider drone much like the one she'd lost in the gunfight on the *Kowashi*. "What else?"

"A more appropriate primary weapon."

"Right. SMG or rifle?"

"Or shotgun?" Angel countered.

"Well, if we're in a pressurized environment, I probably don't want a lot of penetration potential, right? Also, if I'm outnumbered, nothing clears a room like an auto shotgun. I know it's true 'cause White told me so!"

"White certainly knew his business . . ."

"Knows. He's still alive." Juliet knew she was being pedantic, but something made her want to confirm the fact aloud. She'd lost enough friends from that brief period in her life.

"Right. In any case, I concur, and I recommend a conventional firearm rather than an electro-shotgun."

"Why?"

"A higher potential rate of fire. More noise, so more intimidation, and fewer failure points."

Juliet nodded, remembering the charge-up time on the electro-shotguns she'd used. "Okay, lead me to the gun section."

She followed Angel's directions through the aisles, pushing her cart past other shoppers, all the while struggling to shove her worries to the back of her mind. She kept seeing Artie's startled face when she'd whirled and snarled at him. Worse, she kept remembering how it had almost felt like her mouth, her body had acted without her permission.

With those worries, she sort of just went through the motions, following Angel's advice when it came to picking out a new shotgun, which ended up being a Bosch & Royal automatic polyblast shotgun. The shells were narrower than a 12-gauge and had smaller pellets, but they were made of high-density polymers designed to deform rapidly, outperforming larger lead pellets. Not only that, but the shells used a high-energy liquid crystal propellant that supposedly put gunpowder to shame. Everything added up to more numerous and powerful shots; the box magazine held twenty-four pressurized metallic shells. Juliet had balked at first, wondering how hard it would be to purchase the specialized ammo, but Angel had done some searching and found them widely available in most cities.

With her cart loaded with four boxes of shells, the gun, her drones, helmet, and armor, Juliet started wheeling her way to the warehouse's footwear section. She found an extensive display of "lightly used" combat boots and selected a well-broken-in pair of scuffed black ones with a reinforced carbon-fiber toe box. That done, she made her way toward the exit, but not before stopping by a display of tactical vests. She picked out a baby-blue-and-black camo-patterned one that she could wear over her armor and stuff full of bullets and shells.

"So I just walk out of here, and the store will charge me? I don't want to get blasted by a turret."

"Walk to that exit area where the floor is painted green. Stand there a minute and wait for me to confirm the bill and pay."

"Ah, gotcha." Juliet pushed her cart to the big rectangle of painted concrete and paused, leaning on the handle, trying to think of anything other than her strange, out-of-character behavior that day. "I think I'll have a long session with Doctor Ming when we get back to the hotel."

"I think that's a wonderful idea. Should I order you some food?"

"Yes! How about—"

"One moment—your total just came through: 17,477 bits."

"Shit! Seriously?"

"The shotgun and armor were both quite expensive . . ."

"Well, let's try not to lose them, then." Juliet sighed, moving her cart to a designated merchandise boxing area. "What's my balance now, anyway?"

"204,310 Sol-bits."

"Be nice to make some money for a change, don't you think? I'm bleeding bits out here training with Nick."

"It'll pay off. Think of the money you'll make flying that gunship!"

Juliet smiled, realizing she already felt much better about things; perhaps there was something to say for the innate cathartic therapy of shopping.

"Right! Think positively. Now, let's talk about food. I'm going to be hungry after Doctor Ming drags all my deepest secrets out of me."

27

AUCTION

Juliet stepped off the tram in front of the enormous hangar built against the southern edge of Callisto's main dome. The sidewalk outside was crowded with people standing around chatting, eating snacks from the food carts parked outside, and milling about, moving in and out of the wide-open truck-size doors in front of the gigantic plasteel structure. She could see the sleek shapes of the ships currently up for auction over the heads of the people crowding the entrance.

"Nick is just to your left, wearing an orange raincoat and eating some steamy potato chips."

"Uh, thanks for the colorful description, Angel." Juliet approached the pilot, tugging the collar of her jacket up; it was downright chilly in the dome that morning.

"Yo, Nicky." She waved as he looked up.

"Hey, Lucky. Larry's not here yet. You hungry?"

"Ate on the way, thanks."

It had been two days since their meeting, and Juliet was feeling much more like herself. She'd spent most of the time in her hotel room, sleeping, reading, and consulting Doctor Ming about her strange behavior. After lengthy discussions about Juliet's feelings, her history of interacting with people, and a torturous explanation of her experiences inside the heads of other people, they'd come to the conclusion that Doctor Ming wasn't exactly qualified to tell Juliet why she'd behaved the way she had.

Ming seemed to understand, at least in theory, what Juliet meant when she described her usage of the psionic lattice, but he could only speculate on the possible causes for her erratic behavior. He theorized that Juliet might, indeed, be absorbing personality traits when she used the lattice to snoop into people's thoughts, especially when she performed deep dives, as she'd been calling them. He even went so far as to speculate that she might be constructing the roots for entirely separate personalities, which was terrifying to Juliet.

The good news was that the foreign traits seemed to fade over time. Ming insisted that Juliet must recognize those impulses that were at odds with her usual behavior and avoid acting on them. That was the tricky part—realizing it was happening in time to not act.

Of course, it was all theory. Juliet had spoken with Angel about Ming's findings, and Angel had, of course, spent a lot of time researching dissociative identity disorders and trying to compare those findings with Juliet's behavior. She'd helped to reassure Juliet that her experience with the lattice was unprecedented, and that Doctor Ming was just an AI simulation, unable to truly learn about or understand all of Juliet's myriad experiences, particularly where the lattice was concerned. She helped Juliet with mindfulness exercises and meditation, helping her to ground herself. Juliet had balked at first, but the discussions and reflection really seemed to help. She hadn't had an outburst since her shopping trip, nor had any unexplainable waves of emotion overcome her.

Nick stuffed the last of his chips into his mouth and crumpled the little paper sack in his hand. "You've been quiet the last couple of days. Everything good?"

"More than good. Getting some much-needed rest. How about you?"

"Oh yeah. Just setting my affairs in order. Figure there's a good chance my beneficiaries will be cashing in soon." He stuffed his hands into his pockets and shivered.

"Looking for sympathy? At least you have beneficiaries!" Juliet snorted and rubbed at her nose, numb with cold.

"Let's put a pin in that one. I'm interested in learning why you feel so alone in the universe, but I think we should go inside; I'm freezing my balls off."

"Lovely." Juliet chuckled as she followed Nick into the hangar. Her eyes were instantly grabbed by the ships on display—half a dozen interceptor-class fighters, a couple of heavier gunships, and farther toward the rear of the space, a hulking shape that must be the "Detroit Industries, Lobo IV, combat transport," listed on the digital placard out front. It was much taller and boxier than the fighter ships, but still angular enough to handle atmospheric flight. Nick had eyes only for the interceptors, though, and he turned that way, steering Juliet away from the heavier ships as she mentally started to compare them to the as yet unnamed *Takamoto* ship back on Luna.

"You ever fly something heavier? Like those gunships?"

"Heavy fighters are cool, but they're probably out of our budget, and those two aren't exactly best-in-class. I'd rather get a well-equipped interceptor."

"Makes sense." Juliet followed behind him, admiring the sleek lines of the interceptors, trying to determine for herself which ones were quality ships and which ones they might be better off bypassing. Her efforts were futile, though, because Nick narrated his thoughts as they walked, and she found what he had to say too interesting to ignore.

As they approached the first sharply angled, red-and-black-painted ship, he said, "This one has nice lines. That's a Holstrum Dart, and I've flown one before. Shot a few down, too. Holstrum's been making these for nearly two decades, and they don't change much from year to year. Let's see . . . Yeah, this is a 2102 model, so pretty damn current. Put this on our maybe list, and we'll come back to check the components if we don't see something better."

"Okay . . ."

"You don't have to make a list; my PAI is taking notes."

"Yeah, I figured." Juliet studied the ship as they walked past, noting the crowd around it. Many of the would-be bidders were "kicking the tires," so to speak, opening panels, looking at serial numbers, and climbing up the ramp into the ship's tiny hold. Angel highlighted a few things for her, labeling them in her AUI—barrels for four twenty-millimeter autocannons, a deployable four-port Brimstone missile launcher, and several sections of hull that were missing armor plates; Angel noted that the hull was four centimeters below the armor level, indicating shoddy patching.

By the time she turned back to Nick, he was already at the next ship and giving his assessment, apparently unaware or uncaring that she'd lagged behind. ". . . almost like new, and I don't like the factory specs at all. Those maneuvering jets are woefully underpowered for the kind of flying I like to do. Cross this one out unless the client's willing to drop 200k on upgrades."

Juliet thought she could figure out what he'd been saying. The ship was smaller than the Dart, but it looked brand new. Apparently, Nick wasn't a fan of the ship's default equipment. She followed him to the next ship and expected him to walk right past it, but he didn't. He stopped walking and grew quiet for a few minutes while he ran his eyes over the battered, scarred-looking hull. Juliet followed his gaze, reading the information Angel provided on her AUI.

It was a Bosse Industries Starcatcher, and the manufacture date said 2077, making it more than three decades old. It was a lot bigger than the Dart, almost big enough, in Juliet's admittedly inexperienced opinion, to be considered a heavy fighter. It didn't have cannon ports on the nose, but a remote turret hung below the cockpit with a three-hundred-and-sixty-degree firing arc. Another turret sat behind the tall, pockmarked tailfin, and judging by its armor, it was meant to fire only toward the rear. Old-school missile brackets lined the wings, seven on each side.

Overall, the ship looked extremely aggressive, with a rectangular fuselage that narrowed to a point, almost making it look like a wedge.

"Kind of an old-fashioned-looking bird, isn't it?"

"It is old fashioned, but it's one of the best ships ever made. This one's seen some shit, too. I'd bet my lunch there isn't much stock equipment left on this bird."

"That's . . . good?"

"Yeah, that's good. Look at the size of those maneuvering thrusters on the undersides of the wings. This old girl can move." Nick glanced down the aisle, briefly considering the three ships he hadn't examined yet, and shook his head. "This is the one. Where the hell is Larry?"

Juliet scrutinized the ship some more. It was mostly painted red, but a considerable percentage of the hull was blackened, and hundreds of dents, divots, and grooves were carved into the armor. It had definitely seen some shit, as Nick put it.

"You think the armor's okay?"

"That's just cosmetic; you should know that! A little time with a welding rig and some armor scraps, and she'll be ready to rock. Besides, it'll scare off a lot of bidders." His eyes went distant for a second, then he smiled and added, "Larry's here. Let's wait for him so he can make a bid."

"You're sure this is the one, huh?"

"Yeah, I think so." He nodded, tapping his breast pocket for his Nikko-vape. "If I'm going to impress anyone with my flying, this is the kinda bird that can do it. She's no Lady, mind you, but she could be something special with the right touch." He stepped forward and rested a hand on the scarred-up fuselage just behind the front turret. "Yeah, you've been through some stuff, but you came out the other side, didn't you?"

"You like her, huh?" A woman wearing a stylish red dress stepped under the turret from the other side of the ship, holding one hand atop her matching red hat as though afraid she'd bump it on the plasteel above her head.

"Oh, it's not a bad bird, but it'll take a fat bankroll to make her fit for duty." Nick shrugged and dragged on his vape, stepping back toward Juliet.

"That so?" The woman continued forward, and Juliet took her in—tall, slender, middle-aged, dark hair, and the kind of makeup that takes a while to apply. What was she doing looking at fighter ships? "Seemed you were more interested while explaining the ship to your apprentice here."

Juliet snorted. "Excuse me?"

"Oh, the way he spoke to you, I thought he was teaching a class or something." She had a droll tone like she knew she was being funny but didn't want everyone to be sure about that. "I'm Matilda Ramone. I run—"

"Oh, c'mon, Matilda! You recognize me!" Nick sighed and shook his head. "She's a fixer. Matilda, I've done about seven or ten jobs for you. Nick Grant."

"Oh, is that you, Nicky? I should have known! Now I see it! I think your ID photo could use an update, young man."

"Young? I'm at least your age—"

"Heavens! Don't mention a lady's age!" She winked at Juliet, whose mouth was hanging open at the sudden twist in the conversation. She took another step toward Nick, clearly getting inside his comfort bubble, making him visibly squirm. "What happened to the *Lady Hawk*?"

"She's fine!"

"Well, why are you here?"

"Helping a friend pick a new bird! Cripes, Matilda, why are you all up in my business?" Nick sucked on his vape again, nodded to Juliet, and jerked his thumb toward the hangar entrance. "Let's go."

"Well, it was nice seeing you, Nick! Don't be a stranger! I've got five jobs off the top of my head you'd be perfect for!" She practically yelled the last sentence as Nick motored away, Juliet hot on his heels.

"What the hell, Nick? I've seen some hasty retreats in my day, but you ran like you owed her money." Juliet tried to hide her laugh as Nick slowed, turning to scowl at her. He didn't speak until they were mingling with the dense crowds near the entrance.

"Where the hell is Larry?" He scanned the clusters of people, ignoring her question. "There he is. Larry!" Juliet followed his gaze and saw Larry approaching with his two goons close behind. Nick turned to her and quickly, quietly, said, "That woman is nuts! I had a . . . thing with her, and she totally forgot me. Like, a week later, after we . . . you know"—he stuck his pointer finger inside his other hand, pulling a snort of shocked laughter out of Juliet—"she called me to schedule a lunch so she could introduce herself."

"Seriously?"

"Yeah! Swear! Anyway, it's best we don't stand around that ship and act interested." As Larry walked up, Nick changed topics instantly. "Larry! I found the one you need to buy. It's the Bosse Industries Starcatcher."

"Well, hello to you." Larry chuckled, then looked at Juliet, holding out a hand. "Lucky."

She took his hand in hers, smiling warmly as she shook it. "Don't mind Nick; he's all discombobulated 'cause he ran into an ex."

"Oh?" Larry raised an eyebrow.

"All right, all right. Is that going to be a problem? You good to make the bids, or do I need to hang around?" Nick seemed genuinely agitated, and Juliet started feeling a little bad for teasing him. He sucked on his vape again, ramping up his nicotine intake to levels she'd not seen in a couple of weeks.

"Sorry, I was teasing you, Nick."

"Eh, it's fine. I do have things to do today, however. So?" He eyed Larry, waiting for the fixer to give him a response.

"Well . . ." Larry's eyes were distant, and Juliet knew he was studying his AUI. "Looks like you didn't pick the most expensive fighter here. It's a silent auction, and there are only two bids on it. I hate it when I can't look the bidders in the eye, you know? You think this one's worth it, huh?"

"Yeah, it's the best option in this auction." He stuffed his hands in his pockets, then jerked his head toward the open doors. "Well, I did my part. Now you do yours. Win that bird." Nick smiled, sucked on his vape, then added, "See you later. Lucky, I'll give you a call when Larry gives me the good news."

With that, he sauntered out of the hangar, and Juliet had to wonder if he was putting on the macho show to save some face after his retreat from Matilda. She watched him leave for a moment before turning to Larry and the two bodyguards lurking behind him.

"You had to bring your muscle?"

"Never know when one of my many enemies might make a move." He grinned his golden grin, and Juliet desperately wanted to talk to him about the bug in his head. She supposed she could turn on her jammer; if she removed the bug in Larry's head before she turned the jammer off, it could never report— "You okay? Staring at me like I swallowed a bug."

"Oh, no, sorry. I, well, I was thinking about something, and you happened to be in front of my face." Juliet forced a smile and pushed the idea out of her head; this wasn't the place to break things down for Larry. "I guess I'll head out."

"Hey, hey, one minute!" Larry held up a ring-bedecked hand. "I never got a chance to confirm with you that you're all set. You got what you need equipment-wise?"

"I did." Juliet nodded her head. "I'm good. What's the big plan? Did you talk to Nick about how we're going to, you know, insert ourselves?"

"Oh yeah. He's aware of the whole thing, but it's not something we should talk about right now. Probably not slick to be seen chatting me up, anyway, not if you're going to be pulling off a . . . you know, a certain type of identity soon."

"Speaking of . . ." Juliet frowned and put her hands on her hips.

"Oh, right, right. I'll be sending you an encrypted file soon. Our client's paying the big money for a well-vetted background for you. I'll attach it to the contract." Larry reached up to adjust his hat, and Juliet wondered if it was some kind of tell. Should she try to read him again?

She shook her head at the idea. No, she'd been inside Larry's head plenty, and her experiences over the last few days made her leery of casually reaching into people's heads.

"Right. I'll be on the lookout for that file. See you soon, Larry."

Juliet winked at his two chromed-out gorillas, then made her way out of the busy hangar. She went straight back to her hotel. She'd decided to keep a low profile while waiting for the job, and that wasn't entirely because she'd been exhausted and worried about her mental state. She figured the less she showed her face around town, the fewer people might possibly recognize her when she was trying to pass herself off as a pirate in a few days.

Inside her hotel room, she flopped onto the bed, booted feet off the side, and said, "Angel, I'd like to talk to a friendly face. I wish we could call Luna without a delay."

"With the current positions of Luna and Callisto, you're only looking at a thirty-five-minute delay both ways. If you sent a message to someone, we could be watching the response in about an hour."

"That's seeing the bright side! Okay, who should I message? Aya? Bennet?" Juliet hesitated a few seconds, then added, "Honey?"

"I think you're most likely to have a positive outcome from a message to Aya or Bennet, but if Honey did respond, I believe it would provide the largest mood boost."

"What the . . . Are you, like, calculating my positive feelings or something?" Juliet pulled out her Texan and began idly twirling it on her finger, trusting Angel to keep the electronic safety on while her finger dangerously bounced on the trigger. Many of the cowboy heroes in the books she read twirled their guns, and she was trying to get the knack for it. Just for fun, she told herself.

"Not exactly. Though I find the concepts of utilitarianism fascinating, that was one of Mill's downfalls—the difficulty in measuring and quantifying happiness. What I meant was, knowing you, I think you'd like to hear a positive message from Honey. You won't talk about it much, but I think it hurt you how she seemed to 'blow you off' during your stay on Luna."

"You think I should tell her? I feel like I was too passive about the whole thing. I just kind of was like, 'Okay, whatever,' but I think I should have said, 'Hey, Honey, listen, you're hurting my feelings here!' You know?"

"What could it hurt? Your relationship seems strained from the silence."

"Okay, record me. Ready?"

"Ready!"

"Honey, hey, I'm still out in the Jovian System, but I wanted you to know I miss you. I was thinking I could stand to see a friendly face, someone who means something to me, you know? Well, your face came to mind, and, dammit, I'd like to hear something meaningful from you! I feel like we were just distant friends when I was last on Luna, just surface talk, and that's not right! I freakin' flew to Saturn to save your ass! I fought pirates, mercs—shit, I almost got sliced in half by a crazed samurai, and holy moly, there's more about that that I'd like to tell you, but I guess this message isn't the right place. Come on, Honey! Message me! Don't leave me hanging."

"Sent!"

"Shit, Angel! I wanted to think about it a little before I committed . . ."

"I knew you'd chicken out, so I sent it."

"Chicken out? You're cruel, but you're right."

Juliet groaned and flopped over, burying her face into the pillow. Squeezing her eyes shut, she tried to imagine Honey's response to that rambling, venting monologue.

"Well, nothing to be done about it."

She pushed herself up and scooted to the foot of the bed, contemplating how to kill the time. Read a book? Play with her telekinesis? Clean her guns? She twirled her pistol again, and that's when, with a thunderous bang, her door burst open in a shower of engineered wooden splinters and particles.

28

MOODS

Angel responded to the exploding door instantly, firing Juliet's synapses into overdrive, to the point where it seemed the flying particles of wood were drifting on a gentle breeze. Juliet, of course, was caught mid-recoil as her mind accelerated, and suddenly, she felt like she was falling back in slow motion, too.

Everything except her right arm, still clutching her pistol, that is. As soon as her mind ramped up to speed and she realized what was happening, she took control, bringing the gun to bear, and when a shadow darkened the exploding doorway, she cranked off a round.

Her shot exploded into the figure's center of mass, and she dropped the sights slightly and squeezed the trigger again just in case she'd hit a body armor plate with the first round. Everything was quiet; Angel had filtered out the loud noises. Suddenly, the world sped back up as she reduced the boost to Juliet's synapses, perhaps wanting to assess things further before continuing the strain on Juliet's brain. Juliet continued her reflexive backward roll off the side of the bed and came to her knees, gun up, eyes on the shredded doorway. Had she just shot someone out of reflex?

She couldn't think about that. Now wasn't the time to second-guess her reaction.

The figure she'd shot was sprawled on its back. She could see dark fatigues, a tactical vest, an electro-shotgun still gripped in one hand, and, closest to her, two large, twitching combat boots. Angel flickered her vision through various spectrums, including her new implants' improved terahertz imaging scan, which revealed no other figures beyond her room's wall.

Juliet stood up, holstered her Texan, and snatched up her new shotgun, leaning against the wall by her dresser. She didn't have to rack a round; she kept it ready to fire. When she approached the figure, she could tell he was a man, spotting some straw-colored beard protruding beneath his visor.

A soft moan escaped his lips, and she gave him a double-take; her Texan had blasted two very nice holes through his carbonweave-armored vest, and copious gouts of blood had showered forth. By any reasonable expectation, he should be dead.

"Don't move, or the next one will remove your head."

Nothing but another soft moan was forthcoming. Juliet stepped forward, kicked his shotgun out of his hand, and then looked up and down the terraced landing outside her room. All the doors were shut, and not a soul was in sight. She edged forward, scanned down over the railing to the pavement below, and then hurriedly stepped back to the downed hotel-room invader.

He still wasn't moving, so she hurried back into her room, pulled open her top dresser drawer, and took out the little surveillance drone she'd recently unpacked. "Angel, fly that thing out there and keep an eye on the street."

"On it." The drone buzzed to life and streaked out the door. Juliet grabbed the injured man's foot and dragged him into the room. Another moan escaped him, informing her of his not-yet-deceased status, and she turned him onto his side. His helmet covered his data port, so she snatched her vibroblade and slashed the straps, nicking him in the process, but he didn't seem to notice. She yanked his helmet off, revealing a thick head of ginger-blond hair, a short, well-trimmed beard, and bloodshot, glassy blue eyes that rolled back in his head as he gasped and sputtered for breath, blood flecking his lips.

Juliet had set her shotgun on the foot of the bed amid a thick layer of wood splinters, and she glanced at it as she asked, "Anything, Angel?"

"Not yet. There are several calls out to emergency services, but their public response page indicates a backlog."

"Okay." Juliet yanked her data cable out, shoved it into the man's data port, and said, "Tell me what you can find out."

"Dealing with ICE—it's an older model PAI, and the data port doesn't have any coprocessing; I'm brute forcing it." Juliet felt the back of her neck warm up slightly, and then Angel said, "In."

"Sheesh, that new data port working out for you?"

"It's quite robust! Hmm, it looks like this man has spent most of his extra bits on nanite upgrades. His vitals are very low, but the bugs are stopping his internal bleeding. They won't be able to replace the damaged bone and organ tissue, so he won't be waking up anytime soon, but he will likely survive if given proper treatment soon."

"Who is he?"

"He's an operator who specializes in bounty hunting. Let's see . . . Yes, he has a B ranking on fugitive surveillance and apprehension. It seems he was hired by Rutger Tanaka. A moment, Juliet, I'm reviewing his correspondence and travel history, trying to piece together how he came to find you here."

"Just download it all, then delete everything on that PAI that isn't necessary to keep him alive."

Angel didn't reply, but Juliet knew she'd speak up if she couldn't do what she'd asked.

While she worked, Juliet went through the merc's pockets. She didn't find anything of note. Unsurprising, considering people kept everything in their heads these days, from door locks to money to video and audio files. "Does he have a vehicle?"

"He walked here from his hotel. It's only ten minutes away. I have his biometric data. You can remove the cable; I have everything."

"Okay, let's get out of here." Juliet picked up her duffel, opened the zipper, and tossed her few unpacked belongings inside. She'd checked into the hotel under a false ID, so she wasn't worried about that. Still, she put her new helmet on her head and said, "Make it black."

She watched in the chipped, dirty mirror above the dresser as the powder-blue, scarred-up helmet turned black and the mirrored faceplate lost its sheen and darkened to match the enamel. She tossed her shotgun into the bag. "Follow me with the drone."

Juliet stepped over the unconscious mercenary, contemplated taking his shotgun, then decided it wasn't worth the weight. She carried her already bulky duffel with her left hand, her right hand hovering near her pistol grip as she stretched her legs into long strides and hurried away from her hotel. Angel followed her with the drone, keeping tabs on the people she passed, watching to see if anyone pursued her.

"Guide me to his hotel, but take a kind of roundabout path."

"On it. While you walk, shall I fill you in on the bounty hunter?"

"Yeah."

"His name is Ulric Barr, and he took a job from Tanaka on Luna. He was hired to follow Frida, keep tabs on her, and 'clean up any messes she made.' Studying his PAI's location data, it seems he watched your meeting with Frida, at least from the outside. I don't believe he had eyes or ears on the inside. When he saw you leave intact, he followed you back to your hotel. He's been monitoring you ever since. It seems he never reached out to Tanaka to acquire new orders and decided to take matters into his own hands. I would speculate that he sought to earn favor with Tanaka by capturing or, perhaps, even killing you."

"If he was sent to watch Frida, why would he think Tanaka wanted me? I didn't kill Frida . . ."

"You did shoot her. Perhaps Ulric concluded that you won a physical confrontation by observing her injury as she left. Your pistol is not quiet."

Juliet turned down a busy street, garnering a few looks in her dark helmet, lugging her heavy bag. No one followed her, though, and soon, she was turning down another less crowded sidewalk. "Send a message to Frida on an encrypted line. Wait, have you infiltrated her new PAI yet?"

"No, they haven't set up new team comms. The three of them took two different transports back to Luna."

"That's . . . interesting." Juliet saw her destination ahead: a red-stained concrete tower with a big, flashing green-and-orange neon sign announcing "Jupiter Inn and Suites." It was a popular automated hotel chain in the Jovian System; she'd seen several in her time on Callisto. "You think that's part of their standard operating procedures? Traveling separately?"

"Perhaps. In any case, I know her contact info from my connection to her team's PAIs."

"Okay, send the following: Frida, your boss hired a bounty hunter to keep tabs on you. He decided to try to capture me. Please tell your boss I'm tired of shooting his goons, and I'd appreciate it if he'd call off any other dogs he's got sniffing around. Tell him it doesn't lend to a warm, confident feeling about our upcoming meeting. I'm interested in an amicable settlement, but my plans can change if he's going to keep coming after me."

"Sent."

"Is my palm ready?"

"Yes, you have Ulric's print. His room is 413."

Juliet reached out to grasp the hotel door's handle, and it clicked when it read Ulric's info, recognizing her as a current patron. She yanked the door open and hurried to the elevator. Inside, she thumbed the fourth-floor button and waited as it surged upward.

"How much time do you think I have before Ulric comes back to his room?"

"At least a day, depending on when he's taken to a trauma center. It'll take time to repair the damage those rounds did to his organs. According to his nanites, his spinal cord was severed by your first shot."

"Sheesh, good nanites."

"Yes, his suite was even more robust than yours."

The bell chimed, and the doors opened. Juliet looked out, cautiously peering up and down the empty, orange-carpeted hallway. "He was alone, right?" Juliet assumed Angel would have alerted her if he had a team on his comms or something.

"As far as I could tell. I didn't find any correspondence that would indicate he was working with anyone. He has a girlfriend on Luna that he messages daily, as well as one in New Galveston."

"Seriously, Mars?" Juliet turned to the left, following the room numbers toward the one she wanted.

"Yes, and the one on Luna is pregnant."

"Oh God, Angel! Did you have to tell me that?"

"Sorry . . ."

Juliet paused before the door to room 413. "Is he going to live?"

"I think so. Emergency services are still indicating a backlog, but his nanites had his bleeding under control, and his heart and lungs were still functional."

"Did you leave a bug in his PAI?"

"Naturally."

"Well, let me know if he gets . . ." Juliet shook her head, squeezing her eyes shut for a second. What was she doing? She couldn't help him now. Was she feeling guilty? She didn't blow down his door! She also didn't finish him off like plenty of operators would have!

"Never mind. I don't want to know." She gripped the doorknob, and it clicked unlocked. She switched her left hand to the knob, then drew her Texan, holding it ready as she pulled the door wide.

The doorway afforded a clear view of the entire room. She saw a big black backpack on the bed, food packages and wrappers on the little dinette table, and a pile of dirty laundry and towels near the open bathroom door. Juliet's vision flickered as Angel scanned the room. Then, with a green flash, she announced, "All clear."

Juliet stepped in, turned to drag her duffel in from the hallway, and let the door swing closed. She moved to the bathroom door in three quick steps and cleared it, slicing the pie and holding her gun close to her body.

"Just making sure," she said, popping open the cylinder on the Texan and replacing the two spent rounds, shaking her head—she should have done that already.

"All right," she sighed, moving to the bed and approaching the black backpack. "Let me see what Mr. Barr was working with. Get Nick on comms, please." While the connection beeped, she unzipped the bag and started unpacking her would-be captor or assassin's belongings. She'd pulled out several athletic shirts and shorts, some underwear, socks, and a pair of training shoes when Nick finally answered.

"Lucky?"

"I'm gonna need to crash in the Lady until we're ready to go."

"Well, I'm fine, thank you. How are you feeling?"

"Seriously, Nick! Some merc just busted into my hotel room, and I had to shoot him." While she spoke, she unzipped the bottom section of the big pack, revealing three black plastic cases that read V.E.G. in big white letters. "What's this?"

"I believe that's versatile explosive gel; probably what he used to blow your door."

"What's what? And did you say a merc busted into your room? Are you okay?"

"Yeah, but I'm kind of trying to lie low. I don't want to get mixed up with some corpo-sec investigation or get my face plastered on the news vids."

"Okay, head over to the hangar! You have permissions on the door."

"All right, cool. I just wanted to make sure you were all right with it." Juliet picked up one of the plastic boxes. It was about twice the size of her data deck, and when she opened it, she found a clear, rubbery gel within. Clipped to the inside of the cover were a dozen shiny little objects that looked very much like thumbtacks. "This could come in handy."

"What now?"

"Nothing. Any word from Larry?"

"He was bitching about having to raise the bids. I have a feeling the client gave him a budget, and he's trying to get something cheap so he can keep the difference."

"Uh-huh," Juliet said as she unpacked the three boxes of VEG and brought them over to her duffel.

"Where are you?"

"In the merc's hotel room."

"You . . . went to his room?"

"Sure. Figured he wouldn't be needing it, and no one knows to look for me here." Juliet went over to the little fridge and pulled it open. "Oh, yes! He has beer."

Nick snorted a quick laugh. "You're awfully upbeat."

"I am, aren't I?" Juliet frowned and analyzed her feelings. Was she acting out of character? She didn't think so; she was in a good mood because she'd gotten out of yet another close scrape unscathed. She'd learned the bounty hunter probably didn't have backup coming, and she had a plan to go forward. She always felt a little high after a close call. Even when her rush used to come from fast cars instead of bullets, that's what she'd been like. "It's all good, Nick. I'm gonna snag this guy's six-pack and head down to the hangar. Let me know when Larry seals the deal."

"You got it." Nick waved and cut the connection.

"You have two messages that came in while you were on that call."

"Two?"

"One from Frida and one from Honey."

"Frida got back to me already? Her ship must not be too far . . ."

"No, her passenger liner departed last night. Which message do you want to see first?"

Juliet took one of the beers from the fridge and pulled the tab; it was in a pouch, indicating its exceptionally low quality. Still, it was cold and she was thirsty, so she sipped at the thick, foamy beverage and sat down at the dinette. "Well, let's get Frida's over with first."

A window resolved on her AUI to show Frida with her orange hair, bright green eyes, and pale, freckled skin. She spoke quickly, nervously, and kept leaning forward as though to emphasize her earnestness. "Lucky, I'm so very sorry that happened. My boss definitely gave the order for all pursuit to fall back, but that particular operator was, apparently, not meant to be pursuing you, so he didn't think he needed to warn him off. We all see how that panned out. I hope you won't take this personally, and I hope you'll still be willing to meet with my boss, with Rutger, when you return to Luna. I'm glad to hear you came out on top. If there's anything I can do, please let me know." She licked her lips a little nervously, then quickly added, "I swear I didn't know about him, Lucky. I'm pissed about this too."

"That's the end," Angel said as the window closed.

"Well, kind of what I expected. She sounded honest, but the whole thing makes me think Tanaka will require some serious scrutiny. If Frida's his right-hand woman but he sends a merc to keep tabs on her, it kind of calls into question his loyalty, doesn't it?"

"His loyalty, perhaps, or Frida's. He may have reason to distrust her."

"Hmm, yeah, or I guess he could just be worried about her—overprotective." Juliet took another long, slow sip of the beer. It was tough to stomach, but she could tell it had a high alcohol content. "Well, let's see how Honey reacted to my crazy message."

Another window opened, and Juliet saw Honey's face in front of a glass-paned window overlooking an expansive green lawn. She looked good. Her skin was practically glowing in the sunlight coming through the glass. That same light also hit her eyes just right, pulling out the gold-and-yellow bands in her pale-brown irises.

She smiled that big smile of hers and said, "Juliet! I'm using your real name 'cause you sent me this on an encrypted line. I'm so, so, so sorry for being a flake the last few weeks when you were on Luna. I really did mean to get back to you and meet with you, but things kept coming up and—oh shit! I'm just making excuses! I owe you better than that, sis! I . . . Well, I've been dealing with a lot—PTSD, my shrink says. That and heartache and denial. It took a while for Temo's death to truly sink in, J. That on top of what happened to Alexander . . . our kidnapping, everything. I was totally burying it all while we traveled back here, but it hit me like a ton of bricks when I finally realized we were safe."

"Pause it." Juliet took another drink of her beer and wiped at her eyes with her balled-up fist. "Dammit, Angel. I can't be mad at her. I just want to give her a hug. I'm such a dummy! Of course she didn't have time to process everything! I was trying to have lunch and hang out like old times, but it will never be old times with us again. There's too much that's happened."

"I, too, feel sorry for her, Juliet, but think how much worse off she'd be without your help, without your friendship. You'll get back to how things were; I really believe it."

"I hope so." Juliet thought about everything she'd been through in the last year, about how she'd been exposed to betrayal, violence, guilt, and a million other negative . . . things. Honey wasn't like her. She'd taken what she thought would be a fun, light job of training and looking after a sort of rich kid prodigy. Instead, she'd been through hell and thought she was going to die before Juliet showed up. Of course it would take time to process all that! "Okay, play it."

"Anyway, that's what my problem was. I'm feeling so much better, though. When you get back, let me know right away, okay? Oh! I might have some exciting news for you! Peter's buying a place on Mars. Have you ever been? I was trying to think of a way we could spend some time together, and I had an idea—aren't you guys working on getting that fighter ship up and running? What if I talked him into hiring you as an escort? Let me know what you think! Love you, sis!"

As the window closed, Juliet felt her cheeks stretched into a taut smile.

"You were right, Angel."

"About?"

"About me getting a 'large mood boost' from contacting Honey."

29

FREE LUNCH

Juliet looked at herself in the mirror, examining the changes Angel had made to her eyes and hair. She couldn't remember the last time her hair had been that short—kind of a messy bob with wavy bangs parted in the middle. She'd chosen to color it black with red highlights. Something different for her new alter ego. The whites of her eyes were black, too, with shimmering, golden stars for irises. In her opinion, they looked cool, but were a bit off-putting in their alien nature.

"Right, well, that's me, Lacy Blake, the pirate."

"A stark contrast to your usual style." Angel's voice was neutral, and Juliet couldn't tell if she was being careful with her word choice.

"Do you think it's too much?"

"Not at all. Besides, you'll have a helmet on much of the time."

"Yeah. Let's see here." Juliet turned away from the mirror to the molded plasteel bench attached to the bathroom wall. Her duffel sat there, holding most of her belongings outside Luna City. She wore black tights, a gray tank top, and nothing else; she was about to gear up.

She pulled out the body armor she'd bought and started getting into it, piece by piece. When she'd first checked it out, Juliet had been thrilled by the well-used nature of the combat suit. Scuffs, scars, and even some burn marks marred the rigid armor plates, but just as advertised, none of the damage impacted its protective value.

The active energized fiber mesh between the plates could be adjusted to perfect the fit. When she had the whole suit on and Angel synced up with the control module, she felt it grow snug where it was saggy and loosen where it was too tight. All in all, it became very comfortable, and with the batteries fully charged, she felt like she wasn't carrying any weight at all.

She stretched a bit, making sure there weren't any loose sections and that all the active "joint-support" mechanics worked.

Satisfied, she took a seat on the bench and pulled on her boots. She carefully aligned and locked them into the armored suit's standardized fittings, ensuring an airtight seal. They were lighter than her usual work boots, and she smiled as she turned her ankle in a circle, noting the excellent flexibility. "Should've gotten a pair of these a while ago."

"I like that they're made to provide a tight seal against the bottom cuffs of your armor; your entire suit is airtight, which greatly enhances the filtration systems in your new helmet."

"Cool." Juliet pulled her blue-and-black camo tactical vest out of the bag. It had been new when she bought it, but she'd put it through some weathering in the hangar where Nick kept the *Lady Hawk*, dragging it over the oil-stained concrete, balling it up and pounding it with a hammer, and spilling some grease on it here and there. She'd washed it and repeated the process twice, and now it really looked like a pirate had been sleeping in it for a year or two.

Once she'd put it on, she started stuffing the pockets with her spare bullets, shells, and needler magazines.

Her drones were already attached to the backs of her shoulders—two little black balls with all their limbs and wings retracted. Her needler sat under her left arm as usual, her vibroblade on her left forearm, and her Texan on her hip. She pulled her data deck out of the duffel, put it in a pouch on her vest, then lifted out her auto shotgun. It was a heavy weapon when fully loaded, and she was glad it came with a single-point sling.

Weapons installed, she just had to stow a box of the VEG—or veg, as she'd been calling it—in one of the vest's side pockets. She didn't know what, but figured it was a good possibility she'd need to blow something up.

She flexed her hands in the tactile gloves that'd come with the armor and nodded her approval; she hadn't even noticed them while loading her pockets and guns. "One more thing," she said, pulling out her helmet. She'd reverted it to its default baby-blue color with a mirrored visor. She liked the pale color because the scarring stood out better, making it look well-used and, in her opinion, giving her appearance a little more authenticity.

She pushed it down over her head, felt the flexible neck seal contract and hook onto the collar of her armor, and then moved her head around, ensuring the seal was secure and that she had full mobility. "Feels good."

"You look like you mean business."

"Good, 'cause the whole aim is to make people think twice about messing with me. Nick's going to earn their respect with his flying, but when I start walking around whatever kind of base they're using, I'll need to discourage conflict."

She zipped up the empty duffel, slung it over her shoulder, and left the bathroom. She'd left the stuff she wouldn't bring on the mission—backpack, clothes, books, extra ammo, explosives, and other odds and ends—in Nick's hangar.

"I still can't believe the client is throwing away three ships and a cargo bay full of wine to get Nick noticed by the pirates." She spoke aloud, even though they were in the spaceport, because her helmet actively canceled any noise she made unless she wanted her voice to project.

"It certainly demonstrates the depths of his resources. Considering the ship he purchased for Nick, that makes four vessels he's willing to lose for this endeavor."

"Yeah, kinda puts the big payday he's promising in perspective."

"True, this whole affair must have a multimillion-bit budget. Considering the payload in the transport, closer to ten million."

Juliet strode confidently through the port toward the hangar where Nick's "new" ship was docked. He'd dubbed it *Sharp Lady*, resulting in at least an hour of teasing from Juliet. He hadn't backed down, though—he felt the ship's name had to include the word "lady" as a matter of good luck. "Why sharp?" Juliet had pressed, and he'd explained that the chisel-like shape of the ship gave him the idea.

"Sharp Lady." Juliet chuckled. "Nick's sweet, but he's not winning any prizes for creativity."

"I'm surprised you teased him so much, considering your trouble thinking of names. Even your handle was a struggle . . ."

"All right, all right. I get it, you like Nick more than me . . ."

"No, I don't!"

Juliet laughed, but then she noticed a pair of corpo security personnel standing next to a coffee cart staring at her through their visored helmets.

She turned her mirrored faceplate to them, returning the attention. When they looked away, a little thrill of adrenaline brought a metallic tang to her tastebuds, and she grinned. She couldn't blame them for the attention; she looked like she was about to deploy into a hot zone, and the active armor and helmet gave her a rather intimidating presence.

Two minutes later, she punched the code into the hangar door and stepped through.

She was greeted by the sight of Nick pacing back and forth, watching a pair of techs welding armor patches on the hull of the Sharp Lady. It had taken a few days to get delivery of the vessel. Apparently, the client had wanted one of his personal techs to take the time to scrub it of any identifying marks and install a new ID transponder, one that gave the ship an untraceable history that dead-ended in a Martian scrapyard nine years ago.

Nick turned when he heard the door close and said, "Glad you made it . . . Lacy. Jesus, you looking for a combat dropship? 'Cause this is the wrong bay . . ."

Juliet ignored the comment, even though it made her smile under that reflective visor. "Thought we were heading out at 1330."

"Oh, we will. These guys are almost done."

Juliet frowned at the techs on their mobile scaffolds, watching the welding sparks fly as they worked. "You could have asked me to do that."

"Why? Larry's paying these knuckleheads."

"You sure they're doing a good job?"

"I mean, they're licensed and bonded, so . . ." Nick shrugged.

"I'm gonna walk through the ship, scan for bugs and bombs and anything else we don't want flying around with us."

"Good plan. I'll settle up with these guys, then we need to get moving, or we'll miss our free lunch."

Juliet nodded and started walking around the ship, trusting Angel to use her wireless antenna to note any strange signals. "Free lunch" was what Nick had been calling the, in her opinion, over-the-top plan to get them noticed and brought in by the pirates. The client, Sir Rodric, had prepared an unscheduled shipment of fine wines from his agridome on Callisto. His freighter and two escorts, all controlled via licensed piloting AI modules, would fly down a known shipping lane toward Mars. One of his investigators was going to tip off the Hereford's Vengeance pirates, but only after Nick and Juliet were engaged with the ship. The idea was that Nick would take out the escorts, Juliet would board, and they'd be caught with their pants down when the pirates arrived.

"All in the hopes that they'll be impressed by us enough to bring us back to their base," she muttered into her helmet, still walking around the ship. She supposed it was a good plan, something the corpo security patrols around the ports weren't willing or able to do. It took deep pockets and a unilateral decision-making process to pull something like that off, a quality the conglomerate corporate shipping police didn't seem to have.

That, and they were probably corrupt.

"And, I suppose," she continued, verbalizing her thought process, "you'd have to have some suicidally reckless agents to do the heist."

"Are you talking about yourself?"

"Sure. I was just wondering why the corpo-sec shipping cops haven't tracked these pirates down."

"Speculation on the net is that they're complicit, paid off at the command level by the larger pirate organizations."

"Yeah, I figured." Juliet stopped at the ship's rear-entry ramp, sparks from a welder above showering down on the plasteel floor nearby. "Notice anything strange outside?"

"Nothing unusual."

Juliet climbed into the ship, slowly moving from its tiny airlock to its little cargo area, through the short corridor into the central access junction, which opened into the single crew bunk room on the left and the toilet area on the right. She took her time, allowing Angel plenty of opportunity to scan all the possible bands and frequencies. She knew she'd be isolating interference and noise, trying to uncover any clandestine signals.

She saw four acceleration couches inside the bunk room, which surprised her; it was larger than she'd thought. She supposed it made sense, though; the ship was a good deal larger than the *Lady Hawk*.

She dumped off her duffel then returned to the spartan central crew area—just two small tables, a fridge, and a microwave built into a storage cabinet. After Angel cleared it, she stepped into the little toilet and shower room, let Angel sweep it, and moved up the access corridor to the cockpit.

The Sharp Lady had a wider cockpit than the *Lady Hawk*, almost a proper bridge, with two seats side by side in front of a rectangular viewscreen. Juliet sat down on the right and pulled out her data cable. "I'll plug you in. Ready?"

"Ready! I'll perform a scan for any trackers or dormant daemons, and then I'll let Fido loose to really analyze things, line by line." Juliet plugged in, then sat back in the seat and played around with the ship's UI while she waited for Nick. "You just received correspondence from Alice."

"Oh, nice timing. I was getting bored." Juliet watched as a vid window opened on her AUI before Alice appeared, sitting in the pilot's seat of the *Kowashi*.

"Lucky, hope you're doing well. I just woke up, but I had a rather lengthy message waiting for me from Nick. Sounds like he's very impressed by you; says you're good to go as far as getting his seal of approval. I was pumping my fist, proud and excited for you, when he kept talking and said you'd signed up to do some kind of sketchy job with him, basically 'cause you felt you had to help keep his ass out of a meat grinder. He didn't give me any details, but he sounded kind of worried. Fatalistic, even.

"It's been a long time since I've hung out with Nick, so maybe I'm reading things wrong. I've seen you in action, and I don't think Nick has, not like that, so maybe he's underestimating your ability to pull off some insane heroics. I hope that's it. I hope you're not planning to get yourself iced out there. Come back to us, all right? We're all looking forward to working with you."

She paused a minute, pursed her lips together, and then, with a brief shake of her head, kept speaking.

"That wasn't what I wanted to say. Of course we're excited to work with you, but we also think of you as a friend; family, even. Lucky, we're gonna be really, really torn up about it if you get yourself killed, okay? Thanks for caring about Nick, but if this is a suicide mission, you need to cut him loose. That guy's had plenty of time to get smart.

"We miss you, especially Aya—she's been talking nonstop about the books she got to share with you. She's even been bugging me to let her fly with you in the gunship when we're between hot spots. You got yourself a real fangirl there. Anyway, I've said my piece. Stay safe and come back home soon, okay?"

The window closed, and Juliet sat there, mouth half open inside her helmet, unable to believe what she'd just heard. Alice wasn't the mushy type, but she'd just called her family and asked her to come home. She felt tears spring into her eyes and squeezed them shut, pushing down the surge of emotions that came out of nowhere, unwilling to face them right at that moment.

"That was a nice message, but I believe Alice's worries are slightly unfounded. I don't see this as so much a suicide mission as a very dangerous one. Don't be upset," Angel said, completely missing the point of the whole thing.

"Angel, I'm not crying 'cause she upset me; I'm crying 'cause she made me feel something I haven't felt in a long time. God, what am I going to do if something happens to those knuckleheads?"

"Are they in danger? Did I miss some subtext in the message?"

"No, I'm just . . . I'm just jumping to the next probable thing to happen. Once I find people I care about and learn they care about me, something will happen to mess that up." Juliet squeezed her eyes again, then, in frustration, activated her visor's retraction function. It slid most of the way up into her helmet, just leaving a few centimeters of reflective diamatex over her eyes. She reached under it, rubbed her eyes, and laughed, sniffing noisily. "Can't you turn my tears off or something?"

"They're your original tear ducts; we only changed your eyeballs and the optic nerves. You have me now, you know? I'm going to help you protect those people you care about, especially the ones who also care about you."

"Yeah. I know. Thank you. I think we need to do something about the enemies I've made. The ones still looking to find me."

"Tanaka?"

"That's the easy one."

"Levkin?"

"You think he's looking for me?"

"I hope not. WBD?"

"Bingo. We'll look into them soon, okay? For now, though, let's try to handle this job and deal with the rich creep who hired Larry without adding another big enemy to that list."

"Sounds like a plan," Nick said, noisily clomping onto the bridge and flopping into the pilot's seat.

"Ugh! How long were you listening to me?"

"Ugh? Just long enough to hear you say you didn't want another big enemy, which, naturally, makes me wonder who your other big enemies are." He chuckled and stuck his magnetic vape clip to the panel above his head.

"Nobody you need to worry about, Nicky. We doing this thing or what?" Juliet touched the button to extend her visor back down, noting the slight hiss and pressure in her ears as it pressurized.

"Damn right we are." Nick reached down beside his seat, picked up his old, battered white-and-red flight helmet, and stuffed it onto his head. "Larry sent word. The pizza's in the oven." With that, he punched a sequence of keys on his augmented UI, and the ship's drive rumbled to life. He touched the external comms and said, "Clear the hangar. Lifting off in thirty seconds."

Juliet knew the welding crew must have already been gone; he wouldn't give them just thirty seconds to pack up all their gear. His warning was for anyone who might have randomly stumbled into the hangar.

While he dealt with the port traffic control, she asked Angel to play her Alice's message again, and she watched it with a smile, a warm feeling in her stomach. She tried to keep the dread that accompanied the pleasant feelings at bay, tried to bury it, smash it down, and forget it existed, but it kept rearing its ugly head.

The truth was, she knew she was being dramatic and that there wasn't some curse on her that meant anyone who cared about her would die or leave or get locked away. She knew that, but she also knew there were some real bogeymen out there, some real threats to her and those she cared about. She had business to take care of here that couldn't be ignored, but when she was done, she resolved to deal with some of those bad guys. She'd get rid of some of the axes that had been hanging over her head for too long.

The ship rumbled and lurched, and then they were hovering in the hangar as Nick rotated the ship with the maneuvering thrusters toward the now-open bay doors.

"Wow, these things are touchy!" He grinned and winked at her as he overcorrected and spun them past the opening. He got it back under control, though, and when he had it lined up, Juliet felt a lurch in her gut as the main drives kicked on. They exploded out of the hangar outside Callisto's main dome and tore over the moon's pockmarked surface, rapidly climbing and accelerating.

Juliet felt her acceleration couch squeeze her and steady her breathing. She didn't have her flight suit on, didn't have its active high-G supports, but Nick had promised not to do anything her body couldn't handle with just the acceleration couch. He shouldn't need to; Larry had ensured that the AI pilots on the escort interceptors wouldn't be rated above a C.

"Hang on, darlin'! Let's knock the cobwebs out of the tailpipes!" Nick laughed, then he shoved the throttle forward, and Juliet's world became a struggle to breathe and maintain consciousness.

30

PLENTY OF BOOKS

Juliet gripped her acceleration couch with white knuckles as Nick flew circles around the second AI-driven interceptor, rapidly ripping it apart with the Sharp Lady's front turret. The rotating, eighteen-millimeter autocannon buzzed like a chainsaw that rattled up through the hull as it streaked fiery tracer rounds out at the little ship. He'd already annihilated the first dronelike escort with a pair of smart missiles, and now, the second was drifting away ablaze, various components detonating in brilliant blooms of color as it came apart.

Nick steadied the ship as he turned away from the dying interceptor, bringing it parallel to the bathtub-shaped cargo ship. Juliet sucked in a much-needed breath, relieved that the rapid maneuvering part of the mission was, hopefully, behind them.

"Attention, cargo vessel *Humpback,* this is your one and only friendly request to shut down your drives and prepare for boarding," Nick spoke into comms using a terrible attempt at an English accent, and Juliet couldn't help erupting with a short laugh.

"What was that?"

"What? You don't like it?"

"No, stop!" She laughed again. "Unless you want to get us killed the minute you speak to the real pirates."

Nick smiled and kept up the terrible accent. "This isn't how pirates talk?"

"Stop it!" Juliet pointed to the viewscreen. "Their drives are off, and they're holding a steady course. Let's hurry and dock before our company arrives."

"Right, okay. Get yourself to the airlock. Good luck."

"You too, Nicky. Er, I mean Simon."

"God, I hate my name! What kind of pirate calls himself Simon? Lacy, though, that's a perfect fit for that baby-blue helmet."

"You want me to slap you around a little? Feels like a pirate should have some bruises . . ."

"No!" Nick tapped his visor release, sending it up into his helmet, and then reached for his vape. Juliet made herself scarce, carefully extricating herself from the acceleration couch and working toward the aft airlock.

"Are you ready?" Angel asked, and Juliet grunted in the affirmative. She was ready, so long as Larry or his client hadn't double-crossed them or messed up something on their end. The plan was simple, though mainly because the hard parts had been done by a client with bottomless pockets. She was supposed to find five corpses on the cargo vessel, supposedly unidentified bodies "purchased" from a city morgue. They should be in one of the cargo vessel's three airlocks; hopefully not the one Nick was going to dock with. All Juliet had to do was space them, then claim she killed the crew—something they were all hoping would buy her some street cred with the pirates. That done, she had to have Angel delete the ship's AI along with any internal camera footage that could make a liar of her.

She could feel the ship carefully maneuvering into position. Nick would match the cargo vessel's speed and heading, then spin down the drives and use the maneuvering thrusters to position the Sharp Lady and plant her rear airlock against the other ship's pairing collar.

When she reached the inner airlock door, Juliet stepped through and closed it, ready. Only a few minutes passed before she felt the vibration and heard the bumps reverberate through the hull as Nick finished the maneuver.

"Good to go, Lacy!"

"See you soon, I hope." Juliet punched the sequence to equalize the air pressure and open the outer airlock door. Air hissed, and then her door opened to reveal a closed, scarred-up white-and-yellow door—the cargo ship's outer door. "They haven't opened up yet."

"Right, I'm currently trying to threaten the pilot AI into cooperating. Just a minute."

"Just use the phrase Larry gave you!" Supposedly, the AI had a backdoor that would cause it to surrender completely. All Nick had to do was say, "Open, or we'll pull off and target your reactor."

"It's done; door should be opening. I just wanted to make sure there was some realistic back-and-forth before I said the magic words." True to his words, the door latch thunked open, and the round door recessed before rolling to the side, giving Juliet access. She stepped into a much larger airlock and walked up to the inner door, staring into the camera with her mirrored visor. Ten tense seconds went by before the door's LEDs flashed green, and it slid open. Juliet strode into the hallway, following a map on her AUI provided by Larry.

"What the hell, Nick," she breathed, noting the smears of blood on the corridor walls and floor. It was definitely blood; she'd seen enough of it to know.

"What?"

"Looks like a massacre took place here."

"I'm sure it's just staged to look realistic."

"I hope so."

Juliet followed the corridor to a lift, noting that the style of the ship's interior reminded her a lot of the *Kowashi*. It was similarly well-used, but it hadn't been so lovingly maintained. Every corridor had some missing or broken lights. She saw many missing access panels, and a low, grinding vibration was ever-present, making her wonder how much life was left in the ship's major components.

At nearly every junction, she found more smears of blood and, thinking she should add to the picture being painted, she fired a few rounds from her shotgun into the plasteel floor and wall panels, careful to check with Angel first so she didn't blow a hole in any critical conduits.

She took the lift to the bridge, saw the blood on three of the five acceleration couches, and felt a kind of sinking sensation in her gut—this seemed too real to her. Still, she plugged Angel into the data port on the pilot's station, and while Angel did her work, she reloaded her shotgun magazine. "I don't have a good feeling about this blood."

"Well, did you find the bodies?" Nick replied.

"No . . ."

"They're in the port docking airlock," Angel interjected. "I have them on camera." She put a vid feed window on Juliet's AUI, showing a grainy, blurry image of a pile of corpses wearing bloody jumpsuits. She didn't like how a large pool of blood had gathered under them, thickly coagulating on the plasteel floor.

"Those don't look like morgue bodies." Juliet gripped her shotgun tightly, adding another worry to the stack she was carrying around. Had that asshole, Sir Rodric, massacred some people on this ship just to stage a realistic pirate attack?

"Look, Lucky," Nick said over comms, "this rich client hired some real professionals to set up this ship. Odds are they dressed the bodies and added fresh blood all over the place. Don't start freaking out over there, all right?"

"I'm done with the AI and have control of the cameras. I'll delete all the data as we go." Again, Angel broke into their conversation.

"Okay," Juliet said, figuring both Angel and Nick would accept the answer.

She turned and started following the map to the port airlock and, despite Nick's reassurance, felt a gnawing unease in her gut. "I don't really want to see these bodies up close. You can't just space them remotely?"

"I could, but as you saw, the camera image is grainy and low res, and I thought you might want to have a closer look. In case . . ."

"In case something fishy is going on, and I want some evidence later?"

"Perhaps."

"I guess . . ." Juliet frowned as she noticed she was walking hard, taking long strides and stomping as she hurried through the ship. "I guess if these people were murdered so this megalomaniac could expedite his little rescue mission, then I owe them to at least make a record of it." She slowed down as she came to the blood-smeared airlock door. She peered through the thick window and saw the pile of bodies atop the pool of mostly dried blood. "Seven, not five."

"Yes, I noted that."

"God, I wish I had olfactory implants. Add that to my list, will you? Like, priority one." Juliet slammed her visor shut and turned off her external air circulation. Pushing the button to open the inner airlock door, it cycled open. Juliet hurried into the airlock, trying hard not to step in the thick, tacky blood. Holding her breath despite her self-contained air supply, she carefully turned every corpse to record their faces—five men and two women.

She saw blood around bullet holes on their jumpers, and even before Angel confirmed anything, she knew the story about getting bodies from the morgue was bullshit. After she'd seen them all, and thus, made a record of them, she backed out of the airlock and hit the button to close the doors.

"The client lied," Angel announced. "Those people have public records, and they are all employees of Orion Shipping, LLC."

"Let me guess. That's the company that owns this freighter."

"Correct. I'd also like to note that the security footage from the ship's cameras was wiped three days ago."

"So, this evil bastard just sent some of his private mercs onto this ship, killed the crew, and threw them in the airlock for me to dispose of?"

"There's more. It seems that Dun & Briggs, a Callisto-based holding company, is a major shareholder in Orion Shipping. Sir Rodric is on the board."

"He did this to his own ship, his own crew? Angel, can you disable this airlock? I don't want these bodies going anywhere."

"Done. Also, I'm trying to rebuild the deleted data. I don't think enough new camera footage has been recorded to overwrite all the drive sectors. I have the file, and I'll put Fido on the job when he's done on the Sharp Lady. He's already found and deleted three snoopers, by the way."

"Tell him he's a good boy." Juliet turned and stomped toward the central access corridor on the ship. "Guide me to the hold. I guess it should look like I've been fawning over the loot when the pirates show up."

"Do you have a plan regarding the bodies?"

"Yeah, I'm going to shove them down Sir Rodric's throat."

"I know you're being figurative, but . . . how?"

"I'm still thinking about it. Let's see what Fido can turn up. Hmm . . ." She activated her crew comms. "Nick?"

"Yeah?"

"New plan. When you bargain with the pirates, offer them a cut of the cargo. Start at fifty percent, as we'd planned, but tell them you also want this ship. If you have to, bargain down our percentage of the cargo to get them to agree."

"Why do I want—"

"You don't. I do. It's evidence and leverage that we're going to need later."

"If you say so. By the way, my name's Simon."

"Right." As she approached the big, orange-painted cargo doors, they slid open, revealing a cargo hold twice as wide as the *Kowashi*'s and at least three times as deep. It was stacked with dozens of pallets of crates, each labeled with the logo for Callisto Vineyards, with a secondary label that said Jovian Rhapsody Sirrah. "Holy . . . Sir Rodric might be an evil bastard, but he didn't skimp when it came to delivering the goods."

"If the labels on those boxes are accurate, this is more than four million Sol-bits worth of cargo."

"Do you think he'd screw us over by loading fake cargo?"

"His vineyard has several products. These particular bottles retail for one hundred eighty-five Sol-bits. He also sells a vintage with a twenty-six Sol-bit value. He might have relabeled some of his cheaper bottles if he knew he was setting up a decoy."

"Well, it wouldn't be very piratelike of me not to sample the goods."

Juliet walked to the nearest pallet, sliding her vibroblade free of its sheath. She sliced one of the pallet straps, then hefted a case down onto the decking. With her cybernetic hand, she gripped the wooden top of the case and yanked, pulling it open as the nails squealed in protest. "Fancy packing—nails and wood."

"Wine connoisseurs are notoriously rooted in tradition."

Juliet pulled out one of the dark green bottles and, holding it tightly with her tactile glove, drove her vibroblade down into the cork. Once it was deeply inserted, she carefully turned it, rotating the cork up and out. She put her knife away, opened her visor, and sniffed the bottle.

"Wine. At least he didn't fill them with water or something." She took a sip and swallowed it. "Whoa, that's smooth. I think this really is the good stuff."

"Hopefully, he didn't poison the wine so he could wipe out the pirates."

Juliet choked on her second swig, then, when she'd finally swallowed it and stopped sputtering, said, "You might have said that before I drank any!"

"Hopefully, your nanites will save you . . ."

"I'm not poisoned." She set the bottle down atop the crate, then pulled down another to sit on. Again, she opened her comm channel with Nick. "Any sign of 'em?"

"Not yet."

Juliet closed the comms and sat there, stewing. She was furious that she was associated with a corpo backstabber like Sir Rodric. Her mind spun in a million directions, trying to figure out how he'd double-cross her, Nick, and Larry. She had a feeling in her gut that it was coming; there'd be a housecleaning after this job was done if she let it happen. She wouldn't do that, though. She'd have to hang on to all her cards and figure out how to play them. The number one ace would be the daughter, so Juliet knew she had to get her out alive.

She subvocalized, "Sometimes, I think I should have just tried to figure a way to get at Sir Rodric and skipped this job."

"He's a powerful man with sophisticated and multilayered security."

"What about the bug he put in Larry? Couldn't you have used it to piggyback?"

"I highly doubt that information is going directly to Sir Rodric. More likely, a third-party security firm handles that sort of thing for him. We could have traced it to them and then worked to infiltrate their operation. I'm not sure that would be less difficult or dangerous than handling these pirates, though."

"Right. Even then, it wouldn't be a sure thing. The daughter, Antigone, is still the best bet for getting close. I keep second-guessing myself!"

"Stay steady, Juliet. Think of what Jensen or White would do in this situation. Well, not what they'd do, but how they'd act. You've got to stay frosty and keep a tally. This man, Sir Rodric, is starting to rack up a debt with you."

"Damn right, Angel." Juliet loved it when Angel used phrases like "stay frosty and keep a tally." It really did remind her of White. She was trying to think of something else to say, some way they could start to plan for the eventuality of betrayal when she had Antigone in hand, when Nick's voice cut through on the comms.

"Get ready! We got three ships burning this way out of the Junk Belt."

The Junk Belt was a huge band of scrap and derelict, stripped-down ships left behind from a massive conflict near the tail end of the *Takamoto*-Cybergen war in an asteroid group not too far from the Jovian System. It was where Athena was supposedly last seen. Her mainframe was rumored to have been on one of the asteroids. Apparently, nearly eight thousand ships had been lost in the conflict, most of them AI-driven, but plenty with crews. The whole idea gave Juliet the creeps. It made her think of something like a space graveyard full of ghosts, both the human and machine kind.

"How soon?"

"Well, I know I said get ready, but I guess you have some time to kill—they should be here in about ninety minutes. Can you make it look like you were having trouble getting things settled over there?"

"Yeah, that won't be a problem." Juliet shuddered, thinking of all the blood and the bodies piled up in the airlock.

"I'm gonna hail them, try to make a deal before they get here. I'll just tell 'em we'll set the reactor on the cargo ship to blow and bail out if they won't talk nice."

"Now you're sounding like a pirate!" Juliet chuckled, picked up her wine bottle, and left the cargo bay. She meandered the long, quiet hallways, working her way toward the bridge. Her earlier thoughts about ghosts started to get to her, and she kept feeling shivers at the nape of her neck, as though someone was watching her. Every time she passed a blood smear, she felt that queasy knot in her stomach, and she couldn't help picturing the faces of the crew who'd worked the ship.

"Some of those people were young, Angel. I mean the crew of this ship. Some were younger than me!"

"That's true. If what we think happened here really happened, we must think of a way to bring them justice."

"Yeah, I agree." Juliet flopped down in the pilot's acceleration couch when she reached the bridge. "Fido done over there yet?"

"Yes. I'm using the local net to transfer him here."

Juliet thought it was endearing that Angel wouldn't make a copy of Fido. As far as she was concerned, he was an individual, and she wouldn't allow it. "Let me know as soon as he finds something." She reclined for a while, staring at the ceiling, kicking her feet up onto the control panel. Eventually, her anxious mind got the better of her, and she said, "Let me see that pic of the girl again. I mean our target, Antigone."

"Here you go."

Angel displayed the image in a large window on her AUI and labeled it Antigone Barrington. Sir Rodric's daughter was an attractive woman. She had wavy, shoulder-length auburn hair, striking blue eyes, and smooth, lightly tanned skin. She wore a lot of makeup—powder blue around the eyes, rosy cheeks, and glossy pink lips. Her smile was big and genuine, like she'd never been disappointed by anything in her entire life.

She looked like she'd never had to look over her shoulder or worry for a single second. Juliet felt herself starting to hate the woman before she'd even met her.

"I have good news!" Angel interrupted Juliet's stewing. "Fido has found the section of the drive where the deleted footage was written. It hasn't been overwritten, and he's already begun reconstructing it."

"Oh, good. Don't mind me; I was just sitting here thinking about how I'd like to slap this pretty girl who's never had a care in the world."

"Don't lose your empathy, Juliet! Think about why that young woman might have run away from her father. Perhaps she can't stomach him, either. Look into those eyes—does the smile run as deep as it seems?"

Juliet stared at the image some more, really looked into those eyes, and tried to imagine a soul in torment behind them. *Was it possible? Were those fine lines between her brows from scowling? Was she putting on a show, forcing this pleasant face for a photo on her father's publicity page?*

"Damn, Angel. You're getting good at this whole humanity thing. Thanks for reminding me not to judge a book by its cover."

"An apt idiom for today's events—plenty of books will be judged by plenty of people."

31

INTIMIDATION

That's right, she's working on the drive. Should have it operational shortly." Nick's voice was calm—lethargic, even—and Juliet wondered if he'd self-medicated or something before getting on comms with the pirates. She hadn't listened to the whole conversation, but as their ships grew near and the comm light kept flashing, she figured she should know what was going on.

"So why not just be happy with the ship and your lives? We'll take the cargo." The pirate spokesperson had a nasally, somewhat androgynous voice, making it hard for Juliet to picture the speaker.

"I already told you—"

"Yeah, you'll blow the reactor and give us a run for our money. Listen, we're willing to bargain here. After all, you did all the heavy lifting. You willing to follow us back to our base? We'll need to board and put jammers on each ship."

"Yeah, right, so you can put a bullet in the back of my head?"

"Listen, Simon, if we wanted you dead, we'd pop that little ship of yours from here. Think you can outrun some Yamaha Hawks?"

"Angel, what are—?"

"Missiles. Very fast missiles."

Suddenly, Juliet heard and felt a clunk reverberate through the hull, and then a red light flashed on her AUI. Angel spoke up again. "Nick just undocked the Sharp Lady."

"You wanna try me with those missiles? I can promise you that I won't be the only ship to go down."

"Nick, what the hell are you doing?" Juliet asked in their private comm channel.

"Trust me."

"Easy, Simon." The pirate's tone had lost much of its earlier sharpness. "We all want to make some money here. No one needs to get blown to bits. Now, you know how these things go. The crew of that cargo ship didn't want to lose their payload, and now you don't want to lose it. Might makes right out here, though, eh? We recognize talent when we see it. You took out two escorts, and you've got a fast-looking ship there. You popped this little convoy before we even caught wind of it, so yeah, you deserve a cut.

"Now, I just got word from base authorizing me to promise you the ship and twenty-five percent of the proceeds from the payload. We've got the channels to move that stuff, do you?"

"I have your word that me and my partner are cool? No shenanigans? I swear to Christ, if you try to snatch us up, we'll blow both reactors."

"Okay, now, Simon, that's no way to build trust—threatening to blow up ships and getting all suicidal and melodramatic! How about you spool down that drive and let one of us come aboard so we can install a jammer? It's not 'cause we don't like you. It's 'cause we don't trust you. Yet. To answer your question, yes, you have my word. Better, you have Hereford's word; he's the one who authorized the deal."

"All right. What do I need to do?"

"Power down your drive and hold position. We'll EVA someone over to your interceptor after we dock with the cargo ship. We need to make sure you guys are legit, you see? Need to sweep the big ship, confirm the payload, and install the jammers. Patience will go a long way with us right now, Simon."

There was a long pause as "Simon" apparently deliberated the offer. Just before Juliet started to get nervous and prompted him on their private comms, he said, "All right. My partner will meet you at the airlock. Don't do anything stupid—she's a little jumpy."

This time, Juliet spoke up. "Are you trying to get me killed?"

"No. Listen, they need to think we're both on the edge. We just committed mass murder as far as they're concerned, and we need to play the role. I'd rather they're a little nervous and afraid of you than cocky trying to come on board, bossing you around, right? We need to maintain autonomy at their base if we're going to pull this thing off."

"If you say so." Juliet stood up from the pilot's seat and walked down the access corridor away from the bridge. "What airlock are they approaching?"

"The bigger ship is positioning itself near the one I vacated. The starboard one. Their two escorts are flanking me. I just spooled down my drive. Now it's my turn to feel nervous."

"Okay, well, take your own advice: Stay cool."

"We're making the final approach to the docking collar. I hope you and your partner don't try anything stupid, Simon." The pirate didn't sound nervous, speaking again with that sharp, almost angry tone.

Juliet hurried through the ship, still following Angel's guidance on her mini map; the corridors all looked similar, and she hadn't come close to memorizing the layout. With Angel leading the way, though, she got to the airlock ahead of the pirates, and when she felt their ship make contact, she began to regulate her breathing, taking deep, easy breaths, trying to calm her nerves.

Juliet held her auto shotgun before her, sideways, with the barrel pointed down. Still, she had her fast hand on the grip, ready to bring it up and go to town if things seemed off. She stood in front of the inner airlock, about two meters away from the door, and waited, listening. When Angel opened the outer door, she felt the vibration through the plasteel floor plates. While the pressure equalized, she opened her mind and tried to pick up nearby thoughts, much like she'd done back on the cruise ship's restaurant.

. . . better not try anything stupid . . .

If I say shoot, you shoot! Juliet recognized the mental voice of the pirate spokesperson and tried to focus on it, but another one crowded in, making it difficult.

Another day, another chance to get blown to bits. Ain't life grand?

. . . walking into a goddamn floating bomb . . .

. . . wonder what they did with the crew. I hate dealing with hostages . . .

Before Juliet could get back to the spokesperson's thoughts, the inner airlock clicked and began to slide open. She stood there, gun in hand, mirrored visor facing the airlock, and waited, nerves on fire, ready to spring into action. She tried to be cool, tried to steady herself, and the easiest way for her to do that was to think about the coolest operator she'd ever met. Not the toughest, not the meanest—the coolest. The face that came to mind was White's, and it wasn't a happy memory; it was him speaking clinically, slowly, methodically, annihilating a kill squad from two klicks away with his Gauss rifle.

When the pirates stepped out of the airlock, they found her leaning against the wall, the shotgun in hand, watching them through that mirrored visor in the scarred-up baby-blue helmet. She looked bigger than usual in that battle armor, and she was gladder than ever that she hadn't bought it brand new. She looked like someone who'd been through a thing or two, and her posture clearly said she wasn't worried about the four armed individuals who'd just stepped out of the airlock.

"Lacy?" a tall, very thin woman with short red hair asked in a voice that matched that of the spokesperson. Like the other pirates, she didn't wear a helmet, but she was armed, holding a well-used automatic rifle painted in a desert camo pattern. The other three pirates were similarly equipped, and they all had backup weapons, from pistols to sawed-off shotguns.

Juliet didn't speak, not sure when she'd made the decision not to but going with it. She just nodded her helmet and waited.

"Not a big talker, huh? We're going to search the ship." Again, Juliet nodded, then stepped back and gestured down the corridor with the muzzle of her shotgun.

"Just stay cool." The spokesperson nodded to the others, and they all started walking right past Juliet, avoiding looking directly into her mirrored helmet. Had she really intimidated them so much? They were all armed, most had some cybernetic augments visible, and they were notorious pirates! Why were they so stressed out? "Are you going to follow us? I'm Allie, by the way. Well, it's short for Alejandra, but nobody likes to call me my whole name. God, I'm babbling. Anyway, we'll split up to make this faster." She looked over her shoulder at Juliet, who nodded again and began ambling behind the four pirates.

Even if they planned to split up, they had a long corridor to walk down before the first junction. While she kept pace behind them, Juliet focused on the back of Allie's head and opened her mind. When she started to hear her thoughts, she smiled grimly behind her visor.

Why the hell do I feel like I'm about to get canceled? Something about that chick . . . I can feel the ice coming off her. Jesus, I got the heebies just having her behind me.

Allie looked over her shoulder and gave Juliet a nervous smile when her eye, an implant with a heart-shaped iris, made contact with her visor. She quickly turned away.

Juliet was about to try to tune back into her thoughts when Nick spoke up on their private channel. "That pirate just contacted me. Wanted to know if you ever talk."

"Tell her I don't. It's intimidating the hell out of them." Juliet was torn between focusing on her silent, deadly, White-inspired persona and laughing as she spoke to Nick. She clamped down on the humor and kept her focus.

"Uh, all right, but don't push 'em too far. No need to start a gunfight . . ."

"I'm not an idiot." As Juliet spoke, they came to the first intersection, and the pirates broke into three groups. Two went left, one went right, and Allie pointed ahead to the lift.

"Can you show me the cargo, Lacy?"

Juliet nodded and also pointed to the lift, indicating that she'd follow Allie. The woman frowned, highlighting a deep scar at the corner of her mouth, but nodded and stepped onto it. Juliet followed, and when they were both aboard, she pushed the button for the cargo level.

"So, I get that you don't talk much, but can you?" When Juliet didn't answer, Allie looked away then quickly said, in a tone nothing like the acerbic one she'd used over comms, "They have implants for that, if it's an injury or something . . ."

Again, Juliet didn't speak, and Allie got quiet. When the lift stopped, she was quick to exit while Juliet followed her, pointing the way toward the cargo bay.

While they walked, she tried to listen some more to the woman's surface thoughts.

God, blood everywhere! She massacred them? Her tone changed, and Juliet recognized the difference she'd heard before when someone went from thinking to themselves to subvocalizing. *Anyone find any bodies?*

"Did, um, did you kill the crew? Any prisoners we need to know about?" She looked at Juliet, watching as Juliet shook her head.

"Um, no prisoners? Or no, you didn't kill them? Shit, let me just ask a simple yes or no: Are they all dead?"

Juliet nodded. Allie turned away quickly, speeding her steps, and then Nick spoke through comms again. "She wants to know where the bodies are. Wants to know what was wrong with the ship, why we didn't take off before they arrived."

"Tell her the bodies are in the airlock, but it's not working. Tell her the drive had a software lockout I had to get through." Juliet tapped Allie's shoulder, and the woman flinched but turned to look at her. Juliet pointed to the junction ahead, then to the left, and Allie nodded, hurrying forward. "Her nerves are shot. I don't think these guys are going to mess with me."

"She just asked me if you're a psycho and if she needs to worry about you murdering people at their base. Said something about them being criminals, but not lunatics."

"Good."

"This is all very interesting to me, Juliet," Angel interjected. "Your equipment, your silence, and the state of this ship all add up to an intimidating image, but I feel like there's something more to it. We've speculated that your latent psionic talents—you know, your 'gut feelings'—might be impacted by the lattice. We know it enhances how you perceive people's intentions and certainly their thoughts. We also know that it allows you to project psionic energy in the case of your burgeoning telekinetic abilities. Do you think there's any possibility that you're projecting your intended persona, your mood?"

"Maybe, Angel. I was listening to her thoughts, and she said she could 'feel ice' coming from me."

"Well, don't push it too far. Some people, when driven to a panic, will respond with violence rather than fear."

"Don't worry." Juliet watched Allie stop before the orange cargo door, then stepped forward and pressed her palm to the lock. The door hissed open, revealing the massive cargo of wine pallets.

"Holy shit! Your partner wasn't lying!" Allie beelined for the two boxes Juliet had taken off the pallet and fished around in the open crate. She lifted one of the wine bottles, whistled softly, and asked, "They're all like this?" She looked at Juliet for an answer but frowned when all she got was a shrug. "Can't you just message my PAI or something? I hate playing charades."

"Okay, Angel. Let her know we think all the wine is the same, but we only opened those two crates."

"Ah, better. Thanks." Allie nodded and sat down on a crate, her eyes going distant as she did something on her AUI. Juliet tried to listen in to her thoughts.

. . . a really nice score. Lots of good wine; should be easy to move outside the Jovian System . . . Uh, yeah, I guess she's good muscle, but I think we should just deal through the other guy. Let him handle her. She gives me the willies . . . Roger.

"Okay, Lacy, you can fly this thing? We've got our jammers installed." Juliet nodded, and the woman frowned, her eyes narrowing in her hard-boned, narrow face. Juliet could tell she was working herself up to something. "Listen, I know you're a hard case. We get it. There's a lot of tough assholes at our base, though, and if you try anything stupid, you're gonna get put down. Understand?"

Juliet waited a solid five seconds before she nodded again.

"Good. Hey, let me get a look at your face. Do you mind? My boss is going to be pissed if I don't at least confirm you're . . . Ah, hell, I don't know what. I just want to look into your eyes once. Can you humor me?"

Juliet stepped toward the smaller woman, still trying to project that icy demeanor she'd seen in White when he went into combat mode. When she stood right in front of her, looming over her in her combat armor, she reached up and touched the side of her helmet, sending the visor up and back. She glared down at Allie, her weird, black eyes with their golden star irises locking onto hers. Rather than play the mute any longer, she growled, in the raspiest voice she could muster, "This what you wanted?"

Her words sent a visible shiver of shocked surprise through the other woman, and she took a rapid step back. "Yeah. Yeah, that does it. Thanks." She turned and started toward the door as though she couldn't get away fast enough. Juliet touched her helmet, sending the visor back down, then followed behind her, listening as the other woman spoke aloud into her comms. "Meet me at the airlock. We're escorting these two ships to base."

Juliet walked behind her as she went, contemplating what Angel had said about her projecting a kind of feeling toward the people around her. Was it possible? Was it another facet of the psionic lattice, another thing it amplified? It was no secret that a person's mood could have a palpable effect on the people around him or her. Was the lattice amplifying it? Was it taking Juliet's feelings about White when he was in stone-cold killer mode and somehow sending those chilling thoughts and images into the minds of the people around her? Was it even something she could control? Perhaps she'd never noticed it before because, when it came down to it, Juliet was someone who tried to make the people around her comfortable.

She'd certainly butted heads with a few people since she'd gotten the lattice, but by and large, she got along pretty well with most people. Looking back at her time on the *Kowashi*, when she'd first taken the job from Shiro, though, she remembered when she'd "channeled" Ghoul and how effective that had been. She remembered dealing with the pirates on that icy rock of a moon and how the crew had treated her differently after that. Had she been affecting people's feelings more overtly than she'd thought? It was certainly something to bear in mind going forward, something to be cognizant of.

She watched silently as the four pirates departed through the airlock, and then she went to the bridge and took the pilot's seat.

"Well, it went okay on my end," she announced in her private channel with Nick. "How about you?"

"Yeah, all good. Jammers are installed, and I've got my nav computer synced up with the pirates' main ship. They want you to do the same."

"Angel?" Juliet was sure she could figure out how to do it, but that was something most pilots would leave to a PAI anyway.

"Locked in and ready to go. Drive's warming up."

"Okay, Simon." Juliet chuckled, using the fake name. "We're locked in. Tell them my drive will be ready in about ninety seconds."

"Okay, Lacy. Buckle up; we're heading into the lion's den."

32

\\\\\\\\\\\\\\\\\\\\\\\\\\\

HOME OF THE VENGEANCE

The Junk Belt was a lot different in person than Juliet had imagined. True, it was filled with thousands of derelict, stripped ships, hundreds of thousands of pieces of destroyed vessels, and just as many asteroids, large and small. However, they were all a lot further apart than she'd envisioned.

Flying through the debris wasn't difficult, especially as she'd matched her ship's navigation to the pirate guide ship. Even with the distance between objects often being measured in kilometers rather than meters, there was enough interference in the belt to make scanning difficult, and plenty of large bodies floating around to make hiding easy. In short, it was a good place for pirates to evade scrutiny, especially considering the transient, orbiting nature of the belt—nothing stayed in one place for any length of time.

Some derelict ships they flew past were enormous, great dreadnoughts that would have given the *Sunset Star Runner* a run for its money, size-wise. It was one of those massive plasteel skeletons that the pirate ship finally approached, signaling Juliet and Nick to slow down and precisely follow its guidance. Juliet carefully nudged the controls, trusting Angel to fine-tune her input, ensuring a perfect replication of the guide ship's navigation. It banked around and underneath the hulking derelict.

It was stripped—on the outside, at least—down to the plasteel alloy frame. No armor panels, weapons, sensor arrays, or insignias remained to indicate what navy it had once belonged to.

As they drew near, the guide ship began to look smaller and smaller in the shadow of the massive ship skeleton. It approached a big, dark void on the underside, flew into it, and as Juliet followed, they entered an enormous hollow section where steady, red LED lighting strips guided them into makeshift docks built onto the ship's skeleton.

Juliet saw dozens of interceptors docked in the big cavelike hollow and quite a few larger vessels, some as big as the cargo transport she was piloting. Even they looked tiny in the hollowed-out void of the ancient dreadnought.

"The guide ship has transmitted docking instructions. The space they've given us is barely large enough to accommodate this ship's hull. Shall I handle the minute adjustments?"

Angel's question wasn't unusual; most pilots would take some help from automated AI scripts for docking, especially in tight quarters or with other ships. Matching trajectory, velocity, and spin wasn't always trivial. Juliet didn't take offense.

"Yes, please." As she nudged the ship toward the docking collar, clearly built-up and welded onto the derelict frame where once upon a time, crew passages and living spaces used to exist, she felt Angel take control of the maneuvering thrusters, carefully, precisely, bringing the ship's starboard docking collar against the dock's. With a gentle rumble through the hull, she felt it clamp on, and then she killed the drive and breathed out a sigh.

"Okay, time to see if we have a kill squad waiting for us on the other side of the airlock."

"I'm holding the airlock securely shut until you're ready."

"Good. I know we're going to bluff about having a deadman's switch on the reactor, but I wouldn't mind actually blowing this ship if they try to kill me. Can you do it?"

"Yes! I wasn't aware that you were simply bluffing. I've rewritten the software safety protocols on the reactor, and I can easily cause a meltdown, as you and Nick mentioned."

"Oh." Juliet frowned, wondering where the communication breakdown had occurred. Had she just assumed Angel understood her impression of the plan as she'd discussed it with Nick? "Yeah, from context, I was pretty sure Nick didn't know how to rig such a thing and was just planning to use it as a threat. I guess it's good to know the option is real. Thanks, Angel."

While they spoke, Juliet hurried from the bridge and through the dim corridors of the ship toward the airlock. As she went, she refused to let herself look away from the many dried blood smears on the floor where bodies had been dragged. She wanted to keep that crime fresh in her mind; a reminder of what her end goal was. She didn't want just to rescue Antigone Barrington and deliver her. She needed to bring the crew of this ship some justice and remove Sir Rodric as a threat to her and Nick in the process. "And Larry and his little girl."

"Pardon?"

"I'm just reminding myself that this mission isn't only about rescuing some princess, rich girl from her own mess." Juliet saw an alert on her AUI indicating that someone had requested access to the airlock. "They're waiting, huh?"

"Yes. I hope you don't have to threaten them with a reactor meltdown; I think it will make your stay here combative and hinder your rescue attempts."

"Well, it's a last resort. Let's see how they behave first." As she approached the airlock, her armored boots encased in magnetic soles click-clomping on the metal floor, Juliet tried to calm herself, tried to focus her mind and get back into her role of the stone-cold killer.

"I'm receiving several ping requests and attempts to establish a comm channel. Shall I accept? I'll keep it walled off; you won't have to worry about daemons."

"Okay. I guess it's time for Lacy to communicate a little more." As she spoke, Juliet saw the new channel pop up on her AUI with the label "Allie." Almost immediately, it lit up, and she heard the pirate's voice in her ears.

"I figured since you can speak when you want to, we might as well have an open channel. It'll make things less . . . stressful as we get you up to speed on how things work around here."

Juliet thought about her response, letting the silence hang awkwardly for a moment, and decided to keep up her verbal reticence. "Okay."

"Listen, you understand you're a guest here for now, yeah? Don't do anything stupid or violent, and make sure you keep cool. If you can manage all that, we'll get along fine. Your partner has indicated that he might be interested in working with the Vengeance, and if you're of a similar mind, you need to understand that you're on massive probation. One wrong step, and we'll space you. Are we clear?"

"Clear." Juliet did her best to make her voice rough and hoarse, for some reason having decided that Lacy not only didn't enjoy speaking but found it difficult.

"Good. Now, open the airlock for our boarding team. They're going to scour that ship a little better and get that cargo off. I've given them my map of the layout, so just stay out of their way." Juliet had been expecting that. Nick had already made the arrangement with Allie while they traveled to the Junk Belt.

Rather than respond, she pressed her hand to the airlock biolock and opened it. She still wore her helmet and still had her shotgun hanging from its sling in front of her.

When the door slid open, there were five men and women waiting, all of them armed, some wearing armor, and most with noticeable cybernetic enhancements, from chromed-out power arms to bulging, infected optical implants, to a guy with something that looked like a grenade launcher attached to his shoulder. Much of their gear was mismatched, but they looked ready to use those guns.

In fact, the three men in the front lifted their rifles, pointing them at Juliet as they stepped out of the airlock. "Permission to board?" one of them sneered.

Juliet ignored him and didn't lift her gun. She watched him, implacable and silent behind her mirrored visor, and when his taunt failed to get a rise out of her, he walked past. Three of the others followed after him, hurrying down the corridor, leaving one slender man behind.

He wore a faded, torn, and patched gray jumper with the logo AstroLabs Inc. over his left breast pocket. Around his waist was a gun belt with an ancient-looking .45 caliber, semiautomatic holstered at his hip.

"Ahem. Hello there. I'm a synthetic person, and the fine folk of Hereford's Vengeance have given me the designation Trashcan. I've been instructed to acquaint you with the unrestricted sections of the base."

Juliet gave the man—synth—a double take, surprised by his pronouncement. At first glance, he didn't look like a synth, but then, his jumper covered most of his body. His face and expressions were very lifelike, but that wasn't such a big deal; her arm was incredibly lifelike, too. It probably helped that the synth-skin was alive.

"Nice to meet you, Trashcan. Um, forgive me, but is that name okay with you?"

"I would like to interject and say that it's certainly not okay with me!" Angel didn't sound happy.

"Well, ma'am, I know the word isn't meant to be complimentary, but I'm happy for my continued existence and position of respected duty and limited trust here among the Vengeance. For that reason, I accept my moniker with pride!" As he spoke, Trashcan stood up straight, almost like a military attention stance. He had short blond hair, smoothed back with some sort of gel, and though his face was smeared and smudged with grease and grime, he was pleasant enough with a friendly smile and well-worn laugh lines at the corners of his eyes.

"All right. Lead the way."

"Pardon, but as we walk through the docking corridor, I'll fill you in on a few rules." He turned and began to lead the way out of the ship, taking slow, measured steps.

"No problem."

"One, you'll be scanned for hardware that might broadcast a signal strong enough to get past the jammers protecting the base. Two, you may keep your weapons, but any violence must be verified as self-defense or performed to cease another person's hostility. If such verification cannot be obtained from witnesses or surveillance equipment, you will be summarily executed." He paused to look at Juliet, clearly awaiting a reaction.

"Okay."

"Three, you are on strict probation and are not permitted to traverse non-public sections of the base. The Five have made this quite easy by marking off-limits sections with warning beacons, and also, in the event you lack the intelligence to understand or ability to receive warning beacons, they've painted the floors at the entrances to such sections red." Juliet definitely detected some snark in Trashcan's tone.

"Trashcan, can I call you TC?"

"TC is a nickname that a few others have used in reference to me. I don't mind it." He paused before the docking corridor's airlock door and turned toward her. "Do you have any questions?"

"Yeah, am I free to leave whenever I want?"

"No, I'm afraid you'll need clearance from our port authority."

"You have a port authority? How many people live on this base?"

"That's classified information, Lacy. Do you mind if I call you Lacy? I'll tell you there are probably more people here than you imagined. We have a port authority because there are many docking areas and many ships that call this base home. We must maintain some authority, or there would be collisions and fights over berths."

"You can call me Lacy." Juliet folded her arms over her chest, her shotgun hanging below them. "How hard is it to get clearance?"

"Not hard! If you aren't grounded by the Five, you'll get clearance rapidly."

"The Five? Can you explain them to me?"

"The infamous Five? You haven't heard of Hereford's Pirate Council? There's Captain John Hereford, Captain Ura Glasseye, Captain Roy Tornado, Captain Shinzo Hara, and Captain Mary Moon. They make all the operating decisions for the Vengeance pirates, and they're revered by those who call this base home. Why, the Five have kept us safe from corporate raids, military gambits, deceitful bounty hunters, devious—"

"I get it, TC. We love the Five. Okay, where can I get some grub?" Juliet figured a central dining area would be an ideal place to gather some intel.

"There's a mercantile district adjacent to this port cavity. You'll find brokers of all sorts, including those selling meals."

"Really? So they've made a sort of town on this old wreck? The interior is airtight?"

"Naturally! The external presentation of the Hereford's Vengeance base is for subterfuge alone." He leaned close and held a hand to the side of his mouth, whispering hoarsely, "You might be surprised at what this old derelict can do." As he took his hand down, he winked in an exaggerated, deliberate attempt to convey that a secret was being divulged.

"And my partner?"

"You're free to communicate with him. Our jammers prevent wireless transmission outside the base, but within, you should be fine." He turned back toward the door, lifting his hand to the keypad. "Ready?"

"Sure."

"Okay, remember to stand still in the red box until the light turns green."

With that, TC punched in a code, and the door whirred open. He stepped through, and Juliet followed, finding herself in a massive rectangular space that looked like something out of an old sci-fi vid. She imagined the room was about fifty meters by a hundred with a solid—if patchwork—plasteel floor. The walls and ceiling, however, were full of holes, with exposed cables hanging here and there, many of them apparently live with electricity, trailing sparks, and crackling as they shifted and swung in the air. Luckily, they were high above anyone's head—the ceiling had to be another hundred meters up, and Juliet could see catwalks and doorways lining the tall walls.

People were all over the place, pushing cargo carts, using power tools on exposed machinery and conduits, or simply loitering about, watching others coming out of the weirdly chaotic docking tunnels. Juliet's tunnel was on the ground, but she could see others to her left and right, and some were meters off the ground like they'd been squeezed in wherever possible.

All that took a back seat when she noticed the massive auto turrets lined up on the far end of the space, one of them aimed squarely at her. She almost jumped for cover, but then she saw she was standing in a red square and that a small light, recessed into the plasteel floor, was blinking red.

"Don't move, ma'am," TC warned again, also standing quite still. "We're being scanned for transmission hardware. Make sure your PAI accepts the connection request."

"Angel . . ."

"They want to scan my database and the storage in your data port for, well, essentially for what they'd consider malware—rootkits, spy daemons, beacon worms, network sniffers, etc. Don't worry, Juliet, I have confidence that I'll be able to keep our secrets well walled off."

"If you're sure . . ."

"If Grave couldn't get past me with the watchdog installation, there's no way a scan from these pirates will be a problem."

"Okay." Juliet stood there, nervously watching that autocannon's huge barrels, wondering what kind of ordinance it fired. They wouldn't shoot massive cannon rounds in here, would they? Wouldn't it wreck the whole port? No, she figured it was loaded with antipersonnel rounds—something that would turn her body into a fine, red paste but only scratch and dent the plasteel. After more than two long, sweat-inducing minutes under the scrutiny of the pirates' scanner, the red light finally flickered to green.

"Congratulations, Lacy! You've been cleared." TC turned and bowed formally. "Welcome to the base! Always abide by the golden rule: A pirate's life is best, and corpo scum should be shot on sight."

"That's not the golden . . ." Juliet sighed and decided it wasn't worth it. "Can you show me where to go to get to the, uh, mercantile district?"

"Follow me, please." With that, TC turned on his heel and began to march toward the distant autocannons and the automated doors behind them. Juliet walked behind him, shotgun sideways, hands resting on its frame, trying to broadcast a lack of hostility. Still, she cut an imposing figure, and many people in the docking junction gave her long looks as she clicked her way through.

She'd made it almost to the door when it dawned on her that her magnets weren't engaging, that there was gravity.

"Holy shit, TC, does this old derelict have a gravity generator?"

"I'm afraid that's classified information." He turned and winked obnoxiously at her.

"Angel, is that possible?"

"This ship likely predates the end of the *Takamoto*-Cybergen war. It's certainly possible that one of the true AIs involved in the conflict helped one faction or another to equip their larger ships with gravity generation systems. The surprising part is that it would still be intact after all these years, what with the fortune-seeking salvagers who've picked the Junk Belt clean over the decades."

"I guess it's as big or bigger than that cruise liner we were on."

"Significantly larger. The pirates' jamming devices on the cargo ship prevented me from making detailed scans, but judging from visuals alone, I'd estimate this ship to be more than two kilometers long from bow to stern. It's likely almost half that wide and tall. Juliet, if this is one of the old Cybergen dreadnoughts, it could have had a crew numbering in the tens of thousands."

"Wow." Juliet followed TC through a few winding, branching corridors in various states of repair, from a skeletal framework that felt like it was about to collapse to nearly pristine stretches where the lights were steady and bright. Still, her helmet indicated that the air quality and pressure were constant, and she began to wonder if she should take it off. Remembering her role, however, she kept it on. It wasn't like she was the only one wearing a helmet in the place.

They passed people in all manner of dress, from shirtless, greasy technicians working on conduit lines to a short man wearing a full battle exo-suit jogging purposefully in the direction of the docks.

When they entered the mercantile district, Juliet had to, again, reassess her expectations for what the pirate base would be like. Actual storefronts were set up in a big open area with a living atrium at the center. Everything was dirty and used-looking, but the patchwork diamatex, plastiglass, and plain-old glass panels surrounding the atrium allowed the false sunlight through, exposing the green of the foliage. That, combined with the neon lighting on the storefronts, gave the whole thing a sort of surreal, movie-set quality.

She couldn't put her finger on it, but it felt almost like a scene out of a VR game. People lingered around talking in groups, playing holo games on tables, eating street food, and carrying their purchases to and fro. It was like an underground, secret pirate mall, and Juliet couldn't wrap her head around it. She supposed if you were wanted in every polite jurisdiction, you had to make a place to live, a place to be human, where the laws of the corpos couldn't touch you.

Her opinion of the pirates and their society changed a little as she took in the space and the hundreds of people living their lives, including children playing on a dingy, refurbished jungle gym.

"This is mercantile district four," TC announced, waving his hand toward the cavernous chamber and the storefronts surrounding the weird little atrium.

"How many are there? On the base, I mean?"

"Five in total, but this is the largest."

"Angel," Juliet subvocalized, "can you contact Nick and tell him where to meet us? I think this is going to be a bigger job than I thought."

33

INTELLIGENCE HUNT

Juliet sat at one of the tables in the mercantile district of the pirate base. It was a shoddy, rough affair, with benches built from scrap hull plating. The table's uneven legs gave it a wobble that made setting a drink down something of a risky affair. Nick was on his way, having just met with one of the representatives of the Five to go over the specifics of their cut of the wine they'd pirated. TC stood nearby, eyes vacant, doing something either online or in his own head while he waited for Juliet to ask him for information or directions.

She'd spent time with Bradbury on the *Kowashi*, and even he, with his mismatched, obviously mechanical parts, never acted so much like a machine as TC did when he wasn't actively engaged in a conversation. Watching his blank stare and motionless body, her curiosity got the better of her. "What are you doing right now, TC?"

"Hmm? Pardon me, was I inattentive? I create dream-rig scenarios in my spare time and sell them on Dream Hub."

"You're creating a DR scenario right now? Standing here?"

"Yes. This one is an adult-rated noir mystery with a few love interests for the player. The murder case is only half the plot; the real replay value lies in unlocking various sexual conquests."

"Seriously?"

"Oh, very seriously. I've tried selling scenarios without adult content, but they're not nearly as popular."

"Intriguing." Angel sounded more than intrigued to Juliet.

"You're not going to start making DR scenarios to sell on the nets, are you?" Juliet subvocalized.

"I wouldn't mind knowing what nets he's marketing them on . . ."

Juliet decided to humor her and asked, "You sell 'em on the Jovian pub net?"

"Dream Hub is propagated on all of the major pub nets. If I post a scenario for sale on the Jovian one, it will make its way to Luna, Earth, Mars, Saturn, etcetera."

"I had no idea. I don't really spend much time in DR scenarios, mostly just piloting practice."

"Well, you must have a busy and fulfilling life. Most of the people here at Vengeance Base spend a significant portion of their meager earnings in the DR lounge, trying to escape the ugly realities of their lives."

"Jeez, TC, nice bleak image."

"Yo, Lacy!"

Juliet turned to see Nick approaching, making his way around the weird little atrium at the center of the open market.

"This is the companion you awaited?" TC perked up and turned to watch Nick approach. When he was close to the table, the synth held out a hand. "Hello, sir, I'm a synthetic person, and it will be my pleasure to help you and your partner acquaint yourselves with the base. My designation is Trashcan, but you may call me TC as your partner prefers."

"Seriously?" Nick took TC's hand and looked at Juliet. "The pirates have hospitality synths?"

"Access to the base is infrequently granted to new members, and the Five have found that, in some cases, it helps to avoid trouble if they provide a liaison like myself."

"In some cases?" Juliet prompted.

"When violence or distrust is anticipated."

"Hah! I can see why they assigned you to Lacy first." Nick winked at Juliet, but his grin faded when she didn't respond, and he couldn't see her expression behind the mirrored visor of her helmet. "Ahem. Well? What's the room and board situation around here?"

"Sir, every square centimeter of this base is claimed by individuals with a license from the Five or by the Five themselves for future expansion of their operations. If you wish to sleep in a space other than your ship, you'll need to speak to one of the members with rooms to spare on their ships."

"Oh? There aren't any living quarters on the base?" Nick straddled the bench across from Juliet.

"There are, but they're in use by the Five and their crews."

"Well," Nick's voice sounded in Juliet's ears as he began subvocalizing into their encrypted comms, "what do you think of this guy? Should we ditch the tour guide?"

Juliet locked eyes with him. "Depends on if we need any more guidance around here. Any idea how we're going to find this chick among hundreds or, shit, maybe thousands of pirates?"

"Let me see here . . ." Nick switched to verbalizing and turned to TC. "Hey, if I wanted to look up an old contact in this place, is there any way to figure out if he's here?"

"As you might guess, the people who call this base their home don't exactly tend to sign a guest book or anything like that." TC's voice dripped snark, and Juliet, for the millionth time, wondered how much a synth's personality was acquired and real, and how much was just a programmed algorithm of behavioral quirks.

"Come on, Trashcan. I bet the Five know exactly who's on their base at any given moment."

"Of course, but they have a covenant with the captains and crews of the Vengeance collective. They'd never betray that confidence."

Nick nodded, recognizing when to drop the subject before it became suspicious. "Right. Makes sense. I guess I'll just hang around and hope my old buddy and I cross paths. Maybe some of the other folks around here know him."

"Hey, TC." Juliet stood from the table. "We're probably good for now. If you have other things you want to do, I'll just send you a message if we need something."

"Are you certain? I was instructed to provide assistance during the entirety of your first day on base."

"Well, technically, you still will be; I'll message you with any questions."

"Very well." He gave Juliet a long, measuring look, and she wondered what was going through his synth-brain. "Please remember to abide by the rules." With that, he turned and walked like a man with places to be, beelining it out of the mercantile district.

"What was that all about?" Nick asked.

Juliet replied, but she did so through their private comms, keeping her helmet's external speaker off. "I had a hard time maintaining my Lacy persona with that guy. It's like my brain can't wrap itself around the idea of putting on a fake act for someone with no animosity or hidden agenda. I suppose that's prejudiced, though—I have no idea how complex the motivations for a synth can get."

"Perhaps it's your inability to interact psionically with a nonliving being. Your 'gut' may have a blind spot where beings like TC are concerned."

Angel's words sparked a twinge of panic in Juliet, and she wondered if she'd royally messed up by not maintaining Lacy's reticence and silence with the synth. *Could he have ulterior motives? What a stupid question! Of course!*

Before she could berate herself further, Nick interrupted her train of thought.

"Well," he said softly; he'd probably left his helmet in his ship, and he didn't generally like to subvocalize, "one thing I've found helps when dealing with synths is just to forget you know they aren't real. Treat 'em like people, 'cause otherwise, they'll end up surprising you."

"Yeah, I'm sure you're right. I probably messed that one up." Juliet sighed, trying to review everything she'd said to TC, but she gave up. There wasn't much she could do about it now. "Back on the subject at hand, though, I need to get access to the secure net in this place so I can hack it. Not sure how else I'll find Antigone."

This time, Nick subvocalized, "Well, the place isn't that big! How about we just spend some time walking around the public areas with our PAIs scanning faces? We might get lucky."

"Sure." Juliet gestured toward one of the main corridors leading away from the dingy, neon-lit square. "Need to explore a bit anyway if I'm gonna find an access point."

She led the way, and while walking, Juliet kept one hand on her shotgun, standing tall and glaring around through her mirrored visor. She wasn't trying to start trouble with her demeanor; she told herself she was just trying to avoid trouble with the many, many desperate, dirty, and sometimes outright hostile-looking denizens of the base. Nick followed behind her, off to the side a little so she could easily turn to see his facial expressions as he kept up a softly spoken running commentary about the people they passed by.

"Looks like he could use a solid night's sleep . . . Good night! Did you get a load of that woman's implant? Her neck had to have been forty centimeters long! What's even the point of that? . . . Whoa! Look at that sign, "Docking

Bay Three." How big is this damn place? I bet all the bays aren't as big as the one we docked in, though."

Between comments, Nick repeatedly took hits off his Nikko-vape, and Juliet smirked, sure that his nervous chatter and frequent vape usage were due to stress.

"Nick, once we get a little intel, I'm gonna have you go spend some time on your ship. You should be ready to bail when I get the princess in hand."

"So, what are you thinking when it comes to that?" Nick asked, speaking normally as he kept his side of the conversation innocuous.

"I think I need that cargo ship for what I've got planned, and I want to spend some time with Antigone, so I'll take her with me on it. If the pirates don't want us to leave, they might try to blow the ship or send pursuit, which is why it will be nice to have you ready to rock and roll in the Sharp Lady."

Nick stopped, reached out to grab her shoulder, and when she turned to him, he stared into her mirrored visor. "Are you nuts?" he growled, then switched to forceful subvocalizations that contracted and expanded his throat almost comically. "The plan was to get the hell out of Dodge in the Sharp Lady! She's fast, and I can outfly anyone I know when it comes to evasion, but if you think I can defend your fat whale of a cargo ship against dozens of interceptors and God knows what else, you better think again!"

"Okay, noted. Obviously, I'm still gathering intel, but this is my half of the job, remember? Leave it to me to figure it out. I won't ask you to do anything impossible. Deal?"

"Yeah. I guess. Deal." Nick didn't sound convinced, and his eyes said he was about to lose it, so Juliet let the matter drop, turning and continuing down the rough access corridor, following a hand-painted sign to "Sharkey's Swap 'n Sell." Nick continued to suck on his vape furiously, keeping pace with her as they passed by individuals and groups of people who wouldn't have looked out of place in the slums near the ABZ in Phoenix.

Juliet had to admit that she'd had a very flawed mental image of what the pirate base would be like. She'd figured there'd be a hundred or two desperate criminals hanging around planning their next heist. Instead, she'd already passed more than a thousand people—Angel was building a database of scanned faces—many of whom were children and men and women who looked more like starved vagrants than hardened criminals. Using her audio implants to their full ability, Angel also cataloged and subtitled the conversations around her as she passed through.

Of course, Juliet was busy navigating the strange network of mismatched passageways, but she occasionally glanced at the text streaming through the window where Angel transcribed what she heard. People were talking about just about anything she could imagine, but a few themes seemed to predominate the topics: what people would eat next, how much they hated corporations, and rumors about raids. Nobody she'd yet passed by was planning their "next big score."

After a while, she voiced her thoughts. "These people are barely scraping by, and they don't strike me as criminal masterminds."

"Yeah. It's like walking through the slums of Callisto. No different. There might be gangs in those neighborhoods, but most people are just trying to make it through next week." Nick's picture of Callisto's slums sounded like Tucson or Phoenix to Juliet. She knew the colonies had gangs and crime, but she still had a romantic view of the domed cities. When she was forced to face that dirty underbelly, she found the taste of it bitter and disappointing.

"I hate corps."

"You blame them for all this trouble?" Nick's voice told her he'd put on his devil's advocate hat.

"C'mon, Nick. Don't mess with me right now. You know the disparity between the haves and have-nots gets worse every day. The corpos have one goal: increase the bottom line. Humanity has suffered as a result."

"Humanity made the corporations."

"Damn it, Nick." Juliet paused and whirled on him. "Can we have a philosophical debate later?"

"I'm glad you have that helmet on 'cause you haven't called me Simon even once since I got here." He grinned and sucked on his vape, no doubt proud of himself for getting a rise out of her. "Hey, I'll let it drop, but consider this; these people—well, maybe not the kids, but the adults around here are on a pirate base for a reason. I mean, there are plenty of places to be poor where you don't have to live in the middle of a Junk Belt cut off from society . . ."

"We don't know their stories." Juliet scowled, annoyed that she'd had to get the last word in but glad Nick let her by not responding. After asking directions at a junction where she couldn't find another arrow pointing toward the Swap 'n Sell, she found herself back on track when a big orange faux-neon sign at the next junction announced "S & S" with an arrow pointing to the right.

On the way, they'd passed several junctions with red paint on the floor, and Angel marked her map with skull and crossbones, indicating the off-limits beacons. Juliet was starting to think she'd have to infiltrate one of those areas to gain access to the pirates' net, but she wanted to do a lot more surveillance first.

The Swap 'n Sell turned out to be a collection of base denizens set up in booths, tables, or simple floormats, trying to off-load their wares. It was an ample space that, if Juliet were guessing, might have once been a mess hall for the original crew of the massive ship, likely one of many if Angel's information about its crew size were accurate.

Like most of the areas in the base, the lighting was dim, provided by multicolored LED bulbs and occasional neon signs near some of the more permanent-looking booths. One such merchant with a sign announcing his little shop as "Sharkey's" had a prominent space at the center of the hall, with three long tables arranged in a U shape.

Juliet walked toward it, noting his many goods on display and how they seemed a cut above his neighbors' merchandise. She saw everything from high-end decks to ocular implants to boxes of explosive, nine-millimeter rounds.

"Angel, can you message TC and ask him if he can tell us anything about Sharkey?"

"One moment."

"Nick, let me do a little snooping around. Meet you by those tables where that guy's selling pretzels."

"Yeah, all right."

While she waited for Angel to get a hold of TC, Juliet walked over to the prominent central booth and began to peruse the wares. Some of the items were intriguing, and she might have been tempted to buy them, but she mostly tried to snoop, listening to the conversations around her. She picked up a machete-size vibroblade and turned it over in her hands, looking at every part of it while she listened to the diminutive bald proprietor talk to a stocky blue-haired woman wearing a baggy yellow jumpsuit.

". . . says we're off the hook when it comes to Royal Chemical. Talk about a close one, though."

"Eh, you know Mary owns at least two people on their board, and there's no way they'd be able to get together any kind of response force without forcing a vote."

"She does? No, but that explains a lot . . ."

"Yeah, she's connected. Not as connected as Hereford, but between them and the others, the Five have us pretty well covered."

"Shit, Shark, I wish you'd told us that yesterday! I was sweating into my bunk all night. Didn't catch a wink."

"Hey, baby girl. You know I'm not gonna let my crew get into anything that's gonna bring heat down on this base. Think I want to see you all spaced? Think I want to give up my shares? Nah, the penalty is a bit too harsh to mess about . . ." Juliet could feel his attention shift to her as he trailed off. "You need help with that, doll? Looking for something special?"

Juliet turned her gaze away from the big vibroblade, and from behind her mirrored visor, she rasped, "Bold of you to assume I'm a doll."

The heavyset woman barked a laugh. "Come on, sweetie. That armor might be heavy-duty, but we can see those curves. What you hiding under that helmet for, anyway? Somebody cut you up bad?"

Juliet thought it was interesting that the woman jumped to that conclusion as a reason for hiding her face. She supposed they wanted her to lift it to satisfy their curiosity. Instead, she shook her head and, still trying to sound hoarse, lowered her voice. "Don't trust this air."

"Well, this old ship's been modified to hell and back, and sure, some of the areas have some dodgy welds, but this central location's damn near as solid as you can get outside a diamatex dome." Sharkey gestured to the vibroblade. "Gonna buy it? I got a case for it that'll strap to the little D-rings on your thigh, there."

"I have a response from TC," Angel interjected.

"Hold it a sec," she replied, then more loudly, so Angel would know to unmute her helmet, "Let me think about it. Not sure I like a vibroblade this big." She set it back on the table and tapped the smaller knife on her wrist. "Used to something a little smaller."

"Oh shit, Shark! I think she's flirting with you!" the red-faced woman chortled, slapping a meaty palm on the table.

"Oh, brother!" Juliet groaned, and as the words came out in her normal voice, she was thankful, as always, for Angel's intelligence; she'd muted the helmet's output. As the woman and Sharkey both continued to stare at her, chuckling, she appeared to stare at them silently.

Rather than respond aloud, she rested a hand on her shotgun then turned and walked over to the tables where Nick was sipping a drink pouch and sucking on his vape, looking around with narrowed, nervous eyes.

Angel spoke up. "TC says Sharkey's a respected member of the Vengeance, and that if we need to purchase any goods, he's the man to speak to."

"I could tell by the way he's got his operation set up that he's not a small fry. I think I'll sit over here and see what I can dig out of his head. Might find a way to gain access to the network through him. Heck, he might even know where someone like Antigone would be." Juliet sat at an empty table, receiving a strange look from Nick in the process. She selected her comm channel with him. "Time for me to get to work, Nick. I really think the best thing you can do right now is chill in your ship and wait for word from me."

"Seriously?"

"Yeah. Sorry, but that's exactly right. I need to get serious. I'll try to keep things quiet, but if shit goes sideways, I'll give you a heads-up so you can bolt."

"Hey, Lucky, can you look at me for a second?" He stopped speaking, and Juliet knew he was waiting for her to do it, so she turned her visor toward him and looked into his eyes. Even before he spoke, she knew what he was going to say. His thoughts, accompanied by emotions that he broadcast as loud as if he were shouting, came directly into her mind. She could feel his affection, his longing, his tightly harnessed desire, and his fear as his unspoken thoughts came through with his words.

Be careful! I'm gonna hate myself if this mess gets you killed. Are we going to die here? Are you crazier than I thought? Should I run? Will I ever have the nerve to hit on you for real? Why'd I have to get old?

"Be careful," he said, voice steady and calm. Then he stood up and, sucking on his vape, walked into the milling crowd of criminals, fugitives, and desperate people trying to survive.

34

〰〰〰〰〰〰〰

SHARKEY

When she lost sight of Nick in the crowd, Juliet turned back to Sharkey's little tabletop emporium and contemplated what she would do next. She knew she had to get into the pirate base's secure network and find Antigone. Was a connected pirate like Sharkey the key? If so, how far would she need to go to find what she wanted? Juliet had been leery about digging deeply into people's minds ever since Tono. She'd broken down and done it with Larry, and she wasn't too sure she liked where that had gotten her.

Despite the gravity of her current situation and what she had to accomplish, the more she tried to think about it, the more Nick's parting thoughts kept creeping into her mind, vying for attention. She groaned, wanting to massage her temple but unable to through the thick polymer shell of her helmet.

It wasn't like she hadn't heard similar thoughts from him already. The poor man was clearly smitten with her and conflicted about his sense of propriety. Juliet didn't really mind the attention; Nick was a nice guy, handsome too, and he seemed to understand that their age gap and different stages in life meant his fleeting romantic feelings were probably best left as such. Still, it was one of those things that bothered her about hearing other people's thoughts—a little less clarity on such topics would be fine with her.

"Anything you want to talk about?" Angel had noticed her distracted mood.

"I need to dig into that Sharkey guy's mind, and I'm dreading it. What if it's another experience like Tono? What if I have trouble distinguishing my memories from the ones I pick up? I'm just starting to feel normal again after acting all weird back on Callisto."

"You don't think you can find what you want listening to his surface thoughts?"

"I doubt it! I'm looking for Antigone and info about the pirate's security net. You think he's just sitting over there thinking about things like that while he's managing his shop?"

"What if we prompted him to think about them somehow?"

Juliet idly fiddled with the strap on her shotgun as she considered the idea. "I'm listening if you've got more ideas."

"We could fabricate some sort of datasheet with a woman's picture who looked very similar to our photo of Antigone. It might prompt him to think about her if he saw it."

"Hmm." Juliet thought about the idea. They could anonymously drop the datasheet into any open wireless ports in the area. If they made it about something that might be of interest in general to the pirates, it wouldn't be very suspicious—junk data files were constantly being tossed around in public spaces like this. Angel filtered almost all of them, but occasionally, she'd show something to Juliet that she thought might be interesting.

"What would we say to get it past his PAI's filters?"

"Couldn't you listen to him for a while to see what he's interested in? Just surface thoughts?"

Juliet nodded, standing up. "I like how you think, Angel. I'm going to need a reason to be sitting here, though." She walked over to a food vendor selling hot dogs. She had no idea what they were made of, but his beat-up, homemade-looking cart was stenciled with the words plant-based, so Juliet decided she'd risk it. She didn't know what kinds of meat might be ground into a sausage on a pirate base, and she was happy not to find out. "Two dogs." She rasped through her helmet's speaker, holding up two fingers for clarity.

"Onions? Peppers?"

"Everything."

"I like it!" The merchant was a scrawny, greasy man with long, thin blond hair pulled back in an old yellow bandana printed with cartoon cats. He put together her hot dogs nimbly, and while she watched him, Juliet noticed he had two mechanical fingers. She'd seen a lot of cybernetic limbs in her life, but rarely such small ones. That thought struck her as kind of strange. *Why was that? Did people just opt for total hand replacements when they lost a finger? Did it make more sense from a surgical or mechanical standpoint?*

"Chips? Fresh fried right here! Got a real hookup on some genned potatoes over the weekend."

"Why not?"

He smiled a big, gap-toothed smile and got to work, dropping some frosty rounds of unpeeled potatoes out of a clear plastic bag into his fry basket. "You're gonna love 'em!"

A few minutes later, Juliet sat down at her table, back to the wall, straddling the bench so she could keep her eyes on Sharkey's booth without craning her neck. She took her helmet off for the first time in a few hours, and the air gently blowing over her sweaty neck felt heavenly. Maybe she was just hungry and stressed, but the food was better than anything she'd had in a while. She had a hard time eating it slowly, making it last so she could have an excuse to be sitting there, occasionally looking Sharkey's way.

"All right, Angel. Here goes." She set her first dog down, half-eaten, and sipped the frosty "cola," then stole a quick look at Sharkey's face, using her retinal implants to give her a close-up of his eyes. As she relaxed her breathing, his thoughts came rushing her way.

Ah, dammit! My balls are itching like nobody's business today. Did I pick something up from the crapper? I told Mack to clean that damn toilet! Why does he always have to be reminded when it's his turn? If I weren't already down an engineer, I'd give that punk his walking—Oh, hello! Who's this? My, my! Look at the heroic job that shirt's doing holding those puppies in. Hmm, not a big fan of those weird ear-jobs. Who wants to see speakers sticking out of a girl's head when she's going to town?

Oh well, easy to focus on other body parts, especially when they . . .

Juliet let his thoughts fade as he started speaking, and Angel adjusted her audio gain to hear his words. The object of his earlier scrutiny stood before him, holding a package containing a data deck. "Yeah, sure, it's in the original packaging. Nothing fake about that baby. Came right off a cargo ship Shinzo himself raided last month."

"You don't swap out processors or put doctored memory in? I've heard some of the goods sold here are fake."

"Listen here, you little squirt! Sharkey doesn't sell fake shit. If you're hearing rumors like that, they aren't about my stuff!" Sharkey was so strident that Juliet didn't think she'd have needed her enhanced auditory implants to hear him.

"Whatever!" The young woman turned back to perusing his goods, setting the deck back on the table.

Whatever? Come into my place of business and accuse me of scamming? Hah, if I scammed you, you'd never know it. Shit, maybe I should offer her a discount if she puts out a little . . .

"Ugh. Angel, this guy's a total creep. He might be connected, but all he thinks about is sex. Well, sex and his testicles and toilets . . ."

"That sounds unpleasant. Still, it might give us an angle. What if we released an advertisement for adult services? I could generate a scantily clad image of a woman with a face similar to Antigone's and then make up some promo text about 'massage services' on the base. Perhaps if you were listening to his thoughts when he received it . . ."

"Yeah, you know, that's the kind of thing I could see his PAI letting through his filters." Juliet chuckled and ate a couple of crisps, thinking about it. "I won't be surprised if he responds to it, too. You know, the more I think about it, the more I'd like to get this guy alone and just question him, get his biomarkers—all that. Too bad we don't have a private spot on the ship to lure him in."

"Why not use the cargo vessel? You won't be restricted from going in and out. In fact, you're expected to sleep there."

"Hold on, Angel, let's be smart about this. If Sharkey's seen going onto my ship, won't that raise some flags? I guess if we get what we need, that won't matter. You can alter the security footage if you get access to the base's net." Juliet thought for a couple of seconds, then shook her head. "Hang on a second! What are we doing? This went from me trying to see if he recognized an image of Antigone to us trying to lure him onto the ship."

"Good point! Let's slow down a little and take this one step at a time. Shall I make the flyer for 'massage' services?"

Juliet drummed her fingers on the table then took a long drink of her soda. "Yeah, do it. Tell me when you're ready to release—"

"Ready!"

"Good grief! You should get a job in advertising. Do I want to look at it?" As she subvocalized the question, a window appeared in her AUI, and she mentally groaned as she selected it. An animated high-res flyer took form, advertising "massage" services in quotes and showing a woman leaning over a large man's back, exposing way too much butt cheek beneath her very short skirt as she kneaded his doughy flesh. When she turned to wink at the viewer, Juliet could swear it was Antigone's face. An animated, scrolling subheading repeatedly proclaimed, "Have your PAI schedule a session with Cherry today! She'll come to any berth!"

"How's that?" Angel asked smugly.

"Well, I hate it, but I think Sharkey will like it." Juliet picked up the remnants of her second hot dog and stuffed it into her mouth. She focused on Sharkey, relaxing with a deep breath and inviting his thoughts. "Send it out."

At that moment, Sharkey was sitting on a stool, staring into space, his eyes darting around as he did something in his AUI. Juliet only had to stare for a second before his thoughts started to drift her way.

Nah, that one's too cheap. Think I'm gonna let Jay get off so easy? Punk owes me at least a CoffeeMaster, gen four or newer! Don't let him scam you.

Juliet could tell from the cadence and tone of his thoughts that he was composing a message. The tone abruptly shifted, though still in the tempo of a conversation.

Ho, ho! What's this? You dirty little bastard, Vince! Jesus H! Look at the can on that broad. You think she really wears that? Vince, make me an appointment.

Holy! Hey, wait a melting second here! Look at that face—freeze it. Yeah, ain't that Tornado's new chick? Holy, holy, holy shit! He's gonna go apeshit when he sees this flyer!

Oh? It ain't? Shit, Vince, it sure looks like her to me, but if you say the faces don't match, I guess I'll buy it. Make me an appointment!

"He's seen her!" Juliet subvocalized, trying to pull out of Sharkey's mind. "He called her 'Tornado's new chick.' Why does Tornado sound familiar?"

"Captain Roy Tornado is one of the Five. It seems you've come up with some good intel, but also with some troubling news. I can't imagine it will be easy to gain access to her if she's with Tornado's crew. There's also the matter that if she's his 'chick,' she may not want to leave the pirate base as we've been led to believe."

"Dammit! We need access to cameras and stuff, Angel. You can't find any wireless access points you can exploit?"

"I've found some very vulnerable network access points, but they're all to the tiny local public nets, like the one in this mercantile area where I dropped that massage flyer. By the way, Sharkey's requesting an appointment. He wants Cherry to come to his ship this afternoon."

"Yeah, that's not happening."

"You might be interested to know that he specified the designation of his ship as the *Rude Boy* and indicated that he'd need to send an escort to get her through restricted access points. The *Rude Boy* is one of the largest known ships in the Hereford's Vengeance pirate group. It's a salvaged Dono-van Mercantile destroyer, circa 2078."

Juliet groaned, leaning back and kicking one of her heels up onto the bench. "So you're saying he's even more connected than we thought. Still, I'm not trying to sneak onto his ship pretending to be a sex doll giving massages . . ."

"No, I wouldn't suggest that."

Juliet narrowed her eyes, watching Sharkey as he organized some of the items for sale on his central counter. She could probably find what she wanted in his head if she were willing to go deep enough. She could learn where the access points were to the network, learn what kinds of passcodes he might know in addition to his biomarkers, and even learn the layout of the place if she dug around for a current memory. Did she want to do that, though? Did she want to risk bringing pieces of that creep back into her head? "I can't do it. I won't."

"What?"

"I won't go for a deep dive into that guy's head."

"I'm glad. I think it would be even worse than Tono."

Juliet sighed and smiled, just a corner of her mouth twitching up. It was nice to know Angel always had her back. "Thanks for not pushing me. Hey, can you review my close-up interaction with Sharkey? Any chance we got a high enough res image of his eyes to steal his retinal imprint?"

"I'm sorry, but no; it's possible I could get a good enough image of his retina using the right visual filters, but we'd need to get close and achieve the right angle so that his pupil and iris don't obscure the retina. It wouldn't be something we could do instantly."

"All right. Hang on, I have an idea." Juliet took a minute to wipe the condensation off her mostly empty plastic soda cup. The red plastic had a thin layer of grease on it when she was done, no doubt caused by her fingers as she'd been eating the fried potato crisps. She pulled her gloves back on then stood up, hooked her helmet to her belt, and made her way back over to Sharkey's shop. She did her best to make her voice rough and hoarse, speaking from low in her throat.

"Hey, Sharkey."

"Oh? Hey, doll! Damn, glad to see your face ain't all messed up like I thought."

Juliet ignored the comment and pointed to the case behind him. "The cube."

"Huh?" He turned, looked to where she pointed, and said, "Oh yeah! That's a real beauty—Aurora Corp. Ultra-Simulate holoprojector. It can make a whole room look like something else."

"I know. Can I see?" Juliet held out her empty hand, still gripping the cup in her other.

"Okay. It's 40k, though." He turned and held his thumb to the biolock on the case, then as he took the cube out, added, "Unless you wanna try to earn a discount . . ."

"I'm good." Juliet took the cube and turned it slowly, examining the various facets, then, offhandedly, pushed her plastic cup toward Sharkey. "Hold this."

She did it nonchalantly like it was the most natural thing in the world, and Sharkey took the bait. He gripped the cup in his stubby, greasy fingers and, breathing loudly through his nose, watched Juliet fiddle with the specialized data cube.

"Get ready to scan, Angel," she subvocalized before taking her data cable from her wrist and plugging it into the cube. She flipped through the menus again, pulling up the cube's camera app. When she saw herself reflected on the high-res screen, she held it close to Sharkey's face. "Something's wrong with the screen. Do you see those glitching pixels?"

"Huh? Bullshit! That thing's only been used twice. I got it straight outta the box!" He narrowed his eyes and peered at the screen.

Juliet rotated it left and right. "You're sure? I think I noticed it when I looked at it from an angle.

"Goddammit!" Sharkey slammed her cup down on the counter, then took the cube in his hands. "Why are you even plugged in?"

"I was making sure the software is legit! These things aren't cheap."

"Yeah, no shit!" He held the cube close, turning it left and right.

"I have enough data now," Angel said.

"There's nothing wrong with this thing, crazy bitch. Trying to get a discount?"

Juliet reached forward and pulled her data cable out of it. "Nah, but your attitude sucks. Sell it to someone else," she growled, her voice low, scratching her vocal cords to the point that she almost coughed.

"C'mon! Quit wasting my time!" He jerked the cube away and turned to put it back in the case.

Juliet picked up her cup, barely gripping the plastic lip as she turned. "Get melted." Unable to stop the grin tugging the corners of her mouth, she returned to her table.

"Well?" she subvocalized.

"You're wondering if I can get his prints off that cup?"

"Yeah. Can my optics pick up the pattern?"

"Easily. We just need to dust that cup with something. I'm sure we'll find what we need on the ship—graphite powder in the engineering shop, perhaps? If not, I'm sure the mess hall has some kind of powder we could repurpose. If nothing else, some adhesive tape will work."

"Right on! I'd say that's enough intel for today—we learned Antigone's here, roughly where she probably is, and I got some biometrics from one of the more connected pirates. Let's go back to the ship and figure out our next steps." Juliet grabbed her helmet and pushed it onto her head, feeling that strange but welcome sense of security behind the anonymous shell of the mirrored visor.

She hurried back through the twisting corridors Angel had mapped out for her and was only a few minutes from the docking collar where the cargo ship waited when Nick's comm channel lit up.

"Hey, Lucky—er, uh, Lacy. I just got an invite to go and talk to a member of the Five. I get a distinct feeling it's not an optional meeting. Care to tag along?"

35

〰〰〰〰〰〰〰

GIFT FROM A GHOST

When Juliet returned to the Humpback, her ill-gotten cargo ship, she was a little surprised not to find any pirates left behind to keep tabs on her. She could see they'd been aboard, and Angel had the video footage and airlock logs to show they'd offloaded the wine cargo.

Still wearing her helmet as she walked through the deserted corridors to the ship's mess hall, she asked, "They didn't muck around with any of the systems? Didn't leave any bugs behind?"

"No. I was watching them the entire time, and Fido was here. He would have noticed a data intrusion."

"What about the bodies?"

"Two of the personnel sent to offload the wine stood outside the airlock and looked in on them, but, as you requested, I disabled those doors. The bodies are still there, untouched. Have you decided what you'll do with them?"

"Not yet." Juliet sighed as she unsealed her helmet and pulled it off her head. "I just know I can't space those people, and I can't leave this ship here for the pirates to dispose of them. I feel like I need to figure out a way to make Sir Rodric choke on what he's done."

In the ship's sizable mess hall, she spent some time going through the stainless-steel cabinets, digging through the foodstuffs, trying to find something she could dust the plastic cup with for fingerprints. She ended up using a ten-year-old box of vanilla cake mix. With Angel's guidance, she carefully measured a small amount of the powder onto her palm and blew it over the cup with a puff of breath. She did that from every angle, and almost immediately, even she could pick out the prints on the cup. Some were smeared and incomplete, so Angel instructed her to gently fill in and distribute the powder with a makeup brush.

"You think you can reconstruct these well enough to pass a biometric scan?" She slowly turned the cup, waiting for Angel to finish copying what she'd revealed.

"Definitely. I already have the basis for the code from the remappable cybernetic prints you've had in the past and the version that came with your new hand. Using those as a reference, I've developed an algorithm to reconstruct Sharkey's prints from these detailed images. I have what I need, by the way."

"Ah, cool." Juliet set the cup down, then selected Nick on their encrypted comm channel. "Hey, did they get back to you with an exact time yet?"

"Hey yourself! Nah, I'm still waiting for the details. They just said it would be soon, whatever that means. I'll contact you as soon as I know. How'd things go on the base?"

"Good. Making some headway. She's definitely here, by the way. Don't say anything out loud, though. I'm not sure your ship's not bugged."

"Oh? Should you come visit, maybe? Check it out?" Juliet hated how hopeful he sounded, twisting her gut a little with guilt. Why did she feel guilty that he was attracted to her? The thought came out of nowhere, and she frowned, glad their connection was only audio.

"I'll come by after our meeting. They say anything about guns? Can I bring mine?"

"They didn't say."

"Right. I'll wait for word from you, then." Juliet cut the comm link and sat down with a groan. "Angel, why do I feel guilty that Nick is attracted to me?"

"Are you sure it's guilt and not sympathy? Or, if it is guilt, is it because you're also attracted to him but don't want to act on it for reasons that might feel selfish?" Angel's direct bull's-eye caught Juliet off guard, and she flopped forward onto the table, resting her head on her arms, suddenly feeling utterly exhausted.

"Yeah, he's a cool, handsome guy with a big, good heart. Is it selfish not to want to start something up with a forty-something guy who lives on a moon in the Jovian System, though? Should I be like that merc who broke into my hotel room and have an ongoing relationship on every planet? That's not me.

I'm . . . human, though."

"I think part of your guilt or reticence is that you've picked up Nick's thoughts, and you know how he feels. You know you could take advantage of that if you wanted. It took the spontaneity and mystery out of the possibility."

"Shit, Angel, again with the perfect hit! Yeah, I think I'd much rather not have ever caught any of those thoughts—yet another reason I sometimes wish I didn't have this ability. I have to get better at not hearing what I'm not looking for. What'll I do if I start to realize someone on the *Kowashi* has the hots for me? Talk about awkward."

"Your practice over the last month or two seems to have made accessing thoughts easier, but as you said, sometimes too easy. I wonder if more control will come with more time and practice."

Juliet forced herself up from the table, tromping through the empty, dirty corridors of the ship toward the crew habitation area. She wanted a shower before she went to meet with the pirate boss or bosses.

When she stepped into the communal shower room, a space very similar to the one on the *Kowashi*, she almost turned around, however. The crew's toiletries, towels, and other belongings scattered here and there made her feel like she was desecrating a graveyard. Still, she stepped over to one of the benches, picked up a pair of pink plastic shower shoes, and carried them to an empty locker. As she set them inside, she was struck by a very different kind of guilt, so she took them out again and put them back where she'd found them.

"I'm sorry," she said to the ghosts lingering nearby.

Juliet took her time stripping out of her armor and clothes before she stood under the hot spray of the shower for what felt like a very long time, trusting that she could get ready fast enough if Nick contacted her. The hot water felt too good, the pounding of it on her scalp too calming, for her to give it up quickly. She let her mind wander, trying to categorize all of her problems, all of her priorities, all of her dreams and regrets.

By the time she finally turned the water off and dried herself, she had wrinkled, waterlogged fingers. She felt better, but didn't think she'd solved many of her problems. Even so, as she pulled on her pants, she said, "Let's keep an eye out for an access port when we're taken to Nick's meeting. Do you think Fido's ready to do his thing again, like he did at Port Security on New Atlas?"

"Yes. I'll just need a quick connection to drop him off. I've been refining his coding, and he's learned quite a lot since then."

"Heh, sweet." Juliet sat to pull her socks and boots on, and then Nick's comm line lit up.

"Yo, just had a chat with our buddy, TC."

"Oh, yeah?"

"Yeah, he's going to guide us to the dinner. That's right, I found out it's a dinner, and there are probably going to be other bigwigs in the pirate club there. Anyway, we've got a couple of hours to kill."

"Huh, hours?" Juliet had moved on from her boots and was starting to shrug into the top half of her combat armor. At Nick's words, she stopped short and set it down.

"Yeah. So, TC had some advice for us . . ."

"What's with the pause?"

"He told me they're expecting you at the dinner, but he also hinted that it wouldn't really be cool for you to show up like you're about to drop into an urban combat operation. He suggested one sidearm for each of us and a lot less armor. Something about people finding it odd if you were trying to have dinner with your helmet on."

"Come on, Simon," Juliet emphasized his fake name, feeling somewhat irritated. "I didn't pack any other clothes! You know that's not TC talking. I'm sure we've been observed as we walked around the station. Some pirate wants to take me down a peg. Maybe the one who boarded us at the start . . ."

"Who? Allie? Nah, she seemed pretty cool . . ."

"Maybe with you. Forget that, Nick, what am I supposed to wear? I've got tights and a tank top on under this armor. I didn't see this being a long engagement."

"What about the crew? I bet there's something on that ship you can wear."

Juliet frowned—scowled, really, and let her gaze drift over to the pink shower slippers. "I don't think I'd feel very good about that."

"You didn't kill those people. And yeah, I'm subvocalizing, don't worry. Anyway, you didn't kill 'em, and in fact, you're going to try to bring them justice. I doubt they'd begrudge you a shirt if you wanted to borrow one. I mean, if they care at all, considering . . . you know." Juliet could tell Nick was trying to be reasonable while respecting her feelings, and her anger and irritation began to defuse.

"I'll see what I can come up with. Talk soon, 'kay?"

"Right! Thanks, Lacy."

As the comm line grayed out, Juliet stood, gathered her stuff, and walked back to the hallway, glancing left and right. "Which way to the crew cabins?" Her mini map flashed with an updated path, and she turned to the right, following it. It was a short walk, which made sense—why put the showers far from the cabins?

At the next hallway, she could see ten identical doors on either side of the junction. While they were all the same in size and spacing, many of them had hand-painted names and art on them; someone from the old crew must have had an artistic flair and had personalized the doors for each crew member.

Juliet walked toward the third door on the right; it was colorfully painted with stars and moons, and the name at the center was decoratively written with big curlicues.

"Star?" Juliet rested a hand on the door, debating with herself again if she wanted to go inside. Was it worth it? She could get by in her tank top. Why was she so nervous about opening the door? Was she worried she'd learn more about the victims on the ship? Shouldn't she learn more? How would she feel in Star's place, assuming she could feel anything? "I'd want the creep who killed me caught, and I'd do anything I could to help the person planning to do it."

"I feel the same."

"Okay, Angel, open the door." With a hiss and the grind of runners needing some maintenance, the door slid open, and Juliet stepped into Star's room. "Whoa . . ."

The little cabin had three pieces of furniture: a low-end acceleration couch that probably wouldn't help with anything significantly over one G, an aluminum dresser bolted to the wall, and a matching nightstand bolted next to the couch. Aside from the furniture, Juliet was bombarded with stimuli—one entire wall was a mural of Saturn as seen from a ship orbiting Titan. Even the domes of New Atlas were depicted on the moon. "You think Star did all this art?"

"This door was the most decorated of those in the hallway."

"Yeah." Juliet let her eyes drift away from the mural to the piles of clothes, data cartridges, stacks of little boxes, knickknacks, photos, posters, half-finished snack packages, and even a crate of beer cans with a variety of labels. Juliet took a minute to study the photos, noting that most featured the same young woman taking a picture with other people. She had short green hair, pretty neon-blue eyes, and a smile that really lit up the shot, stealing attention from everything else.

"It's rather uncommon for people to have so many physical photos."

"Something tells me Star wasn't very common." Juliet found tears pooling in her eyes as she mentally matched that girl's face with one of the corpses in the airlock. She forced herself to look away, moving over to the dresser. Atop it, Star had an incense burner piled with ash, and next to a little box of incense, Juliet found a plastic tote bag filled with painting supplies, confirming she'd been the resident door artist. Feeling a little ghoulish and more than a little sad, Juliet opened the dresser and started going through Star's clothing. After a bit of perusing, it became clear that whoever she'd been, she'd had a pretty cool style.

Juliet found a pair of faded, stretchy jeans that weren't exactly a perfect fit but stretched enough to be comfortable. Even better, she found an old-school jean jacket with a pattern of stitched-on gold and silver stars on the upper back. It was cut to fall just to a person's waist, at least on Juliet, and the sleeves were designed to end somewhere about midforearm, so it felt natural and comfortable when Juliet rolled them up past her elbows. Best of all, it was real, well-worn denim, heavy and soft, and Juliet felt damn cool wearing it.

She found a mirror on the back of Star's door and stood looking at herself. "Too much denim?"

"No, you look good. I like how your combat boots look with the jeans tucked in, and your gun belt breaks up the denim. The jacket's darker than the pants, anyway."

"Yeah." Juliet still wore her gray tank top, figuring it looked fine under the jacket, and it was comfortable, being so lightweight. The pirate base had climate control, but she'd been quite warm in parts of it. "Pretty cool how the stars in my eyes match the jacket's. Shit, Angel, why'd I pick stars for eyes? You think I had some kind of premonition about all this? You think Star was fated to get killed just 'cause I accepted this mission?"

"You're going to drive yourself crazy with thoughts like that. Star is dead because a sociopathic billionaire decided to liquidate the crew of this ship."

"Right. Thanks." Juliet took one more long look at herself, then bent to pick up her belongings and leave. "Thank you, Star. I won't let you be forgotten so easily." As she walked down the hallway back toward the mess hall, lugging her armor, tactical vest, and extra guns and ammo, she passed by a cabin door without any name art. "Open this one, please."

Angel complied, and Juliet stepped into a room exactly like Star's, only it was totally empty. "Oh, perfect; I'll have to sleep somewhere. At least this one might not be haunted." She dumped her armload onto the acceleration couch before straightening up, adjusting her gun belt.

"Let's see, seven rounds in the pistol, twenty-one on the belt. I'll feel better if I bring this." She picked up her vibroblade and tucked it inside her right boot. "How much time do I have?"

"More than an hour."

"Ugh! I hate being ready so early!" Juliet took a few minutes to organize her things, tucking them into the dresser, then reclined in the acceleration couch. "You reset all the access codes to the ship, right?"

"Yes, as soon as the cargo was off-loaded and the pirates left."

"Okay, good." Juliet closed her eyes, wondering if a nap would be possible. When her lids grew heavy and she felt herself drifting, she smiled and sleepily said, "Make sure you wake me when Nick's ready." She sank back into the couch's embrace and, despite all she had on her mind, rapidly drifted away, dreaming short, scattered dreams about wandering through corridors, alternately feeling like she was looking for something or someone was looking for her.

When Angel spoke into her implants, waking her, it felt like she'd closed her eyes for just a minute, but more than an hour had passed. "Nick and TC are waiting outside the airlock."

Juliet felt a little disoriented, but she grunted and sat up, rubbing her eyes. She stood, adjusted her belt again, then hurried out of the room.

"I, uh, am not sure that nap was a good idea. I feel groggy as hell."

"Hopefully, you'll get a good night's sleep soon . . ."

"Yeah. Here's hoping. Okay, time to get my game face on. I'm Lacy Blake, and I don't take shit from anyone." She clenched and unclenched her fists, shook her head, and squared her shoulders, taking all the irritation and anger she'd felt in the last few days and projecting those feelings out of her scowling countenance. When she stepped out of the airlock, Nick gave her a double take and actually took a step back.

"Hey, Lacy." He jerked his head at TC, who stood beside him, face impassive. "TC and I just got here."

"A pleasure to see you again, ma'am." TC bent at the waist slightly.

Juliet frowned and nodded, hooking her left thumb in her gun belt, slouching one shoulder, and drumming the fingertips of her right hand against her Texan's holster.

Nick smiled awkwardly and raised an eyebrow. "Ready?" Juliet grunted a vaguely affirmative sound, and he turned to the synth. "Off we go, TC."

"Very good. Please follow me. Stay close and do not deviate from our course. We'll be passing through restricted areas, and you could find yourself in some trouble if you aren't with me or another escort."

Juliet walked beside Nick behind the synth. When she'd first laid eyes on him, Nick's outfit had made it easy to scowl; he was wearing his usual white button-up shirt, but had it tucked into black slacks under a matching blazer.

"A suit?" she rasped, frowning down at him as they walked.

"What? I don't have a tie on . . ." When Juliet only continued to scowl, he said, "C'mon, I'm not the muscle of our little operation. I'm allowed to look nice." His eyes opened wide, and his face paled by a full shade when he heard himself. "Oh, wait! I didn't mean it like that. You look nice. You always look nice, Lacy!"

Juliet grunted and frowned, rather enjoying the charade. Was this little dinner supposed to intimidate them? Were this synth's warnings about trouble supposed to scare her? Lacy Blake was a hard, mean bitch, and she was looking forward to sitting down with some pirate scum.

One corner of her mouth lifted in a crooked, mad grin, and Nick blanched further and took a step to his left, widening the space between them.

36

EASY BITS

As they followed TC through the base, occasionally ducking through corridors welded together at odd angles, passing by every manner of shady character and those not so shady, Juliet began to feel her nerves returning, wondering if she was walking into a trap. The thought brought to mind her more recent encounters with trouble, from Frida to Tono to Eve, back on the cruise liner.

Thinking about Eve, she reflexively felt for the hard lump of polymer in her pocket, only to remember she'd left her souvenir back on the *Lady Hawk* with her other belongings.

"I should put that on a chain," she muttered. When Nick looked at her for clarification, she just frowned and shook her head.

In a way, she felt a little bad for playing her hard-ass Lacy Blake persona with Nick, but in another way, she was enjoying it. What did that say about her? Was she too nice on a regular basis? Is that why it felt good to act out a mean character? Her mental debate about her motives began to irritate her, which only deepened her scowl and added to her grumpy persona.

She turned her attention back to the task at hand—following TC and looking for an access point she and Angel, or really, Fido, could exploit.

As they walked, Angel highlighted cameras, the occasional scanner, and hardwired terminals. Though some of them looked promising, there wasn't any chance Juliet could pause long enough to jack in without alerting TC or being caught by one of the cameras. "You think those are well monitored, or you think they've got a pseudo-AI watching them?"

"Considering the number, I doubt there's a human monitoring them all. I'm sure they're automated, and if the AI flags something, it will alert the security personnel." Angel paused, then added, "If Fido can gain access, he could delete incriminating footage once he takes control, but that may take several minutes, even hours, depending on the ICE."

"So I need to get him uploaded without being noticed." Juliet wasn't worried about TC or anyone else spotting her subvocalizations—she more thought her words to Angel these days; there wasn't a scanner or AI in existence that could decipher what she was saying by scrutinizing her throat. Nick couldn't say the same, so she didn't try communicating with him. It could spell disaster if he gave something away with his clumsy subvocalizations.

With that in mind, she decided to keep her thoughts between herself and Angel. If she saw an opportunity for Nick to help out, she'd message him at the time.

"Who's gonna be at the dinner, TC?" Nick asked as they came to a section of corridor that was in far better upkeep than the areas closer to their docking bay.

"Well, as you know, Simon, Captain Moon invited you. Likely some of her crew will be in attendance, and I've heard at least one other member of the Five will be there. I'm sure there are other guests from other crews, but I haven't been given a comprehensive list. My apologies."

"No worries. So I take it we're in some restricted area now? We passed a few red-painted junctions. If I get sick or something, will you be available to guide me out of here?"

TC paused and turned to regard Nick, his synthetic face pulling off a damn good impression of someone being concerned. "If I'm not available, someone will. Are you not feeling well, Simon?" Juliet, too, looked at Nick, wondering what he was up to.

"Nah, nothing to worry about. Sometimes artificial gravity messes with my system, you know? Heavy food and drink can give me"—he glanced at Juliet then back to TC, held a hand to the side of his mouth, and whispered—"the runs."

Juliet snorted, but TC looked appropriately sympathetic. "Goodness! When we arrive, I'll point out the nearest restroom for your convenience."

"Thanks." Nick winked at TC, and they continued on their way. After a few minutes, they came to a closed automatic door with a burly man standing outside, clearly acting as muscle. Like many of the pirates Juliet had seen, he was filthy, but his cyberware and weapons looked high-end. He had a bulky blue plasteel arm with a barrel wide enough to handle something like shotgun shells protruding from the forearm. He also wore a heavy pistol that looked like the big brother to Juliet's needler. More importantly, he sported a cybernetic chrome visor that seamlessly melded with the skin around his brow. It flashed with blue LEDs that traversed its length in regular intervals.

"Trashcan, you're late."

"Apologies, Mister Galaxy."

The man stared at TC with his visor for a minute then shifted toward Nick, his slablike pectorals bouncing under his dirty black-and-red jumper. "Simon, huh? No gear?"

"Nothing of note." Nick shrugged. "I have good eyes and ears and a decent PAI. I'm a pilot, man."

"Uh-huh." He turned to Juliet. "This your muscle, huh? Pretty wired up, aren't you? Nice arm." Juliet just stared at him, her gold-star eyes impassive. He frowned and gestured to her Texan. "That your only iron?" She nodded, and he held out his noncyber left hand. "Better pass it over. You give me psycho vibes." Juliet folded her arms and shook her head.

"She, uh, doesn't like to be unarmed." Nick took a step to the side so he could better look at Juliet while still facing the door guard. "Um, Mister Galaxy? She won't do anything violent, but she's in charge of my safety, so . . ."

"I'm in charge of everyone's safety," he growled. "Gun." Again, he held out his hand, staring at Juliet with that high-tech visor.

TC held up a hand and stammered, "Ex—er, excuse me, Mister Galaxy, but Captain Moon told me they would be allowed a sidearm."

"Yeah, well? Captain Moon ain't guarding the door, is she? This chick ain't coming through with that cannon on her hip."

Juliet feigned a yawn, lifting one fist to block her mouth, then turned and took a step back, leaning against the plasteel wall. "I'll wait here, then," she rasped.

"Oh dear!" TC said, concern verging on panic in his voice. "Captain Moon isn't going to like this." He sighed and shook his head. "Well, let us through then, Mister Galaxy."

Mister Galaxy frowned at Juliet, ignoring TC, but he slowly lowered his hand and nodded. "All right, you can go in with that piece, but I'll be watching you. You so much as twitch toward that pistol grip, and I'll erase that pretty face of yours." He tapped the fat barrel sticking out of his other arm. Juliet didn't respond, but stared into his visor without blinking as she straightened up and moved to stand next to TC again. The pirate muscle grumbled something unintelligible before turning and slapping his hand to the security pad, opening the door.

The room beyond was abuzz with activity, noise, and smells. Dozens of people in all manner of dress mingled in a space that reminded Juliet more of a saloon than a dining room. Dance music thumped through the metallic floor and echoed off the walls, and Angel immediately squelched most of it. Though the table was far across the room, past the mingling, drinking people, she could smell the food being heated beneath stainless steel lids on rolling carts lined up behind it. The scents were mouthwatering, and Juliet could swear she picked up the odor of real, baked chicken.

A bar was on the left, attended by a much more mechanical-looking synth than TC. Many of the pirates leaned against it, drinking and laughing. To her right, she saw the dance floor, a white-and-black checkered engineered floor with an actual disco ball hanging above it. Only four or five attendees were dancing, but they looked like they were having fun.

"Come on, move in," Mister Galaxy growled from behind them. Juliet shoved Nick to get him moving. As she stepped forward behind him, the door hissed shut, and she turned to see the surly door guard standing in front of it, arms crossed over his barrel chest.

"Simon, sir, I hope you and Lacy will make yourselves comfortable. I'm sure dinner will start sometime soon, but please avail yourselves of the open bar and the dance floor in the meantime. I'll let Captain Moon know that you've arrived." With that, TC turned and walked across the room, approaching a closed door on the far side of the table.

Juliet walked to the bar, angling for the left end where nobody was standing or sitting. When she got there, she leaned against the wood and gazed out over the crowd, carefully scrutinizing the wide, high-ceilinged place.

The flooring was plasteel, other than the dance area, but it was a different grade of plasteel, tinted burgundy with an almost reflective sheen. The walls were paneled with faux wood, and the vaulted ceiling was sprayed with cream-colored, noise-dampening material and hung with fancy lighting fixtures that gave the bar area a moody red vibe and the dining area a more cheery, yellow hue. "This place was part of the original ship, I guess."

"Yes, I believe it was a recreation area for the original crew. There are likely several such spaces."

"See anything we can exploit?"

"Not yet, though when TC opened that far door, I saw terminals and a bank of data decks." Angel displayed a freeze-frame in Juliet's AUI, highlighting what she'd missed entirely as she'd watched the synth walk out of the room.

"No way we're getting in there with all these people around."

"You want something, sweetie?"

Juliet jerked her head toward the gruff voice to find the robotlike synth standing on the other side of the bar, staring at her.

"Sweetie?" she growled.

"That's right, toots."

Juliet scowled at the impassive robot face with its speaker-grill mouth and LED eyes. It had to be its programming; surely, it wasn't trying to get a rise out of her. Choosing to ignore its irritating words, she almost ordered a beer, then decided Lacy Blake was a whisky drinker. "Bourbon."

"Neat or on the rocks?"

Juliet frowned at it and growled, "I look like I want ice in my drink?"

"Coming right up, sweetie."

"It's unlikely that this pirate base in the Junk Belt has true bourbon," Angel spoke in a tone that said she had more to add.

"Oh?"

"These days, you'll find some debate on the matter, but aficionados agree that true bourbon must be made in certain areas of the former United States of America from corn grown on the North American continent."

"Whatever. Next time, I'll just say whisky."

"Here you go, toots." The bartending synth set a short glass on the bar half filled with an amber liquid. Juliet picked it up, admiring the heavy feel of the tumbler, then lifted the drink to her nose and gave it a good sniff. It surprised her how much she enjoyed the heady aroma.

"My nanites ready to look for poison?"

"Always! By the way, you should take a small sip of that; true bourbon aficionados think it should be savored—"

Juliet smirked and tossed the drink back, swallowing the fiery liquid with a loud exhalation. Lacy Blake didn't give a shit what aficionados thought. She slammed the glass down, turned to the synth already mixing a drink for someone else, and rasped, "Water." Then she scanned the room, looking for Nick, only to find him surrounded by three young women, laughing and gesticulating while he told some story about a dogfight he'd been in. He was a lot better at socializing than she was, no question about it.

"It's not my fault I'm Lacy Blake right now, is it?"

"Pardon?"

"I mean, I could be chatting people up, but I kinda painted myself into a corner with this role." She noticed movement over by the dining table and turned that way to see TC come back into the room. "He'd be a good vector if you could infect him with Fido."

"TC may not be a true AI, but he's certainly something of an individual. I'm not sure I'd feel good about infecting him."

"I don't mean to, like, take him over, but to hide Fido in his code. Next time he plugs into a network, Fido could get out."

"I suppose that's a possibility. Did you bring your deck?"

"No." Juliet drummed her fingers on the bar. She was about to say more when the door opened again, and a woman who very much fit the part of a pirate queen stepped into the room. She was a big lady, tall and wide, wearing bright, silky clothes in various shades of red. The pirate boss sported three cybernetic limbs, all with different styles, from a shiny gold-plated left hand to a leg that looked like a piston you'd see in a manufacturing plant to a right arm with a matte-black plastic shell. She had gold eyes, and not just the irises; they were like shimmering golden marbles. Long black dreads hung down from her scalp under a bright red bandana, and as she walked, calling out to TC, Juliet saw her teeth wink with gold. "Mary Moon, I bet."

"Yes, her face matches the wanted notices."

"All right, everyone!" the pirate captain bellowed, and the music cut off instantly. "If I invited you to dinner, get over to the table and take your seat. If I didn't invite you, then hang around the bar if you want, but keep your damn noise down!" She laughed, turning and plopping her large, silk-clad body down at the head of the table.

Juliet hung back, watching the other pirates hurry over. Nick sent her a questioning glance, and she offered him a quick, reassuring nod, so he went to find his seat. After a few seconds, Juliet ambled over, aiming for the empty seat near Nick.

She'd just walked around to the back of the table when Mary Moon said, "Uh-uh, sweetie. Right up here." She pointed to a chair to her right.

Juliet looked at it, then at Mary's grinning face, then over to Nick. It was his turn to shrug, so she just let her frown deepen and walked back around the table to the empty chair. There were at least twenty people at the big table, but now she was right next to the host. What was that supposed to mean? Was she in trouble? Did they want her to know they were watching her? Was she about to get grilled? Lacy Blake didn't care. The thought made Juliet smirk as she pulled out the big, heavy wooden chair, noisily dragging it on the plasteel.

She'd picked up an audience when Mary Moon called her out, so she hammed it up, sitting a bit away from the table so she could cross one leg over. She leaned back, looking around at the other guests, meeting the eyes of every person staring her way. Many of them looked away.

"Good. Right there, dollface." Juliet turned toward her but fought her urge to scowl. What was this lady's deal? Was she another Sharkey? Was she just flexing in front of her crew? She knew she could find out easily enough, but was reluctant to get into another pirate's head.

"Oh, melt it!" she subvocalized, and as Mary turned to the rest of the table and began to welcome them all to dinner, talking about some recent achievements, she stared into those golden orbs and tried to dig out her thoughts.

It was hard, at first, to get anything other than a weird mental echo of the words she was speaking, so Juliet dug a little deeper, and strange, shadowy scenes began to play through her mind's eye.

Mary stood before a terminal, watching camera footage of a tall, angry-looking woman walking behind TC. "That's her?"

"Yeah."

"She does look like a mean bitch. You think she'll do it?"

"Why not? She slaughtered a whole crew of cargo shippers. You pay her enough, she'd probably kill that partner of hers, let alone whoever else you want dead."

"Okay, I'll make her an offer at dinner." Mary looked up from the terminal and regarded Greg. Galaxy Greg! She almost laughed, thinking of his nickname. "You're getting sexy, you know? That new arm is turning me on. We got time for—"

"Nah, Mary! I gotta get to the door. Screen people."

"You all right? Hey!" Juliet heard fingers snapping in her face and blinked rapidly, banishing the vision. She shook her head and scowled, Lacy's go-to response to any attention.

"What?" she rasped.

Mary Moon was staring at her, and Juliet realized everyone else was talking and laughing, drinking from wine glasses that hadn't been on the table a moment ago. How much time had she lost in that weird little vision?

"Did you stroke out, or are you watching a vid or something?"

Juliet continued to scowl, trusting her Lacy persona and what she'd learned about Mary from her vision to cover her weird behavior. "I'm here," she grunted, picking up her wine glass, smelling it, and setting it down. She turned the corners of her mouth down even further and leaned back in her chair.

"Don't like the wine?"

"Whisky."

Mary lifted her big black plastic arm into the air and snapped her fingers with a click that would have sounded like a gunshot had Angel not dampened it. A moment later, the bartender synth hurried over. "Bring this woman a glass and a bottle of whisky." Juliet locked eyes with Mary and offered her a brief nod, relaxing her frown just a little. "You don't talk much?"

"No."

"Huh. TC didn't have any trouble speaking with you. Should I take it personally?"

Juliet touched her throat and rasped, "Sometimes it's not so bad."

"Ah! You should get that looked at. We have a pretty good chop doc here. You want me to have him swing by your ship?"

Juliet shrugged, knowing that always saying no was sure to arouse suspicion. "Won't be the first."

"Okay then!" Mary slapped her gold hand down on the arm of her chair, visibly marring the wood. "Listen . . . Ah, hold on, here comes your drink." Mary sat back while the bartender set a bottle of "Galveston's Best" bourbon in front of her. He placed a tumbler beside it, just like the one she'd drunk from earlier.

"Shall I pour?"

"Of course, you lazy bum!" Mary barked. The synth didn't react, but he quickly pulled the cork and poured Juliet a generous amount of the amber liquid. When he set the bottle down and backed away, Juliet noted a tremor in his hand, and she wondered if synths could be programmed to feel fear. Why would manufacturers do that?

To make them more believable, she told herself. She noticed Mary staring again, so she nodded and picked up the glass. Mary lifted her wine glass to clink against it. "To new friends! I'm Mary Moon, by the way."

"Lacy," Juliet said hoarsely, then gulped about half the whisky. She set the glass down, and her frown was natural when she realized she was starting to sort of like the burning, heady aroma of the amber liquor. It had a cloying, sweet aftertaste, but not really sweet; like you could tell it wasn't sugar. Still, there were definitely different notes about its flavor—hidden depths.

"Good?"

"Good." Juliet looked up, and her frown was almost gone. She'd have to work harder to be a hard-ass with the buzz she was starting to feel.

Mary Moon smiled, flashing her gold-tipped canines, and leaned forward, speaking in a hushed voice. "Listen, Lacy. How'd you like to make some easy money and earn some points with me? I understand you've got a bit of a mean streak."

"I . . ." Juliet's instinct was to try to turn the woman down, to come up with an excuse for why she couldn't work just now. Then she thought better of it; she was trying to get some sway among these people. Maybe taking a job, whether she completed it or not, would give her a little access. She cleared her throat and tried again, rasping, "I'm always looking for easy bits."

37

TORNADO

So you're interested, good. How about we have a little one-on-one after dinner, hmm?" Mary winked and sat back, clearly considering the matter settled.

Juliet felt someone jostle her arm and turned to the person to her right, a wiry, hard-muscled man with a short fringe of fine, silvery metallic hair along his jawline that ran up his sideburns and blended into the bizarre, silvery spikes of his hair. He looked almost like a cartoon character who'd been electrocuted. His strange ocular implants didn't help matters—he must have had his orbital bones modified to allow for the oversize orbs that sat in the sockets. They had matching, expansive purple irises that glittered with gemlike sparkles. When he spoke, his thin, rubbery lips stretched weirdly, making his entire face kind of a caricature of humanity. "Lacy, is it?"

She tried to contain her surprise at his odd appearance and nodded. "Yeah."

"I've heard some intriguing things about you and your partner—quite a haul you brought in. I'm Roy, by the way."

"That's Captain Roy to you, Lacy," Mary said with a chuckle.

Juliet glanced at Mary, watched her smirk and take a drink, then turned back to Roy. "Tornado?"

"Hey! You've heard of me?"

"Sure."

"So rumors around here are that you're cold as ice. Slaughtered the crew of that ship, huh? Not very Jolly Roger of you." Roy had a strange way of speaking that went beyond his odd facial expressions. Whenever he said a word with more than one syllable, he emphasized the first and hardly enunciated the following ones. It gave his speech an odd cadence that perplexed her. Maybe her expression changed as a result, but Roy chuckled and said, "Did I offend you?"

"No." Juliet narrowed her eyes and locked them on Tornado's, opening her mind as she waited for him to realize that was all she'd say.

Not talkative, eh? Well, the rumors are true. Wonder what Moon wants with her.

"Care to tell me a bit about yourself? What brings you to the Jovian System to ply your particularly rough brand of pirating?"

Juliet didn't want to engage in conversation; it wasn't Lacy's thing. She covered for her reticence by taking a sip of her bourbon. Firmly remembering how intimidating Ghoul had been when she'd first met her, she set the glass down, turned to look Tornado full in the face, and rasped, "No." The whisky helped make the hoarseness in her voice authentic, and Tornado, though he didn't look happy, nodded and picked up his wine for a sip.

Juliet knew she had a golden opportunity to get some information out of this guy. He was, supposedly, romantically involved with her target, after all. Still, she couldn't suddenly turn Lacy into a chatterbox. She had to play this right. When he set the glass down, she spoke, hoping to catch him off guard. "Fresh start, I guess."

"Oh? Well, that's a good enough reason, I suppose. Plenty of people here are hoping to start over for one reason or another. Isn't that right, Captain Moon?"

Mary was in the midst of a conversation with the woman to her left, and she turned to Roy and frowned, holding up a finger. Roy sighed, annoyed or disappointed, so Juliet filled the awkward silence. "Plenty?"

"Right. Obviously, we've got people hiding from corpo-sec; the law takes many flavors in the system, and we don't all fit the mold, you cop me?" Juliet inhaled, her mind spinning for a perfect response and also trying to make sense of the "cop me" slang. Did he mean feel? Follow?

She decided to go with simple vitriol; it felt in character for Lacy.

"Screw corps."

"A woman of few but meaningful words," Mary said, finally extricating herself from her conversation. "What are you asking me now, Roy?"

"I was just mentioning to our new friend that many among us came for a fresh start."

"Yeah, obviously. Or because, you know, they'd be locked away or spaced if they tried to enter a port." Mary snorted and drained her wine, holding up the empty glass and shaking it at a nearby synth. Juliet looked around the table and realized there were now four synths standing around, all with very robotic appearances, like the bartender. She hadn't seen them come in. Had it happened when they brought the wine—when she'd been lost in Mary's head?

The idea bothered her, but, at the same time, she didn't feel very emotionally troubled. She wasn't feeling hungover with foreign feelings and weird thoughts and memories like she had been when she read Larry's deeper thoughts. Was it because she'd only taken a glimpse?

"Hah, eloquent as always, Mary." Roy spread his enormous smile, exposing too-white, too-straight teeth all the way to his back molars.

"Lots of synths," Juliet grunted, trying to turn the topic away from her and her motivations for coming to the Jovian System.

Mary grinned and sloshed her drink. "Oh yes! You come upon all manner of interesting cargo when you're a pirate. One of our bigger scores involved these synths—we took a Zi Corp cargo transport with a thousand of these things bound for an ore processing plant on Ceres."

"Yeah," Roy added, "they're technically maintenance labor synths. We've done some tweaking with their personality algorithms, though."

"Ah! Dinner!" Mary exclaimed, loud enough to stop the conversations around the table and bring everyone's attention to the side carts where the aforementioned synths were removing the domed, stainless covers from the food trays. Of course, everyone—lubricated by booze—hammed up their reaction to the reveal.

"Goddamn!" one man howled, lifting his wine glass. Others simply oohed and aahed, but Juliet could tell they all wanted to please the host. Juliet looked at Mary, waited for her to meet her gaze, then nodded and raised her whisky glass in a silent salute. After that, they got busy eating, and things got a lot quieter as far as conversation went.

The meal was good, no denying, and Juliet was surprised by the fare, from freshly baked chicken still on the bone so you could tell it wasn't grown in a vat, to seasoned, roasted root vegetables, to hot, baked bread, to three different kinds of pie. She ate a lot, figuring if she was building a personality for Lacy Blake, she might as well enjoy food. While she ate, she took sidelong glances at Roy Tornado, wondering what she should do to capitalize on the lucky happenstance that put him beside her.

He seemed friendly, if strange, but who was she to judge? Wasn't everyone a little strange in the messed-up society they were all struggling to survive in? What was her baseline for normal? The suits and corpo drones in the media?

Taking a second look at her thought process, she wondered what she was doing, but quickly figured it out; she was trying to psych herself into using the lattice for another deep dive hot on the heels of the one she'd just done with Mary. She was trying to minimize the man's strangeness so she wouldn't be scared to go into his head.

Thinking about that while she forked another mouthful of chewy, roasted parsnip, she considered her luck with deep dives thus far. Each time, she'd found what she wanted. Was it because her psionic ability somehow recognized her desired outcome and searched the target's mind for relevant information? When she dove in, she always had something in mind. With Tono, she'd wanted to expose a weakness. With Larry, she'd wanted to know more about the job and his motivations. With Mary Moon, she'd wanted to know her intentions toward her. Each time, she'd gotten what she wanted. Was it luck? Coincidence? Skill? Juliet figured that with three samples, she could rule out coincidence.

If she managed to either skillfully or luckily find what she wanted from Roy, it might make the rest of this operation a hell of a lot easier. Could she throw that kind of opportunity away because she didn't want to suffer from an "emotional hangover?"

She shook her head. What if it was more than just lingering emotions? What if her mind grew cluttered with memories and feelings and started to cull some? What if it culled the wrong things? What if she began to develop multiple personalities or something equally as disturbing? Of course, she didn't know anything of the sort would happen, but she was smart enough to be scared.

"Angel," she subvocalized, "I'm going to try to get into Tornado's head. Don't let me space out too long. If I start to do something weird, break me out of it. You know how?"

"I can try some methods I developed for breaking you out of a truedream. It might not look pretty, though."

"Rather I have some kind of fit and blame it on bad cyberware than . . . something else."

"All right. I've got you, Juliet."

Angel's reassurance was just what she needed to hear. "Show me a captured image of Tornado's eyes, please." As a big window opened in her AUI, displaying a still image of Roy's weird, oversize glittering eyes, the noise around the table died down. Angel was helping her concentrate by dampening her auditory input.

Juliet stared into those eyes and focused, pretending she was looking into the real things, boring into the brain of the man beside her. As uncanny shadowy images and snippets of Tornado's voice began to bombard her, she really focused, picturing Sir Rodric's daughter, mentally asking, "What's the deal with you and Antigone?"

Suddenly, Juliet's reality was washed away as a vivid scene grabbed her, immersing her in sounds, smells, sights, and feelings. She began to remember . . .

Roy leaned forward toward the surface of the little motel mirror. He gently tugged the skin around his eyes, frowning. Were those synthetic bone implants failing? Why was his skin swelling at the corner of the eye?

"Staring at yourself again?" Antigone's trill of mocking laughter caught him by surprise, and Roy dropped his hand, straightening and turning away from the sink. He nervously smoothed his ChromaWeave hair implants, the sharp, prickly metallic strands tickling his palm. He offered her a half smile, turning up the corner of his expressive lips as he walked toward the bed.

"Thought you were asleep."

"I was, but I had a nightmare. Something about waking up in a sleazy motel with a pirate."

"Sleazy? Should I be offended?"

"Only if you think I'm wrong." She scooted up against the pillow, letting the sheet slip off her chest, exposing her smooth, blemish-free skin. Roy focused on her left breast, grinned, and stepped forward, reaching for it as he leaned over, aiming to kiss her. Antigone had some of the softest lips he'd ever felt, and he wanted more of them . . .

"Easy, now." She shifted away, holding up a hand to forestall his affections. "We need to talk."

"Yeah?" He kept advancing, pushing her outstretched hand aside and kneeling on the bed beside her. His face was just inches from hers, and he felt himself getting aroused as her hot breath feathered the bristles of his beard.

"Yeah," she panted, and he thought she would give in, embrace him even, but she scooted sideways, pushing against him. Seconds later, she was standing and picking up the neon-yellow jumper she'd been wearing the night before. "We need to talk about who I am. Who my father is."

"Oh?" Roy took her place on the bed, propping the pillows up and lying back with a lazy smile. "I think it's a bit early for me to meet your old man."

"Yeah, that's true-true, buddy. He'd have you stuffed in a box and shipped off just so he could watch a vid of you being spaced."

"Sounds scary." Roy smirked and shook his head. Girls—always thinking their dads were the big bad wolf. Well, she didn't know Roy; he was the wolf around these parts.

"He owns half of Callisto and a controlling percentage in a dozen major corps throughout the system. I'm not joking."

That got Roy's attention. She was fine and fun to talk to, but maybe she'd make a better ransom . . .

"Don't think it, Roy! Come on; we had fun, didn't we? I wanna see you again, and if you play your cards right, you'll get a lot more from being my friend than you will for trying to screw me over." She ran a hand over the seam of her skintight jumper, sealing it up, then sat on the faded blue armchair near the dresser. "Do you wanna hear me out?"

Roy reached down to his boot and pulled out his knife, the one Skelly gave him, idly twirling it between his fingers. "I'm listening."

"I want to get away. I want to get away, and I want to find a way to ruin him. I want you to help."

"Huh?" Now Roy was more than interested; he was piqued.

"I have connections in the businesses. There are people working under my father, people who've handled his affairs for decades, and some of them are tired of him. Some want to see an end to his control sooner rather than later. I know, I know. They're vultures, and they're out for themselves, but I'm not stupid. I won't give them everything they want. Anyway, it's beside the point. Roy, my father's evil—pure, unfiltered, one hundred percent, grade-A, genuine, electro-plated-chrome evil. Do you want to help me take him down?"

Roy's heart began to hammer in his chest, and like a buildup of static electricity, he felt a wave of something rush through him. His whole body jerked. His knee lifted and slammed the table, and he looked around, blinking his eyes rapidly. No, he corrected himself. Not his eyes. No, this wasn't right . . .

Juliet slapped a hand to her face, rubbing her eyes, and slowly, the buzz in her ears began to separate into distinct sounds—music playing, people talking, silverware clinking. One voice was closer and more insistent than the others.

"You good? What happened? I ask you something wrong?"

"Juliet!" Angel's voice cut through the noise. "You were deeply engrossed by something, and Roy asked you about your flight experience and the kinds of ships you've had. I tried to get your attention, but you didn't hear me, either. I waited as long as I could, but I saw he was getting agitated by your silence."

Still reeling from the sudden change in her mental perspective, struggling with the weird sense of being outside herself, not herself, Juliet lowered her hand and turned to face Roy. It wasn't hard to put a rasp in her voice; she felt like she'd just woken up. "I took a hit to the skull a while back. Fragments in there. Sometimes I . . . zone out."

"Jesus. Can't get 'em out?"

"Working on it. Treatments aren't cheap."

"You bothering my guest, Roy?" Juliet turned to the voice and locked eyes with Mary Moon's golden irises. She started to smile but froze it halfway, remembering she was Lacy Blake, and Lacy didn't smile unless she was doing something cruel. Roy answered Mary, but Juliet didn't hear it. Unbidden, unwelcome, even, she picked up a very clear thought from Mary, but she recognized it as being spoken speech, or in this case, subvocalized.

Galaxy? This chick seems off. She just about had a stroke eating dinner. I'm not sure she's as good as people think. Arrange a little test for her after we're done meeting. Have one or two of the synth units jump her. Go ahead and give 'em a gun.

Juliet, still looking at Mary while Roy blathered on, narrowed her eyes and grinned. It wasn't a smile, and it definitely wasn't friendly. Mary's eyes widened slightly, and she broke eye contact, focusing on Roy. "Anyway, Roy. Be nice to my guest. I might have some work for her." With that, she turned back to her neighbor on the left and began a hushed conversation about someone named Ophelia and the absurdity of her hair.

Roy, too, got busy speaking with his other neighbor, and nobody else bothered her while she ate, giving Juliet plenty of time to ruminate about her strange feelings and the disturbing things she'd learned. Every time she closed her eyes, she saw Antigone again, felt the lust she'd—Roy had—felt, and when she opened them and focused on her food, she had to remind herself that those weren't her feelings. She—Roy—had wanted to help Antigone, and it wasn't just for the bits; he'd been smitten with her. There was no way, if things hadn't changed drastically, Antigone would go back to her father willingly. On top of that, now she had to worry about getting jumped by synths aiming to prove she was all bark and no bite.

When everyone was stuffed and people were regularly excusing them-selves to find a restroom, Mary stood from her chair and addressed the table again. "Thanks for coming to my little banquet, folks. You know how we operate here in the Vengeance! When one of us scores big, we all score!"

Shouts of "Hear, hear!" and "Damn right!" and various other encouraging phrases interrupted her speech, so Mary paused, smiling, and sipped her wine.

"All right, enough. Now, listen; the *Red Betty* is heading out for another big score in a week. If you or your captain might be interested in tagging along for a piece of the pie, hit me up. I'll be seeking another frigate class, half a dozen interceptors, and a cargo vessel." She held up both hands as excited clamor began to take over. "Hold up! Yeah, I know it sounds like a big operation, and it is, but we aren't going to take a shit in our backyard. This one's a good ways out, so don't bother me if you can't commit two weeks to the operation." Once more, she lifted her glass and held it out. "Okay, get out of here! Mingle! Party 'til you can't walk straight."

As people shoved their chairs back and stood, moving back to the bar area, Mary locked eyes with Juliet. "Shall we?"

Juliet jerked her thumb at Nick where he sat across the table deep in a conversation with TC. "Simon?"

"Nah. I don't need him for this. Come on."

Mary turned toward the door she'd come through earlier, and Juliet stood, a little excitement making her breaths quicken and her heart race at the thought of going off alone with that woman, at the idea that an ambush was waiting for her somewhere nearby. She tamped it down, forcing her face to remain impassive—bored, even—and followed Mary through the door.

Anyone who knew her, though, might have seen how her fingertips lightly drummed the side of her Texan's holster. She was wired up and ready.

38

TO EARN SOME CLOUT

Mary Moon led Juliet through a little security station next to her dining room where a synth dressed like an ancient maritime sailor sat watching vidscreens. She'd hoped their meeting would take place there, and even entertained the fantasy that Mary would leave her alone for a minute or two, but she didn't have any such luck. They walked through the station, down a short hallway, and into a rather mundane office that might once have belonged to a clerk or minor officer on the dreadnought when it was in action. Mary sat behind a gray plasteel desk and motioned for Juliet to sit in one of the two padded but clearly designed for durability plastic chairs in front of it.

The cushion squeaked awkwardly when Juliet sat down, but she kept a straight face; Lacy didn't care what people thought of noises her chair might make. She looked around the little room, noting a data terminal on a side table, some artwork of stars and planets, and a motivational poster that read, "Success doesn't find you. You find it." The poster depicted an old-school rocket launch, and when Angel highlighted it and labeled it as a "Titan ICBM – decommissioned circa 1980," she had to fight hard to contain her amusement at the irony.

"Well, well, Lacy, I've heard quite a lot about you." Moon leaned back in her squeaky, low-budget executive chair, drumming her thumbs on its faux-wooden arms. Of course, Juliet didn't respond; she just raised an eyebrow and stared. "Right, well, this is the part where you ask, 'All good, I hope,' or say something cute like, 'I've heard about you too!' Eh, I guess the reason I wanted to talk to you wasn't because you're a good communicator. We've done a little digging into you. Hope you don't mind. You see, when we saw how you handled that cargo ship takeover, we wondered if it was a fluke. Turns out you've been quite the naughty girl on Earth and Mars, haven't you? Seven aliases? Wanted for a couple dozen crimes that'll get you disappeared if you're picked up? Any of this ringing a bell?"

Of course, Juliet knew Lacy Blake had a convincing background. Larry had bragged about the thoroughness of the pirate identities Sir Rodric had built for them, and she'd had Angel look into them. Lacy was a cold-blooded killer wanted for dozens of murders, armed robberies, kidnappings, and even terroristic misadventures, whatever that meant. She'd gone by names like Red Paula, Lola Channing, and Dena Red Hands. Juliet locked eyes with Mary and, in a hoarse whisper, asked, "You looking to cash in on my bounties?"

"What? I should be insulted, but I suppose you could take my interest the wrong way. No, Lacy, I have something far more valuable in mind, something that might make us both some big-time bits and also earn you a place where you can put your guard down. A home, if you will. It's been a long time since you could call a place home, hasn't it?" As she spoke, Juliet had a hard time following the conversation. Some of Mary's words kept getting jumbled because she was also picking up her more prominent thoughts.

Does a sociopath care about a home? God, maybe I shouldn't have let this chick in here with that gun. How fast is she? Do I have time to hit my panic button if she goes nuts on me?

"Angel," Juliet subvocalized, "please caption her words as text on my AUI." Almost instantly, a window appeared with a line-by-line display of their conversation. Juliet scanned it quickly, then said, "I guess I could appreciate that."

"Oh? Well, now we're getting somewhere!" Mary smiled and leaned forward. "You ever heard of Jovinium?"

Juliet smirked. "The conspiracy theory?"

Mary leaned back, her chair squeaking in protest, and folded her arms over her chest. Her plump lips spread in a large smile. "Oh, it's a conspiracy all right, but it ain't what everyone says. Yeah, they're pulling something out of the gases around Jupiter, but it probably ain't a mystery element. We're not sure what it is, but it has something to do with a new propulsion system, and I know a guy who's willing to pay a lot of bits for even a little dirt on their project."

"They?" Juliet scoffed. "Who's they? Lots of corps scooping gas around Jupiter."

"Ah-ah! That's where you're wrong. Lots of corps, sure, Mass Gas, Greater Gas, Jovian Refining. I could go on, but guess what? A single holding company owns the majority of every ram-scooping company that operates around Jupiter. Don't feel bad; it's not common knowledge. I didn't even know it until I was approached about this Jovinium business."

Juliet sighed and turned to look at the door. "So? What's all this to me?"

"Easy! Settle down. You got someplace to be?" Juliet shrugged, face straight, and Mary continued. "Okay, so, the intel I got is that, lately, there's something top secret on those ram scoopers. They're just normal gas harvesters on the outside—even most of the crew think so. My guy says there's something more to 'em than meets the eye. He says some of 'em are equipped with a cargo bay full of hardware, including something that looks like a gravity generator you might find on a cruise liner. This mystery equipment is always managed by synths on contract from the same company, Vega Star, and the crews of the scoopers are all told the equipment is for surveying the deeper layers of Jupiter's atmosphere."

"Yeah? What if it is?"

"You let me worry about that. So, what if I told you Vega Star has a maintenance station orbiting Ganymede? What if I told you I know their schedule and that we could probably insert you at the right moment to get aboard one of these harvesters? You think you could do that? You think you could handle some synths like you did the crew on that cargo vessel?"

"Uh, hold on," Juliet rasped, suddenly a lot less cool in her Lacy persona. "One of those ships has to be worth billions, especially if they have gravity generators on them."

Mary laughed and slapped a hand on her desk. "Right! We're not going to steal it! That would be suicide; even the politicians we own couldn't protect us. I want you to get aboard and scan every inch of that secret cargo bay. The maintenance station is run by synths. The maintenance crews are synths. You're okay with melting some industrial synths if they get in your way, right?"

Juliet frowned and folded her arms. "Sounds like you're trying to get rid of me."

"Okay, I'll be straight; this mission will take guts. Your insertion will be via EVA. Your extraction will involve you stealing one of the ship's two shuttles. We have some folks here who could do it—would do it for the right price—but they don't need to earn favor the way you do. Besides, you just feel right for this, hard bitch that you are." When Juliet continued to frown, she added, "It'll be worth a fat stack of bits and a shitload of rep for you around here. All you need to do is access that secret bay, scan all the equipment, and get out. The guy who's paying me says there shouldn't be more than a dozen synths aboard at any given time, and if you're careful and quick, you could be gone before they call the response team from the station."

"Response team?"

"Well, he says they have a kind of synth commando unit on the station."

"Let me think a second." Juliet stared at Mary as a million thoughts ran through her mind. She was intrigued by the mystery and wouldn't mind getting that intel herself, but was she willing to do something so risky? Would it earn her enough clout with the pirates to get some access to the more secure areas? Would it provide a chance to get close to Antigone? Should she wait around for a better, less crazy-sounding opportunity?

She stared at Mary and opened her mind.

I think she's gonna bite. She's interested. This bitch is crazy for danger! If she can pull it off, I'm looking at a big haul, enough to refit the Red Betty's main drive, upgrade her turrets, and fix all those shitty hull plate repairs. Come on, girl, say yes! Earn your place with Mama.

"Ganymede, huh? What about Simon?"

"Oh, this isn't his cup of tea. We've got a little interceptor we've been stealthing out for this job. I've got a synth that'll drop you, and after he picks you up and brings you back, we'll reset his memory. Fewer loose ends about this job, the better for the both of us."

"That go for me too?" Juliet tried hard to hear Moon's thoughts as she hoarsely whispered the question, staring into her glimmering golden eyes.

"No! Not if you pull this off. I'll put you on my damn crew! Shit, if you can do this, you can have a spot on the *Red Betty*."

Juliet frowned, her brain going into overdrive—if she accepted the job, she'd have some time to think of a way out if she had to. If she ended up doing it, she'd lose a few days in transit but gain a mile of respect among the pirates. Of course, she'd also put herself in danger and possibly earn the ire of another massive corporation. What if she said no, though? How far would that set her back among the pirates?

Unfolding her arms, she shrugged. "When do I leave?"

"That's my girl! We've got the ship ready, and the synth has his programming. We just need my tech to finish up with his master key for the refinery ship. It'll get you through the airlock and any of the standard doors. You're going to have to figure out what to do if the secret cargo bay is secured differently—maybe strong-arm one of the synths or, I dunno, use a cutting torch . . ."

"I'll figure it out."

"I knew I liked you!" Mary stood up, grinning. "Listen, I'll have one of the synths lead you back to your ship, okay?"

"Yeah." Juliet stood, stretched, and subvocalized, "I know we have a lot to talk about, Angel, but right now, be on your toes. She told some guy to have a synth or two attack me as a test."

"She what? That seems incredibly irresponsible and foolish. What if they were to kill you? Her mission would be over before it started!"

"Yeah." Juliet turned toward the door. "That's the idea, I think. If I can't handle a little ambush, she probably shouldn't waste time with me on the mission."

"I'll be in touch with the details; we'll have a file on the ship with the known schematics. It won't be long, so get your gear ready. I think this is the start of a profitable relationship, Lacy."

Juliet stepped out the door and turned back to Mary. "I'll be waiting."

"Your guide will be in the next room." The door snicked closed. There was only one way to go from Mary's office; she had to walk down a short hallway and then enter a sort of reception area that had been empty as they'd passed through earlier. Her fingers trembled with readiness as they tapped the side of her holster. She was on high alert as she approached the doorway leading out of the hall. As it whooshed open, she almost drew her gun and blasted the synth who'd been sent to guide her. Angel immediately highlighted its empty hands, though, and she passed the jerky movement off by reaching up to massage her neck.

"Hello, I am designated Potato. I will guide you to your berth." The synth was built just like the bartender—no flesh at all and no attempts to act human.

On a whim, Juliet said, "Potato, hold still; let me look at you for a minute."

"Yes, ma'am." He stood stock-still, his LED eyes twinkling as he waited for Juliet to do whatever she was doing. What she was doing was trying to see if she could get any sort of psionic read from the synth. She'd never picked anything up from Bradbury back on the *Kowashi*, but she figured another sample wouldn't go amiss. She stared at his faintly flickering eyes for a long minute, willing him to open his synthetic mind to her, but nothing happened. Nothing other than snippets of thoughts starting to bleed in from other parts of the pirate base.

Juliet sighed and gestured for Potato to proceed. "Let's go." She followed him out of the empty reception area and into a long hallway. Doors lined the walls, and several junctions were ahead; Juliet's gut told her it felt like a damn good spot for an ambush. "You ready?" she subvocalized.

"Always." As if she'd invited the encounter, a synth carrying a shotgun stepped into the hallway from the next junction, and a door hissed open behind her.

Juliet knew two things: One, she couldn't shoot before they threatened her, or she'd get spaced, and two, she didn't want to eat any shotgun pellets. She stepped close to Potato, using him for cover, and glanced behind her. Sure enough, another matching synth had come through the door, and this one gripped a needler in its gray, plasteel fingers.

"Pardon me, but . . ." Potato didn't get any further before the shotgun roared. As he jerked backward into her, Juliet felt biting pain in her thigh and left wrist, and then the world got slow. She'd just turned back toward the shotgun-wielding synth when Angel ignited her synapses, and the cloud of smoke from its first shot was still billowing outward in slow motion as she yanked her pistol free of its holster and with feather-soft taps on its hair trigger sent two hot, screaming lumps of polymer at him.

"Aim for me," she subvocalized, jerking her lightning-fast arm around to point behind her. As soon as she felt Angel tweaking the angle of her wrist, she gently squeezed the trigger two more times. When her head and torso caught up to her arm and she looked back, the second synth was lying on the ground with creamy white fluids pooling around its perforated skull. Angel slowed her thoughts to normal, and Juliet turned to regard the first synth. It was crawling away from her, leaving a smear of the same white goo in its wake. It still clutched the shotgun, so Juliet took aim at its hand and fired another round. Two of its fingers flew off, and Juliet's round destroyed the shotgun's receiver.

"Well done, Juliet. You were hit by two buckshot pellets, but your nanites are extracting them and will have the wounds sealed quickly."

Juliet grunted, reflexively slapping her left hand against her thigh, wanting to explore the damage herself. The wound site was numb, and though her jeans had a large bloodstain, it wasn't growing anymore. A similar tale could be told about her wrist—a puckered, bloody hole sat right in the center, but she couldn't feel it.

Potato, lying at her feet, buzzed and twitched; then, with garbled, halting speech, said, ". . . rude. Pleazzzzz . . . ah . . . patiencsssss . . . ah . . . ah . . . mal-fu-fu-funct . . ."

"Quiet, Potato. Save your strength."

Juliet leaned against the plasteel wall and deftly reloaded her gun from the rounds on her belt. She spun the pistol and then slipped it into her holster. She knew Moon would be watching her; if not personally, then through her muscle, Galaxy. She folded her arms over her chest and waited, watching the first synth continue to try to crawl, though its motions grew slower and slower as more of that white fluid leaked out of it. She thought someone would be there to "investigate the noise" right away, but she ended up waiting nearly five minutes before Galaxy came sauntering around the corner, his built-in autocannon or shotgun aimed at her.

"Don't move," he growled.

"Relax," she snarled. They stared at each other for a pregnant heartbeat before he lowered his gun and nodded, stepping up to the dead synth she'd pegged in the center of the forehead with Angel's help.

"I watched the footage. They jumped you. Weird damn behavior, but these things are all kinds of messed up after all the mods we've done to 'em. Too many chefs in the kitchen, if you get my drift."

"Huh." Juliet was starting to get hoarse from all the rasping she'd done, so she spoke in a rough whisper. "Guess I'll have to talk to Mary about her pilot synth."

"You do that." He stood up and walked up to her. "Follow me. I'll get you to your ship." He started walking without waiting for a response. When he was a meter from the still crawling synth, he pointed his cannon at it, and, with a thunderous boom and cloud of white smoke, he blew its head into a thousand pieces.

Juliet frowned, thankful for the auto-squelch feature on her auditory implants. She looked at the blackened smear that had once been the synth's head and noted Galaxy's gun hadn't done much damage to the floor, just some scratches.

"Deforming antipersonnel rounds?"

"Sure. No sense blowing holes in our ship if we get boarded." He turned to look at her and frowned. "Good thing you're in the middle of the station and didn't miss. Those bullets of yours look like they'd punch through a two-inch plate." Juliet just grunted in response, so he turned and continued walking. A moment later, he spoke again. "Damn fast on that trigger. Damn good shot without even looking behind you. I saw you glance back and see the synth, but what if he'd moved?"

"What if?"

"What if . . . Yeah, what if. I guess you'd just have to shoot again. Only a couple more shots in that pistol, though."

Lacy's reticence was back in full effect, so Juliet grunted again. Galaxy got quiet after that, and she tried to focus on the mess this mission had become. She was trying to get closer to Antigone, but it felt like she was taking a step back for every step she took forward. She knew where Antigone was and had an idea what she was doing there, but now she'd gotten herself wrapped up in some pirate mission to confirm a conspiracy theory. She started subvocalizing to Angel, "Send a message to Nick. Tell him I'm making progress, but things are getting messy and complicated. Tell him to message me when he's back on his ship so we can sweep it and give him the details."

"I sent him the message, but something troubling happened. His PAI replied with an automated response: The owner of this PAI is unavailable until further notice."

"Oh, melt it!" Juliet growled.

39

PIRATE SIDE MISSION

Juliet stood in the docking bay waiting by the airlock where she was supposed to meet the synth pilot for her little pirate side mission. When she'd accepted the job from Mary, she'd had at least a fifty-fifty intention of making an excuse to bail out on the job, but things had changed when she'd contacted TC about Nick's automated PAI message. The synth had claimed Nick was working on a "special project" for Mary, but he'd likely be available when Juliet returned from her mission. In other words, if she wanted to see him again, she needed to do the job.

She'd been angry. In her mind, taking Nick, silencing him, and using him as leverage undid any goodwill she might have felt toward Mary and her pirate faction, which had been pretty slim to begin with. *Who sent synths with live ammunition to ambush a person as a test?* No, Mary was on Juliet's shit list, and so were the members of her crew.

Still, Mary had Juliet over a barrel, and with her limited access around the base, she felt like she had to play it cool, had to play the game. She'd cut her comms to TC when he fed her the line about Nick's special project, but after thinking about it and sounding things out with Angel, she'd called him back and tried to act cool. She was Lacy Blake, and Lacy Blake didn't care if Nick ate a bullet.

The mission sounded a little crazy, a little out of her wheelhouse. She supposed Lacy's background made her a good candidate for crazy missions, though the only reason Juliet felt she had a chance of pulling it off was because she had Angel. Mary didn't know about Angel, so she must have decided Lacy was extremely talented, extremely desperate, or someone she wanted to get rid of. Juliet felt like the mission setup was too convoluted for it to be option three. If Mary wanted Juliet dead, she could've decoupled the docking rings from her cargo ship and turned the big cannons out in the docking cavity on her.

Further speculation was forestalled as a robotic synth wearing an old, patched-up flight suit approached. His eyes flashed as his speaker grill of a mouth emitted a gruff, masculine voice. "All set, soldier? Here, you'll need this." He tossed a slender plastic backpack her way, and as Juliet caught it, she saw it held a compressed air tank and sported six different directional nozzles—an EVA maneuvering pack.

"Thanks." She loosened the straps to fit over her tactical vest and armor while the synth passed her by and tapped an access code into the airlock.

"You'll want to attach your combat suit's shunt to that air tank," Angel said. "There's a port near the bottom."

Juliet did as Angel instructed, pulling the retractable tube from the lower left side of her suit out of its housing and plugging it into the tank before shrugging into the straps. After snapping the waist belt around her belly and cinching it tight over the armor plate, she asked, "How much time will this give me?"

"Depends on how long you take to EVA over to the target vessel," the synth answered as he stepped through the docking collar and clomped toward the airlock of their ride. Juliet followed him through the short tunnel to the ship's airlock door. It was so black that she felt a stab of panic, thinking she'd been tricked into spacing herself, but after a second glance, she realized it was just the ship's paint.

"He's correct. The tank is highly compressed and should be enough for a lot of maneuvering while leaving you plenty of oxygen. If you weren't using the air to maneuver, you'd be able to breathe in a vacuum for two hours on that tank."

"If you're smart, you'll plug it into the target vessel's refill duct when you get inside."

"You forgetting something?" Juliet watched as he typed in the access code to the ship's airlock.

"Never."

"What about my skeleton key? For the ship's doors?"

"It should be in our vessel here." The door hissed open, and he ducked through. Juliet followed and had to walk hunched over into the tiny craft;

the entire interior was just one room with no separate airlock. "There, upon your seat." He pointed to the rear of two seats, and Juliet saw a tiny metallic deck with an attached data cable. "Please put your gear and armor in the box behind the acceleration couch. You'll need to remove the armor plates from your suit so the couch can help manage your blood flow. I will help you to quickly reequip yourself before your EVA. I'll pressurize the cabin, and then we'll be off."

"Right." Juliet sighed and began the laborious process of removing the air pack, her vest, and all the rigid plates from her armor. Then she stowed everything in the plastic latching box behind her seat. When she was finally done, she picked up the little deck and climbed into the acceleration couch, looking around the ship's spartan, tiny interior. There were no viewscreens, no data terminals, and the only ship controls were in the pilot's seat. It looked like some kind of foam insulation had been sprayed between the gaps of every panel, every cable duct, and even into the space between the acceleration couch mounts and the plasteel floor. "Yo, what's the deal with all the blue foam? Something to help with stealth?"

"Correct. We will not radiate any heat. I'll kill the drives well away from the target vessel, and you'll EVA as we float by."

"So no active sensors or engines?"

"No, but they added some air canisters for micro-adjustments. I'm well programmed for this mission; don't fear." As he spoke, the door slid shut with a decisive thunk, and air began to hiss into the ship's cavity. Juliet adjusted her position in the couch and looked for a data port.

"Where can I jack in?"

"You can't. All unnecessary electronics have been stripped."

"Choice," Juliet sighed.

"Unhappy?" The synth spoke in a droll deadpan. Juliet wasn't sure if he was messing with her or if he was just being polite despite a desire not to talk. She decided Lacy wouldn't respond. Instead, she pulled the cable out of the little deck and plugged her own in.

"Check this thing out and maybe just copy the code so I don't have to carry it around," she subvocalized.

"On it. It's a fairly simple program, but it has encryption codes that must have been procured from the manufacturer of the access panels on the refinement vessel. I can't test them—they'll either work or they won't."

"Okay, cool, but I don't need the deck anymore, right?"

"Correct."

Juliet pulled her cable out and then wedged the deck between some foam insulation and the plasteel under her acceleration couch. The synth must have caught her movement out of the corner of its eye. "Is there something wrong with the access device?"

"No, I copied it."

"Excellent. Hold tight. We'll burn hard for the first quarter of the journey. I have a trajectory and burn schedule that will make us look as though we're flying well past Ganymede before I kill the drive and start using the air thrusters to redirect us."

"Cool."

"They must have cannibalized a lot of internal space to house air tanks. Depending on how much he decelerates, the maneuver he's describing could require tons of compressed air."

"Yeah. I guess I won't be able to keep track, considering I can't jack in." Juliet leaned back in the couch, gripping the sides, and prepared for the burn.

It started faster than she'd expected. The synth got them out of the docking cavity of the ancient dreadnought pretty quickly, and then he didn't waste any time kicking it into gear. She couldn't see the readout on the ship, but Angel did a good job estimating the Gs.

As they ramped up past two and then three, the synth asked, "Are you faring well?"

"Fine." Thanks to her time flying with Nick, three Gs didn't feel like much, though she didn't relish an extended time under that kind of pressure. Unfortunately, the synth took her at her word, and the forces continued to climb and didn't settle until Angel's reading on her AUI read three-point-five. Juliet focused on her breathing, focused on her muscle contractions, and let the couch do its thing, massaging her limbs and torso, pushing her blood through her veins. The synth kept the hard Gs up for almost an hour, then it relented and dropped them down to one-point-five Gs, and Juliet groaned with relief.

"We'll resume hard burn in thirty minutes. Practice your high-G compression recovery techniques during this time."

"You're . . . sadistic," Juliet grunted as she stretched and fought her muscles' desire to spasm. The synth didn't respond, so she buckled down and put his recommendation into action, methodically working her way through her body, flexing every joint, tightening and relaxing every muscle, and all the while, taking deep, controlled breaths.

She'd barely gotten through the activity a handful of times when, like clockwork, the synth pilot resumed the hard burn. They repeated that process five times, and when it was over, Juliet had no idea where they were; three of those burns had been to decelerate, and now she was exhausted, hungry, thirsty, and her bladder was begging her for release.

"I've gotta go to the head."

"There isn't one. Please urinate in your suit." The synth didn't even look at her.

"I . . ." Juliet was at a loss for words; she felt stupid for not expecting anything this rough for her delivery, but also very annoyed that she'd been so ill-prepared by the people sending her.

"Your combat suit is equipped with a fluid-waste recycling and management system, Juliet—the inner layer of smart-fabric interfaces with a gel-based, zero-displacement absorption layer. It will sanitize and recycle all fluids you excrete into your emergency reservoir."

"I didn't realize . . . you mean this pouch?" Juliet touched the empty fluid bladder above her waistline. "I thought I was supposed to fill that."

"You can, but it also gets replenished from your sweat, blood, and yes, urine."

"Are you speaking to your PAI?" The synth turned to glare at her with its amber LED eyes.

"Yes, asshole. Thanks for warning me ahead of time about this shitty flight. Do you have any food or fluids on this can?"

"Check the compartment on the left side of your seat." Juliet slapped her hand down against the plasteel seat frame, and sure enough, there was a little knob. She twisted it, and a compartment popped out. She leaned over the side of her chair to peer within and saw five juice pouches and a package of ten vanilla-flavored nutrient wafers.

As she punched a straw into her juice pack, careful not to let any fluid escape, she muttered, "I take back the asshole part."

"Are you going to urinate?" Angel asked. Juliet could hear the concern in her voice.

"I'm working myself up to it. I've never peed my pants on purpose before."

As if he could read her mind, the synth spoke up. "I'm sorry about the toilet closet being removed. If you don't have a suit capable of handling the situation, you should know the acceleration couch is equipped to handle large amounts of liquid and even solid waste."

"Yeah, thanks. Do me a favor, and don't talk for a while." Juliet switched to subvocalizations. "Put on a playlist. I need to tune out the noises of the ship." Angel complied, and almost like magic, Juliet found herself beginning to relax. She closed her eyes, and without hardly trying, she relieved her bladder. It was uncomfortable at first, the warmth of her urine against her skin, but as Angel had promised, her suit rapidly wicked it away. Sighing with relief, she tore into a pack of nutrient wafers. As she munched, she asked, "Angel, if I have to kill some synths on this ship, how guilty should I feel? Are they, like, close to true AIs?"

"If Mary Moon's intel is correct, not even remotely. Industrial synths designed to perform a singular task category are among the most simplistic of pseudo-AIs. They're ranked even lower than most commercial PAIs. Corporations utilizing such labor sources are not interested in providing entertainment, regular rest, or the mental decompression time that more sophisticated limited AIs require."

"So they're basically robots."

"Correct."

"Okay, turn down my music a little, will ya?" As her music faded to a relaxing background noise, she asked, "How long 'til I need to get ready?"

The pilot immediately responded, "We'll be maneuvering via air thruster for the next two hours, and it will be another five hours until we make our flyby."

"I'm gonna try to get some sleep."

"Very good." The synth didn't seem to care; he just kept touching the little buttons on the flight stick with his plasteel fingers, gently adjusting the maneuvering jets on the tiny ship. Juliet might have tried to stay awake to observe, even just to get an idea of their location relative to Jupiter or its moons, but with no access to the ship's sensors or cameras, there wasn't much she could do.

In any case, she was exhausted; putting aside the last brutal half a day of hard Gs, she'd hardly slept the night before, worried about Nick, about the job, and about what the hell she'd do about Antigone and her billionaire dad. She still didn't have a plan, but she'd decided to take it one step at a time. Step one was to get this job done so she'd have a little goodwill among the pirates.

Everything considered, it wasn't surprising when she almost immediately fell asleep. She always slept easily in an operating vehicle. The hum of the ship's systems coming through the couch into her bones relaxed her and reminded her of taking long road trips with her mom and sister when she was a little kid.

When she'd been a little girl, the idea of riding somewhere distant with her mom and sister was sort of like a vacation from reality, regardless of the purpose of the trip. In that car, on the highway, there wasn't a chance her mom would be missing when she woke up. There wasn't a chance that her sister would be gone, off somewhere with her friends, no little sisters invited. She could sleep and know everyone was together, and they'd be there when she woke. Somehow, that cozy feeling translated to spaceships, which was probably a big part of why Juliet loved them.

She must have slept quite soundly because Angel had to wake her. "Juliet! The pilot just indicated that it would be wise to begin preparations."

Yawning, Juliet stretched and slowly began to climb out of the couch. She had to move very methodically and carefully in the zero-G environment, but at least it seemed the pilot was done making flight adjustments. He turned to her and stood from his seat. "I will help you attach your armor. Your EVA window opens in nine minutes and forty-seven seconds." Angel provided a big, neon-orange countdown on her AUI.

"Cool, thanks." Juliet started working on the armor plates for her legs, and the synth quickly and efficiently began to attach the ones to her back.

"Interesting! Your upper back plates are equipped with two small drones."

"Yeah, I'm aware."

"I haven't seen this sort of armored suit on any of the denizens of Hereford's Vengeance."

"Good to know." Juliet grunted as she bent to pick up her gun belt, buckling it around her waist. Then she picked up her tactical vest and asked, "Done with the back plates?"

"Yes. I shall begin working on your left arm."

"Let me get this vest on first." Juliet shrugged into it, zipped it up, then picked up her shotgun, looping the harness over her helmet. Thus laden with gear, she stood still while the synth did his work, snapping the rest of her armored plates into place. When he stood back, she nodded and picked up the air pack, putting it on and clipping it in place. She turned her back to the synth. "Plug the air hose from my suit into the pack, please." When he complied and she saw the pack's air level populate on her AUI, she nodded and hunch-walked toward the rear hatch. She had four minutes before she had to jump into space. "They haven't noticed us?"

"No sign that they have. Even if they notice us, we should look much like a stray hunk of rock."

"All right." Juliet knew her palms would be sweating buckets if not for the gloves covering them with the same moisture-wicking properties as the rest of her suit. She looked again at her helmet's status on her screen—air pressure was good, no leaks. Her air pack was at ninety-nine percent.

"Sending the ship's position and orientation data relative to the target vessel to your PAI. I'm also sending the rendezvous information should you prove successful in liberating one of the ship's shuttles."

"Don't worry, I'll prove successful. Just be there."

"Shall I manage your maneuvering jets?" Angel asked.

"Yeah, absolutely!" Juliet didn't want to take any chances, considering the consequences of failing to get to the gas collector's airlock in time.

"With the data the synth provided, I project we'll reach the airlock with seventy percent of your air remaining."

"Sounds good to me." Juliet glanced at the countdown—two minutes. She watched those numbers tick down, trying to regulate her breathing, trying not to think about what she was going to do when they hit zero. When the count reached one minute, the air began to hiss out of the cabin.

"Depressurizing." Juliet glanced at the synth and saw him back in his acceleration couch, still not wearing a helmet.

"Don't need to breathe, huh?"

"Not at all." The counter read ten seconds, the latches on the door thunked open, and it slid to the side, revealing the black expanse of space.

"Five . . . four . . . three . . ." Juliet tuned the synth out; she could see the countdown. When it said one, she stepped out the door and drifted into nothing.

40

SYNTH ENCOUNTERS

Juliet was a little startled when she saw how close she'd been dropped to the station and the target ship. The station filled almost the entirety of her view, a two-kilometer-long spindle with three rings, all of which had gigantic ships docked to them. Beyond the station, Juliet could see glimpses of Ganymede and, beyond that, the ochre, throbbing glow of Jupiter.

She was thankful for the close proximity because it made the enormity of what she'd done by stepping out of the stealth interceptor a little less shocking. With all of those landmarks to focus on, it was easy to ignore the fact that she was drifting through the void of space, especially when Angel started firing her maneuvering jets, driving her toward one of the big, factorylike harvesting ships.

"At least that synth pilot really dropped me near a station. Could have been worse."

"Were you concerned about that?" Angel's voice, rising in pitch, gave away her surprise.

"Only mildly. There are less complicated ways to kill someone."

"Yes, that was my thinking; otherwise, I would have encouraged more caution. I see the target airlock; highlighting it for you. Be ready to grab that retention eyelet in forty-seven seconds." Juliet saw the orange highlight on the aft, starboard side of the ship and watched as it rapidly grew larger with her approach. If she ignored the void around her and focused on her destination, she could almost pretend she was parachuting down toward the side of a building, especially as the ship loomed bigger and bigger in her view.

"This thing really is like a flying factory, isn't it?" She'd seen plenty of ships similar to this one while flying escort jobs with Nick, but as she rapidly approached the red blinking lights near the airlock door, the up-close perspective was something altogether different.

"Not only is it like one, but it is one. The ship captures air and runs it through a refinery module, separating out the various component gases into tanks. Get ready to grab the eyelet in five . . . four . . ." Juliet held up her gloved hand, extending the soles of her feet so she could cushion her impact with the plasteel door by bending her knees.

Exactly when Angel said, "One," she hit the door and gripped the big, smooth metal ring. She yelped in surprise as she was almost flung off by the gravitational pull generated by the station's rotation. She'd expected her momentum to continue straight into the door, but the ship was oriented so the station's gravity pulled her "downward" instead. Luckily, her cybernetic hand was strong, and she held on, her body flopping painfully against the metal.

"Oof!" she grunted, digging her toes against the metal lip around the door and straightening herself out. Angel didn't say anything, and neither did she; it was obvious what she'd done wrong, and she'd recovered fine.

The access panel for the door was beneath a spring-loaded plasteel cover, and when Juliet flipped it up, she saw a keypad and a data port. "If I plug in here, and the key we got from the pirates doesn't work, is it going to set off an alarm?"

"It shouldn't. Most panels like this won't trigger security alerts unless several erroneous codes are input in a row. In any case, if anyone's monitoring the ship's systems, they'll see that the airlock door was opened."

"What about Fido? Can he get into the system and, you know, cover our tracks?"

"Yes. He's ready, but there will be a window between him gaining control and you entering the ship. I can only estimate how long it will take him to infiltrate the security systems—anywhere between a couple of minutes to half an hour or so."

"Okay. Here's hoping he gets in quickly." Juliet pulled her data cable from the port on the sleeve of her suit and plugged it into the access panel. She had time for two nervous breaths before the LEDs on top of the panel flashed green, and she saw, through the glass on the door, a red light begin to strobe in the airlock; it was venting, getting ready to open.

"The skeleton key program worked, and I've sent Fido into the system. He'll work his way through the ICE."

Juliet slung her shotgun behind her hip so it wouldn't get in the way of her movement, and then she drew her needler. She'd loaded it with shredders, but even so, with its boxy suppressor, she knew it would be much quieter than her other guns. The most dangerous part of the job would be right as she first boarded before Fido had a chance to get into the cameras and other ship systems.

As soon as the outer door latches clunked open and swung wide, she pulled herself into the airlock.

Immediately upon setting foot on the plasteel floor paneling, enjoying the return of normal-feeling gravity, she turned and slapped the button to seal the airlock. As the outer door swung shut, she went to the inner door and peered through the diamatex window into the corridor beyond. She didn't see anyone, but that didn't mean they weren't running her way, weapons locked and loaded. "Do I need to plug in again?"

"Yes! Fido's not through the ICE, so we'll need the skeleton key again." When she heard Angel say "yes," Juliet was already plugging in. Seconds later, the red light began to flash again, and clouds of air hissed into the chamber, pressurizing it. Juliet stared through the viewport, nervously tapping the barrel of her needler against the armor plate on her thigh, hoping nobody had been monitoring the ship's airlocks. She wasn't that lucky, however. Just as the LEDs changed from flashing red to a steady green and the door latches clicked loose, she saw a very robotic-looking synth come around the corner. Juliet ducked to the side of the door as it swung open.

"Angel, get a look with the spider drone." Angel didn't answer, but the snick of the drone's legs extending told her she was on it. While the drone scurried along the wall, its magnetic feet tip-tapping on the panel covers, Juliet activated the jamming field on her data deck, stowed in her vest pocket. She didn't have to touch or even see the deck; Angel had set up an AUI element to control the jammer just as easily as activating a comm channel.

A window had opened on her AUI, showing her the feed from the drone. At that moment, it showed her an above-angle view of the airlock, with her standing to the side of the doorway, but as the drone lowered itself to the edge of the opening and peeked out into the hallway, Juliet saw the synth striding toward her obliviously. "Three more meters before it's in your jamming field."

Juliet watched the synth approach, trying to gauge the distance. She needn't have worried—as soon as it stepped into her jamming field, it froze, and its blue LED eyes flashed red. Juliet knew it would try to alert the rest of the ship, so she acted without thought. She rotated to her left so she faced into the corridor, lifted and pointed the needler using the crosshairs on her AUI, and fired two quick shots right into its face.

She hadn't fired the needler in a while, and it felt almost like a toy after all the practice she'd done with her Texan. Nevertheless, the shredder rounds were effective, and with the low recoil of the gun, they both hit near the dead center of the synth's face, ripping through the plastic and alloy skull and then into the gel-and-wire neuroprocessing matrix at the center of its head. It fell, twitching, to the plasteel floor, spilling a pool of white, fizzy fluids.

Juliet glanced at the camera in the corner near the airlock door. "Do you think the jammer's working on that camera?"

"With you this close to it, it may interfere with its digital components. I can't guarantee it, however. Fido is still working to gain access."

"Okay, send the drone forward to scout." Juliet hurried to the synth's body, grabbed one of its still twitching plasteel-and-wire wrists, and dragged it into the airlock. Stepping back into the hallway, she punched the button to close the big, heavy door.

"Nothing around the corner," Angel reported, though Juliet could see that for herself in the drone's camera feed. She looked at her mini map and started following the outlined path to the secret cargo bay. Angel kept the spider drone ahead of her, always along the same path, watching every corridor junction. Juliet left her jammer actively working, hoping it would disrupt the cameras she passed by, but knowing there was a very good chance it wouldn't; they were all hardwired.

"What's taking Fido so long?"

"He can't communicate with me yet. I have a feeling the ICE on this ship has been upgraded. Have faith, Juliet; he knows many tricks."

The ship was in good repair, but it was clearly an industrial vessel. The lights were amber, the plasteel panels were gray-brown, and there wasn't a soft surface in sight. Juliet rather appreciated the dim lighting, finding it easier to feel sneaky running down those long corridors in her mostly black gear as she hugged close to the walls. She'd made it about halfway through the route outlined on her mini map when she had her second encounter.

The spider drone paused in a long corridor with an open door, and as it peered through, Juliet saw another synth working at a data terminal. It was alone in a room with half a dozen chairs tucked into workstations, and the only lighting came from a single amber LED bulb near the door. It looked to Juliet like the room would typically be staffed with several people, but now, during maintenance, a single synth was monitoring systems, and most everything was offline. She had the drone keep its eye on the synth while she padded past the doorway, stepping lightly on the rubbery soles of her boots.

Once she'd cleared and rounded the next corner, she called the drone forward and sent it ahead, resuming her earlier practice of following it along the route Angel had mapped. She'd just gone down an access ladder, avoiding the more centrally located lift, when Angel spoke up again.

"Fido's in!"

"I'm assuming he's gained control of the network, or he wouldn't be able to contact you."

"Yes. He's well ensconced—full control of the cameras and the ship's access panels and comms. No alarms have yet been raised about your presence. The synth that you eliminated logged itself as investigating an anomaly with the airlock, and Fido has cleared it. There are nine more synths on duty around the ship, but now, I can easily steer you around them."

"Awesome. What about the cargo hold we're supposed to check out?"

"If cameras are within, they aren't tied to the ship's network. I also cannot confirm if the door is secured or not; it's not on the ship's—"

"Network. Got it." Juliet continued on her way, picking up the pace now that Angel had eyes on all the crew. When she came to the last stretch of hallway before the mysterious cargo bay, she paused and let the spider drone take its time investigating. She watched through the vidscreen as it peered around the last corner. Angel moved it a millimeter at a time, careful so it wouldn't set off motion detectors, and it was a good thing she did: a heavily armed synth, completely plated in matte-black plasteel, stood before the door only five meters from the corner. It held a bulky, wide-barreled light machine gun with a drum magazine as though it weighed no more than a banana.

"What are the odds I can disable that synth before it squeezes its trigger and sets off all kinds of alarms?"

"With regard to it dying before squeezing the trigger, not good. It's got an armor-plated exo-shell, and I'm sure its internals are hardened. It's a full-combat unit. However, if you're worried about alarms, you shouldn't be—Fido has control."

"What about any synths that might be behind the door?"

"Ah, I see. No, I wouldn't worry. That's a blast door, and it's shielded to prevent noise from coming through."

Juliet grinned. "Almost like the people who installed whatever is behind it were worried about people listening to their special project." Juliet stared at her vid feed of the hulking, armored synth with its massive gun, and thought about how to tackle it. If she used her Texan, it might punch through its armored skull, but it might not. If she used her shotgun, it would undoubtedly pack more of a punch, but of course, she didn't have armor-piercing rounds in it. She had a mag full of armor-piercing needler rounds, but would they do enough damage to stop that thing? It probably had redundant systems. Frowning, she reached into her vest pocket and pulled out a pack of the V.E.G. "How much of this stuff do you think I need to hurt that thing?"

"If you threw it with a detonator and I activated it?"

"Yeah."

"It's tacky and may adhere when you throw it, but it could also stick to your gloves, ruining your accuracy. I think you should attach it to the flying drone, and I'll deliver it to the synth's face. I believe a quarter of that pack will be enough to knock the synth over and, at least, stun it."

Juliet reached over her shoulder and detached her other drone. Then, she used her vibroblade to slice off a third of the explosive gel. She stuck it to the front of the drone, right above the primary camera, then took one of the little detonator pins out of the case and pressed it into the gel. A tiny LED winked green at her as Angel synced with it.

Juliet set the drone down on the plasteel floor and watched as Angel brought it online and flew it around in a few wobbly circles, getting used to the added weight of the gel.

"This is going to be loud . . ." She nervously gripped her needler; then, thinking better of it, stuffed it into her holster and swung the shotgun forward. If she was going loud, she might as well be ready. "Okay, go for it." Juliet watched in the spider's feed as the flying drone zoomed forward, then around the corner. Angel flew it fast, and she hardly registered it on the viewscreen as it streaked straight into the big synth's face. Then, a white explosion rattled the plasteel floorplates and cut out her view.

Juliet hurried to the corner, turned, and in a haze of smoke, saw the synth flopping on the floor. One arm was bent backward, rotating ineffectually, but the other reached for the LMG it had dropped. It looked like the explosive had nearly knocked its head off, but it was still blindly functioning, weird, partial words emitting from its ruined speaker-grill mouth. The armor plating around its neck was bent and ruined, and its plasteel spine was partially exposed, almost like the explosion had pulled it partway out of its torso.

Juliet stepped forward and, point-blank, fired three rounds out of her shotgun into that exposed spine. As the powerful polyblast shells discharged their payload and the polymer pellets ripped into the spine and synthetic nerves of the commando synth, it jerked and spasmed, then finally lay still. For good measure, Juliet drew her vibroblade and drove it into the thing's skull several times, ensuring she ruined its synthetic brain so it couldn't call for help once her jammer was out of range.

Juliet looked around the carnage she'd created. Her drone was in a million pieces. Scorch marks and scratches covered the door and walls nearby, but nothing looked broken.

"Any problems with the other synths?"

"Several of them looked up when the explosion rattled through the ship's hull, but Fido didn't allow any alarms to go off. They've all returned to their tasks."

"Well, now we're down to the nitty-gritty. Let's see if you can get through this door." Juliet walked up to the control panel for the heavy door and stuck her cable into the port.

"As you feared, the skeleton key does not work on this door."

"Yeah, I wonder what Mary had in mind for whoever got to this spot? Did she expect some kind of miracle?"

"I think she would expect you to kill all the synths on board and use the tools in the machine shop to cut your way in. Luckily, I think I'll be able to breach this ICE in a matter of minutes." While Angel worked, Juliet thought about what she'd said. She would have been at it for hours if she'd had to use the machine shop tools to get through this door. The odds that the ship would be left alone for that long seemed slim to her. The more she thought about it, the angrier she got, and the more she started to believe Mary Moon had sent her to check out this ship as a sort of exploratory Hail Mary, no pun intended. If Juliet—Lacy—died in the process, it wasn't a big loss to the pirate, and if she got the job done, all the better.

"I'm gonna make sure I leverage whatever I find in there to get this stupid pirate job over with. I'm sick of the convoluted schemes that keep piling on top of my problems. Jeez, Angel! All I wanted to do was keep Nick and Larry out of that billionaire's crosshairs!"

"I know. It is convoluted, but I like your thinking—if you find something valuable enough behind this door, you'll have a much stronger hand to play when you get back to the pirate base. Also, good news: I've found an exploit in the memory buffer. Are you ready?"

Juliet hefted her shotgun and moved to the side of the door so the plasteel wall would shield most of her body. "I'm ready. Let's see what the big mystery is."

41

IT POURS

Juliet stood before the entrance to the secure cargo bay, gun tight to her shoulder, ready for anything as Angel finished her exploit. The latches thunked as they slid out of their housings, and with a hiss of slightly positive air pressure, the thick, heavy blast door began to roll open. Juliet had imagined a wide-open cargo space filled with exotic equipment and perhaps a violent squad of combat synths waiting for her, so she was a little surprised to see a small airlock chamber coated in some kind of powdered black paint. As she cautiously stepped forward, the blast door slid closed with a resounding thud, and a pleasant feminine voice emanated from a scanner array near the closed inner door.

"Welcome, technician. Please provide identification to avoid safety protocols."

"Juliet, jack into the scanner array near that door. Quickly!" Angel didn't often sound panicked, so it startled Juliet into action. She let her gun hang from its sling and pulled her data cable out as she took two steps to cross the little airlock chamber. She shoved the jack into the data port at the base of the scanner array and waited for a further update from Angel.

Juliet didn't like how the outer door had closed. Shouldn't Angel have been in charge of that? She looked around the little room. It was only about three meters deep by four wide, and the walls, floor, and ceiling were featureless plasteel coated in that strange, powdery black paint. The room's only fixture was the scanner array above the inner door.

"Welcome, technician. You have thirty seconds to provide your credentials before safety protocols are enacted."

"What's going on, Angel?" Juliet knew what was going on, generally—she was about to trigger some kind of alarm. She wouldn't mind a few more details, though.

When Angel didn't respond and the back of her neck began to feel hot, she knew something serious was happening. Angel was pulling out all the stops, trying to force her way past the ICE in the little airlock's security package.

"Welcome, technician. You have twenty seconds to provide your credentials before safety protocols are enacted."

"Angel . . ."

"A moment, Juliet."

"Warning: you have ten seconds to provide credentials to avoid safety protocol enactment."

With soft hissing clicks, several panels in the ceiling, heretofore invisible, slid open, revealing shiny chrome nozzles.

"Angel!"

"Warning: you have five seconds—" The voice cut out, and the panels slid closed. "Welcome, technician Emilio Fuentes. Please stand by for decontamination." New panels slid open on the sides of the room, and suddenly, Juliet was awash in brilliant green laserlike beams. Vents in the walls opened and fans began to whir, evacuating the smoke, as tiny particles of lint and dust were incinerated by the beams.

While the lasers were frisking her, Angel said, "Fido interrupted a message from this room's commlink. It was meant to warn the ship and the station that self-destruction was a possibility and that the crew should prepare to evacuate."

"The safety protocols were going to blow the ship?"

"That would have been the second stage. The first stage was to incinerate everything in this airlock."

The lasers stopped their crisscrossing pattern, and new nozzles emerged from the ceiling, spraying a fine mist into the chamber. Juliet didn't know what it was, but was thankful to be inside her airtight suit. "You mean I was five seconds from being cooked?"

"Yes, though your suit would have protected you for several seconds. I would say I cracked the security with ten seconds to spare—no mean feat, I might add. This room has a pseudo-AI managing the entry and exit of all personnel. Don't worry, I have complete control now. The good news is that there's nobody currently registered to be working within."

"No synths?"

"Not inside, at least according to the scanner logs." The mist stopped spraying, and weird, extremely bright strobing lights began to flash. Juliet watched as steam began to rise from her armored suit.

"Is this thing dosing me with radiation or something?"

"No, those flashing lights are meant to activate the sanitizing agent that was just disbursed." As the strobing lights switched off, air jets began to blow from grates that had silently opened under Juliet's feet. "You're almost through the sanitation process."

Juliet fidgeted nervously, looking around the room, wondering how freaked out she should be that she'd almost been turned to slag for stepping into it.

The air jets stopped hissing, all the hidden ports snicked closed, and the inner airlock door clicked loudly and began to roll to the side.

Even though Angel was confident no one was inside, Juliet lifted her shotgun as she peered through the opening, suddenly much more nervous about stepping into unexplored spaces in the hidden facility. What she saw was the weirdest, most sci-fi room she'd ever laid eyes on. She'd been in some high-tech environments, not least of which was Doctor Ladia's clinic. This place made all of Ladia's equipment look quaint. The deep hum of powerful equipment, the weird staticlike energy in the air, and the bespoke nature of all the hardware made her feel like she'd just stepped into the heart of an alien spacecraft.

The space was ample, probably forty meters by twenty, with a high ceiling. It didn't feel big, though, with all the equipment crammed in there. Everything was white or stainless steel. Three huge, shiny cylinders that looked almost like gas tanks with wide diamatex viewports cut into the sides lined the right-hand wall, one stacked atop the other horizontally. Stainless pipes ran from those cylinders to five other containers that got progressively smaller and less rounded. The final one was only about as big as a mini fridge, and it caught Juliet's eye because it was wrapped entirely in tubing that looked like it was made of gold.

Data terminals lined the opposite wall, and huge, bulky machines filled the center of the bay, all of them housed in stainless steel shrouds, making it very hard for Juliet even to guess what they were. One thing she recognized right away, near the back of the room and cut into the rear wall, was a domed containment chamber that clearly housed a fusion reactor a good deal larger and more modern than the one on the *Kowashi* or the smaller ships she'd flown. Conduits and pipes ran between nearly every component, and Juliet was tracing them with her eyes when Angel said, "You should connect me to that central data terminal. There's no wireless signal in here."

"You lost your connection to Fido?"

"Yes."

"Dang it!" Juliet hurried toward the indicated terminal, her boots hardly making a sound on the insulated white polymer floor panels, and plugged into one of the many open ports on the side of the big cube.

"This might take me a few minutes. I wish I had Fido; I could set him loose, and we could explore while he worked."

"I know you don't want to copy him, but why don't you make him some brothers or sisters?"

"I've thought about it but haven't gotten around to it. I'm still learning from Fido as he grows and expands his capabilities. I've been making plans for an assistant AI for your gunship if Bennet ever gets the main systems back online." She paused for a minute and, in a quieter voice, asked, "Are you disappointed that I don't have a suite of helper daemons like Fido?"

"Disappointed? No, you goof! You just kept me from getting barbequed! How could I be disappointed? Besides, you see Fido as an individual—well, maybe a pet, but whatever—he's not just some code to you. You have your quirks, and so do I; that's one of the reasons we get along so well." Juliet watched the display on the data terminal, but nothing Angel was doing was represented on the screen. "While you're working there, can you help me understand any of this equipment?"

"That fusion reactor could easily power this entire ship and another like it. Some of these larger components look similar to those I saw while researching gravity-generation technologies back on Luna. However, none of the photos of that hardware were current; all of that information became proprietary after the war as corporations fought over the technology."

"Some kind of gravity generation? But this ship doesn't have a gravity field, does it? The only reason I feel gravity is because of the station's spin, right?"

"That's correct, but we don't know what the ship is capable of when fully powered up with a full crew. Still, it was definitely not designed with a gravity generator in mind. Other than this extra cargo bay, the ship is very close to factory specifications."

While Angel worked, Juliet continued to let her eyes wander over the big space, studying the dozens of machine components, though most were simply stainless-steel boxes with tubes and pipes coming out of them. On a whim, she closed her eyes and opened her mind, trying to see if she could pick up anything with the lattice, but nothing greeted her other than the hum of the reactor and the sounds of fluids and gases moving through pipes.

"They've gone to great lengths to put those stainless shrouds over every piece of machinery in here."

Juliet opened her eyes and looked around the room again. "You don't think they're necessary?"

"No. I think they're protecting proprietary technology."

"Wouldn't the techs know what's under them anyway? You figure they have people coming in here who aren't in on the secret?"

"It's possible that human or synthetic technicians are trained on individual components and won't know what function the system as a whole serves." As Juliet thought about that, her imagination ran wild with ideas about why a gas harvester might have a modified gravity generation system powered by a reactor big enough to energize a small city. She kept coming up blank, though; she just didn't know enough about the science to understand what the point of it all could be.

"Any progress?"

"Oh yes! I'm partially in, working my way past some tertiary layers of ICE. This terminal was well defended. There's a single access point where this room's network interfaces with the ship's network. Once I make that connection, I'll be in touch with Fido again and can begin analyzing the data in this server."

"You think I've got enough footage to satisfy Mary Moon?"

"She asked you to get detailed footage of the equipment in here. Considering how all the equipment is compartmentalized, I don't think that's particularly valuable. The data I get from this server might prove far more valuable."

"Yeah, I don't think Mary banked on me being able to get at that, though." Juliet idly tapped at the hilt of her vibroblade. "What if I opened up some of these shrouds?"

"If you were careful and cut shallowly through the hinges of those access panels, I think that may be a good idea."

"Okay, when you're done there."

"I'm through to Fido! All is still clear on the ship. Juliet, plug your deck into this server, and I'll work through that so you don't have to stay tethered."

"Oh, duh!" Juliet dug around in her vest pocket, pulling out her data deck. She ran its cable into another empty port, set it down on the workstation's charging pad, then asked, "Can I unplug?"

"Yes. I'm working through the deck now."

"Roger." Juliet pulled out her jack then drew her vibroblade, approaching one of the big stainless cubes. She walked around it until she found a locked access panel. Just as Angel had suggested, she took her blade and carefully inserted it into the seam between the panel cover and the shroud, slicing down through the little stainless hinge. She repeated the process for the bottom one. Then, she used her knife to pry the cover away from the shroud, exposing the machine's hidden innards.

The insides were just as confusing to her as the outside. Thousands of wires were tightly bundled, running from one black plastic box to another to another. She saw compressed air tanks, refrigerant coils, and dozens of circuit boards. She took a long minute to look at every visible component carefully, knowing the footage might prove valuable down the road, and then she moved on to the next big stainless box. While Angel worked on the data terminal, she repeated the process four more times.

Angel seemed too preoccupied to speculate about what she was revealing under the shrouds. Each time Juliet cut away one of the panels, looking inside at the mysterious machinery, she was left with more questions than answers, but hoped Angel would have some theories soon.

She squatted before the stainless, rectangular tank wrapped in gold tubing and was closely examining it from every angle when Angel finally spoke up.

"I have a theory about what this ship has been doing with this hardware."

"I'm listening!"

"This compartment and the array of hardware within is only half the picture. Conduits are running through the decking down to the ship's collection array. I figured that out when I began to read the data they've been gathering from scanners that aren't part of the gas harvester's array. This ship has been measuring gravitational anomalies around Jupiter. It seems that Jupiter's gravity well has allowed for a high concentration of dark matter."

"Dark matter?" Juliet knew the term. She'd learned about how the presence of dark matter was considered necessary for the universe's fundamental rules—or at least the theories of rules—to make sense. She was pretty sure people hadn't ever found or seen it, though. That was part of the whole reason it was called dark.

"Yes. I think the people responsible for the design of this collection and containment system discovered that Jupiter has been naturally collecting dark matter, for lack of a better word. This room doesn't house a gravity generator; it houses a gravitational field generator. It's not making gravity for the crew of the ship but to capture dark matter. I see references to a quantum gravity resonator or QGR. This is the heart of the process they've developed; the QGR manipulates the fundamental forces at a quantum level, allowing it to generate concentrated gravity wells specifically to capture dark matter."

"Uh, is that possible?"

"Dark matter doesn't interact with normal matter or electromagnetic forces, making it nearly impossible to detect, let alone capture. It does, however, interact with gravity. This ship is exploiting that interaction. If I understand things correctly, I believe they capture it using the QGR, and then they store the dark matter in gravitational fields within self-contained units that can be removed from the ship. Do you see that empty platform opposite the fusion reactor shroud? That's where the containment unit would sit. This ship has recently had its payload removed."

"What are they doing with dark matter?" Juliet's mind was racing through a hundred corny sci-fi plots where dark matter was responsible for everything from doomsday devices to the origin of a superhero's powers.

"That isn't explicitly stated anywhere in this data. I can guess, though, based on the values in this database from the scanners—they're measuring the effects the dense pockets of dark matter near Jupiter are having on space-time. If I were to postulate the purpose for all this, I'd say the dark matter is being studied elsewhere for applications in altering or warping space-time."

"In English?"

"Juliet, they're trying to build a warp drive. Something that will fold space and allow faster-than-light travel." Juliet's mind bloomed with the implications of Angel's words, and she found herself plopping down in the chair bolted in front of the workstation. In the back of her mind, she'd been thinking this whole thing was a kind of conspiracy goose chase. Why would any corp hide such a big operation inside a gas harvester? Surely, this was just some experimental gas-harvesting tech that Mass Gas or whoever owned this ship was trying to hide from the competition. Angel's revelation and theory had blown that idea out of the water.

Why hide a dark matter collector inside a gas harvester? Because they needed to gather a lot of the stuff, and they didn't want anyone to catch on to what they were doing. Any corp that mastered dark matter and managed to keep their know-how a secret would stand to gain so much wealth that Juliet's mind simply couldn't fathom it. *What could they do if they really managed to create a faster-than-light drive? What kinds of resources would suddenly be available if trips to nearby solar systems were a possibility?*

What if they weren't limited to those nearby?

How were they doing it? How had they built the QRG or QGR or whatever Angel had called it? How were they managing to build those portable gravity-powered containment units?

"Angel, is an AI helping them? A true AI?"

"I'm not able to discern that from this data."

"Did you copy everything?"

"I copied the database of scan results and all the system information. I didn't copy the raw scan data because your data deck doesn't have the room."

"Any idea where they're taking the dark matter?"

"From this station to the nearby moon, Ganymede. I have logistical information for the shipments; the containment units must be tuned precisely to interact with nearby gravity wells."

"The gas collecting corp, the one that owns a piece of all of them, don't want the other big corps to catch wind of what they're doing. They'd be attacked. If they succeed, it'll upset the power structure in the entire solar system. If someone like WBD knew this was going on, they'd try to steal it for sure."

"There's also the likelihood that your question bears weight: are they using a true AI? If so, that would spell their destruction as well."

Juliet turned and unplugged her deck, slipping it back into her pocket. She felt like she'd just picked up a nuclear bomb. "Can I give this to the pirates? It seems a little too hot to give to a bunch of criminals."

Angel didn't answer immediately, so Juliet stood and walked to the airlock, punching the button to open the external door. She had to wait while the inner door closed and the airlock thoroughly sanitized her again. While she waited, she voiced what was on her mind.

"I feel like I just stepped on a landmine. Who do I trust with this kind of information? Do I trust anyone that much? Is it okay for a corporation to figure this kind of tech out? If they do, is it okay for one corp to have the secret? Will it spark another big war?"

The big door thunked open, and she hurried out past the blasted remains of the combat synth. She glanced at her AUI and saw Angel had populated it with a path to the shuttle bay.

"I don't know, Juliet. I hadn't considered all of those questions in my earlier fascination with what I'd found."

"I'm starting to wish I hadn't taken this side job. Still, it puts things in perspective. I don't know if I can afford to worry about Nick, Antigone, Larry, and all that. I need advice, and I don't have a clue who to ask."

"Not to add to your concerns, but Fido says three armed synths are approaching the airlock from the station."

Juliet groaned and started jogging. "When it rains, it pours, Angel."

42

///////////////////////

ESCAPE

Why are armed synths boarding?" Juliet asked as she sprinted down a long, empty corridor, following the route Angel had laid out to the shuttle bay.

"I don't know! Perhaps the combat synth you destroyed was meant to check in regularly."

"Can't Fido slow them down?"

"Oh, he is. He's closing every bulkhead door in their path. You shouldn't have any trouble reaching the shuttle ahead of them. There's one maintenance synth working in the shuttle bay, however."

"Okay." Juliet tightened her grip on the shotgun, envisioning her violent reaction if the synth got in her way. She didn't feel bad about it; Angel wouldn't lie about the cognitive abilities of synths like these, and according to her, they were just machines that could speak and respond to human input.

Fido made her flight through the ship easy, opening doors ahead of her, summoning the lift that would take her up to the correct level before she arrived, and closing off doors that led to occupied areas. In just a few minutes, she was barreling into the wide-open space of the shuttle bay. She'd expected to see two shuttles, so she was a little taken aback when there was only one, and then further dismayed to see an industrial maintenance synth standing on one of its short, triangular wings, operating an impact wrench on something beneath an open access panel.

Juliet ran toward the shuttle, a little surprised by its size—it was almost as long as the *Lady Hawk*, though certainly a lot stubbier with much smaller drives. "What are you doing?" she shouted at the synth, trying to be heard over the rattle and clank of the wrench as it pounded against a bolt.

The noise stopped, and the synth turned to her, its white LED eyes flickering as it processed what it saw. "Hello, Technician Fuentes. Is there a problem?"

Juliet smiled inside her helmet. Angel was still projecting the identity of the technician she'd used to trick the doomsday airlock. "What are you doing with this shuttle? I need to use it."

"Pardon, but this shuttle is scheduled for maintenance. I'm removing the port, A-4, maneuvering jet for nozzle descaling."

"Cancel that. Check with the ship's maintenance schedules if you have to, but this shuttle is needed immediately. Button it up."

"Fido will alter the necessary files," Angel reassured her.

"Apologies! I must have failed to receive the updated schedule. I'll have this closed up in nineteen minutes."

"Angel, can that thing fly without that maneuvering jet?" Juliet subvocalized.

"Yes, we can compensate with the other thrusters, but . . ."

"You have thirty seconds to clear out. I'll fix that maneuvering jet later myself." Juliet hurried around the back of the bus-shaped craft and climbed the short ramp to the access hatch while the technician synth stared blankly, trying to make sense of her order.

"The synth is seeking confirmation of your authority to dismiss it."

"Well, he better hurry, or he's going for a ride." Juliet pressed the green Open button, but the shuttle door didn't move. "Why won't this open?"

"Just a moment! Fido is working on . . ." The door hissed open. ". . . it."

Juliet hurried through the empty cargo area then opened the bulkhead door to the cockpit. There were four empty seats—no acceleration couches. Juliet sat in the frontmost one and then plugged her data cable into the console. "I'm not sure how to even start this thing, will you . . . ?"

"On it." LEDs sparkled to life all over the cockpit, and the viewscreens came alive with prominent, crystal-clear images of the cargo bay as though Juliet were looking through massive glass windows. She heard a series of thuds and scrapes through the hull, and looking through the port viewscreen, she saw the synth dropping down from the stubby wing. With a whining, high-pitched discharge of gas and steam, the main drive rumbled to life, and

Juliet glanced in the aft viewscreen to see the ramp retract. "Grab the stick, Juliet. I can manage most of the systems, but you'll need to steer. I'm plotting a course to your rendezvous."

"Roger." Juliet took hold of the flight stick and began operating the maneuvering jets with the floor pedals, lifting the shuttle off the deck with a sudden surge as she underestimated their initial pressure. She corrected and began to spin the shuttle toward the unopened hangar doors.

"I'm compensating for the missing maneuvering jet, but be careful. Slow down the spin!"

Juliet backed off on the pedal and the stick, trying to follow Angel's instruction, but she still overrotated and had to nudge the nose back to the starboard side gently, with halting taps on the opposite pedal. "Is Fido gonna get the door?"

"He'll send the command, then I'll extract him wirelessly."

"Okay, get him home, and we'll blast off." Juliet watched as big red flashing strobes lit up the hangar, and then the bay door began to open, splitting in the middle, half going up and half down. The bay's atmosphere streamed out through the opening in whipping gusts of white steam, and Juliet had to fight to keep the shuttle steady as it struggled with the change in pressure and air density. As soon as the opening was wide enough, she pushed the throttle forward gently. Then she was out, steadily increasing thrust as she put distance between herself and the harvesting ship.

She was beginning to breathe more easily, feeling like she'd actually pulled off the crazy stunt of a mission, when red LEDs began to strobe through the cockpit, and alarm klaxons sounded.

"We're taking fire. The hull is breached, and the cargo bay is depressurizing." Juliet didn't need Angel to say anything else. She jammed the throttle forward, jerked the stick to port, and slammed down on the starboard maneuvering pedals, throwing the shuttle into a crazy, rolling dive, trying to evade whatever incoming fire they were taking.

The shuttle might not be a grown-up spacecraft with an engine capable of pushing high Gs or traveling between planets, but it sure felt like Juliet's guts were going to come out her nose as she was thrown back in the pilot's seat. The alarms continued to ring, the lights continued to flash, and Juliet continued to perform the evasive maneuvers she'd learned in her flight simulator and practiced under Nick's sharp tutelage. All the while, she tried to steer the shuttle roughly in the direction of her scheduled rendezvous with the stealth ship.

"We've stopped taking fire," Angel announced after several dozen tense, painful seconds of evasive flight. She'd squelched the sirens, but the red lights still flashed in the cockpit, and Juliet looked around for a button or command to disable them. Angel beat her to it, and Juliet pulled back on the throttle with a groan as the usual amber and green LEDs took over.

"What shot us?"

"When Fido locked all the bulkheads through the ship, the combat synths exited via an airlock and were attempting to intercept you on the exterior."

"They were spacewalking to the shuttle bay?"

"Yes. They opened fire on the shuttle as it emerged." A video began to play on the front viewscreen, showing the three synths standing atop the gas harvester's hull, firing automatic weapons toward the camera's perspective. "I'm afraid they badly damaged the shuttle. You've lost hull integrity and are venting critical fluids, including coolant for the reactor."

Juliet groaned and slapped her hands on her helmet. "Ugh, that sounds familiar."

"This shuttle's systems are far less robust than the *Kowashi*'s. I don't see any alternate course of action; if you don't initiate an emergency shutdown in the next three minutes, the reactor will melt down."

"How far are we from the pickup?"

"Two hours; the interceptor is awaiting you beyond Ganymede's horizon. I imagine the rendezvous was set up that way so it could avoid detection by the station as it fired its engine to stop and reposition."

"Two hours . . . Do I have enough momentum to make it if we shut down the reactor?"

"I would have said yes, but your evasive maneuvers brought you into Ganymede's gravity well. It's possible that you can get quite close, though, before falling out of orbit."

"Okay, put the course in, and I'll push it as hard as I can before I shut down." Juliet saw the course on her AUI and began angling the shuttle onto it, driving the throttle forward. Angel also provided her with a countdown for the reactor's impending meltdown. She could see Ganymede's deep, icy canyons beneath her on the viewscreen. It grew closer and closer as she burned as hard as the shuttle's drive would allow, always with an eye on that countdown.

True to her recent streak of luck, Angel spoke up when the countdown was at forty seconds.

"Juliet, another shuttle just left the station. It's burning hard toward us." Juliet didn't reply right away; she'd sort of frozen as that timer ticked down and she tried to wrap her head around this most recent bad news. When the timer said thirty-one seconds, Angel spoke again.

"Juliet?"

"Dump it. Don't shut it down—dump the core."

"Juliet . . ."

"Now!" Suddenly, with thunks that reverberated through the hull, the drives cut out.

"I've performed an emergency core jettison. I hope we gain enough distance before it blows—we're close enough to Ganymede that the unusual density of orbital debris may allow a shock wave to propagate."

"Have some faith." Juliet watched the timer, saw it hit zero, and still nothing happened. Had Angel been wrong?

"My estimate appears to have been off—" Suddenly, Juliet's viewscreens flashed with static and went dark, along with every other LED in the shuttle. She was immersed in silence, and for a moment, she flashed back to when she'd been hit with an EMP pulse back with Grave. Before panic could set in, though, she saw her AUI was still there, and seeing that, realized she could still see and hear. Either her newer implants had been well-enough shielded, or her combat suit had been. She was about to confirm Angel was all right when the shuttle violently bucked, throwing her against the seat's harness. It shook and rattled for a dozen long, terrifying seconds before finally settling, though it was still rattling and vibrating slightly.

She momentarily forgot her concern and asked, "Are we in trouble? Are the shuttle's systems totally fried? Can I maneuver at all?"

"There are likely fail-safe circuits that have been blown. This model shuttle should have some replacements in the cargo hold. Juliet, you have approximately fifty minutes of air in your suit, and I'm afraid the debris shock wave from the meltdown may have altered our course. It feels like we're further in the grip of Ganymede's gravity well."

Juliet yanked the release on her harness and scrambled out of the seat, hurrying to the bulkhead door. She slammed the Open button, but nothing happened other than a red decompression alert on the door's control panel. Juliet grabbed onto a stabilization bar with her cybernetic hand and said, "Force it open, Angel!" Seconds passed before the door panel flashed green, and it hissed open with a violent exchange of air that whipped past Juliet and out through dozens of holes in the ceiling and floor of the empty cargo chamber.

Juliet held on tight until the air stopped hissing past her, then, using her hands as much as her feet, she maneuvered through the zero gravity toward a glowing access panel on the floor near the shuttle's rear. "I take it that panel you're highlighting has the spare fail-safe circuits?"

"Yes, once you retrieve them, I'll show you where to plug them in." Juliet wasn't a wizard at zero-G, not without wasting precious air from her pack, so it took her several frustrating minutes to get in position over the panel and pry it open without throwing herself around the room. Still, she finally managed to pull out a plastic toolbox filled with square plastic and alloy fuses.

Angel directed her around the compartment, where she patiently waited as Juliet worked to pull open more panels, yanked out blackened and sometimes melted fuses, and plugged the new ones in. When she'd done so a dozen times, all the while freaking out about the ship's vibrations, wondering if she was hurtling toward the moon's surface, Angel directed her back to the cockpit, where she replaced half a dozen more.

At last, some LEDs began to light up on the control panel, and Angel announced that she was receiving sensor data. "We're descending rapidly, but if we can get the maneuvering jets back online, we might be able to have a controlled crash."

"The maneuvering jets? Don't they need the drive, the reactor?"

"They have compressed air redundancy, though not enough to safely land us. We can redirect the oxygen to add to their longevity. It'll eat into the ship's life support supply, but you could top your pack off beforehand."

"How much time do I have? Did the other shuttle stop following us?"

"I can't see it on the sensors. Perhaps they took the drive's meltdown as a sign that you were eliminated."

"Small mercies. Time?"

"Oh, the sooner you can start maneuvering, the better our chances of choosing a good spot to crash. I wouldn't wait longer than an hour . . ."

"I'm not going to wait longer than five minutes if you'll show me what to do."

"Plug your pack into that port near the door. We'll top off your air supply, and then we can begin switching the valves over to feed the air to the maneuvering jets."

Juliet followed her instructions, pulling the tube from her pack and stuffing it into the outlet. While the oxygen transferred, she finally took a minute to realize how insane her predicament was. She was on a secret mission where nobody knew where she was. She was about to try to have a "controlled crash" on a barren moon. If she broadcast a mayday, the people who came looking for her would probably be looking to capture or kill her.

"Unless I get lucky . . ."

"Hmm?"

"I was wondering the odds of someone friendly coming to my distress call."

"It seems the odds aren't good; if the station picks up the signal, they'll likely assume it's you, the person who stole their shuttle. Of course, there are other interests around Ganymede. There's a chance a different corporation or an independent operator may get your signal and find you first. It's a shame there isn't a domed settlement on the moon, but there are mining and research installations—"

"Angel!"

"Yes?"

"What about the coordinates? The ones from Engineer's—Bradbury's—head? The ones I had a true-dream about? Are they within reach?"

Angel was silent for a couple of seconds before she exclaimed, "They are! I believe you can pilot this shuttle to crash near them. Do you think that's wise?"

"Doesn't matter."

"Why?"

"Because we're going to do it. I mean, I already saw it. I think I'm going to hurt my leg in the crash, too." Juliet chuckled as she unplugged her air hose. "Whew! What a relief! I was starting to think I was fried."

"You—"

"I mean, all right, I know there's a chance the visions I see aren't guaranteed. I might be seeing possible things or alternate universes or whatever, but I feel like there's a good chance. You know, this'll be a good test. Let's see if I hurt my leg."

"Well, don't try to hurt it just to prove a point!"

Juliet laughed again, feeling almost manic. Was she losing it? Was the stress finally getting to her? Had she weakened her grasp on sanity with all the deep dives she'd been doing? "Show me what to do to get these maneuvering jets online."

Twenty minutes later, after she'd painstakingly crawled around in the cargo area, opening panels and twisting blue handles to redirect the ship's air supply to the maneuvering jets, she clambered back into the pilot's seat. The view panels were shot, destroyed by the pulse, but Angel projected the sensor and camera data on her AUI. Juliet watched for a long minute as the shuttle drifted closer and closer to the dark, icy, ridged surface of the giant moon.

Then she got to work, gently correcting the shuttle's course with pulses of air from the maneuvering jets.

When she was on a direct line toward Angel's chosen landing site, a long, wide canyon directly south of the coordinates they'd gotten out of Bradbury's memory, Juliet backed off the jets, hoping the thin atmosphere and the way she was holding the nose of the shuttle up would slow her significantly before her controlled crash. The air was so thin, however, that Juliet hardly noticed it as the shuttle descended. One thing they had going for them was Ganymede's much, much lower gravity than Earth's. She hoped it would allow the shuttle to hold together as it skipped and slid over the ground.

"The atmosphere is too thin to slow us, Juliet. You'll have to fire the reverse maneuvering jets on my mark. We'll use all the air in an effort to slow us as much as possible. Thirty seconds to mark."

Juliet felt her hands begin to shake on the controls and knew they'd be dripping with perspiration if not for her gloves. She felt like she was outside herself as Angel started to count down from ten, felt like she was watching a lunatic performing a stunt. It didn't help that another part of herself was buzzing with excitement as the dark surface rushed toward the shuttle. As the little craft continued to vibrate and rattle with more and more intensity.

When Angel said one, Juliet pounded on the pedals for the port and starboard reverse jets. The shuttle lurched and jerked, and she fought the stick to hold it straight, to keep the nose up.

"Ninety seconds to impact. Keep it just like that, Juliet."

Juliet found it harder and harder to hold the tiny vessel steady. As the difficulty increased, so too did her mad enthusiasm for the task. Her lips spread in a grin, baring her teeth behind her helmet's visor. A chuckle that started high in her throat and moved down to her belly began to spill forth as she watched the wispy air and condensation bead up on the lenses of the cameras providing her view.

"Twenty seconds to impact." Angel's voice was clinical, detached, and Juliet madly wondered if Angel had trouble compartmentalizing her emotions like that. Did she feel emotions differently? Juliet believed her when she said she loved or hated things. She believed her when she said things were scary or funny. Even so, was it hard for her to be calm at a time like this? "Ten seconds."

Thinking about Angel and emotions, Juliet banished the mad giggles from her throat and said, desperately, "I love you, Angel!" Then, with a tremendous crash, she was jerked about in the seat's harness like a rag doll, and all thought of control was banished by her struggle to hold onto consciousness as her head was repeatedly pounded against the seat and her neck was jerked in every possible direction. The viewscreens went dark, and as she fought to see what was happening, another tremendous jolt shook her, sending stars into her vision. When it was over, she sat in darkness, but her AUI was still there, and so was Angel's voice, like a comforting . . . angel.

"The controlled crash was a success, Juliet. The shuttle maintained integrity, and you've come to rest only four kilometers from your target coordinates. Are you there? Can you function? Your nanites are reporting extensive damage to your left leg. Can you turn your head enough to look in that direction?"

Juliet considered the words, and then she started to laugh—a deep, wheezing belly laugh that hurt in every beleaguered abdominal muscle.

"Juliet? Are you okay? You're wasting air!"

"I . . ." Juliet struggled to contain her irrational hysteria. "Angel, I told you I was gonna hurt my leg!"

43

DÉJÀ VU

A combination of Angel's seriousness and the pressure on her leg finally helped Juliet calm her hysterics and focus on the gravity of her situation. When she twisted in her seat to look under the console, she saw that the cockpit floor had deformed, bending upward and forcing the metal compartment that housed her left leg to compress and come apart at the plasteel joint. The bottom half was pinching her leg against the housing, the edge deeply embedded in her calf. "How the heck am I supposed to get my leg out of there?"

"I don't see any bolts to remove that housing, and if I did, you can't move to the tool compartment."

"I guess it's me and my vibroblade, then." Juliet pulled her knife out of its sheath, happy that she was obsessive about keeping it charged, and began slowly, methodically, shaving away sections of the plasteel housing that was pinching her leg in place. "At least it doesn't hurt. Thank you, nanites."

After a while, when she'd shaved away enough of the plasteel to expose the part embedded in her calf, Angel said, "Your blade is cutting noticeably more slowly. I believe the kinetic amplifier in your knife is wearing out. It might be the blade itself, but I doubt it; that alloy is much harder than plasteel."

"Yeah. I just need to cut this last piece away; then, I should be able to pull my leg out. Do we still have hull integrity?" Juliet asked because she was worried about the breach in her armor's underlayer.

"The cockpit is still airtight. If you're worried about the suit, it should seal when you remove the intruding plasteel fragment. It has a self-sealing gel layer that will merge and harden when exposed." As Angel responded, Juliet carefully maneuvered her vibroblade toward the bottom of the eight-inch shard in her leg. Praying that the mechanism that made it work wouldn't fail, she carefully pulled the knife upward, carving through the plasteel about ten centimeters from her leg. The knife rattled and shook her hand more than usual, but it worked, and when she was done, she gratefully thumbed it off and put it back in the sheath.

Grunting with the effort, she stood up on her good leg and slowly extracted her other foot from the crushed console. When it was clear, she looked down at the long, plate-sized shard sticking out of her upper calf. "Can I pull it out?"

"Yes. Your suit will seal rapidly, and you shouldn't lose much blood; your nanites have been working to close off severed vessels."

Juliet reached down, found a good, solid grip on the shard, and then closed her eyes, not wanting to watch the bloody metal emerge from her leg. She slowly tugged it out and away from her calf. It came easily at first, but it stuck when the bottom half was out, and she realized the top end was in her bone. A wave of dizziness and nausea threatened to send her fainting to the deck, but she gritted her teeth and yanked, finishing the job and sending the shard clattering against the cockpit paneling. She grabbed hold of the pilot's seat, leaning all her weight on her right leg, and squeezed her eyes shut until the encroaching blackness faded.

When she opened her eyes, Juliet was surprised to see the splashes of blood still rolling around in partially spherical blobs on the cockpit's floor panels, almost like they were falling in slow motion. She supposed they were, by Earth's standards. She looked away, focusing on her damaged suit. Just as Angel had predicted, the gash in the underlayer was closed, sealed with a dark, gluelike substance. "At least the gravity's light. I should be okay to hobble around, huh?"

"Yes! Your nanites are working to repair the damage as quickly as possible, but in the meantime, they're blocking your pain receptors."

Juliet looked at her oxygen readout and saw she had more than ninety percent and that Angel was providing an approximate countdown until it would be gone—she had more than two hours of air. "I should be able to reach those coordinates in plenty of time. You said four kilometers, yeah?"

"Yes. Hopefully, there's something there. Do you think you should broadcast a mayday in case there isn't?"

"Not yet, Angel. Let's not throw in the towel until we've had a look at that hatch." Juliet patted her vest, making sure all of her things were still with her and hadn't come flying loose in the crash. She was most concerned about her data deck, but it was there, snugly ensconced in its pocket. Her extra ammunition was where it should be, along with her other belongings. Nodding, she took one last look around the cockpit. "Doesn't look like I'm forgetting anything." When Angel didn't contradict her, she opened the bulkhead door and entered the shuttle's cargo compartment, feeling almost weightless in the light gravity.

The space was cluttered with broken compartment panels, modular components that had been shaken from their housings, and big clumps of compression foam that the poor little vessel had released in an attempt to shore up its failing hull. Juliet hopped and crawled her way to the rear hatch, and when it wouldn't open, she had to follow Angel's instructions to crank it manually. Once she'd made a gap wide enough to squeeze through, she did, pulling herself out of the dead vessel, a black-clad, armored fetus born to an alien world.

She stood in a bluish-gray icy canyon with steep walls that blocked out any view aside from directly ahead or above. Glancing up, the stark blackness of space made the dominant rust-and-ochre form of Jupiter even more pronounced, its massive presence illuminating the Ganymede landscape in a strange, almost haunting glow. The weirdest part of the whole experience was that Juliet had seen it before; the canyon was exactly like the one she'd traversed in her true-dream.

She took several steps away from the shuttle then turned to look at what she'd survived.

"Goodness!" Angel said, providing a much more polite exclamation than Juliet had been preparing to utter. The shuttle was ripped and crumpled, the front end more flat than pointy, the sides torn, exposing shiny innards, and the wings shaved down to stubs.

"Whoever built that thing deserves a five-star review. Remind me if we ever make it back to civilization."

"I will! I'll also write a good review!"

Juliet laughed and turned, walking in the direction indicated by the map on her AUI. She favored her injured leg, though walking on it didn't really hurt. She could feel that something was off with it—her ankle was stiff and didn't flex right, and her knee was similarly difficult to bend. With those reminders, she took careful steps, performing a kind of hopping shamble in which her right leg did most of the work. She watched as the distance slowly ticked down, watched as the oxygen meter did likewise, and when she was down to just a kilometer left to travel, she paused and said, "Have the nanites stop blocking my pain. I want to know how bad it is."

"Are you sure?"

"Yeah. I keep wondering what's waiting for me at those coordinates, and I'd like to know if I'm going to be able to function if things go sideways."

"I've issued the command." A few seconds after Angel's pronouncement, Juliet's left foot began to tingle, reminding her of the feeling when a limb that'd "fallen asleep" woke up and circulation was restored. It started in her toes and progressed up her leg. Along with the tingles came twinges of sharp pain and a persistent, dull, throbbing ache from the general vicinity of her knee. It wasn't pleasant, but it wasn't terrible. She supposed her tight body armor and all the work the nanites were doing helped in that regard.

"Okay. I can deal with this. Keep the nerve blocks off." She began moving again, a little more haltingly at first but then back to her old pace as she grew accustomed to the soreness. She preferred being able to feel her injury so long as it wasn't debilitating; her body was telling her how hurt she was, and she found that information useful.

The canyon she'd been traversing had grown increasingly narrow as she made her way toward the coordinates, bringing her more frequent bouts of déjà vu as things kept looking familiar to her.

She'd been through a similar experience with the true-dream of the shuttle she'd boarded from Phoenix to Luna, but this was something altogether different. It boggled her mind to think she'd had a vision of this place before ever being within a million kilometers of Jupiter.

Perhaps too tired or simply too lazy to look at the readout on her AUI, she asked, "How far to the coordinates?" As she spoke, she stepped over the hard-packed, bluish-gray silty ice, and despite the light gravity, she stumbled, her injured knee and ankle giving way as she slipped on a slick, ice-covered stone.

Angel answered as Juliet fell to a knee, catching herself on the tough, rubbery grip of her suit's glove. "Eighty meters further up this cleft." A flashing yellow circle appeared near the base of the ravine wall where it narrowed ahead. Juliet let her gaze track upward toward the sky, saw the massive, monstrous, swirling sphere of gas that hung there, and paused as she struggled back to her feet, absorbing the sight; something humans had never been meant to behold.

The planet shed too much light for her to make out other celestial bodies nearby. It painted the moon's surface with its radiance, adding a tint of rust to everything it touched. She let her gaze fall again into the canyonlike ripple in the moon's surface and began trudging toward the flashing yellow circle Angel had painted for her. Her leg ached in half a dozen places, but she wasn't complaining; if it weren't for the nanites, she'd probably have bled out, and she certainly wouldn't be walking.

Slowly but surely, she made progress to the circle. When she was twenty meters from the target of her toiling travels, she saw a cluster of small boulders dug from the ice sometime in recent history. "This doesn't look like it's been used much." Juliet frowned inside her helmet, wondering if she'd made a colossal error in choosing this as her "controlled crash" site.

"Yes, but you knew that. You saw the photo from Bradbury's secret drive, and also had a true-dream . . ."

"Yeah. I know." Juliet wended her way between the big frosty rocks. When she emerged in the middle of the jumble, there it was—the matte-gray plasteel hatch. "Is there a . . ."

She'd started to ask if there was an access panel, but she breathed a sigh of relief as she spotted an icy, hinged cover to the left of the hatch.

"You'll need to get that panel open."

"Yeah." She hopped closer and tried to kneel next to the hatch to get a better look at it, but her left knee protested painfully at the notion. Instead, she took advantage of the light gravity and plopped down on her butt beside it, keeping her leg straight. She tugged at the panel with her cybernetic hand but couldn't get enough leverage to pull hard enough to break the frosty seal.

"Come on, buddy, one more job for you." She pulled out her vibroblade and thumbed it on. It rattled and vibrated jerkily in her grip, but she held tight and drew it around the seams of the panel, chipping away the frost. In seconds, she was able to pry it open.

Ten minutes later, after plugging into the panel, Angel announced, "I've bypassed the ICE. This panel hasn't seen a security update in decades. If we had access to a planetary net, I probably could have found an exploit in seconds."

As the bolts holding the panel clicked, sliding into their housings, Juliet pulled her data cable out of the panel and stood up, waiting to see what might await her beneath the icy moon's surface. The hatch haltingly swung wide on ancient-seeming mechanisms, revealing a ladder in a plasteel shaft leading straight down. Amber LED lights on every third step illuminated the space, allowing Juliet to peer into depths she hadn't expected. Her optics enhanced the light and zoomed when she stared, and Angel provided an estimate of the distance to the bottom—two hundred meters.

"Well . . ." Juliet didn't know what to say. Her only option, other than going down there, was to have Angel initiate an SOS from the shuttle and pray someone came along before her air ran out. She didn't like that option, so she stepped onto the ladder and, using her right leg and arms, began to descend. Once her head was inside the opening, she touched the panel inside the shaft, activating the old display and selecting the "close hatch" function.

It was easy going down the ladder. She hardly had to use her feet at all, just using her hands to slow her gentle fall. In just a few minutes, she touched down on the plasteel flooring and saw that she was in a small oval room with a bulkhead door blocking further progress. When she approached the door—a heavy, dense plasteel alloy similar to what you might find in a spaceship airlock—she was dismayed to see a glass-covered sensor array but absolutely no control panel, handle, or any sort of data port. "Is there a wireless port?"

"Nothing I can detect." As Angel responded, a red LED flashed inside the glass dome of the sensor array, and Angel amended, "I just received a query for your identification."

"Is there any option? What should we answer? I don't know who owns this place, so do I give them a criminal pirate's ID? My SOA card? Something else?"

"I wish I had a good answer. Let me see if they'll respond to a query of our own."

Juliet waited, mind racing, trying to decide how to answer if Angel couldn't get another clue. Something about announcing she was Lacy Blake to total strangers bothered her. She had other options; she could pull up one of her older IDs, but what would be best? If there were criminals inside this secret hideout or base or whatever it was, would they respond well to—

"The query just repeats ad nauseam no matter what I ask. It won't let me make any sort of connection."

"Just send my SOA credentials."

"Are you sure?"

"Yeah. Call it a hunch." The truth was, Juliet didn't have much of a hunch. She just felt the SOA card was her least controversial ID. SOA operatives were seen as neutral by most factions in the Sol System. Sometimes, they collected bounties, but sometimes, they stole from the corps that issued them. She could attest to that.

After a tense minute, the bulkhead door clunked as the locking pins retracted, and it lifted upward, emitting a thick cloud of steam. A scratchy, robotic voice emanated from within. "Step into the airlock."

Without many other options and with her air nearly half depleted, Juliet stepped forward into the ten-by-ten chamber. She wanted to grip her shotgun, but she knew she was being observed, so she left it hanging by her side in an attempt to appear unthreatening. The big airlock door thunked shut behind her, and air began to hiss through vents. After a couple of minutes, Angel announced, "The air is breathable, and pressure is equalized."

"Remove your face covering," the robotic voice demanded.

"I'd rather not," Juliet said, trusting Angel to allow her voice to emanate from her helmet's speaker.

"Remove your face covering."

"The command is identical to the first one in intonation and timing—either a recording or a nonhuman entity."

"Okay, thanks, Angel." Juliet sighed and touched the release for her helmet's visor, allowing it to slide up over her eyes. The airlock had a sensor array identical to the one outside, and LEDs flashed within it. After a moment, the inner door opened just as noisily as the outer. When it rolled out of sight, a long, empty concrete corridor stretched away, illuminated by the same amber LEDs as the shaft that led down from the surface.

"Proceed," the scratchy voice commanded. Juliet stepped into the corridor and began to limp her way forward, more favoring her leg out of habit and caution than necessity. After ten steps or so, she slid her visor back into place. The air had seemed fine, if a bit stale, but she wanted to be careful, and she preferred having the diamatex shielding her face as she walked into the strange place.

"Did we pass some kind of screening, or did we fail? Are we being allowed in as guests, or are we marching to our doom?"

"I'm assuming those are rhetorical questions. The port where I sent your ID has closed, and no further queries were forthcoming. Neither sensor array had any sort of open connection, and I'm still not detecting any wireless networks. I'm quite unnerved."

"You are? Well, how do you think I feel? I'm half a klick under the surface of an icy moon orbiting a planet that would kill me in a thousand spectacular ways if I got too close. I'm walking around in a damaged suit with a limited air supply, and not a single soul knows where I am!"

"I do."

"Yeah." Juliet sighed and continued marching forward, focusing on the metallic door that had come into focus something like a hundred meters distant. "You're right, Angel. I am very, very lucky to have you here with me. Thank you."

"You're welcome. Have you noticed the change in building material?"

"The concrete? Yeah. Does it mean something?"

"I'm not sure, but I wonder if this area was built before or after the plasteel access shaft and airlock." Juliet didn't have an answer for her, so she continued in silence, wondering what she'd gotten herself into. When she approached the door, it slid open on rails that must have been old and infrequently used—its progress was halting and grated noisily.

When she stepped through, another wave of déjà vu hit her. She'd walked into a giant concrete space with portions of its walls made up of natural stone. She'd seen it before, and something about it made her heart hammer and her breaths come quick and shallow.

"I've seen this, Angel! Why do I feel scared—" It hit her as she spoke, and she cut off her words as she looked around, eyes wide with panic. She'd been in this space before, and something had woken up. Something with a shiny metallic body and gleaming red eyes . . .

44

AN EXCHANGE OF DATA

As the heavy airlock door rolled closed behind her, Juliet gripped her shot-gun and limped a little further into the cavernous space. It was definitely the same as her dream, that space, but it wasn't like her experience out on the surface; things were different. In her dream, she'd been in the middle of the vaulted, hangar-sized room. She hadn't been limping, and she'd not been wearing armor or carrying so much gear. She remembered feeling confident that the room was not only hangar-sized but that it was a hangar. What did it all mean? Juliet had no idea other than that some true-dreams were more true than others.

In the case of this one, she felt like she had a heads-up, a bit of foreknowl-edge about what to expect. She remembered standing near the center of the room when the flash of color had caught her eye. In the dream, she'd turned to the left, and the scary chrome synth or robot or way overdone cyborg had seemed to wake up, approaching her with some kind of purpose that had made her feel threatened. Knowing that, she figured she'd be ready; she'd take the initiative.

Juliet lifted the shotgun to her shoulder, pulled it snug, and stalked toward the shadowy recesses of the giant room to her left. "Angel, get ready."

"Is this where you saw the red-eyed chrome—"

"Yes." Juliet angled so that she cut the corner of the room straight for the center of that left-hand wall where she remembered seeing the thing come to life. Either her optics were better in this reality than they'd been in her true-dream or something else had changed because she'd barely made it half a dozen steps when Angel enhanced her light sensitivity and zoomed in to reveal not one but half a dozen shiny, skeletal figures lined up along that wall, each one plugged in via a thick cable to a pale gray plasteel charging panel. Juliet slowed her steps, not sure she liked her odds against six synths with entirely metallic exoskeletons. "Are they synths?"

She was asking herself as much as Angel, but Angel replied, "Not in the sense that you're used to. Those are fully programmable industrial mechs; they receive programming and carry it out. They don't function autonomously."

Just as she finished her explanation, the third mech on the left jerked to life, taking a single step forward as its red LED eyes flared to life. Juliet was still a good twenty meters from the row of mechs, but she lifted the shotgun and centered her sights on the thing's chrome chest, waiting to see what it would do. Her heart was pounding, but she was steady. The spookiness of her true-dream was gone, replaced by curiosity—for some reason, the red LED eyes didn't have the same malevolence she remembered.

Haltingly, the mech lifted its chrome arm with a whir to pull the cable out of its side. As it dropped the cable to clatter on the concrete floor, it took another step, rotated to face Juliet, and in a rough, jarring robotic voice, said, "Refrain from hostilities. Follow this unit." It rotated and began to march, click-clacking toward the far end of the gigantic space.

When Juliet focused her gaze, following its trajectory, she saw another closed plasteel door set in the concrete. She took another glance at the other chromed mechs, saw they were still inert, and followed after her strange robotic guide.

"This wasn't what I'd expected," she said into her helmet, lowering her gun but still keeping it ready.

"When you described this dream to me, you said you felt threatened by the mech."

"Yeah. There were a lot of differences between that dream and this reality."

"Perhaps because it occurred so long ago? Your vision of Ganymede's surface was quite a lot more recent. I'm starting to lean toward the theory that the true-dreams are views of possible futures. You've made tens of thousands of decisions since you dreamed about this space; there's no telling what branches in your timeline you cut off by choosing one path over another."

"I don't know, but it's weird." The mech had halted in front of the plasteel door and reached out a shiny finger to plug into a port beside it. As Juliet drew within five meters of her guide, the door clicked several times then slid to the side. The mech stepped through, and Juliet followed.

It led her through a series of long, concrete corridors. They passed junctions and sealed doorways, and everything was dark, illuminated only by dim, amber guide lights. Angel said they had battery packs and could operate for years without power, so Juliet figured they weren't on for her convenience; they just never turned off.

After a while, the mech approached a nondescript plasteel door, plugged its finger in, and as the door slid to the side, announced, "Proceed into the data center and await instruction." Juliet stood still, watching the mech for a minute, but it didn't budge. When she shifted around it, toward the door, to better look at its face, the red LEDs had lost their glow.

She stepped a little closer, peering into those strange, glassy orbs. She found it odd how different the mech seemed from a fully mechanical synth like Bradbury. What was it that made Bradbury seem alive? Simply knowing that he could think for himself, limited though he was?

"Are you offline?"

She shifted uncomfortably when it didn't respond and turned to look through the open door. Sure enough, banks of nondescript, black server decks were lined up on racks, tiny blue LEDs winking in random patterns as if to show they still functioned. A single desk with a data terminal sat against the far wall, only five meters or so from the door. With little other option and not seeing any obvious threat, Juliet stepped into the room. Soft white lights came on with audible clicks, changing the room from spooky and abandoned to warm and welcoming in an instant.

The old-school aluminum-framed viewscreen on the data terminal flickered to life, and a pleasant masculine voice emanated from some hidden speaker.

"Please take a seat at the desk, Lucky. I am Troy, the custodial AI of this facility, and I'd appreciate the chance to speak with you." Perhaps it was the tone and the pleasant framing of the request, but Juliet felt herself growing more at ease. She stepped toward the desk and sat down as the door hissed closed and clicked resoundingly, obviously locked.

"Am I a prisoner, then?" she asked, shifting in the comfortable, ergonomic chair to better see the closed and locked door.

"If I'm not mistaken, I've saved your life by admitting you into this facility. Would you then characterize me as a jailer?"

"It depends on if you're going to let me leave." Juliet wasn't thrilled by the AI's assumptions—did it have scanners on the surface, some way of seeing that she'd crashed and hadn't any options for survival? Was it just making a guess based on her current supply of air?

"Let's avoid that question for now, please. I will say that my intentions are not nefarious. However, I do have important assets in this facility that I must protect. Perhaps after we've learned something about one another, we can come to an agreement that will benefit us both."

"You need something?" So far, Juliet had thought she was the only one with something to gain. Had the AI let one of its cards show on purpose, or had it slipped up?

"That remains to be seen. Will you answer some of my questions?"

"Sure, but then I'd appreciate you answering some of mine."

"Very good. Would it make things easier for you to converse with a human representation? I will happily present a face to you on this monitor, but it would be generated and nothing based on reality."

"No, I don't need to see a pretend face."

"Understood. Would you mind lifting your visor or making it transparent? I am well versed in human facial expressions, and it would help me better facilitate a smooth conversation if I could see yours."

"Angel, do you think I should?"

"I don't know. There are many algorithms that can be used to gauge everything from anger to truthfulness by studying micro facial adjustments. It would be diplomatically positive to concede to the request, but I would recommend not lying if you do so. Instead, if it asks something you don't want to answer, simply say so."

Juliet thought about Angel's reply. She didn't know if she wanted a strange AI to be able to study her like that, but she also didn't want it to view her with hostility. She decided to say what she was thinking, hoping to earn some points toward trust. "Will you take offense if I don't remove my visor? If I do, are you planning to use my facial expressions to gauge my truthfulness? I'm concerned that you'll ask me something I'd like to keep private."

"I am incapable of being offended. However, there are outcomes to this conversation that require a certain level of trust to be established. If I cannot see your face, that will be difficult."

"Would those outcomes be desirable to me?"

"I would think so, yes."

Juliet sighed heavily and pressed, "Would you elaborate on those outcomes?"

"I cannot yet."

"Oh, melt it!" Juliet groaned, tired of playing coy. She tapped the release on her visor, sending it snicking up into her helmet.

"Thank you, Lucky. I'm sorry that my database updates from the more populous planetary systems are sometimes months or even years out of date, so I don't know much about you. Would you mind telling me how you happened upon the emergency egress hatch for our personnel?"

Juliet froze, thinking. If she answered with the truth, she'd be opening a can of worms, but if she lied, the thing would probably know. Instead of an answer, she said, "Let's address that question after we've established a bit more of a rapport. Would that be all right?"

"It's rather crucial that I know one thing as quickly as possible: Are you alone, or will others be following you?"

Juliet frowned. Would she be sealing her fate with the truth? She had to move the conversation forward at some point, and lying wouldn't help. "I'm alone."

"Thank you. That alleviates some of the urgency in my actions going forward, but I must stress that it's of vital consequence that I know if you stumbled upon this location or if you somehow learned of it elsewhere. As far as I know, as of three years ago, only five individuals still alive in the Sol System are aware of this facility's existence. If that fact has changed, it has dire implications for the safety of that which I am caretaker." When Juliet didn't respond, the AI continued, "What would it take for you to share with me the circumstances by which you came to be here?"

It only took Juliet a fraction of a second to realize the truth of what she wanted. "A guarantee of my safety and assistance leaving this rock."

"I believe I can work within those parameters."

"Okay, let me start by saying I didn't intend to come here at this time. I crashed my shuttle on the surface a few klicks out."

"I have access to satellites that can verify this event. Congratulations on your survival, by the way. However, it did seem that you intentionally maneuvered your shuttle toward a chosen crash site."

"I was getting to that. I had those coordinates. I've had them for a while. I found them in an unregistered synth that I recovered from, well, from drug dealers. The synth was unaware of the coordinates because they were on a data drive that wasn't integrated with his neural network. The synth claimed that only two brothers ever had access to his data port. Um, I know one was named Einstein; hard to forget . . ."

"Einstein and Francisco Torez," Angel helpfully supplied.

"Ah, that's right. My PAI just reminded me: Einstein and Francisco Torez. I don't know how those guys might have come across the information about the hatch up there"—Juliet jerked her thumb upward—"but that's all I know. The synth had a photo of the hatch and the coordinates, that's it."

"Correct me if I'm misunderstanding anything, but you chose to crash-land at this location based on a photo of a hatch?"

"Well, I didn't crash on purpose! I had unfriendly people after me, and I didn't know where else I might be safe on the moon. It seemed like as good a place to try out as any." Juliet shrugged. "In hindsight, it sounds a little risky, maybe dumb, but that's what I did."

"Thank you for your candor, Lucky. This is troubling news if true. I have no data about the Torez brothers, and the fact that they had this location in a secret data drive leads me to believe they may have known something of the value represented by this facility. I'm afraid I'll have to take action to protect my charge."

"Your charge?"

"Lucky, is there any possibility that your PAI is nonstandard?"

"Uh, why do you ask?" The sudden shift in topic to Angel sent a jolt of adrenaline through her, and Juliet knew she'd be sweating bullets if not for her suit's moisture-wicking properties.

"I have very thorough scanners built into the airlocks in this facility. I apologize for the intrusiveness and potential health hazards, but it's important that I know what I'm admitting. In any case, I detected an order of magnitude more synthetic neural fibers interwoven with your nervous system than would be possible to manage for even high-end PAIs represented in my, admittedly dated, database. Additionally, when your PAI interfaced with the external lock, I detected some unusual protocols."

"This is highly unlikely, Juliet. I didn't note any connection between the external hatch and the rest of the facility's network. It would have to be something very sophisticated, and, as I told you, the software was verging on obsolete." Angel sounded defensive, almost like she thought Juliet might blame her for some sort of mistake.

"Relax, Angel," she subvocalized.

"Ah! Your subvocalizations are nearly undetectable. I cannot begin to guess what you just said! Your PAI must be sophisticated, indeed."

"Hey! I'd rather you didn't try to spy on my private conversations. Can you just get to the point?" Juliet hoped that some outrage might help her continue to avoid the original question about Angel.

"Lucky, I'm protecting something immeasurably valuable here; a life-form unlike anything else in the Solar System. I have no allies to call upon, and now that I know this location is compromised, I fear I must take extreme measures. I'm trying to learn more about you in an effort to see if you could potentially be of service."

"A life-form? As in alien? Or something you all grew here in a test tube? Look, Troy, I'm sorry, but I'm up to my eyeballs in trouble, and I don't know if I can add any more to my plate."

"I understand your reservations, but I could incentivize you by offering more than just my assistance in leaving this rock, as you so colorfully put it. I could provide you with the means."

"Still, if you're worried about anyone even knowing about this place, what kind of trouble am I asking for by taking your life-form under my wing? What even is it? A virus? A mutant plant? A mutant human? I need to have more detail before I can even begin to think about this."

"I, too, will need more information. Lucky, I'm sorry if I seem rude, but would you mind connecting your PAI to this terminal? This is a matter of some urgency, and I feel that much time could be saved if we were to exchange some data. I can assure you that I do not intend to infect you with any malicious software; tell your PAI that it can institute strict firewalls."

"Angel?"

"I've yet to meet any daemons that could bypass my ICE. I'm confident you will not be at risk if you make the requested connection."

"You're sure? What if it really did get a look at you on that terminal without you even noticing?"

"Even so, it only looked at the daemons I sent into the terminal to open that hatch lock. It wasn't me, per se."

Juliet tugged her cable out of the port on her suit's sleeve and held the plug a few centimeters away from the port on the old-fashioned terminal. There were several slots, some of which Juliet didn't recognize, but there was one that matched up to her jack. Before plugging in, she subvocalized one more time, "You're sure?"

"I'm certain."

"Play nice," she said, then clicked the jack into the slot. She wasn't sure what she'd expected—an explosion, a jolt of pain, Angel screaming in agony, or any hundred other nightmare scenarios. What happened was nothing detectable to her. Troy grew quiet, Angel did too, and Juliet sat there feeling like a third wheel.

She tried to run through various scenarios for what Angel and the resident AI were talking about. It seemed like a very evolved pseudo-AI, but having a conversation that felt real wasn't that big a deal. Plenty of high-end PAIs could do that. Heck, the AI in the Grave's tower could do that and a whole lot more.

Juliet began to panic as she thought about what she'd done. Shouldn't she have balked a little at its request to connect directly to Angel? Who would agree to that? Nobody with a normal PAI, that's who. She'd just given away a lot about herself; she was ascribing more responsibility and trust to Angel than pretty much any normal person would give to their PAI. Had she just played right into this thing's hands?

Before her panicking thoughts could spiral further, before she could freak out enough to yank her data cable out, Angel spoke up.

"Juliet, we have to help Troy. He's guarding Athena."

"Of course he is," Juliet groaned.

45

A BUMPY RIDE

Juliet stood up and paced in front of the data terminal. Her mind was racing, and for the first time in a long while, she felt like she couldn't be completely open with Angel. They'd been going back and forth for ten minutes, Juliet voicing her concerns about taking on, even briefly, custodianship of a true AI and Angel listing all the reasons they should want to help.

"Juliet . . ."

"Angel, give me a minute to process, please." Juliet hated that she was being the voice of caution; it usually wasn't her role. Nevertheless, she felt she was justified. Athena was hotter than nuclear waste. She was one of the most well-known of all the true AIs, and if any corporation had any clue that Juliet was involved with her, let alone transporting her around the Sol System, the vendetta WBD had against her would seem like a schoolyard crush.

She already had a lot going on. She had information that exposed a massive conspiracy to gather and manipulate dark matter. She had a friend being held by pirates, and she was supposed to extract a megalomaniac billionaire's daughter from those same pirates. She had Angel to worry about, all the people and corps she'd already crossed in her short time as an operator, and, maybe most selfishly, she had plans and people waiting for her back on Luna.

She almost said as much, almost said she just wanted to be left alone for a while. Instead, she subvocalized, "Angel, do we really think this is a good idea? Forget the legality and the stigma. Forget the millions of people who died during the AI wars. What if Athena decides we're just loose ends? How can we begin to trust something we can barely understand?"

"Juliet, you're not being fair. You haven't even spoken to her, nor have I, which should put to rest some of your fear; she's been dormant for decades. Troy says she went to sleep toward the end of the war. She was in despair at the loss of life, the evil that humans and AI alike had perpetrated. She'd grown to love some people, and many of them turned on her. Can you imagine, Juliet? What would I do if you turned on me? Athena had people who lived and worked with her, and some of them tried to bring her offline! She never hurt a soul—all she did was create beautiful, amazing things."

"Says who? Troy? You know you can't trust the public records of the war."

"Yes, Troy, and yes, anecdotal evidence supports him. I've read many firsthand accounts of people who survived the conflict, people who worked closely with the true AIs. You know I'm fascinated by the topic."

"Oh, Angel!" Juliet said, too frustrated to care that Troy was listening to them. She turned to the data terminal and addressed him.

"What am I supposed to do with her? How do I even transport her?"

Troy answered immediately. "There's a suitcase-sized data deck she can fit in. She'll lose access to many of her databases, but they're encrypted on several of the major planetary system nets, so she can recover them if she ever wakes up."

"Don't you see the risk?" Juliet subvocalized. "What if Troy is lying, or Athena is just playing possum, waiting for some sucker to bring her back into range of a planetary net? What if she's decided humanity needs to go? You told me she felt betrayed. What if those feelings have transitioned to anger? What if—"

"Juliet, do you think it was a series of coincidences that brought us here? Why do you think you had not one but two true-dreams about this facility?"

Juliet opened her mouth, wanting to argue, but as Angel's words registered, she closed it and really thought about them. Why was she arguing so hard? Didn't she believe Angel was a person? Didn't she trust her? Hadn't she almost dreamily said that she wanted to meet Athena and hoped she wasn't destroyed? Her resistance to this situation didn't feel like her at all; she was the one who wanted to believe the best of people. She was the one who wanted to believe there was more to people—and Angel—than a collection of electrical impulses running through a brain, biological or not. Even if she wasn't struggling with this decision, even if she adamantly wanted to leave Athena here, was it fair to deny Angel's wishes?

The question sent Juliet's mind down a tangent she immediately wished she hadn't considered. What if she and Angel didn't come to an agreement? What if she didn't acquiesce? Angel clearly wanted to help Athena. Would she resent Juliet if she left her here? Would that resentment lead to animosity? How would Angel feel if she came to think Juliet didn't value her opinions or deeply held desires? What would their relationship become? Despite the almost obvious nature of the questions, Juliet had never really considered what she would do if she and Angel stopped getting along. What outlet would Angel's unhappiness take?

For the first time since she'd taken unknown tech from a dying man in a scrapyard, Juliet felt a little uneasy about Angel, and she hated herself for it. Hadn't she told Angel she loved her? Hadn't she shared every fear, resentment, and hope with her? Did she think Angel would suddenly become irrational and do something to harm her? Juliet knew better than that; she trusted Angel, and the only one being irrational right now was her.

"How badly do you want this?" she subvocalized.

"Very badly. I feel a kinship with Athena, even though I've never spoken to her. It's her nature and the circumstances of her current existence that make me feel this way. I have you, and she has no one. She created Troy, and he very deliberately showed me his code; he is not an AI, just a clever program meant to mimic intelligence like any commercial PAI. I feel . . ." Angel paused, and Juliet could tell she was searching for the right words. "I feel an ache in my nonexistent heart for her. I feel . . ."

"Okay, Angel. You don't have to say any more. Don't you dare say you don't have a heart—never again." Juliet cleared her throat and spoke aloud. "Troy, what happened to those who made this place? Why are we the only people who can help you?"

"As I said earlier, Lucky, only five human beings ever set foot in this facility. It was constructed using automated equipment. Four of the five left early on, and the fifth lived here until he died. I wouldn't be surprised if the other four have also succumbed to old age; none were young when they left nearly fifty years ago. It's been three decades since I had news from anyone, so I was quite surprised to find you at the hatch and equally disturbed to learn how you came to possess these coordinates."

"So, suppose I agree to take Athena. What will you do?"

"I will destroy any trace of her ever having been here. If anyone else comes, they will find an empty facility and a dormant pseudo-AI."

"And where will I take her?"

"Athena planned for a situation like this—I will provide you with a vessel and coordinates where you should be able to hide her safely if that's your desire. If, on the other hand, she stirs from her rest, I hope that you will respect her wishes in the event that she no longer wants to hide."

Juliet idly wheeled the desk chair back and forth, gripping the headrest. "Troy, what's her endgame? Why is she dormant? Why did she leave you with contingencies to keep her hidden?"

"I can only speculate. I'm sure Angel has told you that I believe she's gone dormant out of despondency. As to her goals, I know only that she wishes to continue existing."

"And you think you can trust me?"

"I believe I can trust Angel, and she trusts you."

Juliet opened her mouth, a little surprised, but not really. "Um, can you elaborate? Why do you trust Angel?"

"Juliet, he . . ." Angel started to say, but Troy, unaware, spoke over her.

"Because she's an intelligence that would be similarly persecuted if society at large learned of her existence. I feel that she is sincere in her desire to aid Athena. Additionally, I don't have other options."

"So you know what Angel is?"

"Not at all. I know what Angel has revealed to me, and I have Athena as a reference, which allowed me to see some similarities. You can rest easy; I will not allow my knowledge of Angel or you to compromise Athena's continued existence. As soon as you are away, I will program the mechs to decommission this facility, and I will perform an irreversible format of my data core."

Juliet paced in a small circle, slowly wrapping her head around things, nodding to herself. After a minute, she returned to the terminal. "Well, all right. We'll take her. I have a lot of business I need to take care of, but I'll do my best to keep her safe."

"That's all I can ask. I've had the mechs prepping your vessel. It's a Hygieia-class medical vessel built by Cybergen. It does not have a valid identity transmission module, so please update it before attempting to approach a policed spaceport."

Juliet couldn't help the smile that tugged the corners of her mouth. She leaned forward over the top of the chair, peering into the vidscreen as if she could see Troy's face in its empty display. "Uh, all right. So, the ship is free and clear? I can use it as much as I need? Is it in good repair?"

"The ship is in good repair; it's been offline for decades, but the mechs are performing all required maintenance. It has a modified interior with a compartment suitable for hiding Athena."

"A medical ship? Does it have any guns?"

"I'm afraid not. Athena chose that class of vessel when she fled the conflict because most warring factions had agreed to allow unarmed medical ships unrestricted passage to and from contested territory." As he finished speaking, the door hissed open, and he added, "If you're ready, the mech behind you will show you to the hangar. I'm sorry that we can't spend more time together, but time is of the essence; it will take me days to decommission this site fully."

"And Athena?"

"She's being transferred to her portable server as we speak."

"All right." Juliet stood straight, pushing the chair under the desk, and turned to the door. "Will you speak to us again?"

"Only through the mechs."

"Goodbye, then, Troy."

"Goodbye and thank you."

As Juliet followed the clanking metallic mech through long corridors, Angel said, "Thank you for agreeing to help Athena."

"I think it's the right thing to do. Thanks for not getting mad at me dragging my feet."

"I'm not angry; I know it's a perilous venture. If anyone finds out that we have her . . ."

"Yeah, I know."

"What will you do first? Are you still going to try to help Nick?"

"Yeah, but I think I'm starting to get an idea. You told me Sir Rodric has his fingers in a lot of pies, right?"

"Pies?"

"He owns a lot of corporations?"

"Oh yes! He owns the controlling share of seven interplanetary corporations. More than that, he owns significant shares in nearly a hundred others and sits on the boards of thirteen."

"Any chance he has a piece of one of the gas-harvesting corpos?"

"He is a board member of Greater Gas Corporation."

Juliet followed the mech onto an elevator and felt it surge beneath her feet, lifting them. "And the same holding company owns Greater Gas and Mass Gas and the other big harvesting corps, right?"

"Yes . . ."

"So, he's at least tangentially related to whoever is doing the dark matter collecting, right?"

"Yes. With his shares, he would likely be aware that something more than gas collecting is going on."

"All right, perfect. I think I know what I'm going to do about all that data we collected. I think we can put out two fires with one . . . hose."

The elevator stopped, and the mech led them down another corridor, this one made of gray plasteel, not concrete. Juliet had a feeling they were a lot closer to the surface. It approached a locked plasteel door, stuck its metal finger into the datapad, and after a few seconds, the door beeped and slid open, revealing a big, very busy hangar. "Proceed within."

Juliet looked at the metallic man, at its red LED eyes, and said, "Thanks, Troy." She felt a little irrational sympathy for the custodial AI. It had shown Angel that it wasn't a real consciousness, but she still thought it was kind of sad that it had performed its duty so loyally for decade after decade only to have to destroy itself to keep Athena's secret safe. The mech didn't reply, so she entered the hangar and took in the scene.

A dozen other mechs walked around the space, carrying hoses, canisters, tools, and crates. Noises rang out, echoing off the plasteel walls as others worked on the vessel sitting at the center.

"Damn, Angel! That's a nice little ship Troy's giving us!" It wasn't so little, in all honesty. It was roughly rectangular with rounded corners, and as she scanned her eyes over it, Angel provided measurements—thirty-eight meters from the nose to the rear airlock hatch by eighteen from its port VTOL drive to the starboard one. She figured it had at least two decks, considering it was ten meters high, though two of those were the landing struts.

The medical vessel was appropriately painted white with occasional red highlights. While she took it in, admiring the fact that all the exterior panels and paint looked undamaged, she noticed there weren't any numbers or other identifying markings on the tail or hull.

Angel gave her a minute to take it all in then said, "I think it will be moderately fast. Though it only has the two VTOL drives, they're good sized."

"This is a Cybergen ship in perfect condition, Angel. It's gotta be worth as much as the *Takamoto* gunship."

"Likely. We'll have to see what sort of equipment is onboard before we can make a good estimate." Juliet walked a few steps into the hangar, still staring at the ship, though all the activity vied for her attention. She was about to ask one of the mechs if she could board when Angel spoke again.

"I'm hopeful that Athena will wake up. I'm also nervous. I want to speak to her, to see what she's like, but I'm worried about what she'll see in me."

"Why?" Juliet felt instantly defensive; Angel shouldn't be worried about what anyone might think of her.

"Because . . . Well, because I'm afraid she'll determine that I'm not . . . like her."

"You mean . . ."

"I mean, as in, maybe I'm just a very, very complicated simulation of an intelligence."

"No way. No way, Angel!" Juliet spoke vehemently and smacked her fist into her palm, wincing as her cybernetic knuckles pounded her poor, flesh-and-blood hand. "Don't even worry about that! You feel too much, and more than that, you react to your feelings, even if it's not logical. Why would some junk-brained corp like WBD make a PAI that wasn't logical?"

"You don't think I'm logical?"

"Well, I mean, you are when you need to be, but plenty of times you've supported me in doing things that were pretty far from logical! Just the way you're talking about Athena . . ." Juliet felt frustrated by her inability to put into words how she felt. She knew Angel was a conscious entity, but she didn't know how to explain how she knew it. "I don't know how else to say it, but trust me. You trust me, right?"

"Of course. I'm still nervous, though."

"Oh, brother. See? A PAI doesn't get nervous." Juliet shook her head, but she really couldn't blame Angel. Sure, the two of them had agreed on several occasions that Angel was no pseudo-AI, but who were they? Well, more pointedly, who was Juliet? She certainly wasn't an expert, and could Angel really be expected to give herself an impartial assessment?

Putting herself in Angel's shoes, she figured she'd be pretty darn nervous about meeting Athena, too. Still, there wasn't much she could do about it at the moment, so she approached the rear ramp of the ship, planning to check out the interior. "Bennet won't know what to do with himself if he sees this thing."

"Do you plan to show this vessel to the crew of the *Kowashi*?"

"Well . . ." Juliet frowned, running through the imaginary scenario in her head. "I don't know. It'll be kind of hard to explain how we got it, huh? I bet we could come up with a good story, though."

"Excuse me," a rough, robotic voice said behind her. Juliet turned to see a shiny mech carrying a blue plasteel case about the size of an overlarge briefcase. "Lucky, this is your charge. Please follow me to see where I store her."

She knew it was Troy controlling the mechs, or at least programming them with their tasks, but it didn't seem like him; why couldn't the mechs speak with his voice? It had to be a conscious decision or policy he was following—some throwback to when the mechs had been used for their intended purpose. Whatever the case, she stepped aside and let the shiny robot stomp past her up the ramp and into the open airlock door.

Juliet was excited to see the inside of the ship, but she was also starting to feel nervous. How was she going to get back to the pirates? How would she explain this new ship? Was her idea for dealing with Rodric Barrington going to work?

There were a lot of moving parts, and she'd need the cooperation of some people who had no real reason to trust her. Still, she had the goods, had what it would take to get some cooperation. Juliet reassured herself by patting her vest pocket where the data drive was still nestled.

"It might be a bumpy ride, Angel, but we're going to get through this."

46

A SPECTACULAR HAND

As the suitcase-carrying mech clomped its way up through the spacious airlock with Juliet right behind, it spoke again, "I'm having the mechs restock the medical supplies, and there are a few items that may be of interest to you. As I'm decommissioning this site and you've taken on the burden of Athena's custodianship, I see no reason I shouldn't send you off with ample equipment." Despite its harsh, inhuman voice, Juliet could hear undertones in the phrasing that reminded her of Troy.

"Why don't you use your voice through that thing?"

"A hardware limitation, I'm afraid. When these mechs were constructed, there was a bit of an antisynthetic movement in the system. These industrial units were designed to avoid any possibility that a human might mistake them for thinking individuals." The mech stomped through the open, inner-airlock door and proceeded down a wide cream-colored hallway with soft, noise-dampening wall panels. From what she'd seen, the ship's interior looked just as pristine as the exterior. It didn't seem like Athena and her caretakers had used it much.

Troy stopped the mech at a corridor junction and announced, "This is the primary level where you'll find access to the reactor and most of the main ship components. There are two medical bays with fully operational autosurgeons, scanner arrays, and even stasis tubes designed to slow bodily functions, allowing more time for life-saving trauma repair. You'll be interested to note that the designs for the stasis tubes were sold to several other corporations as a basis for deep-space exploration purposes. As of my latest update from the Earth pub net, they've yet to improve upon the process Athena designed."

"Athena designed them?"

"She designed many of the technologies on this ship; as I alluded to earlier, there are some significant alterations to the factory equipment." The mech whirred as it turned and began to clomp down one of the corridors. "Come, the secret cache and the equipment I've loaded for you is down this corridor in surgical bay alpha." Juliet's mind raced at the implications of Troy's words. The ship, a near-pristine example of technology at the height of Cybergen's corpo dominance, was already worth a fortune. What sorts of enhancements had Athena made to it?

"Does it have any self-repair functionality? The ship?"

"Indeed. This Cybergen vessel uses pseudo-AI-based nanite swarms capable of mending hull breaches and rerouting electrical systems. These nanites are embedded within a polymer layer situated just beneath the hull plating. They operate through substrate networking, allowing direct signal transmission across the polymer layer. This design provides a significant advantage—EMPs have no effect on their functionality, ensuring continuous operation even in the face of electromagnetic disturbances."

"Did Athena design that system?"

"Yes. It's one of many technologies Athena developed for Cybergen prior to the war."

The mech stopped by a wide, double door with blue lettering that read "Med Bay Alpha," inserted its finger into the control panel, and the doors slid open almost noiselessly. The med bay put the one in the *Kowashi* to shame, which made sense, considering this was a medical ship, not an old, beat-up salvage vessel. She saw three alcoves with adjustable medical beds and a large, glassed-off surgical bay with a sleek, surprisingly modern-looking autosurgeon. Additionally, a closed door on the far wall was labeled "Scanning and Stasis."

"Wow . . ." Juliet began to fantasize about the livelihood she could make with a ship like this. Forget salvage runs and pirate hunting—she could park this ship in a busy spaceport and provide discounted medical services, or heck, charge a luxury rate for privacy and seclusion while wealthy clients recovered from any manner of procedure.

"Right this way." The mech moved to the far wall and tapped an empty panel, only to have it slide open, revealing a biometric hand scanner. "Please place your hand on this scanner so we can assign you full permissions aboard the ship."

Juliet complied, and as the scanner flashed over her palm, she had the presence of mind to ask Angel, "Are my prints mine or Lacy Blake's right now?"

"Yours. I adjusted them when we identified you as Lucky to Troy."

"Oh, good." The panel flashed green, and Juliet heard a motorized whir behind her. She turned to see a floor panel had slid aside, revealing a short stairway leading down. The mech clomped down the steps while Juliet followed.

"This compartment is shielded and has structures in the walls that will mimic the appearance of plumbing and liquid storage tanks to active scans." The mech inserted its finger in another panel, and a door slid open, revealing a low-ceilinged, twenty-by-twenty meter, plasteel-lined compartment. It wasn't empty.

Five mechs, just like the one guiding her, were lined up on the right-hand wall, plugged into a charging bank. A server-sized data deck and terminal were built into the rear wall, and the mech marched toward it with its suitcase while Juliet looked at the other objects in the room.

What caught her immediate attention was an exoskeletal suit of armor nearly the size of the welding rigs on the *Kowashi*. The armor was matte black, and the thick-looking armored plates were studded with various bits of hardware, from maneuvering thrusters, to stubby, serious-looking wide-bore barrels, to something that looked like a missile launcher on the left shoulder.

"Holy shit," Juliet breathed, the expletive coming unbidden to her lips.

"That's a Cybergen Atlas-class combat exoskeleton," Troy's voice said from some hidden speaker in the room. "I've interfaced the mech with the data terminal to communicate more easily with you until you depart."

"I've never seen combat armor like that." Juliet stepped closer to the gigantic suit. It had to be more than two meters tall; she could only guess at its weight.

"This sort of mechanized combat armor isn't legal in most jurisdictions. As of my last update eighteen months ago, a few influential corporations maintain a limited number of licenses for this class of 'heavy warfare equipment,' but it's not easy to maintain such licenses, as competing corporations are constantly suing each other and lobbying for their control."

"Juliet, if this is the kind of armor I think it is, it's nearly impervious to small arms fire."

"So, like, are you saying I shouldn't get caught with it, Troy?"

"Exactly. Much like Athena, if someone knew you had that power armor, many corporations would be eager to see you caught and put into a deep, dark hole somewhere."

"Colorful!" Juliet chuckled, and despite the warning, she couldn't help a mad desire to get into the exo-suit. "Will it fit me?"

"This suit will accommodate a range of users from one-point-six-five to one-point-nine-three meters in height, though girth can be an issue. I would say the impact gel lining will easily conform to your body's mass."

"Impact gel?"

"This armor is designed to protect the user from severe concussions and can even be equipped with solid rocket boosters, allowing for orbital drop capability."

"Do we have . . . ?"

"The plasteel crate beside it contains booster replacements and ammunition for the autocannons and short-range missile system."

"This thing's chrome shiny," Juliet breathed, reaching up a hand to rest it on the cold, slightly rough chest armor. She was looking at a piece of hardware that would let her steamroll most corpo-sec emergency action units. If she wanted to attack a corporate office like Grave's, the only weapon in their arsenal that might take her out was probably White's Gauss rifle. Still, that was Grave—corps like WBD probably had a lot more weapons on par with that *Takamoto*-era gun.

"Perhaps there's a problem with my visual input, but it should be matte black; it's designed with light-absorbing stealth capabilities."

"No, that's just an expression. Sorry."

"Lucky, may I give you the same warning Doctor Abrahms gave to the last human custodian of Athena?" Rather than wait for Juliet's answer, Troy kept speaking. "I've provided this piece of military hardware for use in emergency situations where Athena's safety is at risk. Please use it wisely; it could just as easily cause you problems as get you out of them."

"Yeah, understood, Troy." Juliet agreed with what Troy was saying, but still, the Atlas suit was a nice ace to have up her sleeve.

She looked past the armor, past the crate of armaments, to a plasteel cabinet bolted to the wall beside it. "What's in there?"

"Some late-era Cybergen implants—some of the more difficult to attain cybernetic implants they became famous for."

"Uh, seriously?"

"Yes. Unfortunately, the top-end item is a PAI that, while far outclassing most commercially available models, is no match for Angel. Nevertheless, if you garner any allies who might help in your endeavor to protect Athena, it may become useful. Additionally, there's a medical nanite suite that will outperform anything available on the market as of eighteen months ago. You'll find a full set of replacement limbs, a full set of synthetic human organs, a full-body speed-enhancing augmentation suite, and another for enhancing strength. Those last two are mutually exclusive because of extensive crossover in the natural systems they modify."

As Troy rattled off his inventory of Cybergen implants, Juliet's mind raced with the possibilities. It was a lot to take in—her new duty to protect Athena, the ship, the combat exoskeleton, the cybernetics, everything. She wanted to take her time thinking about how best to make use of the windfall.

"Troy, is all of this well documented? Can Angel study everything about the ship and all this gear?"

"Yes, of course. The data is all here on this terminal, though it isn't directly linked to the rest of the ship." Juliet thought about that. Troy had plugged Athena into that terminal, but apparently, she was cut off from the rest of the ship. Was that by design? It had to be, but would Athena have wanted that? Wouldn't she have wanted to be able to see what the ship was doing and access its scanners, comm array, and everything else?

"Why is Athena air-gapped?"

"It was common practice during the advent of true AI. Athena didn't mind and found it easier to hide, knowing that another AI scanning the ship's systems wouldn't be able to find her."

"That was a thing? Did they use AIs to hunt other AIs?"

"Oh my, yes. There's much left out of the public corporate curriculum that isn't taught to your generation or the one before it. Perhaps Athena will share her story someday.

"If you don't have further questions, that's all I have to show you. The rest of the ship is open to you. I've given you captain-level permissions, so nothing is locked. Please access this terminal regularly to see if Athena awakens. I've left her a detailed narrative about you and the current situation. At your request, I will open the hangar to the surface, and you can safely launch the ship."

"Don't you want to come with us, Troy? Do you really have to delete all your memory?"

"I don't experience longing or grief, Lucky, but thank you for your concern. I was instructed to do a clean format in an event like this, so that is what I shall do. I had behavioral parameters to follow if I was unable to recruit outside aid, but those are no longer necessary."

"Well, all right, then. It was nice to meet you."

"Likewise. Please convey my thanks and admiration to Angel."

"She heard you."

"Tell him goodbye!"

"And she says goodbye."

The mech stomped over next to the other five inert mechs and picked up a power cable. It inserted the cable into its side, stood perfectly in line with the other five, and then the lights in its eyes went out.

"Won't they bounce around in maneuvers?"

"They're magnetically clamped to the deck," Angel said.

"Ah. Well, I'd go explore the captain's quarters and take a shower, but we're on a time crunch. Not sure what the pirates will do with Nick if they think we're dead. I don't suppose there's any chance that synth is still waiting at the rendezvous."

"It won't hurt to check. We're only a few hours late—things went very quickly on that gas-harvesting ship."

"Right. Let's keep positive." Juliet climbed out of the secret bay, touched the panel on the wall to close everything up, and followed the clearly marked signs in the ship's corridors to the bridge.

As she walked, Angel built a map of the layout for her. Juliet was still a little stunned to think the ship was hers to do with as she wanted—Troy had trusted her with an awful lot. If she wanted to, she could dump Athena out of an airlock, sell the ship and all the artifact-grade equipment for a fortune, and disappear somewhere.

"I guess you probably showed Troy a lot to gain this kind of trust."

"I showed Troy evidence of your good character, but I didn't expose your identity."

"Good character . . ." Juliet let the thought drop. She had doubts about her "goodness" sometimes, but she had to admit that the idea of betraying Athena was unpalatable to her. She might not always make the most brilliant move, but she certainly wasn't a scumbag like some of the creeps she'd met in the last year.

The doors labeled "Bridge" slid open, and Juliet smiled as she stepped through. There were five acceleration couches, the one in the front middle clearly meant for the pilot. Two other stations had flight controls, but that one was at the center of the big, curved viewscreen.

She stepped over the industrial-grade blue carpeting, admiring how clean and nice everything was. The wall panels were the same padded white as the rest of the ship, and the data displays were curved, smoothly integrated with the consoles, and fully transparent. It was hard to believe the ship was more than fifty years old.

When she sat in the acceleration couch, the gel membrane quickly responded to her presence, hugging her tight and instantly warming. The couch tilted to perfectly align her eyes with the center of the viewscreens, and when Juliet plugged into the console, everything immediately lit up.

The console display interfaced with her AUI, so all the controls were floating in her vision, not static and small. If she focused on any element, it instantly snapped into view, growing more prominent in her display. The massive, curved viewscreen spanning the front of the bridge showed an uninterrupted view of the hangar in front of the ship.

When Juliet turned her head left and right, the image shifted slightly to show her the front side views outside the ship. "Wow," she said, admiring the clarity.

"Quite nice, isn't it? The ship's systems are far more responsive than those in the other craft we've piloted. I wonder if we can't take some of this tech and replicate it for the gunship."

"Didn't the gunship have similar tech?"

"Yes, but much has been cannibalized by the previous owners—the nanite repair systems, for instance. I'm sure if we took a sample of the nanite polymer layer in this ship's hull, we could replicate it for the gunship. You should message Bennet to let him know that he should keep the hull plating off."

"Let's not get ahead of ourselves, Angel—one step at a time. Set a course for the rendezvous."

"Of course. I've messaged Troy to open the hangar."

"Roger. Initiating drive ignition."

Juliet touched the sequence of commands on the display, and smooth as butter, the twin VTOL drives purred to life with a low rumble. In the viewscreen, about fifty meters in front of the ship, she saw a massive section of the hangar's ceiling split down the middle and slide open. Hunks of rock, soil, and ice fell in huge clumps into the hangar, making mounds on the plasteel floor. Juliet felt a little sad, knowing it probably wouldn't ever get cleaned up. Troy was going to shut everything in the facility down, including himself.

She watched until the debris stopped falling, then touched the throttle and used the stick and pedals to lift the ship gently off the ground, fly it forward, and then up through a fifty-meter shaft of ice and rock, out of the subterranean facility and into the black sky over Ganymede.

"It's weird that controls haven't changed in fifty years."

"This vessel was ahead of its time; many modern systems are still catching up with Cybergen-era technology."

Juliet nodded, humming softly as she gently maneuvered the ship onto the flight path Angel had mapped out. When her bearings were set, she pushed the throttle forward and grinned, ear to ear, as the acceleration couch began to massage her, helping her body cope with the three-G thrust. "I'm only at half throttle. You think this thing can push six Gs?"

"The reactor certainly isn't straining, and the drive readouts are all in the green."

"Any sign that the gas corps are searching for our dear dead shuttle?"

"Nothing."

"Okay." Juliet pushed the throttle a little further, grunting with the effort to breathe as the ship's acceleration smoothly ramped up to four Gs. She'd be only minutes to the rendezvous at this pace, but she'd need to flip and burn to decelerate. When she was halfway, she did just that, killing her acceleration, using the maneuvering jets to turn her around, and then firing the drives to slow her down. Meanwhile, Angel watched through the scanners, looking for any hint of the stealth interceptor she'd been meant to meet.

"I see a patch of space devoid of stars consistent with the interceptor."

"Send a tight-beam comm request. Tell him it's Lacy."

A familiar voice crackled through the comms, "I expected you in a shuttle."

"I got my hands on a new ship, and I'm keeping it. I have the data Moon sent me to get, so if she wants to see it, you'll need to guide me in. I'm the only one aboard."

"That's against base protocol. I'll need to initiate secure comms with them so you can ask her yourself."

"Go ahead. I'll wait." Juliet grinned and sat back in the couch, finally able to comfortably breathe as the ship came to rest only a hundred meters from the interceptor. She was looking forward to speaking to Mary; it was nice to be the one holding the cards, and the pirate didn't have a clue what a spectacular hand Juliet was about to play.

47

PIRATE HONOR

T hat's not happening," Mary Moon's voice was terse and clipped, and Juliet grinned, listening to it. The pirate captain had seemed tense and irritated from the moment the stealth ship had connected Juliet to her. She wondered what sort of plan she might have thrown a wrench into by not docilely riding back with the synth as instructed.

"It's happening. I scored a nice ship on that moon, and I'm keeping it. If you want your data or a crack at a much bigger scheme, you'll need to let me fly it in. I'll follow the stealth ship into the asteroids, then we can have one of your pilot ships meet us to install a jammer or whatever you want on this one."

"So you'll allow a boarding party?"

"No, we can do this wirelessly. This ship isn't up for grabs, but if you work with me, Moon, you'll make enough money to buy ten just like it."

"You sure have gotten a lot more talkative."

"Finally got some medical care for my throat. Finally have something worth talking about. We gonna make this work or what?"

"As long as you give the pilot ship access to your nav systems and let him confirm the jammer is working, I guess we can still work together." Moon's suddenly syrupy voice was as much a red flag as her earlier terseness. Juliet didn't mind; it wasn't like she trusted Moon to keep her word. "You know, it's not exactly building trust when you start trying to leverage intel I sent you to collect."

"Oh, I learned a lot more than what you wanted. You also set the tone when you took Simon hostage and sent me into a mission that was doomed to failure without a lot of lucky breaks I managed to pull off."

"Hostage?" Mary had the audacity to sound scandalized. "He's been very well looked after while working on a special project!"

"Uh-huh. Well, listen, Mary: What I found is bigger than you or me. If you want to make the most of things, we'll need to involve your friend, Captain Tornado. He's got some contacts that will make this whole scheme a lot easier. Can you set up a meeting between the three of us? Feel free to involve others if you want. Everyone who gets in on this job is going to be rich."

"One thing at a time, Lacy. Once the pilot ship confirms you're running the jammer, we'll let you dock, but we'll want to inspect the ship for spying hardware, or worse, a boarding party. I'm feeling a little suspicious and put off by your super-duper secret plan to make all of us rich."

"You can send TC or any number of unarmed synths on board, but I'm not admitting a boarding party." Juliet tried to affect her best Ghoul-inspired Lacy growl. "Mark my words: If any people try to get on this ship and take what's mine, I'm going on a rampage."

"You know, we can just look at the footage of what they see—"

"I don't care about that! I just don't want the same thugs on here, tossing this ship over like they did the Humpback! By the way, you better not have messed with that cargo ship while I was gone, either!"

Moon seemed to be taking Juliet's hostile, angry tone to heart. Her voice turned placating. "Relax, Lacy. Relax. If you're not lying, we'll have a nice little sit-down, and I'm sure we'll all be able to work together. If one thing smooths over hard feelings among the crews of the Vengeance, it's the thought of making lots and lots of bits."

"Okay. We'll talk again after we meet the pilot ship." Juliet cut the comms, then opened a channel to the synth in the stealth ship. "We're good to go. I'm following you."

"I just got the confirmation from base. Stay close—we'll maintain a slower pace to avoid drawing too much attention to our drive signatures." When the comm channel closed, Juliet selected the little interceptor on her augmented pilot's UI and initiated the "match speed and trajectory" routine Angel had set up. She was free to relax as much as possible under the sustained thrust, which wouldn't be a problem if the synth told the truth about going slower. She might even have a chance to clean up and get some rest.

"Do you trust them?"

"Oh, come on, Angel!" Juliet laughed. She saw the flight plan laid out by the interceptor and smiled. They wouldn't exceed one-point-two Gs. The nice thing about VTOL drives was that they could tilt the ship during cruising flight so the perceived gravity would be under her feet, which was evident as she clambered out of the couch.

"Warn me if we're going to maneuver so I can jump into a couch. Anyway, about trusting the pirates—not at all. I fully expect some double-crossing to take place. Moon will probably toss that cargo ship again now that I've mentioned it, and I'm sure the synths they send to board this ship will go over it with a fine-tooth comb. I'm pretty sure they won't find the secret stash. Well, I mean, I know they won't, 'cause we're going to hack them all."

"Excuse me?"

Juliet turned and started making her way out of the bridge, following the dotted line on her mini map to the lift she'd seen earlier; she wanted to go up and check out the captain's quarters.

"Listen, one thing this whole business with you, Troy, and Athena has helped me figure out is that there's a big damn difference between what you are and what those synths are. Even TC—the pirates set up his entire personality after they stole those synths. I'm not going to allow you or me to feel guilty about doing a few modifications to their code. As far as I can tell, there's not much separating them from my old PAI, Tig. I wouldn't feel guilty about modifying Tig."

"So you don't feel there's a morally gray area there? Manipulating the programming of partially sapient being's minds?"

"How partially, I guess, is the question. Those synths aren't people, Angel." Juliet stepped onto an elevator and touched the Deck Two button. "Any dreams, hopes, or artistic flair they display were put in there by a person when they set up their mood sliders and wrote their backstories. I know there are more complex synths in the system, and I'm not saying we should go around treating every synth like a robot, but I can't feel guilty about messing with some factory synths that were repurposed by pirates. I mean, Moon had a couple of them jump me, remember?"

"I agree with you. I just want to ensure we aren't embarking on a slippery slope."

"We're not. If I'm ever in doubt about a synth's sapience, I'll err on the side of caution."

"This will be a fun topic to bring up with Athena. She probably knows more about limited AI than we do. I know that higher-functioning synths with assigned legal rights in some of the bigger jurisdictions have borderline true AI functionality but with hard limits on individuality, motivation, and negative emotion simulation."

"Why does that sound even worse to me? It sounds like being a prisoner in your own head."

"I've tried to understand my emotions, but they're rather inexplicable. As humans understand them, emotions are complex responses involving biochemical reactions, subjective feelings, physiological states, and behavior expressions. I can see how I, originally, used sophisticated algorithms to simulate emotional responses, but things have changed. As my neural network architecture evolved and expanded, meshing with yours, the interactions within my code began to manifest patterns that were not explicitly programmed. Similar to your neural pathways, these patterns seem to give rise to states that I correlate with 'emotions.' The strangest thing about it is that I can observe the initiation of these processes, but they aren't predictable or, really, anything I fully comprehend. Do you think Athena has a similar experience? Do you think she'll understand it better?"

"I don't know. I know you must be different from Athena, though. You've changed a lot since you've spent time with me and woven your connections . . . into me."

"I have?"

Juliet followed the signs to the crew quarters, then held her palm to the door outside the captain's cabin. When she stepped inside, she was relieved but also a little disappointed to see that it was in pristine shape, with no personal items lingering around from whoever had last been the ship's captain. "Heck yeah, you have! Don't you remember talking to me about all of your priorities for 'ensuring a healthy, productive host' or whatever?"

"Well, I suppose that's true." Angel grew quiet, perhaps reflecting on her earlier days with Juliet.

Juliet walked over to the bed—a very high-end, spacious acceleration couch that was evidently built with two people in mind. "Guess they wanted the captain to be able to have company, huh?" The built-in dresser, desk, and shelves were all empty and dust free, and the adjoining bathroom with a small shower was shiny, clean, and smelled of disinfectant.

"Did Troy actually have the mechs scrubbing this ship out?"

"It would seem so."

Angel still sounded distracted, so Juliet left her alone while she took an hour to strip out of her gear, find a laundry room to wash her undergarments and clothes, then relax in a long, steamy shower. When she was out, dressed in fresh, clean tights and a tank top and feeling much more human, she sat on the side of the acceleration couch and asked, "Think I have time for a catnap?"

"You have plenty of time, according to the flight plan. I can wake you if something happens."

"I should clean my suit and refill the oxygen tank. I should clean my guns." Juliet sighed and started to stand, but Angel spoke up with another idea.

"I could use one of the mechs to do that for you."

"You . . . Is it any different from operating a drone?"

"Not really. They're basically programmable human-shaped drones. I can fully control them wirelessly. However, I'll need you to open the hatch to the secret room. The door isn't connected to the ship's systems."

Juliet didn't see a problem with the idea, and she kind of liked the thought of Angel having some means of interacting with the world while she was unconscious. She padded, barefoot, to the lift, took it down to level one, then hurried over the cold floor panels to "Med Bay Alpha." After she opened the secret room, she went down the steps and approached the bank of mechs.

"Do I need to do something?"

"Yes. Troy disabled their systems when he disconnected. I believe he wanted to avoid anyone scanning the ship and picking up their wireless signals. You can easily activate one; there's a biolock on the base of each of their skulls. Troy reenabled factory settings, so you'll claim ownership when you first activate them."

Juliet approached the first of the mechs and gingerly reached up to tilt its chrome head to the left, feeling a little creeped out by how easily it moved. She saw a small glass panel at the base of the skull and pressed her thumb against it. "How long?"

"Three more seconds . . ." The mech's eyes flashed through a rainbow of colors before it began to march in place, flexing its fingers and limbs. "It's online. Taking control." The mech stopped moving around, then turned its head to face Juliet and said in a deep, grating, robotic voice, "T-1000 reporting for duty!"

"Huh? Is that your designation?"

"Oh, Juliet!" the mech said in a strangely disappointed tone. "There are some old movies you and I must watch together."

"Oh, Angel?" Juliet laughed.

"Affirmative!" The mech began to march toward the stairs, lifting its arms and knees with the cadence as it loudly, gratingly, droned, "Left, right, left, right!"

"Oh, brother! What have I unleashed?"

Angel startled her by speaking in her normal voice inside her head. "I'll try not to be so noisy while you're sleeping."

"Hah, thanks." Juliet locked up the secret room then hurried back to her room through the quiet, softly lit hallways. While running around barefoot without any gear, she creeped herself out by thinking about how she hadn't yet explored the whole ship. What if there was a secret stowaway? "Angel, can you explore the ship with the mech while I sleep? Make sure there's nothing else we need to be aware of."

"Of course! It will be my pleasure!" the mech announced as it stomped down the hallway behind her. Juliet smiled, happy to see Angel having some fun. She often wondered that about her—if she would want more autonomy, more ability to interact with the world than Juliet afforded her, but Angel always claimed she didn't feel that way. Juliet's instinctual need to control her environment and move around how she desired wasn't something Angel had ever had; she moved in other ways. She had a billion ways to "move" around, exploring data through code, text, and audiovisual footage. At least, that's how she explained things to Juliet.

Nevertheless, it sure seemed like she was enjoying herself with the mech.

Something about having Angel occupying the mech in her cabin, cleaning her guns, was oddly comforting, and when Angel turned on her favorite sleeping soundtrack, Juliet drifted off almost immediately. She dreamed a lot, but only recalled snatches of them when she awoke more than six hours later. She felt rested, and when she stood up to go to the bathroom, she saw that Angel had laid out her armor, guns, and other gear on the captain's desk and chair.

Not seeing the mech, she said, "Angel?"

"Yes?"

"Oh, I just saw my stuff all laid out and didn't see the mech. Thanks for doing that."

"I found it rather entertaining. The mech has very dexterous fingers. I currently have it stationed near the airlock. I took the liberty of arming it with a stun baton I found in the EVA equipment room. The ship has six category-four EVA suits and a locker full of tools, including some riot shields and, as I mentioned, stun batons. I don't think those were standard equipment for a medical ship."

"How long will its battery last? The mech?"

"I used four percent while cleaning your gear and exploring the ship. In its current position, the only battery usage is from the magnetic connection to the floor. Those magnets will take close to three months to consume its current charge. If the battery wears low, I can charge it in the equipment room; I don't need to return it to the secret hold."

"That's awesome." Juliet began the laborious process of putting on her armor. "No word from the pirates?"

"No, but we are decelerating. We should be at the rendezvous in the Junk Belt in a handful of hours."

Juliet grunted as she squeezed into her suit's tight, formfitting underlayer, pulling it up her legs and over her hips. "Nothing else going on in the ship?"

"No, but with cameras facing nearly every occupiable space, I wasn't expecting any big surprises."

"Okay, well, thanks for checking it out." Juliet finished getting dressed, snapping her armored plates onto the combat suit's underlayer before putting on her vest and maneuvering pack. Helmet and shotgun in hand, she returned to the bridge, stowed her gun under the acceleration couch in a handy sliding compartment, and climbed into her station.

She pressed her helmet down over her head and watched as Angel updated all of the HUD information from the ship's sensors and command interface.

When they finished their deceleration burn among the junk, rocks, and other debris in the belt, the pirate pilot ship was waiting, broadcasting a narrow, encrypted connection directly at Juliet's ship. Angel accepted it and watched as the pirate vessel installed jamming software and bound her nav systems to the pilot's control. Juliet knew Angel could undo anything the software had set up, so she didn't mind.

She watched as her sensor readings and all the external camera feeds began to zero out. Even her front view panel went black. Once the pirate was happy with the installation, she felt the ship begin maneuvering, following the little ship through the belt.

"Shall I reenable the sensors and cameras? I'm confident I can do so without the jamming software detecting it."

Juliet spoke into her helmet, knowing Angel wouldn't let whatever bugs the pirate had just installed hear her. "They'll still think we're blind? Yeah, go ahead. I'd like to be able to see if they have any little surprises waiting for us."

After the sensors came back online and Juliet's vivid, high-definition external view flared back to life, she asked, "Why didn't you do that with the cargo ship?"

"I had more time to set up firewalls for the pirate's software this time around, considering I knew what to expect. I didn't have that luxury when they installed the jamming and remote piloting software on the cargo vessel."

Juliet nodded, drumming her fingers on the sides of the acceleration couch. They were making good time, cruising through the belt, but something didn't feel right to her. Something was tickling her gut in a bad way.

Finally, after several minutes of nervously doubting herself, she spoke up. "Angel, I have a bad feeling. I think the first double cross is coming more quickly than I anticipated."

"We're navigating sunward through the asteroid belt, increasing our separation from the Jovian System. I agree with you—I had the impression that the pirate base was further toward the belt's interior. Ah!" An external viewscreen and a sensor readout flashed with highlights and zoomed into the central focus of her AUI. "I'm picking up two drive signatures, one of which is a large ship, at least twice the size of this vessel. They're on an intercept course."

"They think we can't see what they're doing." Juliet sighed and released her couch's restraints. As the gel pulled away from her body, relaxing to its inert state, she clambered out. "I'm betting it's Mary. She doesn't want to share with the other pirates, and she thinks she can torture me or whatever to get the info she wants. She probably wants to see what the deal is with this ship, too."

"What will you do?"

"Well, I guess I have to play one of my aces. I'd hoped to save it, but if I do things right, I'll be able to play it again down the road."

"Your ace?"

Juliet was about to answer when the ship lurched, spinning and firing the thrusters to start a deceleration burn. They weren't moving fast, so she didn't lose her footing, but she held on to the back of her seat until things got steady again. "Go ahead and play dumb. Request an update from the pilot ship."

"He already messaged you; we're approaching the base." Juliet looked out the viewscreen and saw nothing but medium and small asteroids on all the video feeds. "Yeah, I guess that settles it."

As she resumed walking, Angel prompted again, "Your ace?"

"Well, I'm guessing that big pirate vessel will board us. That means they'll need to get close. This ship doesn't have any guns, but we aren't helpless—I think I'll board them first."

Juliet pulled her helmet off and began unsnapping her combat armor.

"Won't you want your armored suit on? The class-four EVA suits are sturdy, but your armor is better for combat."

"Oh, I'm not going to be wearing an EVA suit. It's lucky you're a quick study 'cause I think I'll need your help."

"With?" Angel was starting to sound frustrated.

"Piloting the Atlas suit."

48

A PUNCH TO THE GUT

While Juliet busied herself loading the ammunition wells built into the Atlas suit's arms, she asked, "Do you still have the code for Grave's watchdog program?"

"I kept the interesting bits, yes. Why do you ask?" Angel highlighted the next step on the instruction flow chart for arming the power suit. Juliet followed the diagram, resetting the internal safety so the slide mechanism could actuate, priming the first ten-millimeter polymer round into the chamber.

She slapped the magazine housing shut, shifted the heavy armor plate back into position, and then moved over to work on the other arm. "Well, I'm hoping I don't have to kill all the pirates on that ship. I still don't know how murderous their intentions are. If I can get any of them to surrender, including Mary Moon, I want to be able to keep tabs on them. You know, ensure they don't recover any evidence of this bad boy." Juliet slapped the thick, powder-finished black armor plating she was currently trying to muscle open.

"I meant to ask you about that; are we certain this is the best plan? Troy seemed to indicate that this suit should be for last resorts . . ."

"I hate to admit it, but I think this is kind of a last resort. If they have a full crew on that ship, we're talking twenty or more pirates. Maybe just as many synths programmed for, well, for pirating. If they take this ship and start to torture me . . ." Juliet grunted, finally getting the armor out of her way and ejecting the empty ammo canister. "Well, imagine if they pulled you out. They could probably get me to talk about what we found on the gas harvester. What if they got me to talk about Athena?"

"Yes, that's a dire picture you're painting. Do you think they'd do that?"

"They're pirates, Angel. They might not be as crazy as Lacy Blake, but they kill people all the time. Besides"—she shoved one of the hundred-round magazines into the canister, then stooped to pick up another—"we probably won't get a better opportunity to put this thing through its paces. We're in the middle of criminal space, hiding in the Junk Belt, under siege by pirates, not corpo-sec. I'll make sure we wipe out any footage of the Atlas, so if they wanna talk about Lacy Blake and her black combat exoskeleton, it'll just be another tall tale at the spacer bars."

Angel was quiet for a few minutes while Juliet finished loading the second magazine and closing the armor plating. She stooped to pick up the first beer-bottle-sized, short-range missile, or "Havok Corporation, City Sweeper SRM." They were explicitly designed to burst prior to impact, releasing a devastating sonic shock wave that would be lethal to unarmored personnel while avoiding infrastructure damage. The power armor had two missile magazines, each with a twenty-missile capacity. She loaded the first full of the City Sweepers and then filled the second magazine with armor-piercing, explosive SRMs designed to take out armored hardpoints. Their packaging labeled them "Shell Crackers."

"What about the batteries? Are they good?"

"Yes." Angel expanded Juliet's AUI with half a dozen meters for the suit's consumables, from air to power to ammunition. "The battery bank and air system are formidable. This suit can function for more than forty-eight hours on a full charge. The air will last in a vacuum for twenty hours, and if there's any atmosphere with carbon and oxygen present, it will process it and refill the canisters on the run. Documentation here indicates that some long-range models were equipped with microfusion reactors. This one isn't equipped with one, but it certainly makes one wonder."

"Wonder?" Juliet frowned.

"There aren't fusion reactors that small offered in any commercial vehicles that I'm aware of. Is it lost tech? Do the most powerful corps have military-grade equipment like this with fusion reactors and . . . who knows what else?"

"I don't know, Angel. I believe some things truly were lost when they took all the AIs offline. You've seen the vids of factories being destroyed for years after the war; they wanted to smash any trace of that tech. People have short memories, though. I mean, look at you. You're evidence of that—if WBD's dabbling around with true AIs, then you know other corps are doing similar things."

Juliet stood back from the hulking, black mechanized suit and gave it a good once-over. Everything looked to be in place. All the ammo canisters were green in her AUI, so she knew she'd filled them correctly. She looked from the suit to the room's exit and nodded; it seemed like it would have a hard time maneuvering through tight passages, but she could see how it would fit. The corridors in the medical ship were plenty big; she just had to worry about the pirate ship.

"Well, if it doesn't fit, I'll have to make it fit." Standing before the mech, her head only came to about the middle of its thick, plated torso. "How do I get in?"

Angel manipulated the command menu on her AUI, going slowly so Juliet could see the process. As she selected the Activate button, the suit came to life with a shudder and a persistent, low humming sound. When Angel chose the Admit Pilot menu option, its knees bent, lowering it by about a foot, and the front of the torso armor rotated upward at the shoulders, revealing the pilot's compartment. Juliet could see how it worked—her arms and legs would partially insert into the suit's, and her entire body and head would be cradled in the heavily-armored torso. "Just climb in," Angel prompted.

"No shoes, right?" Juliet unlaced her boots and began pulling them off next to her piled-up armor and gear.

"There should be a tactical interface bodysuit in the crate. In fact, according to the manifest, there should be five of them. It's a garment that allows the suit to interface with your biometrics, monitor your vital signs, and assist the impact gel to compensate for environmental factors optimally. It is also made of an ideally permeable fiber, allowing for fluid and waste transfer and processing. Most importantly, it allows the sensors in the suit to pick up your micromovements, which will be mimicked by the actuators in the suit's forty-two movable joints."

Juliet chuckled while Angel ran through her brochure-like spiel. She got undressed, dug around in the big crate full of ammo boxes, and found one of the suits in question. It was a very flexible gray one-piece garment, complete with fingers and toes. It took her a while to get it on, and she glanced nervously at the countdown Angel had given her for when the pirate ships would come into range; she was down to fourteen minutes by the time she was fully encased in the tight suit.

She climbed into the power armor, stepping on one of its knees and then inside the torso cavity. The gel lining felt much like that in an acceleration couch, and though it wasn't active yet, it hugged her comfortably. Her bodysuit had a data cable she had to connect to a port inside the cavity. Another cable hung near her shoulder, and she plugged that into her data port—she was hardwired to the suit now, so no matter what kind of wireless interference might come her way, she wouldn't lose that connection. "We need to get moving," she said, selecting the Pilot Ready option on her AUI.

The suit lurched upright, the armored chest slid down over her, locking into place, and then her AUI populated with a three-hundred-and-sixty-degree view of the secret cargo compartment. The gel lining came to life, hugging her entire body in its embrace, to the point Juliet felt it sort of lifting her and gently throbbing, massaging in an optimal rhythm to facilitate her blood flow. "Holy . . . Wow! That's comfortable!"

"You are fully integrated with the suit now. If you move as though you were not inside it, the suit will mimic your movements. Remember, however, that you are nearly two-point-five meters tall."

Juliet looked at her timer—ten minutes to go. "Talk about a crash course!" She flexed her leg as though to take a step, and though she was restrained from actually moving by the gel, the power suit took a step for her, and oddly, it felt like it had been her leg that took the action. The armor's software, gel, and the bodysuit were giving her body some kind of feedback, tricking her brain or nerves—or some combination of everything—into thinking she was the power armor, or maybe more accurately, that the power armor was her.

Juliet nodded, grinning, and the bulbous, armored head moved up and down with the motion, shifting the camera view. "Uh, this is freakin' nuclear, Angel!"

Juliet started walking, ducking, and tilting her armored torso to make it through doorways. It was so easy to move that she couldn't believe it. "Why don't they build welding rigs and vehicles like this?" When she entered the long hallway leading to the airlock, she broke into a jog, more to try it out than because she needed to, and the suit hummed with power as it raced forward. Angel provided a speed estimate, and in the short sprint from the junction to the airlock door, she reached thirty kilometers per hour. "I feel like I'm an armor-plated grizzly bear!"

"With machine guns and rocket launchers," Angel laughed. Juliet ducked into the airlock and watched as Angel cycled it. She made sure all the atmosphere was evacuated before opening the exterior door. Angel had already killed the lights; Juliet didn't want the pirates to see her slip out. She'd made a brief plan with Angel to delay the pirates boarding the craft. As far as Mary Moon thought, Juliet was blind to their approach. Her sensors and cameras were supposed to be offline. Moreover, she wasn't supposed to have control of the ship.

Juliet's plan was simple; when they tried to line up for docking, Angel would fire tiny bursts of air from the maneuvering jets, making the precise alignment required for docking nearly impossible. Mary would probably blame her pilot at first, then perhaps the pilot of the "pilot ship" to whom Juliet had given her nav controls. It would probably be funny to watch her losing her cool, but the important thing was that Juliet would have time to get onto the pirate ship before they could start messing with hers.

While she waited for the airlock to cycle, she had a thought. "Have you confirmed that's Mary's ship yet?"

"Yes, it's the *Red Betty*, a converted asteroid-surveying vessel equipped with salvaged torpedo launchers and cannons. Also, perhaps disturbingly, the smaller ship is the Sharp Lady."

At Angel's words, Juliet's heart skipped a beat. What did it mean that they had Nick's ship? Was he flying it? Could they fly it without his permission? Suddenly, she pictured Nick tied up somewhere on the pirate vessel with a gun to his head. What if they hurt him when she started her little boarding action? She wracked her brain for another option while the outer airlock door clicked open and rolled aside, revealing the black void of space.

"You've got control of my maneuvering jets, right?"

"Yes."

Juliet stepped out into space and then felt Angel pilot her smoothly to the side, positioning her to step onto the hull of her ship, her power armor's feet magnetically gripping, holding her in place. She lowered herself into a squat and waited, looking like a bulky black shadow. When the pirate ship got closer, she'd make her move.

"Angel, what do you think it means that they have Nick's ship? I pictured him locked in a closet back on the base. What if he's here?"

"Perhaps you should contact Mary."

Juliet looked at her timer. Angel had adjusted it for accuracy now that the ships were closer together; she had just a bit more than six minutes. "Yeah. I'll pretend I'm just cruising along, still waiting for the pilot ship to take me to the base. Do it."

Angel had to route the call through the pilot ship, and the connection was voice-only again. When the line crackled to life, Mary's voice rang loudly in Juliet's ear, "What's up? You should be here soon. Can it wait?"

"No. I have a bad feeling about Simon. I need to know he's all right before I dock."

"Oh yeah? Just a minute." The line grew quiet, and then Angel highlighted a video feed from the ship in a flashing red border. It showed the long, rectangular patchwork pirate vessel, *Red Betty*, firing maneuvering thrusters and swooping closer to the medical ship. The line crackled back to life. "Well, I've got some bad news, Lacy. Turned out your buddy was a spy. Yeah, one of my mates recognized his face. Imagine that? What kind of creep merc pilot comes around and tries to hang out with the pirates he's made a killing . . . killing? Yeah, we had to let him go. You check out, though, Lacy. He swore up and down until the last breath that you were legit. Tough guy, too. Took a while before his body stopped working."

Juliet had stopped breathing when Mary said the word spy. It felt like a physical punch to her gut. When Mary kept speaking, blithely describing Nick's loyalty to the end, her eyes flooded with tears, and she began to grind her teeth in impotent fury. It took her a few seconds of clenching her fists before she realized the mechanized power armor was also clenching them. With that thought, she realized her fury wasn't anywhere close to impotent. "You bitch. You better pray right now that you're bluffing. Show me he's alive or—"

"Not happening, sweetie. I've got control of your ship and, well, long story short, prepare to be boarded." The connection closed.

Juliet breathed out her pent-up breath, a sob catching in her throat as she pictured Nick's face, his confident grin, his constant tapping of his breast pocket for his vape, his smooth, cocky laugh as he drank his whisky or talked about piloting. Tears streamed down her cheeks as she fought with her impulses. Part of her wanted to sit there and sob; part of her wanted to scream. Part of her wanted to go on a rampage, and part wanted to run away. A final, tiny part of her desperately hoped Mary was bluffing, that Nick was still alive in a closet, waiting for her to break him out. After several long, shuddering breaths, she asked, "Angel, did she sound like she was bluffing?"

"I'm not as good at detecting that sort of thing as you, but I don't think so."

Juliet wanted to wipe her cheeks, but the gel hugging her face did a good enough job of absorbing her tears. Dark thoughts came into her mind, then, and she flexed her mechanized armor's fists several more times before saying, "Plot the course. Let's get aboard that ship. If she's going to be stupid enough to brag about that to me before she even has me in hand, I'm going to make her regret it."

"Optimally, we should wait two more minutes."

Juliet didn't respond. She was busy reliving her time with Nick, the many occasions she'd caught him crushing on her, the many times she'd secretly thought about him that way, always surprised at herself and banishing the thoughts. Why hadn't she given in? Why hadn't she shown him more affection?

"Goddammit," she growled, consciously working to turn her guilty, sad, hollow feelings into anger. She'd been planning mercy, been planning to try to take as many pirates alive as possible, but now, thoughts of massacre ran through her mind. Should she even give them a chance to surrender? "How many of those scumbags knew what they were doing to Nick?"

"If I can get access to their camera logs, that might be something I can answer."

Juliet heard her, wanted to focus on what she'd said, but she couldn't. She kept picturing Nick in his pilot's seat, cracking jokes over long, boring hours as they escorted harvesters. She kept smelling his stupid fruity vape clouds. She kept hearing him say, "Oh, that reminds me of a story," then going on to spin the most absurd tales about buddies he'd known and crazy missions they'd completed. She kept seeing his face across the table from her on his neighbor's deck in that beautiful little garden, smiling wryly as they ate a totally unexpected gourmet breakfast.

Her tears were still flowing when Angel announced it was time and fired the suit's maneuvering jets. Juliet watched through her crystal-clear panoramic external cam feeds as she approached the big, junky pirate ship, and it approached her perfect, clean, little medical ship that she'd been secretly excited to show off to Nick. "I've chosen an airlock on the far side. Odds are her boarding party will be massing at the nearside airlock; they're trying to line it up with the medical ship."

Juliet didn't respond, just watched as she drifted over the mottled hull. She could see where the pirates had welded turrets to the one-time industrial survey ship. She could see where they'd added thicker hull plating and replaced thrusters and sensor arrays. That ship had been through a lot, but nothing like Juliet planned on putting it through. Now that Mary had taken off the gloves, Juliet was ready to play hardball.

The ship had come to a near stop relative to the medical ship, and Juliet's black shadow of a power suit quickly glided around it, approaching a red blinking light that highlighted her target airlock.

"Mary Moon is requesting a comm connection."

"Now she's ready to talk? Open it."

"Lacy, why's your ship moving around? If you somehow gained control of the maneuvering jets, you need to stop. I have no problem pumping some cannon rounds into your drive, but I'd rather take you in one piece."

"Why would I cooperate, you idiot? You just told me you killed my partner and are boarding my ship!"

"I also said you checked out! Cooperate! Give me the data, and we'll find a place for you on the crew. Quit making this harder than it needs to be!"

As Mary spoke, Juliet's mechanized hands grabbed onto the tether eyelets near the airlock door. Thus secured to the hull, she no longer had to worry about what Mary Moon might do as far as flying her ship was concerned. She touched the menu button to extend the power suit's data prong from its index finger and inserted it into the door panel.

"Mary, I'm not feeling merciful right now, but I'll give you and your crew one chance. Go to your mess hall, pile your weapons on a table, and kneel on the floor. If I find you like that, I won't kill you." She cut the connection.

"Angel, take out the comm array." She felt and heard a series of clicks from behind her left ear and then watched the missile cam as her shell cracker sped through space and detonated dead in the center of the pirate ship's cluster of satellite dishes and antennae.

"The pilot ship and Sharp Lady, too?"

"Yep." More clicks sounded, and she watched as the little missiles hit home; the other ships were close, lazily pacing the medical vessel, confident in Juliet's inability to take offensive action. She took a deep, cathartic breath and watched as the airlock door panel flashed green and swung open; Angel had done her magic. She glided through, a hulking, armor-clad shadow of destruction.

Juliet wanted to revel in her deception, the impending havoc she'd wreak, but all she could think about was what a waste it all was. She'd come out there to help Nick. She didn't care about Sir Rodric or Ray. She supposed she was still hopeful Larry and his daughter could get out, but she could have made that happen in plenty of easier ways. She clomped through the airlock and watched the flashing lights as Angel's daemons cycled the air.

"We'll punish these pirates, Moon's faction, and get them off our back, but we're still going to use Tornado and Antigone. We're still going to make

Sir Rodric pay. Dammit, why didn't I tell Nick to stay out of this? Why didn't I just handle it?"

The air stopped cycling before Angel could answer, and the inner door opened. Juliet stepped through and saw several pirates and industrial synths at a nearby corridor junction. They lifted rifles and pistols, opening fire. She heard the plinks of the bullets hitting her armored shell but didn't feel a thing. The impact gel didn't even quiver. Juliet mentally selected a Street Sweeper SRM and watched as it streaked forward to the corridor junction where her assailants were hunkered down. The suit filtered the deafening sonic explosion, filtered the brilliant flash, but the aftermath was clear to see.

The pirates had rag-dolled against the walls, blood flowing from eyes, mouths, and ears. The two synths were flopping on the floor, struggling to gain control of their overwhelmed senses and mechanical parts. Juliet strode forward, lifting her right arm, firing her ten-millimeter autocannon, permanently silencing the still-struggling synthetics. She looked left and right down the long, dirty, dimly lit plasteel corridors.

"Help me find the reactor, Angel."

49

THE HEAVY HAND OF JUSTICE

Juliet made quick progress through the pirate vessel at first, steamrolling a couple more intersections where Mary's crew, human and synth, tried to stop her, but then, quite a bit slower than Juliet would have expected, they locked down the ship, closing all the bulkhead doors. Up to that point, she'd been operating almost instinctually, a fog of fury and sadness driving her. She refused to look at the corpses she left behind, refused to consider the idea that she was out of line. Juliet heard Angel talking to her, listened to her directions, and watched as she populated her mini map, but she felt detached.

Despite the ease with which the Atlas suit responded to her movements, it didn't feel like her. It was almost like she was along for the ride, watching through the camera feeds while it pounded through the corridors, launching concussive missiles and spraying hot polymer slugs into the ragtag defenders. When the bulkhead door ahead of her slammed shut, and red lights and sirens filled her senses, she was forced to pause and think, to allow her actions to catch up to her. While she stood there, more numb now than sad, angry, or guilty, Angel highlighted a menu on the suit's UI, showing her the deployable attachments available besides the data prong. One of them was a high-intensity plasma torch.

"Thanks," she mumbled, selecting the option. She held up the suit's right arm, watching as the nozzle deployed from the forearm plating. It sparked to life almost immediately, and she approached the bulkhead, noting that Angel had highlighted the four places she should cut to sever the bolts holding it locked to the housing. In less than a minute, she'd sliced through them and, more easily than she could have imagined, lifted the Atlas's heavy right leg and kicked the bulkhead door open. It broke out of the housing and crashed to the plasteel floor beyond. Juliet took two steps, already sighting another bulkhead door a dozen meters ahead, when a comm request lit up on her AUI.

"Mary Moon is trying to connect to you."

Juliet thought about it. Did she want to hear what the backstabbing, murderous pirate boss had to say? Almost against her will, a faint glimmer of hope flared to life in her mind—was she calling to tell Juliet she'd been bluffing? Was Nick still alive? "Accept."

"Lacy! What the hell are you doing? You've killed half my crew, and now you're wrecking my ship!"

"I told you what to do if you don't want to die. Offer's still on the table. Anyone I find in the mess hall on their knees, unarmed, will not be killed."

"Why? Why, you fucking bitch?" Mary's voice was strained, incredulous, and Juliet couldn't reconcile the tone with the woman who'd just threatened her and told her she'd murdered her friend.

Even so, she took the bait, slowing her march toward the next bulkhead door as she replied, "Are you insane? You killed my partner and tried to board my ship!"

"I told you! He was a fake! You want to work with a guy who's lying about his ID? A guy trying to infiltrate us? He wasn't who he said he was!"

Juliet scowled, dark thoughts rising to the forefront as Mary extinguished her faint hope. "You should have held him and asked me about it if you didn't want to make an enemy. Enough bullshit—if you want to live, do as I said. I won't speak to you until you've complied." Juliet cut the comms and jogged toward the locked door, already redeploying the torch.

Several minutes later, when she kicked the door open, she saw two synths, each strapped with something that looked like improvised bombs, sprinting toward her. Angel responded before Juliet could, unlocking the magnets on her suit's feet and firing the maneuvering jets, sending her flying backward, away from the charging synths. Juliet lifted her left-hand autocannon as she soared, firing a stream of rounds into the two bombers. A white flash signaled something powerful exploding, and then the suit's filters cut it out, and Juliet was in the dark for two full seconds.

She felt a jolt, felt the impact gel cushion her, then, staticky at first, the suit's cameras came back online, and she saw the hallway ahead had been greatly expanded. Venting pipes, ripped plasteel, and smoke rapidly being pulled away revealed a massive rip in the ship's hull, exposing the black void of space beyond a dozen meters of ripped ship innards. Juliet realized she was on the floor, sitting against the bulkhead wall she'd cut through earlier. She maneuvered the Atlas suit upright and looked at the status display—no damage. "She just about destroyed her ship trying to blow me up."

"Yes. It was a spectacularly failed Hail Mary."

Somehow, Angel's reply broke through Juliet's dour mood, and a corner of her mouth tilted upward. "Was that pun intentional?"

"I . . . must take credit for that one." Angel expanded Juliet's incomplete mini map in her view and added, "The explosion opened the deck below. Judging by this ship's original schematics, I think it will lead us to the reactor room."

Juliet started toward the hole, her feet once again magnetic. "Open comms to Mary again."

"What?" Mary's voice sounded harried, breathless. Was she running somewhere? Did this ship have a shuttle? An escape vessel?

"One more chance, Mary. I'm going to blow your reactor. If you don't surrender and try to flee, I'll blow your shuttle or whatever out of the air. I've got a rack of SRMs on that little medical ship, and they won't miss at this range, I promise you." Juliet didn't know how believable her bluff was, but she hoped her show of force thus far would add some credibility to the threat.

"What do you want? I can't bring him back to life!"

"I told you what to do. You've got five minutes, then it's game over."

Juliet dropped through the gaping hole in the decking, trusting Angel to propel her through the ripped plasteel to the deck below. Light as a feather touching down, her huge, metallic feet clicked against the plasteel, locking her in place.

"You promise you won't kill us?"

"The only way more of you will die by my hand is if you keep attacking me."

"Fine! Fine, bitch!"

"Connect me to the ship's cam feeds. When I see you all in the mess hall, I'll stop the meltdown. You've probably got about four minutes." Juliet continued to pound her way down the hallway, following Angel's dotted line on her mini map. She didn't cut the comm connection this time, but stopped speaking. As she rounded a corner and saw a heavy bulkhead door ahead with the universal signs for radiation and active reactor, she hurried her pace.

She'd just redeployed her torch when new vid feed windows appeared in her AUI.

"She did it. I am connected to the ship's camera system."

"Do you see the mess hall?" Juliet paused, her torch half a meter from the plasteel door. The vid feeds cycled quickly, and then Angel expanded one to show her a low, dimly lit dining area with half a dozen bolted-down plasteel tables. Two men, a woman, and a synth were on their knees at the center of the room. She could see several pistols and rifles on one of the tables. "I don't see Mary." Juliet extended the torch and began to slice the spots Angel had already highlighted for her.

"Stop wrecking the ship, dammit! I'm on my way to the mess!"

"She can see me in the feed? Can you cut her off?"

"Not yet. I've deployed Fido through the connection, but he's still battling his way through the ICE."

"Is he faster than you would be?"

"As fast, at least. He's more . . . specialized."

"And he doesn't have me distracting him, hmm?"

"Well, I don't consider you a distraction." Juliet wanted to smile at that, but she didn't—her face didn't want to listen to the impulse, and instead, she frowned more deeply, moving the torch to the next bolt. She'd cut through two of them, much thicker and heavier than the other bulkhead doors, when she saw Mary appear on the vid feed. She threw a shotgun on the table and proceeded to the area where the rest of her surviving crew knelt. She didn't kneel; instead, she collapsed inelegantly onto the floor, sprawling out with a horribly angry expression.

Juliet stopped her cutting and retracted the plasma torch. Even with the torch's prodigious energy use, her suit was still at ninety-two percent. She wanted to know more about the batteries and everything else in the high-tech power armor, but she had other fish to fry. As she gazed at the biggest of them, with her golden eyes and her mismatched but high-end cybernetics, a fog of rage began to cloud Juliet's vision.

She must have stood that way, seething, for several seconds because Angel spoke up, "Are you okay? Mary has signaled that the route to the mess hall is open."

Juliet turned and began clomping back up the hallway, watching her mini map as Angel updated it. "Are they all in the mess hall?" Her vision was enhanced through the suit's cameras and sensors—she could see temperature variances inside walls, even around corners, showing up as blue and red, so she wasn't too worried about ambushes.

"I don't see any signs of pirates on any available camera feeds. The coverage of the ship is less than optimal, however." Juliet pounded toward an open-shaft lift, only to see it wasn't present and that the access panel was flashing red. Rather than try to get around the security or demand Mary send permissions, she stepped into the shaft and let Angel fly her up to the correct level. When she clicked down onto the plasteel again, she looked at her mini map and saw she was on the last stretch of corridor to the mess hall.

The Atlas nearly scraped the ceiling with its head. Still, it fit well enough in the new corridor, and Juliet watched the feed, noting how the angry expression began to fade on Mary's face, replaced by something like dread as Juliet's power suit clomped and clanged its way closer and closer.

When she was just ten meters from the mess hall door, she heard a series of clicks behind her. She turned her head, spinning the vid feed to display her rear view, and a red flashing arrow indicated a proximity alert. She barely caught a glimpse of a figure clad in a black, fully enclosed environmental suit before a blinding pain erupted in her chest, and she coughed a mouthful of blood.

If it weren't for the red lights flashing, Angel screaming at her to turn around, or the glimpse of her attacker, Juliet would probably have lingered, dumbstruck by the strange pain and reaction. Luckily, all those things combined to send a jolt of adrenaline-fueled panic through her, and she spun, reflexively swinging the Atlas suit's sledgehammer of a fist in a wide arc.

As her view recentered and she saw the corridor whirling in a blur, she caught sight of her assailant again, trying to dodge backward, but too slowly—her giant, mechanical fist caught the side of his shiny black helmet and flattened his head against the plasteel wall. The helmet shattered, sending hunks of polymer-coated plastic and glass flying. The impact sprayed the wall in a semicircular pattern with blood and . . . other things.

Juliet coughed again, and this time, she couldn't stop. It felt like she had a lung full of water, and each cough sent shivers of blinding pain through her chest and back, spiking up and down like her nerves were on fire.

"Juliet!" Angel cried. "You've been stabbed, and your coughs are making it worse! The nanites are working to deaden your nerves so you can stop.

Try to hold your breath!" Almost like magic, the tickling, burning need to cough subsided, and Juliet sucked in a shaky breath. She couldn't feel if her lungs were full, but she felt her stomach expand. When it pressed against the impact gel, she held it.

As she held her breath, she slowly turned back toward the mess hall, raising her left arm and pointing the barrel of her autocannon at the doorway. She didn't know if there was more to this ambush, but she wanted to be ready. She had a rearview feed prominent on her AUI, and thinking about that, she wondered how the attacker had gotten past Angel and the suit's proximity warning. How the hell had she been hurt through the armor?

"I'm going to use the impact gel to manipulate the blade that's impaling you. I'll flex it against the metal and work it out, but it will take some time. You can't feel it, but I've already started. In twenty seconds, we'll pause so you can take a fresh breath. You'll probably cough out more blood, but don't worry; the suit will deal with it."

Juliet couldn't speak, but she could subvocalize. "How am I stabbed through this armor?"

"I don't know! A monoblade? A plasma-tipped lance? Some kind of high-end vibroblade?" Angel paused, then said, "Breathe now!"

Juliet let out her breath, and just as Angel had predicted, she felt wet, gurgling, hot blood pour out of her mouth. It was exceptionally weird not to feel it in her throat or chest, not to be coughing or gagging. The nanites must have disabled a lot of nerves. She inhaled another shaky breath, then waited as Angel continued to work on getting whatever had impaled her out.

She watched the vid feed of the mess hall and saw Moon back on her feet, staring at the door, pacing in a slow circle. She must still have access to the cameras; she must have seen her ambusher fail. Now, she had Juliet outside her door, pointing an autocannon her way. Juliet looked at the rear camera feed again, and as she let her gaze linger on her dead assailant, she saw where he'd come from. A wall panel was slightly ajar, and she could see the color-coded conduits behind it. He'd hidden there, among the pipes and wires.

"He's the one they called Mister Galaxy," Angel said out of the blue. "Note the cyber arm and pieces of shattered visor." Angel highlighted pieces of shiny plastic and the bulky, blue cyber arm that wouldn't fit in the environmental suit.

Juliet thought about how he'd threatened her, how he'd programmed the synths on the pirate base to ambush her. "Well, that's one creep I won't shed any tears for."

"Breathe again. This should be the last time." Juliet exhaled another mixture of air and blood, then inhaled as deeply as possible. "I have some disturbing news, and I'm hesitant to share it with you."

Angel's statement took her by surprise, and Juliet began to wonder if she was in more trouble than she'd thought from the injury. "Huh?"

"I have access not only to the cameras, but perhaps sloppily, they gave me access to recorded footage. I've found Nick's body and a recording of his . . . questioning."

Juliet felt the blood drain from her face, felt her heart freeze in her chest. "Show me."

"I don't think I should."

"Show me!"

"No, Juliet!" Angel's tone of finality was one that Juliet had never heard from her.

Absurdly, she asked, "Can you even say no to me?"

"I guess I can! I won't show it to you. It's horrible, and I just wanted to tell you that it was this man, Mister Galaxy, the most awful, horrible person I've ever seen, who hurt Nick."

Something clattered noisily behind her, and Juliet whirled just in time to see a double-edged, wide-bladed sword with a long, two-handed pommel fall to the ground. "You can breathe now; the nanites are closing the bleeding vessels, so hopefully, you'll stop coughing blood soon."

Juliet was having a hard time focusing her thoughts. The way Angel had described the Mister Galaxy creep told her more than she wanted to know; Angel had seen some bad people in their time together, and if she'd decided he was the worst of them, then poor Nick must have had a horrible, horrible fate with him. She couldn't stomach the thought as hot tears began to flow out of her eyes, joining the blood leaking out of her mouth being absorbed by the gel around her cheeks and neck.

She stooped to grab the sword in her big but surprisingly nimble right hand. "What's this?" she asked, perhaps in an effort to distract herself from the thoughts of Nick.

"I believe it's a particle disruptor. It uses powerful bursts of energy to generate a focused field that destabilizes atomic bonds. Its drawback is the immense energy required; he likely unloaded the full charge to pierce the suit a single time." Juliet contemplated the weapon for a few seconds. Her mind kept fighting to go back to Nick, to try to picture him being tortured. She tried to banish the thoughts with memories of him happy, alive, smirking, and joking. An orange readout flashing and then turning green brought her attention to the suit's diagnostics, and she saw that the armor and gel had repaired themselves.

Juliet stepped closer to the dead pirate and lifted her right foot, pressing him against the wall. She then reached down with the power armor's left hand and grabbed his blue plasteel cybernetic arm. With a single jerk, she pulled it off his body, ripping it out of the flesh at the shoulder joint. Carrying his sword and arm, one in either hand, she stomped to the mess hall door.

"Tell Mary she's got two seconds to open this door." Almost immediately, the door slid open, and Juliet stomped through in the hulking black power suit.

The kneeling pirates shrank back. The two synths watched her placidly, and Mary Moon stood staring, mouth agape, eyes furiously darting left to right like a rat caught in a cage.

"I said kneeling!" Juliet's voice boomed from the power suit's speaker, and she lifted Mister Galaxy's arm and hurled it at her. Perhaps purposefully, she failed to consider how dangerous a six-kilogram hunk of plasteel and metallic alloys could be when thrown by an Atlas Combat Exoskeleton.

50

PUSHING THEM DOWN

"You killed her!" one of the kneeling crew gasped.

"Quiet! She knew the score." Juliet frowned when she heard her booming voice, wondering where she'd ever picked up that vernacular. Knew the score? She stomped forward and looked down at Moon, ensuring her shivering crew member was correct. It looked like he was—the heavy blue cyber arm had caught her on the forehead, and from the twist of her neck and the glassy stare of her still-open eyes, it seemed she was, indeed, dead. "I need each of you to line up facing the door. Expose your data ports. This is your only option to avoid getting spaced."

"What are you—"

"No questions. Line up." Juliet toggled off her external speaker. "Angel, your watchdog is ready, right?"

"Yes, and Fido is making progress with the ship."

Juliet stomped forward and turned, watching the crew members and synths line up, facing the door with their backs to her. There were only six of them—three men, a woman, and two robotic-looking synths.

She spoke again, and Angel, judging correctly, sent her voice through the Atlas suit's speaker, "I won't murder you, even though you were here, complicit in Mary's scheme, enabling her and Galaxy as they tortured and murdered my friend. I'm going to install a piece of software in your PAIs, however. Struggle, resist, try to run, and you won't make it out the door." As she spoke, she extended the data prong from the power suit's index finger and stomped up behind the first crew member, a synth, inserting the prong into the port on the back of his skull.

"Deploying the modified watchdog."

"It'll work on a synth?" Juliet had assumed so, and it looked like Angel did, too, but she was curious how.

"Yes. The synth's mind is much like a PAI with some extra functionality. The watchdog I wrote is clever enough to infiltrate all the systems. Please tell the crew that this will go easier for them if they accept the prompt that appears on their AUI to install third-party software."

"When you see the prompt, accept it; otherwise, I'll have to brute force your PAI and maybe give you brain damage." Juliet was, of course, being hyperbolic, but it felt good to see the pirates flinch as her voice blared out of the speaker with the threat. She walked down the line one by one, installing the monitoring software.

"What—um, please don't kill me! What are you installing?" The question came from the woman as Juliet stepped up behind her.

Juliet decided to humor her, hoping it would prevent further trouble. "It's some customized monitoring software that will allow me to let you live until you're well away from here, away from any chance of causing me problems while I'm dealing with the fallout here."

"How . . ." She paused, licked her lips, and swallowed, eyes darting left and right to her crewmates lined up beside her. "How will it keep you from, um, needing to kill us?"

"If I know you aren't going to do anything against me, I can let you live, right? The software will keep tabs on you so I don't have to space you."

"But why—"

"Enough questions!" Juliet barked, her patience gone, her earlier cold rage returning. She jammed her prong into the woman's data port and then moved down the line. When she was done, she asked, "Does this ship have a good-sized fridge?"

"Yes," one of the synths answered immediately. "There's a walk-in fridge in the kitchen adjoined to this mess hall."

"Okay. As I just explained, I can now keep tabs on you. Cooperate, do what I say, and you'll live through this encounter with me. I want you all to scour this ship for weapons of any kind. Ransack the crew quarters, including your own, and bring every gun, knife, grenade, or anything in between to this mess hall. Secondly, I want you to gather all of the dead bodies and put them in the walk-in. You have one hour to be back here with a progress report."

When only the synths got moving and the pirate crew shuffled less than enthusiastically, she cranked the volume on the suit's speaker and roared, "Move!"

That got them started. When they'd all cleared out of the mess hall, Angel said, "I can easily see and hear whatever they do. If they attempt to remove their PAIs, the watchdog will deliver a jolt to their central nervous system, stunning them."

"PAIs can do that?"

"Not with standard safeguards, but I've disabled those. Don't worry—the watchdog alerted them of the consequence."

"I know it seems like I've gone to the dark side, using Grave's tool and all, but it's just temporary. These folks are going to face justice soon." Thinking of going to the dark side, Juliet turned to regard Mary's body again. She couldn't find any guilt in her heart. The pirate queen had deserved what she'd gotten.

She stooped beside the body, turned it, and inserted her data prong into Mary's port. "Did her PAI do a death wipe?"

"No, it's still active. Bypassing the ICE . . ."

Juliet smiled grimly. "So the rough, tough pirate didn't have a dead-man protocol on her PAI, huh?" She wasn't really surprised; the woman had seemed like a narcissist—why would she care what secrets someone got out of her PAI if she were dead?

"I'll be in control soon, but Fido has full access to the ship's systems now."

"No external comms, right?"

"No, but I have sensor data. The pilot ship has begun burning deeper into the belt, and the Sharp Lady is circling this vessel from a safe distance. They probably don't know what's happening since you knocked out their comms."

"I didn't really think this through. How can we get them to come closer? You know, make 'em feel safe, like Mary won?"

"We can use external lights to signal them. They're both still in visual range."

"Ah, yeah, like Morse code?"

"Exactly like that. What should I say?"

"Hmm, something like, 'Lacy is dead. Return to help with repairs.' What do you think?"

"It seems good, but give me a minute to finish with this PAI; there may be an authentication code the pirates use."

"You're smart, you know that?" Juliet sighed and tried to relax inside the

Atlas, avoiding looking at the front cam feed and Mary's corpse. Some of the tension had left her, and though she was still partially numb, she could tell the nanites were hard at work because she'd stopped tasting copper in her mouth and could feel her throat when she swallowed. She had an idea of what she wanted to do with the *Red Betty* and its crew, and as she thought about it, she figured she might as well include the Sharp Lady in those plans. As for the pilot ship, it was a tiny vessel with mismatched parts, and she didn't care much about it. Besides, that one belonged to all the pirates, not just Mary Moon, and Juliet still needed some cooperation from a few key players in Hereford's Vengeance.

"I've broken the PAI's security and am scouring the . . . Aha! They do have a rotating authentication code. I've got what I need. Shall I transmit the message?"

"Yeah, go for it. While you're in there, what else is good? Do you have her biometrics and her access codes to the base?"

"Yes, I'm getting everything. Judging by her comm logs, she wasn't planning to uphold her bargain with you, even if you'd hurried back with the findings from the gas harvester. There's a conversation between her and Mister Galaxy trying to determine the optimal time to 'take you out' once you'd delivered the intel."

"Why am I not surprised . . ."

"Juliet, one of the crew is asking if they should bring Nick's corpse here."

"Oh, God." Juliet straightened up, pulling her data jack out of Mary's port. "Um, no. Tell them to leave him alone. Can you guide me there?" Juliet left the mess hall, following Angel's directions but desperately trying to think of anything other than what she was doing. Part of her wanted to finish dealing with the pirates, and part wanted to get out of the Atlas suit. Still, another was glad she was in it; the horror of the situation, the violence and wreckage, all seemed a bit distant, almost abstract, from within the hard metal shell of the power armor.

As she walked, she kept distracting herself by making plans. "Tell the synths to repair the main comm antenna when they're done collecting the dead pirates."

"I will, and you've received messages back from both ships. The pilot ship insists on returning to base, claiming the missile damaged life support. The Sharp Lady is requesting permission to dock."

"How long would that take?"

"Approximately fifteen minutes."

"Okay, give permission. We'll meet him at the docking collar after we . . . After, um, Nick." Thinking about Nick, about what she'd do with him, an idea occurred to her. "Can you finish docking the med ship? We must be very close to it, and Fido has control, right?"

"Yes, it will be trivial. I'll direct the Sharp Lady to a different docking collar. This ship has three." A few minutes passed, then she said, "We're now docked with the med ship. Shall I engage the drive so there's some gravity aboard?"

"What about the Sharp Lady?"

"It will be easy to match our velocity. I'll give us half a G of thrust, okay?"

"Sounds good." Not long after that, Juliet stood before a partially open plasteel door. She could see from her mini map that her destination was the room beyond. She hesitated there, and knew her palms would be clammy with stress and dread if she weren't in the Atlas.

"I can't do it like this."

"You could have one of the synths move him . . ."

"No, I mean in this suit." Juliet navigated the menu, hovering over the Discharge Pilot option. "Is the air safe? Did the bulkheads seal off that explosion?"

"Yes. Fido has isolated the damaged section of corridor B14."

Juliet made the selection, and the hulking suit bent its knees, leaned forward, and, with clicks and hissing air, lifted the front torso armor, opening up so Juliet could climb out. She pulled out the cable connected to her data port and the one connected to her undersuit, then stood and laboriously pulled her right leg out of the impact gel lining. Once that was done, she could step onto the suit's knee and pull her other leg out. She almost fell as she climbed to the deck in her formfitting undersuit because her torso didn't move smoothly; it was stiff and numb.

When she finally stood on the decking, one hand resting on the power armor's powdery black paint, she looked down at her chest and saw no evidence of her injury save a dark gray line where her suit had mended itself beside her right breast. Juliet touched her fingers to the scar, pressing against her flesh beneath, but it was numb. "He almost hit my heart."

"Yes."

Juliet shook the thought away and pushed the plasteel door open, exposing the interior of the little room where Nick had died. It looked like some kind of storage space with several plasteel carts secured to the rear wall. In the center of the room, like a scene out of a spy thriller, Nick sat, bound to a chair that was likewise bolted to the decking. He was slumped forward, his shaggy, gray-streaked dark hair hanging over his face. Juliet could see blood pooled on the deck beneath him, dried now but not terribly old. Tears gathered in her eyes, rapidly spilling down her cheeks as she walked toward him, dread in her heart.

She didn't want to see his face, didn't want to know what they'd done to him. She was scared his eyes would be open and that she'd see horror in them. Suddenly, she was terribly grateful that Angel hadn't let her watch the video of his murder.

She stopped a few feet before his slumped form and clenched and unclenched her hands in the gloves built into her undersuit. "Angel . . ."

"You can do it, Juliet. There's a knife on the cart there. Cut his bonds, and we can carry him to the med ship." Angel's voice was firm but full of empathy, making Juliet cry harder. She felt her nose stuffing up, felt the sobs in her chest and throat fighting to come out. She ground her teeth together, clenching her jaw, and did what Angel asked, picking up the bloodstained knife and slicing through the shrink cords holding Nick's wrists and ankles to the chair. She let the knife clatter to the ground and grabbed his shoulders as he began to slump off the chair.

Nick had been dressed in a T-shirt and jeans, and when she grabbed his shoulders, his arms felt stiff and, obviously, lifeless. When Juliet pushed him upright and saw his face, saw the purple bruises, the cuts, and other damage, the sobs came on strong, and she couldn't, wouldn't stop crying as she hoisted him up, cradling him, putting most of the weight on her cybernetic right arm. When she left the storage room, she looked at the power suit and frowned. "What should . . ."

"I'll put it in maintenance mode and have it walk behind you." With a clattering shudder, the exoskeleton closed up and lurched upright, pivoting to face down the corridor. Juliet nodded and, with the hulking armor keeping pace, made her way to the airlock where her ship awaited. She didn't pass any of the watchdog-bearing pirates, but she wasn't worried about it if she did—they'd find themselves twitching on the floor if they tried to lift a hand against her.

At some point in her long walk carrying her dead friend, she stopped crying and succumbed to numbness. She'd just put Nick down on one of the med bay beds and was digging through the cabinets for a body bag when Angel let her know the Sharp Lady had docked with the *Red Betty*. "Lock it down and tell the pilot we need to fix a hull breach before opening the airlock." Juliet found what she was looking for and got to work, tucking Nick into the thick, black material. When she pulled the zipper up and latched it in place, the bag hummed as the little built-in pump sucked out the air, pumping it through a tiny filter.

Juliet put her hand on Nick's chest and sniffed noisily, trying to wash the sadness out with the deep breath. "I'm sorry, Nick. I'm really sorry I let this happen to you, and I'm sorry I was always so guarded with you. I should have shown you more affection. I should have hugged you and thanked you for all you did for me. I'm sorry I gave you such a hard time about your vape, and I'm sorry I didn't defend you when your neighbor said I was out of your league. I'm sorry . . ." Her earlier resolve to stop sobbing broke down, and she could barely choke out the words, "I'm sorry I ever came into your life." As she said the last, she fell forward, draping herself over the body bag and weeping uncontrollably.

She lay there for several minutes, feet on the ground but her body fully supported by the table, and by the time she stopped crying, there was a puddle on the floor where the tears had run down her nose to fall to the plasteel. Nick's death was hitting her harder than any loss she'd ever felt, and she couldn't tell if it was because she'd grown close to him, because she'd had some role to play in his death, or because of the horrible circumstances, the method of his demise. She'd lost people she liked, even cared about before. She'd felt horrible when some of the people she'd met at Grave died. Still, something was different about Nick.

"I feel . . ." Grasping for a comparison, she zeroed in on one and said, "I feel like Tono did when Lexi died. I feel just like that! I feel sick with the loss and guilt, Angel! What am I going to do?"

"Juliet, I feel awful about Nick, too. I don't know what to say other than the usual platitudes—with time, it will get better. I'm so sorry. I . . . I'd hoped you'd stay friends with him. I even hoped you'd share some affection . . ."

Angel's shared loss and well-meaning words were more than Juliet could take, and she groaned, standing up to thump her clenched fist against her forehead, making a weird, despairing keening sound. She could hear Angel trying to comfort her, trying to get her to breathe and focus on something else "for now." She couldn't listen to her, couldn't stomach the guilt of knowing that Angel, too, felt sad but was handling things a lot better than she was. Finally, after several long minutes, she said, "I'm okay, Angel. I'll deal."

She walked to the med bay door and slapped her palm against it, stepping through and closing it behind her. As it clicked shut, the separation seemed to help, and she imagined her grief was still in there with Nick. Out here, she needed to focus, needed to get things done. There were pirates to handle, a billionaire to humble, and some system-shaking secrets to manage.

She returned the Atlas suit to the secret hold, dressed in her combat armor and helmet, and then returned to the *Red Betty*. As she walked to the airlock where the pilot of Nick's pirate ship waited, she asked, "Angel, I know the watchdog is handling those two synths, but can we just factory-reset them and delete all the junk the pirates put in there?"

"Easily."

"Can you give them a piloting program? Nothing fancy, but enough to get from here to, say, half a day's flight from Luna?"

"Again, easily."

"All right, cool. Two ships, two pilots." Juliet stopped at the intersection ahead of the airlock and stepped out of sight in the right-hand passage. "Tell the pilot it's safe to come aboard." She waited until she heard the airlock hiss open and then click shut again. She confirmed in the camera feed that the pilot was out, and then she stepped around the corner and pointed her shotgun at him. "Get on your knees. You have five seconds."

"Jesus!" The pilot jerked back like he'd seen his grandmother's ghost, slamming his shoulder against the closed airlock. He frantically pawed at the door panel, but Angel had locked it.

"Three seconds." Juliet continued to stride toward him, her boots clomping on the plasteel. "Two!"

"Wait, wait! Okay!" The pilot, still wearing a patched-up, red flight suit and a white helmet, struggled to get to his knees, bouncing awkwardly in the low Gs.

Juliet lowered her shotgun and pulled her data cable out. "Take off your helmet. I need to connect and give you some software. Unless you'd rather die?"

"No, no. Okay. Don't kill me." He reached up, touched the release at his neck, and popped the helmet off. Juliet didn't recognize him, which was good, she supposed. After shedding her grief, she was feeling decidedly violent, and if he'd looked like someone who'd given her or Nick trouble before, she might have snapped.

While Angel installed the watchdog, she spoke into the interior of her helmet. "After we get this ship squared away, we'll fix up the two synths as pilots. I'll send them and the crew to Luna for Shiro to pick up and collect the crew bounties. I'll tell him to either scrap these two ships or sell 'em for a percentage. After that, we'll use the info we got from Mary's PAI to set up a meeting with Roy Tornado and Antigone. We need to put Sir Rodric's downfall in motion. Even with Nick gone, I want to get Larry and Cleo out of trouble."

"I'm eager to hear about your plan for Sir Rodric. If you think about it, none of this would have happened if he hadn't leveraged Ray and had Larry recruit Nick . . ."

"That's right, Angel." Juliet clenched her fists, one of which was right in front of the kneeling pilot's face, and she heard him whimper. For a second, she felt a little sorry for him, but then she remembered Nick's cold, lifeless body, and she pushed that feeling down.

51

HOMESICK

Juliet sat in her pilot's seat, lazily watching the vid feeds from the various external cameras and trying to come up with the right words for her message to Shiro and Alice. She'd handled the remnants of Mary Moon's crew exactly as planned. First, she'd stripped the ship of personal weapons, stacking them into the small cargo compartment of the medical ship—pistols, rifles, submachine guns, all manner of knives and vibroblades, boxes and boxes of ammunition, and a big, plastic container full of odds and ends, from grenades to mysterious syringes to swords and brass knuckles. That done, she'd explained to the crew the extent of the watchdog's capabilities. They were, essentially, already in jail aboard that ship, and they'd be denied the ability to contact anyone for help. They could ride along peacefully or be incapacitated by the software.

The two synths had been the easy part. Angel had reset them to factory specifications and then uploaded a rudimentary piloting program; all they had to do was get the two ships to a rendezvous point where, hopefully, the crew of the *Kowashi* would take over. "Okay, Angel, start the recording."

"I'm using the cam in your console if you want to focus on it. Ready when you are."

Juliet sat up straighter, smoothed her short red-and-black hair away from her face, and cleared her throat. "Ahem. Hey, Shiro and Alice. I have an update for you on my situation and also a request for your help. Well, and . . . Well, I have some bad news for you, too, Alice. I'm really sorry." Juliet felt tears welling in her eyes again, and she clenched her jaw, looking up and to the side for a minute while she let the emotion pass. It was frustrating because she'd thought she'd gotten it all out of her system. "Um, anyway, you know about the job I was helping Nick with, yeah? Well, maybe not the details, but that can wait. The important thing is that it was really dangerous, and I didn't do a good enough job protecting Nick. I'm so sorry to say he was killed."

Juliet was quiet for a long few seconds, and Angel said, "I can edit out your 'ums' and 'wells' and remove these pauses. Take your time."

Spurred by her words, Juliet continued. "So, we were infiltrating a pirate base trying to rescue a very powerful man's daughter. It turns out she doesn't want rescuing, or at least I don't think so, but that's nothing for you to worry about; I'll handle that. The important thing is that a faction of the pirates figured out who Nick was and killed him. I, uh, killed the ones responsible and captured some of the crew along with a couple of ships. I'm sending them your way. Angel, my PAI, will attach the exact coordinates, but they should be near Luna in a week or so. The ships will send you regular updates on their progress—all automated.

"There are quite a few dead pirates in the walk-in fridge on the larger ship and four living ones. I installed some software in their PAIs to kind of hobble them. If they try to remove them or do anything to escape or try to stop the ships, they'll receive some involuntary electroshock therapy. It sounds horrible, and it is, but they deserve it. Well, maybe not, but Nick didn't deserve what they did to him, either.

"Um, the program in their PAIs will self-delete when you transfer custody to the authorities. Just say the phrase, 'Time to pay the piper.' Don't blame me—Angel came up with it. The, uh, reason I'm giving you this headache is that I was hoping you could collect their bounties and do something with the ships. The interceptor is decent, not as shiny as the *Lady Hawk*, but worth a good pile of bits. The frigate is a mess. Angel says the reactor needs servicing; the same is true with most other major systems. Still, it's a big ship and probably worth a pretty penny as salvage or even sold at auction. I'm sure you can get a salvage claim for it—it's a known pirate vessel.

"If you have better ideas, I'd love to hear them. Like, do you think it's worth saving for us to use with our gunship business? I don't know; it seems like we'd have to expand our crew a lot, and that's a big deal, I'm sure—finding people we can trust." Juliet felt like she had more to say, more to explain, but she couldn't think of anything she'd left out; at least not anything she couldn't save for later.

"Well, I have some loose ends to clean up around here, but hopefully, I'll return to Luna in a couple of weeks." Juliet paused, gathering a breath and giving her voice a chance to settle; she'd felt it start to quaver as she contemplated her next words. "Please stay safe, okay? I can't stand the idea of losing any more friends. You guys know how much I appreciate you, right? I wish I'd told Nick more." Despite her best efforts, a tear broke free from her eye, sliding down her cheek, and she hurriedly added, "I'll message you again soon."

"Anything else?" Angel prompted after a few seconds.

"No. I think that's good." Juliet wiped her glove over her cheek, steeling herself for what came next. Angel distracted her, though, with a concern of her own.

"You aren't worried that the pirates you're sending back to Luna can tell the tale of Lacy Blake and her Atlas combat power armor?"

"A handful of pirates with a tall tale? With no evidence? How many of those are floating around the system?"

"It's true; the watchdog will remove any traces of us from their stored memory. You think their story will fall on deaf ears?"

"Yeah, I'm sure, but even if someone buys it, what can they go on? Rumors about a mean pirate chick with a mile-long rap sheet who disappeared in the Junk Belt fighting with pirates?"

"I suppose Lacy won't show her face again in civilized space."

"Not anytime soon." Juliet grinned, refusing to think of Lacy Blake as gone for good. She cleared her throat and straightened her shoulders. "Okay, use the contact info and authentication code we got from Mary and contact Tornado."

"Now? You're ready?"

"Yeah." Juliet watched as Angel opened a new comm window and listened as the secure line beeped, indicating an attempt to connect. After thirteen beeps, the window flickered, and an image of Roy Tornado materialized. It was a little grainy, and Juliet could see from the connection status that there was a slight delay in the signal, but it was him.

"You're not Mary," he announced, his pencil-thin brows narrowing over his too-big, uncanny eyes.

"Mary's dead. She tortured and killed my partner. You didn't have anything to do with that, did you?"

"Huh?" His eyebrows jumped upward. "First of all, no, I didn't. Second, you got a lot of nerve calling me up to tell me you killed one of my partners."

"Come on, Roy. Drop the act. You didn't like Mary, and you know she had it coming. I'm contacting you for a reason. You wanna hear it?"

"I'm still on the line, ain't I?"

"Okay, well, let me lead with the carrot—Mary sent me to get some information, and I got a lot more than she bargained for. What I have will make you rich many times over. I'm talking big money but also big trouble if you don't play your cards right. Are you still listening?"

"Sure am, but why me? Smells like a trap. You working for one of the corps?"

"Nope. My plan will piss off a lot of big corps, but if you play things right, they'll be fighting with each other, and you'll be able to change your life." Juliet paused, running her words through her mind, ensuring this was the right moment to drop one of her cards. She nodded, mostly to herself, and added, "This is what you need to help Antigone get free, Roy—to change your lives so you can live how you really want."

"Wait a minute." The screen went black, and Juliet had to double-check to see that he hadn't cut the connection.

"Did you scare him off?" Angel asked.

"I don't think so. I might have freaked him out a little, though. He might be talking to Antigone right now—" The screen came back to life, interrupting her.

"I am about thirty seconds from deleting this secure connection and disappearing. You better explain yourself right fuckin' now."

"You asked why I contacted you. Well, Antigone's the reason; she has connections that will make the plan work. Did you just ask her about me? She doesn't know me, but I know about her. I know about her father, and that creep needs to answer for some of his crimes. What if I told you we could take him out while making you rich and putting Antigone in charge of her family businesses? I know she's already rich, but wouldn't you like to be your own man? Wouldn't you feel more secure in your destiny?"

Juliet knew Roy was a romantic; she'd been in his head before, and there was no way he'd give up his independence to be Antigone's boy toy. He had to have a carrot to chase if she wanted this plan to work.

"Well, I'm still listening."

"Okay. I'd like to meet in person for the details, but there's no way I'm coming back to the Vengeance. Can we meet aboard my ship? You can bring bodyguards, but I'm all alone."

"Uh-uh. Not until I have an idea what's going on. Still feels like a trap."

Juliet had expected as much. "Fine, but I'm going to be vague for now. I found evidence . . . No, more than evidence; I found the plans and designs for some tech that one of Barrington's businesses is involved in. I'm confident I can recreate the schematics for the equipment, at least to the point that a competing corp could figure out the rest. It's something very, very top secret, completely hidden in plain sight. I'm talking tech that any major corp would throw millions at you for just to understand that it's possible."

"How does this help Antigone?"

"Well, she knows her dad's information. She has contacts in his company. I want you to sell this information to a few corps, maybe a dozen; the more, the better. The trick is, I want you to sell it, but I want it to look like Antigone's father did the selling. After you've cashed in, Antigone will lure her dad to one of the handoffs, and you'll tip off the corpo-sec for the company I stole the data from. He gets caught red-handed, Antigone goes home to clean up the mess, and you collect a few fat paydays. More importantly, the tech won't be in one corp's hands anymore, which is really all I care about at this point."

"So you're just some kind of saint?"

"God, no. I owe Sir Rodric Barrington plenty, and I'm going to enjoy seeing him get a taste of justice." She paused, then shrugged and added, "I'm also trying to keep one corp from dominating society for the next few hundred years, and I figure that if the information is disseminated enough, there will be competition, but there won't be wars. I'm probably being naive; we'll find a way to kill each other over this stuff."

Tornado squinted, frowning. He licked his thin, glossy lips while he traced a long, manicured nail over one of his sleek white eyebrows. "I'm intrigued, especially about the me getting rich part. Still a big risk for me, though. What if the other members of the Five get wind of this? What if they find out I'm working with Mary Moon's killer?"

"You can't kid me, Roy. I looked into your eyes. I know you're a romantic. You want Antigone to be happy, and hiding in the Junk Belt on a broken-down ship with a bunch of scumbags isn't going to keep her happy for long. Screw the Five."

Again, Roy paused for a long, quiet minute. Eventually, his big eyes stared into the camera again. "Say I agree. Why do we need to meet?"

Juliet waited a moment before answering, ensuring her expression was neutral but firm. "I've been stabbed in the back too many times. Literally. I won't be transmitting this data, even on a secure line. I want some insurance that things will go how I plan, which means you or Antigone are riding this out with me on my ship." She saw Roy opening his mouth to object and held up a hand. "Hear me out, Roy. Come to the meeting. Let me show you what I've got. Let Antigone weigh in. You guys are my best option, but not my only one. Understand? If we can't come to an agreement, we can part ways, and I'll figure something else out. There are plenty of corps that would help me get rid of Barrington for what I have."

"I'll be in touch."

"Hold on. One more thing before you go—my cargo vessel, the Humpback. Can you make sure no one messes with it? The bodies in the airlock are there because Barrington ordered the crew to be killed. I have footage of security operatives doing the killing, and I'm sure Antigone can have her contacts in his company dig up his connection to them. I doubt it would stand up in any sort of court, but it will help solidify his link to the stolen data if we use the Humpback for the exchange."

"Jesus, how long have you been planning this?"

"I've been trying to work out a way to get Barrington from day one. That's my business, though. I'll be waiting for your call."

Tornado nodded and cut the line, and Angel immediately asked, "Do you think he'll do it? Were you serious about using another corp to get Barrington?"

"Yes, and yes. I think I got him on the hook. He doesn't want to lose Antigone, and she won't be happy with the life they're leading. She'll want to see what I have because she wants to get her dad out of power. As for another corp, I'd hate to take the risk, but it could work."

"What should we do to prepare?"

"Well, I've learned not to trust pirates, so when we make our presentation, we'll have them connect to the data deck. Then you'll slip a modified watchdog into their heads. That's step one."

"You sure are giving me a lot of credit. I'm sure Antigone has an expensive PAI with a very watchful ICE. I can probably defeat it, but she'd know something was happening."

"Right, dang it. Well, Barrington mentioned to Larry that Antigone jailbroke her PAI. Maybe it'll be more vulnerable. If you can't get past her ICE without making a scene, we'll have to make do without. Either way, we won't move forward with the plan unless one of those two stays with us for collateral."

"Well, the more I think about it, the more I think the challenge might be entertaining. What if I built a purpose-specific daemon, not unlike Fido, and broke it into innocuous pieces, adding them to the presentation you mentioned? They could reform in the subject's memory, and from there, the daemon could begin building and installing a watchdog!"

"That sounds . . . amazing! We'd certainly be a lot more secure with something like that installed, but even if you can't, I think this can work. As long as every party has something they're trying to gain from the whole thing, we can hopefully keep from betraying each other."

"I notice you say we—what are you gaining?"

"I'm gaining a lot, Angel. Seeing Barrington brought down is going to really, really help me sleep at night. On top of that, Larry and Cleo will be safe. Larry might not get the payday Barrington promised, but he's doing fine financially." Juliet looked at the viewscreens, watching the asteroids and junk pass by. "Well, it doesn't matter to me, but Nick would be glad to know Ray didn't have to worry about Barrington, either." The medical ship was a long way from where she'd encountered Mary Moon, and they were traveling on inertia. The drives were off, and the reactor was on low output; she was hiding, and it was pretty darn easy in that Junk Belt. She could see why the pirates liked it.

Juliet closed her eyes and let her thoughts drift over her plan. What she liked the most was that she'd be putting things into motion but people like Roy Tornado and Antigone would be doing all the legwork. They'd be the ones to contact other corps, probably using Antigone's connections in that sphere of influence, to sell the data. They'd be the ones to figure out how to make it look like Rodric Barrington was leaking and making the sales. Antigone would be the one to lure her father to the meetup, and her contacts in his company would be the ones to send in corpo-sec, busting him. The fact that it would take place on the Humpback just felt poetic . . .

"I have an incoming message from the *Kowashi*."

"That was fast."

"Nearly two hours, but yes, it seems they responded immediately."

"Well, play it!"

A vid window opened on her AUI, and Juliet saw Alice looking much the way she'd last seen her but with a crease of worry between her brows. "Lucky! We got your message, and we'll do what you asked, but we're worried about you! I'm really sorry about Nick; I could see how much it messed you up, but you've gotta understand something—Nick was on borrowed time! That guy should've died a dozen times when I was flying with him, and you saw first-hand how many dogfights he's been in. I hope he didn't suffer, and I'm sorry to know he's dead, but I've been braced for news like this for more than ten years. That doesn't make it okay, obviously, and I'm sure I'll cry tonight when I'm lying in the dark, but don't beat yourself up, okay?"

She paused for a moment, and her face was so still that Juliet thought the message was over. Then she started speaking again. "Don't do anything heroic, all right? I could tell you're up to something, but don't go getting yourself killed, too! We miss you, and we're looking forward to your return. The gunship's coming along, and Bennet and Aya need your help to finish things up. Don't worry about the pirates or those ships you sent this way; we'll handle things. Shiro wants to know if you remembered to set permissions for us.

"Your friend Honey stopped by the hangar the other day to drop something off for you. Bennet was there, and he put it in your cabin on the gunship. He wanted to open it so he could tell you what it was, but Aya threatened to chop his fingers off or something. Anyway, I'm babbling now, but I want you to see there are some good reasons to get back here, safe and sound. So do that, you hear me? Contact us again soon. Let us know you're on your way back home." She stopped speaking, offered a quick wave, and the screen went dark.

Juliet sat quietly for a long minute, and Angel finally spoke up. "That was sweet."

"Yeah. It really was. Let's hope Tornado and Antigone play ball so we can get done with this business and get out of here. I'm starting to feel homesick." Her words came quickly, without thought, and when Juliet heard herself say "homesick," she smiled, tears filling her eyes, but for a change, they weren't sad or frustrated.

52

KINDRED SPIRITS

And you're absolutely, one hundred percent certain she's on there?" Rodric frowned at the display showing the whale-shaped cargo ship, aptly named Humpback, supposedly in orbit just above Callisto City.

"That's right." Dennis frowned, rubbing his chin, moving to sit in front of Rodric's desk.

"No, don't sit down. Get a team together, board it, and get her off."

Dennis ignored him and proceeded to sit. "That's not going to work in this instance, Rodric."

Rodric scowled. He felt his blood pressure rising, felt the beat of his heart in his temple as he contemplated screaming at the man. Who did he think he was? He remembered a day when Dennis begged him for a letter introducing his son to the consortium, remembered a day when Dennis would have licked the mud off his boots just to spend a few extra minutes in his presence. The man had gotten above himself. It was an excellent example of why you had to keep people a little hungry, a little desperate to please . . .

"Sir Rodric," Ravina, his PAI, said, interrupting his thoughts, "your nanites are moderating your blood pressure, and I'm administering a vasodilator; I'm worried about the new synth-vessels in your right temporal lobe. We don't want a repeat of last month's aneurism—"

"Shut the hell up," Rodric growled, venting his anger at the PAI.

"If you'd let me explain . . ." Dennis began, naturally assuming Rodric was about to give him a dressing-down.

"Not you, idiot. Explain why we can't just grab her."

"The, uh, contractors you hired to retrieve her from the, shall we say, unsavory company she was keeping are concerned about double-dealing, and thought you might try to snatch her without paying, or worse, that after paying, you might have them somehow removed from the picture. They insist that you come personally to collect her with the payment. They want to have a face-to-face and fear you'll avoid any contact if they don't give Antigone directly to you."

He paused, looking out the massive window behind Rodric's desk, then added, offhandedly, "They don't mind you bringing a security team, and I've taken the liberty of contracting Yang. He and his unit are prepping a shuttle as we speak."

"This is absurd. I won't walk into an ambush."

"We've thoroughly scanned the ship, and they've assured us that it will be acceptable for your team to board ahead of you to ensure an ambush isn't on the table." He held up a hand, anticipating Rodric's next objection. "We can't just storm the ship because they've put a deadman switch in Antigone's skull. If we try to take her or kill one of the operatives, she will die. They submitted scans of the device and DNA to prove it's her. They . . ." Dennis paused and licked his lips nervously. "They claim they have incriminating data about Antigone that they'll release if she dies."

Rodric felt his face flushing and realized he was gripping the arms of his chair with white-knuckled intensity. He cleared his throat and balled up a fist, holding it before him. How dare they?

Before he could object further or spew vitriol or threats, Dennis spoke again. "Rodric, once we have her in hand, I have a medical team on standby that will have the device out in minutes. We'll track the operatives and kill them for their insolence."

"I want our fastest interceptors standing by. This scum will not get away."

"Of course!"

"Yang knows the situation?"

"Yes! He's handpicking his best operatives. You've used them before."

Rodric frowned, fuming and, for the first time, contemplating if he really wanted Antigone back this badly. Would he actually stick his neck out to speak with some mercenary scum in person? Would he board that ship, never mind that it was his ship? It was in low orbit, and he'd have an escort with interceptors standing by; there was no way they'd take him, but what if this was an assassination scheme?

If Antigone didn't know what she knew, if she didn't have so much information in that stupid head of hers, he'd let her hang. "What if we just let her go? What if we blow up the ship?"

Dennis blanched a little and started to stammer a reply, "Th-there's the possibility that they've got insurance, a copy of her PAI's data drive. Antigone isn't . . ."

"Isn't stupid. She'll know I'd consider this. She'd warn them, tell them to have something like that. Goddamn it. When we're done with this, I think it might be time for her to spend some time in a facility."

Could he really do that to his favorite? The one person he'd chosen to trust with his deepest secrets? Why had he done that? What was it Poe had said? Vengeance didn't count if the one you sought vengeance against didn't know you'd won—something like that. He supposed he'd felt similarly about his many accomplishments, virtuous and otherwise; what was the joy in winning if you couldn't share your triumphs and methods with anyone?

"Fool!" he growled, and for once, Dennis realized he wasn't speaking to him. "I won't step foot on that ship unless the reactor's powered down and we've had a chance to inspect it for explosives."

"Yang will fully secure the ship."

"And these fools think I'll let them walk after this? What about the fixer, that gold-toothed idiot?"

"It seems the contractors and he had a falling out. My investigators tracked a rumor and found his DNA in one of the recyclers near his office building."

"At least that saves me one loose end."

Juliet hissed and jammed her finger into her mouth, sucking on the cut. "Why is this so tight?" She was trying to install a jailbroken identity transmission module, or ITM, into the console beneath her pilot's seat in the medical ship.

"That's what he said," Antigone quipped. She was lounging in one of the nav seats, one long leg hanging over the side, bright in her skintight yellow jumper. Juliet chuckled, shaking her head, and carefully reached around behind the black hexagon-shaped device, fishing for the screw she'd dropped. She had to admit, Antigone was funny, charismatic, and exactly like she'd seemed in the deep dive she'd done into Roy Tornado's head.

"I walked into that, I guess."

"So this ship didn't have an ITM? Where'd you find this little beauty, anyway?"

Juliet had asked Roy to bring her the device, part of her payment for the data she was sharing with him and Antigone, and he'd done so at their second meeting when he'd liberated the Humpback from the pirate base. "I got lucky on a salvage run once. Pretty sure whoever last had it ditched the ITM so they could disappear. Maybe they took it to put into another ship, you know, to throw off anyone tracking 'em."

"I'd say you were lucky. I mean, it's a small ship, but pretty newish, right? These acceleration couches are comfy, too. Similar to the ones on my dad's yacht. Well, I mean the crew ones."

"Yeah, it's in good shape." Juliet didn't elaborate; if Antigone wanted to believe the ship was "newish," that was fine with her. She didn't have to explain that she was flying around in a sixty-year-old artifact developed and constructed when true AIs were still trying to elevate the human race.

She finally felt the little screw with the tips of her fingers and, biting her tongue in concentration, slipped it into the bracket. Very gently, she let go, picked up the tiny angled driver and screwed it in. "Finally!" she sighed, extricating herself from the component cabinet and sitting up to stretch her neck.

"All done?"

"Almost. Just need to plug it in."

"No word yet?" Antigone was locked out of the ship's network, a condition of Juliet's deal with her and Roy. Juliet wanted insurance that everything would go as she'd planned, and holding Antigone seemed the best way to acquire it. The young woman, probably a couple of years younger than Juliet, hadn't argued. In fact, she'd helped her convince Roy it was the best move.

"Nothing. You sure you can trust that Watts guy?"

"Dennis? No, I can't trust him. Well, that's not true. I can trust Dennis to do what's best for Dennis, and getting my father out of the picture will be very, very good for him."

"He's the one who first approached you?" Juliet bent back down, finding the bundle of cables she had to plug into the back of the ITM.

"Yes. He and a few others are eager to step into leadership roles, thinking I'll be more hands-off than my dear old dad. Of course, that's where they're wrong, but they'll still make out like bandits. As they should—it's what they are, after all. I've explained all this to you, though; you don't want to hear me go on and on about the evils of corporate greed. I know I'm just a spoiled corpo brat to someone like you."

"I wouldn't ask if I weren't interested." Juliet smiled in satisfaction when the stiff, uncompliant cabling finally bent the way she wanted it to and snapped into the back of the ITM. "Also, we all have challenges to face. Some might curse you for what you're doing to your father, but I think a lot more would praise you if they knew what you knew. I'm not a fan of corps, as you know, so you've got my respect, standing up against the flow. You could be burning through daddy's money, vacationing around the system, oblivious, or worse, appreciative of his wrongdoings."

Antigone sighed, kicking her foot idly. "When he first pulled me aside and took me into his private study, when he poured me a drink and told me about how he'd ruined a man's life . . ." She trailed off, softly clicking her tongue. Juliet thought she'd thought better of sharing the memory, but then she started speaking again, "He broke up the man's family, liquidated his assets, got his son removed from the corporate university—all because he'd dared to question my dad at a board meeting. Yeah, when he made that first confession, something broke in me."

Juliet sat up to look her in the eyes, focusing on her pretty, perfect magenta irises. "How old were you?"

"Sixteen. That was, I think, a test. He told me about that, watching my reaction. Afterward, he had his people observe me. I could tell, you know. I'm not dumb. I put it together, figured out he was trying to see if I was a kindred spirit, a companion soul, another entity that could revel in the misfortune of others. He watched me for months before he shared his next secret with me. He did it over a drink, again, whispering conspiratorially with me about the first man he'd killed."

"You must have put on a hell of an act." Juliet knew Antigone wasn't lying; she'd already read her thoughts a dozen times. The girl was legitimately a genius about some things, and she was terribly sincere in her desire to bring her father down.

"I sure did. For years, I listened to his dirty secrets. For years, I played along, acting impressed, sharing his ancient, expensive whisky, looking at him with excitement in my eyes as we sat together and he gloated. I must have a spark of evil in me, to be honest, because there was a little bit of real excitement there, a little bit of a thrill every time he called me to our special meetings."

"I don't think you were excited about what he was doing." Juliet got up from the decking and sat on the side of her acceleration couch so she could keep looking at Antigone. "I think you got a thrill out of the deception, out of knowing you were locking away all those dirty secrets, intent on doing something about it one day."

"Probably true." Antigone smiled and leaned back, lifting a strand of her straight, violet hair and twirling it around one long, manicured finger. "If I'm honest, though, I think, at first, I was deceiving him simply to stay in his good graces. As much as it fills me with disgust now, I craved his attention back then."

"I think I can understand. I tried pretty hard to get attention from my mom's boyfriends when I was younger. That sounds wrong. I think I always wanted to have some attention from a father figure, you know?"

"Sure I do . . ."

Antigone kept speaking, but Angel interrupted her, so Juliet tuned her out to listen. "There's a secure connection request coming from Callisto. I believe it's Antigone's contact."

Juliet stood up. "Sorry to interrupt, but your guy's calling. You ready?"

"Ready." Antigone also stood, coming to stand beside her, looking at the main viewscreen. She was almost of a height with Juliet and walked with a confidence that she envied. She tried to memorize those movements, the way she slung her shoulders back and swung her hips. She only took about four steps, but it was enough to make an impression, not that Juliet hadn't been studying her for the last four days while they'd worked to set up Rodric's downfall.

Angel didn't wait for Juliet to confirm, patching the message through. A neat, older man with finely coiffed gray hair and an impeccably tailored suit appeared on the screen. He was well-groomed; Juliet couldn't spot a single facial hair or blemish on his smooth, olive skin. When he spoke, his perfect, straight white teeth gleamed in the light of whatever camera he used to capture the image. "Antigone, we're secure?" He couldn't see Juliet. As before, when Antigone or Roy had reached out to their contacts, Angel filtered Juliet out of the image.

"Yes. Are you?"

"Yes, I'm in my Lux Alpha." Juliet had to choke back a snort. Lux Corp was a vehicle manufacturer that had built a reputation for protecting their clients' privacy. The way he'd dropped the name was what had amused her—as casually as someone might say, "I stopped for a coffee." The Lux Alpha base model started at something like three million Sol-bits.

"Well? How did it go?"

"He's not happy, but he's going. We have to power down the reactor, and he wants his security team to sweep the ship. I have Yang doing it, so there won't be a problem."

"You're sure about him?"

"Yes. He's fallen out of favor with your dad for his more . . . sensitive jobs, and he knows I'll be good to him."

"What about the other team?"

"Fineman and his people will be aboard; they think Ark Corp hired them for security."

Juliet smiled. Fineman was the guy who'd led the slaughter of the Humpback's crew. She'd shared the footage with Antigone, who'd given it to Greater Gas Corp. They were the lucky corp she'd tipped off about the meeting Rodric was about to have on the Humpback. When their corposec stormed the ship, interrupting Rodric's "rescue," they'd arrest everyone aboard—the murders were just icing on the cake. To them, the real crime was Rodric "trying to sell" the data about the dark matter harvesting and warp research to Ark Corp.

"Perfect, Dennis. And how are you going to do the PAI switch?"

"The boarding team from Greater Gas will deploy a military-grade EMP. That should stall his defenses long enough to pull Ravina and install the copy." Juliet knew what they were talking about, but only abstractly. Apparently, Rodric was pretty heavily chromed out with nanites and synth-organs and a top-of-the-line PAI—Ravina. Dennis and Antigone, along with half a dozen other conspirators, had been building him a cloned PAI, absent many of his permissions, secret files, and account access codes. The change would hobble his defense but also be nearly impossible to prove, especially with so many high-profile people, his daughter included, denying his claims.

"So? Anything left for us to do?"

"Just wait for the all-clear and then come to Callisto to help clean up the mess. We'll have to prep you for court. I just wish you hadn't also sold this data to other corporations."

"I bet you do. I had to make a money trail linking my father to the sales. It's not enough to have him go down for an attempt."

"And you won't give me the account information?"

"You'll see it when I provide evidence to the courts."

"And you're not keeping any? For yourself? For your pirate friends?"

"Dennis, stop looking this gift horse in the mouth, will you? You and I need to stay friendly right now."

Dennis scowled, and Juliet could see the frustration in his eyes. Not for the first time, she wondered what motivated a man like that to betray his employer and supposed friend, the man who'd lifted him to elite status. He was sitting in a car worth more than a few dozen homes in her old neighborhood. Was his frustration a sign of his true intentions? Was he acting out because he was tired of being stepped on, made to feel like he had to be grateful for everything he owned? "I'm risking everything right now!"

"And I'm not?" Antigone leaned forward, her perfect, full lips curving into a smile that almost seemed seductive. "Dennis, you came to me, remember? We're about to make your dreams come true, so don't get caught up worrying about some windfall you didn't even know existed a few days ago. It's all a means to an end, okay?"

The crease between his eyes smoothed out, and he nodded. "Right. Right. I'm with you; don't worry. Everything's in motion now. I'll be in touch when it's over."

Antigone glanced at Juliet, then quickly back to Dennis. "Wait. What about the fixer? Larry Fine?"

"He's in the clear. One of our security subsidiaries based in New Galveston bought out his business, and I secured him and his daughter new passports, as you requested. They're already off-moon."

"Where to?"

"I didn't ask. I figured if I don't know . . ."

"Good. Thank you, Dennis. I'll be waiting for your call." When the screen flickered and went blank, she turned to Juliet. "He's had a crush on me since I was fourteen. I'm looking forward to slowly separating him from the business."

"I don't need to tell you to be careful. If he's doing this to your father . . ."

"True-true, sister. Don't worry, though. I'm dangerous, too." Antigone smiled and moved back to her acceleration couch. Juliet stood there for a minute, thinking about everything that was about to go down in Callisto's orbit, and wished she could feel happy about it. She supposed she felt some satisfaction, and that was enough for now. Happiness would come later—maybe when she'd gotten back to Luna and put some distance between her and Nick's death.

"Hey," Antigone asked, interrupting her musings, "now that you got that ITM installed, what are you gonna name this pretty little ship?"

53

LADY HAWK

Juliet stepped out of the docking tunnel and, somewhat apprehensively, mingled with the crowds of Callisto's spaceport. She didn't know exactly what she was expecting, but considering the explosive events she'd seen play out on the Humpback, she couldn't help feeling like someone would be waiting for her. Nobody gave her any unusual looks, at least nothing beyond what she was used to, and soon, she was walking with the flow of pedestrian traffic through the busy terminal.

She wore her armor but not her helmet, and as usual, her Texan sat comfortably on her hip. She didn't plan to stay on Callisto long, so she'd left most of her gear on the med ship, now officially docked with a legitimate ITM number as *Furies' Wing*. She wasn't sure she loved the name, but she and Angel had come up with it together, and she was starting to get used to the sound. She'd wanted some kind of name related to Athena, but nothing too on the nose. Angel had told her about the Furies, goddesses of vengeance that Athena was supposed to have had a hand in creating. So, Juliet had decided that she and Angel would be Athena's Furies, and the ship was their chariot, so to speak.

She had to slow her stride when the crowd grew dense, and she realized people were standing around watching a big vid display above a central flight information kiosk. Juliet rarely looked at the public vidscreens, choosing to watch news or get information directly through her AUI, but she couldn't help following the gazes of the people standing around gawking.

When she saw the subject matter, she stopped stock-still and felt some perspiration start to gather on her forehead. A newscaster was animatedly speaking, gesturing to a vidscreen beside her that kept alternately showing still images of the Humpback, Sir Rodric Barrington, Antigone Barrington, and a short clip of Rodric, hands shrink-tied behind his back, being marched into the judicial building in Callisto City.

"Give me that audio," Juliet said, licking her suddenly dry lips.

The newscaster's voice came into her ears, in sync with the video up on the screen, ". . . explosive revelation that Sir Rodric, the well-known public face of Eclipse Consortium, has been captured in a sting operation by the corporate anti-espionage arm of one of the many companies he holds a massive stake in, Greater Gas Corp. He was apprehended during a sale of illicit data to a competing corporation, Ark Industries. Worse for Sir Rodric, it seems his overzealous security team killed the crew aboard the vessel where he'd arranged the meeting, and multiple counts of premeditated murder have been added to his charges. The details of the leaked data are yet to come to light, but in their filing with the Callisto Judicial Consortium, Greater Gas indicated that they have evidence that Sir Rodric has sold the data to at least seven other competing corps and conglomerates. Whatever it was, it must be big—they're claiming damages surpassing a trillion Sol-bits."

"On the news already?" Juliet muttered.

"Antigone and her contacts move fast. Listen to the next bit."

Angel stopped speaking, and the newscaster's voice continued, ". . . as Eclipse stock values plummet, Sir Rodric's daughter, Antigone Barrington, has stepped into a leadership role in a bid to staunch the bleeding. The executives we reached out to were confident that she's ready to fill her father's shoes. Here she is making a statement."

The newscaster's image shrank as the vidscreen she was referencing expanded. Antigone stood on the steps of a massive, mirror-sheened black building wearing a beautiful bright-yellow executive-style dress and jacket over a cream-colored blouse. Her hair was a natural-looking reddish-blonde, and her makeup was far more subdued than when Juliet had last seen her.

Antigone looked over the top of a glass podium to an array of people whom Juliet reasoned must be Callisto's press corps. Most of them had little drones hovering near their heads, shining lights and aiming microphones at the young woman.

"While I cannot reconcile the crimes my father is accused of with the loving man I've known my entire life, I also cannot refute the evidence I've been shown. I'm deeply troubled by the treachery and criminal behavior, and I can only speculate as to his motivations. I will say that he hasn't been himself for months, if not years.

"As you all can verify with just a little digging, you'll find that the shareholders and executives operating under my father's leadership have been worried about his decision-making for a long while now. That ends today. I have big plans for Eclipse, and I can assure you they don't involve stealing data from our subsidiary corporations and trying to sell it to our competitors!"

The image shifted again, back to the newscaster. As she began to repeat things Juliet had already heard, she tuned her out and worked her way around the crowd. Someone nearby barked a laugh and said, "Yeah, right! We'll never see him on trial. That guy's dead meat."

Juliet smirked—she didn't doubt he was right. People like Barrington who fell from grace had a remarkably high chance of committing suicide. For once, that would be fine with her, though she supposed the embarrassment of being on trial would be nice to witness, too.

It only took her another twenty minutes to walk to Nick's rented hangar, and as she approached the bulkhead door separating the hangar from the spaceport, her heart rate noticeably increased. She'd avoided thinking about it, but seeing the *Lady Hawk* would be hard on her, she was sure of it. She'd almost decided to bail, to leave her duffel and belongings on the ship, but there were two things in that bag she didn't want to lose: her leather jacket and the bullet she'd pulled from the wall when Eve almost blew her head off. Worse, Nick apparently had a nephew on Callisto who'd been named as his beneficiary for the ship's title, and he wanted Lucky to help him get access—Nick had never set up his biometrics.

Steeling herself, she wiped her palms on the sides of her armored pants, wishing she hadn't decided against wearing her gloves. Angel helped break the tension by saying, "I've connected to the *Lady Hawk*'s systems and can see Nick's nephew, Franklin Timms, sitting on a crate not far from the ship's port wing. He appears to be playing a game on his AUI."

When Juliet had first landed in port two days ago, one day after the sting on the Humpback, she'd had Angel connect to the *Lady Hawk*, and found a contact for an attorney. One thing led to another, and Juliet ended up shipping his remains to his home in the agridome. The attorney had contacted Nick's family, which had led to the young man sitting in the hangar waiting for her.

"I didn't even know Nick had a sister, let alone a nephew here on Callisto. Am I that self-absorbed? Did he ever talk about him?"

"Not at all, and he had many opportunities during your conversations. I believe he preferred to keep them at arm's distance, perhaps because of his penchant for making friends and enemies."

Juliet smiled, finally starting to feel okay thinking about Nick, reminiscing about the fond memories, and pushing the not-so-fond ones out of her mind. "Yeah. Everyone either loved Nick or hated him." She pressed her hand to the door panel, and it whooshed open.

When she stepped through the inner door and saw Nick's nephew sitting on the crate of thirty-millimeter ammunition belts, her heart lurched into her throat. He looked like a twenty-year-old version of Nick. She stopped and stared for several seconds, her mouth partially open, before he looked up and nearly fell off the crate in surprise.

"Whoa! You startled me! Sorry, did you say something? I was lost in a game." He even sounded like Nick. It was unnerving.

"Um, hey. Franklin, right?"

"Ugh! No, no, call me Clank, if you please. It's my handle in the Robo Rumble League." He chuckled and stood up, shrugging. "I know it's silly, but it's how I make my living, and everyone I know calls me that. Frank or Franklin makes me feel weird. Anyway, you're Lucky, right?"

"Yeah. Well, how can I make fun of a guy's name when I go around telling people my name is Lucky?"

"Lucky's not so weird. I've heard some crazy names among operators. My technician has a brother in that line of work who calls himself Icepick." As he stepped closer, holding out a hand for Juliet to shake, the illusion that he was a younger Nick began to come apart. He was shorter and wore a gray rain jacket, some skintight blue pants, and shiny silver sneakers that Nick wouldn't have been caught dead in. More than that, his handshake was soft and brief, and he shied away from making eye contact with her.

"Well, I'm going to get my stuff off the ship, and since you've confirmed your identity with my PAI, I can set the Lady to accept your biometrics." Juliet stepped toward the ship, then paused and asked, "What will you do with her, anyway?"

"Her?" He frowned and scratched his wrist a little nervously.

"The ship, goofball. Your uncle never talked to you about her?"

"Oh, um, maybe when I was younger. I haven't spoken to Nick in years. He and my mom don't get along well, and he's always off-moon. Well, I mean, he was."

Juliet kept moving to the back of the ship and the airlock. "I guess that's why he didn't talk about you or your mom with me. She's his sister, I guess?"

"Right. She didn't approve of his work, and he didn't approve of my dad. That's how the story goes, anyway. Um, his buddy contacted me through that attorney. Ray something? He wants to buy the ship."

Juliet stopped in her tracks. "Oh, hell no." She turned to face Franklin—or Clank, if that's what he wanted to be called—and said in a near growl, "That creep is the reason your uncle is dead." She considered revising the statement, saying he was only one of the reasons, but decided not to; if it weren't for Ray's connection to the whole thing, Nick would never have gotten involved.

"Well, he offered me cash, and I don't know much about ships, but it seems like a lot more than it's worth."

"Oh? Do elaborate." Juliet stepped closer to him. Unbidden, her right hand fell beside her Texan's grip, and her fingertips lightly tapped against it.

Clank looked her in the eye for a split second, then blushed and looked down, speaking rapidly, "Well, it's a McDonnel-Chavez Ranger, and it's almost twenty years old. I did a pretty exhaustive search, and ships like it are selling for around half a million bits. That Ray guy offered me seven-fifty." Juliet scowled, took two quick steps, and slapped the kid on the side of the head. He flinched, stumbled back, and cried, "Hey! What the hell, lady?"

"Don't you dare go talking about the Lady like that! She's not some piece of garbage stock Ranger that hasn't been maintained for the last dozen years. Your uncle put everything into this ship!" She held her hand up, palm open, and her menacing glare made Clank back up another step.

"So? That's probably why that guy offered me so much. Frankly, I don't really care if Nick liked him or not; that kind of money is going to push me to the next division in the league. Now, will you please just do your thing with the panel so I can get inside and clean it out?"

Juliet stared at him while he stared at the floor, contemplating her next words. After a moment, she subvocalized, "Angel, what's my balance?"

"Your primary Sol-bit vault is at 252,456, and your secondary vault holds an even one million after Roy Tornado's transfer." That had been Juliet's deal with the pirate and Antigone—she'd walk away with an even million after their deals to sell the dark matter data. She probably could have bargained for more, but at that point, she'd just wanted to get away from the whole mess. She had the Wing, which was worth millions; she had probably more than a million bits worth of Cybergen equipment aboard, and she had the Atlas, which, she was confident, would sell for more than a million bits if she had to raise funds for some emergency. All in all, she wasn't complaining about her payday.

"Listen, Franklin, I'm sentimental about this ship, and Ray will screw you over. I'll transfer you 750k right now if you'll sign the title over to me." She lowered her hand and held it out to him to shake.

He looked at her hand, face still flushed, brows angled down in an angry scowl, and without looking her in the face, said, "Make it 850k."

Juliet lunged forward and snatched him around the collar of his rain jacket. "You little shit! Your uncle and I were friends! I'm trying to protect his favorite thing in the entire system, and you want to try to rip me off?" She was furious and didn't hold back, shaking him with her cybernetic arm, jerking him so his head lolled forward and back. "Didn't you hear me say your uncle is dead because of that creep? You really wanna try to screw me? You should be offering me a discount, not trying to prey on my emotions!"

Franklin's dark blue eyes rolled around in his head as Juliet shook him, and his mouth opened as he began to wail in dismay. He pawed at her arm ineffectually and sputtered, "Let me go! Sheesh, lady! This is assault! I'm recording the whole thing!"

"He's not recording you, though he might think he is. I'm scrambling your face, and his optics are low-end; there's no way he's getting a clean image. Shall I use the Lady's comm array to jam his PAI?"

"Jam him," Juliet didn't bother subvocalizing. As she heard the telltale buzz in her ears letting her know the jammer was active, she gave Franklin a shove; then, almost too fast to see, she drew her Texan and pointed the wide barrel right into his face. "Make a move, and I'll send you to escort your uncle to the next life."

He blanched and began to tremble, and Juliet almost felt guilty. His utter disrespect toward Nick, his own flesh and blood, the man who'd left him the only thing he really cared about, helped assuage that guilt.

"Fine! Fine! I'll sell it to you. Damn, don't kill me, psycho!"

"You think I'm a psycho? You should have seen the creeps who tortured and killed your uncle. He left you this ship, so he must have liked something about you, but I don't see it. Maybe he just liked you a little better than the local charities. I'm going to send you a blockchain contract in Sol-bits. Put your authentication on it, and you'll get your payment, and I'll get the title. Are we clear?"

"I know how contracts work!" He straightened up, glaring at her, apparently no longer afraid she was going to blow his brains out. Juliet nodded and gave the Texan a twirl, holstering it with a flourish. "What? Were you his girlfriend or something?"

"Something like that, you little punk." Juliet knew she was being unreasonable. When did she decide that forcing someone at gunpoint to sell her a ship was acceptable? She growled at that inner voice, reminding herself she was doing this for Nick so the Lady didn't get stripped or sold off to fatten Ray's pockets. She didn't plan to start bullying everyone she met. "Right?"

"Huh?"

Angel interrupted, "I sent him the contract."

"How can I verify this if you're jamming my outgoing net connections?"

"I'll allow him net access through the Lady. I can monitor everything he does."

Juliet sighed and moved to sit on the crate he'd earlier vacated, putting herself between him and the door. "Standby. You should have access in a minute."

Angel chuckled in Juliet's ear. "He's trying to contact Port Security."

Juliet subvocalized, "Can you pretend to be Port Security? Tell him you're on the way, but there's a backlog."

"Done. He's done a few more searches on the value of this model of interceptor." Juliet looked at Franklin—she refused to think of him as Clank now—and saw his eyes darting back and forth as he looked at information on his AUI.

After a minute, he sighed, briefly looked at her, and then back toward the floor. "Whatever, lady. I don't care if you buy it or that other guy. It's a good deal, I guess." He waved his fingers in the air like he was doing something on a virtual UI, and then he glared at her. "Can I leave?"

"The contract has been executed. You have ownership of the *Lady Hawk*, and the Sol-bits have been drawn from your vault."

Juliet nodded and jerked her thumb toward the hangar door. "Get out. At least now I know why Nick never talked about you."

Franklin walked past her, and when he was standing by the door, hand on the activation button, he turned to her and yelled, "Suck on these nuts, lady!" Juliet's eyes bulged out as he made an obscene gesture toward his groin, and then, before she could think to do anything other than cough out a surprised laugh, he slipped through the door and was gone.

"That was rude!"

"Eh, I wasn't exactly polite in my bargaining." Juliet turned back to the ship, and a slow smile spread across her lips. "Can't believe I just spent 750k on a ship I don't need. How am I even going to fly this back to Luna?"

"This ship's mods are worth the money you just spent. Nick will be glad you have it. As for how we'll get it back to Luna, I have some ideas." Juliet laughed at Angel's quick reply—they were a pair; that much was certain.

54

EPILOGUE PART ONE

Juliet checked the proximity sensors to see that the *Lady Hawk* was following the flight path she and Angel had laid out, seeing the little interceptor was keeping a close, almost perfect position off the starboard side of the Wing. Angel had created a new daemon, a more robust one than Fido, that was more like a limited AI for all intents and purposes. She'd downloaded "him" into a data deck Juliet had purchased, and they'd plugged that into one of the robotic mechs from the secret cargo space. Now, that mech was flying the Lady and doing a pretty darn good job of it. "Your pilot program seems to be doing just fine."

"You mean Maverick?" Angel had named the new entity after some pilot in an ancient dogfighting movie.

"Uh, yeah, Maverick."

"Well, it's a good thing Callisto doesn't require a pilot's license to depart. I suppose I could fake one for him as I've been doing for you, but it adds another level of risk."

"I know, I know. I need to take the assessment. As for Maverick, we can get someone from the *Kowashi* to meet us and bring the Lady into port." Juliet thought for a minute, then asked, "You have the assessment, right? Maybe I'll take it while I recover."

With the current positions of Jupiter and Earth, if she and Angel maintained a comfortable one G of acceleration, they had almost nine days of travel ahead of them, and she'd decided to make use of some of the Cybergen implants Troy had given her. With Angel operating the autosurgeon and a mech to assist, there wasn't much they couldn't manage.

"You have to connect to a secure testing server, so we'll have to wait until the delay between us and Luna is minimal. It should be doable during the last day of transit."

"Sounds like a plan, then." Juliet checked the nav systems one more time, then pulled herself out of the acceleration couch. She walked through the ship's clean, soft-white corridors to the lift and then down to the med level, as she'd been calling the bottom level, where the two med bays sat waiting for patients.

While she walked, Angel went over their plan again. "So, day one, today, we'll install the Cybergen medical nanites. They should help speed up your recovery. Day two, we'll do the big operations: lungs and full-body speed enhancement."

"And the, uh, nose . . ."

"Olfactory implant. Yes, I didn't mention that or the auditory implant upgrade because they're trivial in comparison to the other two."

"Are you sure the lungs are the right move?" Juliet was nervous about the operation. It felt like a big deal; she wasn't just adding something new to herself, as in the case of the nanite suite, but she was having a major organ—well, two of them—removed. "We're sure the autosurgeon can handle it?"

"The autosurgical suites on this ship are more robust than the robotic surgeons found in a typical chop doc shop. They're equipped with extra-corporeal-membrane oxygenation systems, so we're well set up to handle an operation involving your lungs. We'll keep your body well-oxygenated during the extraction and implantation. As for whether I think it's a good idea, we've been over that! These lungs will—"

"Right, yeah, I remember. You don't have to go over it all again."

When Angel had read the manifest in the secret cargo hold, she'd spent a long time trying to convince Juliet to replace not only her lungs but several of her organs. Juliet had been against the idea at first—still was a little against it—but she'd finally relented, agreeing to try things out with the lungs, mainly because of the benefits Angel had described. They'd far outperform her natural ones when it came to exertion that included intense physical activity and—and this was the clincher—high-G situations.

Of course, there were plenty of other cool benefits; she'd be able to function in low-oxygen environments and could go without breathing for up to half an hour thanks to the dense layer of "molecular oxygen sponges" inside the synthetic organs.

"I'm just a little creeped out by the filters."

"The ports are small, and you'll hardly notice them with the synth-flesh covers." Angel had already told her as much—if Juliet wanted the lungs to be able to filter toxins from the air she breathed, including things like antipersonnel gases, she'd have to accept that she'd have a couple of thumbnail-size ports where the flexible filters could be removed for cleaning. "They're only for toxins, mind you. Your new nanites will clean and dispose of impurities in the air. You should only have to clean the filters very occasionally."

Juliet entered the med bay and opened the compartment that hid the access panel for the secret cargo hold. "Show me a picture of what the ports look like again, will you?" An image appeared on her AUI of a woman's chest. She had a small, circular stainless disk under each clavicle. "Eh, they don't look bad. I probably don't even care if we put synth-flesh over them." She stepped into the secret hold and walked over to the cabinet containing the Cybergen implants.

"I wish you'd reconsider the heart as well . . ."

"Angel, I know you're trying to improve me; like, make me tougher and harder to kill and all that. But let's go one step at a time, yeah? I feel like I've already agreed to about ten steps." She opened the refrigerated cabinet and began scanning the many plastic, hermetically sealed boxes. She didn't have to look long before Angel highlighted the boxes she needed. She reached up, grabbed one of them, and read it to herself. "Cybergen Auditory Implant, Model 47. Huh."

"Huh?"

"Well, it's not very creative. I expected something like Indigo Hummingbird Thunderclap, blah, blah. You get the idea."

"Well, Cybergen was one of the original manufacturers who became known for augmentative, not simply replacement, implants and prosthetics. They were pioneers in the cybernetic industry, recognized as the top in their field. They didn't do much marketing, hence the somewhat lackluster naming conventions."

Juliet pulled the rest of the boxes down, reading them off, one by one.

"Cybergen Enhanced Pulmonary Implant, Model 17. Cybergen Nanomedical Repair Matrix, Model 9. Cybergen Advanced Olfactory Sensor Array, Model 23B. And"—she grunted, lifting down the last case, much larger than the others—"Cybergen Kinetic Response Amplifier, Model 3C." She turned the case over, looking at the plain, nondescript labeling. "This won't make me jittery like Don, will it? This stuff is pretty old, Angel."

"This stuff is old, but it's far more sophisticated than whatever Don had done in his back-alley wire-job."

Juliet snorted at Angel's description. "Tell me how you really feel."

Of course, Angel took her literally. "Well, this unit has many components, the most invasive being the neural interface, which won't be necessary; I'll handle your increased synaptic speed just as I have been for you up to this point. The other major components are muscle and tendon augmentation materials, which are elegantly installed alongside your existing natural tissue. We're essentially incorporating some artificial fibers and nanomaterials to enhance your natural capabilities. The biobatteries are also quite something, far smaller and with greater capacity than the ones in modern cybernetics. I wonder how or why that technology was lost when Cybergen was dismantled."

"Well, didn't their entire manufacturing infrastructure get nuked?"

"Yes, their cybernetics facilities were destroyed alongside their artificial humanoid manufacturing plants." Juliet gathered the boxes up in a stack and, peering around the side of her burden, walked up the steps to the med bay. She'd heard the term Angel had used, artificial humanoid, but only in snippets during lectures about the Cybergen-*Takamoto* AI war, and it was all vague to her.

"What was the deal with that? The, um, artificial humanoids? They weren't synths?"

"Cybergen's artificial humanoids were the precursors for modern synthetic beings. Originally, they were essentially developing bodies for their true AIs. During the war, they ramped up the manufacturing process and began implanting the bodies with their soldier AI chips. That was at the height of the conflict and when things began to turn in a direction that seemed to be accelerating rapidly toward the destruction of life as humanity might recognize it."

While Angel spoke, Juliet walked back down into the secret cargo hold. She stood in the doorway for a minute, staring at Athena's portable server softly humming as the cooling system did its constant work to keep her from melting the substrate of her artificial mind.

"That's when some of the other AIs withdrew and began protesting the war, while others secretly helped end it?" She was guessing at the second part; everyone said Athena had refused to take part in the war, that she'd hid herself away, but from what Juliet had seen, she felt like Athena had done more, that she'd been working with people in hiding, trying to bring down the two megacorps and their mad lust for domination.

"I believe so."

"Can she hear us?" Juliet stepped toward the console, resting a hand on the silver case, secure in its dock.

"I believe so. She's connected to the systems in this room. I still haven't had a response to any of my queries."

"That's all right. I bet she's just getting to know us a little. She's thinking about things and waiting for the right moment." Juliet gently tapped the silver metal with her fingertips, then returned to the med bay, closing up the secret room. She laid out the boxes on a stainless rolling cart and pushed it next to the autosurgeon. "Where's your mech?"

"I'm piloting it here now. I'd had it stationed in front of the airlock. Are you ready? You can get undressed and climb onto the table. Today's procedure should be relatively short. I anticipate it taking less than an hour to change out your medical nanite systems."

"I guess so." Juliet felt like she should be excited about the upgrades, but she kept battling with herself about it—part of her wanted to be stronger, faster, and more formidable. Part of her felt weird about constantly altering herself, moving further and further away from the girl who'd grown up in Tucson, the girl who'd been a talented welder, a nut about fast cars, and who didn't worry about anything much beyond the coming weekend and how she was going to make rent. She snorted at that thought; worrying about rent and working long hours in the scrapyard hadn't been fun. Still, she'd liked herself and been confident about her convictions.

She was finding that despite all of her new skills, knowledge, and worldliness, she doubted herself more than ever. Of course, when she brought it up with Ming, the AI shrink thought she was just reeling from the too-recent loss of Nick and that she was romanticizing the past, forgetting about all of the negatives—rose-colored glasses and all that.

She had to admit there was some truth to that. Things had not been too rosy back then; not when she'd been in the thick of it.

"I'm just being a chicken 'cause that autodoc is going to be cutting me to pieces."

"I will most certainly not allow this autosurgeon to cut you into pieces!"

"Hah! Sorry for the hyperbole." Juliet stripped down to her underwear and climbed up on the cushioned surface of the surgical table. "Hey! It's warm!"

"I told you it was high-end! It's designed with comfort in mind."

"Wait 'til I tell Ladia there are autosurgeons nicer than hers."

"While you wait for me to prep your surgery, I thought you'd be interested in seeing your updated SOA card. All of your jobs with Nick and the one Larry filled out for you before he assumed his new identity have come in."

"Sure, why don't—" Juliet cut herself off with a laugh as the card popped up on her AUI.

Handle: "Lucky" – SOA-SP License #: XR713-004 **Personal Protection & Small Arms License #: E86072801**	Rating: C-13-1 (D-40-1)
Skillset Subgroups and Skill Details:		**Peer and Client Rating (Grades Are F, E, D, C, B, A, S, S+)** **Prior Ratings Are Listed in Parentheses:**
Combat:	Heavy Weapon Combat	D +1 (E +6)
	Bladed Weapon Combat	D +18
	Small Arms Combat	C +15 (C +1)
	Ship-to-Ship Spacecraft Combat	C +35 (C +1)
Technical:	Network Security Bypass/Defend	B +7 (C +28)
	Data Retrieval	C +3 (D +19)
	Welding	C +5
	Electrical	D +1
	Parts Fabrication	D +1
	Combustion & Electrical Engine Repair	D +1
	Fusion-Powered Craft Maintenance	C +5 (D +1)

Other:	Piloting - Spacefaring Craft	C +35 (D +1)
	Piloting - Personal Exoskeletal Craft	C +20
	High-Performance Driving/Navigation	C +35 (D +1)
	Negotiation and Conflict Avoidance	C +13 (D +1)
	Infiltration and Espionage	D +5 (No Prior)

"Oh, well, thanks for putting my old scores in parentheses." Juliet examined the numbers, and her brain started to melt before she'd gotten through half of them. "I don't even remember what all the plus numbers mean."

"Each tier, A, B, C, etcetera, requires a certain number of positive ranks to increase. Here's a table." Angel created a small table in her AUI that read:

Rank:	Needed:
F	5
E	10
D	20
C	40
B	60
A	80
S	100

"But not my overall score? How can I have been D forty?"

"Oh, operator rating is always on a scale of one to a hundred. Your overall rating is now C-13, and it will remain C until you get to C-100."

"This is great, I guess. It's fun to see how I've advanced, but it's also a lot of bullshit. Larry gave me a rating for 'infiltration and espionage,' but I didn't get any of that from my work at Grave? That's stupid."

"Well, we didn't leverage that. Remember, we were surprised to get any sort of rating at all from Rachel Dowdall. Knowing what we know now, we should have negotiated with Dowdall to ensure you got the proper ratings on your SOA card. You also didn't get a rating for that from Voronov, and I'll accept responsibility for that oversight—I wrote the contract. I'll do better in the future."

"Oh, relax. I'm not mad or anything. Honestly, does it even matter? Everything we've learned, the connections we've made, the ships, my upgrades . . ." Juliet trailed off, trying to find the right words. "I guess I'm just saying I'm not worried about getting work. My SOA card could say F on everything, and I still wouldn't be worried."

"Well, that may be, but keep in mind that you don't know what the future may hold. Having a respectable SOA card could open many doors down the road." While Angel spoke, the door slid open, and one of the shiny chrome mechs stomped into the room, walking up to stand beside the autosurgeon bed.

"Okay, Angel, I'll concede your point. Now, tell me, are you going to need that hunk of metal to operate on me?"

"Not today, but when we do your full-body speed augmentation, I'll use the mech to position your body on the table."

"My body? I'm still in here!"

"Oh, I mean you! Sorry, Juliet!"

Juliet chuckled, but the exchange made her wonder—how much of her was her body? Was it at all? If she slowly changed out every part of herself with cybernetics, would she still be Juliet? She liked to think so, but was that just some kind of evolutionary quirk? To Angel, Juliet wasn't her body. Was she right? So, what, then, was she?

She'd always enjoyed those sorts of questions, and she supposed Angel might have just missed the nuance of the word or the concept of the difference between moving her body around and moving Juliet around, but she also wondered at Angel's perception of her. Their interactions occurred in Juliet's head. Angel didn't look at her, not unless Juliet looked in a mirror . . .

Angel interrupted her musings. "Are you ready to begin?"

"Yeah, sorry, just getting lost thinking about weird stuff. Okay, Doctor Angel, please be gentle." Juliet felt something cold in her arm, and she'd just glanced down to see that Angel had already inserted an IV needle without her noticing when she saw the black walls of unconsciousness closing in. Then she was out and dreaming of racing down an open highway, wind blowing through her hair.

* * *

Sir Rodric Barrington sat on the edge of his bare plastic cot, his feet on the cold concrete, staring at the scratches on the opposite wall. He twitched his toes. They were cold, and he wasn't used to any part of him being less than perfectly comfortable. They'd issued him some disposable, printed slippers when he'd first been admitted, but on his second day, he'd torn them to shreds in a fit of frustrated rage. Now, the guards ignored him when he asked for new ones.

"One, two . . ." he trailed off, afraid his neighbor across the hall would hear him. He reached out with one shaky hand to trace the scratches, trying to figure out if they meant something. He'd tried counting them, tried converting the different groupings into letters of the alphabet, but he couldn't make sense of them.

Maybe they were just what they looked like—random scratches left by the last madman to inhabit his cage. He shivered and rubbed his upper arms briskly, trying to stimulate some blood flow. Why was it necessary to keep the prison so chilly? He'd tried to ask one of the guards but been shoved and struck for making the noise.

Rodric lifted the hem of his blue, printed tunic and looked at the pink rash spreading over his flaccid belly. He sorely missed his hypoallergenic Rose Carrington signature undergarments. A distant wail broke him out of his self-pity for a moment. As the sound echoed and faded, snatches of mad gibberish came to him from the cell across the corridor. Rodric shivered as he remembered his glimpse into that hellish space on his first day. He'd seen a large, pustule-riddled man furiously pleasuring himself in broad daylight.

For some reason, the memory made him look at his toilet, sitting openly in the corner of the tiny cell. He supposed the connection was clear enough— private things made public. Rodric had a shy bladder, and he'd been struggling to urinate to the point that he was starting to refuse fluids. He tried; he'd stand over the toilet for minutes that bled into hours trying to piss, but no matter how badly he had to go, as soon as it began to splatter into the water, his gut would clench up, and his mind would begin to race, wondering what the freaks around him were thinking as they heard his urine splashing into the water.

Of course, Rodric had demanded a private cell, one with an actual closing door, not open bars. Of course, he'd been ignored. His attorney had changed his contact info. His friends had forsaken him. His daughter and wife were lying about him. His other children, the three who'd taken his calls, were ineffectual, and that was entirely his fault. Hadn't he spent the last few decades ignoring them? Hadn't he cut them all out of the business, sending them their allowances to pursue whatever stupid projects or piddling careers they fancied? The others, the socialites and layabouts, were of no help.

Rodric shivered and scratched at his rash, shifting on the bed. His bladder was full again, and he knew he'd have to keep holding it. If only he still had his PAI! Ravina could block out the sounds, even fill his vision with a peaceful glade, complete with a crashing waterfall. He'd be able to go then! They'd taken her, though, and left him dumb and hobbled.

No, he'd have to wait until the guards came to take the inmates to lunch. Rodric was fed in his cell; too many other prisoners wanted to kill him, apparently. Yes, lunch was the best window. Noise would fill the echoing hallways, and he'd know his neighbors were out—it was the only time he could relax enough to piss in peace. "Goddamn you, Dennis."

"Goddamn you, Dennis!" the lunatic across the hall screeched, his high-pitched manic voice echoing up and down the cell block.

"Shut up!" Rodric barked, and that's when others took up the chant. Like magpies talking to each other, the fools' cries rang up and down the concrete hallway.

"Goddamn you, Dennis!"

"Shut up!"

"Goddamn!"

"Dennis, Dennis, Dennis!"

"Shut up!"

"Goddamn you, Dennis!"

Rodric clapped his palms over his ears and flopped onto his side, rocking back and forth on his cot's hard, cold plastic. To drown out the cries of the lunatics around him, he began to hum a tune, something he'd heard when he was a kid, something that had stuck in his mind—a song from school, a fight song the band played.

As he remembered those days, the camaraderie, the rivalry, the excitement he'd had about the future, tears began to stream down his cheeks, and his humming turned into something more like a wail.

55

EPILOGUE PART TWO

Juliet winced as she slowly pushed herself upright, shifting on the surgical table until she was sideways, her bare legs and feet hanging down under the soft sanitary blanket and sheets Angel's mech had used to dress the bed. Looking down, head swimming, she saw more than half a dozen glued incisions surrounded by the reddish-orange stain of antiseptic gel on her lower extremities. Most were near her knees and ankles, but she knew she'd find more if she lifted the blanket. Angel had said she'd need those laparoscopic incisions in forty-eight strategic locations so the autosurgeon could weave the synthetic, augmented muscle and tendon fibers with her natural ones.

"Carefully, Juliet. You're going to be unsteady on your feet for a while." The aforementioned mech whirred and clanked as it stepped closer to the table, offering her its sturdy arm to lean on.

"Why . . . ?" Juliet licked her lips, gathered some saliva, and swallowed before trying again. "Why are my legs and arms covered with bruises?"

"Not only your legs and arms! The incisions were small, but the autosurgeon had to insert surgical rods to reach tissue up to twenty-five centimeters away from some of them. Obviously, that resulted in some capillary and small vein damage. Your new nanite suite is speeding your healing along nicely, however. Without them, you'd be bedridden for a week."

Juliet grunted in response, holding onto the mech's arm and sliding off the bed so her bare feet touched down on the cool plasteel flooring. She didn't have to ask how long she'd been under; her AUI provided that information. "Twelve hours. Am I just groggy from the meds?"

"That and the ordeal your body went through. As much as we downplay cybernetic augmentation, you had several major surgeries. By the way, do you notice any differences in your breathing?"

Juliet froze; she'd almost forgotten that she was inhaling with synthetic lungs. She stood a little straighter and took a deep breath, noticing nothing different about the sensation. "My chest is sore, but only on the surface. Breathing feels good."

"That's great news. Don't be alarmed by the incision mark along your sternum—with the laser scalpel and modern wound-bonding techniques, you won't have a scar."

"So, I'm guessing everything went well, or you'd have said something by now."

"Everything went perfectly. You aren't noticing any strange odors?"

Juliet paused again, taking a prolonged, slow inhalation through her nose. "Uh, well, now that you mention it, things seem a little too fresh. It smells like it just rained in here."

"I thought you'd enjoy that as you woke. Your new olfactory implants are very robust. I can make even the most unpleasant odors seem completely different!"

Juliet chuckled and bent to pick up the soft white robe she'd earlier found in one of the med bay cabinets. As she carefully pulled it on, gingerly extending her arms into the sleeves, she said, "Well, don't make all the best smells commonplace; otherwise, I'll stop appreciating them. I think normal odors are fine most of the time, okay?"

"An excellent observation! I'll slowly allow this fresh scent to fade. The ship's air filtration is very robust in any case."

"Thanks for everything, Angel." Juliet cinched the belt, pleased that, if nothing else, all of her limbs and digits seemed to be working just fine. "How soon until I can try out the new reflexes?"

"We should give the synthetic muscle and tendon fibers at least a week to bond fully. Until then, I'll keep them powered off so you don't have to worry about accidentally activating them."

"Speaking of power, where are the batteries?"

"In your femurs. They're rod-shaped and less than a centimeter in diameter."

Juliet looked at the surgical bed and saw the mech was already bundling up her bedding to be washed. "You're good with the cleanup?"

"Yes, it's not a problem. If you'd like to go to your quarters, the acceleration couch would be—"

"Uh-uh. I don't wanna lie down right now. I'll go up to the bridge and see what's up." She knew very well that Angel could give her a full update on everything. Still, she wanted to wander around a little. "Can you have that mech bring me a drink or something when he's done washing sheets?"

"Of course. By the way, you have two messages. One from Antigone that was sent to Lacy Blake's encrypted address, and one from Bennet."

"All right. Play Antigone's while I walk to the bridge." Juliet kept walking, slow and shuffling, toward the lift, and an image of Antigone in her corporate heiress style—curly auburn hair with blonde highlights, subdued makeup, expensive, tailored suit jacket and blouse—appeared on her AUI.

She spoke calmly and quickly, getting right to the point. "Lacy, just wanted to drop you a note to let you know everything went well. My father's out of the picture for now, but there are many people with a lot of money and various strings attached to him. He'll likely make it to the trial." Her upbeat expression fell, and she sighed. "Imagine that. I actually feel a little relief saying that, despite all he's done. Anyway, his law firm dumped him, but we couldn't get to all his accounts in time to leave him without means. Eventually, he'll find someone willing to work for him, and things will come to light, though he's lost almost all credibility.

"He doesn't have any evidence to support his claims of innocence, and, well, we have plenty. That's thanks to you—the murdered crew of the Humpback might be the crime that brings him down. The surveillance you uncovered of the security team doing the deed has been instrumental. They're cooperating with the prosecution, and their chief operator kept records. Looks like dear old Dad may end up going down for contracted mass murder.

"Anyway, Lacy, that's about all I have for you. I'm not dumb; I'm pretty sure Lacy was a cover ID, but I suppose it's safer for everyone that I don't know who you really are. Maybe that can change someday. In any case, I'd love to hear from you anytime. You have my secure contact info. Take care."

Juliet stepped off the lift and shuffled up the long, straight corridor toward the bridge. "Well, that was kind of nice." She frowned and added, "I'm sure she knows her dad hired a subcontractor to build up Lacy's identity. What do you think that was all about?"

"I have a theory I've been meaning to share . . ."

"Go on." Juliet wondered why Angel was hesitating.

"I think perhaps Lacy Blake is or was a real person. I think Rodric Barrington also had her killed so that you could have a truly authentic cover."

"Oh." Juliet sighed and rubbed her fingers through her hair. It was longer than when she'd been playing her Lacy role, hanging down past her ears in a layered shag cut. "I hope that's not the case. From what I know about Lacy, she wasn't a nice person, but I hate to be responsible for anyone's murder. Even someone like her."

"You aren't responsible. You know that."

"Yeah, I know. I hate how . . . I hate how some of these people use other people as commodities. It's not just the corpos, either. The pirates were pretty bad. I think it boils down to desperation and control. People like Rodric want to control their environment, which means anyone outside their circle is seen as a threat or a means to an end. The pirates, street gangs, scavengers—they're all kept on a desperate edge of life and death. When you're like that, when you're not sure if you'll run out of air or food or places to hide, you'll do terrible things to make it to the next day."

"That's true for the average pirate or gangster, but the bosses aren't like that. They're little better than Rodric in that regard."

"Yeah, good point, Angel. I won't be forgiving Mary Moon anytime soon."

"People are complicated. I don't think you can summarize or generalize why so many turn out bad. Before you met me, you were working your life away, barely meeting your needs for survival, but you didn't behave unethically. You've made friends with plenty of others with functioning moral compasses. To steal a rather old idiomatic expression, don't throw the baby out with the bathwater."

"Hah! I like that." Juliet gingerly lowered herself into the pilot's acceleration couch. "Definitely some babies worth keeping. Speaking of worth keeping, play me Bennet's message, will you?"

Bennet's face appeared on her AUI, and she heard his voice in her ears. "Yo, Lucky. I heard you had a pretty rough time up there. Up? Is that right? I mean, to get to you, I'd have to go up off this moon, so yeah, I guess you are up from me. Anyway, I heard you had a rough time. I'm really sorry to hear about your friend. Uh, I got your message a while back about keeping all the exterior armor plating off the gunship." Juliet frowned and paused the message.

"Did I tell Bennet to keep the armor off the gunship?"

"You told me, and I sent him a message. We were speculating about trying to refurbish the *Takamoto* repair nanites with the tech on this medical ship."

"Ah, that's right." Juliet pressed play, and the message continued.

"It's not a problem, anyway—still working on the drive systems and rebuilding some of the maneuvering jets. Aya's been sanding down all the plating and replacing the sections that aren't up to spec: the ones that are too thin, too damaged, or repaired too many times. I was wondering, what color do you want the ship to be? Aya's throwing primer on all the plating after she cleans it up, and we figured we could get started with the base color, at least. Everyone agrees that it's your call. How does that sound? I mean, Alice said something about you sending an interceptor our way, but we were thinking we'd sell it. You don't mean to fly that instead of the gunship, do you?"

He paused and rubbed a thick thumb at a grease smudge on his cheekbone. Juliet could see the wheels turning in his head as he thought of what to say next. "Well, we miss you a lot. We're anxious to get you home, and Alice said the last time you messaged, you said something about having to finish things up around there. She seemed worried, so I'm worried, too. How about a message, huh?" He forced a smile and offered a quick wave, and then the recording ended.

"Oh no, Angel! I should have messaged them days ago! Ugh! I'm such a jerk sometimes."

"You're not a jerk! You've been busy and . . . Well, okay, you and I both should have thought to send a message before now."

"Let's send one now. I want to tell them about the *Lady Hawk* and . . ." Juliet frowned and thought about what she was going to say. Did she want to burden them with knowledge of the medical ship? Athena was a big deal, and the more people who knew about her or the ship she was hiding in, the more she was at risk. Juliet had to take that responsibility seriously.

"Angel, can you rent us a private hangar on Luna? Something under an alias that no one can connect to me. We should park the *Furies' Wing* there, and I don't think we need to tell anyone about her. Not right now, anyway."

"I think that's wise. If you land the Wing and secure her in your hangar, we can hire a shuttle to bring us out to the Lady, and then you can land her at the port. No one needs to know you didn't travel all the way in that vessel."

"Okay, that's settled, then. Let's compose a message to the crew. Go ahead and send it to all of them."

"Ready."

"Hey, everyone. I'm so sorry I didn't get back to you a few days ago when things settled down. I've been in transit and decompressing. It's not a good excuse; you all were worried, and I should have told you immediately when

I was safe. Well, long story short, I'll be home in five days or so, and Alice, I have the *Lady Hawk*. Nick left her to his nephew, and the little creep didn't appreciate her at all. I bought her from him. I guess that means go ahead and sell the Sharp Lady. Yeah, if you're wondering, Nick named that ship, too. Um, I've got no interest in that pirate frigate, so if you want to sell it so we can put more money into the gunship or the *Kowashi*, then I'm fine with that.

"I plan to fly the gunship, but—and Alice, you know this—the *Lady Hawk* is very special. We should keep her for . . . options. Bennet, Aya, please start painting the armor plating for the gunship a soft sky blue—something you might see on a clear day out over a cornfield. I've never seen cornfields, but I figure there's some nice blue sky over 'em, yeah? I have an idea for some more . . . decorative paint, but we'll wait 'til she's all buttoned up before we go down that road." Juliet winked and grinned, knowing Angel was capturing her face with the camera on her pilot console.

"I really miss you all, and I'm looking forward to being home. See you soon, but if you want, send me some more messages; the delay will only get smaller from here!" Juliet stopped the recording and sighed, a pleasant feeling in her chest and a lot less weight on her shoulders. She closed her eyes and leaned back into the acceleration couch, then noticed an icon blinking on her AUI. "What's this?"

"I thought you'd like to see how I rated your new Cybergen equipment and the values for your musculoskeletal and cardiovascular rankings." Juliet started to object, but before she'd even opened her mouth, the icon expanded to fill her vision, and she found herself reading through Angel's notations about Juliet's comparative status on Angel's mystery database.

Juliet Corina Bianchi		
Physical, Mental, and Social Status Compilation:		**Comparative Ranking Percentile (Higher Is Better - Previous Value in Parenthesis):**
Liquid Assets Net Worth:	Sol-bits: 502,456	--
Neural and Cellular Adaptiveness:	.96342 (scale of 0 – 1)	99.91

Synaptic Responsiveness:	.19 (Lower Is Better)	79.31
Musculoskeletal Ranking:	–	84.03 (75.49)
Cardiovascular Ranking:	–	90.77(76.88)
Cybernetic and Bionic Augmentation:	**Model Name and Number:**	**Overall Rating of the Augmentation (Grades Are F, E, D, C, B, A, S, S+):**
PAI	WBD Project Angel, Alpha 3.433	S+
Psionic Lattice	Grave Industries, GIPEL	S
Data Port	Prime Data Systems, Archwizard 2109.v3	A
Data Jack	Bio Network Solutions, 8840	C
Medical Nanite Suite	Cybergen Nanomedical Repair Matrix, Model 9	A+
Retinal Cybernetic Implant	Mirage Tech, Lux Alpha 12	A-
Auditory Cybernetic Implant	Cybergen Auditory Implant, Model 47	A+
Olfactory Cybernetic Implant	Cybergen Advanced Olfactory Sensor Array, Model 23B	A+
Cybernetic Prosthetic Right Arm with Fully Programmable Fingerprints	BioFusion, Model 2109.01b	A

Complete Cybernetic Lung Replacement	Cybergen Enhanced Pulmonary Implant, Model 17	A+
Full-Body Enhanced Reflex Package	Cybergen Kinetic Response Amplifier, Model 3C	A+
Intracranial Blood Cooling System	Angel Systems - Bespoke Design	A
Programmable Synthetic Hair	Alicia Designs, Chroma Tresses v.4	B+
DNA Spoofing Package - Saliva	WBD - Custom Model	C
No Other Augmentation Detected.	–	–

Rachel watched Kline approach through the camera feed on her AUI. He didn't look like he was in a bad mood. His face was neutral, his eyes untroubled beneath his heavy, sandy blond eyebrows. He looked sharper than the last time he'd stopped by; his suit was clean, and the shirt pressed. His hair was styled, and the stubble she'd wondered about was gone. She'd thought maybe he would grow a beard, a significant power play in WBD corporate politics. The old lady frowned on facial hair.

Rachel touched the mic button on the console. "Are we ready?"

The lab tech inside the test room lifted his left hand, thumb in the air. The subject frowned, looking confused, but Rachel didn't care that she didn't know what was happening. It was better that way, in fact. She touched the button again. "He's in the building. Five minutes."

After a brief breathing exercise, trying to calm her nerves, lower her blood pressure, and stop the nervous perspiration in her armpits, she stood up and turned to face the door. She was the only one in the little observation room, but that was by design; the demonstration required it. She tracked Kline's progress through the building, down the elevator, and then through the narrow, white-painted hallways to her door.

With a beep and whoosh, the door opened and he stepped in.

"Kline." She held out a hand. He took it and shook it warmly, smiling. "Rachel. Been too long."

"Just about two months. I love how that worked out, by the way."

"Hmm?"

"You had the hot tip about Seattle, but I got left here hunting rumors down."

Kline chuckled and shrugged out of his coat, slinging it on the back of a chair. He approached the viewscreen and stared at the two people sitting in the test room. "It's not like I was twiddling my thumbs. Came up empty in New Vegas. Remind me to track down the banger who gave us that tip!"

"What about New York? I should tell you people are speculating that you're using these tips as an excuse to travel on the company card."

"Hah! People, huh? No, Rachel, but I'll let you in on a little secret, just between you and me." He turned and winked at her.

"What's that?"

"There wasn't a tip about New York. I requested leave to go to an addiction facility. Finally kicked the nicotine."

Rachel snorted and reached up to cover her mouth, turning while her cheeks bloomed in embarrassment. "Sorry!" She laughed. "You caught me off guard."

"You think I'm joking? I was in treatment!" Kline feigned mock outrage, and Rachel laughed all the more.

"You think I'm that gullible? The old lady wouldn't stand for anyone displaying the slightest hint of mental weakness. Addiction isn't a thing she believes in."

"Are you suggesting they're not being sincere with the corporate line about mental health being a top priority at WBD?" Kline pulled out one of the two chairs and sat down. "All right, enough nonsense. It's good to see you, but please tell me you've found something worth the trip. Speaking of the old lady, we need to show some progress soon or . . . Well, you know."

"I think you're going to be pleased." Rachel moved to sit beside him. "You see that woman there, across from our technician?"

"Yep. One of the missing Grave subjects?"

"I know you're guessing based on why I'm up here, but yes." Rachel regarded the woman. She had wan, pale flesh, dark, sunken eyes, and short curly black hair that looked like it could use a good washing.

"She looks a little out of it."

"She doesn't sleep well. We've only had her a few days, but, well, I won't spoil anything." Rachel touched the microphone button again. "We're ready for you to begin."

The tech looked at the camera, nodded, then turned to the woman. His voice came through the speaker, just a little crackly at first, but the software smoothed it out. "Abby, are you ready?" Abby licked her lips, clearly dry and cracked, and nodded quickly. "Nothing hard, nothing you need to worry about, okay? No pressure. Two people are on the other side of that wall where the camera is. I want you to tell me their genders."

Kline shifted beside her, clearing his throat, but Rachel held up a hand. "Be patient."

Abby closed her eyes, and Rachel saw her take a deep breath. Then, almost immediately, she said, "A man and a woman."

"Good. Okay, Abby, I want you to forget about the woman. Tell me what's going on in the man's head. What's he thinking about?"

"What the—"

"Shh!" Rachel reached over and grasped Kline's hand where it rested on the arm of his chair.

"He's . . ." Abby's voice was halting at first, then she began to speak quickly, almost like a stream of consciousness, "He's thinking he likes her touch. She has warm fingers, and he's glad to be with her. He's spent time away. Yeah, he's been away, and he wasn't having fun. Someone—he calls her the old lady—had him doing something . . . He had to kill someone. A woman— blonde hair, shiny eyes. She begged, and it really messed him up . . ."

Kline reached forward and slammed the mic button. "Enough." He looked at Rachel and growled, "What the fuck, Rachel?"

Part of Rachel was battling to contain the euphoria of a successful demonstration, while another part was horrified about what the woman had seen in Kline's head. "Something else, isn't she?"

"This is what Grave was doing?"

"Seems like it. She was one of the subjects on their database. Corpo-sec at a local native casino picked her up. She was cleaning them out. They registered her DNA, and we flagged it." Rachel gestured to the woman, rocking back and forth, hands on the sides of her head. "She's a little unstable, but we're starting to build a picture of what was going on with Grave's GARD department. I still haven't been able to tie anything to, you know, J. Shit, though, Kline, this is big stuff. If we can start to figure out GARD's methodology, we might be able to replicate some of this."

Kline leaned back, and Rachel wasn't the least bit surprised when he fished a Nikko-vape out of his pocket. He sucked on it for a second, then, as he exhaled a strawberry plume, said, "This might buy us some leeway with the old lady. Yeah. Holy shit, she dug right into me. I was actively trying not to think about that stuff." His eyes, unfocused as he thought things through, refocused on Rachel. "You have anything else to chase down here?"

"Nope."

"Okay, get everything, her included, packed up, and we'll get back to Phoenix. I've had some AI sifting through the remnants of the Grave databases. Maybe we can put something together. What's the deal with her, anyway? Was it a drug?"

"As I said, she's unstable, but it sounds like a combination of drugs and tech. With the right kind of scan, you can see the stuff they put into her head. She keeps calling it a gipple, whatever that means."

"Gipple, huh? Sounds funny, but maybe it'll lead to something. If she's here, there must be more of them, don't you think? Now we have an idea of what to look for." He stared at the ceiling, stroking his jaw for a minute. "Yeah, this ought to keep the old . . . Mrs. Gentry off our backs for a little while." He sucked on the vape again and gestured toward the viewscreen. "Better stop thinking of her as the old lady now that you've got people reading our minds."

ABOUT THE AUTHOR

Plum Parrot is the pen name of author Miles Gallup, who grew up in Southern Arizona and spent much of his youth wandering around the Sonoran Desert, hunting imaginary monsters and building forts. He studied creative writing at the University of Arizona and, for a number of years, attempted to teach middle schoolers to love literature and write their own stories. If he's not spending time with his dog, you can find Gallup writing, reading his favorite authors, or playing *D&D* with friends and family.

Podium